A Game of Two Halves

Anthologies published by VUP include:

Great Sporting Moments: The Best of Sport 1988–2004
(edited by Damien Wilkins, 2005)

Middle Distance: Long Stories of Aotearoa New Zealand
(edited by Craig Gamble, 2021)

Six by Six: Short Stories by New Zealand's Best Writers
(edited by Bill Manhire, 1989, 2021)

Sista, Stanap Strong! A Vanuatu Women's Anthology
(edited by Mikaela Nyman & Rebecca Tobo Olul-Hossen, 2021)

Monsters in the Garden: An Anthology of Aotearoa New Zealand
Science Fiction and Fantasy
(edited by Elizabeth Knox & David Larsen, 2020)

Short Poems of New Zealand
(edited by Jenny Bornholdt, 2018)

Twenty Contemporary New Zealand Poets
(edited by Andrew Johnston & Robyn Marsack, 2009)

The Best of Best New Zealand Poems
(edited by Bill Manhire & Damien Wilkins, 2008)

Some Other Country: New Zealand's Best Short Stories
(edited by Marion McLeod & Bill Manhire, 1984, 2008)

A Game of Two Halves

The Best of *Sport* 2005–2019

Edited by Fergus Barrowman

Victoria University of Wellington Press

Victoria University of Wellington Press
PO Box 600, Wellington
New Zealand
vup.victoria.ac.nz

ISBN 9781776564316

A catalogue record is available from the
National Library of New Zealand.

Printed in Singapore by Markono Print Media Pte Ltd

Contents

Introduction

Sport was conceived in the back of Damien Wilkins' yellow Ford Escort—he tells the story in the introduction to *Great Sporting Moments*—and born in spring 1988.

It has died three natural deaths. The first came after five years with the slender and tired issue 10, the cover of which features the large face of Jack Knox Barrowman, born in spring 1992. *Sport 11* was nearly a farewell best of—the 1st XI—and thank you Forbes Williams for a good idea that we didn't use—because resurrection came in the form of great new writing—'The Poet's Wife' by Bill Manhire, 'Not Her Real Name' by Emily Perkins, 'After Bathing at Baxter's' by Gregory O'Brien.

The second death was in 2014, when after 41 issues of unbroken support Creative New Zealand declined a grant application without notice or discussion. Pooh to that (as Barbara Anderson would have said).

The third death was in 2020, when the pressure on me and everyone else of keeping the VUP show on the road in the pandemic meant there was no way of putting on a sideshow. And as the year turned we thought, yes, it's time.

*

We were driving around the Basin Reserve—I can remember that, but not where we were going, or what produced the thought at that particular moment. But the pressure behind it was a degree of dissatisfaction at VUP. I was in my fifth year (good grief), and although with Bill Manhire's leadership we had begun to open the press up to publishing more new writers—first books by Dinah Hawken, Elizabeth Knox, Jenny Bornholdt and Barbara Anderson in 1987–89—there was only so much a firm with a staff of 1.5 (Damien was the half) publishing 6–8 books a year could do, and I was getting to know lots of terrific new writers. How could I publish more of them?

The local litmag scene was in a low state. *Islands* hadn't appeared for a while, and while it hadn't closed—Robin Dudding made that clear when we visited him to ask for his blessing (see pp62–64 below)—I saw an opportunity to copy what Robin did and take *Islands'* place. The other long-lasting mag, *Landfall*, was being edited uncertainly by committee and turning down the very writers I wanted to publish. Meanwhile two stylish interventions had come and deliberately gone again. *And* was the kind of bracing intervention every literary scene needs from time to time, and stayed exactly its prescribed course of four issues, while *Rambling Jack* was more of a good-time coterie mag, which was having too much fun to stop at four and added a fifth issue.

And out in the world there was *Granta*, the mighty quarterly that after its reinvention in 1979 became the showroom for literary glamour: Dirty Realism, The Best of Young British, James Fenton riding into Saigon on the back of a North Vietnamese tank . . . That's what we wanted to be: a fat paperback book of new writing on the front table of Unity Books every quarter. Or every six months, which was a considered decision: we wanted *Sport* to last the distance, as well as to be glamorous, and to have room for long stories as well as short ones.

And it wasn't going to have a manifesto. It was clear to all of us that experimental writing—or postmodern writing, call it what you like—was just as rulebound as literary realism, and no more likely to be any good; that experienced writers took as many risks as beginning writers; and that older beginning writers—Barbara Anderson!—were just as alive in the moment of self-discovery as young writers.

*

It happened quickly. Elizabeth and Damien and Nigel said 'Let's do it'; Bill Manhire, Alan Preston and Andrew Mason offered loans; and, crucially, the Literary Fund quickly approved a first-issue grant to a magazine with no track record. (Wouldn't happen now.) Damien and I looked in the VUP 'under consideration' file; we wrote to writers we knew, to writers whose work I'd admired while assessing Bill's creative writing course folios, and to some writers we didn't know. We went as far as two Australians, Les Murray and Gerald Murnane, both of whom sent work, and it was a thrill years later to see the story Gerald sent us, 'When the Mice Failed to Arrive', first up in *Stream System: The Collected Short Fiction*. It was the opening story in *Sport 2*, and the inspiration for Catherine Bagnall's terrific two-colour cover (the budget would have fainted at the thought of CMYK back then).

In fact *Sport*s *1* and *2* filled up almost immediately, and it felt like only weeks before *Sport 1* was published, although it must have been longer, because the publishing process was to edit in red pen and blue pencil and send the manuscripts to a typesetter in Christchurch, who would take four weeks to typeset them and a further four to correct the errors that had been introduced, and printing in New Zealand took five weeks.

I investigated making *Sport* an official VUP magazine, but book publishing and periodical cycles are very different, and at that time I was engaged in extricating VUP from its share of responsibility for four university periodicals, so the Publications Committee wasn't going to let me create one of my own. Also, I didn't know how long I'd be at VUP. Nevertheless, *Sport* wouldn't have been possible without VUP: the contacts, the facilities, the skills, the confidence. But I kept the finances strictly separate, and the hours for that matter—for years *Sport* was what I did in the weekends.

One by one my co-editors fell away. They were writers and had better things to do. I never quite solo edited—I would always circulate manuscripts for opinions—but it was a happy day when James Brown came on board as guest editor or co-editor for issues 12–25. James shook things up nicely. He could never be one of those editors who can quickly breeze through a large pile of submissions and reduce it to the likely 15%. No, James got to the bottom of every piece. In those days we communicated mostly by writing notes to each other on the covering letters. These of course can never be seen by the authors, so when accepting

(10%?) or rejecting I'd detach and file them. They're in a box somewhere secret.

The problem is easy to spot. Fine for me to donate my time, but James is a poet, so after Creative New Zealand twice rejected my application for an increased grant to pay him something, he retired. Subsequent editors—Catherine Chidgey (23–26), Sara Knox, Kate Camp—did it for love, mostly once.

Sport 15 was guest-edited by Greg O'Brien and was the first to feature photographs: 'White Horse Black Dog' by Peter Black. Greg's idea, the move also reflected my love of photography, then and now usually regarded as inferior to painting and sculpture, and *Sport* went on to publish work by Bill Culbert, Alan Knowles, Bruce Connew, Mary McPherson, Andrew Ross, Bruce Foster, Peter Black again, and finally Harvey Benge, in issue 33, the first to be featured in this book. It wasn't always popular—C.K. Stead cancelled his subscription because he wasn't going to spend his money on dingy black-and-white photos of Wellington, which I took as a tribute to Andrew Ross—but it was fun.

We stopped because of the economics. *Sport*'s funding came roughly in thirds: donated time; income from bookshop sales, subscriptions and a few ads; and the Literary Fund/Creative New Zealand grant. Circulation settled at 400–600 copies depending, and on that basis each 'normal' issue made a small surplus, which we would spend every two or three issues on photos. That no longer worked after *Sport 31*, when the twice-yearly magazine became an annual, and the issues got bigger, and the budgets got tighter.

*

We founded *Sport* early in the Golden Age of New Zealand Publishing (1983–2008). While researching *The Picador Book of Contemporary New Zealand Fiction* (1996) I found that of the 11 (!) New Zealand fiction titles published in 1979, six were published internationally and three of the five published locally were author-funded; and that by 1995 the annual totals were over 40, all of which were published locally, many of them profitably.

The Golden Age was fuelled by the hunger for local stories—Maurice Gee's *Plumb*, Fiona Kidman's *A Breed of Women*, Sue McCauley's *Other Halves*, Janet Frame's autobiographies, and above all Keri Hulme's Booker Prize–winning *The Bone People*. The British publishing industry noticed and increased their investment in New Zealand branches; the fourth Labour Government opened the economy and increased support for the arts; and before long VUP was selling out an 8000-copy first print run of a Barbara Anderson novel every two years.

The Golden Age was doomed by the loss of local industry market share to offshore internet retail, which really got going around 2004–5. British publishers saw that they didn't need local warehouses to sell their books to New Zealand readers, so they closed them—and hasn't the pandemic shown us how robust just-in-time supply from Australian warehouses really is? What has developed since then is in many ways more modest and local, but also more lively and open to a diversity of new writers, as the financial and technological barriers to publishing a book or setting up as a publisher have got lower. These have turned out to be ideal conditions for a risk-taking small-to-medium-sized publisher with a university's support to thrive, and they have changed *Sport*.

*

Becoming an annual made *Sport* less magazine-like. There were fewer interviews and reviews, no photo-essays, fewer oddities and experiments, fewer personal essays even, despite this being the age of the personal essay. Instead, the larger issues became new writing anthologies, dominated by fiction and poetry. There are so many ways for writers to get new work in front of readers—in print and online magazines (such as the IIML's own *Turbine|Kapohau*), on Twitter and Insta, in chapbooks and collective publications, at festivals and readings—why wait for something that only comes around once a year? And the line from a first-draft manuscript to a first book is shorter and straighter than it used to be too.

Sport also became less international. In the early years we exploited our connection with Writers and Readers Week at the NZ Festival of the Arts (founded 1986) to ask for work from visiting writers, who often sent something. However, once the international festival circuit got fully into gear and coming to New Zealand was no longer anything special for the writers, publishing them didn't feel special to us either.

The exception came in 2012, when New Zealand was guest of honour at the Frankfurt Book Fair. I went to Frankfurt with other New Zealand publishers in 2011 to set up German translations for 2012—Germany being the stage and the rest of the world the audience—but the lovely German publishers I met told me that we had been a late substitution and I was two years too late, so I came home with a new idea: to publish a special issue of contemporary German writing in translation, and make my Frankfurt 2012 a two-way cultural exchange. With the enthusiastic and expert help of guest editor Sally-Ann Spencer, and generous assistance from the Goethe Institut, who insisted we pay all of the translators commercial European rates, we produced something really good.

It tuned out that our 450-page *Sport*, which put young New Zealand writers next to some of the best contemporary German writers, didn't really fit the New Zealand export drive, which can best be summed up by remembering that inside the pavilion it was too dark to read and too loud to have a conversation, and the books were hung on butcher's hooks. Nevertheless, five of those 24 writer–translator combinations are here, and I'd love to have kept them all.

And *Sport* grew closer to VUP, which had grown to a team of seven (FTE 5.5) publishing about 30 and as many as 42 books per year. Editing became a collaborative process involving other VUP staff, especially Ashleigh Young and Kirsten McDougall; and so many more writers in the whānau were obviously going to take up more space.

*

Most of all, *Sport* grew closer to the IIML—the International Institute of Modern Letters at Te Herenga Waka—Victoria University of Wellington. If anyone wants a pragmatic answer to the question 'Can creative writing be taught?', this book is it. The first issues of *Sport* were full of unknown writers who had recently done Bill's undergraduate course—Dinah Hawken, Elizabeth Knox, Jenny Bornholdt, Barbara Anderson . . . and a few years later those were our leading writers. As the undergraduate course became an MA class of 10, then under Damien Wilkins 20 then 30 students per year, those numbers flowed through to *Sport*. Pip Adam, Airini Beautrais, Hera Lindsay Bird, Eleanor Catton, Tayi Tibble and Ashleigh Young are just half a dozen of the new names that appear in this book.

My first connection with Bill's course was before my job at VUP. In 1983 I was a teaching assistant in the English Department struggling with an unfinishable MA thesis comparing Seamus Heaney and A.R. Ammons (a publishing job with deadlines saved me) and Bill asked me to help assess the folios. It was really hard because there were no other opinions to benchmark against. Then he asked me to write a reader's report on a collection of short stories by a New Zealand postmodernist. I gave it a thumbs-down. I guess I passed the audition.

It seems to me now that my involvement with this university's creative writing course—writing assessments of the folios in 1983 then every year since 1985—has been at the heart of everything I've done. That's nearly 40 years of Novembers devoted solely to reading the best work that those writers can do inside the best workshop in the world, and reading it without any of the usual crutches like covers, blurbs, track record, publisher imprints and genre signifiers. I feel like Shift in *The Absolute Book*: periodically reduced to a condition of radical innocence, having to learn everything all over again.

And *Sport*, it seems to me, has been a practical application of that editorial negative capability. Over the years, it has been an exercise in open-hearted reading, extended to an at times exhausting number and range of submissions from across

Aotearoa New Zealand, and producing both a record and a prefiguring of the literature of this place.

*

A Game of Two Halves finds room for about 15% of the million or so words that were in the 15 issues from 2005 to 2019. Reading all of those pages last summer was fascinating. I remembered everything, and still liked it all, and found it painful to leave so much on the bench. I based my selections on how immediately rereading each story, poem or essay rekindled the excitement I had felt when I read it the first time. I tried not to second-guess myself.

Some of my favourite things are the longer stories: Eleanor Catton's chilling 'Descent from Avalanche', published shortly after her first book, *The Rehearsal*, and not reprinted until now; but equally the stories by Cate Palmer, Maria Samuela and Sylvan Thomson, whose first books we keenly await.

And the poetry is amazing. If *Sport* struggled with anything it was how to do justice to the extraordinary number of excellent poets who have been writing here over the past 15 years. In hindsight, I wonder whether we tried to squeeze too many poems into some issues, or too few poems by too many poets. Here, the mostly solo poems shine.

Several writers get two pieces, because I couldn't resist, and one gets three. Altogether, and with due modesty, this is a staggeringly rich offering. Huge thanks to all of the writers who have sent us their work over the years, and to those who have allowed us to reprint it in this book.

*

Early this year, when I was asking myself whether it was a good idea to resurrect *Sport* after a gap year—could we go from publishing *Sport* every six months, to every year, to when it was ready?—I looked at a copy of *Sport 47*, the vibrant pink issue edited by Tayi Tibble. That was fun. That was different. But did it make sense to go on doing it that way, reinventing *Sport* every year? When would it stop being *Sport*?

I have regrets—all year I have been on the verge of changing my mind—but it is time. Our collective energies at VUP will now go into the books we're publishing, especially by new and emerging writers, and into pushing our boundaries out with anthologies: beginning with 2020's *Monsters in the Garden: An Anthology of Aotearoa New Zealand Science Fiction and Fantasy*, edited by Elizabeth Knox and David Larsen; continuing with *Middle Distance: Long Stories of Aotearoa New Zealand*, edited by Craig Gamble and published alongside *A Game of Two Halves*; and looking forward to a book about animals in 2022. And after that? You tell us. Send us your ideas. Send us your work.

*

And now it is time for

THE SECOND HALF

Pip Adam

The Kiss

At six o'clock on the morning of the sixteenth of December, the soldiers of Echo Company woke in Dili, showered, dressed in civilian clothes and made their way to the vehicles that would take them to the plane that would take them home. There was towel-flicking and a shared feeling of excitement and joy. They had packed the night before and their rifles would travel separately. In Darwin they changed planes and boarded an Air New Zealand flight. They laughed at the safety instructions, ate small bags of peanuts and drank complimentary beer. Several air hostesses declined to give their phone numbers. The flight home was noisy; there were jokes and horse-play, head-rubbing and play-fighting. In all the noise a few soldiers looked out the windows at the clouds and felt their eyelids drop.

As the plane flew over Canterbury some of the men shouted out landmarks that became apparent as they continued their descent. From the plane they could see the airport and a large sign saying 'Christchurch'. They couldn't see the crowd of family and friends in the arrival area, but they felt it. On the ground, and as the seatbelt sign went off, they felt the weight of the people waiting for them. They disembarked, saying thank you to the air hostesses.

Before the doors through to the arrival area there was a duty free shop. The first off the plane stopped at the shop and the others, one by one, five by five, fell in. Recognisable as soldiers by their short haircuts and tidy jeans, they tried on sunglasses and looked at bottles of spirits. The married soldiers smelled perfume and asked the women behind the counter about them. Three soldiers, almost the last off the plane, stood at the entance of the shop until they saw another soldier looking at a shelf of aftershave. Wyatt, a broad man who wanted to be a chef and was everyone's first pick for anything needing weight and force, joked that even the most expensive aftershave wouldn't help the soldier have sex with anything resembling a woman. The others laughed. They started looking at the aftershaves, joking about the names, spraying each other with the testers. Lennon wore his glasses. Knight, the third man, called him 'my blind foot soldier' when they were on patrol. Lennon said he was fine unless it was raining or humid which, Wyatt pointed out, was all the time in East Timor. Knight said, 'Exactly, a blind assassin—stay in front of me.' The first soldiers stayed as long as possible, then began to disperse into the arrival area. The soldiers left in the duty free shop heard the shouts and cheers and screams of excitement. They looked toward them as the shop fell silent for a moment.

As they walked through, Wyatt was grabbed by his mother and sisters who covered him with kisses and hugs, whoops, small jumps and claps. Knight was met by several women who called themselves his good friends; they hugged and kissed him, except the ones who were in the army as well, these women stood back, shook his hand, then walked into sportsfield hugs. They thought this meant more than thrusting their chests forward and wet-kissing his cheek. Knight didn't.

Lennon was the last to come through the double doors, his mother was there. His girlfriend ran to him, grabbed his face in both hands and kissed him on the mouth. She looked odd. He'd forgotten about her. He'd seen her name on the letters she sent, called her a couple of times. He'd mentioned her name and had her name mentioned to him in strip bars and mess tents but he'd forgotten about her—the her that stood in front of him now, smiling broadly and wiping tears away like something he was sure she'd seen on television. She was something waiting for him—what could be done with her now? He kept his distance. Lennon wasn't frightened of anything but he kept his distance, unsure of what she could tell or smell or sense. He smiled at her carefully from beside his mother. Wyatt and Knight came over, said something about a party in the afternoon. Wyatt was going to have breakfast with his family and Knight said he was going to have sex with one, or more, of the women. They left.

Eventually everyone left. Lennon kept saying, I just need to see so-and-so, and ducking off but eventually everyone had left and he was there with them so he said, 'Shall we go for some breakfast? I could murder some food.' He would travel with his girlfriend, his mother would come in her own car.

On the way to the restaurant there was a long silence. Lennon put his hand on his girlfriend's thigh and said, 'Good to see you.' She glowed and beamed, 'Oh Mike.' He didn't have to say anything else or touch her again for the rest of the journey.

They talked at breakfast, told him someone had died, someone else had got married and the weather had been warmer than last year. Did he like his mother's new haircut? It was shorter. Lennon ate and looked at his watch and the clock on the wall behind his girlfriend. He paid the bill and met them in the carpark. His mother said goodbye. He thought he would mess around in town until the party but his girlfriend held out her car keys and asked if he wanted to drive. She meant back to her place, to drop his stuff off, and he realised she expected him to stay there. He was going to crash at the party or catch a lift back to barracks but he didn't tell her that. It could still turn out that way, but not if he told her. He hadn't driven for nearly a year. He'd been awake for almost twenty-four hours, traveled hundreds of kilometres and she wanted him to drive, so she could feel like a war-bride. It would get him into town and there wouldn't be a fight. Concurrent activity, he thought, eating and marching. It was money in the bank, easy money.

At her flat he took another, longer shower and dressed in the humid dampness of the bathroom—blind. She offered to take him to the party and he said no, Wyatt was picking him up. She said okay, and looked out the window. He told her not to start and she said sorry, it's just that he only just got home. He said just don't fucking start and she said yeah, she wouldn't start, she had stuff to do. She had no money. He could tell. She was listed as a dependant on his record. They'd lived together for a year in the housing area. She'd left while he was in Bougainville for a week. She'd taken lots but left more. She took the cat. Weeks later, when they were back together, it had to be put down after it broke a hip. She got another cat. He offered to look after it when she moved into this place. He told her to get a collar on it because they shot cats in barracks and she'd said you have to keep it inside for a couple of weeks. It disappeared within days and she didn't say anything about it. He suspected she was saving it up and about a month before he went to East Timor he was right. He'd wanted to go out for dinner and a movie with someone and she said she didn't think it was appropriate for him to go. He said he was going and don't start, and she said, 'What about the cat?' He took forty dollars out of his jeans pocket and left it beside the basin for her. She'd put on weight. Shitloads of weight. Every time he went away she put on weight. When he got back she put on more. She looked fat. One thing about Indonesian women—they weren't fat.

Wyatt arrived fifteen minutes prior to parade with Knight in the back seat, slightly drunk in the arms of one of the women from the airport; she was also quite drunk. Lennon saw his girlfriend see the woman with Knight and as she opened her mouth to say something he said, 'She's a hooker. It's only strippers and hookers at the party.' As he jumped in the front seat his girlfriend told him to text her and she'd meet him in town and something else as Wyatt drove him away from her.

In the car Knight said the woman he was with gave good head. She hit him on the arm and sat slightly taller. Wyatt asked how was brunch and he and Lennon laughed, saying, 'Fuuuuck!' and shaking their heads. What was up with them, they asked. It was doing Lennon's head in, he said, and Wyatt agreed it was also doing his head in. Knight said a surf would be good as they passed the beach and Lennon said surfing was a pussy sport and Knight was a pussy. Knight said it was better to be a pussy than pussy-whipped like, for instance, Lennon. Lennon leaned over and slapped him. Knight slapped him back. Lennon told Knight not to make him come over there and turned back to the front of the car. There were people on the golf course, men and women playing golf like it was an ordinary Saturday afternoon. Wyatt pulled into the mall at Shirley so they could all buy alcohol. Knight bought the woman a lollipop. The mall was full of people

Christmas shopping. Tinsel and snow hung off everything. The woman with Knight stopped to try on sunglasses and said, 'Buy me some sunglasses, Knight.' Lennon said, 'Buy me some sunglasses, Knight,' and told Knight to sort it out, for Christ's sake. Knight said quietly to Lennon that he, Lennon, didn't understand just how good the head was she gave and handed her a fifty dollar note. The woman kissed Knight on the cheek, took the money and, while the men were in the bottle store, didn't buy sunglasses.

The party was on Bealey Avenue, a long road with tall trees along the middle of it. It was daylight when they arrived. On the front lawn of the row of flats Kimbell was chasing Wyman and Miles was yelling at Davids. Some other soldiers were sitting in the sun, drinking. Wyatt, Knight and Lennon nodded at the men on the lawn and Knight, with his arm round the woman, tried to catch Wyman as he ran past. Wyman yelled something like 'pussy' at him, so Knight joined Kimbell in the chase. The woman who was with Knight stood and laughed and opened one of Knight's beers and drank it.

Inside the flat the curtains were drawn and the stereo played loud music. There were soldiers in every room; lying on couches, sitting on the floor—all drinking. The host, Doe, was in the kitchen with his hand up his girlfriend's skirt. When he saw Lennon and Wyatt arrive he smiled and slapped them on the back. His girlfriend pulled down her skirt and emptied a bag of chips into a bowl. Doe led them to the living room where they were welcomed with a volley of hoots. Someone made room for them on the couch and they sat and drank and no one said much to anyone except quotes from *Full Metal Jacket* and *Terminator*. When it finally got dark, the lounge was cleared a bit and the strippers arrived. Doe's girlfriend and the woman with Knight joined in. Lennon was offered several women but said he was home now and everyone said 'pussy-whipped' and pretended to be on leashes. Doe's girlfriend chose one of the strippers and Doe said for everyone to look after themselves for a couple of hours. Someone shouted more like a couple of minutes and Doe emptied the bottle he was drinking from and threw it so it hit the wall and exploded.

Around nine, Lennon's cellphone rang. It was his girlfriend. He let it ring. He turned and asked if Wyatt wanted to go into town. Wyatt said sure, maybe, in a bit. Lennon stood up and went down the hall to find a quiet room to ring her back. The first one he tried had people in it, and the second, but the third was empty and dark. He closed the door behind him, keeping it dark, and rested his weight on the door. Sudden movement coming toward him startled Lennon. The man, who he couldn't make out, said, 'You came.' Hands pulled Lennon's face close and kissed him. The hands held his head, his neck, his jaw, pulling him closer and further into the kiss. Then pulled back and pushed Lennon away. Cold rushed in. Lennon's phone rang green and illuminated but the man was gone. Lennon closed his eyes and felt it all over him, again and again—the stillness of the room. Quiet and alone—it was all he wanted. Someone was calling his name from another room, Wyatt, asking where the fuck he was and had anyone seen Lennon.

Although the rest of the house was only dimly lit, it was blinding. The right thing occurred to Lennon—to run from the room shouting that some faggot tried to kiss him. All eyes were on him, saying, Wyatt's looking for you and slapping him, shouting 'pussy-whipped' and saying she could smell him up to no good. Wyatt was with Knight when Lennon found him, on the front lawn holding his cellphone to his ear. When Lennon saw them he wiped his mouth with the back of his hand. It took him like falling—the sensation that hung on him pushed deep inside, filling him, trying to escape out every pore. Wyatt raised his eyes, pushed the phone into Lennon's chest and told him to fucking sort it out. It was her. She'd tried his phone and couldn't get through so she'd called the barracks and someone had given her Wyatt's cellphone number. Lennon looked at the empty sky. He said he'd been trying to call her from a quiet room but she was engaged so he'd stayed there for a bit and tried again and dozed off and way too much. She wanted to meet him in town.

She was out with a few friends. Did he want to meet at this bar? Wyatt was standing beside him drinking his last beer. Lennon asked if he wanted to go to the bar. Wyatt said sure, yeah. Knight said, 'Don't fucking humour him, he's got to sort that bitch out.' Wyatt said he was out of beer so he needed to go somewhere and Knight could talk—where was his missus? Knight said she wasn't his missus and he told her to go home when he found her and Doe's missus having sex with about ten guys watching. Wyatt pissed himself laughing. Knight said he would go to the bar, not because he wanted to but to show Wyatt what a fuckwit he was, and that he, Knight, wouldn't be alone for long, but Wyatt would be alone forever. Wyatt said he would rather be alone forever than not get invited to his girlfriend's live sex show. Knight said shut up and for fuck's sake hurry up, Lennon, if they were going let's fucking go, for Christ's sake.

Lennon got off the phone and handed it back to Wyatt without saying anything. They began to walk away from the party when Wyatt said, 'Where's your fucking jacket, Lennon?' Lennon had taken it off inside somewhere. He walked back over the lawn, picking his way over the soldiers who were lying there. On patrol, at night, no one slept until it was their turn and then they slept well. During the day, through the strangle of Indonesian bush, each man watched the one directly in front, never needing to look back or to the side. When the militia opened fire they retreated and hid together in the small spaces they found down low and were quiet. He should find the faggot and tear him apart. Davids and Wyman leant on either side of the door, beers in hand. They nodded and met his eye. There were soldiers everywhere inside. He had to push past to get to the lounge. They were pushing on him, leaning on him, heavy and drunk. He said sort it out a few times and with every push on him his body swam and the margins where his skin stopped broke like shrapnel had opened them. When the shooting stopped several of them were crying. They crawled out of their low places to find Deering missing. Lennon's body was leaking out his skin and the pushing and the leaning was leaking into him. Washing in like a tide and he was getting fuller and fuller and could feel every pore of the skin on his face.

Miller was on his jacket, a topless woman in a g-string was on Miller. Lennon leaned down to pull his jacket out and his cheek grazed the woman's breast. He turned and kissed it. She held his head close to her. Someone grabbed his arm; it was Wyatt come to see where he'd got to. Lennon turned quickly. Wyatt looked him in the eye and said, 'Have you got your jacket?' Lennon looked around to make sure no one else had seen and pulled his jacket out from under Miller. On the way out Lennon's girlfriend called Wyatt's phone again and he told her they were on their way and they would be about half an hour. As he hung up he told her to lose his fucking number. Knight met them outside and asked where the fuck Lennon had got to. Wyatt raised his eyes and said let's walk to the bar.

They walked and kicked things and jumped over things and hit things but none of them were looking for a fight. Lennon's phone rang, he didn't answer it. Wyatt said, 'Oh fuck, Lennon, she'll just call me—for fuck's sake.' Lennon said, 'All right,' told them to go ahead and pretended to answer his phone. Knight said, 'I'd do her.' Wyatt looked at him like you've got to be joking and Knight said, 'She must be fucking amazing for Lennon to put up with all this shit.' They both laughed and Lennon caught up with them.

'Makes you want to go to war,' Wyatt said. Knight laughed and Lennon looked around and said he'd get the drinks. There were dress pants everywhere; men their age with stupid civvie haircuts drinking stupid drinks and chatting up ugly hairdressers and sales assistants. The doorman had said he didn't want any trouble. Knight said, 'Mate, there's only three of us.' The doorman had let them in, repeating he didn't want any trouble. It all operated below them—everything that goes on. Broken shoelaces, lost jobs, car insurance. Not by choice. It was just where they lived now—a couple of feet above it all. Lennon's girlfriend waved at him as he waited at the bar.

Back at her flat, in the dark of her bedroom, Lennon went down on her and she came. Then they fucked and he came. He held her as she got heavier and heavier and then he went to the kitchen to get a drink. He opened the fridge and something fell off the door. It was a magnet he'd sent her from Bali; a carved wooden fish. He turned it over with his foot. The note he'd sent with it was on the floor as well. She'd cut it out like a speech bubble and stuck it to the front of the fish with cellotape. He didn't need to read it because he knew what it said. A car went past outside on the street and he caught himself in the reflection of the glass door, skinny and naked and spent. He could leave. People left people all the time but he wanted her to go. He tried to make it complicated, but it wasn't. He picked up his clothes and dressed. The door was deadlocked. His girlfriend walked toward the bathroom, naked and rubbing her face. She looked at Lennon and said, 'They're by the phone,' and closed the bathroom door.

It was a clear night. The sun would be up in a few hours, until then he would walk around. He'd get some breakfast and call Wyatt for a ride out to barracks. It was what he'd wanted from the start. It was all he ever wanted. He walked past houses and pubs and through a cemetery until he came to the river. He sat beside it and watched it move. The air was still and held his face. As the dark water bit at the shore he ran every man's face through his mind. Trying to match jaws with the one that had touched his. He thought of their hands and then their hands holding their rifles. He eliminated some, shivering in the pre-dawn. He could feel the indent of those hands on the back of his neck. The light had fallen on Deering's face. It shouldn't have but after they'd looked and looked, in a place that was previously dull, a light fell on Deering's calm, still face, where he lay alone and quiet. Knight had said, 'For fuck's sake,' and turned away. Wyatt had vomited, resting his whole body weight on his rifle as he bent over. Out of all of them, Lennon wished it could be Deering. He ran through every man's torso, their chests. He mixed torsos with faces and hands. Someone's right hand with another's left— Deering's head three feet from the rest of him. Carrying him back to camp, holding his head, his neck, his jaw. He went over it all. Trying to remember every time he had touched or been touched by someone in Echo Company.

When Lennon arrived back at Doe's flat there were still soldiers everywhere, asleep now. He walked through the house, through room after room of sleeping soldiers until he found the room where it had happened. It was still empty. He closed the door behind him. The first of the dawn broke through the Venetian blinds as he lay on the bed. He teetered on sleep and felt the weight of everything above him—gravity pushing it down on him. That faggot was bound to come back and when he did Lennon would kill him. Something wrong until now slipped and was almost right. Everything rose in him as he remembered. In his mind he heard Deering breathe—in and out. He breathed in what was left of it. He thought about the fish and the note and how much he'd meant it when he wrote it. From the bottom of his heart he'd meant it and for what he imagined was forever.

Pip Adam

Andy—don't keep your distance

When I was about 20, we knew a guy called Andrew Moore. He made a skateboard magazine called *Yeah Bo* and played in bands. One night he was on stage setting up and my boyfriend called out, 'Andy! Don't keep your distance!' It was a clever joke. A knowing joke. It was 1990. *Songs from the Front Lawn* had only come out the year before. I was impressed—with him for making the joke and with all of us for getting it. The joke reached out of our orbit a bit, it wasn't an obvious one to make. As I remember we were in some grungy basement and Andy's band was loud and destructive and we'd be walking round for days with the dodgy sound mix ringing in our ears. The Front Lawn were artists. I didn't always use that word as a compliment and at that time I felt a certain tension between being impressed with Harry Sinclair and Don McGlashan—they of the short film masterpiece *The Lounge Bar* and concerts which bordered on performance art—and being suspicious. Who had told them they could do this, I thought? Who had told them they could do this in New Zealand? We muddled on casually, we didn't care, we didn't do things ambitiously. *Songs from the Front Lawn* was experimental and clever and polished. 'Andy' was a beautiful song about loss and money. Like the song itself said, though, at that time listening to our weighty, loud, painful music, I thought, None of this is going to last. I imagined everything would fade. Especially, I thought, the Front Lawn's deceivingly slight pop song would make no mark on my life.

Probably the joke is what I thought about more than the song, in the intervening years. Maybe the joke kept the song alive in my thoughts. What did we mean? Making a joke of calling out to a live young man in the words of a song that calls out to a dead young man? At times I thought it was because we knew nothing of death. But that's ridiculous, we were soaked in death—friends OD-ed, friends had car accidents, one person I knew swam too far out from an eastern bay beach and never came back. We knew death—often in those awful years it felt like we knew nothing but death. Was it a death-defying joke, I wondered? Were we laughing in the face of death? Or was it just a recognition that we were the walking dead—that really it could all be over now . . . or now . . . or now. And why not call out to the living as if they were dead?

When I came to write a book about rich people and Auckland, that line about 'making money out of money' came back to me and the view from North Head. *The New Animals* is so much about that harbour. Takapuna Beach felt like a strange and powerful place to me. We lived out east—the whole North Shore was a bit of a mystery. We would go to Long Bay once a year to play in the surf and ride on the ETA miniature train—there was a flying fox. Takapuna Beach is a flat, light-sanded bay bordered by cliffs and rocks you could walk out on. It was vast compared with our short, shelly eastern bay beaches.

So, I listened to 'Andy' for the first time in years and cried and then I listened to it again and again and again. I was so confused. How could such a simple wee pop song bear all this attention? Because, I decided, it's a fucking great piece of art.

During this time of intensive listening, my kid—who was about eight at the time—and I were driving and they said, 'I always start crying before he even starts singing.' I've always been jealous of the way musicians get to use wordless noise to create tone. I talked to David Long on Wednesday; he plays slide guitar on 'Andy'. He was in Six Volts at the time. I was trying to work out what the instruments were in the song.

'Is that a French horn?'

'It'll be a euphonium if it's anything.'

'Why's it so sad?' I asked. I meant the music. David explained that the instruments are played in a naïve way and then the bowed bass comes in and it's kind of devastating. And I realised the specificity of the sadness. Not just sad—innocence visited by tragedy. Fiction tries to do this too—pay attention to the particularity of emotion and find the correct order of words to express it. But imagine having all those instruments to back up your words. David told me Harry Sinclair is playing a concertina. I googled it, it's a small accordion. If you listen closely you can hear the valves being pushed and released and the breathing of the bellows—like lungs.

McGlashan is famously a percussionist and although there are glockenspiel and blocks and cymbals in the orchestration, all the instruments seem to do percussive work in the song—producing beat as well as melody. I love the way this sort of mimics walking. I always imagine the speaker of the song walking up and down that smooth-sanded beach. I thought about it lots when I was writing the walking and swimming parts of *The New Animals*. I realised I didn't have to keep writing—'she is still swimming'—I could show it in the rhythm of the language.

And then there's the lyrics. Don McGlashan said of this song: 'Yeah this is really about my brother who we lost when I was about 15 . . . it's not really an attempt to create a story too far away from that.' This attention to one close event. The genius of the late, casual, easy reveal: 'If you were still alive you'd be just short of 33.' The repetition of 'Andy', after the line explaining 'the rest of the family won't even mention your name'. The lyrics use the change to Auckland as its flashpoint. And we take on that rage for a moment, the rich kids, the buildings made out of glass, only to be cut down by the quotidian and now heavy, heavy almost throwaway line, 'If only you could see your home town now.' The lyrical genius of McGlashan is often this reframing of the everyday. It never feels fussed over. Everything comes seamlessly out of everything else. There's no grand gesture.

On Wednesday 16 September 2016, I walked round Auckland in the footsteps of the characters in *The New Animals*. Around 4pm I took a bus over the harbour bridge. I got off the bus at Shore City realising I was going to get to Devonport too early for Tommy's dinner with his parents. I walked down to Takapuna Beach and sat and watched. I'd decided Elodie would swim past. It was a way out of the harbour. Not the only one but a way that meant she could hear Takapuna Beach waking up. It was a beautiful day and it hit me again. The power of the song to evoke the place. The genius of choosing this place—the happy kids, the cliffs, the change in the architecture that surrounds it, the tininess of us and ours in the horizon. And it cemented in me the conviction that 'Andy' is our national anthem of loss.

Michele Amas

Daughter

The Steeple Chase

Get off my back
daughter
this is not dancing
you have sharpened your spurs.

Get off my back
you are giving me
the fingers
behind my head.

Get off my back
you have me pinned
against the ropes
the ref is on his tea break.

Get off my back
I am not carrying you
to my grave.

Get off my back
from up there you are
taller than me.

I will not race you
to the finish line
race you to freedom
I will not count down.

I am not your competitor
daughter

you signed me up
without my permission.

I am not your
leap frog.

GOLDEN DELICIOUS

She is sunny
she is sunny side up, my girl
running to meet me.
The other girls look lumpy
 with their slumping shoulders
dyed hair and regrowth.
But my one is a beautiful apple
rolling down the drive
out past the school gates.

BLAME

It is my fault
her toenails
her thighs
the hideous
hair on her arms.

My fault
she has too many books
it's making her schoolbag
fat.

Fat is my fault
I don't feed her
correctly, don't limit
her intake.

My fault
the failed marriage
I am simply
unlovable.

No money is my fault
what sort of grown-up
is an actress.

No brothers or sisters
my biggest fault
an unpardonable crime.

BABIES

It's a feast or famine
with sperm
wouldn't you say?
Some days they can lap at your feet
other days are shorter.

I see flakes of babies
on hands
on shirt fronts
on benches
on car back seats

The old guy, toothless and cursing
wearing socks and jandals
is full of babies.

The college boy
has left babies
on his sheets this morning.

The Unborn Ones

The brothers and sisters
how stupid of them
to leave it up to me.

Stupid too
the German psychologist's
advice.

One child will now
bury her parents.

The brothers and sisters
salty baby mammals
have returned to the sea

turning into little grey whales.

Alliteration

Bullshit, she says
and *I better bloody not be.*
I watch her b's bounce off
the breakfast table,
stinging little orange and black
bumbles
stick to my hair.

THE TXT

Mum come upstairz
my throats 2 sore
2 call out 2 u.

In firemother red
I take the stairs
two at a time.

Barbara Anderson

from **Getting There: An Autobiography**

I was fond of dentists as a child. They gave drama to a structured and overprotected life. The first one I met, Mr Tonks, started it with what I thought was a haze of exciting words. 'Open wide while I look for caries.'

I thought he meant fairies. Clutching the arms of the chair in an effort to keep calm I counted the power lines beyond the square sky of the window above his head. Sixteen there were, counting the more frail telephone lines drooping lower and ending in mysterious white china cups, but never a fairy in sight.

Later I was moved to Mr Bob Whyte in King Street. Why I have no idea and probably didn't ask. I was a vague and dreamy child with hay fever, unlike my brother David who was spirited and demanded answers.

Mr Whyte was kind and jokey and told me I was brave which was a surprise. Squeaky clean in his high-necked jacket he was loved by all, including his receptionist Miss Protheroe (NHRN) who sat behind a desk in a starched white cap like an upturned boat, gave you appointments and pined away while Mr Whyte flourished and made his patients laugh. You couldn't help it.

Another thing of interest near Mr Whyte's surgery was the ivy-covered house across the road. Half hidden behind its privet hedge, the house where I was born gave little away. For years I kept hoping for some reaction, some interesting memory dredged up from the time when David and I lived there and Colin was a baby. Nothing happened. Only three memories remain from King Street, Hastings: Miss Morris's mother, the garage across the road, and my fairies.

The last one puzzled my practical mother. I was head down, bottom up, searching among the pansies one day when she appeared to be greeted by my wail, 'You've frightened her away.' This interest in fairies came from my four small books, illustrated and written by an English woman called Cicely Mary Barker. I carried *Flower Fairies of the Spring, Summer, Autumn* or *Winter* long before I could read. None of them were New Zealand fairies but then nothing ever was in the books of my childhood. I studied fairies endlessly, knew each one off by heart and had my favourites, such as the reckless Thistle Fairy swinging about on top of his purple cushion, or the red baby-faced Spindle Berry Fairy shaking his berried branch with force. All the boy fairies had pointed ears, so technically, I suppose, they were elves, but who cared. The only one I never warmed to was the Wild Rose of England. Dressed in a long pink robe with a crown of roses, she was, I felt, beyond me as she sat staring straight ahead on her high branch, holding a gold staff in her hand.

Each fairy painting had its own verse which meant nothing to me before I could read, and was a sad disappointment when I could. The Burdock Fairy remains, washed up on some useless tide of memory.

Wee little hooks on each brown little burr
(Mind where you're going, O Madam and Sir!)

What on earth was a Burdock? Again, it didn't matter as I searched for Snowdrop or Primrose or Bluebell fairies among my father's Jerusalem artichokes.

I learned quite soon that not every child believed in fairies, let alone saw them. It was a shock at the time but I learned to keep quiet on the subject. Fairies, apparently, were sissy, or worse, babyish.

Miss Morris and Mother (my second memory) lived next door. Mother had white hair and was old. I had worked out that the two went together and found it vaguely interesting, but not much.

One day Miss Morris came to ask my mother if she would like to come next door and see Mother before they took her away because she looked so beautiful.

My mother, who always looked beautiful, said that was very kind but thank you no, she had a friend coming to tea and she didn't think Barbara would want to . . .

Miss Morris had a jar of humbugs for boys and girls on her desk.

'Yes, I do.'

Mum looked doubtful. 'Are you sure, Bub?'

'Yes.'

I took Miss Morris's hand and trotted beside her up the shingle path to Mother's house, through the shadowy hall, past the tall clock which bonged the hours away and into Mother's bedroom which was dark, with pulled curtains. The only light was a dim bedside lamp beneath a pink lampshade with silky tassels. On the bed lay Mother. I stared at the face, the closed eyes, the stillness. Something was badly wrong.

'Why's she there?' I whispered.

'Mother has passed away. They'll be coming to take her away soon.'

Worse and worse. What? Where? Why?

'I knew you'd like to see her, dear.'

'No, no, no,' I yelled and ran screeching down the path.

My mother apologised. Miss Morris forgave me. The humbugs continued.

My last memory of the Frederick Street house involved Mr Hursthouse's Garage across the road from our house. I suppose there were cars for sale behind the vast windows, but the thing I loved was a brightly-coloured placard standing upright on the floor near the front. Watched by two cows and a pig, a 1920s roadster sped along a country road, its carefree young driver laughing at the wheel, his scarf flying in the wind. Beneath were words.

'What does it say?' I asked my brother David, who could read but was already car mad, and didn't like me much anyway.

'Ask Dad, dopey.'

I did so.

It is better to be five minutes late in this world than fifty years too soon in the next, intoned my father.

'But what does it say?'

'You'll understand when you're older.'

More puzzlement.

One of Katherine Mansfield's stories I read twenty years later tells of a child's excitement when her family moved into a new house, a dramatic day which involved trailing up the long hill from Wellington city to the developing suburb of Karori.

Nothing like that for the Wrights. Our new house in Robert Street was only a few blocks away from our one in King Street. Hastings, a small country town in 1930, was, according to Grandmother Jackson, 'flat as your hat. Hadn't a hill to bless itself.'

The first people who saw the new house were our grandmothers. They shared the honorary title of Nana, with a long 'a', as in Nana in Peter Pan, or worse, Émile Zola's Nana. Both our Nanas were strong women and I don't know why they settled for the same name as a large hairy dog in a frilly cap pretending to be a Nanny, or Émile Zola's mid-nineteenth-century prostitute.

The Nanas' reactions to 609 Roberts Street differed. Nana Jackson said there was plenty of room out the back for a henhouse and Mum must keep White Leghorns which were the best layers. Nana Wright said there would be more room for us all to frolic.

Fat chance.

For as long as I can remember I was aware that we were not a family who frolicked.

The house at number 609 Roberts Street remains for me as a series of spaces. The best one was the so-called Doll's Cupboard, a small child-sized place behind an odd-shaped door in my bedroom where my People lived when fairies had departed. All of them—Jane, Bunty, Josie, Molly and Bella with the long yellow legs—were never babies. They were not fed or cuddled or put to bed or woken up. They waited in dark nothingness, flat on their backs, with arms at their sides and feet facing outwards, ready to swing into instant Adventures when I opened the door.

I had little interest in the sitting room downstairs except in winter, when the fire gave one of the few sources of heat in the house, and we were allowed to warm our behinds in front of it before sprinting upstairs to bed. No one was ever allowed to poke the fire except Mum. For years I thought there must be some skill in keeping a fire going, a skill known to Mum's Jackson tribe but not the Wrights. I discovered years later any fool can do it. Another myth gone poof.

Grandfather Wright's bookcase and its books now stood against one wall, the King Street sofa and chairs were still covered in flowery linen, padded window seats stood either side of the fireplace, and always, inevitably, a vase shaped like a miniature cattle trough sat on the left hand of the mantlepiece, filled with dahlias, or gladioli, or a Mixed Bowl. Troughs, with chicken wire crumpled inside to support the flowers, were the chosen vases for mixed bowls in 609 and Mum's were much admired. She was good at mixed bowls as well as fires. The thing I liked best in the room was a Tiffany vase, which also came from Grandfather, its curved rainbow colours sleeping inside, definitely not for touching, nor for flowers.

Blinds were always drawn unless people were in the sitting room. The sun was Mum's enemy: it faded the covers if she wasn't careful, and made the flowers wilt sooner.

The dining room, besides the table, chairs and Dad's sofa, held a wind-up gramophone with a cabinet in which were stored His Master's Voice 78s, including our favourites: *Tiptoe, through the tulips, through the tulips, through the tulips . . .* ; *The Laughing Policeman*, who did nothing but laugh so hard that we did too and once Colin wet his pants; and *The Cats' Chronicle*, which prints all pussy cats' news.

And best of all, Frank Crumit and his bum songs. Bums were rude, we knew that, but Frank's bums were alright. They were Americans and were also called 'hobos' and sang about a land that's far away in The Big Rock Candy Mountains. We sang along with Frank.

In the Big Rock Candy Mountains you never wash your socks,
And little streams of alcohol come a'tricklin' down the rocks.
The brakemen have to tip their hats and the railroad bulls are blind,
There's a lake of stew and of whisky too.

You can paddle all around 'em in a big canoe
In the Big Rock Candy Mountains.

And his theme song:

Alleluia, I'm a bum,
Alleluia, bum again
Alleluia, give us a handout
To revive us again.

Innocent as a nest of singing birds we sang along with them all, including what I discovered later to be a bowdlerised version of *Abdul Abulbul Amir.*

Beneath the windows which overlooked the garden stood another bookcase which, beside 'ordinary' books, held dictionaries. These were for looking up words at meal times. 'Knowledge,' said Grandfather Wright, and probably someone else before him, 'is knowing where to look it up.' None of which made any sense for any of us until we could read. Before that was an atlas or two and *Brewer's Dictionary of Phrase and Fable* where I found *Famous Last Words*, the most memorable of which was St Lawrence's, whose martyrdom took the form of being roasted on a gridiron, and ran thus—

This side enough is toasted
so turn me, tyrant, eat,
and see whether raw or roasted
I make the better meat.

Another friend was *Fowler's English Usage*, which was first published the year I was born therefore worth picking up. Dad read me H.W. Fowler's dedication to his brother who 'died, age 47, of tuberculosis contracted during service with the B.E.F. in 1915–16'. He writes, 'I think of it as it should have been, with its prolixities docked, its dullnesses enlived, its fads eliminated, its truths multiplied.'

I liked that, and remember I nagged Dad about 'prolixities', but didn't get far.

When I could read, I discovered that the problem with dictionaries is that you have to know how to spell the word required before you can look it up and find its meaning. There are fair traps in learning.

Beside the dining room ran a long narrow place called the servery, at the far end of which was the smallest space of all, smaller even than the Dolls' cupboard. This was called the water safe and projected beyond the outside wall. It opened above a shiny wooden slab which housed three large bins for sacks of sugar, flour, odds and ends.

The safe had fly-proof netting all around the servery. Shelves surrounded the shallow square pond, into which water ran all day and then disappeared out down the plughole. It never stopped; cool water lapped around a damp brick on which sat a blue plate with daisies and on that sat a pound of butter which never melted, not even in the nineties, Mum told us. The safe's shelves were lined with things which might 'go off' if Mum wasn't careful, but she was.

Years later the Fridgidaire arrived and there was more excitement as Mr Jones wheeled it in to install this miracle, with its ability to make squares of ice enclosing tiny trapped bubbles, its promise of ice creams on tap. Mum was relieved when the door opened and the Fridge swallowed up meat and puddings which sat on shelves. Above was the doughnut-shaped top where the engine was. Periodically its mechanism gave a convulsive shuddering rumble, then calmed down again. The fridge was Mum's friend but the safe was more interesting to me; the coolness of the brick in its square pond, the deep golden butter slab for spreading, the plums cooling and the sound of water falling. When I met the word 'plashing' I thought of the safe.

It was running when we came down each morning and was still running, cool and safe and endless, as we trailed up to bed. It could do this, we were told, because we had an 'Artesian bore'.

'A what?'

'You'll know when you're older.'
Colin loved it too.

On the dining-room side of the servery two huge meat covers hung one beneath the other. They were silvery grey and made of what Mum called pewter, another good word, though Mum says they were too big to be any use and took a lot of cleaning. Near them was a hatch through which food could be handed into the dining room. One of the few games the three of us played together was Slides. When the coast was clear we skidded onto the shelf beneath (with a leg up for Colin), wriggled through the slide, hit ground in the dining room, then ran around for another go. The idea being that someone must be in the wooden hatch at all times. It usually ended with us all singing along with *The Road to Vicksburg*, or one of Frank Crumit's other classics.

We were caught once or twice but the game continued for years.

Beyond the servery was the kitchen, which was of little interest. None of us was ever allowed to help Mum, let alone attempt cooking. Beyond that was a larder, notable for me because it was said I had swallowed a fly there. Another door led to the washhouse with its copper, which was lit from below and boiled its head off every Monday. When the wash was finished the floor was scrubbed with Pearson's sandsoap, which was again of great interest to me. Each slab had two tiny pictures on each of its sloping sides, like those vans which now carry sheets of glass. On one side a tiny lady tended a sick child, saying, 'I WISH I had used Pearson's Sandsoap.' On the other side an equally tiny, but happy lady holds a laughing child, saying, 'I'm GLAD I used Pearson's Sandsoap.'

Sometimes Wrightie came to help Mum on washing days. We all loved Wrightie and she loved us. It was she who translated the Pearson's sandsoap ladies for me before I could read. Near the end of the washing process the cool water was made blue by a little muslin bag containing a lump of solid blue Reckitts, which made your sheets 'whiter than white'. She also told us sad stories in the kitchen after she had finished in the washhouse. The three of us sat in a row on the kitchen linoleum and watched as Wrightie flopped herself in a wicker chair which crackled with fright as she landed. Then she began her stories, all of which had dreadful endings. One was about a little girl who fell in a boiling copper, which I begged for, then wept each time I heard it.

David would point at me in concerned but scornful tones, 'Look, Bub's crying,' and Wrightie would clutch me to her deep and loving bosom and tell me it was only a story, 'Just a story, dear.' Wrightie also read me the messages of advertisements for blue-bags: 'Whiter than White.' And another in which a bubble from a mouth says, 'Don't let Mrs Next Door Sniff at your Whites.'

We all knew Mondays were busy for Mum and Wrightie and we were not welcome in the washhouse. Nevertheless if Wrightie was on duty alone she would let me 'help', until one day a tiny white hand surfaced among swirling soap bubbles. Wrightie and I shrieked together. This time it was her warm wet sacking-apron which caught my terror. Even when she lifted the dripping object from the boiling cauldron with her wooden pole I wouldn't look despite her laugh. 'Look dear, just a poor wee shrunken glove that got in by mistake. It's now no use to man or beast.'

'No, no, no.'

'There, there, love—look, what's Wrightie got in her pocket?'

And out came a soft green jube dusted with damp and slightly hairy sugar.

Angela Andrews

White Saris
for my son

What I knew of their house
was a blue garage door,
kicked-in at the middle.
A buckling dent.

You approach a scene like that
with caution. It takes time
to know whether to pause
or hurry, head down.

Their glowing white saris
on this grey marble day.
Outside the buckled
door, a station wagon, black.

I was thinking of you. How you
will find out. The black suit
you will wear. How the feel
of your best white shirt could hurt.

How silk might hang
in a cold wardrobe. I pushed
you through those people.
I pushed you along the road.

Jane Arthur

Idiots

I've known people who decided
to carry their brokenness like strength

idiots

I'm a tree
I mean I'm tall, I sway

I don't say, treat me gently
No—I say, cool cool cool cool

I say, that sucks but I guess I'll survive it
or, that wind's really strong

but so are my roots, so are my thighs
my branches my lungs my leaves my capacity to wait things out

I can get up in the morning
I do things

Nick Ascroft

Summer's Necrologue
for Kate

The day is bright, the air is still.
Your tooth hurts, and you take a pill
Because another said you should,

But pain is neither neat, nor good
To be thought easily relieved.
The leaves of which no wind bereaved

The branches rest a glaring hue
On lawns beneath the office-view
For one-hand typists eating lunch.

Above, the clouds retreat to bunch
A chasmal edge of blue and loss.
Your boyfriend skim-read Kübler-Ross.

In bed he ventured his belief
That largely it's obsessive, grief.
Your face, in half-light from the hall,

Revolves: that isn't it at all.
The summer grinds another week
To dust and words that they won't speak

When briefing editorial.
We tried at the memorial:
The afterward reception's spread

Lay dormant on its doilied bed,
Condolatory—your smile was numb—
Consoling with a biscuit crumb.

Morgan Bach

Hungry

I always eat
the apple core.
To eat the sprouts
of plants is to eat potential
energy, the life force
of babies. Fill me
with the earth's iron,
I would drink
magma if I could.
One day, when my
insides are made
of steel, I will.
My oesophagus
a mine
of solid rock.
My spine
a sky scraper.
Heart an engine
of bolts and pistons.
Blood,
oil piped
from under ice
and all that
wind and water
will not
touch me.

Hinemoana Baker

The details of her nightmares

It's not enough, apparently
to witness the mutilation with a chainsaw
of a friend at a wedding
to which she has arrived
without a gift.

Now those responsible
having placed the victim in a suitcase
and a hole in the ground
are following her as she hitches a ride
with the oblivious bride
who believes her brother still has legs.

Kapiti Island's black on the black sea
a seam of silver leads to it.
I look from the moon to the page
and yawn, a small howl.

We all watch her now
her shape in the moonlight
the slowing updown of her breath

she's stepping off the bus
making foolish errors
wandering the streets
of Hamilton in a towel.

Antonia Bale

Christmas Morning

A bunch of us were ready for a good night.

We met at the Matterhorn beforehand. The party was a theme party but I can't remember what the theme was now. Keegan didn't dress in any discernible theme though. He dressed as he always dressed: tight black jeans, black leather jacket, black band T-shirt, black Vans, black fingerless leather gloves. He wore them summer or winter, no different. People gossiped. Said he had cuts, welts, burn marks, allergies, regretful tattoos. I imagined the nice things I'd whisper as he peeled the gloves off in the half light, revealing his secret to me.

I was wearing an eighties prom dress I'd got from an op shop: strapless, bright scarlet. Crisp starchy layers of synthetic taffeta bloomed out down the length of my body from boobs to thighs. It was a mullet of a dress that showed your legs but covered your bum. It was sexy despite all that extra material. I wore my favourite sneakers, white high-top Converse. Christmas Eve is a night for dancing.

Me and my taffeta dress and my high-top sneaks were out of place in the sleek bar with its shiny dark wood ceiling, leather-bound drinks' list, metal stools welded to the ground so you couldn't move them. Stools made for tall people in tailored suits and expensive leather pants. The taffeta made a brittle, crunchy sound as I stalked through the bar. I couldn't be sure only I could hear it. The waiters, dressed alike in their counterfeit army uniforms, stared at me. I enjoyed being seen by them this way. Some kind of gypsy girl, not afraid to wear what she liked, threading bright colours through the throng of black leather. Keegan was over by the amp, big and jolly, light on his feet.

Me, him, the others, we drank Falling Waters, Campari Spritzers, wines we couldn't afford. Then we sang ourselves down the long echoey corridor that pitched us up and served us out, another late-night offering to Cuba Street.

We barged our way into a BYO Malaysian with bad lighting
and cheap food. We met more people, gathering them up along
the street until there was a mob of us, cowboys and spaceships,
penguins and lifeguards, naughty nurses, Supermen, Santa
Claus. All of us shrieking and ricocheting across the cement car
park into the abandoned building, down to the place where the
cool kids were.

A musician I knew, Batman for the night, gave me a hug,
taffeta crunching. Over my head he said to Keegan, 'She's so
hot, you lucky devil.' It made me feel warm inside. Not the
compliment; the implication—Keegan was with me, I was with
Keegan, and other people knew it too.

All night we tracked each other's movements through the
crowded room. We always knew where the other was. Cliché, I
know, but it was just like that. I'd feel something on me and I'd
look up and it was his brown eyes fixing mine.

The party was overcrowded and I kept feeling bodies pressing
against my flesh but when Keegan and me met out on the ledge,
in the hallway outside the bathroom, there were ripples of fresh
air between us. We made each other laugh, wedged in by the
door in the kitchen that wasn't a kitchen, its stove ripped out.
The empty alcove where the fridge should be was filled with the
writhing bodies of Batman and Robin. At a certain point Keegan
put his arm around my bare shoulders and I buzzed with his
touch.

I said no to the pills and the rest of it. Hadn't drunk as much
as the others; I had stopped after the Malaysian. That was hours
ago. Maybe half a day ago. It was after three in the morning. No
one had marked midnight, no carols sung, no cheer. Maybe you
only do that at New Year's Eve but I remember feeling that it
mustn't be Christmas yet because no one had said anything.

That it wouldn't be until we did.

My flatmate had lent me her car for the evening. It was small
and dark blue and it drove flat, close to the ground. Its doors
were clangy when you shut them. He asked me if I could drop his
sister home. His beautiful blond sister, dressed like a shimmering

mermaid. In the car we laughed and turned the radio up loud
and he was happy, it was easy to tell. His body was loose, his head
moving in time with the music. We dropped the sister at a big
house on the hill.

'It's my dad's,' he said. 'Check out the view.'

We all tumbled out, my taffeta dress rustling with the wind.
He gave me a quick tour. Big wooden entranceway, stained glass
windows, winding staircase.

'Best view in Wellington,' he said, but the night was so dark I
couldn't really see anything. Just a big black gulf.

'There,' he said, pointing out towards some lights in the
distance. 'That's the wharf, that's the ocean.'

'The sea, you mean?' I said.

'The ocean,' he said.

He was drunker than I'd thought. He slipped down the
stairs, landed in a heap and rubbed his head. The sister made
shushing noises and hopped from foot to foot. The dad was
asleep somewhere in the house. I asked her if Keegan was going
to be all right.

'I'll just leave him here then, shall I?' I said.

'Oh, no, no!' he said from the floor.

'Oh no! Shit no,' the sister said, slipping into the bathroom,
shutting the door on us.

'I'm going home,' he said. 'I don't wanna wake up *here* on
Christmas Day.'

'Why? It's your dad's house,' I said.

'Yeah, I've gotta go to Mum's first. If I woke up here she'd kill
me.'

'What about your sister?'

'Different mum,' he said, 'different rules.'

'Oh,' I said.

We got back in the car and I leaned over his body and opened
a window so he'd feel better. He smiled at me. We careened off,
me pushing my foot down too far because the accelerator was
looser than I was used to. I eased it off until it felt like the belly of
the car was scraping along the road, and we slunk down the hill.

'It's my flatmate's car, so don't be sick, okay?' I said.

'I'm too happy to be sick,' he said, out the window to the city. 'I'm so happy,' he said, turning to me and smiling again. I caught it like a snapshot in the streetlights. He took a big swig from a square glass bottle.

'Me too,' I said.

He shouted, 'I'M HAPPY!'

'HAPPY!' he yelled at the traffic lights that obligingly turned green.

'I'm happy too,' I said and then yelled it out through the windscreen to the flags of green and red whipping in the wind. 'HAPPY TOO!'

He laughed and closed his hand over mine on the gear stick. I was happy.

When we got to his place, I parked in the spot outside the dairy. I'd dropped him off twice before but I wasn't too sure where he actually lived. He flung open the door and the corner edge of it caught on the pavement and got stuck there.

'You need to lift it up a little. Be careful, be careful,' I said, 'it's my flatmate's car.'

He came round the front of the car to my side, pulled a Santa hat out from his jacket with a flourish and put it on the wing mirror. It perched there for a second and then fell off. He was not very steady on his feet, I could see that. He knocked on my window, holding the glass bottle up, waving it at me. The passenger door was still wide open, stuck there by a small triangle of dark blue metal. I rolled down my window.

'Hi,' he said, leaning in.

'Hi,' I said.

'Merry Christmas,' he said. 'The hat's all yours.'

'Thanks,' I said out the window and he stood there mugging at me, his eyes droopy.

'I want to hold your hand,' I said, quietly into the night. 'I want to wake up on Christmas morning holding your hand.'

It was already Christmas morning. His hand was clinging onto the edge of the window. I could've leaned over and kissed it.

'Okay,' he said gravely.

He almost sconed himself getting back onto the pavement. I rolled up the window, got out and then went round to the other side of the car and lifted the door up gently, easing the snagging metal until it gave way. My taffeta layers bounced. I slammed the door shut with a clang. Keegan stood watching me with a funny look on his face. I followed him up the back steps. They were slippery; it must've rained at some point in the night.

'This is the kitchen,' he said. 'This is the bathroom,' he said. 'This is the vinyl but it's bedtime now. So we won't play them.'

'No,' I said.

He didn't turn the lights on in the bedroom. Didn't even get under the covers. Just heaved himself down on the bed, a huge lump in the dark.

I stood there for a moment, not sure what to do. He didn't move, didn't say anything. It appeared that he was asleep already.

I took my sneakers off and carefully sat down on the side of the bed. I wasn't sure if I should really stay. As slowly as I could, I lowered myself inch by inch until my eyes were staring up at the ceiling, my back feeling the doughiness of the duvet underneath. I lay there next to him, my pink dress puffing out around me. I could smell the sweat on my body, the alcohol on his, the eucalyptus laundry powder he must've used in the wash.

At some point I became aware of something. A sound, a movement. I was still asleep but there flashing through my brain like a fire alarm was a message. *Did you lock the car?* I had a sudden sure feeling that someone must've stolen it, driven it away for Christmas. I've got to get up and check, I thought. I've got to get up right now. But I was still asleep and my body was sinking down deeper underneath me. When I woke up he was already on top of me, already inside me.

He was holding my arms above my head, pinning my wrists with his fingerless gloves. I was still wearing my puffy pink dress. It was crunching and rustling underneath him. He was wearing a T-shirt. Our skin didn't touch. Except for there. I could taste blood in my mouth. I must've bit my tongue.

No, a voice said, a soupy muggy voice in my head. No, it said again, clearer, louder. But my real voice was lodged inside my throat, pegged in place. His eyes weren't looking at me, they were flicking along the ceiling. It was light now. A quiet time.

Inside my mind, my body was propelling him up and out to the other side of the room like a superhero would, like Batman or Superman. His back was slamming into the opposite wall, his legs were swinging up and then crumpling beneath him. I wanted to be able to do that to him, to get him out like that, but instead I lay very still. My toes, my armpits, my whole body could hear things. A creak in the roof, the rain on the windowpane, the grunting sounds he was making as he rummaged around inside, ransacking my body.

Slowly, like something thawing, my wrists began to strain against the pressure; to resist. My nails snatched wildly against the gloves, scratching now soft leather, now the pink flesh of the tips of his fingers. His eyes slid down from the ceiling then and fixed on mine. He didn't say a word. Jabbed inside me maybe three more times, one last stab deeper than the rest. And then he rolled off.

I stayed there, still like that, with my arms reached out above my head, my body icebound.

The light crept in the room and stretched out along my pale thighs.

We lay in the silence.

After a time I shoved my dress down, pulling at the hem hard. The sound filled the room.

Sssh, I wanted to say.

Marooned on my back, I could still feel the feelings from inside me. A rawness. I pressed the fleshy heel of my hand down onto my pelvis and pushed hard so that this pain could cover that pain. He made a sound then, a sudden sob. His big paw reached out and roughly brushed down the side of my body, catching in the taffeta folds, searching for something. Fierce and tender, he held my hand on Christmas morning like I'd wanted, like I'd asked him to.

I tried not to breathe.

After a while the pressure of his grip eased off and it felt like he had gone back to sleep.

Or maybe he was pretending. I extracted my hand in one firm slide.

Did I lock the car? I thought.

I left the house quietly, like a thief.

In the car, I wound down the window again. Sipped in the air through my nose. The roads were slick with rain. The shop windows were green and red and closed. The light was thin and raw in the grey sky. My bare feet pushed too hard against the pedals and the car jolted. I wasn't wearing any underwear.

I don't remember parking or getting into my bed, but I do remember going round to Mum and Dad's in the mid-afternoon and Mum saying, 'Oh what's the matter with you, Anna? You're always such a sad sack on Christmas. You ruin it every year.'

I was supposed to go camping on the East Coast for New Year's but I didn't. I spent the holiday in bed. On the fifth of January I took a shower and got dressed for work. I almost tripped getting out the front door. There, sitting in a neat little pair on the step, were my Converse high-top sneakers.

*

Years later I told a boyfriend about it. It was lodged in his head, he said. He couldn't stop thinking about it.

'Could we do that?' he said. 'Could that be our thing?'

'What?'

'That,' he said.

'Our thing? Non-consensual sex?'

'No, like you're asleep and I wake you up like that. I think it could be hot.'

I grimaced.

'Like you won't know when until I do it. You won't know when it's coming.'

'You know what you're asking, right?' I said.

'I think it could be hot,' he said.

'I won't be able to sleep.'

'Sure you will, that's the point.'

'You want to take something without my permission? That's what you want to do?'

'No. We're two consenting adults. It's not like that. It'd be an arrangement.'

I started putting my coat on, moving towards the door.

'Don't get huffy,' he said. 'It was just an idea. I thought it could be hot.'

*

The other day, I saw Keegan. Fingerless leather gloves feeding coins into the meter. We never even kissed, I thought. He saw me, standing on the street outside the library, staring at him. I didn't mean to but my hand raised, quick, like a wave. His eyes flicked away and I kept on walking.

Fergus Barrowman

Robin Dudding 1935–2008

Robin Dudding died on 21 April 2008, as this issue was going to print, and just two days before he was to be awarded an Honorary Doctorate by the University of Auckland.

When we started *Sport* in 1988 ('we' being me as editor, Nigel Cox, Elizabeth Knox and Damien Wilkins as contributors and assistant editors, and Bill Manhire as contributor and wise counsel) (and please tell me it isn't really 20 years) our model was *Islands*. *Islands*, edited and published by Robin Dudding from 1972 to 1987, was a classic little magazine, the best New Zealand has seen, and there were rumours (unconfirmed, denied) that the November 1987 issue, no. 38, would turn out to have been the last. With *Landfall* in the doldrums someone needed to do something. And—let's be honest—perhaps we saw an opportunity.

There was a delicate manoeuvre to perform. I wanted one of the cornerstones of *Sport 1* to be Elizabeth's autobiographical essay 'Origins, Authority and Imaginary Games', but she had sent it to *Islands* late in 1987. There had been no reply, so, on 3 July, Elizabeth and I wrote separately to Robin. I asked for his 'blessing and advice', telling him unconvincingly that 'this venture is complementary rather than in competition', and Elizabeth asked for her essay back. I don't think I deserved a reply, and if I got one it's gone from both memory and archive. In his reply to Elizabeth, Robin gently mocked the style of her essay:

Dear Elizabeth Knox,

Robin. First Person. Peculative.

Or perhaps petulant. I am sorry to let this go, but it is my own fault for being slow . . .

Timeline for ISLANDS. Third Person. Pretty Tense.

Or perhaps Terse.
August 1988. ISLANDS 39
November 1988. ISLANDS 40.
Hopefully.

In the years when there was so little serious publishing here that with a few exceptions literary writers had to send their books to London or privately subsidise a local boutique publisher, *Islands* was where the conversation of New Zealand literature took place. It never pretended to be the mouthpiece of the final word. The first issue set a dizzying standard: Allen Curnow's return to poetry after 10 years alongside James K. Baxter on living with junkies. In other words, deeply in the tradition and completely up to date. And *Islands* was vital up to the end. The second to last issue, for instance, opened with stories by Anne Kennedy and Bill Manhire; Jenny Bornholdt's poems were alongside C.K. Stead's. Throughout, there are the names that define those 15 years, but there are also names that have scarcely been heard of again. And there are the loyal mistakes! We admire those; any editor who doesn't make their share of mistakes is playing it too safe.

When interviewed by Iain Sharp for *In the Same Room*, Bill Manhire said of Robin's editing: 'I think it was partly that he had time to shape an issue. He wouldn't lumber it with a great thematic idea; he just let it slip into place as an arrangement of parts with somehow its own shape and logic, which wasn't an obvious logic . . . But you do need a lot of time for that to happen.' Therein lies the rub: in one of his infrequent editorial notes Robin lamented that another 1000 subscribers would mean he could afford to make *Islands* the full-time occupation it effectively was, but in a country the size of New Zealand?

Elizabeth and I visited Robin and Lois in Torbay in August 1988. We talked and talked, so much that we failed to notice the bus go past as we stood talking at the Torbay bus stop, and Robin generously drove us back into town. I don't remember much talk about literary magazines. I didn't know much, and I guess Robin wasn't giving much away. What I remember most is the warmth of his enthusiasm for writers and books. He had recently discovered 'New Zealand's greatest story teller'—Margaret Mahy. He was so excited by the human insight and political engagement in Nigel Cox's *Dirty Work* he thought Nigel should immediately be given money to write another novel . . . Robin will be sorely missed, but the tangible results of his passionate enthusiasm will always be with us.

David Beach

Self-portrait 4

A poem is an opening line plus work. My
forte is the opening line but I toil
too. I bang my brain upon the page, read
through as far as I have got again and
again. That might seem too tortuous for Keats'
'If poetry comes not as naturally
as the leaves to a tree it had better
not come at all' but leaves grow slowly and
experience who knows what erasures. And
I'm confident I pass the botany
test, a blossoming bough, in the throes of
writing liable to undergo something
like the arboreal fate which the Greek myths
relate could befall maidens fleeing from gods.

Airini Beautrais

Bug Week

At a certain age I began to think less about sex and more about tableware. I thought about wide-rimmed martini glasses and bulbous brandy balloons. I thought about crockery: matching dinner plates with small side platters and round soup bowls. I thought about the tinkle spoons make when stacked together and the subtly erotic act of sliding a perfectly sharp knife into a receptive knife block.

I dreamed my dreams in a home with scraggly wallpaper and peeling linoleum. At night I dreamed them in a bed that seldom stayed properly made, between pilling polyester sheets, next to a man with a balding ponytail.

Phil and I were not particularly wealthy. We partly owned a reasonable house. We had known each other for a long time and, having tangled and entwined year in year out, having created two curly-haired kids who often had sand or jam on their chins, the current lack of physical passion between us did not seem like so much of a lack. It was a reality I was unconcerned by.

Mine was the natural age of accumulation. My body was accumulating constantly and my kitchen cupboards were never stocked with the full complement of entertaining possibilities. My bookshelves, although groaning, spoke of need for shining covers closely pressed together, for beautiful colour editions whose prints seldom reflected light. The hot water cylinder whispered of linen and the pipes sang of the luxurious free-standing bath they longed to trickle into. Evenings and weekends I wiped cupboard doors and shined faucets, I laid shoes large and small in matching pairs by the door. I arranged fruit in my pièce de résistance, the cast glass fruit bowl – banana over orange, or orange against pear?

At work, Kelly, who was my age and should have known better, fantasised about people she wanted to sleep with. 'Last night I went into this bar and thought, Whoa, did I stumble in on a modelling convention?' she blurted. 'Every guy in the place looked positively Swedish.'

'I looked at a Swedish chair in a design store yesterday,' I said. I had looked at it, although I couldn't afford it. It had been plastic yet natural, modern yet elegant. It was made from a single sheet, with legs that bent back in perfect submission.

'I need a lover,' said Kelly, putting on her lipstick, or rather smearing it in the general vicinity of her lips, using the coffee plunger as a mirror. 'I so need a fuck.'

I have never understood people who apply makeup in company. 'Watch out,' I said, 'you could end up married or something.' It was perceptible that marriage and children were the things Kelly really wanted – and fast – fucks aside.

'Not necessarily,' she said. She smoothed her shirt and went back to her computer screen. 'It's the twenty-first century, and I was never particularly romantic.'

'Phil is trying to be romantic.' I didn't really want to discuss my personal life, but I felt it was expected. Suddenly the library catalogue in front of me looked very absorbing. Bug Week was approaching.

'That's nice,' said Kelly, with the hint of a question mark.

'He thinks we need more spontaneity in our lives,' I said. 'He's trying to be unpredictable. His hair keeps getting longer and it's driving me nuts.'

'Unpredictable how?'

'Oh, surprise picnics, random gift-giving. He's unpredictable in a predictable kind of way, if you know what I mean. Breakfast in bed.'

'I love breakfast in bed!'

'I can't imagine anything worse.' Crumbs get between the sheets, coffee gets spilled on the pillows. Grease is wiped on the bedside table. People who relish such things bemuse me. How is it pleasurable to wallow in one's own scraps? How does a devil-may-care attitude to cleaning lead to happiness? There is nothing romantic about filth.

'What else is happening in the bedroom?' Kelly asked.

'The bedroom is where we sleep.'

'Aha.' A knowing smile. Of course she didn't know. A welcome silence. Then: 'Does he ever break into song?'

'Not yet. I'm scared that one day I'll get home and there'll be an air ticket to Rarotonga sitting on the table, and I'll be expected to sort out my luggage in ten minutes, and leave without doing the washing.'

'Rarotonga!' Kelly said. 'Fucking hell, why wouldn't you want to go there?'

'Oh, you know. It's not that I'd rule it out forever, but I just wouldn't want to go at a moment's notice.'

Kelly shook her head. I have given everyone I work with a secret hairstyle nickname. Kelly is Hedgehog. Better, Albino Hedgehog – short, blond and spiky. 'I've never understood you,' she said.

I had to stop the conversation before she delved further. 'I'm going up to the bug room. Is there anything you need taken upstairs?'

I went up to the bug room, partly to get away from Kelly, and partly to spy on my colleague Don MacCreedy, the entomologist. Lately I had noticed that he was walking around in a state of permanent semi-sleep. His eyelids would flicker like he was on drugs; he would meander through a room and not see anything in it. I didn't know Don well but I had picked up a few things about him. He was able to focus intently, and while peering down a binocular microscope would enter a sort of trance that could last half an hour. He rarely engaged in conversation. On the other hand he was always impeccably presented, with crisp shirts, clean shoes and dignified colour schemes. He never wore the garish ties or revolting striped shirts that screamed, for some men, 'I'm going to WORK.' He shaved his face and kept his hair short and tidy, with no signs of a mid-life grooming crisis. People often infer that a well-presented man has a woman somewhere forcing him into it. However, Don lived alone. He was a divorcee and his mother was sufficiently ensconced in the Outer Hebrides to prevent her from ironing his trouser creases.

Don's appearance and behaviour were so anomalous as to be interesting. He was, I told myself, a rare genus I had yet to identify. I doubted the influence of substance abuse in his case, but I decided to keep an eye on him.

That day I arrived home with my heart in my throat, thinking about spontaneity. My one superstition is that saying things aloud can bring them into being. The table top was covered in bits of paper, which I screened anxiously. A picture of a giraffe by my son, Nicholas. A grocery receipt, two local papers, three empty envelopes and flyers for a Jamaican restaurant, a drycleaner's and a weight loss programme with a money-back guarantee. Last month's phone bill, some notes of Phil's, a couple of children's books from the public library and a copy of *Greatest Love Ballads arranged for Piano*, with an airbrushed rose on the cover. Part of my brain felt relief and another part quickly became absorbed in formulating the disappearance of the latter item. But fortunately the piano key was still hidden from the fourth birthday party.

'Darling,' came my husband's voice from the kitchen, 'how daring are you willing to be when it comes to pizza?'

Confrontation in a marriage is often best avoided. 'It's up to you, Phil,' I said, heading up the stairs. My mind raced with imagined horrors – steamed broccoli, pineapple, tinned kidney beans, crabsticks, piled into a cheesy mountain of unnecessary chaos. Fuck. I looked at the turned wooden stair rail and hated it. I thought about clean lines. I thought about ripping down the spew-patterned nineties curtains and I thought about minimalism, colours that were hardly colours. I went into the bathroom, wiped down the mirror, washed my face and thought about tiles. I thought of the tiler laying each one precisely, the years of development of the craft. Then I heard a familiar voice saying, 'Come on, it can't be that hard. I'll do it myself.'

'I just want some semblance of order in my life,' I said to my reflection. She blinked the water out of her eyes. She looked sullen, mousy and dishevelled.

*

I was enjoying myself at work one morning, making a dichotomous key for children to identify invertebrates. I thought about how everything in nature has a place, how everything is a component of a larger thing that fits into an even larger thing. I hoped the universe was like that, but infinitely. I thought about the mosaic vision of insects.

'You know what,' said Kelly. 'What'll happen next.'

'Next in what?'

'In your relationship. If things are stagnating or if neither of you are happy, one of you will have an affair. You will or he will.'

'I hope he does.' Someone else could be afforded the pleasures of R.E.M. piano renditions and jazzy shirt fabric.

'What about you?'

'I don't have time to meet anyone,' I said. 'Besides, I am completely unthrilled by the prospect of fornication.'

Kelly snorted coffee out her nose. 'How do you think of all the crazy shit you say?'

I pushed my glasses up my nose in a way I hoped was supercilious, and carried on with the *Guide to the New Zealand Forest*. Kelly was obviously reading lots of semi-teenage glossy magazines, or the type of novel that only sells because it fills the large vacuole in women's brains with sugary sustenance.

'Don the bug man has the hots for you,' Kelly said.

I felt a warm shudder go through me. It felt like the flu coming on. 'Bollocks.'

'It's true. He totally wants to fuck you. He's always coming in here and giving us stuff.'

'Kelly, in case you have forgotten,' I said, 'next week is Bug Week. We have twenty schools booked in to learn about entomology. He is a national expert.'

'Oh, how many beetle books do we really need?' Kelly has an arts background. I ignored her and thought about taxonomy. I thought about the beauty of phylogenetic trees. The thin calligraphic branches.

Later that day – perhaps this relates to my one superstition – a strange thing happened. Our office is opposite the lift, and as I went to shut out the draft, the lift doors opened. Don was standing in there, holding a stack of brown parcels. I thought of the tiny glass tubes that might be in them. Then for a split second he looked up. His long eyelashes lifted, the trance state wavered on the point of breaking. His eyes met mine for a brief millisecond and then looked down again. Janet from front of house walked into the lift, the doors closed, I went back to my computer, and a voice inside me said, 'That was the most erotic moment you have had in years.'

A song went through my body, not the kind that is sung but the kind that is felt, too low a frequency for the human ear. Sometimes distance is more intense than closeness. The knowledge that someone is thinking of looking at you, but deliberately stopping himself, can be a million times more provocative than any lover's touch.

At home Phil said, 'Honey, what do you think about Hawai'i this winter?' The Rarotonga scenario came back to me. My blood pressure rose slightly.

'Hawai'i is a long way away,' I said to my plate. Phil was experimenting with vegetarianism and had made soy cutlets. The children had used them as table scouring agents and most of their meals were on the floor. 'Where would the money come from?'

'Well, I figure it's such a horrible autumn this year, six more months of this can't be healthy. Why not have a week off in July and just let the bathroom renovations wait a couple of years.'

'I don't know,' I said. 'There is a mouldy smell in there. The whole thing needs gutting if you ask me.'

'Think of the kids with fresh coconuts, drinking the milk,' Phil said. His eyes were starting to twinkle. 'And we could see real lava.' The kids themselves did not look up. They were too young to have any concept of a planet or the Pacific Ocean. Phil shrugged. The twinkle died down. I could sense I was hurting him but felt too stubborn to stop. 'Just an idea,' he said quietly. 'Where would you like to go on holiday?' he asked Scarlett.

'Nana's,' said my daughter, adjusting her doll on her lap.

'Me too,' said Nicholas.

Their filial duty impressed Phil. I didn't want to mention the bottomless jar of jubes that Nana kept in her cupboard.

On the Monday of Bug Week, Kelly came in on tip toes. She uttered a few exclamations, then said, 'I got laid on Saturday night.'

'Really,' I said, no question mark.

'Guess how old he was. You'll never guess.'

'Seventy-two.'

She made a face. 'Twenty-three! Can you believe it?'

'I suppose so.' I have known twenty-three-year-olds to thrust themselves into inanimate objects while inebriated, but I thought better of mentioning this. 'Will you see him again?'

'Of course not,' she said, delightedly. Clearly she had already planned the next five years, the moonlit spa baths, the fireside sex, the declarations of eternal fidelity.

I knew the questions a woman was supposed to ask about such things. Was he any good? Did he have a big dick? How did it happen? Was he hot? But I couldn't face even polite enquiry. 'I'm going to get a cup of tea,' I said. 'Would you like anything?'

'Nah, I'm all right. I'll give you all the details when you get back.'

I didn't go to the kitchen. I went to the rooftop and looked out over the city. I felt high up and small and suddenly lonely. I thought about earthquakes and cloud formations. I thought of words like 'epicentre' and 'cumulonimbus'.

'I've never seen you up here,' came a Scottish lilt from a few metres away. Don the bug man had crept up on me. Or he had been there all along. 'I come up here about this time every day,' he said. It was before nine. 'Just to get some air.'

'Oh,' I said.

'I'm a creature of habit,' he went on. His eyes were fully open. The trance was momentarily suspended. I had the sense of a pond waking in the spring, shoots emerging from the mud. 'I like each day to follow a pattern.'

'Do you.' I couldn't breathe properly.

'Every morning I get up at seven. I have my breakfast at seven thirty. I get here at eight. I like to do my reading in the morning. I'm better at organising things after lunch. I always have about five cups of tea, at fairly regular intervals.'

'I like to eat breakfast alone,' I said. 'I get up early while everyone else is sleeping. I like to have all my clothes sorted out the night before, and I hang them over the end of the bed.'

'A sensible idea,' Don mused. 'I put on my clothes in the dark. I can't even see what they are.'

'I don't believe you.'

'Well, all of my clothes are much the same colour. As long as it's a shirt and pants I'll be fine.'

'Not enough people pay attention to colour,' I said. 'People think they understand it, but very few actually do.' I felt a little in danger of ranting but kept talking anyway. 'Colour can be overdone. Perhaps one small item of bright colour is enough, such as a scarf, or shoes, but the rest should be understated. The trees in this country mostly have small white flowers. If you look at the native forest, there is that lovely, soft, uniform green . . .' I could feel him watching me. 'I suppose I am talking shit,' I said. We had never had a conversation like this. I wasn't sure if the things we were discussing were entirely normal for acquaintances of our standing. 'I had better go back downstairs. We have a class arriving in half an hour.'

'Yes,' he said. He was standing closer to me now. 'Small white flowers with a pronounced nocturnal scent. Many of them are pollinated by moths or lizards.'

I risked looking at him. I hoped I didn't appear pensive or flushed.

'Admittedly I care about my clothes,' he said. 'A man who spends all his spare time scrambling up hillsides after insects shouldn't need to, but I do. I will only wear certain fabrics, for instance.'

'I am a stickler,' I told him, 'for cotton, silk and wool.' He nodded. We both stared ahead, quiet, unmoving. Should I stop there? Should I talk about the view or the terrible architecture before us?

'What kind of sheets do you sleep in?' he asked.

There was a sick, plummeting feeling in my abdomen. I coughed. 'Is that an appropriate question?' I asked.

'I'm sorry. I just believe that a lot of inferences can be made about a person, from these small details.'

I was already walking away. 'I would never sleep in anything but linen,' he said. 'Belgian linen. And it has to be white.'

Children chattered around me all day, made feelers out of pipe cleaners, cellophane wings. That evening I felt disorientated. On the way to the bus stop I walked into a shop outside of my budget. The blond assistant stared at my shoe hole, my wind-styled hair. Aggravated by her apparent deduction of my financial status, I walked out with an ostentatious paper bag containing a set of red wine glasses and a set of champagne flutes. I stayed up late at night removing tissue paper and standing the glasses on the bench, twirling and admiring them. Phil wasn't exactly furious about my purchases – fury was an emotion he never expressed – but he seemed morose. 'I thought we agreed we'd leave these things till the kids are bigger,' he said. 'That there's no point having fancy stuff with small children around.'

'I want my surroundings to be tasteful,' I told him.

'I thought they were.'

I looked at his fading Monet reproduction over the fireplace and was too tired even to scoff.

'You know,' he said, fingering the end of his ponytail, 'I think it doesn't matter what stuff you have or what your house looks like, if there is a loving family that lives in it.'

Something caught in the back of my throat. He was sounding a call to guilt.

'I don't want to bring up my family in a pit of squalor,' I said. 'I want to live in a clean house with smooth floors and curtains that aren't mouldy. I want a refrigerator that doesn't leak and a washing machine that doesn't sound like a jet plane taking off.' My voice was starting to rise, a thing I loathed in women.

I cleared my throat and continued in a deeper tone. 'Yet you somehow insinuate that I am callous or shallow to want these things. There is nothing unreasonable about a few new glasses from time to time.' Phil was about to reply as I exited the room. I knew he would say 'But we have heaps of glasses already' and it would incense me too much to point out that not a pair of them was the same.

Don and I circled each other for the remainder of Bug Week, neither of us moving from our series of choreographed steps. I thought of the lyrebird with its tail over itself. I thought of the kākāpō, green in his hollow, of blue-footed boobies waving their oversized feet. I thought of stag beetles battling with their strange antlers. I pretended nothing was happening. Our conversations became shorter and more infrequent.

On Friday a teacher brought in a jar containing a bright green beetle, thinking one of her students had made a rare discovery. 'You can leave it here for our entomologist,' I told her. 'We'll get back to you.' Our entomologist replied to my email almost immediately. I was short of breath when I reached his floor, even though I had taken the lift.

Don was in a microscope daze and didn't look up when I walked in. 'Show us this beetle,' he said.

'You don't even know who you're talking to,' I told him. 'You have an eyeful of pond life.'

'I recognised the sound of your shoes.' The room was piled to the ceiling with filing drawers, each with a little pinned death inside. Don unbent from the microscope, took the jar and smiled. A joke I wasn't party to.

'People don't know their Coleoptera,' he said. '*Stethaspis suturalis*. This one is reasonably common in pine plantations and native forest.'

I wasn't concentrating. I touched his waist. I could feel warm flesh through his thin ironed shirt. This is not what you want, I told myself. You like neatness. You like distance. I pressed him against a wall.

'Let's not do this in here,' he breathed, close to my ear. 'There are one hundred and ninety years of collecting in this little room and I don't want to damage anything.'

'Okay.' I swallowed. I thought about how I could extricate myself. I thought of the antlion in its funnel of sand.

'Look, the mammal room,' he whispered. There were other people in the lab next door who may or may not have been aware of our presence. 'No one ever goes in the mammal room.' It was true. We never put the mammals on display because they turned people's stomachs. Most of them had mange; some of them had missing limbs.

'I'll meet you in ten minutes,' I said.

'This can wait. I can be there in five.'

In less than a minute we found ourselves in the mammalian storeroom, in the controlled coolness between the tall shelves. A few hundred small glass eyes stared down at us. The smell of death, dust and preservation was overpowering. We couldn't touch each other.

'This is ridiculous,' I said, and Don agreed. 'These things shouldn't happen in a workplace,' he said. 'Come to my house tonight.'

'I can't.' I had two little heads to coax onto pillows. 'Some other time.'

'Will you kiss me?' he asked.

I looked up and saw the Tasmanian wolf looking back at me. Its lips were peeling. I couldn't.

Bug Week was over. The holiday in Hawai'i transmogrified into a week in Thames with Phil's parents. It worked out well for all of us. Phil enjoyed seeing his family, the children were content with the prospect of lollies, and I had a week at home by myself. It was luxurious. I cleaned and sanitised and ordered everything in my house, and then I went to Don's house at his invitation. We had sex a few times, which he seemed to find overwhelming. Afterwards he lay in silence with his hands folded on top of his chest, eyes unfocused. Don without his clothes was strange, pink and damp, like a peeled crustacean. I realised quickly that the desire I had initially felt had not been for him. I enjoyed his company, but it was mostly a necessary preliminary to spending time sitting on new leather couches, drinking decent wine, eating off flawless plates and sleeping between the aforementioned linen sheets. The sheets were always clean – it was as if there had been nothing bodily happening in them. I liked it that way. Don also had a slipper bath that one could slide into and remain slid. When I turned the taps with my toes to add more hot water, they made no sound. Afterwards I wrapped myself in huge thick towels the colour of stone. I saw my reflection in the large mirror over the basin. Her hair was damp and she looked older and less attractive than I felt. 'What are you doing?' she wanted to know. I couldn't tell her.

Don's house was sparsely decorated and completely compartmentalised. There were no hidden corners where dust could gather. There were no places to lose things. There was nothing burnt on to the ceramic stovetop. Nothing biodiverse lurked at the back of the fridge. The wooden floors shone and the ceilings were immaculate.

'I've lived alone for a while,' Don said. 'A couple of years, in fact. Shirley, my ex-wife . . .' He looked out the window. There was a view over moving trees and distant water. 'She was pretty unstable. When she left she trashed the entire place. Totally ruined it. That's why everything is new. She even ripped out the fucking plumbing.' A smile hovered on his face. Was it embarrassment or some form of humour?

'I can't understand how anything could prompt someone to do that,' I said. 'People do terrible things to each other but I can't see the point of getting that angry about it. I can't see how you could justify the waste involved.' Wine was making me talk.

'She was pretty angry, all right.' He put down his glass. 'I'm going to look in my cellar – would you like another drink?' And with that the book was shut. The story had been traced out but would not be embroidered. In some ways it was a relief.

*

'Something is going on with you,' Kelly said at work. 'You're even more agitated than usual.'

'I'm not usually agitated,' I said. 'And I feel fine. Nothing in my life is remotely different. Except I have a new dinner set.'

'You're a useless liar. Spill.'

'You make it up. I did whatever you think I did.'

'I know what you did,' she said. I knew she didn't, but part of me wondered if the Tasmanian wolf had been talking.

The week in Thames ended. The children came home and drew on the walls. Phil applauded their creativity and their articulation of their ambitions – Nicholas the future astronaut had scribbled a spaceship in the corner of the lounge. Kelly met a Spanish tourist with a beard and very little English, and came into work moaning that she was saddle sore. Don and I met occasionally for cocktails on Fridays, which could be justified as work drinks. Once or twice I let him caress my back on the rooftop. He was becoming reticent again: his eyelashes were beginning to droop. Soon he would either tell me we should cool it or tell me he loved me. I was afraid of both of these things.

One day I came home anticipating an evening alone. Phil had taken the children, along with his sister and her kids, to see some juvenile comedian. I put my bag on the hall table and walked into the kitchen.

It had been a mess when I left it, but what had happened now? Every plate – not just the new ones but every single plate – was in pieces on the floor. Every glass was smashed. The fruit bowl was in shards in the sink. I was too shocked to weep over it. My chest of drawers was emptied. All my clothes were off their hangers. The bookshelves had been disembowelled. In the bathroom all my makeup was emptied, scattered, smeared, strewn. In very small writing in dark grey eyeliner pencil the corner of the mirror read, *There is no order in the cosmos.*

'Who the fuck would do this?' I said. My heart was knocking around. I rang Phil on his cellphone – there was high-pitched laughter in the background. 'Phil, our house has been broken into,' I told him, voice cracking. He was genuinely horrified at what I described. Clearly he had nothing to do with it. Don was equally taken aback when I informed him. I rang Kelly just in case and succeeded only in disentangling her from Tomás and confusing her horribly. Who could have done this to me? Could it have been the resurfacing of the misfortunate Shirley? But she had long since moved home to Minnesota. I was sick with fear not knowing who knew enough about me to have made this melodramatic point. Would I be believed if the crime were reported? A garden variety housebreaker does not normally inscribe philosophical statements. Nothing appeared to have been taken. They will say I am nuts, I thought. They will say I have done it myself.

I sat on the bottom stair. I hated crying. I hated the trail of snot that slicked from my nose, I hated redness and swollen skin. I hated the small, timid sound of stifled sobbing. I thought about holding my husband. I thought about stroking the hair of my children as they fell asleep. I would replace everything exactly. I would put every book in its rightful place. No order. I thought about the honeybee doing its round dance and its waggle dance. I thought about the fish that home to the streams their parents came from, streams they have never swum. I thought about how our galaxy is spiralling around a fixed point. And then I thought of the atom and my head throbbed. The image of it whizzed before me. The electrons moved back and forth and filled up sub-shells. Their paths were impossible to follow. They were just a cloud of light.

A nice night

What went through your head, Neil,
waiting at the Stratford bus stop, for three and a half hours?
Did your dog, Umbrella, sniff something gone awry,
nosing your steel-capped toes? Dogs know.

What went through your head,
putting Umbrella on the bus to Auckland,
seeing the Whanganui bus pull up?
Doors sighing apart. The future, opening up.

How did you feel, in your rabbitskin vest,
buying a battery, asking the cashier
to test it for you? 'I put a screwdriver
across the terminals,' he told the papers,

'and it sparked quite nicely. He seemed like a nice guy.
The last thing I said to him was "Have a nice night".'
You drank your last can of drink.
You went to the cinema, bought a ticket

to a movie half-over. Cradled your pack,
its unseen contents. Did you watch the action
on the screen, or just sit there, passing minutes?
You must have had a time in mind.

What went through your head, Neil, leaving the cinema,
moving through the back alleys of the Old Town?
There are lots of blank walls there, they echo well.
What went through your head taking out a spray can,

writing on the wall? The text strikes me
as having been written with a steady hand. Also,
it was a fitting choice of quote, then and now,
though written in 1809, in the Junta Tuitiva.

La Paz, peace, must have been in your mind,
when you added 'Anarchy: Peace Thinking.'
Some might contest the connection.
'One day,' writes my friend Sam, in a zine on anarchy,

'it may be unnecessary to begin
every piece of writing on the subject of anarchism
by pointing out that anarchism
is not about violence and chaos,

but about organisation and cooperation.
Somebody please give me a yell when this happens.'
What went through your head, Neil, crossing Bates Street?
Did you look at the building, or at your feet?

Were there lights on in the windows?
In Willie Keddell's short film 'The Maintenance of Silence'
we see an actor's legs, from the knees down,
walk the carpark, a pair of hands place a red knapsack.

I was struck by the similarities
between my imagined scene and the film,
except that in the film the footsteps ring ominous
and Keddell's bomber crouches side-on to the building,

while I imagine him facing the doors. What went through your
    head,
stooping there? Did you know about the men,
two of them, on the other side of the armoured glass?
There wasn't time to talk. Did you know about the six

sitting at terminals? What went through their heads,
working there? What I wouldn't do for a beer.
What I wouldn't do for a couple hours more sleep.
BANG! The explosion sears through your head,

molecules rearranging, structures unforming.
I have a dream in which I hear the sound
of body parts landing. They make a small noise: blick.
An ambulance arrives, but it is much, much too late.

Miro Bilbrough

I'll never get a poem from this neighbourhood

Discarded sandals on doorstep & verandah say
otherwise, something so Sunday in their attitude

lying where cast, the jubilance of being without feet.
I make a mental note, cross the park and forget

to check the window where once I saw a woman's
head parallel an ironing board, the flash of metal

tongue licking straight brunette falls. I pause at the
former butcher's old glass door, islands of paint thinned

by the strain of being so looked upon by would-be poets.

Yearling beef
sides   hinds
fores   butts

I *thought of your line on my walk* sighs Alice,
sardonic as a bittern, as I follow her up humid streets.

It's my new criteria for renting a house. And right then
I sight it, crackling and clapping its wings, the poem.

Hera Lindsay Bird

Oh, Abraham Lincoln, kiss me harder

In poems you can do anything you like. You can start fires, or break the law. You can break the law by starting fires. You can set fire to the house of your worst enemy. In poetry, you can have worst enemies. In real life, I don't really have any worst enemies. There's that dickhead at the salad bar who always puts walnuts in my salad, and there was that girl who used to ring me up and scream at me, but I've got a new phone number now and as much as I hate the salad guy, I'd like to think that I'm a conscientious citizen who wouldn't intentionally try to burn his house down. Besides, I don't have his address. But I'm totally onto you, salad bar guy! In poems you can make out with whoever you like, even if they died forever ago. In poems you can say, 'Oh, Abraham Lincoln, kiss me harder.' I have a friend who is angry at poetry because he says it makes life more beautiful than it really is, which is a stupid reason to hate anything. Hating poetry because it makes life more beautiful is like hating ketchup on your burger because it makes your burger more delicious than it really is, or hating the swans on the lake, for making the lake seem more peaceful. Fuck off swans! How am I supposed to make an accurate emotional assessment of the lake with you gliding around all serene? Sometimes all I want is to read poems that feel a bit more like real life. Something a little bit directionless and frightened. Something without any literary subtext, or clever double meanings. Clever double meanings are like those magic eye puzzles that were popular in the nineties. You can get really good at seeing them, but in the end you're still the arsehole sitting in the library at lunchtime saying 'I can't believe you guys can't see the fucking dolphins' to no one. Sometimes all I want is the poet to come clean and say, 'I have no idea what I'm talking about.' Sometimes in a poem I want to just list some good things that I like. The solar system. The names of lipsticks. Poached eggs and mushrooms on a little stack of potato cakes. Houses. Satellites. Swamps and the monsters who live in them. The internet.

Jenny Bornholdt

Medical

She listens
to your chest
with such
concentration . . .

There's all the loud
machinery of course
and June—do you mean the month
or her name?
Her name is inside you
and audible, and the dream, too,
in which you try to fax your publisher
a cake.

She hears us remember
the cats and their soft fur
birds going ape
in the trees.

She can hear
the domestic
rattle around
like small change—
cake call
from the oven,
sigh of the tired
pots and pans, rice
slip into water
like a swimmer.

She hears
your upset.
The watermelon bought
to cheer you up
from a place with an aisle
marked 'instant dissolve food and drink'.

Erratic door,
a lack of iron,
the fence
creaking in the wind
like your knees.
Everything hurts
if you *hitch a hip*
says the physio
as her fingers wade
the river of muscle
which runs the bank
of your spine.

She hears your watch cough
politely, bellow of weather
appease the garden's thirst.
Lone plum on the tree,
long soft body of the stick insect
traverse the rampant rose.

She hears the love you have
for your husband.

Hears you kiss the baby
then drive across town
in your pyjamas
in the early morning, past
planes in a queue

on the runway. The man who
leans across *here, have a chocolate*
person.

Anger rise
like steam
off hot asphalt
on the runway.

Your friend, her dodgy
neck, her low
morale.

Listening, she can hear
the spades as they dig down
for the elderly beloved
cats. She hears children and adults
weep, 'all things bright and
beautiful' sung
over the graves, then the car doors
close as we head
for the beach.
A week of sun, then
the weather moves on.
We don wetsuits
the dinghy rocks
on the porch
tree saws
on the roof
the baby says
no no no no
and refuses to get
to her feet.

All night
insects flip and click
while the wind roars

suck and blow
suck and blow

and the curtains rattle
on their tracks.

It Has Been a Long Time Since I Last Spoke To You, So Here I Am

All day
cloud has hovered in a vee of hills
just below the snow-covered
Pisa range. It's nature's joke—
snow / cloud / cloud / snow?
Unfeeling nature, to which we bring
our joys and sads.   Wanting . . .
as if staring at a mountain or a lake
will ease loss.

It has been a long time since I last
spoke to you. Since then
his mother has died
and my uncle. Each Christmas
this kind, gentle man would build
a centrepiece for the table—one year
the Eiffel Tower, the menu
French. Next, for Italy,
the Colosseum. Our middle age
is one long goodbye. Even nature
is in danger.

Like in summer
when the hawk struck the sparrow
from beside us on the riverbank.
We were talking, still damp
from swimming, heads
turned to each other so we saw
nothing, just heard the wings' rush,
the smaller bird sound its brief alarm . . .

It has been a long time
since I last spoke to you.
When we were children, our fathers
wanted to be mountains
our mothers were the sky.
So here I am, the dry hands,
steady in fog, waiting by the not-there
trees, the holes birds make
in air.

William Brandt

Broken

for Jaime

Her husband had only recently died. He'd been through a long painful illness, and she'd been with him every step of the way, walking with him, hand in hand, down that long dark tunnel with no light at the end. Two years she'd been staring it in the face, watching the man she loved die.

It can get grim towards the end, but she didn't flinch. Hers was the face he saw, hers the hand he felt. She took unpaid leave, kept him at home as long as she could. She pushed him through the park in a wheelchair, propped him up with pillows in the sun. She read to him. She fed him, spoonful by spoonful, wiped his chin, held the bowl for him when he had to throw up. She helped him to the shower when he couldn't walk and she washed him when he couldn't wash himself, and when he couldn't wipe his own backside she did that for him too.

She was with him right up to the last moment, sitting by his hospital bed and holding his hand, and at that very last moment, as his body gave up the fight to breathe, she saw or felt or felt that she saw something leave his body, and then he was gone. The nurse came with a sponge and a bowl but she took it and she washed his body herself. Then she kissed his cooling forehead and said I love you and goodbye. She buried him. She chose the funeral parlour and she chose the coffin and she chose the flowers and she delivered the eulogy and afterwards she threw a big party for him and invited all his friends and all her friends, and they all came and she drank whisky and couldn't get drunk.

But when all that was done, she found that she was still right where he'd left her; she was in the dark. She was standing at the end of that long tunnel they'd walked down together, and now she was alone. And she realised that she was desperate for the light. She was desperate to feel something again, to be with the living. She was like a diver striving for the surface, lungs bursting.

And I guess this is where I come in. I was at a party. I didn't actually know anyone at the party, except for the host. He was a guy I'd met at work, Jeff. I can't even remember why I went. I think Jeff thought I needed cheering up or something. Which I did. It was a big loud party with lots of drinking and dancing and knots of wildly laughing people spilling across the lawn, so I ended up in the kitchen of course. And there was Shelley. She was washing cutlery. I picked up a tea towel and we got talking, and we clicked. Straight away. Instant. We knew where we were headed pretty much right from the first word.

It was sex. Pure unadulterated sex. Just this wild, intense affair. We couldn't get enough of each other. It was incredible. She was so hungry, and I was too. We'd meet up whenever we could and we'd just fuck, and fuck and fuck until we could fuck no more. We'd spend entire weekends in bed. I'd never experienced anything like it. Literally, days in bed, fucking. We'd fuck for hours, then we'd order Indian takeaways. I'd pad to the door in a towel, pay, take it straight back to bed. We took regular shower breaks and sometimes we'd maybe go for a short walk, or we'd watch an old movie on TV, but generally it was just the sex.

At the same time, though, she kept a certain distance. She wasn't in a hurry to introduce me to her friends and she didn't seem keen to meet mine. I could understand that. Maybe she felt guilty. Maybe she thought her friends would judge her. Maybe she just couldn't face the thought of introductions and silences and the thundering presence of her dead husband.

We didn't go out either, to parties, or movies or restaurants. And we never went to her place. Not once. It was pretty much my place, takeaway food, and sex. We got on really well, though. There was nothing cold about it. We talked, we laughed, we tickled. We went the places lovers go, or most of them.

But a lot of the time she was—absent. Somewhere else, somewhere far, far away. And she didn't like to talk about herself too much. Sometimes I'd ask the wrong question and she'd smile and her eyes would slide away and I'd know I'd irritated her, or not exactly irritated her but blundered in somewhere I wasn't welcome. Or I'd say her name, when she was looking out the window or brushing her hair, and she'd be so far away in her thoughts she wouldn't even hear me. So I'd call her name again, more loudly, and she'd start and look at me, and for just that split second I could see in her face that same thing—disappointment, irritation, impatience. Almost dislike. I suppose she was angry at me for not being him. For being alive.

Sometimes I'd look into her eyes, in between bouts, or even when we were right in the middle of it, fucking, and it would be like looking into the eyes of a fish. Blank, cold, glassy. Horrible. But then, at other times, for the briefest moments, just for a second, she would turn, or make a comment, or put out her hand and touch me, and it was so present, so immediate and tender and alive that it was really beautiful and my heart just ached.

Once I had a dream about her and she was underwater, in the dark ocean, drifting through great forests of kelp, her eyes wide and staring and her lips blue and her long black hair blooming around her head like a cloud of ink. I told her about it and she said if it was all the same to me she'd prefer that I didn't put her in my dreams and I said no problem won't happen again.

It wasn't supposed to last. This is the point. That was the thing. And I understood that. It was an affair. A fling. Intense, all-consuming, brief. If it had been up to me—well, it wasn't up to me. She had her reasons, and I understood that. I really felt for her and I wanted to help if I could. She was in a terrible position. I told myself my part was just to be there. For as long as it lasted. Whatever it was she was looking for, she would find it, or not find it, and then it would be over. There was a level beyond which she could not go and that was only natural and completely understood. I promised myself only this: that when the time came there would be no bitterness, no regret, and whatever happened, no matter what, I wouldn't try to change her mind.

And that time was approaching. I felt it. Often she was edgy. She was moody, restless. Her absences were getting longer, and more frequent. She was sinking back down into those dark waters.

Saturday evening, we were at my place. I'd taken a Viagra.

I had to, to stand the pace. We'd been going about it with determined concentration and resolve. We'd hardly spoken. But I could see she wasn't getting there. She was getting frustrated. All afternoon she'd been distant, preoccupied. Finally I plucked up courage and I asked her what was wrong. This was exactly the sort of question I wasn't supposed to ask. It was the sort she never answered. But this time she thought for a moment, then looked at me almost timidly. 'I don't think I can do this much longer,' she said.

So the moment had come. Okay. I took a breath. I shrugged. 'That's okay,' I said. 'I totally understand.'

'We can still be friends.'

'We can absolutely still be friends, or we can even not be friends, just whatever you think is appropriate to your situation.'

She smiled. She looked relieved. She pushed me back down on the bed.

*

She was on top. It was dark now, but there was some light coming from a street light outside my window. I remember looking up at her and she seemed magnificent. She was a mermaid. Small beads of sweat were glittering on her chest and her neck like fish scales and her black hair was flying. She'd started slow, but she was building, and now she was coming down hard at every stroke, hovering and striking, and starting to build up speed. She was completely lost in it, in the rhythm, and I was holding still and being a rock for her. She was building and building, getting faster and faster, and it was all coming together for her and for me and then, I don't know why, for just a split second she lost concentration or I twitched or something happened and as she came to the top of the stroke she went an inch too far and I slipped out.

It all happened so fast. I felt myself pop out and then she came back down again, the whole weight of her body behind her, slamming down. She didn't notice or even if she did she couldn't possibly react in time, she couldn't stop or even slow, and she came down with full force right on the end of my penis which was now lodged hard up against her perineum.

God it hurt. I heard a sharp popping sound, and there was just this sudden incredibly intense pain. I screamed. We switched on the bedside lamp. I sat there and stared. It was like a bad dream. There, in a pool of light, was my penis, bent over in the middle at ninety degrees, like an old drinking straw. Shelley gasped and said oh my God, and that we should go to the hospital, but it seemed to be slowly straightening out so I said no, I thought it was going to be okay, and let's just wait and see what happens. We turned off the light and lay there in the dark, side by side, not touching, and she kept saying over and over how sorry she was and I kept saying it wasn't her fault and not to worry it would be fine, though it was actually throbbing like hell and I felt panicky. But after a while we drifted off to sleep.

I woke up an hour later, and now I was in agony. I switched on the light again and my penis was the size and colour of an aubergine. It was swollen up into this giant purple thing. It was so painful it felt as if it was about to burst. I couldn't get dressed. I could hardly move. Shelley wrapped her dressing gown around me, and somehow we got down the steps and out to the street and she drove me straight to casualty. I lay on the back seat staring at her profile with the city lights flashing past and she drove fast and all she could say was I'm sorry, I'm sorry, I'm sorry and all I could say was not your fault not your fault not your fault.

The nurse at reception took one look and just the look on her face. That's it, I thought. I've lost it for sure. It's gone. She put us in a little examination room and called the house surgeon who called the consultant. The consultant said I had suffered major penile trauma with a rupture of both the left and right corpora cavernosae. He'd seen this sort of thing before—it happens a lot more than you might think—but he'd never seen a case as bad as this. He explained that when Shelley came crashing down on the end of the penis it bent so far that it ruptured the internal sheath which is normally watertight and holds in the blood during an erection. Normally after an injury like that the erection would be lost, the blood vessels would shut down, and the bleeding would at least be minimised, but because I'd taken a Viagra, the blood supply didn't shut down—that's what Viagra does, it keeps the blood flowing. And that's why it was so severe. Even after the injury I didn't lose my erection, and the blood flow didn't stop; it just kept on haemorrhaging away until my penis was one giant haematoma, a swelling balloon of blood.

The consultant asked if he could some take photos for research purposes. I said okay, so he got out his mobile and snapped a few, which didn't seem very official to me. Then he said he was going to have to operate. I started crying again. I couldn't help it. It was all just so awful, like waking up on the wrong end of a Tarantino movie. They wheeled me off to theatre, prepped me, sedated me, and got stuck right in. He explained later that they peeled the whole penis, like a banana, fixed it, put it all back together.

Of course I didn't want to see any of that. I was awake but they did it behind a little screen. I actually begged for a general but I'd eaten dinner and he said I could choose between a stomach pump and then a general or just straight to a spinal block. I took the block. Putting in the block hurt like hell, but I didn't feel anything after that, just a distant pushing and pulling, like they were vigorously rearranging my underwear. Anyway I was so sedated I hardly knew what was going on—and then about the time they were finishing time telescoped completely shut.

Next thing I remember I was in a ward with a lot of other cot cases, strapped up and catheterised. It was throbbing, throbbing, throbbing, but I was heavily drugged. Shelley was nowhere to be seen. A few beds away someone was muttering. Someone else was snoring. I drifted in and out of consciousness for what remained of the night, dreaming strange vivid dreams and waking, time and again, to the same recurrent nightmare of that darkened echoing ward, the smell of disinfectant and my own tacky mouth.

I remember one dream in particular. All the women I had ever slept with gathered round me as I lay on a white bed in a white room with a single high window through which could be heard the sea. They wore white gowns and kept calling me Patrick,

though that is not my name. I realised the women were all virgins
and they were smiling and I knew that they had forgiven me.
Then they turned into sea birds and flew away, singing sweetly.
I looked between my legs and saw that I had a vagina. It was
the most beautiful vagina I had ever seen. It glowed with inner
light. I realised with inexpressible relief that I had actually been
a woman all along and everything in my life up to this moment
had been a terrible misunderstanding which was now cleared up.

I woke up next morning and there she was. Shelley. She had
some flowers and she was smiling down at me. 'Sorry,' she said.

'Not your fault,' I said.

I was in hospital for another two days. Shelley was there
the whole time. She had asked me on the first night, before I
went into theatre, if there was anyone I wanted her to call. But
I realised there wasn't. My family were all overseas, in different
cities, so I didn't see any point in worrying them. I'd wait until I
had some good news, or at least some news. I had friends in town,
of course, but I didn't want to call them either. Not yet. Actually,
the truth was I only wanted Shelley. I didn't say that, but maybe
she understood, or maybe she just felt responsible. Whatever the
reason, she stuck around and she was wonderful.

On day three they took out the catheter and changed the
bandages and sent me home. The consultant came round for a
final look. He unwound the bandage himself. I didn't know what
I was going to see and I was nervous as hell. Shelley held my
hand. When the gauze came off, it looked awful. It was blotchy
and yellow and purple and strangely chalky and flaky, and all
flattened out like an inner tube. I thought I was going to be sick
and I said so, and instantly she had a kidney dish under my chin.
It was like magic.

But it was good news. The operation had gone well. I was
going to be on painkillers for a while longer, and I was going to
have to take it very, very easy, but he was confident I would make
a full recovery, probably in six to ten weeks.

Shelley drove me home. We were both quiet in the car. We
were awkward and formal and overly polite with each other. It

was as if we'd never met. When she spoke she was chatty, but I could see a muscle in her jaw working, and she kept her eyes fixed on the road ahead. I understood, of course. Now that I was on the mend it was over. Again. This was goodbye and I had no problem with that at all. She owed me nothing, after all. I even had a vague idea that I could somehow take something from all this, make a new start of some kind.

We got back to my place and she helped me upstairs. It was a small flat but it had a view of the sea. I lay on the couch. I closed my eyes. I could hear her moving about the kitchen, unloading the dishwasher. Every rattle of a plate, every tinkle of a glass, seemed to be a sound only she could have made, as personal as her own voice.

I became acutely aware of time. It was passing. The interval between now and forever was dissolving, crumbling away. But somehow there is always a second, a half-second, in which to shelter from the inevitable. I lay there, safe in that ever-crumbling moment, thinking about all the things I had lost and all the things I had thrown away. My personal history seemed to me a junkyard, a great pile of unsorted and unusable objects, none of them paid for, none of them mine. I slept.

When I woke it was getting dark. The orange light of the sun glowed strangely on the pea-green walls. The flat was hot and dim and silent. A light was on, the window was shut. Shelley must have closed it before she went. Perhaps she had left a note. Perhaps I would never see her again. Perhaps this was her way of saying goodbye. Perhaps it was the best way. Perhaps she would be back tomorrow. It didn't matter.

I was terribly thirsty and I had to urinate, but if I moved it would hurt, and if I urinated it would hurt even more, so I lay a while longer.

Suddenly there was a noise across the other side of the quiet room, halfway between a rustle and a tearing sound, and I shouted in surprise and leapt to my feet. Much too quickly; through a flash of pain, I saw her sitting cross-legged on a nest of cushions in the corner, a book in her lap, the page she had been in the act of turning still grasped between forefinger and thumb. Her expression was comical, eyes wide. Then I half fainted and sank back onto the couch and lay down. She came to kneel beside me. Our eyes were on a level. Her breath, smelling lightly of cloves, was warm on my face.

'Stay,' I said. 'Please stay.'

Amy Brown

Jeff Mangum

I played all I could remember
of *Aeroplane*—fans bought me beer
but didn't treat me like the Messiah.

Awesome show, Jeff, they'd say, friends
not apostles. There was just one
woman with magenta hair, dilated

pupils, who said, *'Religion itself,*
any religion, keeps a person on the right
path. Not the fear of God, but

upholding your own sense of honour
and obeying your own conscience.'
I'm not afraid of you, Jeff Mangum,

but you keep my conscience strong
and my eyes from wandering.
Aeroplane *is kind of my religion.*

I listen to it on Sunday mornings
to soothe my hangover
while I eat corn chips and smoke.

I think you're amazing.
Usually this sentiment would send me
straight to the airport, back to my sofa

away from the stage.
It would put me off the smell
of beer and tobacco for years.

But, not her. *You quoted Anne*
Frank, I said.
Yes! You made me

read it—it's part of my worship.
I felt ill and wanted to yell
Worship Anne not me

but could only say *Excuse me.*
I was Anne's apostle,
this pink-haired woman was mine.

I didn't want her. Did Anne
not want me? I felt sick. Outside,
someone passed me a joint.

Cat drum tree truck car petal breath lie water tea trickle baby
scream dog wind snore television Beach Boys maraca kettle birds
(always birds and traffic) cars teenage-girls laughter giggling
(always giggling) fiddle kick drum snare tom bagpipes singing
saw voice my own my love's sex breathing friction car horn toots
footsteps creaking doors teeth grinding (bruxomania—good
word) words poetry birds smashing snail shells woodchopping
lawnmowing vacuuming indoor and outdoor sounds the
beginning of *Under Milkwood* read aloud by a twelve year old
limping running capering jumping fawning sulking impressing
caring caressing humouring listening humming whistling

a thousand sounds in a minute: that's my goal.
Laziness looks inviting, but only work gives you
true satisfaction. It takes four hours to record one minute.

If I work more than three hours a day, I forget
how to talk to people, how to eat and how to sleep
(not that I've ever been an expert at any of these).

I'd work in a trance and never stop
if it were possible. I'd do nothing but make sound
montages for my friends.

But I can't—the results would be disappointing.
So I take a break each afternoon
to collage acoustic Fenders. Black and white

photos glued in a harmonious pattern all over
the instruments' bodies. It is
a beautiful occupation until morning.

James Brown

What the very old man told me

That he had regrets. That he didn't like saying
things were better in the old days,
but they probably were.
That god existed, but only as an idea.

That most people had rocks for brains.
That Wordsworth was right about emotion
recollected in tranquility, but wrong about nature.
That one should never turn one's back on the sea.

That vehicles shouldn't be allowed on beaches.
That I should be careful about shellfish.
That he liked form. That his joints ached
when it was overcast.

That asked to choose between the devil and
the deep blue sea, he'd take the deep blue sea.
That Roger and Simon were his favourite characters
in *The Lord of the Flies.*

That automatic cars were hopeless
because you couldn't crash start them.
That his jet-ski cuff-links were a present
from one of his sons. That they were a joke.

That the mind is first a maze, then a treadmill.
That he preferred classical music.
That dogs should never have thrown
their lot in with humans.

That he could barely recall
the strange young man who wrote
Daddy   from the author   9/4/37
in his book *Enemies: Poems 1934–36.*

That he missed glass milk bottles.
That he loved his wife.
That he liked walking.
That he liked watching water.

The Pitfalls of Poetry

I grow old.
The world is mould.
The dreams I held
were cheaply sold.

My shoes have holes.
My feet are cold.
I mark my pages
with a fold.

The sharp mind forks
the tongue for gold.
A likely story
poorly told.

Stephanie Burt

Fifth Grade Time Capsule

Having given the sun and school
      their expected, ceremonious farewells,
I can start to envision my future, my big reveal.

      By that point everything I have kept
between my boards, in my polyurethane seal,
      will have acquired fresh appeal

as evidence from another age:
      a glitter-pen sketch of a tubular rocketship;
an origami-cricket notebook page,

      a jadeite earring, the *Boston Globe*, and a scallop-
necked T-shirt graced with an entourage
      of names in Sharpie, in graffiti script.

I know I am too young to date.
      My answer to everything is 'It's too early to say'.
Though I am ready to lead a long-delayed

      or even a buried life, I dream of the day
when I am decoded and vaunted, of a floral float in a parade
      if not a chauffeured evening on the town.

The people who pick me up can never be
      the same as the ones who put me down.

Rachel Bush

Thought Horses

Some things to think of between 4.30 and 6.30 are:
The sleeping computer, how its green eye opens and closes.
Then how the heels of shoes can be stacked and steep and you
will never wear them or buy them or desire them.
So you remember the small woman with glittery eyes who
said outside Dick Smith's, 'Your shoes look like you're going
tramping.'
Then the friend who is worried because maybe the growth is
back again.
You lie as if you take savasana in yoga, your feet apart, your
palms facing up so that your shoulders are spread, your fingers
curled. You will let go of your thoughts, just concentrate on
your breathing as if you watch someone else breathe in and out.
Another woman who is sick will have a hysterectomy on 13
June and you work out that will be a Monday and you know the
operation is to be in Christchurch.
There is a chance to think of death.
You think about baking gingernuts.
You think about baking ginger crunch.
You think about whether you want a new bed or new spectacles
first.
You dream you can take wooden bookcases from the downstairs
room of your old house. They have adjustable shelving and you
dream you use them again.
You think how that is the first dream of the old house and that
now those dreams must be starting.
You think about the dawn chorus which does not happen at
your new house, though one or two birds seem to be doing their
individual best to pull up the sun.
You think about emailing the friend who is worried her cancer
has returned, but then think it is probably better just to let it go
because almost everything you say could be wrong.

You think about the woman who returned a plate on which
you had given her some ginger crunch. She'd left this painted
African plate with four persimmons in your letterbox.
You think about the cousin who said he would ring you this
weekend. Your thought is not of him, but about him ringing
and he has not rung.
You think about the *Brighton Rock* film where Helen Mirren
still manages to look like Queen Elizabeth, especially when she
wears a headscarf.
You think of the poem you wrote about leaving a house, and
how houses we have owned will come back to us in dreams.
You think about taking your computer into the next room.
You think maybe you ought to try to sleep.
You think you should just think about your breathing. You do
this for several breaths until the thought horses ride over and
look at you and you turn to them with their big protruding eyes
and you forget about the movement of your breath.
You think how, if you are careful, you could move very quietly
to the computer.

'All my feelings would have been of common things'

All my feelings are of common things
of the clock going on, of the next
meal or the last one, of the washing
on the line and if there's enough heat
to dry it, of how to clean a lawnmower
just enough to make the Salvation Army
man want to take it away, with old grey
grass stuck to the blades, the tyres that hold
dirt, like cleats in walking shoes. Also
a dryer I bought forty years ago,
I stick the manual and the expired
guarantee inside the metal drum.
All those clothes it turned and churned, the lint
that it trapped in its door. I once thought
many things would make my life happier
and now one by one I will let them go.

Zarah Butcher-McGunnigle

Late to my appointment because my ex-boyfriend was like, Do you want to scam Airbnb with me? You can make a hundred dollars out of this. I colour-coordinated my outfit to my medication. I want something to bite me. On the way home my phone falls out of my hand and breaks. I tell my housemate about my broken phone, she says, 'Oh, that's difficult when you are poor and you can't afford to replace it.' Last year I went on a date with 56-year-old man from a sugar daddy website. I got paid a hundred dollars to talk to him while he ate lunch at the botanic gardens café. He asked me if I knew what a 'gif' was. A bird kept jumping on the table trying to get his food and he got really stressed about it. I took photos of the bird.

I tell my friend I'm stressed because I can't afford to buy food for the next few days. He says, Yeh, me too, same, I only have X amount of money in my account till I get paid tonight. But he just moved to London and he lives rent-free with his dad and he has a full-time job. I tell him about how my shoe started breaking when I was just sitting at a computer, and then it fully broke, the sole came off completely. I had to travel home for an hour without shoes. He says, Oh yeh, me too, my shoe is breaking too, I'm just waiting for it to break fully before I get it repaired.

*

Everyone is getting married. I'm eating these disgusting chocolates that have melted and re-formed five times while sitting in my friend's hot car. My sister has fallen in love with a $64 fish. I'm really depressed, maybe I should have a baby. I already feel like a mother because I've dated a lot of immature people. I think I need to have an emotional experience with a dolphin. I think that would help me, if not a baby. Dolphins always seem happy and like they are smiling. However, the blubber under their skin disconnects facial muscles from skin, so they are incapable of facial expressions. A lot of people have advised me not to focus on romantic relationships and to focus on friendships instead but . . . I don't have any close friends. The last time I had a close friend I hung out with and enjoyed spending time with was when I was eight.

The last guy I dated was still officially married to his ex-girlfriend. He said that he hadn't wanted to get married and he'd told her that he didn't want to get married. But then she proposed and he didn't know how to say no. I don't understand, I said. If you didn't want to get married why did you get married? It's not that easy, he said. Have you ever been proposed to?

*

I'm very cold and I can't concentrate on anything but also I feel existentially embarrassed about wanting to be warm. The only thing keeping me warm this winter is period blood soaking in to my underwear. I finally bought a heater but it is small and doesn't warm up my room properly. Three days later I'm still experiencing cognitive dissonance regarding the heater I bought and the heater that the people at the shop tried to sell me. The heater that would have warmed up my room properly was too expensive because I don't have a job. I want to tell someone I love them but there is no one to tell. Except my sister, maybe. I want to pick blackberries on a farm and then die.

Kate Camp

Snow White's Coffin

Tom Waits records the sound of frying chicken
that's how he achieves his pops and crackles.
Our old unit had a hooked grey arm,
it was a trunk of wood with woven speakers.

As a child I worried about forgetting:
the hexagonal handle, a creamy honey cell,
that flaw in the lino resembling Donald Duck
while the others of its kind looked like grey bells.

Sometimes life would seem too big, even then
an empty Sunday where you drifted as a ghost.
I saw *Bonnie and Clyde* on such a day,
as I recall, in black and white

when the bullets came
they died like oceans
full of slow turbulence
as if brought by death to life.

Why preserve one's childhood memories?
So, like Egyptians, they might be packed into the grave?
That I would sit up nights, eating from the Haworth mug
spoonfuls of plain sugar mixed with cinnamon.

Is there room in the sarcophagus for that,
for the feeling of the covers of paperbacks,
in which girls survive, among great trees,
girls who make mistakes in forests.

One thing I loved was to pick the scabs on my knees
while sitting on the toilet.
Do I need to say, I ate them?
Who is taking this down?

*

The Dutch, I believe, have built a car one molecule long.
I've seen its silly form, its atom wheels.
It looks nothing like a car, it looks to be a pupa
some kind of baby bee surprised by disaster in its cell.

The problems of this world will not be solved by tiny cars.
Everything is small enough already
and there is too much, too much of everyone.
To understand your life you need another whole life.

I think we are sitting here on the axis my friend
that is why we feel a bit unwell.
Buried in us are minutes, days, mornings slept late
nights of no rest, turning to one side

turning again like a tide
sweating into the bodies of hot beds
those bucketfuls of moisture.
I think that futures might be in us too

driving in tiny cars, they are opening their minute glove
boxes and with infinitesimal hands
draw out maps too small to imagine
but they imagine them, they look at the lists of streets

all arranged according to the alphabet.
And then I think they throw the book away.
And they get out from the car
and they throw the keys into the ocean

howling. They do not want to go to places in books.
They will not drive
in their molecule cars
those ridiculous cartoons.

*

Snow White's Coffin
is an integrated radio and record player
that introduced Plexiglas to the domestic interior.
Relieve yourself of the excruciating clutter of the world

is what it says to you
everything you thought was *being alive*
is revealed as a problem
which can be solved by good design.

Eleanor Catton

Descent from Avalanche

What next? A double room at the lodge down in the pass village. Maybe a steak dinner at the hotel after the climb. Harriet's wind-worn cheeks shining in the yellow shudder of the candle flame, and then a walk up to the Devil's Punchbowl in the dusk with unlit torches strapped across their foreheads, in case the night fell sooner than it ought. Later her red-knuckled hands would find him in the darkness, and her small chapped mouth would open, and when she raised herself on her elbows above him, the slack weight of her worn-leather breasts would fall onto his chest as if she had transferred to him some burden, and pin him there.

What next? Richard thought. And after that? He watched a pair of fantails dip and duck between the birches and he heard the train sound its mournful bray from the river, far below. It had rained in the night, so the veins glittered red in the wet mottle of the rocks and their boot-prints softened and sank in the clay. Harriet was leading. From where he stood he could see only the fine spray of ochre up the backs of her gaiters, the rounded khaki ball of her arse, the two blue veins that bisected the backs of her knees. She hauled herself up over a net of roots and disappeared.

Richard stopped and slipped his arm out of his backpack to sling the bag down onto the track, and as he stooped over it he felt the sudden chill of his own sweat cooled by the wind. The stain on his back always formed the skull of a ram.

He unscrewed his water bottle quietly. He had shucked his bag quietly too. He wanted her to get far ahead before she half-turned and realised that he wasn't there. She'd wait for him sitting on a stone at a switchback farther up and when he appeared she'd say, 'We could have stopped together,' and he'd say, 'I only wanted a drink. I didn't want to spoil your rhythm,' and even though she wouldn't be sullen, even though she wouldn't care, it would still be his triumph, and he would chalk it up in his mind.

It had long since begun, that underwater feeling of retreat, that slow drift away from her, that grey pre-dawn of possibility each time he caught another woman's eye. He yearned for renewal. He yearned to annihilate his defective, disappointed self by simply leaving her behind. Newness would be his restoration. The next woman would be his cure. He had already walked around their flat and mentally parcelled everything that was his, and moved away.

They were selfish about the outdoors and so they holidayed mostly in the wintertime, when the peaks were lonely and the summit shale was splintered bright with ice. The lodges dropped their tariffs and the road through the shrunken gullet of Otira Gorge was often closed. It was July, and no longer school holidays—they'd checked. The car park by the visitor centre was filmed with slush and empty. The forecast was poor. As Richard filled out an intentions card and slipped it behind the elasticated wire that ran across the notice board the ranger said, 'Reckon you'll be all alone up there today,' and Richard said, 'Good thing too, we never learned to share.'

He drank, and took a moment to watch the tumble of a rivulet that had swollen into a cascade. The mountain came alive after the rains. The track became an artery and the earth shone like something raw. The wetness was glorious to him: it lent such a potency, a life, even to the smallest of the birch leaves, each of them focused and pricked by a spot of light. As a boy he had found a green-flecked worry stone in a riverbed, perfectly oval and buffed to a gleam by its endless journey down toward the sea. He plucked it from the water and held it and watched the damp film shrink to nothing until the stone was quite dry in his hand, no longer brilliant or even green. He took it home and held it under the tap occasionally, to watch it shine.

Beneath the cascade, seeded in the slender near-vertical furrows between the strata of the schist, a fern clung darkly to the overhang. Richard watched the leaves shudder beneath the rush of water, and marvelled: such a poor place to seed, he thought, such a sorry prospect for a rooted plant, and yet there it was, alive, and living. He was suddenly overwhelmed by the fecundity around him, by the fierce and blinded propulsion of life—how this most tiny of fissures, the determined anchor of these shallow-rooted ferns, made a foolishness of his question *what next*.

Long ago he might have stored this observation to share with her, to exclaim over, to thread like a small bead of glass beside all the other strung treasures they picked out to remember and to own. Not now. What had they lost? Richard exhaled. The question was too huge. It was not a matter of disconnect—she was *there*, well enough—it was that her soul was so complete, so conclusive and concluded—her pragmatism was deathly and total and cold—he could not hurt her. That was it. He could not alter her, or shake her from herself.

In the last few weeks Richard had found himself forgiving her, being patient with her, performing small measures of kindness with the generous and expansive indifference of a man who would soon be gone. What was once an act of grudging investment was now an act of philanthropy—a dispensation, like a kind of welfare for the very poor. He was impressed by his own instinctive move toward pity, and calm—it showed such a tender streak in him—oh, how warmly he would caress her cheek, how gently he would place those copper pennies over the cold curve of each eye, how touched he would be by his own goodbye, when he left her.

By now his heartbeat had returned to normal and the soreness in his legs had quieted to a kind of hum. Lactic acid gave Richard a profound satisfaction. He was oriented by any kind of pain, and physical exercise disappointed him if it was not rigorous and cruel. This mountain was his measure. He had known the peak in all weather, in all seasons, as a boy, and as a man. When he became old, it would be Avalanche that told him so. He swung his pack up again and turned from the valley and the view.

Soon he would start looking. He knew that he would not leave her before he had found somebody else. He would be a fool to give up the promise of regular sex and the detached comfort of their symbiotic life. But Richard was in his late forties now, and the flood of anxious lonely women in their thirties had become a sudden smorgasbord of opportunity. He knew to wear the relationship on his chest like a badge of internship—'I dated a woman for seven years'—and he knew how quickly he would find another, a woman who would count herself among the lucky and the few.

Harriet was a plum of a woman, round-cheeked and stocky in the trunk, with stout little legs, and ball-shaped calves, and wrists that dimpled. Her brothers were long since barrel-chested. In their years together she had broadened and compacted under his hands—her skin was firmer now, and the scatter of freckles over her arms and across her back had darkened and bled. She had morphed from looking like somebody's unmarried sister into looking like somebody's unmarried aunt. Richard had always felt a peevish self-congratulation at having settled for a woman who was not as attractive as he was capable of winning. He had always felt that she was indebted to him, indebted to his progressive spirit, more than she knew—but she would know it soon enough, of course. When he left her, she would realise how wholly she would have to downgrade.

He was not an arsehole. He did not measure her against those dyed, starved, and brainless women who laughed too loud and flashed their teeth too brightly. But Harriet seemed to care so little about the way she looked—she was not defiant, simply unmoved—and it disappointed him. There was a peculiar thrill to the idea that when he appraised a woman's body, a part of her was appraising too. In Harriet there was nothing of that touching self-effacement, no profound doubt of her own claim to beauty, no profound fear of her very right to doubt. In such women, Richard thought, beauty was something so fragile, so fugitive, so desperately precious, that every touch became an act of worship, a gift. Whenever Richard told Harriet she was beautiful she laughed.

She kept fit. In bed she bobbed energetically and came with a dutiful regularity, always with the same double-glotted gasp and then a release like a murmur. When she undressed, she stripped herself with a capable unthinking quickness, shaking down her shirts from the collar and whipping them over the back of the armchair on her side of the bed. After she bathed she towelled herself with such a vigour that her skin turned pink in patches. He watched her perform these daily administrations through the cracked half-inch of the bedroom door and wondered at her. She bent naked from the waist to rub talcum powder into the rounded sheen of her calf. She brushed back her short hair with hard lashing strokes and seemed not to notice the way her breasts jounced up and down, her nipples lax and puffed and only ever so slightly fawny, like they were overlaid with an umber gauze. She arched out with her leg to flick a pair of underwear off the floor and scoop it into her hand. She hooked her bra together in front, at her navel, and then spun it around and climbed into it like a harness.

He longed to catch her, just once, staring at her own image in the full-length mirror on his side of the bed. He longed to catch her standing there with heavy helpless shoulders and a reflected expression of such girlish resignation and sorrow that his heart would surge into his throat and he would want to crush her soft head against his chest and hold her there. He longed for her to throw down a casserole dish, tear up her tax forms, burst into tears on the motorway—anything, anything. Anything to make him feel mistrusted, or angry, or misunderstood. Each kiss, a murder or a miracle—he didn't care.

But she was generous with him, and patient. Often she came up behind him when he sat working at his study desk and released the hiss-valve on his swivel chair. He sank with a quiet compression of air until the desk was level with his nipples and then she spun him carefully around and gave him head with her strong little hands kneading his hips and his hand cupped around the back of her skull so the heel of his palm crushed the shell of her ear. She was indifferent to his semen and spat it briskly into the sink like a wad of toothpaste before she rinsed.

God, there was something so *adult* about their life together, some-thing so efficient, so mature. She was a woman. He wanted a girl.

Nearly an hour passed before he caught up with Harriet again. She had stopped just above the tree line, where the flank of the mountain emptied out suddenly into a ragged horseshoe of peaks—Bealey through Cassidy, curving around to the summit of Avalanche, still out of view—and gave a sudden vista down into the flat-bottomed cradle of the pass. The tussock was flattened beneath a shelf of broken snow. The foulweather markers started here, and Richard could see the first three, orange-topped and angled acutely like a line of acupuncture needles standing out of the white. They bore southwest up the ridge. Harriet had changed already into a windproof parka and a woollen hat, and when he trudged up through the topmost fringe of the bush she was breaking a bar of chocolate into squares.

'You took your time,' she said.

'I just stopped for a drink.'

'Sure you aren't getting old?'

He swung his pack down beside her and stretched. 'Weather's held out so far.'

'Bet it's raining on Scott's Track right now though.'

'Be savage up on the tops too.'

'Shake us up a bit.'

He found a bag of brazil nuts and shook a half-dozen into his palm. 'I still want to do the round trip,' he said. 'I hate coming down the same way I've come up.'

'Me too. Isn't it funny? It's a bit ridiculous, really. Isn't it ridiculous?'

'Yeah.'

'Isn't it funny,' Harriet said again. Her chocolate had picked up tiny veins of wool fibre from her mittens. She took off one mitten with her teeth and tried to brush the squares clean with her fingers. 'With a round trip you can fool yourself you're *getting* somewhere.'

Richard zipped up his own parka and pulled a balaclava over his head. They ate and looked at the view. The turquoise streak of the Bealey River, vibrant from the snowmelt, threaded east to splice with the fibres of the Waimak and then spill across the plains to the eastern sea. The river was flattened by their perspective and it shone like a lode. Westward, beyond the saddle of the pass, the rivers and the runoff gullies all flowed toward another ocean, bottoming out in the marshy land at the heel of Deception Valley where they joined the ugly bronze rush of the Buller and the Taramakau. The island was an upturned keel after all. A shipwreck. He remembered quipping once, 'That's the thing about Arthur's Pass—it's all downhill from here'—to Harriet, most probably, standing here as they were now, a little younger, a little happier, looking out at a slightly different view.

'I need to get moving,' Harriet said. 'My temperature's dropped.'

'I'll set the pace for a while, okay?'

'Sure. Go ahead.'

Harriet waited as Richard zipped up his pack and set off into the snow, following the path of yellowed boot-prints, days old and gelled by the recent rain so the impress of each patterned sole in the snow was blurred to nothing. She tried to guess the number of people that had passed since the last snowfall, and then for a while she tried to walk exactly in Richard's prints, to match his stride exactly. The movement was unnatural for her, too broad and mannish. She felt herself unfurl. The snow would become fresher as they climbed higher. It might even be unbroken at the top.

They rarely spoke at length while they were tramping. Richard's communion with the land was something dogged and private, a ritual in service of a myth he never disclosed. Even when he explained something that was wonderful to him—bent to cup the scooped white head of an alpine buttercup against his palm, or hushed her with the flat of his hand when he saw the green breast of a bellbird shivering on a pod of flax—even when he laced her boots for her, tighter than she could manage on her own, or rubbed sunscreen into the freckled skin at the nape of her neck, Harriet remained an outsider, a foreigner lost in that vast expanse of negative space between Richard and the world.

Some twenty paces ahead, Richard bent and reached down

with his mitten to fish for a stone and toss it underhand onto a cairn as he passed. The stone was discernible only as it tumbled: the moment it stopped moving it became invisible against the rest. Harriet smiled. She thought of how many of the buried stones in the pile were already Richard's, hoarded up here against the sky as a slender proof of his passing, over the years. The thought was condescending. She was treating him like an invalid, like a widower in mourning for his own youth, like a terminal patient guided to the mountains to rehabilitate and reclaim something crucial he had lost.

She watched him stamp up the ridge away from her and saw, in his whole person, the crushing mighty weight of his midlife crisis—but that term was flip and even gaudy, and the shorthand image of a red Porsche cruelly diminished the profound and particular horror with which Richard had now come to view his future and his life. Harriet shook her head. She felt for him. He had always understood his body as a machine, as a vehicle, as a hobby-project that could be tinkered and tested and improved, and now, at last, it was failing.

Richard's body was a subject that had always been mutually taboo. He refused prostate checks at the doctor's. He was intensely secretive about the ointments and medicines that he kept in the drawer on his side of the bed, and flew into a rage if she remarked on any shadow of infirmity about him, any defect, any rash. He called himself a liberal and voted to the left, but whenever a man kissed another man on television he would get up and leave the room—always under pretext, of course, stacking the dishwasher, boiling the jug for a cup of tea—and if she tried to tease him about it he would look past her, look through her, and frown slightly, as if what she was saying simply didn't make sense. Whenever he fell ill he would tremble and creep around the curtained darkness of their bedroom in a withered state of despair.

She thought: poor Richard. If only he didn't take himself so seriously.

Harriet placed her own stone upon the cairn. It quavered and then rolled over and came to rest. She did not cherish her own skin as Richard cherished his. All her life she had enjoyed that peculiar invisibility of an average-looking woman with no real charm to recommend her and nothing to lose. It was liberating, to be able to enter a room and disturb nothing, affect nothing, while other more attractive women were pursued with straining bloodshot attention every time they bent, or reached, or touched. How exhausting it would be to be stripped and stalked and raped by eyeball, every day. Harriet saw women forced to withdraw, to give less, to protect some secret patch of unbounded skin below their navel with the cup of their hand as they spoke, and after it all, to end in despair before the mirror, crying out, as her friend Marge had cried in the changing-sheds at the department store, 'My breasts—my breasts—like two cookies in a pair of socks.' Harriet pitied her. She was proud of her own equanimity. She was even proud of her plainness, in a way—it was a freedom. She wore it like a badge.

She kicked out her leg and felt the sharp coin of the blister forming on her heel. It was amazing to her how the mind condensed any recollection of a physical act—in her memory Avalanche Peak was a mere series of slides, vistas picked out at intervals and strung together in such a brisk sequence that the tax and the cruelty of the journey entirely dropped away. But that was the way of all effort: it vanished into abstraction on either edge of the present moment. All you were ever left with, Harriet thought, was the summit view, the before and the after, and above that, a vague and hovering sense of whether the journey had been hard or easy—whether it had been worth it—whether it had been a waste of time.

Harriet had never really been tramping before she met Richard, only squash and swimming and yoga classes on the dusty floor of the community hall. Richard brought her to the alps. When they first met he took her to the climbing wall at the YMCA and said, 'It's a way to learn to trust someone.' On the wall they were polite and tender with each other, and whenever Harriet lost her hold and swung out over the gym with her shoulders trembling and her fingertips on fire, Richard would say, as he paid out the rope and she descended, 'It's harder for you—you haven't got the reach, that's all.' There was something infinitely touching about the way that his harness gave a triangular emphasis to the slack pouch of his groin. She had been surprised by his embarrassment. He clasped his hands together in front of him whenever he could, and tugged the hem of his T-shirt down below the belt of the harness so it formed a ruched little skirt and his collar was dragged downward at his throat. She looked away, to be kind. He kissed her in the car afterwards and chucked her under the chin with the pad of his thumb.

Richard's smallness was something they had never talked about aloud, then or now, but privately Harriet was fascinated by it. How had he coped as a boy? Had he been bullied or shamed? What about brothers, father, uncles—had they seen, and did they know? It was tempting to view the whole of Richard's projected self—the way he swaggered, the way he sat with his knees well apart, his loud scoffing laugh, his moods and sudden silence—merely as symptoms. That was unfair. But she did think of the rest of his body as a kind of consolation: his broad square shoulders that tapered to a narrow, tightly muscled waist, the handsome sweep of his hair across his shoulders, the fine breadth of his cheeks and his brow. And she liked that he had this private handicap. It made her love him all the more.

A kea wheeled above them and cried out. The sound trailed to an eerie nothing. She looked up the slope and saw Richard lift his head and follow the bird with his eyes as it swooped up the cleft of the valley and shrank against the sky.

The truth was that his handsomeness disturbed her—as if the genetic accident of his face was some kind of ruse, some cunning stratagem to advance his position in the world. Beauty was only ever a deception, Harriet thought. The unlovely were frank, and honest, and they were *real*. Richard's beauty gave him only frailty, insecurity, guile. Harriet had dated increasingly unlovely men through her twenties and thirties—Richard was a rare exception—in a trajectory that was wholly conscious, for close to her heart she still believed that an ugly man might be less inclined to leave her, in the end.

Harriet had never once ended a relationship on her own terms. This was a piece of information so traumatic, so intensely private, that she had never spoken of it aloud to anyone, not even once. She was vague with Richard when she spoke of former lovers. She contrived to make each split sound mutual and even inverted the roles of the most painful partings—'I just didn't want that kind of a life,' she said, and 'I guess I'd left him behind, emotionally,' and 'One day I woke up and looked at him, and it was like all my love had drained out of me, and I simply felt nothing at all.' By now they had all become husbands and fathers. For three of them, she had been the dead patch of air that launched them into marriage, the vacuum beneath the wing.

She crested a false summit and paused to breathe. Ahead the ridge dropped into a shallow saddle and then climbed again. Richard was walking determinedly, without pause, as if he meant to keep a distance between them. She thought: he is so parcelled up in his own failure. Each year drives the kernel of his self still deeper, embeds it still more firmly in the lonely fog of his sinking chest. She thought: soon he will be too far away even to see me. He will look out from the murk of his studded, oystered self and only see his own wasted chances, poor, wisping, mirrored back.

And yet that was just the way she wanted it to be. How strange that was. She craved his insecurity—rewarded it—coaxed and nurtured it. It warmed her heart when he showed a weakness. His failures made her ache. She would never admit it, to Richard least of all.

By now the weather had begun to turn. The clouds thickened and paled and if she looked directly at the sky the glare seemed to cower and contract.

It had begun to spit with rain by the time Harriet pulled herself through the last teeth of the ridge and found Richard wedged in a cranny with his back to a flat-sided boulder, fussing over lunch. Richard smiled at her and pulled her down for a kiss (his lips were cold and stiffened from the wind, but the dart of his tongue was hot) and when she dropped down next to him and dug in her bag for another layer to stop the wind he said, 'It sounds funny, but I'm glad the weather's turning.'

The thing about bad weather, Richard was thinking, was that it brought the land and the sky together—it forced you to understand your environment both as something quick and as something still. He had been thinking about this as he walked up the ridge. Good weather could fool you. Good weather let you believe that there was a middle zone, some untouchable limbo between the elements, as if the world was cloven at the point of selfhood, that atmospheric belt of consciousness some five feet above the ground. In bad weather you could not imagine such a divided, isolating world. Land and sky were all around you. The elements conspired.

He turned to Harriet to ask: when you call Avalanche Peak to mind in abstraction, in its typical form, how do you imagine the weather? The question was already formed in his mouth, but when he looked at her he felt suddenly exhausted, smothered by the vast effort of merely sounding the words, and so he said nothing. She smiled at him. The kiss had pleased her—another betrayal. He smiled back.

They lunched on waxed sticks of sausage and papered rounds of cheese. Richard ate a cold apple and threw the core to the west. The pips sat dark on the snow. The kea that had tracked them up the ridge returned now, and strutted on the rock just beyond the toes of their boots, waiting for something to steal.

'I wonder how old he is,' Harriet said, watching as the bird cocked its head and snapped its beak to show the scored grey root of its tongue. 'Parrots live for years, don't they? I wonder if we've met before.'

Scott's Track came down a different ridge, curving off to the west and closer to the flat saddle of Arthur's Pass proper. This ridge was more exposed. The wind was fiercer, the tussock was coarser. If the cloud lifted they would have a stunning view across the valley to the eastern flank of Mt Rolleston, across to where the rumple of the glaciers sat high above the bluish face of snow. The track ended abruptly on the side of the highway just beyond the village, and it was a short walk from there, past the filling station and the lodges and all the curtained windows of the roadside shanties, back to the visitor centre where they had begun.

The kea blinked its bright eye and swaggered. 'Bet you've seen it all, mate,' Richard said. The kea seemed to consider them, and then with a half hop and a strong thrust of its wings, launched itself and beat off into the cloud.

They tucked their lunch away. Richard clapped his hands to his body and moved his weight from foot to foot, stretching. He had bivvied up here once as a young man, long before he met Harriet, one windless night in summer when the moon was fat and the silver dust of the Milky Way was bright enough to glister. He left the pass at sundown with a head-torch and a bivvy bag. Above the treeline it was glorious. The tussock was raked by the moonlight and everything shone. His shadow was so black. He reached the summit soon after midnight and then went back down the ridge a bit to look for a bare patch of level scree to spread his bivvy bag and sleep. He dropped down off a boulder and tripped over a doubled mound cuddled against its lee. Someone yelped. He grunted an apology and backed off, slithering away over the rocks. 'Got the same idea as us, bro,' came a cheerful voice out of the dark, after him. 'Cracker night for it.' Richard tried to find a site to bivvy a good distance away but he was irritated, and after several minutes creeping over the stones he gave up and left. He was boiling coffee on a dewy picnic table in the village in the early morning when he saw the couple emerge from the track and return to their car, mussed and happy and craning together as they walked.

The descent was easily as difficult as the ascent. By the time they reached the village his knees would be trembling at such a frequency they would seem to hum. Sometimes it took days to recover from the stiffness, and Richard had to haul himself up the stairs to his study by the banister rail. He was leading. 'Be my guest,' said Harriet. She was being especially kind today. That meant sex later at the lodge. Richard played it out in his mind. Harriet would be soothing and attentive to his orgasm and afterward she would purr and say, 'That feel better now?' as if she had administered some small dose of a cure.

The cloud completely filled the valley on the western flank of the mountain. When he looked back up the ridge he saw that the summit had long since disappeared into the white. Harriet was still a fair way behind. He saw her slither down a small outcrop and reach out to grab a handful of tussock to right herself. She saw him looking and gave him a thumbs-up. Across the valley, where the Crow glacier should have been knuckling out of the snow on the flank opposite, there was only a howling grey fog.

As they got lower Richard began to hear the sound of the falls across the pass more clearly. The rocky amphitheatre around the punchbowl focused the sound across the valley, and the pounding roar was quite audible although the waterfall itself was only very dimly visible, a tiny dagger-splash of white spearing thinly through the mist.

He was looking out across the valley when he suddenly came across a young Japanese girl, standing with her arms folded across her chest and swaying in the wind. She was standing just off the track, facing down the mountain, and she was alone. Richard stumbled to a halt and stared. She was wearing only a thin cotton zip-up sweatshirt with a limp hood that whipped around her neck and a pair of blue jeans, and she was soaked from the soles of her canvas sneakers right up to the slick shank of her hair. She had a shiny synthetic bag slung over her shoulder. Up here in the driving sleet, against the tussock and the white sky, she looked transported from another world.

The girl turned to face him and Richard saw at once the dull uncaring glaze of early hypothermia. He stared and she stared back. She might have tried to smile—her mouth quivered, and her lower lip thrust forward and back. She was so thin.

Harriet came up behind him and saw the girl. She acted swiftly, shrugging off her pack, releasing the clasps, digging for hats and woollens and food. The girl was still looking at Richard. Her lips and her eyelids were blue.

'Were you coming up or coming down?' Harriet said, seizing

an oversized polypropylene and forcing the girl's hands into the arm-holes without invitation. Almost in the same movement she whipped off her own beanie and pulled it well down over the girl's ears. The girl didn't try to resist. She dropped her gaze away from Richard at last and said quietly, 'Coming down.'

'Bloody well done, then,' Harriet said, breaking off a wedge of chocolate and pressing it into the girl's bloodless palm. 'Eat that. You got to the summit?'

The girl looked aghast and tried to give the chocolate back. 'I can't take your food,' she said, and Harriet said briskly, 'Of course you can. We were just about to stop for a break anyway. You got all the way to the summit?'

'Yes,' the girl said. 'It was beautiful.' She dropped her eyes to the ground when she spoke, like she was being disgraced.

'You had a better view than us, then,' Harriet said. 'By the time we got there you couldn't see ten feet. We might have been anywhere. Was anyone with you?'

'No.' She whispered it.

'Just on your own?'

'Yes.'

'You don't have any other clothes?'

'No.'

'Been up here before?'

'No.'

'Anyone know you're up here?'

She considered. 'At the YHA they might,' she said faintly. 'But I don't know if they were listening.'

'That's fine. Tell me what you had for lunch.'

Harriet continued in this way for a while, bossing the girl about and forcing a conversation, as she wrapped her up tighter and tighter, after each layer clapping the girl on the upper arms and giving her a little half-hug and a shake. Her voice was bright and hard. Richard came to his senses. He shucked his bag too, and found an emergency windbreaker, a pair of mittens, a scarf. The girl followed the movements of his hands.

Harriet said, 'Richard, she needs a hug.'

He hovered. His elbows twitched. 'Ancient Kiwi ritual, dress up the tourists,' he said, trying to make light of it, but Harriet shot him a look and he realised too late that she might not be a tourist. Now he looked like a racist. He wasn't. He was a liberal and teppanyaki was his favourite. He just didn't know very many Japanese. He tried to make up for it by unwrapping a muesli bar and inserting it into her blue little fist. Her skin was dry and very cold to the touch. He smiled and gave her a thumbs-up and then awkwardly, like a teenager on a first date, he stepped forward and put his arms around her. His chin came down on to her shoulder, gently at first, and then he sank into her and he felt the bones of her shoulder through his mouth. He held on.

Harriet was scrabbling in the bag for more food and still talking. When she straightened she said, 'Go on, eat it, eat it,' to the girl, and 'Give her a rub, she needs to get her blood moving,' to Richard. He began to rub the girl's shoulder blades with his hands. It was strange to embrace a form so unlike Harriet's—so angular, so insubstantial and cold. Harriet stooped and placed her mittened hands around the girl's thigh and began rubbing vigorously through the damp of her jeans, up and down with such a force that the girl staggered. 'That's it,' Harriet said. 'Do a little dance. Get moving. That's it.'

'Thank you,' the girl murmured, against his ear.

Richard was still rubbing her back. He shifted his head slightly so his mouth was now almost in the crook of her neck, or it would have been if Harriet had not already wrapped the scarf around the girl's face twice and jammed it into her collar. Over his shoulder the girl lifted the muesli bar to her mouth and began to eat. He could feel the muscles of her jaw tense against his ear.

'We're going to get you out of the wind,' Harriet said firmly. 'All right? And you're going to have to walk quickly.'

'Thank you,' the girl said again.

'Let's move. Come on, Richard. Let's move.' Harriet made a little pushing movement with both her palms and began to shoo the girl down the mountain. She trotted behind, clucking to make the girl hurry, and Richard hovered alone for a moment.

He was cold without his backpack on, and a little dazed.

'Looking better already!' Harriet was saying, her voice thinned by the wind and the distance. 'How on earth did you get to the summit in canvas sneakers? I've got proper boots and I bitched and moaned the whole way up!'

'My name is Umeko,' Richard heard the girl say.

Harriet gave their names. The girl slithered and fell and Harriet hauled her cheerfully up by the arm. 'Easy does it,' she said. 'Quicker the better. Don't mind if you fall.' She looked back and shot Richard a quizzical look.

'Coming,' Richard said. He swept his backpack up into the crook of his elbow and moved after them.

Harriet forced the girl to talk about her life. They learned that she was studying to become a museum curator in Japan. She spoke elegantly but hesitantly, like she was trying out the words for the first time. She said that she had come to New Zealand for a year's experience as a foreigner after her degree, before she married and fixed her fortunes on a place and a family and a man. She had been in Taupo for six months, she said, working at a fish and chip shop, the only job that she had been able to find.

'You have an arts degree?' Harriet said.

'Yes,' Umeko said. 'I am a good student. But it did not matter.'

Harriet glanced back at Richard and they shared an odd and unfamiliar look of national guilt. Harriet shook her head and drew her lips between her teeth; Richard winced and looked away.

'Your English is very good,' Harriet said after a moment.

'Thank you,' Umeko said. 'It is hard to practise. Harriet, you are the first person who has spoken to me here, beyond the customers.' She spoke musically and without bitterness.

'Shit,' Harriet said. She was uncomfortable. 'So what are you doing down here at Arthur's?'

'After six months I left my job,' the girl said. 'I had only six months remaining on my visa, so I bought a ticket for a bus.'

'On your own?' Richard said.

'Yes.'

'Shit,' Harriet said again. 'So you've been backpacking?'

'Yes. I have met many foreigners,' Umeko said. 'Many Japanese.'

'And how do you like it?' Harriet said.

'It is very beautiful,' Umeko said. 'It is a beautiful place.'

Below the tree line Richard pointed out a fantail in the trees and she smiled graciously and nodded. Again he realised she must already know the bird. They couldn't walk side by side on the narrow track so she turned to look at them often, picking her way delicately between the roots and the rocks, her gloved hands paddling a gentle semaphore as she spoke.

'You are very kind,' she kept saying. 'You are very kind.'

They talked all the way down. Every time Umeko slowed or fell silent Harriet prodded her with another question, or broke another square of chocolate for her to eat. After an hour the blueness had left her face and there was even a pink blush in her cheeks. They stopped for a drink and a rest at a switchback, and Harriet darted back up the track a bit to pee.

'Are you staying in the village?' Umeko asked. 'May I take you both for a drink tonight?'

'Maybe later on,' Richard said. He was thinking about the lodge, and Harriet, letting his legs float up in the bathwater, easing his sore back onto the bed, feeling his whole body loosen and flood with warmth as he came.

'I am staying at the YHA,' Umeko said.

'We could come find you later maybe,' Richard said.

'Yes?'

Richard nodded and shrugged at the same time. He drank.

'Where are you staying?' Umeko said.

'Haven't decided. One of the lodges.'

'The YHA?'

'Oh,' Richard said. 'No, probably not.'

'There is a walk to the Devil's Punchbowl,' Umeko said shyly. 'Not long.'

'We've done it many times,' Richard said. 'Very pretty.'

'Would you like to walk there?'

'Maybe later on,' he said again. 'I'm not sure. We'll all be pretty tired, after today.'

'Maybe in the morning?'

'Maybe. We have to drive back pretty early.'

'All right.'

'And the weather is turning,' Richard said. 'Going southerly. Going to rain. It might not be right for a walk.'

Harriet returned and drew Umeko off into a conversation about museums for the rest of the climb. As they got lower the grey seam of the highway began to show through the trees, larger and larger, and then finally they emerged on the roadside and walked single file down the hard shoulder into the village. Outside the YHA they waited while Umeko undressed. She peeled off each layer with exquisite care and folded each item before handing it over. Richard was embarrassed.

'Thank you,' she kept saying. 'Thank you.' She seemed to be taking a long time, drawing out the moment. Richard looked at the trees and stuffed his hands into his pockets and smiled at nothing.

The true beauty of the wilderness was that it had no real proportion. He had often thought that. Its beauty inhered in macrocosm and microcosm at once. A view from a summit contained the same measure of splendour as the pale splay of a flower, or the parchment curl of a stick of birch. He thought about fractal beauty: a fist-sized lump of schist enlarged to the size of a mountain will have the same level of detail, the same fissures and crystals and grains, the same colours, the same strata, as a mountain itself. You could shrink Avalanche into your hand, he thought, shrink it to the size of a nugget, and it would just be a rock like any other.

At last Harriet pumped Umeko's hand and said, 'Goodbye, Umeko. You must buy some warmer clothes.'

'Thank you,' the girl said. 'Thank you, Richard.' She did not ask about the trip to Punchbowl, or whether they would come to meet her later at the YHA. She dropped her eyes and said, 'Goodbye.'

They walked back to the car in silence. When they got back to the city, Richard thought, he would start looking for another woman. He would find one. He would take her to the climbing wall and teach her to trust the harness and the rope.

'What a sad story,' Harriet said as she fished in her bag for the keys. 'What a waste.' She squeezed Richard's hand. 'Now what?' she said. 'Shall we order a steak at the hotel? We could walk up to the falls after dinner if you wanted. Just you and me.'

A truck rumbled past them over the bridge.

'I wonder if she would have died otherwise,' Richard said. 'I wonder if we saved her life.'

Harriet cocked her head and gave him an odd look, drawing her lips together and frowning ever so slightly, as if she had just been surprised by something true. The lock-release lights on the car blinked twice and they separated, Harriet moving to open the driver's door and Richard walking around, behind the hatchback, to the other side.

Geoff Cochrane

The Last of Bashō

i

Bashō writes of the purple wine he likes.
Of the barman's slim syringe and black nail-polish.
Of the ten-dollar note burning in the ashtray.
Of the silver airship moored above the pines,
the tethered airship going nowhere slowly.

ii

The snide sirens dive and the rain catches fire,
but what of the Bengal engine's mango afterglow?

iii

Bashō alone and walking some high path.
Bashō alone and climbing the concrete steps to heaven,
a flask of gin in his satchel.
A flask of gin and a spring roll gone cold.

The Great Wall Café

The major gave us a chit
and we took it down the road
to a basic Chinese joint in Ghuznee St.

1974? Our not entirely wholesome covenant
would end when I got drunk,
bought two bottles of Glenvale's sweetest sherry
and caught the train to Auckland.
Meanwhile, we had a room and not much else.
Meanwhile, we had one another.

Eggs and chips and white bread in abundance.
Worcestershire sauce in a faceted, pressed-glass shaker.
And we paid with our Salvation Army voucher.

Her breasts were small but boldly, starkly nippled.
She was avid and game, my golden-skinned nymphet,
and she had great faith in me. She had great faith in me,
and together we'd admire my splendid erection.
Her breasts were small but loudly, brownly nippled,
and I fucked her frequently, but frequently.

Nigel Cox

from **The Cowboy Dog**

When I was eighteen I came into my anger. It had been buried deep, along with my gunbelt, my spurs and my coiled whip. Now, equipped with a long-handled shovel I climbed the mountainside, dug, and there it was, as red-eyed as a Gila Monster. It got its teeth into me. I was shaken as the anger flooded through me; I knew that there was no turning back. I buckled the guns onto my hips and stood with my face to the gritty wind.

In truth it's wrong to say that they were my guns. These things matter and legally it was so, but legal is just another word for nothin' left to lose. They were my Daddy's guns and had come into my hands when he died. When he was cut down. When my Daddy was torn from this world by a coward's bullet which entered him between the shoulderblades and carried him away to the other side. He fell into my arms, and the weight of him was more than I could bear. I was only a boy then. I went to my knees and still he slipped from me, down into the red dirt and that is where he stayed. I wept over him and begged him not to leave me out here. I was twelve years old and believed that he was the one who had talked the world into existence.

I buried him there, high against the shadow of the mountain. No marker, though there was a symmetrical cactus. I didn't want him to be in any one place. He is in the whole of this place; everywhere I walk here is his body, now. This stinking mountain, this spreading, red, burned piece of dirt that goes out to where the searchin' eye cain't see no more; this land the love of which is all I have. I took not a thing from him, nothing that might have him in it. In this way I hoped I might still have him, somehow—it was a sorrowing boy's notion and went where all such notions go. His voice is gone from me and I can never remember, except suddenly, without warning, what he sounded like when he spoke. I have no creased photograph of his face. For several years afterwards I would see the backs of men's heads in the Auckland street and wait, breathing hard, for them to turn around. Sometimes I ran after such men. They all spit on me, and in time I cured myself of this habit.

I saved his guns.

I knew I could not wear them, then, so they were buried too, in another place. I grew up scrambling this mountainside and was never afraid I would forget. I took off my boots and my chaps, my bandana and my sharp spurs and buried them too, wrapped in an old coat. My hat blew away and I let it. The paint horse stood by and watched all this without expression, reins hanging. Barefoot, bareheaded, I went down the mountain and waited by the highway, so lonesome and windswept, and hung out my thumb.

And now I am back here and standing over all I survey. The anger is gone from me and as I watch the tumbleweeds roll across the floor of the valley below, I could settle; I could say to the past, I will let you be, and turn and lead the horse up to the house and tie him there.

But anger never dies. It shifts, it changes shape like a restless shadow that is searching for an earthly form. You look again and it has moved. But not gone. Never gone.

And so as I go to the house I am vigilant. Tying the horse, my eye goes to the red rim of these lands and I scan the horizon. On the highway, trucks roll like barrels. The wires of the pylons sway in the restless wind. But that is how it has always been; how it should be. No riders.

I kick off my dusty boots and turn inside.

A highway vehicle collected me from the white stripe of the roadside and carried me away.

I was twelve years old, barefoot and out there alone and had to do a bit of fancy talking, which in my heartsick state was a struggle. But the driver was kindly and anyway he had his great vehicle to ride and so I was carried away from those lands where my Daddy lay cold beneath the dirt. I felt the turning of the giant wheels on the blacktop and the roaring of the engine underneath me and I lay back in the warmth of the cab and, pretending I was tired, closed my eyes.

Through the hot afternoon we travelled north with the sun in our faces, and I squinted to make out those things which my Daddy had told me of, that lay beyond the rim of our lands. Little hamlets, each one more straggled out than the last, and hamlet people standing open-mouthed beside the roadstead, as though seeing a chariot of fire, instead of the long truck which, on that highway, are as common as jackrabbits. Mean acres of land, all fenced about and fussed over, and shanties which sold comestibles. The driver saw me eyeing these and said, 'Hongry? There's bread in there,' and passed a brown paper sack which contained sandwiches wrapped in newspaper. The drivers of the great highway are of the most human kind, full of understanding and sadness. If ever I was to leave these lands it would be to the great highway that I would go, to ride the mighty vehicles and chase the bunny rabbit's tail of the broken white line.

We came to a place where tracks of iron crossed the black of the highway and, knowing these for what they were, I asked to be set down. 'In Huntly?' said the driver. 'No one ever stops in Huntly unless they threw a rod.' But he pulled to the side.

I came around to his door to thank him. Looking down from his high window, he raised his shades. His eyes were the blue of a summit lake, nestled among broken rock. He passed down the paper sack with the rest of the sandwiches. After a moment he said, "Get some shoes, kid. They like you to have shoes." Then his great engine roared and he pulled away, leaving me there by the side of the road with my hair all tugged this way and that by the afterdraft.

He was the last good man I saw for many a day.

My Daddy had talked of the strangeness of the lands where I now found myself and I was filled by a desire to wander and gaze. But I was not born a fool and so I moved off, slowly, like a cow that is heading peaceably to pasture, so that nobody would mind me.

Not that anybody was minding me except that if I loitered there I knew that somebody would.

The tracks of iron were bedded deep in the black sticky of the great highway and I followed them, away from the trucks and the shanties and into a little place that I knew to be a siding: my Daddy told me about that. Here, wagons of iron were standing, cold, and I walked close beside them, smelling them, which was a rich smell of rust and grease, and placed my hands on their flanks, so pitted and scratched. Weeds grew beneath their iron wheels, they stood as still as rocks and I knew these wagons had been abandoned here and would never move short of a dynamite blast, and so I walked on. But they had filled me with wonder.

Now I saw that, ahead, there were men and I became cautious. Three of them, standing in a triangle near the open door of a great shed, and from the irritation in their voices I knew they were dissatisfied with their lives in the town named Huntly and would welcome the diversion of a shoeless boy to chase. So I hid, and waited, and when their backs were turned, slipped across lines of iron track, behind wagons, behind a broken building, and thus to the boundary fence, which swiftly I climbed. Beyond were fields and I soon had my feet in soft grass, which cheered me. There were bushes, and in the bushes I hid, until darkness began to fall.

I had seen how there were rails of iron lying close within the fence and once the darkness was complete I moved along the fencewires. The town fell behind me and soon I was alone in the night. Above, the stars were the same stars I had seen on the mountain. Daddy and I had lain on our backs while he named them for me. He knew everything, my Daddy.

I climbed the fence and began to walk between the rails of iron. The sleepers were far apart, I had to stretch to reach each one. But the gravel between them was hard on my feet. Ahead, the rails shone faintly in the starlight and, walking between them, I felt guided, as though, ahead, there was a place where the splintered parts of me would come to a point. I strode on, powered by the sandwiches in my stomach, and, working harder, began to make my way around a long, slow curve that carried the tracks up a slope. Then I heard a sound.

From the mountainside it had been possible to see trains passing in the distance and it was this that had led my Daddy to spend so much time explaining the railroad to me. But now the earth began to shake and I discovered that to have seen a locomotive from a mountainside was different from being in the living presence of one. Swiftly, I leapt from the tracks. Around the curve the great engine came. Its searchlight swung before it and found me, standing open-mouthed—immediately an airhorn spoke from within the engine, an immense spear of sound which shafted through my head, making it ring. Then the machine was passing close before my eyes, a rushing wall of metal, and I was afraid. The mountain had always been the biggest thing. The fire inside it had always been the greatest power. Now I understood how the world might have dire forces which would bear down on a boy and shake his bones. That things comfortable and fascinating to be told of on a starlit night might prove overwhelming when they were rushing at your face.

At my ankles, sparks flew. I sensed down there the crushing fall of the iron wheels on the rails. A smell of burning oil and singed air engulfed me like a foul breath. But it was the passing of the wall of the train which was most impressive. My eyes flickered. Slowly, I put out a hand. I knew that it would not be wise to touch this thing but I could not help myself. The rushing wall of metal smacked my knuckles aside. I staggered and nearly fell.

In a kind of swoon, I swayed beside the track, overwhelmed, and thus was delayed in grasping that, labouring up the incline, the train was slowing. The engine had given way to wagons. Now I stepped back and saw that behind the wagons there were flatcars. And behind the flatcars: boxcars.

How like little houses those boxcars were, oblong in the night.

I remembered what my Daddy had told me, that you studied the first car to see what part of its flank might be gripped. Then you looked to see how you might progress from there along the side of the car to somewhere you could comfortably stand. A boxcar with an opening in the side was what you looked for. And now I saw one. I began to run alongside the train. The trackside gravel was cruelly pointed and cut my feet. But in truth I flew. The idea of being able to become one with this rushing monster was so exciting that all pain, all reason were suspended. I saw that preceding the opening in the side of each boxcar was a ladder and that if I once grasped the ladder I would be able to hold to it while I established my position. I fixed my eye on the ladder of the second-to-last car and increased my speed. At the last moment I was suddenly assailed by a knowledge of the slicing power of the iron wheels which fell like hammers on the long anvil below. If I went down I would be cut in half. This knowledge was a weight I had to carry as I jumped. But I was raised in the physical world and from an early age could leap onto a running horse. My fingers seized the ladder. And while it was true that the knuckles of my left hand were bleeding and weakened, still I had strength enough to hold on. My feet swung in a circle in the air but my arms pulled me and soon I was standing upright, pressed against the wall of the train and plunging through the night. How it vibrated! From the engine, far ahead, a second bellow came from the airhorn, as though the beast resented the burden. But now it was a sound in the distance, a lonesome wail which did no more than remind you that one day you would die.

How proud I was, hanging there on the shuddering side of the boxcar, and how full of optimism. The night rushed into my face and I glanced down and was thrilled by the sight of the miles that were passing swiftly, effortlessly, beneath my shoeless feet. Low along to my right there was a projecting flange and I thought it would bear my weight. I stretched a toe towards it. I saw how, if I had a purchase there, I could swing out and along on one arm and thus gain the entrance to the interior of the boxcar. There, I would be able to sit in comfort and gaze out at the splendour of the passing night. This plan meant trusting myself to the strength of my bleeding left hand, but the night air was becoming cold and I felt that if I stayed where I was I would eventually lose all feeling and fall. I had to do it. But I am confident of my physical abilities and so again I launched myself. My toe found the flange, cold metal, and my good hand swung round and grasped the side of the opening. For a moment I was stretched there on the side of the train. Then, holding firmly with my right hand, I bought my trailing leg from the ladder and onto the flange. This was a precarious situation and I did not linger in it, but pressed on to the doorway.

Below the wheels clattered and, as I teetered in the opening, my thoughts were full of triumph at avoiding them. Thus I did not see the booted foot which came out of the interior darkness to hit me square in the chest and send me sprawling on the sharp gravel below.

to be continued

Vanessa Crofskey

To All the Boys I've Loved Before

Y drove a car quiet like the sigh of steamed
bao but wove his hands too close so
I swung that block button like Chun Li

R told me he missed me as he
jacked off to black hair clouding
neon screens

F had a new half-asian babe to replace his old
half-asian ex but I was his current screenshot

T told me my eyes were lovely

J was Korean but
hated himself deeply

M loved redheads and kawaii
. . . lucky I am a mixed breed Ferrari

M surfed asianbabes.net but
I've always preferred swimming

honestly

I suspected S of a fetish cause he
banged an exchange student on a hike once

and also watched One Piece
I suspected J 'cause he liked miniature figurines

For S I pressed my B cups into A grade
décolletage and informed him that his kinks were just
lightly fermented misogyny

A heard I strode around
in latex skirts, strumming on my abacus

C's mum put me in their Christmas newsletter
She'd heard I lost weight and
spoke good English

X loved my pussy for the slant of its eyeliner
how it wore crusty spiked collars
lashes heavy like crushed garlic lids

X heard I could make a dragon
roar like a waterfall
just at the sight of a thigh slit

I came from
down the road
X

guessed my whatever
like a genre of music

my skin white like
. . . rice porridge

my
city of ethnics
unravelled
like a strip tcase

Lynn Davidson

How to live by the sea

Be like the terns crouched on the shore.
Still under an empty sky.

Stake your life on warnings.
The gulls will circle, shrieking, before rain.

Keep one craft at hand.
A kayak out back among nasturtiums.

Walk lightly.
The grey heron will haunt your letterbox.

Cultivate patience.
The orca may pass by here again.

Settle for disorder.
All summer you will swim before you wake.

Uther Dean

Haiku

#0067
Two cannibals eat
Each other until they are
Just two kissing mouths.

#0156
All fluorescent tubes
Are filled with tiny fairies.
Begging for your help.

#0175
Sue tore up her will,
Drank the serum. Fuck the kids.
She'd live forever.

#0176
Remodel your house
By flying into a rage
And smashing her stuff.

#0178
All the sad robots
Pretend to robot smile
At their robot friends.

#0182
Peter Painter smiles.
His watercolour teeth smudge
When he grins in the rain.

#0414
When he ruled the world
Dr Robotz would show it
His sweet, tender heart.

#0558
The complexity
Of everyone else's lives
Is overwhelming.

#0561
My latest mantra:
'None of this is important.
You have enough love.'

#0569
It's very easy
To feel like you're doing things.
(You're really dying.)

#0570
On a sinking ship
The captain embraced the crew
And became their raft.

#0581
I still remember
My best childhood bullies.
They made sure of that.

#0582
Kids can be so cruel.
So we should cave in their skulls
With big cinder-blocks.

#0598
Tim's misogyny
Seemed like ironic joking.
But was genuine.

#0641
When drowning in work
Allow it to flood your lungs
Then: euphoria.

#0644
When my leg brushed yours
On the Strathmore 44
My heart exploded.

#0645
My man-size pillow
Has a single hand to hold
And a beating heart.

#0663
Then he starts crying
Can't stop and turns into sand.
(How we get beaches.)

#0672
The giant pimple
At the centre of your chest
Pops, oozing out love.

Esther Dischereit

Kissing Terry in the Rain

I stepped out the front door
a coffee in one hand
my case in the other
strings of rain fell
like pearls
pattering on
the still hot coffee
I could have drunk
that coffee with the drops in it
clutched the mug
as if wishing to fill it
with pearls
I put the mug down
on the street where else
on the sidewalk
in front of the waiting car

The way he just stood there
the rain streaking
down his face
and pushing between us
as we kissed
his coat soaked
and my neck and hands
raindrops falling
from our eyes
like pearls he wore them
into the house

Translated by Iain Galbraith

Kate Duignan

Letter

Love, we have finished.
Eaten one another's bones,
consumed the kidneys, the liver, the spleen.
We have picked our teeth
and dusted our hands.

Yes, all the books agree,
the history is concluded:
the nights we lay too dumb to speak,
the flutter of hands between wake and sleep,
the shouts and demonstrations,
the tanks rolling down the street.

You have removed the hair from the tub.
I have disposed of your razor and comb.
The shoes have been thoroughly scrubbed.
The names are gone from the phone.

(So if at night
the pillow assumes the shape
of your back

and the tomcat sounds like your
cry—

I will think of this as
a ghost
a residue
my own private matter.)

Breton Dukes

A Lonely Road

Kelly was returning from the supermarket. It was hot. Her shadow was long and thin with drooping bags for hands. She turned onto their road. On one side were houses and a footpath. On the other a long strip of grass abutted a swathe of mangroves. The mangroves bordered the harbour. You couldn't see the harbour from their house, but from this part of the road you could see the claws of land that made its entrance, its sand bars at low tide, its deep, steady blue at high tide, its pylons and narrow channel. Between the footpath and the houses were long ditches that filled or emptied with the tide. There was weed in the ditches. There were ducks and sometimes shags. There were grey herons and sprats and tadpoles. Families of pūkeko patrolled the grass by the mangroves. Sometimes they too were in the ditches. Other times they were dead on the wide, straight road, flattened by cars, half cooked by the sun.

Kelly had been with Shane in Whangārei for three months. He'd been there for four. Shortly after she'd arrived in Northland, he'd used the odometer in his new station wagon to measure the road's length.

'One hundred metres.'

'What?'

'The road. Our road.'

'Oh,' she'd said.

'You walk it all the time.'

'I know.'

'Well, it's a hundred metres.'

'Oh, okay. Thanks.'

'You're very welcome,' he'd said, hugging her.

Spontaneous hugging was still common. So were apologies. Shane would hug her, and then laugh, 'I'm sorry, it's just so perfect you're here.' Then he'd grab her again.

Kelly passed the ditch with the discarded eeling spear. Low

tide, the water was clear. There were little holes in the mud where mud creatures breathed. The spear hung in such a way as to suggest it had been thrown. Sprats milled about the shaft. She kept walking. A hawk kited up from the mangroves. A van went past. PLUMBER. The men inside spoke to each other and laughed. The driver waved. She'd lost weight and gained a tan. Not trusting the local hairdressers, her hair had grown and grown.

Their place was up a private drive, one house back from the road. It had an open-plan living area—wooden floors, lots of windows—and in the back, off a short carpeted hallway, a bathroom and three small bedrooms. Kelly left the house unlocked. It was a good neighbourhood. People smiled and said hello. Men were always out the front hosing down their boats or using lawn mowers and weed eaters. She walked up the drive. Below them the neighbour owned a business that made pools, above were South Africans whose two young children went up and down the drive on scooters. At meal times Kelly often heard little voices leading prayers.

A frozen chicken, bacon, rubbish bags, a Steelo pad, fly spray, and in the other bag flour, fresh tarragon, lemons, milk, poppy seeds and butter. Though Shane wouldn't be home before midnight, Kelly was roasting a chicken and baking a cake. She'd eat a small meal and offer him a plate when he got home—when he saw the food, he'd hold up his hands and say it looked perfect, but there was just no way. Then he'd shower and they'd go to bed. In the morning she'd rise with him and make the meal into leftovers for his lunch.

Past the carport and up the wooden stairs. Sweat ran down her legs. She went into the house. Curtains were drawn to keep the heat out and it was gloomy after the hard, mid-afternoon sun. The bench and oven were against the wall nearest the driveway. She put the bags on the bench. The milk flopped over. Two lemons rolled out. A fly landed and went quiet on last night's dishes.

Prior to Whangārei, Kelly and Shane had spent six months in an informal coupling in Wellington. When they met she was at the tail of a long-term relationship with a tall, unlucky sculptor, who, at their last meeting, had forced her hand up her back, and spat, 'You're *arrogant*. You're *egocentric*.'

Shane had been single and studying and working hard for most of a decade. On their first date he'd said, 'You're what I've always been looking for.' He took her to the five best restaurants in Wellington, to vineyards in Martinborough and Hawke's Bay. He took her for a week in Samoa and flew them to a concert in Auckland and a racing carnival in Canterbury. She forgot his birthday. He bought her a mountain bike. They were both in their late thirties. When his contract in Wellington ended he'd applied for jobs all over the northern North Island. Warm weather and the outdoor lifestyle, that's what he was after. Everyone said she should go for it—he was *so* much better than the last one and my god, Kelly, a *doctor?!* They'd all just presumed it would work out. And of course they were right: he was good to look at, he was bright and generous and successful. She *should* love him.

Kelly finished unpacking, put the chicken on a plate to defrost, and washed her hands. The sink was part of a breakfast bar that divided the bench and oven from the living area. The fly resumed looping the room. Shane's coffee table and laptop, his medical texts, the long leather couch he'd brought north. She'd lie there and escape into her books, resting her iced water on the low table. But her book had moved. After ten years teaching she had a sense of the whereabouts of valued things. She'd marked her page and left it on the coffee table; now it was on the dining table by the window. And the door to the hall was open. She kept doors and windows closed—you worked hard up here to stay on top of the bugs. There was a noise from the toilet: short steps on the rough tile floor and then flushing.

'Shane?' It sounded strange saying his name with any urgency.

She crossed to the window and made a crack in the curtain. The carport *was* empty. The plumbing got louder as someone opened the bathroom door—now they'd be in the hall. Blood gushed through her throat to her brain. Shane was the only person she knew in Northland. She stepped back to the sink. There was a knife she'd used that morning. On the blade was a shaving of apple skin. She was middle-class New Zealand. She believed in rational explanations. She left the knife, gripped the dishcloth, and stared at the door.

A man appeared. He was wearing a yellow T-shirt and carefully wiping his fingertips on the cloth over his belly. Had Shane organised something? Was he a tradesman? But where's his truck, where are his shoes? Rapist. A cord went tight in her groin. Her hands were little birds fluttering for the knife.

The man looked up. 'Oh,' he said. 'Shit.'

'Hey,' she said, and then louder, even though she was stepping backwards, 'Hey there.'

He spoke with his arms raised; he spoke softly like they were together at the movies. 'It's okay.'

The blood to her stomach and chest went cold. 'It's not.'

He came into the room like there was broken glass.

'Hey, no!' With her heart flinging about in her mouth it was like shouting around a wad of meat. The knife felt unfamiliar. It might as well have been a banana. She pressed herself back against the bench.

'My name's Jeff Collins,' he said, 'with a J.' Then he spelt his surname. 'I'm not here to hurt you. I just need a little time.'

She forgot the name straight away. 'Please,' she said, wobbling her knife-hand towards the door. 'PLEASE!'

His hands went higher. When he turned his small feet made a kissing sound on the wooden floor. The hair on his upper arms was black and wiry. 'I'm a farmer from Raurimu—'

'No!' she said.

'I'm sorry to have frightened you,' he said. 'I thought the house was empty. I needed a drink—'

She shook her head and, though he couldn't see, she again pointed at the door. 'Get out!'

The fly landed on his neck and crawled up his ear. 'I'm sorry I'm here. I knocked. When no one answered, I came in. The police are looking for me, but I'm okay. I'm a taxpayer, I'm a decent New Zealander.'

She freed herself from the bench. Moving felt good. She put

down the knife and picked up the frying pan. Making decisions felt good. 'Why are you here?' she said. 'There's no law against farming?'

When he laughed his thin body shuddered.

Angered by his mirth she shouted, 'You can't be here!' Then, carefully, as if unsure how the words would taste, 'You fucking creep.'

Smooth and so slow the fly was undisturbed, the farmer re-raised his arms and went forward onto his knees. 'That's fair enough,' he said. 'That's what I'd say, but please, you could be in my position, anyone could.' He put his face in profile. He was sweating, maybe crying. His eye was wide and white. 'I'm asking you for compassion.'

She felt responsible for his submission and some of the cold went out of her torso. Outside a car went up the drive. Cicadas pulsed. The other rhythmical sound was her breathing. Aiming the pan at him she went to the front door. 'If I go outside and scream—'

'I'll wait here, right here if you want,' he said, then pleading softly, 'But please, just until it gets dark.'

'What if I call the police?'

Something jigged in his throat. He lowered his hands to his knees as if about to pray. 'You're reading Dick Francis.'

Being so near the outside she felt she had choices. 'What were you doing in the bathroom?'

He moved his shoulder to clear the fly from his cheek and then shifted his face from view. A bottle-sized stain of sweat shaped down his back. 'A house burnt down. I burnt a house down.'

'I'm calling the police—'

The man spoke quickly, loud at first, fading to a whisper. 'The owner of the house killed my partner. Tuesday last week, the jury found him not guilty. Gill, my partner's name was Gill.'

'What *jury*? What *not guilty*?'

'The judge called it a tragic car accident.'

The farmer glanced back. Kelly weighed the pan like it was an axe.

'I didn't go into your bedroom. I *did not* go into your bedroom.'

'Why should I believe—'

He spoke so quietly she had to lean away from the door to hear. 'Gill was walking the dogs—the man ploughed into the back of him. Though they say the man stopped to help, Gill died at the scene.' The farmer shifted as if to ease his knees. 'He and the man had history—they'd played rugby together. They didn't get on. Gill always worried the man would do something, but no one listened when I said that. The man owns the local garage. He's known throughout the district—he does his own ads on the radio.'

'And now what? You're a *fugitive*?' said Kelly, experiencing the word as a sliver of excitement.

'After the fire I ran. I just ran.'

He was little: little feet, little features, little head. He shifted again and winced.

'Sit back,' she said. 'Sit back on the floor.'

He raised himself off his knees and sat with his legs crossed. 'Thank you,' he said, turning to look at her.

'I haven't decided,' she said, pointing the pan. 'I haven't decided anything yet.'

'Thank you,' he said again, and sat forward with his elbows on his knees and his chin in his hands.

Lately, lying there on the couch, just beyond where he knelt, Kelly had wished for an earthquake or a fire, some massive thing to bring massive change.

Forty minutes passed with the farmer on the floor, and, frame by frame, Kelly trusted him a little more. When he'd asked for water she'd slid in a bottle and then thrown a bag with bread. The meal sounded dry in his mouth and, watching him closely, she'd delivered a piece of cheese on the underside of the pan.

'Gill and I used to make our own.'

'Your own what?'

'Cheese.'

In Wellington, Kelly had taught science in high schools and, in letting the man describe cheese making, in allowing him to detail the processes used to formulate the different varieties, he'd reminded her of the small boys who ended up in the tough schools because of their background: the kind who were bullied because of their brains and feeble bearing, the kind who, even as fourth formers, had to be reminded to blow their noses.

This comparison caused further relaxation and in noting that, she'd felt even more in command, which put her on high alert: the con-man who sneaks into women's houses and earns their trust. Clutching the pan in a threatening way, she'd made him go through his story from the beginning. Liars tripped over facts. While plot lines were retained, details failed. But he answered sincerely and without hesitation: Gill, the long leash, the quiet country road. And reliving it seemed to hurt. The patch of sweat enlarged. His little body shook.

'You can sit on the couch,' she said.

'Tie me if you like,' he said, pushing his hands back.

'I wouldn't know where to start.'

Meekly, he stood, turned, and sat in the couch, raising his legs and crossing them primary-kid-style. With his elbows in his lap he was rendered even smaller. 'Just like you'd truss the bird,' he said, nodding at the chicken by the sink.

Kelly almost smiled. Instead she shifted the pan from side to side as if about to return serve.

'Gill and I honeymooned in Aitutaki,' he said, looking at the framed photo of herself and Shane in Polynesia.

'That's Samoa, and we're not married.'

'Our civil union was one of the first,' he said, holding the ring on his finger.

'He's a doctor, he works a lot.'

The farmer was quiet. Head bowed. When he looked up there were tears in his eyes. 'It was all thanks to Aunty Helen.'

Kelly didn't know where to look.

After a moment he smiled wetly. 'What sort of doctor?'

In the staffroom, Kelly had had a reputation for picking the bad ones. They held themselves a certain way. Their eyes had that dead look. How many murderers, or robbers, or rapists knew cheese making? How many knew about civil unions or the person responsible for them? More tension went out of her. 'A paediatrician,' she said. 'I guess he's married to his work. Not that I want—' She stopped herself midsentence, and looked into the pan.

The farmer gestured faintly towards the dining table. 'Bring a chair over?'

He looked like what he said he was: a gay man of the land. Cropped hair (she could see him in a cloth hat), wiry, nice even teeth, a crooked nose, a kind sparkle in those sad eyes. Persecuted by a bunch of red-necks; she'd have to work hard not to forget the manner in which he'd appeared. She'd get the phone and keep it close, and from one of the tall chairs she'd be able to stand quickly.

Still holding the frying pan she went to the dining table and slid a chair across the floor, positioning it at a safe distance from the couch. 'Pass the phone,' she said, pointing.

It lived in a port beneath the coffee table. Cat-like he tipped forward and with an arched back retrieved it. The move was swift and efficient. Unsettled, Kelly stayed standing. He seemed to notice. 'You could keep the front door open,' he said, putting the phone at her end of the table.

She dialled 111, and hung up. She held the pan in her lap and kept her finger on redial. Sitting was a relief. She sighed. 'If I open the door there'll be flies.'

'I am really sorry,' he said.

'And you're not a murderer?'

'I used to do yoga.'

She put the phone in the pan and pulled her hair back, binding it into a ponytail with a tie from her wrist. If she'd had sleeves she would have rolled them up. She wanted to confess—she'd thought of it first when the farmer went to his knees. She couldn't stand Shane. His round nostrils, his thick gums, the way he said *perfect* all the time. She was awake all night thinking about escape. She was rotting. But returning to Wellington terrified her: some grotty high school, all those flabbergasted friends and family.

She must have been staring intently at the farmer.

'Check what I've told you on the internet,' he said.

Shane had left her in charge of contracting a provider, but she hadn't got to it yet. Nor had she replaced her cellphone. 'I will.'

'Or there might be something on the radio.'

The fridge ticked loudly and then shook itself into silence. Another car went up the drive.

Exhaling dramatically, she said, 'I'm forty next year.'

He smiled. 'Forty's good. I came out when I was forty. Gill and I met the year before. He taught at the local primary.'

'I'm a teacher,' Kelly said. 'Science. I hate it.'

'And now?'

Morning's she slept—it was easier without Shane there— then she read. Tough talking Scottish cops, humble ex-jockeys infiltrating rings of country folk engaged in foul play. Heroes and villains. To keep her devotion from Shane she left one book out with a bookmark that rarely moved. Afternoon's she walked to the supermarket and then cooked. Dining at home was perfect for the bank balance. She chose complicated recipes and did multiple courses. He thought it was all for him. 'What more could a man want?' he'd ask at the conclusion of a meal, 'I've got the perfect job and the perfect girl.'

'I read a lot,' she said. 'I cook.'

'Hard to find work up here?'

She nodded. She'd told Shane she was looking, but that was a lie—she avoided anything that committed herself to the place.

'Before I came out,' he said, 'Mum and Dad called every week to remind me about wedding bells and the patter of little feet.'

The fly still circled, in the willow at the back of the property the pair of herons made their emphysemic bark, and in Kelly, the balance shifted. He was now more sympathetic listener than intruder. In a rush, she told him about Wellington and Samoa, about the vineyards and concerts.

But he missed her tone. 'Falling in love's fun,' he said.

She stood, taking the phone, but leaving the pan by the chair, and crossed to the kitchen, returning with a printout. 'When I got here, he'd bought a station wagon, and look at this, he's suddenly right into saving.' Accrued money was described in the form of a bar graph. Behind the graph was an image of a large home: a two car garage, a pōhutukawa with a swing. Each month, Shane solemnly fixed the latest printout to the fridge.

'Ah,' said the farmer, 'the white picket fence.'

'Life's suddenly so serious—all he does is work. Double shifts, weekend shifts. Days off he goes in to review babies he's helped resuscitate. I don't even know if I want kids.'

The farmer's head was as still as the Buddha's.

'I stay in relationships too long,' she said firmly. 'You think they'll get better, that people will change. I get stuck.'

'People don't change,' he said.

'I just don't love him.' Distracted by the intensity of her confession she leaned forward and put the phone on the table.

'Have you got friends here? Family?'

She shook her head. There was the sound of the children on their scooters. Pre-dinner they liked to do bunny-hops in the empty carport. 'I shouldn't have come. My instinct said, stay in Wellington, but when it comes to men, my instincts have never been reliable.'

The farmer smiled. 'Bloody men, eh?'

She shook her head and looked at the ceiling. 'When he got the job here I couldn't give him an answer and he came alone, but he was so persistent . . . And I missed all the fun we'd had.'

Somehow he'd claimed the phone. He tapped the end of the antenna with his thumb. 'Just tell him it's not working out.'

Kelly shrugged. She didn't want to get into the things she *should* do. She changed tack. 'My last partner was abusive too,' she said, muddling the direction of the violence the farmer had described. 'He was an *artist*,' she said, making a long curvy motion with both hands. 'Everything had to be so tactile.'

The farmer stretched out his legs and flexed his toes.

'The last time I saw him he almost broke my arm.'

The farmer filled his cheeks with air and bulged his eyes.

There was a beeping—the pool-king's truck as he reversed into his drive. 'It must be six o'clock,' said Kelly, irritated the sculptor's assault wasn't being treated seriously.

With his feet now on the floor and his left arm along the top of the couch the farmer looked larger and more at home.

She pointed at the phone and held out her hand.

He bared his teeth.

From mouth to anus, her every pipe froze. 'I'm going to put that chicken on,' she managed, and then stood, which was when he made his move—springing out of the couch and riding her and the chair down, so that the action ended with him squatted over her, so that when he spoke there was a hint of the DKNY Shane kept in a drawer in their bedroom.

'The real story,' he said, 'is that I need a little money.'

He hadn't made her lie face-down on the couch, but that was how she felt safest, huddled into the leather like a new-born pup. He was at the dining table, slowly turning the pages of her book. He had Shane's credit card and he had a small knife. When the roads were quieter they'd be walking to the supermarket's ATM.

He'd fried eggs and from his place at the table, she'd heard the crispy periphery of the white, the crunch of toast, the sound of his tongue clearing yolk from his lips. After dinner he'd rifled her utensil drawer for the knife.

'Which one's sharpest?'

She hadn't answered, just clutched her hands beneath her chest and counted each breath.

Her bladder was full, but she didn't trust herself to make the words to ask. And anyway the back of the house terrified her. In books and movies, blood was often shaped as numbers and words on walls. She imagined the blade between her ribs, the lining of her lung giving under the point of her paring knife, alveoli exploding like fish eggs. Sweat on her forehead sucked on the arm of the couch. She opened her eyes and stared at the leather. On a Ministry of Ed field trip, extolling the benefits of dissection, a teacher/part-time farmer had opened a pig and scooped out the innards, detailing all the interesting parts with a piece of kindling.

Should she beg or scream? Or stand and confront him? It worked at high school. Tough kids buckled hardest. He farted and then coughed as if to cover the sound. She couldn't remember the self-defence she'd learnt. You shouted a lot. To gouge eyes you went in hard and kept digging. Back in the capital, when she'd shown Shane, he'd made his hand a fin and set it between his eyes. It had made her giggle. He was strong. He'd been into BMX when he was a kid. He had big calf muscles and could walk around on his hands. On Sunday, they'd walked through bush to get to a cove. There was a photograph on Shane's computer of two kākā ring-barking a tree, and there was a self-timed one of herself and Shane arm-in-arm—the ocean behind them, a freighter on the horizon. Part of her missed the conversation she and the farmer had been having.

She'd closed her eyes and was back to concentrating on her bladder when he pushed out from the table. 'Righto,' he said.

Trying to stay small she rolled over and stood. He was in the middle of the room, arms wide, shepherding her towards the front door. Her clothes were damp with nerved-up sweat and her balance was off. She walked as if supporting herself on a railing.

Outside the low sun was still hot. Windless, a muddy sand and foliage smell off the mangroves, cicadas, the pool-man's boat aboard a trailer in his drive, a wet stain on the concrete from water dripping from the outboard motor. No humans in sight. She wobbled out onto the road. It was empty and wide like a runway.

'Easy there,' said the farmer.

The tide had filled the long ditches with seawater. Five pūkeko stitched at the grass by the mangroves.

'What happens when we get there?' she asked.

'Eh?'

Her mouth felt dry, especially her teeth. She swallowed and passed her tongue over them. She repeated herself.

'We take out some money.'

'And then?'

Before he could answer there was the sound of a plane and, when that faded, a hard, windy, flapping. They stopped and looked. Two parachutes. One lemon, one mandarin. The sound was the chutes catching and filling. For a moment Kelly imagined a rescue attempt: the armed offenders, an airborne SAS. And the farmer must have sensed her hope because he came forward, eyes wide, arm raised. Kelly's knees went, she ducked and got her hands up. But there was no strike, no puncture. He tapped her elbow as he'd tapped the phone's antenna and then hands on hips he waited while she gathered herself. 'Lot of picket fences along here,' he smiled.

She turned. They kept walking.

Panic pumped in her heart. She saw her legs taking her in the wild way of a beheaded hen. Adrenaline. The word spaced the white of her brain. In the next house the doors and windows were wide open, breeze moving through white curtains, a smell of seared barbecue meat, and men's voices! Clear, but not close. Not from the house. She scanned the road. Inflatable boats on the harbour? In the mangroves? But they were coming from above— the parachutists shouting joyously. One, then the other, started singing. Behind her, for a moment, the farmer joined them in song.

She glanced back. He was off to her right and a metre behind. His head shiny with sweat, body hair tufting round his neck and up the back of his T-shirt. Furry and wet like something squeezed from a drain pipe.

'What?' he said, coming up fast and shoving her.

She stumbled, but didn't fall.

It wasn't so much the contact as the face he wore.

The road started its familiar incline. The discarded spear. It was in the next ditch. Could she jump in and come up fighting? But he was so fast. And how would she hold it? She moved her hands, trying to figure the best grip. The water was shallow, the road a good distance from its surface. Eight metres until she was level—she shortened her stride, not wanting to decide. Was it best to pay? Isn't that what the police said? There'd be people at the supermarket, kids riding skateboards around the carpark. The lime-green ATM. She'd once found a sausage roll on its keypad. He couldn't kill her there. Now level with the spear, she raised her eyes, stepped a little further into the road, and stared ahead to the intersection. If she ignored the spear, there was no decision. A red wagon turned. Headlights on. He was cautious with things like that. It was Shane.

Run. Across the road. Scream like you're on fire. But just stopping was easier. He was here—a body to fit between her and the farmer. Her bladder let go. It went warm in her shorts, then dripped. Quiet on his bare feet, the farmer came up and put his hands on her shoulders. Shielding her from the road, he made her turn and face the ditch.

'Pretend you're looking at the little fishies,' he said, pinning her arms to her waist and resting his chin on her shoulder.

She looked. There was the knife in his hand, the wetness on her legs, the ditch water, and then the spear. But it didn't matter. 'It's Shane,' she said, as if they were in the playground.

'Shhhh,' said the farmer, nuzzling in.

Kelly glanced past the farmer's ear. Head back, arms straight. Sad and serious. Shane looked, but didn't even slow. What had he seen? Two lovers? With the farmer's hot, eggy breath down her front, she watched the car turn into their drive.

'Actually, I could return couldn't I? You could be my wee bank. Food. Money. *Conversation.*' The farmer nudged her with his stomach as if to knock her in, then let her go.

'Righto,' he said.

But the line had snapped. And aiming just to the side of the spear, Kelly dove into the ditch. Sprats fled as her hands hit the water that was more shallow than it looked. Soft, soft sand, first to the elbow, then to the shoulder—an ooze which welcomed her head and torso with thoughtless and utterly breathless black, and bar the occasional smooth-skinned sea worm, there was nothing on which to get purchase, and it would have taken swift action and the strength and determination of a man in love to prise her free.

Jenny Erpenbeck

Youth

I can't raise my arms so well anymore, she says, gazing down at herself as if at a foreign body. She looks the same as ever, a bit older perhaps than thirty years ago, but certainly not like an old woman. After all, I'll be seventy next week, she says, speaking in a voice that sounds just like her voice thirty years ago. Next week, though, I'm going to the Baltic coast, to a spa, she says. That will be lovely, I'm sure. She says 'the Baltic coast' no differently than she would have spoken these words thirty years ago—to a lover, perhaps.

Really, where does the time go, I once read in letters written by a girl who was forced to live apart from her parents for two years in Fascist Germany. One year later, she was dead, murdered by the Nazis. Where does the time go?

The illnesses that start to befall us fill us with astonishment, they cause our bodies to move in a different way than we intend, they accelerate and delay, they spoil the meter. They astonish us. The years spatter our skin—which just a moment ago was the skin of a child—with the brown spots of age, they make the small print flicker before our eyes, they astonish us, and since all of this occurs so gradually, we don't even understand where the point of transition occurred. Gradually, one hair at a time, the years make off with the youth of men, they imperceptibly crease the skin of women, gently laying it in folds, and there we are, encased in this skin, gazing with eyes before which the small print has already blurred to the point of illegibility, it is only our thoughts that do not appear to us to age, and for this reason we are astonished to find that the years have settled around our shoulders, and we think that actually, if we wanted to, we could shrug them off again, and for this reason when we look at our own arms, we see something that—the older it becomes—appears to us less and less recognisable and becomes more and more removed from us the more it tries to force us by means of pain and shortcomings to acknowledge its closeness, and this is why we are astonished when our own exhaustion renders us defenseless; and when we realise that death is coming closer to us one friend at a time, we would like best not even to know any longer that our lives often outlast our own ability to age.

Translated by Susan Bernofsky

Cliff Fell

Woolshed Blues

Tally-marks on

the woolshed door—

the stuff that can't be said,

he said—

the things we can't undo:

> *when the shearer sliced*
> *the hamstring*
> *of my wife's angora goat*

he said—

> *I blazed my knife*
> *across its throat*

> *and swore*
> *it wasn't true*

Joan Fleming

Wake

This is the chapter where we learn what distance is.
Come in Come in, our eardrums hymn to the television
news. We all want to carry our share of bricks.
The child tosses and turns in the lowest bedroom.

Pictures of trucks and buildings on the sheets
tangle up at the child's feet.
Out, out,
he calls out in his sleep.

Doesn't the world seem solid?
The glass pane ripples like a lake.
We see ourselves in the glitter and scatter.
Doesn't the end of summer feel like a mistake.

The child's eyelids are as big as hills.
We feel him kick out in his sleep.
A man wrapped in a white blanket
walks the broken street.

This is the chapter of the held breath.
We step out, praying that nothing will fall
except for leaves and hail.
His blanket catches the wind, like a sail.

Robert Gernhardt

After Reading an Anthology

The piss stain at the bottom of the escalator in the
Miquel-Adickes-Allee underground station

I don't claim that it's better
than any of the many poems
I've read today
I just know that it says more to me

This piss stain at the bottom of the escalator in the
Miquel-Adickes-Allee underground station

Talks about someone under pressure
Signals that it absolutely had to come out
Testifies that whoever it was who felt this urge
Produced something in a gush:

This piss stain at the bottom of the escalator in the
Miquel-Adickes-Allee underground station

Then I think of the voices
That have spoken to me today: no
pressure, no urge, no
zing, no danger, no
bite, no compulsion, no
urine, no brain.

Translated by Richard Millington

Paula Green

Early

Early intervention
Simone de Beauvoir is measuring time with each sip of tea. She is listening to National Radio on the front deck. Kathryn Ryan is interviewing Fiona Farrell.

Early history
Plato has finally got around to polishing his shoes. It has taken him so long his cup of tea has gone cold—the milk forms a little scum around the rim. He can see his reflection in the luminous black. Soon it will be time to tip the tea down the sink and swap his good shoes for his walking shoes.

Early morning
Copernicus still finds joy in cooking in a foreign kitchen in a foreign country in a foreign time. He made Bircher muesli the night before and a large bowl of fruit salad when the birds started singing. Without knowing why he bursts into a fit of laughter. His body heaving. Tears running down his face. Silliness in small doses, he says, thinking of Horace.

Early signs
Like Winnie the Pooh, you think it is time for a little something. A brain wave, perhaps.

Early learning
Jane Austen is an unexpected guest for breakfast. She favours toast and marmalade at this hour. From silence it is an easy step to politics.

Early years

Horace is sitting next to Jane Austen. He has his eye on her poached egg. He has his eye on the Bircher muesli. He is always ready to seize the day.

Early edition

Sylvia Plath is sitting next to Horace with her back to the kitchen. She is scribbling a poem between the lines of an article on Egyptian riots in the *New Zealand Herald*.

Bernadette Hall

Really & Truly

I took my anger
running on the beach.
She said, 'You've got to
put me on a longer leash, bitch.
How else can I dabble
my tootsies in the water
and roll in the stinking weed?'

I took my anger
walking round the park.
She said, 'You know
I've always been scared
of the dark
and now you've started
the fucking dogs barking.'

I took my anger
out for morning tea.
She sat there as good as gold,
smiling beside me.
'We don't know what you keep
going on about,' they all said to me.
'She's really lovely. Truly.'

Rebecca Hawkes

Glass glitters better than diamond under such splintered
light

rhinestone crystals drip
at her throat like luxury murder
in a cheap copper setting
that stains her skin green

while she sweats through
a ten-hour shift in the clear plastic
straps that nip the aquamarine
arteries lacing her feet

toes pointed past comfort
for maximum casual elegance
over the edge of the damp
faux leather settee

where she makes her quiet
difference by sipping
vodka cranberry
through a metal straw

because she won't risk a
nother slaughtered turtle
for every man who's ever
bought her a drink

and the dancers aren't allowed
to swig straight from the glass
since the steriliser can't clean off a kiss
smeared with unicorn blood
but a strong matte lip is best

for brushing cheeks without marking
in a way that spooks the missus
plus it can go all night

to stain the next day as a bleary smile
on the girl at the vegetable market
filling a bag with tamarillos
paid for in hard cash

Helen Heath

The Owners
(*found poems*)

I. RAY

It's a little embarrassing.
Sechan spends most of her time
in my room.
Being alone with her, in bed
in the early daylight, looking at her
looking at me, regarding me,
it's the difference
between being alone and lonely.
When she first came
into my life it was just
sex, sex, sex. Now that's tapered
off to where we are just there
for each other, we're always
there for each other.
The thing my father finds
really difficult about my relationship
with Sechan is the fact
that she's not alive. She's an anchor
for me. I know
what to expect. With women
you don't really get that.

II. JAMES

I've had a very pleasant morning
in bed with Virginia. I think
she's sleeping it off now. That, of course,
is her sleeping face. I had to change her
over from the eyes open face to the eyes

closed face. She just lies there,
they're very static.

Smile for the camera.
I have an insatiable thirst
for beautiful women, one doll
is not enough. The photos give
the dolls a life, like family photos,
makes them seem more real to me.
The fact that Rebecca is looking
at her book and Louise is looking down,
their attention is directed
at the same thing, while Louise leans
in a more or less realistic way.

III. GORDON

I used to be easy
before I got Ginger and Kelly
I used to be everybody's
doormat but I'm not anymore, it's all
about what I want now.
This is a Glock 40 calibre and this
a Tech 9mm, fires as fast
as you can pull the trigger and
this is a Mag 90, it's basically
a cheap version of an AK47. 3 guns
2 girls.

I don't like thongs or high heels or any
of that weird stuff.
It's a turn-off to me, makes a woman
look like she's been had by a hundred
different guys. I've found that relationships
with humans are only temporary
I've had that poster for 27 years

that car in the garage I've had my
whole life. I just get attached
to physical stuff.

The dolls are everything
to me. I'd rather live in a
cardboard box in a
frozen terrain than in the
biggest castle on the planet without
them. All the lies and deceit,
that'll never happen again.

The only time I gotta do something
I don't want is at the factory but
that's just 40 hours a week. I go
to the store once a month, get my
supplies, that's it. Other than that
I'm here, doing what I want
doing my thing.

I thought about it and I think
maybe I'll have them
buried with me, after all I'm
pretty small and they're not very
big. I think we'd all fit in
a slightly over-sized coffin. Then
we could all turn to dust
together.

Zoë Higgins

The Pests

The last half-hour at work is the longest part of the day. Imo can't see the wall clock from her place at the service desk. Instead, she watches the digital clock in the bottom corner of the sales computer. Four fifty-nine. It turns over. She grabs her things.

The Tararua ranges are sitting on Imo's desk. She's only just started painting. The sculpting took a long time—referring turn by turn to Google Images printouts and her elevations map—but she's happy with the accuracy.

Behind her, on a tall shelf, are Te Rerenga Wairua, Kapiti, the Port Nicholson settlement, Mt Taranaki, Cathedral Cove, a slice of te Urewera, a whaling camp, and Parihaka before it was burned. She's particularly happy with the trees and lamp-posts in the last one.

Imo picks up a 0.8mm brush from the stand. Mum made the stand for her, in her woodwork class. It doesn't fit all her pens and brushes, but she tries to use it. She dips the brush in white and starts to thread in the snowline.

A week later, she's finished a first coat and started on the trees. They're beech—not that you can tell at this elevation, but accuracy is important. Her desk is next to the room's only window. Today is freezing but she props the window open to clear some of the epoxy fumes. There's a knock at the door.

'Immie?'

'I'm here, Mum.'

'Can I come in?' She doesn't wait for an answer, but yanks the door open. She glances at the mountains. 'That's coming along, isn't it?'

Imo nods.

'I'm going to be at weaving tonight, so don't worry about cooking dinner for me.'

'Okay,' says Imo.

'You could come if you want. There are some lovely people in the class.'

'No thanks,' says Imo. Then: 'Have fun.'

She turns back to the beech trees and hears the door close. The spot of glue on the tree trunk has already dried.

'Bugger.'

She reaches for a craft knife. She's holding the tree awkwardly, distracted, and as she pares off the glue she nicks her finger.

'Bugger.'

It's a small cut but it stings, and there's already a bit of blood on the tree. She puts everything down and takes a couple of deep breaths. Working on models is no good if you're thinking about anything else. She stands and stretches, feeling the tightness in her shoulders and back. She should get some fresh air.

The treeline is almost finished. She'll glaze in the waterfalls next, a job she loves. Looking at the forest following the curve of the land, Imo has a strange sensation of movement. Not the pleasant movement of her eye being drawn across a landscape, but something small and scurrying. As if there were insects crawling under the trees. She leans closer toward the spot and tries to see if ants or spiders have wandered in. She quite likes it when large spiders find a model—they lend a War of the Worlds feel, briefly, to Matamata or Quail Island.

No spiders. She fits in the last tree and starts tidying her desk. Ten minutes later she is in bed.

The next morning she spots the tree stumps. Two of them. She has a good eye for detail, but she gets out the magnifying glass to confirm it. Two of the beeches on the bottom edge of the mountain have gone. No, not gone. They have been felled. She moves the magnifying glass closer and leans in. She has a good eye for detail. The tree trunks—made painstakingly from painted segments of split matchstick—have not snapped under pressure, or fallen out of their dabs of glue. They have been cut, or sawn, just above their base. There is no sign of the tree trunks.

Imo has to go to work in fifteen minutes. She finds her phone and uses the camera to photograph the tree stumps. Then she puts the magnifying glass away, changes into her work shirt, eats breakfast, and leaves the house.

The last half-hour of work is longer than usual. As soon as she's home, Imo inspects the model. No change. She begins mixing shingle and ice for the scree slopes, but halfway through she realises the pieces are too big and has to start again. She keeps half an eye on the model for any flash of movement.

That night, she dreams of scuttling claws and half-there noises. In the morning, another three trees are gone. She uses the magnifying glass and finds what looks like a trail, as wide as a cotton thread, disappearing into the forest. She phones in sick and spends the morning poring over the Ranges inch by inch. No more trees have been felled, but she finds another set of trails, none wider than a thread, zigzagging up a portion of the south slope. Although the glass is not good enough to show them, she thinks she sees footprints.

She spends the rest of the day in the public library, using a computer to search model-making forums. None of the threads seem to be what she's looking for. ModLife is reliable on everything from roof-texturing effects to sculpting an accurate gravel slope (she makes a mental note) but no one has mentioned anything about miniature tree-felling pests.

She starts an anonymous new thread in the *Problems* group.

I am working on a landscape model with 2000:1 scale trees. They have been felled and I am noticing other signs of life. I think I have some kind of pest activity. Help?? Thanks friends.

She can't skip work the next day. In between pointing customers toward the right vacuum cleaner for them, she secretly checks for forum activity on her phone. The ModLife forum is the most active around, and there are several responses to her message. The first one reads:

> Thanks for posting! I have had a similar problem when building large-ratio scale models. In my case the pest problem became a full-scale infestation and I had to scrap the whole thing. I'd be grateful for any solutions folks here can offer as I lost months of work.

There are a few useless jokes. Then gold:

> Hey anon, it sounds like you have a nascent civilisation problem. It's not common but it definitely crops up, especially if you're building resource-rich, hyper-realistic landscapes. Unfortunately common poisons won't work, but you can cover the whole model in an airtight cover and fumigate with formaldehyde or similar (purchasable online). Be careful as most fumigants are VERY toxic. I'd recommend dealing with it asap as the infestation can spread to other models.

Her manager almost catches her on her phone, and Imo spends the rest of the day being very careful.

The trails have spread, and Imo finds traces of mine tailings and what look like cart tracks in her foothills. She purchases 500mL of 37% formaldehyde solution off Amazon with next-day shipping.

By the time the formaldehyde arrives, Imo's lost almost two dozen trees. The pests are less wary of her now. She catches glimpses of them, pushing handcarts between the trees. They are no more than a millimetre or two tall, and move incredibly fast. She moves all the other models out of her room.

'Immie, why is the kitchen covered in geography?' asks her mother, on the way to salsa-bachata class.

'I'm cleaning my room,' says Imo. 'I'll move them back in a couple of days.'

'Don't hurry,' says her mother. 'Boiling the kettle feels quite excitingly volcanic with Taranaki next to it.'

When Mum's gone, Imo takes the Tararua ranges and sits them on a sheet of old window-glass in the back yard. She pours the formaldehyde into a milk-bottle cap and sits it beside the model. She fits a 60l plastic tub upside down over the mountains and checks that it sits snugly against the glass. She weights the tub down with a few large bricks, tapes a 'Do Not Disturb' sign to the top in case Mum tries to investigate, and shuts the back door firmly. She washes her hands and goes to bed.

She leaves the formaldehyde chamber set up for 24 hours. At work she is cheerful and manages to up-sell a young couple on their oil heaters. Her manager gives her a thumbs-up.

When she gets home in the evening she carefully disassembles everything. The formaldehyde has evaporated, but Imo wears gloves and washes everything with vinegar and again with soapy water. She wraps the bottle-top in newspaper and shoves it deep in the rubbish bin. She carries the mountains back to her room.

Under the brighter lights, she can see a number of tiny corpses at the edge of the forest. She picks them out with the tweezers and drops them on another bit of newspaper, to burn. She tweezers up the tree-stumps and sweeps away the mine tailings with a camelhair brush. She brings the rest of the models back into her room and arranges them on the shelf, exactly as they were before.

Emma Hislop

Sweet on the Comedown

Crickhowell, Powys, South Wales. They required chambermaids and waitresses, the ad in the paper said, and it was two pounds sixty an hour. Live in. Food and accommodation free. Uniforms provided. They'd not been to Wales before and it sounded like a bit of a crack.

Eve had been trying to get Kassy out of London, away from the scene and Brett and the pills. It started out with just a bit of ecstasy every weekend but he'd got hooked and then in a few months he was having pills for breakfast, just to get him through the day. Then he'd started dealing. Asked Kassy to go to India on holiday with him, but it turned out she was a decoy for his grand drug smuggling scheme. They'd had a huge row in the hotel room in Delhi. He had spent three hours swallowing a hundred Glad Wrapped finger-sized pellets of Indian hashish with yoghurt and thought she was overreacting when she refused to sit beside him on the aeroplane back to London. He'd made a shitload of money from that trip, but he hadn't stopped there. Ended up owing lots of money to bigger dealers and it was all getting way too heavy for Kassy.

Eve had just split up with Felix after five years, deciding overnight that she wanted out and getting her bellybutton pierced before hitching out of Brighton. She hooked up with Kassy in Hereford and they went to a five-day rave in the Welsh mountains. Carry on regardless. Borrowed a tent from another mate and got a ride with some boys Eve had met in the pub in Brighton. She fancied the tall one.

Eve and Kassy took ecstasy that first afternoon. It was hot and they sat high up on the grassy bank looking down onto the outside dance space. The DJ was an elderly woman with long grey hair, dressed in a combination of fluoro gear and ethnic prints. Layer upon layer. She had a hairbrush and was interspersing her DJing with brushing her hair. About thirty people were dancing in the dust to banging trance music. The pills kicked in and everything seemed very funny.

'Are these people for real?' Kassy said. 'I can't tell.' She was having difficulty rolling a cigarette.

Eve snorted and tucked a loose tendril of dark hair back behind her ear. 'They can't be, can they?'

Kassy stared down at them. 'The party people must have hired them. Hired a crowd. For our entertainment.'

'Yeah, that must be it.' Eve leaned back, using her elbows to prop herself up so she could still see the crowd down below.

'Rent-a-crowd.'

'Rent a raver.'

'Ha ha ha ha ha,' on and on, till the group of beautifully blond Scandinavians in sparkly leather jackets next to them were grinning and laughing as well.

They were grinding their jaws now and thirsty. It felt impossible to stop laughing so Eve walked off fast down the hill, pointing in the direction of the beer tent. When she got there, she crowded up to the bar and got her money out of her purse.

'All right mate?' a voice behind said, in that English way that didn't require an answer.

She turned around, with some difficulty. Her legs had started to twitch uncontrollably and a loud ringing in her ears was making her disorientated. Christ, he was tall, he must be at least six foot six.

'Beers,' she managed and smiled up at him, trying to stop her eyes from rolling around. At least she thought her face was smiling; it was hard to tell.

'Here,' he said and passed her a tiny tinfoil envelope, neatly made. It reminded her of origami. 'Get you dancing.'

'Cheers mate,' she said and it was all getting too much and so she paid for the beers which looked strange and enormous and carried them outside. The sun was glaring after the shady cool tent and Eve wanted her sunglasses badly but her hands were full and she had to get back up the bank and all she could think about was having a lie down and watching the clouds.

Kassy was lying down with her sunglasses on, face up towards the sky.

'The clouds are so beautiful today,' she said.

Eve took a big breath, relieved to have made it back. She sat down hard. 'Here's your beer.'

'On your head,' Kassy said.

'Eh?' said Eve.

'Sunglasses,' Kassy said.

'Off your head,' said Eve and flicked her beer froth at Kassy.

'Off your tits. Off my fucking tits.'

They snorted the powder off the foil and tried to finish the beers, which took forever. Clambered their way down the bank, holding onto each other.

The dance space was impressive now, a giant bowl heaving with dusty glamour. They stood at the edge. Eve felt the speed taking hold and looked across at Kassy as she entered the zone, head down, becoming a cog in the machine of human dance. Eve closed her eyes. The transition was not an easy one. The buzz was electric and she was confused.

They'd been the last ones to leave on Sunday evening, the sound of sheep suddenly loud once the generators were shut down. Everything had been dismantled. They cooked up a final pot of baked beans and bread before getting in the car and being dropped off to start work the next day. The tall guy had left her with his homespun jersey and given her his phone number and a hug before he got back in the car. He was heading off to Thailand for a month to buy jewellery to bring back and sell at a market in Oxford.

The manor house loomed up in front of them as they got out of the taxi, all cream and pale yellow—resembling a soft iced cake among the greenery. A manicured garden and vast croquet lawn, surrounded by low border hedges and wooden benches at evenly spaced intervals. To the left, if you were looking towards the house, was the river, you couldn't see it, but you could hear it from here. To the right, the owner's residence and stables, and more gardens and cottages.

Inside, the foyer was all red and gold, with a high ceiling and a sweeping staircase with an enormous polished wooden balustrade. There was a man in a starched blue shirt behind the desk and he looked up as they came through the glass doors, a welcome smile on his face, which faded when he saw them. You could almost see his face computing them and coming up with *Unclean Creatures.*

'We're here to start work. I'm Eve and this is Kassy. We were told to ask for Mrs Bennett?' Eve said, putting down her overloaded pack.

The man tapped the gold bell on the desk.

'Presumably you were also told to find the back entrance.' Eve suppressed a small laugh. A man wearing a shiny maroon waistcoat appeared through a set of doors on the far side of the foyer.

'Show these people to the staff common room,' the man at the desk said, gesturing at them briefly and looking back at the book.

'Welcome to Wankerham Palace,' Eve said to Kassy in a posh whisper, dragging one leg theatrically behind her as they followed the butler back across the driveway and around the side of the building.

Mrs Bennett was a New Zealander. She was an expat who had been living in Wales now for twenty years, but it was still in the girls' favour. She was a no-nonsense, stocky woman who told them straight off that Eve would wear a headscarf over that hair and that Kassy would need to remove her facial piercings before she reported for work every morning. She directed them to a big cardboard box of spare uniforms in the common room, which also contained some miscellaneous items left behind by their predecessors, and told them to report to her in the morning by 7am. Looking respectable and by the side door, not the foyer.

'Carl will take you down to the cottage,' she said. 'It's right back down the drive, you'd have passed it on your way in. You'll need a torch'.

Nobody had lived in the cottage for years. Not since the witchcraft, Carl said. He was a plain, red-faced bloke, from somewhere up north, Manchester or somewhere, Kassy guessed, from his accent. Second chef here, he told them proudly on their walk down to the cottage.

'Witchcraft?' Eve said, in a disbelieving tone, nudging Kassy in the side.

A woman who turned out to be a witch had rented it briefly a few years ago and had held meetings there, Carl said. Someone had found a doll with needles stuck into it and an Anglican minister had been called to do an exorcism. Eighty-three witches and ninety Satanists were living in Wales, according to the 2011 census. He raised his eyebrows. Eve looked at Kassy, who was trying to stay composed.

The building resembled the gingerbread house from the fairy tale, with a winding stone staircase going up to a whole room spanning the length of the roof, so low you had to crouch over when you walked. Little windows all along the front, starting at the floor. Four unmade single beds in a row and rugs and old looking pillows piled up on the end one.

'Welcome home,' said Eve, shining the torch into all the corners.

It was dark when the alarm went off, but Kassy was already up and outside smoking a cigarette. Eve laid out two piles of clothes, making two outfits. By the time Kassy climbed up the stairs she was dressed in her uniform, complete with white pinny with a frill at the hem. Just the headscarf to go.

'Bloody hell!' Kassy said. 'You totally suit that look. Reckon you must have been a chambermaid in your former life.'

'Hurry up and get dressed,' Eve said, putting toothpaste onto her toothbrush, 'or we'll be late.'

Mrs Bennett asked a younger girl, Lucy, to demonstrate how to clean a guest room. She made hospital corners with the king-size bed sheets and Kassy and Eve crowded into the loo to watch her folding the toilet paper into a silly triangle. She dusted the furniture with a real feather duster. Polishing. Attention to detail, that's what mattered.

'How long have you worked here for?' Eve asked Lucy.

'Oh, about three summers,' she said. 'It's just my holiday job while I'm on break from university. I only live down the road. I hear you're in the cottage down the end of the drive. That's brave.'

'We're from New Zealand,' said Eve.

Lucy showed them how to make a high tea for the busloads of elderly people that arrived in the weekends. Crustless cucumber sandwiches and scones and jam and cream. Industrial-sized tubs of butter and jam were kept in a walk-in chiller, which was packed full of local produce, and fresh bread arrived daily on a truck from the local bakery. And huge silver urns of tea. Mrs Bennett emphasised the importance of making sure the tea never ran out. The day went slowly.

Cutting the crusts off a stack of club sandwiches, Eve said, 'I calculated today what I need to save to get home. I just hope that Felix sells the van and gives me half. That would be five hundred quid.'

'Do you reckon he will?' Kassy said. 'You did break his heart.'

'Yeah, thanks for the reminder,' Eve said.

Eve stood in the restaurant, polishing cutlery by the big windows overlooking the river. Most diners had left by now. The owners had come in for a late supper at their usual table and there was one other table of six about to have dessert. Lucy was putting the coffee out.

The owner clicked his fingers at Eve. You wouldn't get away with that in New Zealand. Carl had told her he was a bastard. She put down the cloth napkin and the forks and walked over to their table by the fireplace.

'My steak's undercooked, disappointingly.'

Back in the kitchen, she watched as the head chef took the plate and threw it, frisbee style, into the bin. He kicked the bin onto its side and it rolled across the floor, hitting the fridge and making a hard noise. Carl was concentrating on perfecting the gelato mounds.

The head chef took a clean pan down from the rack above the ovens. He took the steak out of the bin and threw it into the pan. It sizzled for a minute.

'Plate that up,' he ordered Lucy, who was leaning on the bench nonchalantly watching the scene. She might have been on the sidelines of a football match. 'With extra fucking shallots and red wine sauce.'

Eve carried the plate slowly out to the restaurant. She wanted this not to be happening. She looked at the steak, feeling a stab of guilt. This was taking things a bit far.

'Sorry to keep you waiting,' she said, but she hesitated, holding onto the plate.

'Is there something else?' he said.

She met his eye and shook her head. It wasn't like she had done anything wrong. Maybe he deserved it. She needed to look after herself. Keep it together. The candle flickered as she put the plate down on the table. She needed to work and save and get home to New Zealand.

The laundry was in the basement underneath the kitchen, right next door to the wine cellar. Eve, the wine smuggler. It was only scary the first time. She would wait till the night shift was over and head down there with the laundry basket. Steal a decent bottle of claret and hide it underneath the sheets and pillowcases. Into her fraying old backpack. Out the side door and down the long tree-lined driveway. Home to the cottage. They stayed up most nights till two or three a.m., smoking cigarettes out the crooked floor-level windows of the cottage and drinking the wine till it was gone, and they'd go to bed in their funny, lumpy, single beds.

'I'm scared,' Kassy said, looking at the postcard that had arrived that afternoon. On the front was a brightly coloured map of Ibiza with a setting sun and dolphins around it. 'Excited but scared it'll be the same old shit with him. I'm just starting to feel strong again and I'm in a better place. But you know I can't say no to the bastard. And he'll bring pills with him.'

Eve stubbed her cigarette out on the stone windowsill and threw it out the window.

'Shit, Kass. I'm no expert. Look at how I fucked things up with Felix. I was a total headcase about it all. Still am. I just need to get my shit together and save.' She pulled another cigarette out of the packet and held it between her fingers, tapping it against her other hand.

Eve hadn't been able to visualise Brett arriving, but here he was. He got out of the taxi from Abergavenny, tanned and even thinner than he'd been in London and wearing a number of necklaces all different lengths. A fresh tattoo on one forearm.

'Fuck me,' he said, looking up at the cottage before kissing Kassy on both cheeks.

'Five star accommodation, then.' A bottle of Jack Daniel's in one hand and a carton of duty-free cigarettes in the other.

'Get the taxi, babe? I'm all out of change.' Kassy raced inside, pushing past Eve standing in the doorway. Brett wouldn't meet her eyes. To be expected, but it was still awkward. Kassy came outside again and paid the taxi driver and they all sat on the blanket Kassy had put down on the lawn. Brett got out a packet of Port Royal tobacco and a battered looking tin. 'I've been hanging out for a spliff. And I could murder a drink. Got some glasses?'

'Yep,' said Kassy, standing up again. 'I see you got some work done.' She admired his freshly-inked arm. 'Is that another one of your designs?'

'Yeah, I based it loosely on the Mayan calendar,' Brett said, sticking two cigarette papers together. 'Totally sound bloke, the tattooist. We went clubbing together most nights. He gave me the last session for free. I'm going to show him the London scene when he comes over.'

'Nice one,' Kassy said, sticking her head through the open kitchen window and grabbing three coffee mugs off the bench. 'Only the finest vessels, you may be sure,' she said, coming back over and setting them down on the rug. 'The other night we used a knitting needle to open a bottle of wine. Pure class, eh, Eve? Couldn't find the corkscrew in the dark.' Brett poured the drinks.

'Cheers!' Kassy said, holding out her mug and they clinked them together and Eve said cheers and Brett didn't. Eve sipped the Jack Daniel's, noticing some new lines around Brett's eyes.

'Shit, I've got to get to work,' Kassy said, checking the time on her phone.

'Work?' Brett said. 'I've come all this fucking way to see you and you're going to work. Nice one, babe.'

'Only for the lunch shift and setting up for afternoon tea,' Kassy said, leaning over and punching his arm. 'That way I get all of tomorrow off to hang out with you. I thought we could hitch into town and go to the pub, play some pool.'

'Okay,' he said. 'I suppose I'll let you.'

'Eve will keep you entertained,' Kassy said, heading upstairs. 'I'll just get changed.'

Nobody said anything and then Kassy was back, skip running across the lawn.

'Bye,' she said, 'have fun, I still can't believe you're here.' Kissed them both on the cheek. 'I feel half cut already,' she said. 'Hope it's not busy. I should be back around four.' She disappeared behind the huge old oak trees lining the drive.

'Another drink?' Brett said.

'Brett, I haven't been able to get it out of my head. I'm having dreams about it. About being found out.'

'You haven't told her, I hope,' he said. You gave me your word.'

'Word! You're a fine one to talk about giving someone your word! The only reason I haven't told is that it would really fuck things up. Fuck Kass up.'

'Just let it go, Eve,' he said. 'I have. It's done and dusted. Nobody will ever know. Another drink?'

'We should have done something. We just left her there. That fucking girl.'

'Shit, what were we meant to do?' he said. 'I was off my tits that night; I must have had about five pills. I sure as hell wasn't going to call the cops.' He poured himself another Jack Daniel's. 'I don't mind drinking alone.'

'We gave her the pills,' Eve said, pulling her knees up towards her chest. 'With that must come some responsibility.'

The top of her head felt hot. She looked out over the lawn. A patch of grass between the cottage and the driveway had been bleached brown in the sun.

'It wasn't the pills. We'd been dishing out that lot all night,' Brett said, taking a sip of whiskey. 'All the other punters were sweet. It comes down to personal responsibility. That bird just didn't know her limits.'

'Shit, there could have been others. Others like her.'

'You're being dramatic, babe,' he said.

'Brett, she's dead. Dead.'

'And if you choose to feel guilty about that, you're fucked. It was an accident. Not our fault, babe,' he said.

'I'm off for a walk,' Eve said. 'I need to clear my head.'

'Yeah, good luck with that,' he said. 'I suggest a mini break in Ibiza. Chill you out a bit.'

Eve headed up the track, away from the river.

The boat party on the Thames had been held on the Saturday of the bank holiday weekend. Kassy had come down with bronchitis and wasn't able to go. Eve had offered to sell her ticket for her and gone round to get it on Friday after work, but Kassy was off at the chemist when Eve arrived. While she waited for Kassy to get back, Brett had asked her if she wanted to make some extra cash. It had sounded easy enough and Eve was so broke, she just ended up saying yes. He'd throw in two free pills as well. She had picked up the two little bags from Brett's place in North London on the afternoon of the party.

The pills were strong. Eve had shifted most of the first bag by about ten p.m. and could see the change in people, crowded into the main dance area, dancing wildly to techno music that must have been heard halfway across the London night. At one point she saw the boat conductor come down the stairs, a hip flask in his hand, and survey the roof, which was undulating under the crowd dancing on the top deck. She must have taken her pill around midnight, though it was hard to tell, the boat was just approaching the bridge, so about halfway up the river.

Eve found the girl when she went up on deck for some air. She was wedged down between the safety rings and the inflatable raft, almost out of sight.

She had gone to find Brett who was standing at the front of the boat smoking a cigarette and looking pretty wasted and he came to look. They talked about what to do. Eve had wanted to get the conductor to turn the boat around, or dock somewhere so they could call an ambulance but Brett had told her she was overreacting. We're high, he'd said, it's late, the girl wasn't going anywhere.

In the end they decided to put a tarpaulin over her and leave her where she was.

Eve had been waiting on the bridge for the night bus and thought she'd heard sirens. She'd woken Felix up when she got back to the flat and managed to convince him that London was the reason they'd been fighting so much and Brighton was nice and they had friends there they could stay with for a bit. He'd taken one look at her and told her it was the drugs talking. Come to bed, he'd said, and she had gotten in beside him and put her head on his shoulder and thought about the girl and what a terrible thing it was. They'd done a terrible thing.

The next day Felix had agreed a move might be a good thing. A week later it was on the news. The girl had been found by the cleaner after the boat had docked. She was in a coma and died in hospital five days later. Police were trying to trace who supplied the drug and who organised the rave. Eve didn't see Brett again but heard through friends he'd gone back to India for the trance season in Goa.

Eve was leaning on the fence watching the horses in the field beside the stables when she heard Kassy call out to her. She turned around. Kassy was standing outside the manor house taking off her pinny. The sun was hot on Eve's face.

'What you up to?' Kassy said.

'Been for a walk,' Eve said, crunching over the gravel towards her. 'How was work?'

'So boring! Only had ten in for lunch,' Kassy said. 'But at least I got to bail before the geriatric bus tour arrived. I thought you guys would be well on your way by now. Waiting for me, eh?' They started walking back towards the driveway.

'Kass,' Eve said, 'I'm feeling scared.'

'I know what you're going to say. You're going to tell me to be careful, aren't you? That you don't want to see me make the same mistake with him again. Well, I'm not going to. Anyway, he's going back to New Zealand, he let that slip earlier. Well, Aussie first to see a mate on the Gold Coast, then home. And you know what? I'm actually cool with it. That scene in London was nuts. I was nuts. I reckon we probably got out just in time.'

Eve looked hard at her friend. 'Right,' she said. 'Okay.'

'But while he's here, lets have some fun, eh? I reckon we deserve it,' she said, flicking the frill on her pinny back and forth. 'Two pounds sixty an hour! Are they having a laugh?'

More drinks, more stories. Brett brought out a jar of pills and gave them one each.

'For starters.' Grinning at them, in his element.

'Are they strong?' Eve asked.

'That's never worried you before,' Kassy said and looked at Eve. Eve didn't say anything.

'Yeah,' Brett said, 'but clean as. No strychnine in them, so the comedown's sweet.'

*

They stood at the top of the track. Eve's nose felt sunburnt. She looked at Kassy and grinned.

'Gone Boom yet?'

'Argh,' Kassy replied, in an exaggerated West Country accent. 'Let's go! Boom!'

They grinned again at each other.

Eve charged down the dark track through the trees and out onto the large flat area beside the river. Behind her, Kassy laughed. Down here the paddock, or the meadow as Kass liked to call it—so English—had a silvery quality to it. The grass was tall and wispy. Eve carved a track through into the middle and lay on her stomach. She heard Kassy pass by and keep going, towards the river. Her skin began to itch and she stood back up. The pills were taking hold now and everything was starting to shift. Grasses and trees melding together into one amorphous thing, twinkling and soft around the edges. She began the climb up the hill.

The lookout was hidden behind a group of oak trees but if you climbed up to the top of the old tower box you could see through the branches and down over to the river and right up the valley. Kassy was a vivid dot of colour on the edge of the bank, her long auburn plait standing out against her purple T-shirt.

Reaching into her canvas shoulder bag, Eve took out the bottle of cider and the three plastic cups Kassy had stolen from the lunchroom. Set the cups down. She sat, legs dangling over the edge of the lookout floor, for an indeterminable time. Down below, the paddock had become an arena, lit up by the blazing sun. Sitting still, she waited for the gladiators.

Nadine Anne Hura

The Garage Party

The stones were not yet in the hole when Leah turned up. She immediately regretted arriving so early. The street was quiet and the curtains were still drawn inside the house. She had expected to find the place humming with activity, potatoes a-peeling and jugs a-boiling, but when Leah stood still and cupped her ear to the front door she could hear nothing but the gentle suck-wheeze of slumber. The family, she realised in alarm, were still asleep. She dithered at the top of the stairs, cursing herself for not confirming the exact time she should arrive, assuming that 'putting down a hāngī' meant dawn. She was tiptoeing down the steps in an attempt to slip back to her car unnoticed, when out of the garage came a large man in an orange high-vis jacket and work boots carrying a box piled high with shiny, just-washed cabbage leaves.

'Kia ora kia ora!' he said, stopping in his tracks and lifting his eyebrows towards her. Leah cleared her throat and put her shoulders back. She was determined not to be whakamā with her reo like she was in the classroom. Why else was she doing all this study, if not to use it in the real reo-speaking world? She came down the steps waving, then quickly remembered that a chin-lift looked more natural, so lifted her chin as well, giving her the appearance of an excited puppy. 'Tēnā koe,' she said breathlessly.

The man shifted the box under one arm and held out the other in greeting. Leah leaned in with her lips but he was lining up her nose like a plane above a runway and the whole thing ended with a head- butt and the unnatural sound of a kiss landing in mid-air.

Leah groaned internally. How many times had she practised the hongi in the mirror? A hongi always begins with eye contact! The man smiled. He had dark, ropey skin and dimples so deep they might have been carved into his cheeks. It made her think of all the laughter that had shaped his face, like a chisel tap-tap-tapping away day after day, shift after shift. The green eyes, combined with the high-vis jacket and work boots, reminded her of the photo of her father standing next to her pale English mother. She'd found the old Polaroid in a box under the bed while hunting for the Christmas tree and when she'd brought it out and asked her mother about it, Janet had scoffed and said, 'Biggest mistake of my life, that was,' barely looking up from the sewing machine. Though Leah had never met her father, or this man for that matter, it took all her self-control not to reach out and wrap both arms around him and sob into his vast reflective chest.

'I think . . .' Leah stammered. 'I think I'm a bit early. I came to help with the hāngī.' She smoothed down her jeans which suddenly felt too tight. 'I wanted to help but . . .' She gestured to the house and stated the obvious. 'Everyone's still sleeping.'

'Just us up at this time,' the dimpled man said, nodding towards the back of the garage where tendrils of smoke were curling towards the sky. 'Fire's got to burn down. It'll take a few hours.'

He began to walk and, not knowing what else to do, Leah followed.

'Nō hea koe?' the man said, looking sideways at her. Literally speaking, he was asking where she was from, but Leah knew that what he really wanted to know was who she was, and why she'd turned up here at the crack of dawn looking like a foreign exchange student on a tiki tour. Leah wondered quite the same thing. All she could think of was the man with tattoos.

'I'm from . . . nō te Nōta,' Leah said, trying to copy the casual tone of her mate Tarns. 'Ko Ngāpuhi te iwi. Engari, i tipu ake ahau i Te Awakairangi. I study with . . .' She hesitated before saying his name. 'Taneora.'

'Ahhhhh,' the man said. 'So *you're* his new flame?' He seemed to be looking at her now with different eyes.

Leah blushed, feeling the conspicuous weight of her Deadly Ponies handbag and the sleek whiteness of her shoes. She knew she didn't look like the kind of woman Taneora would be with, although she wasn't exactly sure what his type would be. He was hardly what you'd call a *typical* Māori, whatever that was. She'd first noticed him at a noho marae, standing outside the wharenui wearing a headscarf and kandura like he'd just walked out of the desert. She half expected to see a camel hitched up to the waharoa, so bare were his tattooed feet. But the words that came out of his mouth were Māori, not Arabic.

They became friends, bonding over a mutual appreciation of books and language. For some reason, when Leah spoke to Taneora, she didn't stutter or stumble over her words. The language of her ancestors seemed to flow from her tongue without thought or effort, the way it did in her dreams. What's more, Taneora understood everything she said, no matter how many mistakes she made. Their connection was spiritual, Leah was sure of it. She liked his teeth. They were tall and straight like a white picket fence inside his mouth. When she looked at his teeth she wanted to swing open the gate and move in.

Leah's mother was shocked when she turned up with him at the house one weekend for Sunday roast. She'd started telling everyone that Leah was going through a 'phase', emphasising the words 'reconnecting with her roots' while holding up two fingers on either side of her face. She acted like Leah couldn't hear her when she added 'mid-life crisis' and a knowing wink. Of course, Janet had been through a similar phase herself, once upon a time, which is how Leah came along. But that was an accident. Janet was really only trying to get a rise out of her father, a cruel and brittle man who hated anyone who wasn't white and English. Leah's grandfather had spent four years in a POW camp in Japan and the idea that one of his own offspring might have the blood of another race pumping through them was enough to push him over the edge. He'd left his pregnant daughter on the doorstep of St Mary's home for unwed mothers in disgrace.

Leah knew all of this. For years she'd lived with the knowledge that half of her was flawed and better off hidden. She was Māori but not a real Māori. And yet. And yet! Here she was about to put down a hāngī. At dawn!

When Taneora saw her approaching he leaned his spade against the fence and came over. She wasn't sure if his expression was one of surprise or embarrassment. She waved. He lifted his chin.

'Kia ora.'

'Kia ora.'

Taneora pressed his nose to her nose, holding her in a half-embrace that seemed to carry on for minutes rather than seconds. One of the men grinned and said something in an off-hand way and although only one corner of his mouth moved, the inflection of his voice together with the rapid twitch of his left eyebrow filled his short words with innuendo and all the men rocked in their boots with laughter. Leah joined in, not because she understood but because she wanted to be part of the laughter, not standing on the edge of it. She stole a glance at Taneora, who rolled his eyes as if to say *Ignore them*, then took her around introducing her one by one to his brothers and uncles and cousins. Each one squeezed her hand and smiled politely as though on their best behaviour. It made her feel, she realised uncomfortably, like the Queen.

Oh, but how everything changed once the beers started flowing! With the hāngī served and eaten and all the work done and cleared up, everyone began to relax. The rāhui on drugs remained but Cody's in moderation was perfectly fine. By the time the sun began its lazy retreat Leah could feel the alcohol filtering its way to her heart, simultaneously slowing it down and speeding it up. The whole garage seemed to be aglow in the warmth that was now sitting snugly inside her chest.

Taneora reached out and put his thick, calloused hand on her knee. 'Kei te pēhea?'

Leah nodded back with a wide smile. 'Rawe,' she yelled above the sound of Aunty Mavis crooning in harmony with her niece. She didn't know how to tell him, in any language, that she felt more relaxed here in this garage than she ever had at her cousins' house eating scones with jam and cream. She wanted to say that she felt like she belonged here, that she felt a rightness to the world she always knew was missing. She wanted to tell him that she wished she had a family like this, but it was a silly thing to say because she knew she was only seeing what she wanted to see and that Taneora's family had their dramas, plenty of them, too. Only a few minutes ago the cousin with the dreads had been told off for pulling his knife out on the dance floor, an act that seemed far more harmless in the moment than it would have looked to anyone standing outside the garage looking in. But even that—the way Tina had come up to him and put her arm around him gently and said, 'No more nephew, put the knife away,' was done lovingly. Everyone else had laughed but Leah . . . Leah had to fight to hold back the tears.

Just then, one of the Uncles—one of the older ones—started playing the ukelele upside down. With the cousins egging him on, he got up and shimmied into the middle of the garage, strumming his fingers at the wrong end of the shaft. 'Play it Uncle, play it!' yelled Taneora's sister.

Leah wondered what the neighbours must be thinking and an image of her mother flitted briefly across her mind, sitting at home on the couch watching *Dancing with the Stars* right now. The mere idea of it made her feel lightheaded.

'*That's the way, Uncle does the hula!*' the crowd was singing.

Taneora groaned and rolled his eyes. 'Ahh, sheet,' he said, leaning over to Leah. 'You're gunna have to dance.'

Leah's eyes widened. 'What? No!'

'Yeh. Sorry.'

Leah watched as Tina got up after Uncle, swinging her hips and gyrating down to the ground and up again while everyone sang '*That's the way, Tina does the hula!*' After Tina came Moana, flossing hardout, while the kids all cheered and whooped in approval.

Next was Charlie, who dropped to the ground in one swift movement and started doing one-armed press-ups. The crowd went ballistic.

Leah felt sick. There was no way out.

With one arm held high and another slapping her backside, Aunty Mavis rode into the middle of the circle and the crowd fell about wolf-whistling. Taneora was next, moonwalking across the garage and ending in a mighty pūkana in Leah's direction. Leah squeezed her eyes shut and took a deep breath. She could feel everyone looking at her, watching, waiting.

The next day she woke on a mattress on the floor with a pulsing headache and a sore back. She had a vague recollection of dancing the hula with a broom. Taneora was awake, sitting cross-legged on the verandah with his face inclined towards the sun. She couldn't tell if he was meditating or thinking. It was always hard to tell, with him. She got up and tiptoed to the bathroom. Her throat was dry and raspy and the memory of singing *Islands in the Stream* with Aunty Mavis came back to her in snatches. She could have sworn she could still hear laughter coming from the garage, but the party couldn't still be going on, could it?

Leah turned the tap on and splashed her face with water. She looked up at her reflection in the mirror. Her hair was frizzy and wild, untamed and free. It was the strangest sensation, but for a moment she almost didn't recognise herself.

'How was the party?' Janet asked that night on the phone.

'Great,' said Leah, as if settling a bet.

'Hmph,' came the reply.

'What's that supposed to mean?'

'Well,' said her mother, with a little puff. 'They're not always who you think they are.'

'Who?'

'The Maoris.'

'The . . . the Maoris? Jesus, Mum. *I'm a Māori.*'

'Well, yes,' said Janet. 'But you're not a real Māori.'

'How would you know? What does that even mean?'

'I just mean that you're not one of them,' said Janet. 'Are you?'

Leah looked out the window towards the moon, a slim crescent, barely there. She knew it had a name; every phase of the moon had a name and precise tikanga, everything from when to go out with the nets and when to stay in and watch your back. For some reason, though, no matter how many definitions she memorised or wānanga she sat through, the words just wouldn't stay lodged inside her Pākehā-thinking brain. It was as though certain knowledge had an untouchable quality, protected by a boundary or a threshold that she could feel on some molecular level but could not step across. In her mind, she could see Taneora, walking barefoot across the stones, and dimpled men in high-vis jackets laughing at jokes she couldn't hear. The visions were intermingled and meshed together with her own reflection in the mirror, an intricate knowledge of the shape of mistakes, and the dead-weight of a designer handbag hanging from her arm like whakapapa unclaimed.

Leah sighed, feeling the final afterglow of the previous night fully dissipate. 'It's just that . . . I suppose . . .'

'Exactly,' said her mother.

Ash Davida Jane

hot bodies

how does anyone remember anything
in this heat   the cicadas scream
like they're burning alive   the footpath
is scattered with their tiny husks
they crunch when you step on them
               though you try not to   all the plants
have gone to seed too early & there'll be no food
left for March   we're left gorging ourselves
on too-red tomatoes as we race to put our
teeth in them before they rot
               they turn our stomachs   we'll be starving
come winter   how vintage
               this is not the end   this
is only the beginning   the houses
are burning   right down to the roots
of the trees they were built from   every day
there's another story   it isn't going
to get any easier but you still have to
tell the kids   there is hope   you
still have to tell your friends to recycle
their beer bottles at the end of the night
               you have to fill a piñata with apology
notes   & really go to town on it   you know
               you have to open all the windows
on the windiest day & watch the curtains dance
like giant women in beautiful white dresses
               their hands reaching out to collect
the dust motes in golden rivers
               the sun glancing through the windows
as sharp as cut glass   as gritted teeth
at night make our jaws ache   when we bathe in the sun
mid-afternoon   sunglasses on
          bodies stretched out & helpless

Andrew Johnston

The Otorhinolaryngologist

After having asked me to say Ah
after having himself said Ah

the otorhinolaryngologist
guided me silently over the ancient carpet

to a small white room with two low stools
and handed me a bulb on the end of a cord:

this, he said, is a cold light,
and I want you to put it in your mouth.

He flicked a switch and we sat in the dark
lit only by my ghostly face.

*

Suddenly I understood
history, weather, time,

I could see the skeleton
of every memory

the how of war
the knife of every scar;

everything I'd never learned
burned brightly in my mind—

calculus, zoology,
epistemology—

*

I could see the otorhinolaryngologist
seeing me, I could see

how good he was, and beyond him
where evil came from,

the origins of language, and languages,
the splintering chaos

of thought, slowed down
till I could hear its ticking,

the birth of galaxies, planets and stars,
sped up so I could grasp all in an instant

*

but once his eyes had widened to the dark
in which my sinuses glowed

the otorhinolaryngologist
extinguished the light in my head

and turned on the light
in the small white room

plunging me into
familiar mist

through which I swam to
pay him and to leave—

*

a cold wind blew down the street,
I was hungry, and stumbled,

hankering, perplexed,
abandoned again

to hunting for something
in the hollow spaces

in the voiceless spaces
filled with the sound of footsteps

hurrying
into the dark.

Saudade

So Dad (no more
sad songs) happy

to have reached the very idea
after so much arriving:

permanent yesterday. Now
that you're a xylophone,

monsieur, life is soft,
but there are moments of striving

to hear, above the sodden ground,
the sound of padded hammers.

Hannah Jolly

Flood

Water rose in the driveway during the night, and Kirby was scooped out of bed by her father and put in Mr de Roos' four-wheel drive. It was the sound of the raindrops that woke her in the end, smacking loudly on her jacket, and then on the body of the car.

Kirby was driven across the road to the de Roos' house. Water slushed around the tires. Mrs de Roos was standing on the verandah, clutching her elbows. She led Kirby inside the house and up to one of the top storey bedrooms.

The bed had a wooden rim around the mattress, so you couldn't really sit comfortably on the edge—the wood dug into your thighs. The headboard was old and thick with a post at each end. They were pointed; high and proud like chess-set bishops, but there was a string of pink plastic flowers looped over one. Lying on her back, Kirby reached her hand up and wound the flowers around her wrist.

'That was Yolanda's bed,' Mrs de Roos said the next morning.

At the kitchen table, Kirby was presented with three little rounds of crispy Dutch toast. Mrs de Roos plunged coffee for her husband. Then she dipped a wooden stick into a can of golden syrup. It had a knob on the end the shape of a bumble bee—Mrs de Roos held it above Kirby's plate, and the syrup bled off the ribbing.

Mr de Roos piggy-backed Kirby across the road and dropped her at the garage door, where her mother was sweeping at the concrete with a fat-bristled broom.

'Hey Lady,' she said, and gave Kirby a hug and a kiss. 'That's a pretty necklace.'

'Mrs de Roos gave it to me.'

'Did she? I hope you said thank you.'

Mr de Roos raised his elbow, and leaned it against the garage door. 'She did,' he said.

'It's Yolanda's.' Kirby pulled the string up so it covered her eyebrows.

Her mother held the broom with two hands—two fists, one on top of the other. She looked at Mr de Roos, then down at Kirby. 'Do you think you should keep it?'

'Yes.'

Mr de Roos clapped his hands together. 'Well,' he said.

'Thank you,' said Kirby's mother.

Mr de Roos gave them a salute (two fingers, like a scout) then turned and waded back up the driveway.

The radio was hanging from a nail on the wall, next to a blue-green coil of hose pipe. Kirby reached up make the tuning stick slide, but her mother said, 'Don't fiddle.'

'Where's Dad?'

Her mother swept a sheaf of brown water out onto the gravel. 'Shops,' she said. 'He'll be back soon.'

The radio beeped for the news (five short, one long).

The water hadn't got into the house. While her parents went around unstacking all the furniture, Kirby sat on the kitchen floor, on some newspaper her mother had laid out. On a blank sheet she drew a picture of a white crayon cat. She gave the cat yellow ears and a yellow tail, then finished it off with a bold smear of purple dye. When it was dry, she folded it up in a brown envelope.

By mid-afternoon the sky was blue again, and the evening came in clear. Her mother and father were in the kitchen, leaning against the fridge. They both had their heads down—they looked like they were thinking. Kirby stood on a stool, stirring soup over the element with a wooden spoon. The radio was playing the news again because Princess Diana had just died in an accident, and everyone needed to hear.

'Those bloody paparazzi!' said her father in a whisper.

'Shhhh!'

They put their heads down again, and listened.

Sweet tomato soup was Kirby's favourite. Her father cut cheese into hunks and dropped them into his bowl like ice cubes.

'Those bloody paparazzi,' he said.

Her mother sighed. 'Tony . . .'

'You shouldn't say that word, Dad.'

'Look,' said her mother, grinding pepper over her bowl. 'You shouldn't jump to conclusions. There was probably all sorts going on that we don't know about.'

'There'll be an investigation. And I bet you, they're going to say paparazzi.'

'Dad!'

'It's not a swear word, Kirby.'

'What does it mean, then?'

'The paparazzi are photographers,' said her mother. 'They take photographs of famous people, like Princess Diana.'

'They're sneaky, like rats,' said her father.

'Rats are just animals. Paparazzi are people—that's much worse.' She buttered a slice of bread and put it on Kirby's plate. 'There's nothing wrong with rats, sweetie.'

*

In times of great stress, Anja could see clearly into the future. Images of wine-soaked book club meetings came to her in drifts; the women eating olives with their fingers, cutting thick, triangular spokes from wheels of cheap mini brie. All of them saying, one after the other, 'I remember that moment; the moment I found out Princess Di. I remember it exactly.'

In the future, Anja knew, she would not remember that moment at all.

What she did remember were befores and afters.

Before: looping the flowered lei over little Kirby's shoulders. Making seed bread for Roderick's dinner; her hands, long fingers, tucking the dough into a tight ball.

After: those same hands at rest on the kitchen table, either side of a checkered place mat. The left one covered by Roderick's right—big, brown and crack-skinned. The outside of Yolanda's bedroom door. The inside of it.

That was a few days ago now. Had she been a more reckless person she would have scratched a line for each on the side of the bedpost, like the tracks from the claws of a cat. But she didn't have the nerve to ruin the wood. What would she have used, anyway? There was nothing sharp enough in Yolanda's room.

The door was shut, not locked. And still Roderick hadn't tried to get in. Anja had wondered why, at first. Was he not afraid of what she might do, all alone in there? On the first night, he had put a tray of food outside the door. Then he sat in the corridor, changing position every so often. Anja heard his heels shifting on the carpet; cross-legged, straight-legged, knees down, knees up.

Forty-five minutes later, he spoke her name through the keyhole. Then he got up and went downstairs.

On the tray there were three mandarins, some cheese, and a generous portion of seed bread. A cup of water. Nothing hot— nothing that would have suffered from a long wait.

With the door open she could hear him in the kitchen. The sound of instant coffee-making came softly up the stairs. The kettle boiled, the fridge opened and closed. A teaspoon tapped the lip of a mug—ting ting ting—then fell into the sink. He would go out onto the verandah next. He would sit out there and tamp tobacco strings into his pipe with his fingers.

Anja waited for the slap of the screen door, then she stepped carefully over the tray and walked, bare foot, down the corridor to the bathroom.

From Yolanda's window she watched the flood waters recede. The apple trees still stood in a foot of it—they had been planted in the bowl of the back lawn. Roderick spent an afternoon walking about, spearing holes in the ground with a long metal pole. Anja liked watching him from above. If I wasn't here, she thought, this is what his life would be like. If I was dead, and he was on his own, this is what he'd be doing.

Yolanda had died three years ago, at seventeen. It was a car accident, too. Now there was not much left in her room. A few books—all one series, mostly. Fantasy. A girl who wants to be a knight, so she dresses up as a boy. She has bright purple eyes and, when she uses her powers, the magic comes out purple too. Anja bought the first book in the series for Yolanda's fourteenth birthday. She had read it herself first to make sure it was good. There were black cats and demons and martial arts. All the things Yolanda liked.

There was one poster left on the wardrobe door. There used to be scores of them though, the Blu-Tack running rampant across the wall like acne. Roderick had stripped them all down, repainted in a neutral colour. He'd only left one. It showed six different big cats, with their latin names, average weights and countries of origin. Anja studied it until she had learned them all. The tiger was the largest and heaviest. The leopard was the most endangered. The cheetah was the fastest and the most unique, although the poster did not explain why.

That night, when dinner was delivered, she spoke a question through the keyhole. 'Roderick,' she said, 'why is the cheetah the most unique?'

Roderick was crouched in the corridor outside, squeezing lemon onto a piece of baked gurnard. He had not heard her voice in days, so Anja had to wait for his answer. 'I never thought about it,' he said. 'But I suppose they are different.'

'They're the fastest.'

'And they don't ambush their prey. All the others do—they sneak up on it. But the cheetah, he just runs and runs and runs.'

The next morning Roderick put a newspaper on her breakfast tray. Anja read the front page, and learned that the world was still in shock. Outrage in Hollywood. Britain was in the depths of despair. They were angry with the Royals. Where were they, everyone wanted to know. Why did they not come out and grieve in public? Anja felt it was unfair. If a stiff upper lip wasn't good enough anymore, what else did a Queen have to offer?

*

Kirby's parents wanted to give a proper thank you to Mr and Mrs de Roos, which meant wine and a box of Roses. They went across together one afternoon, Kirby wearing the flower necklace and clutching the brown envelope tight against her chest. Her mother had let her stick on a 40c stamp.

Mr de Roos let them in through the kitchen door. He wasn't wearing shoes, which was unusual, and there was no coffee pot waiting on the table. Kirby wanted to ask about a biscuit.

'How are you getting on, Rod?' said her father, very quietly.

'Oh, we're getting on, we're getting on. You didn't need to.' Mr de Roos took the wine and the chocolates in careful arms and placed them on the table.

'It's OK,' said Kirby's mother. 'Look, if you need anything. If you want me to try, maybe? I could try.'

'Maybe,' he said, 'but I'm not sure, if . . . but maybe.'

Kirby watched Mr de Roos' socks. They were brown and long and a bit too old. She held out the envelope. 'This is for you and Mrs de Roos.'

*

An envelope appeared underneath the door, and little Kirby's voice came through the keyhole.

'Hello Mrs de Roos.'

Anja slid off the bed and knelt beside the door. 'Hello Kirby. You've come to visit me.'

'Is it boring in Yolanda's room?'

'Sometimes. What is this you've brought me?'

'It's for you and Mr de Roos.'

'Is it a letter?'

'No. Mrs de Roos?'

'Yes?'

'Do you want to come out of the room?'

'No.'

'OK.'

'Kirby?'

'Yes?'

'Do you know why a cheetah is different?'
'Is it a person or an animal?'
'An animal.'
'Then it's because it has white on its tail.'

That night, Anja met Roderick out in the corridor. She was on her way back from the bathroom, and he was putting a plate full of brightly-wrapped chocolates next to the door. They stood and looked at each other for a while in the dark, then Roderick stepped back. He pushed Yolanda's door open with his fingertips.

Erik Kennedy

The Inertia Poem

You've been in love for so long
that you count your partner's prepositions
for fun, and you know that his favourite Blind Lemon Jefferson
    song
is 'Peach Orchard Mama',
and you'd rather be dropped from a long-range bomber
over Pyongyang than risk what you've got.
But maybe you want to be more than compatible.
One thing to do
would be to stock your bedroom with hoods and clamps and
    whips and ropes.
Another would be to tie your wishes and hopes
into a sexy balloon animal.
Decisions, decisions.
Or maybe, just for once, go to a nice restaurant.
Only two out of seventeen options are vegetarian.
You feel sick looking at the menu's font.
Like one of those nineteenth-century antiquarians
who was also a vicar,
you don't know how to want the new.
Some things are just not what they're not.
Splitting up would be quicker.

Elizabeth Knox

Tata Beach, New Year's Eve, 1974

Tata Beach, New Year's Eve, 1974. Three weeks without rain. The motels have had the water tanker in, but the locals are toughing it out and peering wistfully across the Bay at the clouds that sometimes come and recline on the West Coast ranges. The air at sea level is hazy with evaporation and by four in the afternoon the black grid-work of the oil rig they're building in the shelter of the Bay has disappeared completely.

I'm on the beach with David McDonald, my same-age cousin, who has scraped through school C and is going into the army next year. He and I can still spend comfortable time together if we have a project. We're busy building a trap just below the notch of 'our' track, the one through the empty lot between the McDonalds' house and the beach. David has done all the digging. We cover the pit with criss-crossed sticks, then newspaper, and a layer of sand. It's been my job to imagine what'll happen when our older sisters, Mary and Steph, come back from their walk and fall into it. I can see them taking the plunge together, though Mary will be trailing Steph, eyes squinted, shoulders hunched, talking.

Mum arrives on the unsealed road between the track and the beach. She says to me, 'Don't wander off, Lif, Auntie Thel will need another pair of hands.' She means to help prepare dinner. This evening there's to be a big family barbecue at the bottom of the McDonalds' garden.

Mum says, 'Don't disappear', then disappears herself—wades into the waist-high grass of the empty lot and lies down. We wait for a bit, and then go over. Mum looks comfortable, if incongruous. She says, 'I *won't* take sides.' Then, 'Let's see if anyone misses me.' David and I understand that we're party to an experiment and mustn't spoil it for her. We go back and check the beach again. There's still no sign of Steph and Mary. David is sick of waiting so proposes I go get his little sister and mine, and 'lure them in'. He demonstrates by walking towards the trap, more upright than he ever is, like he's already practising for army drills.

Dad and both uncles have gone out early in Uncle Colin's trailer sailer. I see that they must be back because someone has caught an eel and cut it up. It's on the lawn between the house and the old fibrolite bach—big, grey segments still twitching as if preparing to swim away into the shade under the lemon tree.

The kids are in the bach. They're playing a game with some toys. I climb up on the top bunk and lean over to watch them. One of the girls' dolls has been murdered, and the teddy and golly are taking turns having sex with the body. I ask, 'Where do you get this stuff?' and Sara says, 'Its called *necrophilia*. Mary read me a bit out of a book.' This might be the answer to my question, but really I want to know something else, something that can't be explained by tracing it back to a book. Margaret is just going along with my sister. But Sara's been shocked, and this is an attempt to outstrip that shock by fearlessly flaunting the most preposterously horrible thing she can think of, to be big and electric, like a little cat with all its hair standing on end. It worries me so I say, 'Let's go down to the beach and build a big trap to catch Steph and Mary.' The trap is built already and I want one of them to fall into it, but my insincere invitation has got to be better than these made-up atrocities. They just shake their heads. They're having way too much fun to think of moving. And, because they have a witness the game is getting worse: so I leave.

Dad is back, so I gravitate to the house we're renting. I still have the habit of going to him for reassurance. The day isn't exactly riddled with darkness, but there was necrophilia, and a too-lively dead eel, and a human voice among the cicadas saying *let's see if anyone misses me*.

I find Dad lying down. His back is sore. He tells me he was stupid. When they got to Ururoa he jumped out into the shallows with the anchor in his arms. I test how bad he is by trying to worry him. 'Mary and Steph have been out since before breakfast and they only took apples.' But he doesn't even look interested in this information, so I let him be.

Auntie Thel calls out to me and I go up into the McDonalds' house to see what she wants. She asks me to go along the road to Auntie Joan's to borrow another steamer for the mussels.

Auntie Joan and Uncle Jim Campbell came to Tata about a year ago after several happy summer holidays. Jim's working part-time at a mechanic's in Takaka. Joan doesn't have to clean schools anymore. 'I'm a lady of leisure now,' she says as she fixes me a G & T, my first. She lets me search her bookcase. She says, 'Your mother was always a reader. She used to make us keep the light on till she'd finished her book.' 'By force of will?' I ask, since that would be a story about my mother with a good forecast for me in it. 'Oh no,' says Joan, 'her bed was beside the light switch.' I want to know whether Mum read any of *these* books. I've decided I'll read a book my mother liked and which no one bothers with nowadays. It feels like some kind of adventure. I'm missing adventure. The men were out on the water, with the honeycombed coastline, hidden coves, shags, oystercatchers and little round-finned dolphins. David only got left behind because he slept in. Mary and Steph set out for Wainui, walking around the rocks. The kids are crazy puffed-up little cats. And then there's my oldest cousin, Andrew. Auntie Joan tells me that Andrew's in the back bedroom. He got sunburned hitching home from a rock concert up north. 'You should pop your head around the door and say hello.'

Andrew is lying very still. He speaks softly and slowly. His adventures aren't spilling, only seeping out of him. His plaited leather bracelet has left a white strip on his wrist, like a thin slice of some earlier self. He's transformed, and not just by sunburn.

I take the steamer and my gin buzz and *Anne of Avonlea* from the Campbells' bach, plus an injunction for Thel about No Pineapple Jelly, and go back along the road.

Uncle Colin is standing in the driveway, looking left and right. 'Have you seen your mother?' I shake my head and try to think what I can ask that will get him to say something she'll overhear. If she's even still there. She might have got up, brushed herself off and gone back to our place. Yes. She'll be there, standing at the sink filling a hot-water bottle for Dad's back.

But its Dad who is up. He's in Thel's kitchen shucking paua. Thel tells me to put the steamer on the stovetop and stay right where I am. 'I have another job for you.'

Mary would say, 'What if I don't want a job?' Clever and quizzical. Or, if it was Mum asking, 'Oh, a *job*. You'd think you were giving me a present!' Mary is always resisting convention. According to her, making fussy preparations for entertaining is conventional—something women only do to show off to each other.

When Dad is done with the paua Thel hands me the basin full of them, and a bowl of chopped onions. She sends me down to the garage where there's a moulie clamped to the workbench. I spend the next hour feeding rubbery paua and watery onion into the hopper in alternate handfuls, winding the handle, to make a glistening black rope.

The bowl is full of minced paua when Joan arrives with fruit salad and Christmas cake and, instead of going upstairs to Thel, walks straight through the garage to the backyard, but not before telling me to wash my hands and fetch my grandmother.

Grandma is living in a bach at the very top of the lagoon. There's a sand track between the mats of rubbery weeds that edge the lagoon, and people's gardens. Partway along it I see a weasel and a weka. The weka is highstepping through the grass, the weasel undulating along the track ahead of me like a strip of empty fur pulled on a string. Grandma is ready. She smoothes her Osti Frock and says that she's put on her 'plumb gown' for 'the festivities'. I'm a tone-deaf teenager and can't detect satire unless its me being satirical, so I only tell her she looks very nice. She says she likes my hair tied back. I don't want to be complimented.

I hate having dirty hair. Mary would say, 'Why do you care? Who are you trying to impress at a family barbecue?' But I want to be pretty in the photographs.

When Grandma and I arrive back at the McDonalds' almost everyone is already gathered under the young birches. Sara and Margaret are squeaking excitedly about how David fell into someone's trap. David winks at me over their heads. Mary and Steph have dragged in. They were trapped by the tide, they say, and have spent hours hanging on to flax bushes at the top of a salt-scoured cliff. Mary moans that she's too tired to carry plates. Dad is lying on the grass with a whisky glass balanced in the forest of thick hair on his sternum, wincing wherever he lifts his head to take a sip. Andrew is sitting with David. They might both be boys, but they're boys of different species. Andrew doesn't have any idea what to ask about motorbikes, and David can't get a handle on the rock festival at Ngāruawāhia. They settle on discussing whether Andrew should pop his sunburn blisters.

The aunts are whispering. This is odd. They haven't been completely comfortable with each other since Joan moved to Tata. Dad likes to say that the Campbells and McDonalds are feuding, which is a sophisticated history joke. Mock epic. I shuffle nearer so that Thel and Joan are audible. They are talking about bursitis. Bursitis and bursting blisters. There's always the body. It's a sort of safe topic. Grandma remarks on Margaret's stringy hair. Mary says, 'We all have stringy hair but only Elizabeth minds.' There's a gap where Mum might remark, 'Elizabeth likes to take care of her appearance.' (Which would be followed by Mary taking offence and saying there were more important things, and then some stuff about triviality as if she's in a secret cell making its manifesto and, sometime in the future, making war on the world.) The gap is very strange. I'm not used to having my differences pointed out and then not used to demonstrate something about someone else. Then Uncle Colin pipes up to promise that we'll all go to the Tākaka River tomorrow to wash.

A moment later, when Auntie Joan passes me my paua fritter, she confides. 'Actually what your mother used to do about the bedroom light was stay silent. She just wouldn't hear our protests.'

Once I've polished off two sausages and three fritters I go to fetch Mum. But where she was lying there's a goat. It's tethered by a long chain to a metal stake. It looks at me with eyes like coin slots in a phone box. One of those eyes should be a coin return button, since the phone is ringing and no one is picking up.

It's only a brief panic. Eventually I see that Mum is walking along the tideline, beach-combing. When I reach her she tips a handful of cat's-eyes into my shirt pocket. She comes back to the barbecue with me, only stops to pull all the sticks out of the slumped trap and kick the sand back till it's not a hole, only a hollow, and no one will step into it and hurt themselves.

On New Years Day, 1975, we take all the cars and drive to the river, in our togs, and with our bathroom bags, to wash. I go upstream of everyone so that I can rinse in the cleanest water. And that's how come I can look up *now* to follow my floating lather and see them all, in the river and on the riverbank, everyone washing, except the kids, who are swimming but who will stay in longer and be clean enough. There they all are, still, the three families, downstream.

Michael Krüger

Fair Copy

We reconstructed my childhood
with unremarkable things.
A pine cone, bread crumbs,
keys, a black-veined stone,
anything to hand and portable.
Just that things have a tendency
to act as they see fit,
and the course I wanted to steer
keeps veering forward and back.
I can see what I no longer am,
but I cannot see me.
An apple rolls sadly from the table
and breaks as words break
when one no longer uses them.
Leave it to the birds to
fair-copy this scrawl, on them
one can rely.

Translated by Karen Leeder

Chloe Lane

Tentatively Joined

Now someone has graffitied the pigeon. It has been lying face down in the garden for a week, and now someone has tagged a green international post label and stuck it to its wing. I am standing at the window of my studio watching a fat girl with a cigarette in one hand and a camera phone in the other take a picture of this. She is wearing Dolce & Gabbana sunglasses—huge like a ski mask—that she doesn't remove to take the photo. I wonder what she will do with the photo. Will she show it to a boy she likes? There are pigeons sitting on a nearby fence, also watching the girl. This is what kills me the most. Someone should bury the pigeon, or take it away—there's a rubbish bin out front. Put a bucket over it at least.

I look around my studio. Although I know I will not find one here, I am looking for a spade. I forget about the brush and shovel under the sink, and instead I pick up the ceramic kettle plate sitting on the table.

Outside, with the plate in one hand and an umbrella in the other, I try to lever the pigeon out of the garden and onto the plate. While I am doing this I avoid looking into the eyes of the pigeon. Its eyes no longer look like eyes. The only thing to indicate they are eyes is where they are located on its head. So far my levering is only managing to spread the pigeon across more garden area, stretching it out. The pigeon is more decomposed than it looks from above—it is no longer a tidy unit of animal. It is now many pieces, tentatively joined. I close my eyes to a squint and breathe heavily through my mouth. I don't know how bad it smells and I don't want to know.

I think about the council's plan to kill off the pigeons *en masse*. Can you imagine mercenaries, armed with guns, knocking off the pigeons one by one? While some criminal fulfils his community service by running around after them with a spade and a sack? I hear a door slam behind me and suddenly terrified that someone will catch me doing what I am doing, I leave the pigeon as it is, and dash back into my studio.

Standing at the window, I watch the fat girl walk past again. She is with someone else this time. Neither of them acknowledges the pigeon. I can see the pigeon is sitting up more convincingly now, half on and half off the ceramic kettle plate, almost as if it were a sculpture on a plinth. I am unsure whether to be ashamed or pleased with myself. I watch the other pigeons slowly come down from their fence. Someone has thrown a loaf of sliced white bread into the courtyard. The pigeons take one slice at a time. All crowding around it, they work away at the middle first, pecking out a small hole that grows till it meets the crusts. They do this slice by slice, working collaboratively, leaving behind rings of crusts in their wake.

Anna Livesey

Bonsense

for Heather Tone

Grass kingdom,
higher than headwise, horsewise.
A tree looks down on you from the roadside.

Paddock peopled with tiny horses,
a stirrup, leg-up, leg over,
more tiny size, more
proliferation of tinyness.

Un-joy, a kind of blank seriousness—
it doesn't live among the horses.

You are a long way away, in a library.
You say, if your small library were a body,
poetry would be the head and torso,
fiction a limb, reference a limb.

From the chest of your books,
you enjoin belief
in outposts of miniature sense or nonsense,
or going further, antonym, *bonsense*—
the elaborate folly of the heart and brain,
built curlicued, baroque.

What bonsense is this, a tiny horse, a tiny library?
The great iced cake of relationships,
the ornamental pony of compassion,
the perennial shout (SHOUT) of shared exclamation.

Artificial Intelligence

Often in the midst of whatever, an image rises:
fields of cabbages on the Croatian coast, purple-black leaves
shading to green where the dense hearts peak.
I was a watcher on a bus, passing: a being previous to being
    spoken for.
This whole sheaf of pages is the speech of life after lives.

In this afterworld I find I cannot write what I used to write.
And also I should say, my mother is dead.
So long expected I had ceased to expect to grieve—
but chance, always, is a fine thing.
The tender passing and the tender growing
met and linked arms in my body.
At eight months pregnant, I found, you'll cry at anything.
She died in the morning. We stayed. At six they came and took
    her away.
The metal and blue vinyl of the gurney said something
    utilitarian.
As I trailed the body I thought: *I never have to live this smell
    again.*

At Playcentre the earthquake drill is
fold over your child like a turtle and hold on
or *fold over any child you can grab.*
Whatever selfish instinct might operate,
the tables are too low, the doors too few.
We give ourselves up, bend bridge-wise
over small hearts that judder and fear.
My baby tied to my chest, I kneel, play-acting.
One month post-partum, I find, you'll cry at anything.
Weeks later I dreamed she was still alive when we buried her:
she called, scratched. I saw her face in the dirt.

We're done, I said, *we're done!* There's no coming back from the
    dead!

It's hopeless to include what's really going on.
The poem can't contain it. A friend says
the brain can't do it, paste
what happens to other families
over the shape of your own.
We are quiet for a moment and thankful:
our separate pairs of children ask only that we worry
in plain-wrapped parcels. They bring us the gifts
of domestic misbehaviour, small moral confusions.
They don't wash up on beaches, drowned and symbolic—
though such thin happenstance holds this distinction open.
The mind shys off, pictures cabbages, great dusky pearls set in
    the dirt.

Rose Lu

穷人店, 富人店

Beep! The buzzer in the dairy goes off. I leave the lounge, walk through the kitchen and trot down the corridor, arriving at the internal door that separates our house from the dairy. On this journey I change my 拖鞋 | slippers twice, from the lounge pair to the house pair, then from the house pair to the shop pair.

My mum is sitting on one of the two stools behind the counter. The seat is upholstered with tan faux leather, cracked and patchy. She hands me the car keys.

'小怡, 带爷爷奶奶去买点儿水果。' | 'Rose, can you take your grandparents shopping for fruit?'

'好吧, 去哪儿个店?' | 'Sure, which shop?'

'穷人店吧。' | 'Let's do the poor-person shop, eh?'

'Okay.'

I climb back up the concrete steps and head back to the lounge, observing the slipper ritual in reverse. As usual, my grandparents are sitting in the La-Z-Boys. I've never known what colour they are, as they've had heavy curtain fabric draped over them since they were purchased. Kon-kon's eyes are shut and my brother's baby blanket is covering his knees. Bu'uah is sitting with her hands clasped, leaning forward with her milky eyes fixed to the television.

'Bu'uah, 'ng da ni ken Kon-kon ki 'ma sy-ku.' | 'Bu'uah, I'll take you and Kon-kon to buy fruit,' I say.

With my grandparents, I speak tshon-min 'eu | Chóngmíng dialect. There are three languages in this house, and each generation favours a different one.

Bu'uah stands up, pressing down the creases on the front of her shirt. 'Au, 'ng-li ki jion-nyng-die 'ai-dzi fu-nyng-die?' | 'Okay, are we going to the poor-person shop or the rich-person shop?'

'Jion-nyng-die.' | 'The poor-person shop.'

Her half-moon eyes crinkle as she smiles at me. She grabs the remote and silences her period drama.

No motion from Kon-kon. Maybe he hasn't heard? I give him the benefit of the doubt. His sudden onset of deafness had caught me by surprise, cautioning that I should come home more frequently. Bu'uah takes a few steps towards him. The foam bottoms of her 拖鞋 | slippers make a scraping sound on the carpet.

'Ki 'ma sy-ku lie!' | 'We're going to the shop!' she says. It's not quite a shout, but she speaks strongly.

His eyes open reluctantly. He shifts his farmer's hands from his knees to the armrest, leveraging all four limbs to come halfway out of the chair. A weak cough. Hands back on his knees to keep the fleece blanket from falling. A slow turn. He places the blanket on the back of the chair. Another cough. He tends to speak in dispassionate coughs these days.

I shuffle my grandparents out the door and into the eight-person people-mover that my parents own. It's silver and capacious. It even has a video feed showing the rear view while the car reverses. We got this car after we moved to Whanganui in 2003. Back in Auckland, if we ever went anywhere as a family, I had to sit on the floor between the back of the passenger's seat and the base of my baby brother's car seat. The adults were too big, my brother was too small, and we couldn't afford a new car. 没办法。

Whanganui's streets are luxuriously wide, even for this spaceship car. I would never be able to cruise like this down Wellington streets. Bu'uah sits up front with me, window cracked to stop her from getting motion sickness. My dad isn't allowed to drive if Bu'uah is in the car. His constant halting and lurching causes bile to crawl up her throat. It's just my mum and me whom she trusts. Kon-kon doesn't have the same issue, but he never wants to go anywhere.

We exit the roundabout onto London Street, then turn down Glasgow Street. I can see the building now—bright yellow and black over austere concrete. The poor-person shop looms over the other shops on the corner—Countdown, the Mad Butcher, Subway.

I park the car. We walk into the Pak'nSave.

The wildest deals of the day line the entranceway. Crown pumpkins with waxy blue-grey skin: two dollars. Not for a kilo but for the whole fat thing! Lindt chocolate bars, sea salt and caramel, short-dated and a measly buck each! Stacks of assorted Griffin's biscuits, practically given away at two for four dollars!

Bu'uah has already taken herself and a trolley through the clanging safety barrier that allows passage in one direction but not the other. Kon-kon takes his time entering, metal rods chiming individually as he ambles in.

A stand of white-fleshed peaches catches Bu'uah's eye. Their skins are a perfect blend of pink and white with a thin layer of mottled fuzz. She inspects the peaches, picking each one up and doing a full rotation to check for bruising. Satisfied, she places one in the plastic bag.

'Ge za dao-zi zai la le!' she exclaims, gesturing at the peaches, telling me that they're fantastic. She uses a word that doesn't have a Mandarin counterpart. I used to think that the dialect we spoke was only phonetically different, that I could map the eight tones into Mandarin's four, but I've realised that it has different vocabulary and grammar as well. They're not mutually intelligible.

'Ge za dao-zi ji kuan-nyeah?'| 'How much are the peaches?' she asks. I know she can't read Mandarin, let alone English, but now I'm unsure if she can read numbers. Perhaps she can't match the numbers with the English signs? I tell her they are six dollars a kilo.

She nods, satisfied. The bag steadily fills as more peaches meet the requirements of her thorough inspection. She places the bag in the trolley and moves on to the next fruit.

After they have selected their desired fruit, I take them through the checkout. They wait patiently as each bag is weighed and placed into the new trolley.

'That comes to $23.56,' says the checkout operator. I give her two twenty-dollar notes from my mum. She hands back the change and I put it straight into my pocket.

'Ge dei va?' | 'Is the change correct?' Bu'uah points at my pocket with her crooked finger.

Once, I asked Bu'uah why her finger was like that. She told me that she was the youngest of the children in her family, and she loved eating sugarcane. One day she wanted to eat some, but none of her older siblings could be bothered hacking off a section for her. Exasperated, one of them told her to do it herself. She took a cleaver to the woody cane, and accidentally cleaved off her fingertip. At this point in the retelling, she clutched her injured finger with the opposite hand and pretended to cry out for help. As if she were little again. As if the wound were still fresh.

Bu'uah looks at me.

'Dei ge!' | 'Of course!' I reply, patting my cardigan pocket, not bothering to check.

Technically, my 爷爷奶奶 | grandparents are my 外公外婆 | grandparents—on my mother's side. I never liked how 外公 or 外婆 sounded. 外 translates to outside, foreign, external. As if they were standing outside our family, looking in but never participating. It didn't reflect how I felt about them, so I didn't address them that way.

They came to Aotearoa in late 1999, just after my brother was born. They would have been in their early sixties back then. My mum is an only child, so, unlike my dad's parents, her parents didn't need to split their attention between families.

I don't know many specifics about my grandparents, like exactly how old they are, or how to write their names. None of these details are important. Western birthday celebrations have never been a feature of our home life. They can speak their given names, but, like me, they don't know which characters make them up.

I call them Kon-kon (Grandpa) and Bu'uah (Grandma), and they call me Shiao-nyi-geu, a family nickname that means 'little happy dog'. I assume the middle character is taken from my Chinese name, but I don't know for sure. It's another name that is spoken rather than written.

Back in China they were farmers, the poorest class. It brings Bu'uah endless delight that the farmers here are affluent. She can't understand how it's possible. Her sense of the vocation doesn't extend past the notion of planting crops as the single means to food, supplemented by a few chickens and maybe a goat in a good year.

In Whanganui Bu'uah is farming again, tending to her vegetable garden every day. They have a lot of time on their hands. Before we moved here, my brother hadn't started school, so my grandparents were kept busy caring for him while my parents worked.

My brother and I were born almost a decade apart and have grown up with completely different lives. Matthew goes to the private school in town, Whanganui Collegiate School. I went to the public school, Whanganui High School. Traditionally the 陆 | Lù family have been doctors, but my dad and his brother failed to get into med school and had to become engineers instead. Matthew is redeeming the Lù family line by pursuing health science at Otago University. I was accepted into the same course and hall of residence as him, but at the last minute I pulled out. I didn't know what I wanted to do but I knew it wasn't medicine.

Matthew is never asked to do chores for our grandparents. It's partly because he's too busy with school, but partly because he can't understand much tshon-min 'eu | Chóngmíng dialect. Mine isn't great either, but it's passable. Anything more complex than fruit prices requires me to switch to Mandarin. Thankfully, Bu'uah understands most of what I say. She spends a lot of time watching Chinese dramas with Mandarin dialogue, so she's picked a fair bit up.

Other than our excursions to the supermarket, the main activity I 陪 | accompany my grandparents in is playing cards. They have a set of long, thin Chinese cards. The backs are dark green, while the faces are adorned with black and white patterns according to their suit and value.

There are three suits in the deck—萬、条、筒 | wàn, tiáo and tóng, each running from one to nine. They symbolise different units of currency. Like old bank notes, the higher values are embossed with cursive red patterns. The three suits have shapes associated with them: small solid dots for 萬 | wàn, narrow segmented strips for 条 | tiáo, and patterned coins for 筒 | tóng.

The cards are designed to be stacked vertically, so players need only to glance at the top icons to read the value of the card. Groups of these card stacks are then nestled in the palm and held in place by a thumb across the short side. Because they're so long and thin, a certain deftness is needed just to hold them.

My grandparents play a variant of mahjong, which adapts its tile images from the faces in this deck. Most afternoons, I find them passing the time with this game. I sit down at the table with them.

Bu'uah looks up from her hand. 'Be xiang va?' | 'Do you want to play?'

'Au,' I reply, and wait for them to finish the current round.

We've always been more of a cards family rather than a mahjong family. Back in 崇明 | Chóngmíng, Kon-kon played cards every day with his buddies. The air would be alive with curls of burnt tobacco, chain-smoked in an expression of manliness, and a spray of spittle and sunflower-seed shells fired from mouths. Now it's just Bu'uah he plays with, and me, when I'm home for the weekend.

It's hard to pinpoint when Kon-kon lost his voice. The Kon-kon that I remember from my childhood is a firecracker. We would play cards and he would always cheat, because he loved to win and he loved to make me laugh. The game was more about catching him at his cheating than about winning yourself.

He taught me nursery rhymes that only worked in 崇明话 | Chóngmíng dialect, pinching the back of my hand with his hand, me pinching the back of his hand with my other hand, us repeating the pattern until all four of our hands were stacked and connected with plucked skin, at which point we would chant:

'Ma ha, ma ha!' | 'Selling crabs, selling crabs!'
'Ma dao nin ga!' | 'Selling crabs to other people!'

We could chant this two or three times before I collapsed into giggles, holding my hands up to look at the red markings stamped on the crab's shell.

This kon-kon was stubborn as well as vocal. He would complain about the food here because he thought the meat had a foreign smell. The staples he was used to were hard to come by. Even though what he'd eaten in China was poor farmer food, he preferred it. Western dishes were abhorrent. He had to be persuaded to try the prime steaks my parents bought. After just a few bites he announced that it was okay, but he preferred Chinese beef. This same New Zealand beef would be sold for upwards of 300元 a plate back in China.

He talked about how smart I was, how he still had the certificate of achievement I received in my first year of primary school. He was so proud of me. He unashamedly loved me the most, even though you're not supposed to pick a favourite grandchild, and, if you're Chinese, you're not supposed to pick the granddaughter.

Now he spends his days sitting in the La-Z-Boy, eyes shut with the blanket over his knees. He still opens his eyes when I come home, and for those moments his eyes light up. But on my last few trips I've noticed that after the initial greeting he shuts his eyes again and retreats back into himself. It's been a long time since he was energetic, but he used to at least ask how long I was home for, demand that I stay longer, and wheedle a date out of me for my next visit.

He doesn't get much respite from his daily routine of sitting and doing nothing. For him, there's not much worth engaging with. My parents are busy with the shop, my brother is busy with school, and my visits are limited. Stimulus disorients him, and he's always tired because he has insomnia. Playing cards is one of the only things he does during the day.

Kon-kon wins, so Bu'uah shuffles the cards. She cuts the bundle of cards into two neat piles, then threads one pile evenly through the other. I've tried this many times and have never got it right. The tips of the cards always clump together, resulting in an inadequate shuffle.

She lays the cards face down on the table, spreading them out slightly so they form a neat pleat. Like in mahjong, the cards are not dealt but picked up. Bu‘uah is the leader this turn, and counts to herself as she picks them up.

'Yi ⋯⋯ nyi ⋯⋯ sae ⋯⋯ si ⋯⋯ 'n ⋯⋯ lo ⋯⋯ tchi ⋯⋯'

Sometimes she inserts a rhyme about the number, like a Daily Keno announcer—'Ba zha da yi da!'—before continuing on.

'Jyu ⋯⋯ sa ⋯⋯ sa-yi ⋯⋯ sa-nyi ⋯⋯ sa-sae ⋯⋯'

She announces the last number with a knock of her crooked finger on the table. 'Sa-si!'

Kon-kon hasn't said a word. He no longer tries to hide cards up his sleeve. If he says anything, it's an admonishment for Bu‘uah to hurry up. They bicker because they are an old married couple. Their days are spent with only each other, and outside of our family there is no one in Whanganui who can understand them.

I look at the cards in my hand. After a decade of playing, I still can't determine their value solely by the iconography. Once the bundles are arranged neatly in my hand, I sometimes have to flick the cards forward to check their image for their worth. I have never seen my grandparents do this. They know this game inside out. Even as their other faculties dull, they remain skilled in strategy and card-counting.

Sometimes when we play, Bu‘uah babbles about their old house and her old life back in China. She has no sense of time or sequence when she tells these stories. Her reminiscences about people and places can be nonsensical. Her thoughts are steeped in her superstitions and her lack of education, and she often comes to the wrong conclusions.

She left her entire family behind in Jiāngsū when she came to 崇明 | Chóngmíng to marry my kon-kon in her twenties; I know that for certain. I don't know any of her family members' names, but I've heard their oral obituaries.

She doesn't mean to be macabre in her recounting, the way she talks through precisely what her family members died of and how much they suffered; she simply tells the situation as she understands it. Medical jargon is a part of 崇明话 | Chóngmíng vocabulary that I am weak on, and other than cancer the causes of death are unknown to me. I don't know how she feels about these family members—she must not have seen them very often after she left. They all died at a much younger age than she is now.

Another of her favourite topics is her heavy winter coats. She remembers the 崇明 | Chóngmíng winter—the month or so when temperatures didn't rise above zero, the concrete housing, and the warm coats she wore. They had to leave the coats behind when they came to New Zealand. She pines for the coats, bought with money that was so hard-earned.

Bu'uah picks up a new card. She must like it, as she rearranges the stacks in her hand to tuck it away. With an exhalation, she discards a card, knocking her hand on the table again. My turn.

'Ae ······ 'n di de van-zi la te le ······' | 'Ae, our house is rotting . . .' she laments.

I pick up a card and let her talk. As usual, her Chóngmíng dialect is croaky when discussing the past.

'We built the house with our own hands . . . we were so poor back in those days . . . your kon-kon used to cycle so far to work each day, getting up before the sun came up, and returning after the sun had set . . . we worked so hard and we were so hungry but there was no food so it was better to just go straight to sleep after work . . . those beautiful coats, also rotting in the house . . .'

Bu'uah's wishes are simple but also frustrating. She often has the same conversation with my mother, who gets more annoyed every time she has to explain the practicalities to her. 'You can't just expect us to go and get your coats when we're in China! They're so bulky and heavy, we don't have the space to lug them around! And even if we did bring them back, then what? You can't even wear them here, it's too hot! We can buy you a coat here if you want!'

Bu'uah seems to have become more sentimental about the past in the last few years. Or maybe I've realised that there can't be that many more times I'll be able to hear these stories, this dialect. I think back to when I was younger, when Kon-kon was more vocal. Every time he complained about life in Aotearoa, Bu'uah would rise to its defence. 'You imbecile! Look around you, look how clean it is! Everything is such good quality! This milk would cost a fortune in China! What is there to miss, our grandchildren are here!'

I don't know if she feels so strongly now. Her grandchildren are grown and have vanished into a culture that she'll never be able to know, coming back with tone-deaf ears that don't understand her 土话 | unsophisticated dialect. Talking to her can feel crude and imprecise, like communicating through smoke signals.

Kon-kon picks up his card silently. He has nothing to contribute to Bu'uah's reminiscences, but maybe he can't hear what she's saying.

He discards; Bu'uah picks up. She discards.

I pick up. It's 三条 | three of tiáo, completing the last set in my hand, three-four-five of tiáo.

'Si mo!' | 'I win!' I announce triumphantly.

Bu'uah cheers, clucking with laughter. 'Ni xia-zha lai le, yi ze fe man ji te.' | 'You're so smart, you never forget how to play.'

Bu'uah stops the game to prepare a salt wash for Kon-kon's foot. He has an ingrown toenail. It's the big toe on his left foot. It's made him even less active than he already is. The toe is a smash of yellow and pink, swollen with infection because he keeps picking at it. He's not supposed to. My mum took him to a podiatrist to get it cut, but the flesh was so puffy they couldn't do anything. The podiatrist told him to keep his hands away, soak the foot in hot brine to soften the nail, and they'll see if it's better at the next appointment.

But of course he refuses to stop picking, because he needs that temporary relief. He is a man who lives for instant gratification.

He curses the doctors here. He complains to my mum. 'What's the problem? The doctors here don't know how to do their job! Why can't they just anaesthetise my foot and cut the nail off? It's so simple!'

Kon-kon waits silently in his chair for the salt wash. He remains silent while Bu'uah brings in the orange plastic washtub, steaming hot. With a laboured sigh, he places his foot in the water. After scarcely ten minutes, he leans forward and reaches for the flannel.

'Ae!' Bu'uah makes a sound, but Kon-kon's foot is out now and he refuses to soak it any longer. 'It's not going to do any good!' he barks at her, settling back in the chair and closing his eyes. No one can make him do anything he doesn't want to do.

My kon-kon is an insomniac. When I was a teenager I regularly stayed up until two or three in the morning, and on those nights I hoped he wouldn't notice the light emanating from under my door while he was on one of his night-time excursions. From my room I would hear the scuffle of his footsteps, his staccato cough. Next came the crinkle of soft packaging and the beep of the microwave. He'd say he couldn't sleep because he was hungry, but it's gone on for so long now that it's clearly become a bad habit.

Kon-kon is the only person in our family with a sweet tooth. His midnight snacks are sugary or fried, but preferably both. At his request my mum used to buy sweet fried dumplings on her monthly trips to the Chinese supermarket in Palmerston North. The dumplings were made from chewy glutinous rice flour, filled with creamy red bean paste or delicately salted pork mince, and deep-fried. By the time my mum was back in Whanganui, the oil from the dumplings would have soaked right through the brown paper bag.

Kon kon is a diabetic. Glutinous rice is terrible for diabetics; its high glycaemic index causes sudden spikes in blood sugar, and the feeling of hunger comes back within an hour. After Kon-kon received his diagnosis, my mum stopped buying him the dumplings and other sugary snacks. So he started making his own snacks to eat during the night. Bloated 粽子 | sticky rice dumplings, bamboo wrappers barely containing the glutinous rice within. Flat, circular 汤圆 | tāngyuán, as big as my cupped palm, made from glutinous rice flour and filled with red bean paste. He'll wolf down at least three of these every night.

Kon-kon is eating himself to death and there is nothing we can do about it. Of course, this foot thing is related. His blood sugar levels in the morning hover around 15 mmol/L. A healthy reading is between 4mmol/L and 7mmol/L.

The first time my mum and Bu'uah saw that number, they were horrified. It was all because of his eating during the night, but he couldn't be persuaded to stop.

'I can't sleep if I'm hungry!' he would shout. 'There is no worse feeling than lying in bed feeling hungry! Do you not want me to sleep?'

Scuff, scuff, scuff. My bu'uah pops her head into the lounge, staying in the kitchen so she doesn't have to swap out her 拖鞋 | slippers.

'Shiao-nyi-geu, bang 'n kai-ya-kai shi-yi-ji.' | 'Rose, help me turn on the washing machine.'

My mum's mentioned before that my grandparents can't use the washing machine. I look at the panel. Coloured lights and options for wool and delicates. It can't be that hard, right? As long as they use the defaults.

I show her a few times. The small grey button to turn it on, the large green button to start and stop. She practises, nodding in acknowledgement.

The next time I come home, I see my mum helping Bu'uah with the washing machine again.

'Ng mang-ji te la?' | 'Have you forgotten?'

'Pei! 'ng lao lai le yi yang a ji ve te!' | 'Pei! I'm so old I can't remember anything!'

I used to think that my grandparents could spend a few years by themselves in China. When they were younger, they'd sometimes go back for years at a time. But I didn't realise how much that had changed as they got older.

My mum tells me about all the things they can't do. '我告诉你，你的爷爷每天要打针。他的血糖量一直很高，一起床已经超过十五了。奶奶也不能帮他打，她没受过教育，连洗衣机和吸尘器她也用不来。她每天看的电视也要我帮她打开。所以奶奶不能帮爷爷打针，而且他们药也买不来。还有老家的邻居都搬走了或者去世了，如果有问题也没有人可以帮他们。' | 'Do you know that your kon-kon needs an insulin shot every day now? His blood sugar is so high, you know it's over fifteen when he wakes up. And do you think Bu'uah can give him his shots? Of course not. It's not her fault, she's never had any education. She can't even use the washing machine, or the vacuum cleaner. She can't use the TV she watches every day. I have to go in several times a day to change it to the right setting for her. There's no way she could give him his insulin shot. And where would they get the medication from? Who would they call if they needed help? All their neighbours are long dead, or gone to live with their families. There's no one to help them if they get in trouble.'

She looks out at the dairy, at the fridges filled with candy drinks. It's the afternoon slump, the lull between the lunch rush and the after-school rush. My dad goes inside for his daily nap and my mum tells me things she can't tell anyone else.

'你的爷爷，不知道为什么他胆子变的很小。他不想出去也不想一个人呆在家里。他说，'比如有人来敲门，那我怎么办？' 就想太多呀，谁会来敲门？ 如果他们来敲门，就不打开门就可以了！ 不知道他怕什么。我们家后面住个老太太，一个人安安静静得呆着。我就跟他说，你看这个老太太一个人呆在家里没问题，我们就出去一下，你也可以的，你怕什么呢？' | 'Your kon-kon, he's gotten really scared recently. I don't know why. He doesn't want to go anywhere, but we can't leave him at home alone, even for a short time. He says, 'But what if someone comes and knocks on the door?' And it's just paranoia—why would someone come and knock on our door? And if they do, all he has to do is not answer it! I don't understand what he's so afraid of! That granny flat behind our house, the old woman lives there alone. So I say to him, 'That old woman behind us lives peacefully and quietly by herself. Why are you so scared about being left home alone?"

She can't talk to my dad about these things, because they're her parents, not his. As both sets of my grandparents age, the distance is driving a wedge between them. My dad hardly ever gets to see his parents back in China. My parents have been working constantly for over fifteen years and they want a break. They want to go back to China and see what it is like now. But how do they arrange that, with my grandparents being the way they are?

'哎呀我真的没办法，他们也不能照顾自己。我每天会进去看看他们，有时候他们会忘记把炉子关掉，真的好吓人，也许会发生火灾。说实话，他们自己呆在家里我也不太放心。' | 'I don't know what to do. They can't look after themselves. I go in from the shop several times a day just to check on them. Sometimes they leave the stove on. I'm so worried. What if they start a fire? Truthfully, I don't feel very safe leaving them at home alone either.'

When I was in my teens, Kon-kon complained that there were prickles in his eyes. Shards of debris that scraped his eyes as he looked around. This is how that particular habit started, the one where he spends hours in the La-Z-Boy with his eyes closed. It was to avoid the pain. Almost weekly there was an appointment with another doctor or specialist for my mum to ferry my kon-kon to. Finally, he had an operation, and the doctors extracted several growths from the inside of his eye. One was the size of a sunflower seed.

At some point during this process, my mother and Kon-kon discovered a Chinese doctor in Whanganui. My mum came back from an appointment with him and commented to me, '医生说爷爷有 depression.'

I had expected to hear more about his eyes, his physical health—anything other than this. The English in her sentence sticks out; there isn't a term in Mandarin for this. I kept my tone neutral and asked, '你懂 depression 是什么意思吗?' | 'Do you understand what depression means?'

She repeated some symptoms that the doctor talked about. 'Social isolation, no community, lack of activities that would generate a feeling of self-worth.' Symptomatic of being the only 崇明人 | Chóngmíngnese in Whanganui. She concluded with a plaintive '没办法。'

Back in Auckland, we knew a few other Chinese families with Shànghǎinese elders. On their walks around Mt Roskill, my grandparents would bump into them. My parents spent three years in Auckland looking for work, but despite their education they could only find jobs as cleaners and factory workers. With two kids and two parents to support, they didn't make enough money to do more than scrape by. So, in 2013, they borrowed money from my dad's family and purchased the combo dairy and fish-and-chip shop. Our family moved down to Whanganui and started our steady trajectory towards the middle class. My parents work seventy-hour weeks with no weekends or holidays. It's not lucrative, but it's not minimum-wage, and they don't have many other choices.

I could see how Mum felt like there wasn't anything they can do for Kon-kon. She seemed to know what depression was, but I wasn't sure if she really understood. It was a word for a Western affliction that required the suffering of an individual family member to be equated with the needs of the family as a whole. I didn't know if she could see past the interdependence that held our family together.

In our family we lack the vocabulary to speak about things that are so delicate, to wade through the overlap in our mutually intelligible language to find the nuance for questions like this.

Once, I asked my buʻuah about the scar on her stomach. It runs the length of her belly and makes all the skin pucker and pull together like a badly folded dumpling.

'Ai-yo ni ge buʻuah ca la le!' | 'Aiya . . . your buʻuah is so wretched!' she wailed, rattling off a list of symptoms I didn't understand. It ended with her clenching her right fist, save the thumb, which she drew violently upward along the length of her scar. Her eyes followed the path of the disembowelment, briefly flashing white before she looked back at me.

'Ni kue, ni ge bu'uah ca va?' | 'Don't you agree, isn't your bu'uah wretched?'

Technically, my 爷爷奶奶 | grandparents aren't my grandparents.

My bu'uah adopted my mum when she was two years old. She describes clutching this child, a child she dearly wanted, while my mum screamed at the top of her lungs and pointed down the dirt path. 'Ki! Ki! Ki!' | 'Go! Go! Go!' she demanded, writhing in my bu'uah's arms, urging her to take her back to her biological mother.

My mother was the third girl born into a family that desperately wanted a son. Her birth family couldn't support four children, so they gave her away to my grandparents and tried for a boy child, this time successfully. It was a small village and they were neighbours. They were helping my grandparents out—how wretched it was that my bu'uah couldn't have her own children.

Twenty years later, my mother was one of the few people in Chóngmíng to leave China. And, three years after that, she brought her parents along with her. Her biological family was left behind in rural China.

The first time my mother went back to China was when her biological father died, in 1998. She took me with her. I had no recollection of this grandfather. I didn't know his face, and I didn't yearn to know if I shared it. I remember only snatches of the funeral, gaudy items of red and gold, rice cakes, unknown faces shouting, everything consumed in a smoky fire.

In 2017 my mother's biological mother died. I didn't accompany her to China this time, but I met her for lunch before her flight out of Wellington. I took her to Little Penang, as I didn't think she'd had Malaysian food before. She looked at the unfamiliar menu and asked me to order for her. Knowing our family's tastes, I ordered her a light soup. She ate it with the white porcelain spoon.

I knew nothing about my biological grandmother, not even her name. I wondered if I should feel something about her now, in death. I asked what she had died of, and my mum told me blood poisoning.

'败血症?' | 'Blood poisoning?'

'对，她十二年以前得了中风，从那时候开始一直躺在床上，你大姨照顾她，崇明医院也不能送。大姨也不是护士，不懂怎么照顾她。最近她得了褥疮，一直侧着躺，还诱发了败血症。' | 'She had a stroke twelve years ago, and has been bedridden ever since. My eldest sister has been looking after her, they don't have access to healthcare in Chóngmíng, you know. She's not a nurse. No one knew how to look after her properly. So she got bed sores from not being turned enough, and that turned to blood poisoning.'

I wondered if my mum felt sad about this news, or if she was going to China out of obligation. But there wasn't a way to ask how she felt, not in Mandarin. She continued to speak about how much of a struggle it had been for the entire family to support her mother. The care was a full-time job; it had wrecked her eldest sister financially. Thankfully, the other siblings were in better financial situations and were able to help her out. My mum looked at me seriously. '哎呀 …… 我希望我一辈子不会给你和你的弟弟那么大的负担。如果我需要机器才能活着，最好就拔掉吧，这也不是什么生活。' | 'I hope I'll never be such a burden on you and your brother. If I'm ever on life support, don't hesitate to pull the plug. I wouldn't want to live like that anyway.'

'别这样说! 我们在新西兰，这里的医药服务不一样，如果你生病也不会到这么严重的状况。' | 'Don't say that! Plus, we're in New Zealand. The level of healthcare is completely different. You'll never get into a state like that.'

We continued to eat our food.

I think of my grandparents here, in relatively good health compared with the grandparents left behind. Two years ago, Bu'uah was hit by a car while crossing the road. She waited at the crossing until she saw the green man signalling. She thought it was safe to step out. Stopped at the lights was an elderly woman, anxious to get to her husband in the hospital. She forgot to check for pedestrians as she turned left on the green light. The next day, the headline of the *Whanganui Chronicle* read: 'Seventy-year-old woman hits eighty-year-old woman'.

My bu'uah's ankle was smashed and needed several screws. The hospital operated on her immediately, and she was wheeled to the same floor as the elderly driver's husband to recover. Her recovery was complicated by her persistent problem with her stomach; she couldn't keep down food and medicines. But she had regular check-ups and rehab, and is back to normal now. Her ankle only feels stiff and sensitive on cold days.

When I moved out of home, my brother got my bedroom. Before that, he'd slept in the same room as my parents. At opposite periods of our lives, my brother and I became only children. I was the only child until I was nine, when my brother was born. Then I left home when he was nine years old, and he became the only child.

My grandparents shared the third bedroom in the house. It had always been too small for the six of us. After I left home, my parents knocked down the carport and built a second living room. It was completed in time for my first visit home from university. I slept in the new living room on a foam mattress.

When I'm home, the three generations of our family eat together. Otherwise, my parents don't often eat with my grandparents. One reason is that my grandparents tend to stir-fry vegetables until they go limp. Neither of them have had their own teeth for at least a decade. Another reason is that they prefer to eat at different times. My grandparents eat early, while my parents fit their dinner around the dinner rush at the shop.

When I'm home, dinner starts just after the takeaways close at 7:30pm. Meal prep begins well before then. Between orders of fish and chips and burgers, my parents fit in chopping, salting, soaking and stewing. There will be at least three different 葷菜 | non-vegetarian dishes. Every night I'm home, it's a feast.

The whole family sits around the table and a bottle of wine is brought out. I can't remember my parents drinking in my childhood, but it's become a regular sight in my last five years of visits.

Tonight there's a lamb leg roast and a whole steamed blue cod. We used to eat their cheaper counterparts, chicken and flounder. My mum carves up the lamb leg. She places a full plate of meat in front of my grandparents, so they don't have to reach. My dad picks up the bone and starts to gnaw, urging my brother and me to have the best cuts of meat. I remember another afternoon chat with my mum in the shop, her remarks on Western family dynamics. How odd it was that the parents bought themselves Magnums but gave cheap Popsicles to their kids. Shouldn't it be the other way around?

I try to tell my bu'uah about my life in Wellington. I tell her that I've started a new job recently. I picked up the Mandarin word for 'software developer' when I was last in China, but I don't know how I would say it in Chóngmíng dialect. I simply tell her that I work on a computer.

She nods, seeming to understand. 'Ng vi di li gon-zhan yue va?' | 'Is your house close to the factory?'

I pause. I say, 'Ae, ng ji ja-da-tsheh ki.' | 'Yes, it's only three kilometres, and I cycle there.'

She clucks, laughing at the thought of me choosing to cycle. 'Ng ki lar-di mua mi-tsi? Jion-nyng-die 'ai-dzi fu-nyng-die?' | 'Which shop do you shop at, the poor-person shop or the rich-person shop?'

I think of the first time I stepped into Chaffers New World. The fruit was stacked so perfectly. I wondered what my bu'uah would have made of it. Before moving to Wellington, I hadn't set foot in a New World supermarket.

My family was poor, but we were the type of poor that you could work your way out of. I could see it in the way our lifestyle changed. When I entered the professional workforce, I was astonished when my bank balance kept increasing.

I want to tell Bu'uah that I am rich in ways she can't comprehend. It isn't just that I can spend twenty dollars on a meal consisting solely of eggs and bread, or pay for drinks in a bar. I can read and write. I can travel and see the world. I have independence. I have choices.

I know where I shop every week. Partly because it's the closest supermarket to me, but partly because I can.

'Fu-nyng-die,' I reply.

Tina Makereti

An Englishman, an Irishman and a Welshman walk into a Pā

This is the way of it. Before I have memorised her in a way that will last forever, my mother is gone. If someone asks me to recite my first memory, which consists of chickens in a yard and an old farmhouse and an outside toilet, it will contain this absence. For the rest of my childhood, I don't think it matters.

When I was small I was provided for, though most of the time I found it necessary to keep my head down. I didn't walk out of my childhood bruised or broken in body, but there are other ways a child can be wounded. Films featuring children always worry me. I want to believe a protected childhood is a thing that can be taken for granted, but there's a delicate balance—it could go either way. In the next scene, the mother might look away or the father might lose control and the childhood could be ruined. There are no guarantees.

There were some things bestowed on me by my upbringing that don't make any sense. From the earliest I learnt that people come in categories—separated by skin colour and gender—norms of culture and behaviour defined by what we called Europeans. We were Europeans, mostly, I was told. But there was nothing European about us. We were the straggly descendants of white people who came here generations ago looking to lose themselves, and promptly did. They were running from whatever it was their own cultures were doing to them at the time, running towards some beautiful possibility in another land. That new land was lush, fresh, empty for the taking. When they discovered it was not quite so empty, it was better to put their heads down and keep working. Like most of us, they couldn't let their mythologies go. The cost would have been too much. Great white man at the pinnacle of civilisation. Everything made to bow to that narrative, even if force was needed to keep the narrative in place. They worked hard, my white ancestors, but didn't rise much higher, and it was better not to question the whys and wherefores of that. Better to be a working-class man in New Zealand than elsewhere. Meat and cheese and milk flowing through the streets. Besides, poor people are inherently better than rich.

There were other mythologies we stuck to: Europeans brought order and civilisation with them; good Māoris are happy-go-lucky, bad ones ungrateful; men have no restraint; women are slippery untrustworthy witches. I rather like the idea of that, but can never quite get over the man thing, even when experience suggests otherwise.

I find I disagree with most of this inheritance, but it is inherited just the same.

GRANDMOTHERS

I became one of those girls who take great inspiration and comfort from the stories of grandmothers and great-grandmothers. These stories were missing when I was very young so, while I did not think I was much in need of a mother, I thought the world a bland and frustrated sort of a thing. Something was missing, I knew. It was as if I had access only to a watered down version of things—washed out pastels and black-and-white surfaces.

As a teenager I became reacquainted with the mother I had never known and a heritage that was richer than I had imagined. Mothers brought with them whole tribes, I discovered. Aunts and uncles! A grandmother! And stories about the people who had gone before. There was the one about the great-grandmother who taught her son to pig hunt in the bush because her husband was too busy with the drink; the one about the great-great-grandmother who bestowed her land to the hapū and took my own grandmother to look after when her mother died. We have a sepia photo of this kuia from a film she was in—fierce brow, sharp but nearly blind eyes, strong chin jutting forth a challenge. I named my first daughter after her simply for the staunchness that emanated from her image. You needed that kind of kaha, I believed, to get by in this world. My grandmother, of course, followed in her footsteps. Having been whangaied by others, she looked after everyone, her own and not her own, spending lifetimes between marae and courts and social workers, until her heart gave way.

There were countless ancestors like them, these immediate grandmothers: providers all, warriors some, women who spent their days in service and survival, leadership and sacrifice. They were extraordinary women to look up to. My life has always been too soft and comfortable to make me their equal. This inheritance, though, quickly conquered the stilted upbringing. These grandmothers brought me a world shot through with bold colour—the world that my white ancestors couldn't acknowledge for fear of losing some part of their own mythology. My grandmothers showed me origins that ranged from earth, sea and mountain, to the vastness of space: te pō, they whispered, te korekore. Sometimes they gave me access to te ao marama—the world of light, where one can see clearly.

Still, nature and nurture continue to tug at each other and negotiate some sort of uneasy truce. I'm learning to live with the disagreements between one inheritance and the other. 'Harmony is the acceptance of contradictory things,' says Shekhar Kapur, 'ultimately the universe is a contradiction.'[1]

WHAT WILL BE REMEMBERED

Every day and night I'm in Auckland, I walk past a woman who lies and sometimes sits on a Hello Kitty™ duvet on the street. She is usually in the same doorway: quiet, innocuous, staring. Occasionally she asks for change. I walk past without looking too hard, and offer her nothing. There are stereotypes about homelessness I measure each time I pass. She looks reasonably

1   Shekhar Kapur, TED India, Nov 2009. Retrieved 4 July 2011 from http://www. ted.com/talks/lang/eng/shekhar_kapur_we_are_the_stories_we_tell_ourselves. html.

healthy and sane from the corner of my vision. I think she must be incredibly tough. I think she must have other options. I wonder where she pees and what she eats. I wonder where the rest of her stuff is. I'm aware then and forever afterwards that everything I think and do in response to her presence says more about me, my sanity and my health, than her. To ignore someone who has nothing is not an indicator of personal wellbeing.

We stay at a very fancy hotel. I am surprised that while a novelty, the opulence of the place does not disturb me as much as I might have predicted. Perhaps poor people aren't inherently better than rich. Perhaps it's okay to play at richness since this is not part of our real life. I make jokes about the sumptuous furniture in the lobbies, which is rarely touched—ornate couches and finely crafted sets of drawers that will never hold anything. We could set up our living room there, I suggest, no one's using it. But I don't sleep. There's no rest to be had in such a place.

Both my partner and I enjoy the storied space of graveyards—how a city tells its history through its dead. One of the things we do before we leave Auckland is cross the street to walk through the cemetery. A man overhears us discussing where to go and launches into a strangely friendly rant about how the gravestones have been vandalised by druggies and taggers. We realise the extent of this when we see empty alcohol containers littering a grave. This cemetery has been sliced through to make room for a motorway, like Bolton Street in Wellington. We walk down and read of the bodies disinterred and placed in a mass grave. Back up by the street, we're both curious about some very old brick cemetery buildings, but curtail any investigation when we see that people have left their belongings there, where they sleep. As we leave the graveyard and wash our hands in a public drinking fountain, I wonder what kind of story this tells: the way a city treats its living and its dead.

Ornate and empty hotel furniture can't compare to the riches of well-worn family drawers and cabinets, and cemeteries. Sometimes people still espouse that old prejudice: the history of New Zealand is so recent, so limited. So poor, is the implication.

Have they looked, I always wonder, really looked? Whenever I peek over the brim of the last century to the one before I am staggered by the stories there, the cluster of voices all clamouring for attention. Most of them have never been heard, and they seem much more quirky and lively and bawdy than the accepted histories suggest.

On our last day in Auckland my partner offers the woman on the Hello Kitty™ duvet a couple of apples. She'll take just one, she replies, reluctantly. Later, when I write about her, I wonder how to convey the strength and dignity in her voice, my own inability to comprehend her place in the world. I wonder what her story is, but at the time I didn't ask.

GRANDFATHERS

When my first daughter was a baby my mother made a composite photo for her, comprising photos of six generations of women in her maternal line, uninterrupted since her namesake kuia in the early 1900s, our marae in the background. A powerful legacy in the face of which the story of male ancestors held much less fascination. Until last year. I was on the trail of another great-great grandmother, on the other side of the family. I soon discovered it was not her, but her father who held the mystery, for we could discover nothing of him but the name: Haimona—a transliteration of Simon, a fairly common name. Every other line in the whakapapa travelled back much further, origins and migrations recorded in detail. We wondered if Haimona was the Moriori link. The obliteration of his history seemed to support this theory.

Looking for Haimona meant exploring the whakapapa around him. I discovered more ancestors, more family stories now reaching back seven generations or more. It meant just as much to learn the women's names as the men's, but this time it was the stories of the male ancestors that claimed attention. I had come to understand the kinds of lives my grandmothers had had. Their stories had dominated my imagination for a long time.

I knew little about the men: what kinds of lives did they have? Why were more of them Pākehā than I'd realised, and how did they come to earn chiefly wives? And why did it matter to me?

A loss early in life can be a defining thing. If we want to go to the source of a person's obsessions, it is perhaps best to take a journey through their early years. After all, some things, once taken out of a childhood, cannot be put back. For me, the picture of what a family or culture consists of was never complete. I hungered for stories of origins, and stories of how people make families. 'Stories matter,' says Chimamanda Adichie, 'lots of stories matter':

> It is impossible to engage properly with a place or person without engaging with all of the stories of that place or that person. The consequence of the single story is this: it robs people of dignity. It makes our recognition of an equal humanity difficult. It emphasizes how we are different, rather than how we are similar.[1]

And what if you don't know all your own stories?

I took what I had learned about Haimona and all his in-laws, and charted the whakapapa. I made copies of this chart and gave one to my mother for Christmas.

THE ENGLISHMAN

The first time I encounter James Worser Heberley is in a picture in Trevor Bentley's 1999 book, *Pakeha Maori*. He frowns at the camera, his hand clasped protectively over that of his wife, Te Wai, who sits on a chair beside him. Her face is blurred, though her body is not, as if she were shaking her head slightly when the shot was taken. Heberley sports impressive sideburns that grow down like a beard in the style of the time, but the front of

1   Chimamanda Adichie, TED Global, Jul 2009. Retrieved 4 July 2011 from http://www.ted.com/talks/lang/eng/chimamanda_adichie_the_danger_of_a_single_story.html.

his face is clean shaven. His nose is broad and his lips as wide and full as his wife's. Bentley says he was one of 'Te Rauparaha's original Pakeha toa, [who] as a young man joined Ngati Toa in their intertribal musket battles.'[1] Something about the Heberley name stays with me for a while before I realise where I have heard it. I pull out the whakapapa chart I created only weeks before and find the Heberley name immediately, just above my great-great-great grandparents—Sarah Heberley and William (Pire) Henry Keenan. James 'Worser' Heberley and Maata Te Naehi e Wai (Te Wai) were Sarah's parents. With an ancestry that was Māori, English and German, Sarah, born in 1840, married a man who also had mixed blood, an Irish-Māori.

Heberley's eyes are penetrating and troubled. When I look closely they seem marked by sorrow rather than anger, though I am not sure I want this man to be my ancestor. Bentley's book is full of bloodshed and cannibalism, thieves and mercenaries. His Māori are bloodthirsty opportunists, his Pākehā variations of disreputable anarchists. To be fair, he doesn't demonise either group. They both, it seemed, brought with them unsavoury as well as honourable practices. But the Aotearoa he describes is not one I recognise. Bentley seems to highlight every cannibal feast, every juicy narrative. According to *Pakeha Maori*, Heberley would have taken part in some of Te Rauparaha's most vicious raids on South Island tribes.

I have not read every historical account Bentley references, but of the other sources I've found, none asserts Heberley's allegiance to Te Rauparaha. They tend to emphasise Heberley's more famous pursuits: he helped Dieffenbach climb Mt Taranaki, thereby becoming the first man[2] known to gain the summit; he was Wakefield's pilot and later the first pilot of Wellington, bestowing his nickname on the bay where he lived and worked: 'Worser'. The name is usually attributed to 'his habit of warning

---

1   Bentley, Trevor, *Pakeha Māori*, 1999, p85.
2   It would be reasonable to assume this, given that Taranaki was tapu to Māori. Local Māori who accompanied Dieffenbach and Heberley stopped where the snow-line began.

that the weather would get "worser and worser".[1] This story may be only legend, however, since Worser's own journal states that he was teased about living in a Māori raised storehouse or 'whata' before he had built his own house. 'Tangata Whata' soon became Europeanised to 'Worser'.[2]

Heberley's own account is also unclear on his loyalty to the warrior chief. For the most part his early stories of life in Queen Charlotte Sound consist of making do as best he can. He describes several skirmishes, and the necessity to flee from his home at Te Awaiti. He uses the term 'we' often, though sometimes it is unclear whether he is simply referring to himself and his family, his Pākehā cohort, which includes fellow whaler and employer, Jacky Guard, or the Māori tribes they are living with. Perhaps at different times, he means all, or different combinations of these groups. When they flee attack, they often return months or weeks later to find all their homes destroyed.

There are two revealing references to Heberley's relationship with Te Rauparaha, aside from his matter of fact observations of ritual feasts. His obituary states:

> [Heberley] well remembered his return with 500 prisoners from the famous raid to Kaiapoi 67 years ago; witnessed the murder of the prisoners, and the cannibal orgie that ensued. He afterwards owed his life to that same Rauparaha, who threw his cloak over him just in the nick of time to save him from a Waikato tomahawk upraised to brain him.[3]

This latter event occurred soon after they had fled the Sounds for Te Rauparaha's northern stronghold:

1   Neich, Roger. 'Jacob William Heberley of Wellington: A Māori Carver in a Changed World', *Records of the Auckland Institute and Museum,* 1991, No28, p71.
2   Ibid.
3   'The Oldest Of Old Settlers', *Otago Daily Times,* Issue 11551, 11 October 1899, p 3. Retrieved 4 July 2011 from http://paperspast.natlib.govt.nz/cgi-bin/paper-spast?a=d&d=ODT18991011.2.8

We took our Boats and the Natives their Canoes, the Southern
Natives followed us but they could not catch us, for we could
outpull them, we went across to the other island and stayed
at Kapiti, the Natives were at war again . . . so I took my boat
and two natives to pull with me to a place called [Waikanae]
to land my wife and child among her own tribe, I came back
to Kapiti . . .[1]

Heberley also records that he paid Te Rauparaha with tobacco
for the protection of his cloak. He seemed to have a distant
allegiance to the chief, owing more to the necessity of survival
than a taste for warrior life. Later he is braver in his descriptions:
"he was very troublesome . . . we were not sorry when he took his
departure . . ."[2]

Bentley's narrative, often derived from Pākehā Māori returning
to 'civilisation' who could make a good bob or two from stories
of savages and feasts of human flesh, makes early New Zealand
seem a relentless and nightmarish world. While there is plenty
of evidence of this in journals like Heberley's, it doesn't always
reflect the reality of ordinary people trying to survive troubled,
rapidly changing times. So many must've been trying to get by
in their own peaceful way. Engage in commerce. Stay out of the
way of that uncle or cousin who was on a rampage. Make a deal.
Clearly Te Rauparaha's reality and his legend would have been
similarly disparate. The more mundane details of history are
not the parts that are remembered. Things didn't always work
out—history tells us that. But quiet friendships also don't make
as exciting a story.

On balance, Heberley's narrative is for the most part about
trying to find a way to live in an unforgiving world. Back in
Britain, he was sent to work at the age of 11, and served for years
at a time on various ships, sometimes captained by 'tyrants',
sometimes by men who found him destitute and offered him
food and shelter. He doesn't expand on the hardships in great

1   Heberley, James, *Reminiscences*, Jan 1809–Jun 1843, Alexander Turnbull Library.
2   Ibid.

detail, apart from the beatings with frozen rope or dogfish tail that sent him from one ship to another. It must've been a grimy, frightening business for a boy growing up. There was some light relief when he began whaling as a young man, the rituals of cutting in being quite festive: 'the Steward sang out Grog O— and we began to cut in the first whale . . . we began to get pretty merry . . . they danced away, although the Decks were greasy with the Blubber, every one got drunk but not so far, as to neglect their work . . .'[1]

When at last he came to Queen Charlotte Sound in 1830, he was told 'there were plenty of Houses in Te Awaite and Native Women, and that we had nothing to do but to go in our Boats and catch Fish'[2]. It was not that simple, for there were no houses, and the next ten years were filled with conflicts between warring tribes that Heberley found difficult to avoid. He must have liked the place and the people though, since he stayed amongst the tribes. He soon found himself a wife in Port Underwood, Te Wai of Te Āti Awa, who 'clearly had important chiefly connections'[3] and 'reared a large family'.[4] Says Bentley: 'There is an important Maori woman in the story of every known Pakeha Maori.'[5] On that detail, we agree. He also quotes Markham from the time: 'in fact it is not safe to live in the country without a chief's daughter as a protection as they are always backed by their tribe'.[6] Multiple wives were not uncommon, though Heberley seemed protective of and content with one, and of course 'Maori wives were rarely compliant or servile partners'.[7] Like the other ancestors in this story, Worser and Te Wai have hundreds, if not thousands, of descendants.

1   Ibid.
2   Ibid.
3   Neich, p74.
4   Heberley, James, *Reminiscences*.
5   Bentley, p193.
6   Ibid, p195.
7   Ibid, p201.

The Irishman

When my mother tells me about our European ancestors, it is with the same pride that she describes our tīpuna Māori. Her pride in being Welsh and Irish is at least equal to that of being Ngāti Tuwharetoa or Te Āti Awa. Henry Eagar and Jackson Keenan were among the first ancestors she introduced me to. Eagar is from her mother's whakapapa, Keenan from her father's. She has photos of each, and speaks of them with a fondness I suspect most Pākehā families would retain only for family members they had known in their lifetime.

It should be said that in the robust Keenan line there are many family historians more knowledgeable than I.[1] I can only touch on those elements of our original Irish ancestor's story that correspond with the experiences of my other ancestral Pākehā Māori. Jackson's grandfather, William Henry Keenan (Te Puponga), was born in 1806 in Sydney, but was said to have been from County Cork, Ireland. He first landed in Taranaki in the 1820s, and was among the group of Pākehā, including Dicky Barrett and John Love, who assisted the local Ngāmotu people when Otaka Pā was attacked by Waikato tribes:

> The siege was pressed with great vigour, and the pā would have fallen before the overwhelming number of the invaders, had it not been for the heroic stand made by the whalers. Time after time the enemy succeeded in gaining an entrance, but they were in every case driven out with loss . . .[2]

The whalers had taken their chances inside the palisaded pā, and emerged, with their hosts, victorious. Their fates were

1 Subsequent research has shown Jackson is known in the whakapapa and perhaps to other families as 'John'.
2 *The Journal of the Polynesian Society*,1910, Volume 19, No. 1, History and traditions of the Taranaki coast. Chapter XVIII, The defence of Otaka or Nga-motu. Retrieved 4 July 2011 from http://www.jps.auckland.ac.nz/document/Volume_19_1910/Volume_19,_No._1/History_and_traditions_of_the_Taranaki_coast._Chapter_XVIII,_The_defence_of_Otaka_or_Nga-motu,_p_25-38/p1.

now linked. Although they won the battle at Ōtaka, Taranaki tribes still faced immense pressure from other tribes, and in 1832 began to migrate south. 'Also in the migration were the people of Ngāti Mutunga . . . and Te Puponga (William Keenan) from New Plymouth . . .'[1] During their journey, fighting broke out at Whanganui,

> and in the feast that followed, Keenan inadvertently partook of some human flesh, greatly to his disgust. The natives were highly diverted at this mistake and Keenan came in for a great deal of 'chaff' over it . . .[2]

Māori names and wives were bestowed on most of the original group of Pākehā at Ngāmotu. Tribal protection was returned to them for the efforts they had expended to protect the tribe. Keenan had the good fortune to earn the hand of Katarina Hikimapu Takuna (Catherine). Both the Keenans and the Heberleys married the Māori way, had several children, then obtained Christian marriages and christenings for their children when a Minister passed through the area. Both settled in Queen Charlotte Sound, and, in the late 1850s, saw their families linked through marriage.

The families were, of course, also linked by whaling, and by their presence in the area prior to active colonisation. Keenan's 1880 obituary is effusive and revealing of the time:

> Another of the links has been destroyed, and the chain that binds the present with the past is becoming gradually weaker . . . With the gift of a fluent tongue and retentive memory what tales he could have told about the manners and customs of olden times, before the advent of any but European adventurers in the colony; when the early comers were more Maorised than the Natives

1   Morris Love. 'Te Āti Awa of Wellington—The migration of 1832', *Te Ara—the Encyclopedia of New Zealand*. Retrieved 4 July 2011 from http://www.teara.govt.nz/en/te-ati-awa-of-wellington/3.
2   *The Journal of the Polynesian Society* (see p259 n1, above).

themselves, and might, not right, ruled this fair land . . .

Few residents in this part but can call to mind the tall upright figure that was conspicuous, especially on regatta days, his curt sentences, as if he was afraid to use two words when one would answer the purpose, and his curiosity in inquiring into the use and meaning of anything new or strange . . .[1]

It must have been this combination of irrepressible curiosity and reserve that allowed Keenan to succeed in his new home. I can imagine his horror at the scene in Whanganui, his desire to fit in with his hosts almost undermining his European sensibilities. But there must have been immense, sinewy toughness too. Both Keenan and Heberley lived long lives, despite, or perhaps because of, the challenges faced. Although I don't know about the first Keenan's appearance, his son, William Henry (Pire), was said to have had red hair, twenty children, and been 'dogged by misfortune'.[2] These were men who lived by the fortunes the sea bestowed on them, and the fortunes bestowed on them by the tribes they married into. It is difficult to tell whether the red hair or the many children contributed to William Jnr's misfortune, though it is known that his second wife Piki Love saved him from drowning when all others had failed. Perhaps he was lucky after all, in marriage.

THE WELSHMAN

The photo my mother has of Henry Francis Eagar shows a thin and well-dressed man with a long straight beard that reaches to his chest. His pocket watch is prominent, his back straight. He stares into the distance with an expression that gives nothing away. With him are his daughter, Riria, and his grandson Keremete.

The day I look for Koro Eagar at the cemetery of Rangiatea Church, it is windy and cold, but not raining. It has been stormy for days, frequent thunder and lightning sending the dog spinning

1   *Marlborough Press*, Friday October 1, 1880.
2   Mike Taylor (Picton Museum), Family Research Papers.

on her heels, barking madly as if to scare off her tormentor, hackles raised. As soon as we arrive, a light rain begins. We look at all the older headstones, especially the ones with clasping hands, of which there are many. According to my mother, Koro Eagar has this image carved on his headstone. A gravestone historian might be able to tell us the exact significance of the relief carved handshakes, though the symbolism is fairly self-evident.

We don't find my ancestor immediately, and the rain rapidly becomes heavy. My family take shelter while I continue my search. I go up the hill when I think I have exhausted other possibilities. The downpour becomes wild, sending biting rain at my skin. As the squall whips up around me I wonder whether I am being told to leave, but I am determined to look. I quickly survey all the stones on the hill and then begin my descent, looking at the last few headstones on the way. 'Well, I give up,' I say, when I reach my family. The rain has lightened. 'Have you looked at that one?' my partner asks, pointing to a monument behind me. I doubt it is Koro Eagar's. We look towards the large freestanding obelisk-shaped memorial, separate but not too far from the other headstones. There are two hands clasped in a high relief handshake at the centre of the stone pillar. Better take another look. I jog over, see the words in Māori first: H.F. IKA. Then I know. It's him.

I am surprised at how grand his memorial is. Perhaps this was why I didn't look at first. Sometimes a large headstone can suggest ostentatious wealth. But many things about Eagar's stone suggest his memorial is indicative of high esteem, rather than pretentiousness. It reads:

in
loving memory
of
H F EAGAR
TENA KOE PAKEHA
E TAPU ANA TENEI HEI
WHAKAMAHARATANGA

MO
H F IKA
I MATE IA I TE 13 O AKUHATA 1911

On the plinth at the base of the memorial are the words:

HE TANGATA WHAKAPONO, AROHA HOKI KI TE IWI
MAORI ME NGA PAKEHA TAE NOA KI TONA MATENGA
HAERE RA KI TO MATUA I TE RANGI

There are two things that strike me immediately about this inscription. One, there has been much effort expended to tell this particular story about Eagar. He was 'a man of faith' and also had 'love[1] for the Māori people and the Pākehā until his death'. Secondly, with the exception of the first part of the inscription, the memorial is completely written in Māori. Particularly affecting is the engraving of his habitual saying 'Tena koe Pakeha' inscribed above the handshake, which is almost three dimensional and stands out in white stone.

Official records do not detail Eagar's involvement with Māori communities, apart from his status as secretary of the Ōtaki Māori Racing Club: 'the only Māori racing club in New Zealand, and possibly one of a few truly indigenous horse racing clubs in the world . . .' He was 'the most important individual in the early years'.[2] He was also secretary to the early Ōtaki Library, and:

Harry Eagar was the clerk to both [Te Horo and Otaki Road] boards, also secretary of many different concerns. Dust inside and on the papers of the shelves did not impair the efficiency of the clerk, nor dull the greeting of 'Tenakoe, Pakeha', which was usually accorded a local visitor. Eagar's funeral, which took place on August 16, 1911, was very largely attended.[3]

1   Also empathy, compassion.
2   Retrieved 12 July 2011 from http://www.otakimaoriracing.co.nz/page/our-history.aspx.
3   F S Simcox, *Otaki: The Town and District,* 1952, p188–119.

Says A.J. Dreaver in 'Horowhenua County and its People: A Centennial History':[1] 'The Cyclopaedia (1896) called him "the veritable Pooh-bah" of Otaki.'

Ōtaki at the time was a metropolis of 836 citizens. This might not be impressive now, but back then it had promising prospects:

> OTAKI, the largest township since setting out from the Capital, is well situated, and near the sea coast, and although under Maori rule, as it were, is yet destined to become an important town for . . . the town and district have many elements of prosperity . . . [and] Otaki will become a resort for invalids, globe-trotters, and people seeking relaxation from the cares of city life.[2]

The community at the time was emphatically bicultural, more Māori than Pākehā, and still retains a strong culturally distinct personality. There were shadows in Eagar's life, as there are in any. I don't know what to make of the absence of his wife in our knowledge of him. Apparently he had caused offence to his in-laws, but I don't have the details of that, and with regards to some whakapapa, it is best to tread lightly over unsettled ground.

From the history I can piece together, I can't say for sure what any of this tells us about Koro Eagar. We know him as the Welsh ancestor, though he was born in Sydney and his name is Anglo-Saxon. He was obviously a hard-working community man, but I can't tell if I would've been on his side around the committee table.

What I am left with is a sense that he walked between two cultures, and that he did what he could to integrate both. He wasn't like my older Pākehā Māori ancestors—though he married into the culture and adopted the language just as fast. His was a world that was rapidly becoming Europeanised. Those that paid attention still did well by engaging and adopting Māori views and ideas, by nurturing Māori friends and families.

1   1984, pp125–6.
2   *Cyclopaedia of New Zealand*, 1897, p1090. Retrieved 4 July 2011 from http://www.nzetc.org/tm/scholarly/tei-Cyc01Cycl-t1-body-d4-d121-d1.html.

Perhaps he was one of a new kind of citizen: one who could be accountable to both Māori and Pākehā worlds. Rangiatea urupa carries testimony to this: a pointed memorial, hands clasped in friendship, the cheery greeting—Tēnā koe Pākehā.

Keeping company

We are always looking for what was lost, always trying to map connections. Once I thought I could be an archaeologist, but now I see that what I might become instead is an excavator of stories. Sometimes these stories can be dug out of family graveyards, sometimes found in the wilderness imagination; sometimes it is tempting to pick on the living, but I can see that they won't be happy about it and I'd prefer to go on being loved, or at least, tolerated.

I wonder whether my preoccupations are connected to that first, primal, lost relation in my life, though I wouldn't like to place too much weight on this conclusion. There are no straight lines. There is no clear path. Excavation is the clearing of dirt; patient brushing away of layer after layer of dust; the use of fine tools. A light tap, a slow chipping away. Careful! You don't want to damage the last remnant. Have you done the right karakia? Are the gods on your side?

'Stories define the potentialities of our existence,' according to Kapur.[1] Tangata Whata, Te Puponga, Ika. That these Pākehā were given Māori names, even in jest, shows the intimacy they shared with Māori. They took a different approach to engaging with the 'other'. These first European settlers chose to see what was here already. They looked to the land and seas and peoples they encountered, and decided to bind themselves to the lives and customs that already existed. They didn't try to superimpose their world on the land they came to.

Of course like many good stories, this one touches on the challenge of prejudice, the mediating power of sex, and the

---

1   Shekhar Kapur, TED India, Nov 2009.

triumph of mythology. From the first I was made aware that I came from two peoples, and that these two peoples had a lot of unfinished business to attend to. This was done explicitly and implicitly on many levels through intimate family relationships and impersonal national mediums. Like many mixed-origin people, I've encountered racism from both sides, which is to be expected, since both feed each other. What made me interested in the stories of my Pākehā Māori ancestors was this: if we have been intermarrying since earliest European contact, and if our earliest white ancestors in New Zealand were willing to approach their ethnic identity in a fluid and adaptable way, why wasn't the development of New Zealand culture more representative of the experiences and approaches of these men? Why, when I think of the stories I was bestowed by the Pākehā side of my family, does it not include these kinds of stories, and the white men who became Pākehā Māori? Did the absolute insistence on a 'European' identity come much later in our story than we like to think?

Perhaps a new approach lies in the convoluted mass of stories from our collective past. My heritage has only ever consisted of a multitude of messy, conflicting, surprising stories. The more of them I discover, the more I am content that my personal story of loss and confusion and strange beginnings is not so unusual. I've sought them out, these fiercely independent, alternative-lifestyle Pākehā grandfathers, to keep me company. To keep company with the kauri-brown ancestral wāhine toa I like to visit often. I bet they like it there. They know their place, and it's better than where they came from. They've paid the prices that were asked of them, adopted the reo and tikanga, earned their turf through work and war and the making of babies. Their stories represent an earlier whakapapa, an alternative form of settlement. While Pākehā Māori had their own issues, could their stories represent another model of intercultural relationship for all of us? Could the story of Aotearoa New Zealand develop differently if we recognised all the stories, not just those of conquest and confiscation, of laws and land courts, but the unexpected, the unpopular, the unwritten?

Bill Manhire

From an Imaginary Notebook

The Eye of the Blackbird

A couple of tūī are scrapping in a tree by one of the entrances to the university (Gate 3, it's boldly called), then suddenly they are flying through the air, horizontal, their passage all feathery beatings and thrashings—and they continue their frenzied argument in a small tree to the right of the steps I'm just about to climb. They are black tufts, iridescent, splashes of white throat-feather. The sound of their wings is strong, like one of those whirring Māori instruments.

The odd thing is that, a fraction of a second later, a blackbird zips across after them from the first tree and perches on a nearby branch to watch proceedings. Now I watch the blackbird, and the blackbird watches the skirmishing tūī—for what seems an age, though it is probably only 30 seconds. And then, show over, the blackbird flies back to its original tree, because the tūī have flown off somewhere else entirely.

I'd always thought Wallace Stevens' blackbird was some figure for the way reality shifts, remaining unsettled and unsettling. But perhaps it is some version of the writer: interested, keeping close, keeping a bit of a distance.

Synaesthesia

I'm surprised it's thought to be unusual, and even that it has a name. I assumed that everyone knew words and numbers had colours. It's something I took for granted when I was little. A lot of it has slipped away, but 3 is still yellow, 4 a dark green, 8 some sort of red. Ruth was green, Henry a pale, putty colour, Bill a dark blue. Letters have colours, too. E is yellow, H is gray,

T blacker than black. And now I remember thinking once that perhaps the colours darkened as the alphabet went on.

Locomotion

All those Tarzan movies. Tarzan gets through the jungle by swinging from one vine to another . . .

As a writer, you want to stay in the jungle, but you need to be able to come and go and get about a bit. Sometimes you need to outpace the thousand enemies who are on your trail. So you need something like a vine, strong and functional, and every so often you need to find a new one. You reach out and grab it, and there you are: swinging again. Locomotion!

If you don't reach out, you don't go anywhere. You just hang there. You dangle.

Guided Tours

A story I once planned to write was to have been about a young New Zealander living in Munich, who earned his living as a tour guide. A couple of days a week, he worked at Dachau, taking tour parties around the camp. He also had sporadic work on the Salzburg *Sound of Music* tour. A life more confusing than continuous. And I thought he would also have a love-life, plus occasional mini-surfing adventures across the Iser in the English Gardens. He would have hung out with the whole Australasian ex-pat crowd, and like most of us been really quite muddled about what matters and how the world works.

More Locomotion

Or would that vine analogy work better for poems? Each line is a jungle vine, and it swings the reader on to the next one. So the poem must be the jungle.

A Lost Poem

I also once planned to write a poem about the fact that General de Gaulle died playing patience. I think it was just going to be a sequence of cards, turned over and gathered successfully into order inside their suits. I was going to play and play and play until I got the poem. Crikey.

Punctuation

Since the Rachel Barrowman biography, the power of R.A.K. Mason's early work can be explained by the thing plenty of people knew but lacked the language or social nerve to declare: Mason was bi-polar. Hence the intense, over-excited poems of the young man, the verbal highs and lows, where passion and rage swirl around inside the tough, rigid, containing form. Maybe those steady Georgian models imposed themselves on feeling and experience in ways that made all the difference. They held the mania yet also intensified it.

Mason would probably have been a very bad poet if he had had so-called open form available to him: just one more Allen Ginsberg on a bad day. As it is, there are the great early poems: 'On the Swag', 'Footnote to John II, iv', 'Old Memories of Earth', 'Sonnet of Brotherhood'.

Sometimes I think you could just about reduce Mason's poems down to a sort of punctuation
[!] or [?!] or [!!!]
depending perhaps on the time of day, or the phases of the moon.

A Fine Poetry Moment

'I'm too famous to die!' —Allen Ginsberg, apparently serious, during airplane turbulence.

An Interesting Sentence

'The manor-house, or *herrgård*, in question is to be called Råbāck (pronounced something like Roebeck), though that is not its name.'
(from 'Count Magnus' by M.R. James)

Three Words Beginning with G

Giggles. I grew up thinking this was the name for fish-guts, when you cleaned them out. I thought I had learnt it from my mother. But she consistently denied ever having used the word. I still sometimes look for it, in dictionaries and online. But I can't find it anywhere.

Guddle was certainly my mother's word, though it's hard to find strong instances of it in the world of lexicography. It means a muddle, a sort of giddy muddle, a mess. 'I'm in a real guddle today.'

Gloopy. One of the great onomatopoeic words. It was worth half learning Russian at the age of 17 to find this word. It means stupid. But that 'y' is deep somehow, not high. Gloopy, gloopy, gloopy.

The Vincent O'Sullivan Dream

I'm to launch his book (the four books book), chairing a kind of 'hour with' session, but only because someone far more important has had to pull out, I'm doing this as a favour to the publisher, as a last-minute ring-in, feeling slightly put-upon, and I'm there just in time, after a desperate taxi ride from the university to Te Papa. But I would never take a taxi from the university to Te Papa! I don't seem to have a copy of the book, but manage to borrow one off Tilly Lloyd who happens to be running the bookstall. But Vincent is on the far side of the room—which is the wrong side of the room—and now he starts declaiming something. *What is he doing?* Eventually he realises he's in the wrong place and comes to the front, but now he stands yards away on my right, nowhere near the raised platform with its table and mics. The room is long and narrow, but the four or five rows of seats stretch horizontally. Actually, they stretch forever. I can't see the ends of the rows. Vincent starts making strange gestures; he stays still on his feet, but his body and head and arms move: a mix of gestures from (maybe) deaf signing and break dancing. A dumb show. I can't figure this out at all. But then I look at the book I am holding and see that it is not the one I thought was the point of this event; rather it's a new book entirely—a long narrative poem à la Browning, made up of monologues—and one of the characters is deaf. Vincent is apparently reading one of his monologues. God, he is prolific! That's all right, then. And now it must be time to wake up.

A Note from Robert Louis Stevenson

'Asked what his songs were about, Tembinok' replied, "Sweethearts and trees and the sea. Not all the same true, all the same lie."'

My First Word

Doodledasher.

Visiting Nigel

I remember visiting Nigel Cox in Seatoun a few weeks before he died. Windy, sunny day; the sea just outside. Nigel's childhood friend Doug was there—he had flown in from America— reminiscing about schoolboy escapades.

Doug: *Yes, we cheated death many a time.*

Nigel: *Sounds like a line from one of Bill's poems.*

Mistakes

James Wood on Keith Moon (in *The New Yorker*): '. . . making mistakes is simply part of the locomotion of vitality.'

The Keith Ovenden Dream

I am in sole charge of a very large hotel kitchen: large work-benches, shining stainless steel, much equipment—but only a single small oven, in which there is a lone leg of lamb. Out through some swing doors is seated the full complement of the New Zealand Symphony Orchestra. The players are all dressed very formally—the men in frock coats, the women in ball-gowns. I am panicking in a pretty high level way. The only thing that saves me is that from time to time a waiter bursts through a set of swing-doors crying, 'It's all right: Keith Ovenden hasn't finished speaking yet.' I was telling my friend Kathryn about this dream, and explaining that I thought it was rather shrewd of me to choose a speaker who was renowned for his long, perfectly grammatical sentences—some of them a paragraph or so in length. But Kathryn has made a bit of a study of dreams and word play. 'Oven,' she says, 'Ovenden. You punned your way to safety.'

And Thinking of Ovens . . .

When I interviewed Hone Tuwhare for *Landfall* in the late 80s, we met in his little cottage in Dundas Street, Dunedin. It was about 11.00 on a Saturday morning, and I had brought a couple of bottles of red wine, just to help things along. After a couple of hours of very good talk, there was a smell of burning from the kitchen. 'Cripes!' cried Hone—he had once been a Billy Bunter fan—and he raced to open the oven door. After the smoke had cleared, two well charred shoulders of lamb were sitting forlornly on the oven tray. He had cooked one for each of us.

Wikipedia on the Tarzan Yell

The sound itself has received a trademark registration, owned by Edgar Rice Burroughs, Inc. The official description of the yell is:

The mark consists of the sound of the famous Tarzan yell. The mark is a yell consisting of a series of approximately ten sounds, alternating between the chest and falsetto registers of the voice, as follows—

1. a semi-long sound in the chest register,
2. a short sound up an interval of one octave plus a fifth from the preceding sound,
3. a short sound down a Major 3rd from the preceding sound,
4. a short sound up a Major 3rd from the preceding sound,
5. a long sound down one octave plus a Major 3rd from the preceding sound,
6. a short sound up one octave from the preceding sound,
7. a short sound up a Major 3rd from the preceding sound,
8. a short sound down a Major 3rd from the preceding sound,
9. a short sound up a Major 3rd from the preceding sound,
10. a long sound down an octave plus a fifth from the preceding sound.

Despite these efforts, the Office for Harmonization in the Internal Market (OHIM) in late 2007 determined that such attempts by the estate of Burroughs to maintain such trademark must fail legally, reasoning that '[w]hat has been filed as a graphic representation is from the outset not capable of serving as a graphic representation of the applied-for sound,' said the OHIM ruling. 'The examiner was therefore correct to refuse the attribution of a filing date.' However, the sound recording of the yell is an officially registered trademark with the USPTO. The mark was registered in August 1995 and renewed in December of 2005.

Things I've Wanted to Write

— An essay on the hyphen in Philip Larkin's poetry.

— A 500-page study of the word 'still' in the Romantic poets.

— 'Nothing comes from nothing': *King Lear* and *The Sound of Music*.

— I also wanted to write about the link between Cliff Richard's 'Living Doll' and Sylvia Plath's 'The Applicant', and then I discovered that someone else had done so.

Velvet

I think I must have been about 14 when I realised what metaphor was.

I was reading a review of a Cliff Richard LP in *Truth*.

Anyway, they described his voice as *velvet*. Astonishing: something you could see and touch (but not hear) was the perfect way of describing a sound! I think that helped me realise what poems could do. I didn't know about metaphor, but when I was told about it, probably later that year, it made total sense.

Schooldays

What did I read in my last year at school? Whatever it was, I found it all for myself. R.A.K. Mason, Walt Whitman, Carl Sandburg (*The People, Yes*), a biography (was it in two volumes?) of George Bernard Shaw. The first Curnow anthology? Ronald Hugh Morrieson, from the rental library below the Crown Hotel. Mickey Spillane. Carter Brown. *Peyton Place. Catcher in the Rye. Ballad of the Sad Café. On the Road. Lady Chatterley's Lover.* More Carter Brown.

MUSICAL MOMENTS

— Someone's house, Invercargill, 1953, men and women singing: 'Ha-ere Mai! / Everything is kapai! / You're here at last, / You're really here at last. // You're welcome as the sunshine, / You're welcome as a king! / Pai kare! This is one time / We'll really have a fling!'

— Dunedin Town Hall 1960s: The Everly Brothers. Ravi Shankar. Roy Orbison. Jimmy Shand and his band. The Beatles. Gene Pitney. Peter, Paul, and Mary. Del Shannon. Gene McDaniels. Mr Acker Bilk. Dusty Springfield. Lonnie Donegan. Kenneth McKellar. Andy Stewart. Cliff Richard and the Shadows. The Howard Morrison Quartet.

— Takapuwahia Marae 1986: Kazuo Ishiguro singing *Blue Moon*.

THE MELANCHOLIA CUBE

Somewhere a year or two ago I came across a reference to a melancholia cube. All I can find on Google are references to a gallery piece by Anselm Kiefer. 'The "melancholia cube" is a cube with the corners cut off and is thus seen as incomplete, like human understanding.' Anyway, I want one.

THE SISTINE CHAPEL

There used to be a wall-poster, 'The Floor of the Sistine Chapel', showing a floor covered in discarded lumps of gum, cigarette butts, screwed up napkins, scraps of food, etc. It depended on you knowing what the ceiling of the Sistine Chapel looked like and, I suppose, what it *meant*. I got to the very place once, and joined the orderly queue. I looked down, just in case: the floor was immaculate. In a sense, my favourite poems show you the floor (as in the poster) and the ceiling at the very same time.

Not one or the other, but both at once. I've always liked Carl Sandburg's definition of the poem as a synthesis of hyacinths and biscuits—though it's probably best, I want to add, if the synthesis is never quite achieved.

THE WALL OF SERPENTS

It's a bit like that story by Italo Calvino, the 'Serpents and Skulls' one, where Mr Palomar and a friend are visiting the ruins of Tula, once capital of the Toltecs. The friend knows a great deal, or believes he does, about the ruins they walk among. He confidently explains and interprets everything—while occasionally they cross paths with a schoolteacher, leading his crocodile of children, who points to each column or statue or piece of carved stone and says, 'We do not know what it means.'

A POEM IS

'. . . a prolonged hesitation between sound and sense'
—Paul Valéry

That covers everything that matters really.

EXCEPT

Where does the cat come from?

The one in *copycat*, I mean.

AND

'He paid to save her from the interactive rat.'

Where did I think that was going to lead?

The Schoolbus

This is the place where the schoolbus turns.
The driver backs and snuffles, backs and goes.
It is always winter on these roads: high bridges
and birds in flight above you all the way.
The heart can hardly stay. The heart implodes.

The heart can hardly stay. The heart implodes.
The body gets down and walks across a field.
There are mushrooms—as in stories,
as in songs. They grow near rabbits.
Slope of hillside,

slant of rain—and here we are again:
a green-roofed house behind the trees.
The body gets down and walks across a field.
The house is full of homework fed by sleep.
A boy combs his hair, brushes his teeth,

or climbs to the top of the valley.
The sky is handkerchiefs, a single shirt.
He wants to climb higher, into a cloud.
He wants to climb into a cloud.
Whatever else is somewhere up ahead.

The schoolbus is driving through the night.
Whatever else is somewhere up ahead.
A boy keeps on hitting his head.
The small girls sing. It's nothing.
We don't know what we mean.

Is that another drink the man is pouring?
The boy turns the handle of the separator.
Cream. The boy stands on the railway line,
disappearing in rust and shine.
Goodnight Irene. Goodnight Irene.

The big door closes. A voice in the kitchen
says: Enough's enough. Running a bath.
Always cold water, boiled in pots.
The driver swears, and then he coughs.
The big door closes and you can't get off.

The question poem

Was there a city here?

We were sitting with friends. It was a sunny day.
We were boasting about the local coffee.
Strange self-congratulations, flat whites.
These were friends we had only recently
found our way back to. For a long time
we were far apart.

Did you all survive?

On that first day of school, I mostly remember
being terrified: the dark interior, the children in rows
at their separate desks, and I was now to be one of them.
In a field by the school, there were bales of hay.
I remember inkwells.
That was perhaps a harder day.

Did you hear the bells ringing?

I keep trying to remember.
Somehow I learned to write my way round things.
The teacher made circles on the blackboard
and none of us said a word. Rubble,
then revelation: inside, we were stumbling.
And at the end of the day we all went home.

Did you all survive?

We will never sit in such places again.
A father chasing his small daughter,
both of them laughing.

The girl, a toddler, was calling out, No, no, Matilda!
Perhaps she knew the song from somewhere
but I think that must have been her name.

Eamonn Marra

Dog Farm, Food Game

I met Abby when we were both sad, on the sad part of the internet. Some people don't realise there is a sad part of the internet, and others claim that all parts of the internet are sad, and that happy people just don't spend that much time on the internet. They're both wrong, the internet is not inherently sad, but there are some parts that are sadder than others. Sad people attract each other and form a whole internet galaxy held together by gravitational sadness. The sad part of the internet is where sad people feel normal. It's easy to fall in love on the sad part of the internet. It's easy to connect with others who feel the same internal dread. It's easy to be charming when all punctuation is flirtatious. First you favourite each other's depression jokes—humour that is hilarious to the sad, but scary to the happy—then you message casually, then obsessively, and then you have cam sex.

The first time we had cam sex it was fast and silent. We didn't want to speak so the others in our respective houses wouldn't hear what we were up to, which is how we kept talking for our entire relationship. We turned on our webcams, and soon her top was off and I typed 'wow' on my keyboard. I pulled my pants down around my knees and got my cock out of my underwear. I tried to find a position for my laptop where my cam would show both my cock and my face, but it was impossible in that moment.

'Do you want to see my cock or my face?' I typed.

'Are you going to feel bad about whatever I don't say?' she typed back.

'No.'

'Cock then.'

I tipped my laptop screen forward to focus on that, then further forward again so my double chin wouldn't be in shot.

'Can I see your . . .' I said.

'No, not today,' she said.

She played with her nipples and put her fingers in her mouth, then it was over and I came into my hand and showed her my handful of cum.

'Was that good for you?' I asked.

'Yeah. It was great,' she said.

I went and got myself cleaned up, and when I got back to the computer she was still there. She was still beautiful after I came, even with her clothes back on, sitting in a pile of messy sheets, waiting for me.

'You're beautiful,' I said.

'I am not,' she said.

'You are honestly one of the prettiest girls I've ever met,' I said.

'You're just saying that because I made you come,' she said.

'Am not,' I said. 'I'm ugly. You're way too pretty for me.'

'I'm as ugly as a hairless cat,' she said. 'You're like a big handsome dog.'

'Let's agree to disagree,' I said.

'I've been reading,' she said. 'To make someone like you, you're meant to tell them a secret the first day you meet them.'

'I already like you,' I said.

'Well I think we should tell each other secrets now,' she said, 'so we keep liking each other.'

'Okay, what's your secret?' I said.

'You have to go first,' she said.

'Why?'

'Because I know you already like me.'

'Do you not already like me?'

'Maybe.'

'Okay. I have to think.'

'Take your time,' she said. As I was thinking, she sent me a photo. In it, she was wearing a red-and-black chequered shirt and cut-off jean shorts. She was lying on the ground covered in puppies—eight of them. She was laughing and had longer hair than she had now, but she looked the same apart from that.

'Cute,' I said. 'Where did you get all those puppies?'

'My parents breed them,' she said. 'But in a good way. It's not a puppy-mill. We're responsible breeders.'

'That is really cool. Are there any puppies around now?'

'No, we got rid of them all. We've got seven dogs though. Three breeding pairs and my one.'

'Okay, I'll type it all in one go so it might take a while,' I said. Her eyes glazed over as I typed and I realised she was checking other websites. 'Here it goes. I went to an all-boys high school, and when I was sixteen it had been three or four years since I had really talked with a girl. So when I started going to parties, there would be these girls there and everyone was acting like it was no big deal. And eventually everyone would get drunk and then people would start making out, and I wanted to be the one to make out with a girl but I had no idea how to do it. I didn't even talk to them, so I'd hover around the people kissing because I thought maybe she would stop kissing him and start kissing the next closest guy, which was me. It was like I was queueing up for a pash.'

It took minutes for her to respond. I was worried that I had scared her away with how pathetic I was but then she said, 'Cute. Did it work?'

'No, of course not.'

'Is that really a secret?' she asked.

'Yeah—well, I've never told anyone that before.'

'You should. It's cute and funny.'

I sent her a picture of me at sixteen. I had hair down past my shoulders and was wearing an oversized suit jacket over a Ramones T-shirt. 'Would you have kissed this?' I asked.

'Probably. I kissed almost anything,' she said.

'Thanks.'

'When did you have your first kiss?' she asked.

'Only like a year ago. A year and a half ago'

'Really?'

'Well that was my first real one, but I'd had like pecks before then.'

'Cute.'

'What about you?'

'I don't remember. When I was fourteen or fifteen I'd get

drunk at parties and kiss everyone. I would have kissed you if you were lining up for it.'

'Damn. I was queueing in the wrong place then.'

'Maybe.'

'What's your secret?'

Three flashing dots appeared on the screen which showed she was typing. Then they disappeared. 'I'll let you know tomorrow,' she said.

'That's not how it works. You have to tell someone the first day you meet.'

'But you already like me,' she said.

I let her get away with it, because the mention of tomorrow was exciting. It was a promise that this was going to keep going.

That night, after eleven hours of talking, we recorded a video of ourselves brushing our teeth. I can't remember whose idea it was. I brushed with my right hand, and held my phone to my chest with my left hand recording the reflection in the mirror. She was left-handed so she did the opposite. I wore a green T-shirt that was the same colour as her bathroom wall. She wore a red jersey that was the same colour as my bathroom wall. I brushed for so long that my gums bled and I smiled through the blood, which matched my walls and her jersey. She sent me her video and I edited them together side by side. We both spat more times than necessary and twice our spitting synced up. I uploaded the video to YouTube as unlisted and sent her the link. I never watched it on YouTube, only ever on my computer, so I could check the play count and see how many times she watched it, assuming she never sent it to anyone else. She had watched it seven times by the next time we talked.

Before I met Abby I had a coping strategy to get through every day. I would binge-watch a TV show on the television. It needed to be something with several seasons and long episodes so that finishing it seemed impossible. Then, once I did finish it, it would feel like I had achieved something. While watching TV, I'd play a video game on my computer. It would need to be something that needed constant attention, but didn't make you think much. Some sort of timed puzzle game where you have to match objects. And while I was doing that, I'd browse the sad part of the internet on my phone. Because of the game and the TV I wouldn't be able to give it enough attention to process the sadness, but it gave me a sense of human connection. I had to do these three things constantly, because as soon as I stopped one, space in my brain would open up to dangerous thoughts. I didn't let myself try to sleep until I was so exhausted that I could fall asleep as soon as I closed my eyes. If I lay in bed before that moment and tried to sleep, space in my brain would open up to dangerous thoughts. As soon as I woke up, my mind would start screaming at me about all the things I hadn't done and needed to do, and the only way to stop it would be to put on the TV show, play the game, and browse the sad part of the internet. I hadn't answered my phone in a month. I hadn't checked my emails in a month. I hadn't gone to university in a month. I was going to keep doing this until things made sense again. Then I met Abby.

With her in America, and me in New Zealand, we were only awake at the same time for part of every day. So to combat this, we developed our own time zone, one where we would never have to be awake without each other. We arranged the time zone so it wouldn't work with any other schedules, so no one could take the other away from us. We set the clocks on our computers to it. Our 9am was NZT 7pm and EST 3am. We would talk for thirteen hours every day until our 10pm, which was NZT 8am and EST 4pm. That gave us eleven hours to sleep and to do anything else we needed to get done. Every morning, I would wake up at 8.30 (our time), get dressed and check the count on the teeth-brushing video. In the first week she watched it on average five times a night.

After a week of our time zone, my flatmates started knocking on my door. 'We haven't seen you for a week, is everything okay?'

'Things are good. I've just got a fucked-up sleep schedule right now,' I told them. And things were good. Abby was good for me. Before Abby, I would spend all day lying down. She made me want to sit up. I looked ugly lying down and I wanted to look good for her. She made me want to change my clothes every day. She made me want to talk to another person, even though we always typed.

We tried talking aloud once, midway through the second week. We whispered into our laptops so no one else could hear and it was weird. We had to get right up close to the computers, and the webcams picked up our acne which had been a blur until then. We both hated our voices, and talking caused too much anxiety to be worth it. She said she sounded like a little kid because she talked naturally with lots of up and downs like she was singing. It was cute and not bad at all but I couldn't convince her of that. I hate my voice because I speak in monotone all the time and I always sound bored. If I try to add energy and add some inflection to my voice, I feel like I'm performing and I get stage fright.

After our failed attempt at talking, the only time I heard Abby's voice was when she talked to her dog Daisy. Daisy was the only dog that I saw, because she was the only one who was allowed in Abby's room. She knew how to get in herself—she stood up on her hind legs, pushed the handle down and leaned on the door to open it.

'Come here, Daisy,' Abby would say in her singsong voice whenever Daisy opened the door. Daisy would sit right on top of Abby and put her head on Abby's shoulders. 'You're a good girl, aren't you Daisy,' Abby said. Daisy wasn't a breeding dog like the others, and was Abby's responsibility. Abby got Daisy when she was a kid so Daisy was now getting old. She had grey hair around her mouth and couldn't jump all the way up to Abby's bed anymore. So when she wanted to get up she'd put her front paws on the bed, and Abby would lean over and pull her up by her armpits.

'When we got her, her name was Gretchen. So that had to change because Gretchen is a terrible name, and since she was mine I got to choose, and I was a kid so I called her Daisy.'

'Do you not like the name Daisy anymore?'

'It's fine, it's just a bit generic. It's better than what Dad would have called her. He called the last dog we got Charisma. That's a stupid name.'

We only turned off our webcams once a day, at 5pm (our time), because Abby didn't want to eat in front of me. I ate baked beans on toast every day because they were fast and cheap. I listened at the kitchen door to make sure my flatmates were not in there before I went in. I put an entire can of baked beans in a bowl and put it in the microwave for four minutes on high. Beans exploded and stuck to the roof of the microwave, and I cleaned them up with a paper towel. I ate them with four pieces of toast. The beans at the bottom of the bowl would always be kind of cold. About once a week I'd go to the supermarket after our day was over and buy seven cans of beans and three loaves of bread. I only ate once a day.

'You never told me your secret,' I said one night after our food break.

'You're my secret,' she said.

'I told you a proper secret,' I said.

'You are my proper secret,' she said. 'If you tell someone a secret it means they'll like you, and if you make someone your secret they'll like you even more. Do you like me?'

'Yeah I do.'

'Then it worked.'

'I told you a real secret though.'

'Yeah, about that, I actually lied the other week,' she said. 'I didn't go to any parties when I was fourteen or fifteen or sixteen or seventeen. I only kissed someone for the first time earlier this year.'

'Why?'

'Because I wanted to be the type of girl that you wanted. Is that a secret enough?'

'But I didn't really want them, I don't know what I wanted. I just wanted someone.'

'Do you want this?' she said and undid a button of her shirt and pulled it open. She traced her fingers around her collarbones.

'Yes please,' I said.

She pushed her computer to the end of the bed, and leaned back against her headboard so I could see her whole body. She was wearing a baggy blue shirt and pink underwear. She put her knees up and spread them apart. She put her hand on top of her underwear and rubbed.

'Wow,' I said. Which is what I said every time we started having cam sex.

She pulled her arms inside her shirt and fumbled around, then took her bra out of one of her sleeves.

I pushed my laptop on an angle so she could see my cock throbbing inside my underwear.

She leaned forward, I saw her breasts inside her shirt as she typed on her computer. 'I want to see your body,' she said.

I pushed my laptop back to the edge of the bed. I positioned myself so my neck was up and stomach was sucked in.

She undid another button on her shirt and pulled one side down to reveal her naked shoulder. She leaned forward again.

'Love that view,' I said.

'Take your T-shirt off,' she said

I took it off, which I hadn't done for her before. I was bloated from the beans; I tried to pull my stomach in and I made sure I was facing the camera exactly front on so that she couldn't see my body's depth.

'Mmmm,' she said, undoing another button. She slowly pulled the shirt to the side, to the edge of her nipple. I pulled my cock out of my underwear and let go of it, showing it standing up firm. The door creaked and she pulled her shirt back, jumped forward and slammed her laptop shut.

I put my T-shirt back on, and put my cock back in my underwear and tried to stop touching myself.

A minute later she called me again and I answered. 'Was just Daisy,' she said. She was sitting cross legged in front of the computer. 'Where were we . . .' She opened her shirt quickly and flashed a breast. Then she closed it again.

'Wow.' I pulled my T-shirt back off and pushed my laptop back to the edge of the bed.

She moved back against the headboard and spread her legs apart again. Daisy was there with her front paws on the bed, next to Abby, waiting to be lifted up. 'Not now Daisy,' Abby said and pushed Daisy down off the bed.

I touched myself through my underwear. Daisy's tail wagged in and out of the corner of the screen. I leaned forward and tried to not let my fat hang as I typed on the computer. 'Sorry, Daisy is distracting me,' I said. 'Can you get her out of your room?'

'Just ignore her,' she said. 'She won't tell anyone.' She sat back down and put her hand inside her underwear. Daisy put her front paws back on the side of the bed. Abby pushed her off with her foot.

'I'm sorry, I just can't. It's weird.'

'She knows how to get back in, she'll just open the door again.'

'Maybe we could do this another time then?' I said.

'There are dogs everywhere here. If you like me you have to get used to the dogs.' She pulled her shoulder back into her shirt and buttoned it all the way up to the top button. Daisy put her feet up on the side of the bed and Abby leaned over and pulled her up.

The conversation for the rest of that day was stunted and we spent most of the time sharing links to funny sad pictures instead of talking. Then we stopped talking completely. We stayed on webcam, but didn't interact. The webcam video was tucked away in the corner of the screen as we browsed the sad part of the internet.

The next morning (our time) I got up and saw she wasn't online. I checked the video view count, and for the first time it hadn't gone up since the night before. I thought I had ruined everything, but then she came online. I tried to call her but she rejected the call.

'Sorry, I'm about to eat,' she said.

'What are you eating? I asked.

'Toast.'

'If I went and made some toast now could we eat together?'

Dots appeared to show she was typing. Then they disappeared, then she said, 'k.'

I rushed into the kitchen. One of my flatmates was in there.

'Well well well,' he said. 'He lives.'

'Yeah,' I said. 'I'm okay.' I threw four pieces of bread into the toaster and set it to two so it would be done fast.

'What have you been doing?' he asked.

'You know, just depression stuff,' I said. He looked at me and looked concerned. 'I'm kidding. I've been working on something. Something for uni. I'm catching back up. I'm actually quite happy right now.'

'Good. We're here for you if you need to talk.'

The toast popped; it had barely been warmed. I put big lumps of peanut butter on each piece, then tried to spread it. The bread ripped in several places. 'I've got to go,' I said and took the plate into my room.

I ran back to my laptop and called Abby again. She answered this time. She was sitting cross-legged on her bed with a small plate with a single piece of toast on it, thinly spread with jam and butter.

'Have you already started?' I asked.

'No. I don't eat much,' she said.

I felt very ashamed of my four pieces of warm bread, thick with peanut butter.

'Okay, should we eat then?' she said.

'Yeah okay.' She nibbled on her toast. Chewing dozens of times for each small bite. I folded my bread in half and took big bites, and swallowed it fast. I finished my four pieces of bread before she finished her one. We didn't talk while eating.

'That was weird,' she said.

'I liked it,' I said. 'I miss you when I eat.'

'Me too,' she said. 'But with you.'

'Let's keep doing this,' I said.

'Okay,' she said. She put her plate on the table next to her bed.

'Sorry about yesterday,' I said.

'No, it's okay. I get really defensive about Daisy sometimes.'

'It's just, I think I was feeling a bit uncomfortable about my body.'

'You shouldn't feel bad. I like your body,' she said. 'My dad has always been really mean to Daisy.'

'I think I've always got really worked up about my body. I've always blamed my body for my lack of luck with girls.'

'You're a big handsome dog,' she said. 'I bet lots of girls like you.'

'I have this weird thing. When I like a girl, I never tell her. I just assume there is no way she could like me. Then when I get drunk, I tell her, but I phrase it as an apology, like—I'm sorry I like you.'

'I like that you tell me that you like me. Now tell me you like Daisy.'

'I like Daisy. Tomorrow I'm going to start walking,' I said, 'I need to get into shape. My doctor keeps telling me that getting exercise will help me feel better.'

'I run every day,' she said. 'I take Daisy. Dad makes me, he says she's my responsibility and if she's not breeding it's not his job to look after her.'

'What? When do you run? You never told me that,' I said.

'You never asked,' she said.

'When do you go?'

'After we finish talking. For half an hour. Then I go to sleep.'

'I'll go then too. So we'll be exercising at the same time.'

'Did you know walking isn't really exercise?' she said. 'It doesn't get your heart rate to the cardio level you need in order to lose weight. It's pretty much worthless.'

'I'll walk up a hill,' I said.

'In fact, walking is worse than worthless, because after you trick yourself into thinking you did exercise when you actually didn't, you treat yourself, and you end up eating more calories than you burned off.'

'Yeah, maybe I should jog instead. That's probably a better idea.'

'The best way to deal with weight is dieting,' she said. 'It's easier to not let the calories in in the first place than it is to burn them.'

'Yeah, I'm trying to eat less,' I said. 'Maybe now that we eat together we can do that together.'

'Sorry,' she said. 'You don't have to. This is all about my own bad feelings.'

'No, I want to,' I said.

'As long as I'm running, and looking after Daisy, my parents leave me alone. They think I'm okay.'

After we finished talking that night, I went for a run for the first time in my life. I could only run for about a minute, then I had to walk for two or three minutes before catching my breath. It was 8am and there were lots of other joggers running at the same time and they all looked at me with pity. I turned around to go home, but the thought of Abby running at the same time made me continue.

I came home and had a shower, and ran into my flatmate when I was coming out of the bathroom.

'Have you been running?' he said.

'Yeah, the doctor said I should,' I said.

'I guess that's good,' he said. 'Good work.'

'Yeah. I gotta go to bed now. Haven't slept yet,' I said.

I went back to bed and struggled to sleep. I had too much energy in my blood, and I felt like I had to keep shaking all my limbs. I walked to the petrol station near my house and bought an ice cream. I wouldn't tell Abby about this because we were only meant to eat with each other.

Abby and I ate twice a day. Each time, one piece of toast with peanut butter. I tried to spread it thin, but it always looked thick compared to hers. It was an unspoken competition who could eat it slowest. We sat in silence, sitting cross-legged in front of the computer, staring at the webcam, with a small plate in our laps. I took small bites and counted my chews: thirty for each bite. By the thirtieth chew, the toast had completely disintegrated and I was chewing saliva, then I'd swallow. Somehow she still always won.

'Sorry I'm such a slow eater,' she said, but it didn't matter because she was beautiful when she was eating. She sucked the crumbs off the ends of her fingers.

'I am getting better at running,' I told her. 'I can run for five minutes without stopping now.' It was a lie, but it would be true soon.

I stood up and took my plate to a table across the room. I did this so my crotch would be in shot and Abby would see that I had an erection without it looking intentional. She either didn't notice it or ignored it, so we didn't have cam sex that day.

'Did your parents ever do things that messed you up, but they never really knew?' Abby asked when I got back to my bed. 'Like things that hurt you real bad and they never realised how much?'

'Yeah, definitely,' I said. 'I've been thinking about this for a while. When I was a little kid, I really wanted a desk. Because my parents got my brother a desk when he started school, when he was five, so I would have been three and I wanted one too.'

'My one is about Daisy.' Abby said. 'We actually originally got Daisy as a breeding dog. We got her all the way from Canada to widen the gene pool.'

'But isn't Canada right there?' I said.

'Yeah but it's a whole other country. We had to do paperwork and everything.'

'Anyway Mum told me, "You don't need a desk, you've got this coffee table,"' I said.

'But what happened was, she was only two or three, and we organised a breeding partner for her. And she got pregnant, and when the puppies were born they were completely white with red eyes.'

'Because in my bedroom there was a coffee table. It was painted bright green and it was really smooth. I used to sit there and touch it and feel how smooth it was.'

'They were all blind. Dad took them and shot them all. I heard the shots from my bedroom.'

'So I thought that this coffee table was mine and I really loved it. Then when Mum and Dad got divorced, Mum took the table with her to her new house.'

'And the breeding partner dog, he had perfectly fine puppies with another dog, so the problem was with Daisy.'

'And I was fine with it, because Mum's new house was empty so I thought it was okay for me to let her borrow my coffee table for a while.'

'Dad was so angry. We had to pay thousands of dollars for her to come here and she was worthless to him.'

'So my table was in the lounge at Mum's house. Then one day the table disappeared for a while and it came back sanded down. They got rid of the green paint and varnished it.'

'But Mom convinced him to give her another go, so the next year she bred again, and the same thing happened. All white with red eyes again. And he shot them all again.'

'I was so annoyed no one asked me. Because it was my table and they changed it and got rid of the smooth green paint without even asking me.'

'And I loved Daisy, more than any of the other dogs, I guess because we got her right when I was the perfect age. I called her Daisy from the beginning, but Dad called her Gretchen still. He wanted to shoot her too.'

'I didn't make a fuss because it did look nice varnished and it was better suited in the lounge than in my bedroom.'

'I cried for days and days and Mom and Dad had a big fight, and Mom convinced him to let Daisy stay. But Dad told me she was my pet, and my responsibility, and he wouldn't walk her or feed her or take her to the vet.'

'Then when my stepdad moved in—he always put his feet up on it and would move it around. And I never liked him anyway, but that really annoyed me, how disrespectful he was about it.'

'They got her spayed so she couldn't accidentally have any more pups. I had to walk her every day. And I had to feed her. Dad wanted me to pay for her food myself, but I didn't have any money so he said that I'd just have to give her half of all my food.

And I did for a while. Mom was furious when she found out Dad told me that.'

'Then one day I came home from school and the table had gone completely and there was a new one. And no one had consulted me about it. And I said, "What happened to my table?" and my stepdad laughed at me and said, "It wasn't your table," like it was his table.'

'Dad still hates her. When I went to college last year he told me I had to take her with me. But Mom let her stay and looked after her. Since I've been back she's with me again. That's why I got so defensive about her last week.'

'But the table was there before he was, and it was mine. And now that I think about it, it probably wasn't mine, it was my mum's, but it still made me feel useless, like me and my things weren't important. I think that was the day that I stopped feeling at home in that house.'

'My story was worse,' she said.

'Yeah, it probably was,' I said.

Then one day, after five weeks of our time zone, she said, 'I have to go back to college next week.'

'Okay,' I said. 'What does that mean for us?'

'I don't know. I need to start sleeping at proper times soon though.'

'Will you still talk to me?' I asked.

'I'll try.'

'I need to go back to school too. I have probably failed the year but I'll talk to my teachers and my doctor and see what I can do.'

'Please do,' she said.

'I am going to miss you,' I said. 'You're looking good today by the way.'

'Am I?' she said and smiled. She pushed her laptop to the bottom of her bed, kicked up her legs and slowly pulled her shorts off.

'Wow,' I said.

She leaned forward to type, and I saw her bra through the

hanging neck of her T-shirt. 'Sorry,' she said. She shut her laptop. She didn't come back online that day.

The next day she sent me a message. 'I can't do this anymore. I'm going to block you for a while, just until I get things sorted. Please don't delete me.' Then she appeared offline.

I checked the view count on the brushing video every day. It went up by one every day, but I wasn't sure if that was from me checking on it, or her watching it. I paused the video before it even started playing, so I didn't think it was me. Some days it went up by two, which was a nice feeling. Then it stopped going up at all.

Kirsten McDougall

Clean hands save lives

No, I said.

The eldest was climbing over the front seat and standing on the shopping and I was buckling the baby in at an angle where my back would go any second and it was stinking hot. The sort of heat where you want to shave all the hair off your head and body and lie on the bathroom floor.

You can't have a biscuit until we get home and you wash your hands, I said.

We'd just lost a week to puking and loose bowels. I wasn't risking another round. I'd given in and bought the biscuits. I was weak, and in need of some peace and quiet.

Fuck you, said my first born.

The one that took thirty-six hours and a knife to come out.

I looked him square to make sure I'd heard right. He's only four. He had that look, the one handed down from his mother and his mother's mother. A heavy-lidded self-righteousness.

The two-year-old started banging his feet against the back of my seat and calling out, Mine! Bicksit! Mine!

That's the thing with the youngest; they can't even talk properly, yet they have an instinct for fueling a situation. I did my best impression of my mother.

No one is having anything until everyone has washed their hands, I said.

Hear that voice—I was no one's mother, just a maniac with a hygiene fetish. The idea was growing in me, taking on a greater importance than it deserved. In the interests of peace, I should have let it go but I wasn't that flexible. I was the iron rod of law. I was a failure of imagination. After all, I argued to myself, clean hands save lives. But here we go, they're both crying, even the four-year-old, who should have been quietly anxious.

Right. No one is having any biscuits, I said.

This only increased the volume.

A car pulled up beside us, with some friends in it. They don't have children. As a consequence they don't drink until six o'clock and have good digestion. They smiled and waved. I smiled and waved back. My heart wasn't in it. All the windows were down, so everyone could hear the kids indulging their sense of injustice.

Lucy said something to me. I saw her lips move but I couldn't hear a word over the racket.

I held up my hands to show her it was no use.

There was dirt under my nails and the fake tan I'd slapped on that morning had developed into orangey blooms between my knuckles. It was my attempt at personal grooming. I'd read it in the Sunday magazine—shave years and kilos off with fake tan! Having said that, my hands have always been a bit wrinkly. A boyfriend once held them up like specimens and called them little chimp hands.

Lucy, who is English and always polite, touched her smooth hair with her white hand. I realised at once that the magazine was wrong and Lucy was right.

She said something to Grant, probably something like—You see—and they smiled again and waved goodbye.

I reversed the car out of its park.

We drove home the long way, around the sea. I wanted to give us some horizon to focus on. We were on the edge of a beautiful city. The south coast, where I'm trying to grow these baby mongrels into happy men, looks like the sea ripped the land off with its bare teeth. Ships had sunk off here. Fishermen died. Once walking the baby, I found a dead penguin. I wanted the kids to know this, to offer up a wider perspective and find a way through the developing bad mood. I've also discovered that sometimes if you surprise a crying child with information, they go quiet.

I pulled the car over and pointed at the water pump station.

This is where they put the ship wreck victims, I said.

The four-year-old sniffed and said, What? The two-year-old almost stopped crying and looked at the four-year-old.

When their boats smash on the rocks and they have to swim ashore, I said.

I was emphatic about the smashing.

They've lost all their worldly possessions and half their families, and this is where they stay, I said. I gave a little sniff too.

We could all feel it; a wave washing over our car. We held a brief, respectful silence. That's a good thing about kids, the way they'll readily change direction.

The four-year-old looked suspicious. What do they eat? he said.

He is practical, with an instinct for survival. He'll go far, even with me as his mother.

Biscuits, I said.

I unbuckled the kids and we walked over to the dangerous rocks. I lifted them up and we sat in the afternoon sun, our bare arms turning red. The sea breeze lifted our hair which is exactly the same colour so that's what we looked like—three in a row, a family.

We were quiet while we chewed on a few biscuits. The Interislander was coming in. It was shining and almost too bright to watch. I let the kids tip the rest of the biscuits onto the rocks, in case it sank.

Aorewa McLeod

The Harmonious Development of Man
Chapter 1 of a novel

1959

At first I was placed at the end of a conveyor belt, packing ice cream lollies with sticks and lurid paper wrappers into cartons. The older women beside me packed swiftly, their hands blurring with the speed, but I was slow and inept and the ice cream lollies piled up, finally spilling onto the floor.

'I think dear,' said the forewoman, as she shuffled through the spilt lollies, 'that I'll move you to icing ice cream cakes. That's the elite end of the factory. And you can be as slow as you are. Now, you pick up the lollies from the floor and take them to the bin out the back. Rosie here will take your place.'

How kind they were. I'd expected to be fired for incompetency and here I was, proud of my pre-Christmas holly decorations, my calligraphic swirls as I laboriously wrote *Happy Birthday Johnny* in pale blue, or *Happy Birthday Mary* in pastel pink.

It was a summer of roses—cream, pink, yellow, scarlet—pouring over fences, cascading down trellises, climbing up drainpipes. School was finished with forever. We walked to the factory from our flat in Sandringham through the scent and petals. Every Thursday we got our money in a brown paper envelope with a pay slip inside. Real money; folded notes and jingling coins that you could see through the holes punched in the envelope. Every Friday, as a bonus, we could take home a quart of ice cream, any flavour, wrapped in newspaper. I liked hokey-pokey best, with its tiny crunchy honeycomb candy balls dotted through the vanilla. I'd eat my way through the quart every Friday night. My four friends would make their more sedate choices, like chocolate or Neapolitan, last for the whole week. It was many years before I could eat ice cream again.

One of the group, Jane, didn't flat with us. She lived with her mother near the ice cream factory. She'd been good at maths as well as English and was school dux and head prefect. We all liked her anyway. Often all five of us went to lunch at her mother's flat where we devoured a huge bowl of steamed green beans fresh from the garden. It was the best food I had ever tasted. We didn't often have vegetables at home and they were always old. That summer I alternated between feeling queasy from hokey-pokey and the relish of those beans, soaked in butter, both against a background of the scent of roses. An odd mixture, not altogether comfortable.

Jane's mother was divorced, which was romantic. None of us knew anyone else who had divorced parents. But she was a short stubby grey-haired ex-farm woman, which was not at all romantic. Whereas Jane's father was most romantic. He was a Welsh remittance man who seemed dashingly bohemian to us flatmates. His name was Herman and he rented a red brick two-storey terrace house in Wynyard Street just down from the University. We gave up our suburban flat, where the four of us had shared one bedroom, and moved in.

Herman belonged to an esoteric philosophic group based on Ouspensky and Gurdjieff and we used to go together to their meetings. Ouspensky was the disciple of Gurdjieff, a mystic philosopher from Armenia with impressive curled mustachios in the frontispiece to his book. Their philosophy was a mixture of Zen Buddhism, psychotherapy and Christian mysticism. I read his *Fourth Way* in bed at night with the same diligence I applied to my zoology texts. I hoped I would develop a higher level of consciousness, some sort of spiritual wakening.

'Self-remembering', Gurdjieff called it. Katherine Mansfield had been a disciple of Gurdjieff, had in fact died at his 'Institute for the Harmonious Development of Man'. I couldn't decide if this was in Gurdjieff's favour or not. The leader/guru of the Auckland group was a short, fat, red-faced, retired engineer from India, a kind of modern Buddha, who chuckled as he read from Gurdjieff and made enigmatic, wise-sounding statements about how to lead a transcendental life: 'Man lives his life in sleep and in sleep he dies', which led onto 'When one realises one is asleep at that moment one is already half awake.'

I felt humble and inferior as I sat on a hard wooden chair in the circle of acolytes in the dimly lit room swathed in scarlet curtains. I was sure I was asleep, and that he seemed to be chuckling because what he was saying would be obvious if only I were higher on the evolutionary self-development scale. The other flatmates seemed more impressed by Ouspensky and Gurdjieff than I was. I supposed they were more spiritual than me. I couldn't find any inner certainty, any awareness of the purpose of it all, which they seemed to have.

My boyfriends came and went. None lasted very long. Waiting for the bloodstains to appear, and panicking about being pregnant was a monthly phenomenon. No way did I want to end up like my mother. Jane and the flatmates said it would be good for me to go out with a fellow Gurdjieff disciple: plump. thirtyish, Brylcreemed mathematician Leonard, who sniggered rather than chuckled when the guru pronounced. He talked to me about inner growth and self-development and after a few outings to movies and on bush-walks, we slept together on the sofa in his flat. He had difficulty putting the condom on as his penis was only half-aroused and I had to help him press it into me. I disliked the feel of his fingers, slimy with anti-contraceptive cream, squeezing himself in. I felt claustrophobic, imprinted into the lumpy sofa, under his continual wet kisses. He was heavy and sweaty on top of me. I was worried the condom might slide off, and despite his moans I didn't think he had come. I didn't feel I knew him well enough to ask him.

The next day was clear and sunny, an inappropriately beautiful day after the night before, and he took me on the back of his 150cc motorbike to an east coast beach. He had a flagon of golden Dalmatian sherry in his saddlebag and we lay on the sand against the marram grass, with a peanut butter jar each, drinking our way through it. The mathematician had a sweet tooth. I was thinking about how to tell him I didn't want to go out with him again without being impolite about the unpleasant sex, when he proposed to me with semi-drunken sincerity, frowning and pursing his lips.

'We only have a few moments of true self-awareness. This is one and last night was another of them. We will work together to increase them. I asked Gregory and he thinks you would suit me.' Gregory was the guru.

The sun had warmed me and the sherry had made me feel pleasantly woozy, but in no way numinous or spiritual. Leonard was not attractive or sexy and last night had been a damp fiasco. His hair was untouchably greasy. Gregory had a nerve mating us up and Leonard had been presumptuous asking Gregory about my suitability.

When my friends next went to the Ouspensky–Gurdjieff group I refused to go with them. When Leonard rang I told them to say I was studying and mustn't be disturbed. After this I went out with a fellow student named Colin, whom I met at the Film Society. He supposed there must be a God and an afterlife, but was not particularly concerned about either and certainly couldn't describe them. He believed one should be a virgin until marriage so being with him was restful.

The flatmates and I also tried the Church of the Golden Light and the Spiritualist Church. The Church of the Golden Light was in New North Road, just opposite Tongue's Funeral Parlour. It was a small nondescript brick building, painted white with amber glass windows. The Spiritualist Church, which was upstairs in a photographer's studio, seemed to have interchangeable congregations and mediums with the Golden Light. As far as I could work out from their sermons the main difference was that the Church of the Golden Light thought their spirits were unhappy and in limbo, needing to communicate before they could move on, whereas the Spiritualists were more optimistic and felt their spirit guides had altruistically returned from a higher level to help us. The mediums were grey-haired women, who would give a short exposition on the souls who still surrounded us, trying so desperately to be heard. Then they would stare intently around the congregation, finally saying who was there with a message for whom.

The departed soul would be standing behind the person focused on. The waiting made the atmosphere dense with anticipation. I once felt a presence behind my right shoulder. I didn't dare turn round and look, but the medium didn't notice it. I had thought it might be God, although I was scared it could have been my father. I had always hoped for a message—it would be a relief to know there was life after death—but was terrified I might receive one. Liz once got an elderly man whom she thought could have been her great-uncle. He was worried about her. There was indeed a lot to worry about in Liz's life, but the spirit was never more specific. Several times Maria got a Māori warrior in a grass skirt and feather cloak with a mere, telling her to stand strong. But since Maria was dark skinned because of her Spanish mother, it was my opinion that the spirit had got confused and had intended to stand behind someone else.

All my friends had been brought up with some sort of conventional religious belief which they had all rejected. Each was searching for a more alternative one. I assumed my father's atheist indoctrination had proved the validity of the Jesuit maxim: 'Give me a child until he is seven and I will give you the man,' and had left me permanently stranded on godless shores. I wanted some sort of belief, wanted the comfort and security of being able to say, like Jane, 'Of course there is a God. I know it.'

If only my parents had pretended that Matthew, Mark, Luke and John had protected the bed I lay upon. Instead, my father had taken me and my brother out from the warm comfort of our beds onto the back lawn and told us about the geological clock. We were tiny specks on a tiny insignificant planet on the edge of one of many galaxies, waiting for the end. 'We're right on the edge of the outside of the Milky Way,' he said, 'the cold of nothingness at our backs, and soon our sun will go out and that will be it for mankind. One day our universe itself will be wiped out. But don't worry, you will both be dead long before that. Your death is just as certain as the irrefutable fact that you'll wake up tomorrow.'

The sky was crowded with thousands of galaxies, infinitely distant but pressing down upon me as I pressed up against my father's legs. When I was depressed I knew that less than a second separated me from the black cold of oblivion, that one day everything I knew would cease to exist as I ceased to be conscious. When I was a small pigtailed girl clutching my heavy woollen blankets around me so that nothingness could not get in through any accidental openings, I was afraid to go to sleep in case I never woke up. I had to stay awake. Fifteen years later, under my down comforter I was still afraid to go to sleep. The flatmates looked puzzled when I tried to explain this. They were fascinated by the various forms of belief, but could not comprehend unbelief.

Living in Jane's father's house meant we spent hours sitting round the dining table drinking coffee and talking. In our third year at university Jane's father married a woman not much older than us and moved into the bush where he built a gloomy log cabin lined with esoteric philosophy books and Russian novels. She had a pale thin mean face and none of us liked her much. Every time we went out to visit Herman in the dense second-growth bush there was a new disgusting, wet, grubby, baby. It must have been hard for her with no electricity and no running water but we thought she was not worthy of Herman, who smoked a pipe and had a beard and would talk to us for hours. No one else's father had a beard, or read philosophy, or would talk to us as if we were rational beings.

As soon as exams finished, four of us drove in Liz's sputtering V-Dub down to Nelson. An ex-schoolmate's father was someone high up in the mental health service and he had suggested that nurse-aiding in psychiatric hospitals was a lucrative way of earning money in the holidays. And it was. Double-time, time-and-a-half, triple-time at Christmas and New Year. We applied at the mental health offices and were allotted positions down in Nelson. None of us had been to the South Island, so it seemed as if it would be a holiday as well as a way to make money.

We were given rooms in the Nurses' Home and each allotted a bundle of starched pink uniforms with white collars and two stiff white nurses' caps. There were three sizes. Medium was too tight, so I had the large size uniform and had to bunch it up under a safety-pinned belt, which was humiliating as I didn't think of myself as fat.

I'd read Janet Frame's just-out *Faces in the Water* and had assumed mental hospitals would be like that—'the raging mass of people performing their violent orchestration of unreason'—but the first thing we naïve nurse aides were told was that we would not be working with the mentally disturbed. They put us in the hospital in town, which contained badly handicapped children in two wards and senile old ladies in another. We didn't know where the senile old men were. Were there any? I was first put in the ward with the bed-ridden children. It was a long room with three rows of large cots and big windows, too high for anybody outside to look in. At first I could not comprehend the reality of what I was seeing; it was like something out of some impossibly cruel horror film. Most of the children were grossly deformed. There were enormous cephalic water heads, tiny pinheads, huge slobbering mouths, bent bodies, contorted hands waving in the air, grasping blindly, clutching as if there was something to reach for. They could grip me with such desperate strength that I had to pry their fingers off. Many were blind. I couldn't tell how old they were.

'He's twenty-one,' the head nurse said of one boy whose rigid body was set in a foetal position. 'He came here as a baby. Here, put your hands under him and lift. He's not heavy.'

I did. He was completely stiff; his twisted limbs were tight, with yellowed skin covering skeletal bones. He was so light I was scared I might drop him and he was twenty-one, the same age as me. I turned him as directed and put him down in the reverse position. I did it three times a day. Nurse gave me a bowl of soapy water, a shaving brush and a safety razor and told me to shave him. I'd never shaved anyone before, not even my own legs, so my hands shook. After I'd nicked him twice the nurse said,

'Here, I'll do it. Don't worry about it. He doesn't bleed much. Not much blood there. You just wash him down. Can't do much damage with that. Not too much soap and try not to get the sheets too wet.'

Like the others he needed constant changing, wiping down and encasing in huge nappies. We threw the soiled cloths into canvas containers suspended on frames on wheels, and an aide in a brown uniform would take them away at the end of each shift. Someone, somewhere, must have hosed them down and washed them. Some, not many, of the children could stand, clutching onto their cot or the nurse, and stagger blindly for a few steps, but the nurses were usually too busy changing the sodden nappies or wiping the faecal, shrivelled bottoms to encourage this. They'd pick them up and plonk them back in their cots.

'You don't want them underfoot, dragging on us. We've enough to do without falling over them.'

There were three nurses on each eight-hour shift. We'd start at the top of the row and work our way down, then, if there was time, start over again. It was exhausting, filthy work. I had to keep asking advice: 'She's got a raw rash on her bottom. What should I do?'

The other nurses were patient with me.

'That cream there, on the trolley, that'll do for anything where the skin's broken. Happens all the time. Constant abrasion. Don't worry about it.'

The only regular events were feeding times, when a kitchen aide in a green uniform wheeled in a stainless-steel bin from the main kitchens, ten minutes away. They'd stop for a smoke on the way so the food arrived barely lukewarm. All the staff, nurses and aides, smoked whenever they could.

'Just off for a fag. Back in a minute.'

The food was soft pap. Sometimes mashed potato or scrambled eggs were distinguishable. A few children would grunt and slaver with excitement at the sound of the approach of food, but many had to have their mouths pried open and the food spooned in. They'd often spit it out onto the white wrap-around aprons we wore, or let it dribble out. They could bite, clamping down with astonishing strength. After being caught a few times I would insert the spoon, scrape it against the usually decaying teeth or the bare gums of the upper jaw and whip it out quickly. I asked the head nurse whether some of the moans and screams might come from toothache.

'You must remember they don't feel pain the way we do. The dentist comes to do extractions once a year. Messy business. They have to be knocked out of course. Anaesthetised. Don't worry about it.'

'Don't worry about it' was the nurses' refrain.

We were usually too tired to do more than shower and collapse on our beds after finishing our shifts. We comforted one another by adding up how much money we were making. We kept repeating the nurses' comment that they don't feel the way we do. I wasn't at all sure I believed that. I was willing to believe it of the oysters I swallowed fresh off their shells, they had a different nervous system. But I felt the children might feel it more and be unable to tell us. Maria couldn't stand it and left. I went down with her to the small grubby bus stop in the centre of Nelson where we embraced clumsily and I patted her back while she snuffled, mumbling, 'We're only twenty. We shouldn't know that there's life like this. What if I have a child and it's like them? The money's not worth it.'

In the two months I was on the children's wards no one came to visit. I wasn't surprised. If my child were one of these I would not want to visit. It confirmed my belief that there was no way I would have a child.

One thing that made life at the hospital more bearable was the trellises laden with sweet peas outside the ward and the nurses' home windows. Bright, fragrant, variegated colours and wafts of scent against the garish blue summer sky. I'd inhale them when I walked to the ward in the morning, hoping my increasingly grubby uniform would last another day. The flowers hinted at something more than the rows of befouled ugliness in the wards. Thin consolation though.

Then I was moved to the old women's ward.

'Short staffed here, nurse, too many taking Christmas time off.'

I thought the old women would be preferable but they upset me even more. The women, Mrs Norman, Mrs Guard, Mrs DeJeune, thirty of them, had once lived normal lives, had loved, had been married, borne children, baked and iced cakes. Now they were mindless. Or their minds had gone somewhere else, into incommunicable depths from which they would never surface. Most were silent. Some chattered incessantly and meaninglessly. Some were tied to their beds to prevent them escaping, looking for the home that was long in the past. Most were incontinent.

On morning shift, I pulled back the bedclothes and lifted their legs up and put their feet onto the floor. I guided them, holding an arm, to the communal bathroom where I showered them, washing between their legs, lifting their flabby breasts to wash underneath, putting antiseptic cream on whichever bits were festering in the heat. Then I'd help them dress, pulling the clothes over their head, supporting them as I lifted their legs for the bloomers.

'How do I know which are their clothes?' I asked the nurse the first time.

Some items in the pile of crumpled clothes had nametags, but the names had faded into blurs with the ferocious washings of the industrial strength washing machines. 'Doesn't matter,' said the nurse, 'they don't care. Just check they're big enough. Don't worry about it. There's a bundle of new bloomers if the elastic's gone.'

On my first evening shift the nurse told me to collect the teeth and clean them. Almost all the women had dentures. I brushed away the soft yellowing detritus. The children's ward had hardened me against gagging at the smell, and then I rinsed them clean. 'Oh dear,' said the nurse, 'you should have put their names on their mugs.' I woke in the night worrying about those women, with the wrong teeth that didn't fit, uncomfortable in their mouths, rubbing on their gums. I woke worrying years later, long after the women would have died. The nurse didn't seem worried about it though. 'That's the way the cookie crumbles,' she'd said. I'd never heard anyone except my American mother use that phrase.

Once a niece visited, but she couldn't pick out which was her aunt from the group of baggy, wrinkled women in faded dresses sitting outside the ward. They all had red-black, sun-hardened faces from months, years sitting alongside the ward wall. I had to go fetch the head nurse who took the niece to a Mrs Guard. The niece stared, tried to smile, went up to her and said, 'Hello Auntie Gwen, remember me, I'm little Gwen, your sister Doris's daughter. Doris and Hughie.' She put her bunch of flowers on Mrs Guard's knee and backed away from her aunt's vacant unrecognising stare.

'Hasn't been before,' said the nurse. 'She won't be back.'

Back in Auckland I was dazed. Those three months had been so vivid, so real, so appalling. We were all quiet and we avoided telling horrifying or amusing anecdotes to our friends who'd worked in factories or shops. We had to find a new flat. All the student flats, shut up over summer, were full of flea eggs waiting for us to hatch them. The eggs would lie there between the cracks of the wooden floors, under the carpet squares, waiting for the thump of our feet. As the one who felt there were a lot worse things than fleas, I would volunteer to take off my jeans, walk round the prospective flat, stamping heavily. Then they'd hatch and spring up, heading for the blood they needed. But they were newly born and confused so it was easy for me to pick them off my legs, while I stood in cold water in the bath tub.

I had to forget the implications of the summer holiday, get rid of fleas, begin to learn Anglo-Saxon, read very long eighteenth-century novels and mate fruit flies. And I did forget, until

November and the end of exams, when we were due down in Nelson again.

Those wards contained a truth about the short time I was going to be alive, far beyond anything Ouspensky or the spiritualists or the churches could offer me. What did it mean when Jane said, 'Of course there is a God. I know it'? How could she reconcile that belief with those children, those women? Jane didn't go back, despite the money we'd all made, which meant we could buy small cheap cars and expensive books, smoke Sobranie Black Russians and drive out to the Western vineyards to buy flagons of Dally plonk. Next summer, it was only me and Liz who drove my Morris Minor across the flat tobacco-growing plains from Picton to Nelson, eating juicy red-black cherries out of brown paper bags and spitting their pips out the car window.

The letter confirming our appointment told us to go three miles beyond Nelson, through the village of Stoke and up the Stoke Valley. The valley was among low, round hills whose grass was cardboard-coloured burnt ochre, even this early in the summer. Stretching up the valley were six buildings, which we learned were called villas, a nurses' home and an administration block.

'You're in Villa 2,' said the administrator, a short, very fat woman with a gigantic monobrow. 'The matron is Sister MacFarland. She's strict, but as long as you keep on the right side of her you'll be tickety-boo.' She handed Liz and me each a bundle of pink uniforms. 'We seem to have run out of belts, but don't worry, you'll be fine.'

Next morning Sister MacFarland, tall, narrow and tight-lipped, took me to meet the more important patients.

'Maggie, she runs the kitchen, don't you Maggie?'

Maggie, fiftyish and chunky, grinned and said, 'I do too.'

'And Shirley, she's head gardener, aren't you Shirl?' Shirley's flabby mouth worked and she mumbled something indistinguishable.

'And here's Annie, she's in control of the laundry. We're practically self-sufficient here. Annie's such a hard worker.'

Annie ducked her head and offered me a swollen, reddened hand.

'Now, we don't need that do we Annie? Nurse is a nurse, not a visitor. And nurse, make sure you have a belt on tomorrow. We have to keep up standards.'

There were thirty-two patients, all women, and they all seemed able, with some encouragement, to wash and dress themselves. They all had tasks, which Sister Mac read from a roster at breakfast each morning. There was a certain amount of chivvying for the nurses to do, to find the patient doing the task, say, peeling potatoes or cleaning toilets, and then to watch as they did it. However, after last summer, this was a friendly, even convivial environment. The patients were either jovial, trying to ingratiate themselves with the staff, or somnolent, as they dozed, drugged on lithium, on benches or sofas.

My first job was to cut long strips out of sheets of gold tinsel paper and, balancing on a wobbly ladder, tack them in a criss-cross pattern over all the wooden panels of the dining room. Then I had to add a sprig of tinsel holly to the centre of each diamond. It was like icing ice cream cakes and it took several days. This was more than a month before Christmas but Sister Mac liked to see the ward looking festive 'bright and early'. The Christmas tree from the forest up the valley had already arrived, brought by a work party from the male villa, with their male nurse.

The next day I was assigned outdoors supervision. It was sunny so I sat beside the swimming pool, supposedly supervising some of the younger women splashing in the shallow end. What a cushy job this is. Then I saw the head of a mongol girl going under, surfacing, going under, at the deep end. I ran to the edge and jumped in, pushing her to the steps. The other nurse, hearing the shrieks and laughter—'Look, look at nursie. She's in the water!'—strolled out. 'Oh dear. Now you'll have to go and get changed. Don't worry; I'll hold the fort. Sister should have told you she always does this—she's like a balloon—unsinkable. You just need to grab her hair and drag her along.'

I had momentarily felt heroic. Now, as I went dripping to

change, I repeated to myself, 'Think before you act. Think before you act.'

On Christmas day the head nurse from the male ward came, outfitted as Father Christmas, with a Ho-ho-ho and a lop-sided cotton-wool beard and a pillowcase of presents chosen by Sister Mac. Maggie had prepared a lunch of roast chicken and Christmas pudding under Sister Mac's close surveillance. Relatives were invited but only one couple came, the tiny tentative parents of a very large woman who worked with Shirl in the garden. Maybelle was proud of them. 'These are my mum and dad.' I was shocked. They seemed younger as well as a lot smaller than Maybelle.

'Such nice people,' said Sister Mac. 'They had enough sense to stop. Most don't. They just keep trying. Look at Ruby and Pearl and Emmy. And they have a brother up the valley.' I looked at Ruby and Pearl and Emmeline. I hadn't realised they were sisters. All inarticulate and often incontinent. It was impossible to tell how old they were. No one visited them.

Moana, the other nurse on duty, served the Christmas lunch with me. I got a comb as a present from Father Christmas and swapped it for a plastic Minnie Mouse, before Joannie—'Look. A bloody stupid toy, I'm not a baby'—threw her Minnie Mouse into the ice cream.

I was a wide-eyed innocent compared to the psychiatric nurses. Really wide-eyed, staring at their style and flamboyance and insouciance. They were probably no older than Liz and me but they seemed so much more sophisticated and they were undeniably tough. They'd been through everything we were going through and had come out bravely. The nurses' home reverberated with Elvis and the Everly brothers, Buddy Holly and Johnny Cash, Chuck Berry and Little Richard, played on portable multi-coloured record players. Particularly Elvis. One nurse put 'Heartbreak Hotel' on repeat full blast, locked her door and went down to the hotel. None of the nurses minded. Next day another reciprocated with 'A Whole Lotta Shakin' Goin' On'.

The clothesline was festooned with skimpy scarlet lacy knickers and black lacy bras, blowing in the warm valley breeze. Liz and I had never seen undergarments like these. We both wore white cotton underpants with elastic in the waist, which would deteriorate in the wash and leave you walking tight-kneed to keep your underpants up. The nurses invited Liz and me down to the hotel in the village and shouted us beer with 'top shelf' chasers. They played pool with the local shearers. The first time Liz and I played I beat the local champion, a dirty sun-bronzed hero. I'd played billiards with my father at home but he always beat me so it was exciting to be a champion and to be praised by the nurses who laughed and cheered me and bought me drinks.

Once the nurses realised that both Liz and I would drink as well as play pool, they asked us to their evening soirées; ten or so would crowd into one of their rooms, cram on the bed, sit on the desk and floor, put the player on and smoke and drink and drink and drink. They joked about the patients, the matrons, their jobs and one another. They laughed at us 'little scared white rabbit student girls', but affectionately, so I felt included and even loved. They all rolled their own, which seemed both tough and suave. And dance! Wow, thought Liz and I, could they dance: 'We're going to rock around the clock tonight' and they would. 'Don't be no square / if you can't find a partner use a wooden chair,' they shouted along with Presley, at me. Next to them, I was indubitably square.

One night, sitting on the corner of a bed, squeezed up against Liz, I watched Moana, a handsome Māori woman, crooning to the song on the player. Then she leant into the woman next to her, wrapped her arm round her neck and kissed her. On the lips. On the lips. All those songs that pulsated through the nurses' home daily and echoed through my mind on the ward took on a new significance: 'I can't think straight'—'I'm living right next to an angel, I'm going to make that angel mine'—'cutest little jailbird I ever did see'. My God, these women were gay. Or at least some of them were. These songs were gay songs. I grabbed

Liz's arm and pulled her, protesting, out into the corridor. 'Did
you realise that Moana and Rachel are lovers?'

'I'm not sure. They might just be being affectionate. But I
think Jo and Robyn are. And I think they think we are.'

'Oh no.'

'I think that's a good idea. It means none of them will try it
on with us.'

That's when I realised. I would like one of them to 'try it
on' with me. They were so glamorous and at the same time so
competent and wise to be able to handle this terrifyingly other
world. I'd like to be like them. I'd love one of them to feel I was
worthwhile. So I went back in.

'Hey, here's our little timid, white, pool-playing rabbit.' Moana
poured me half a tumbler of Jack Daniel's, topping it with a slosh
of Coke.

'I wish you all'd stop calling me a white rabbit.' My discovery
and the bourbon had made me brave.

'Well you most surely are not brown.'

That night was my first blackout. I wavered to my room and
collapsed on the bed, the ceiling swirling in huge elliptical arcs
above me.

'You drank most of us under the table sweetie,' said Jo as we
dished up the porridge. 'I thought you'd be too under the weather
to turn up this morning. You might be a lousy dancer but you're
sure a champion drinker.'

The endearment and the combined insult-compliment made
me feel I'd been accepted. Despite my hangover I dished out
globules of sticky porridge with enthusiasm.

Three nights later, with 'Great Balls of Fire' drowning out any
attempt at conversation, the door of Rachel's bedroom burst open
and whacked into my knees. When I looked down I saw the
black boots of the door-kicker then, looking up, I saw a short
solid Māori woman in a red shirt and black leather biker's jacket.

'Hey Suzy, no need to be so butch. You've just slammed the
door into our white rabbit's knees.'

I wanted to draw her attention to me, but the best I could come up with was 'Ow!'

The woman grinned at me. A wicked grin and glinting slitted eyes.

'Sorry baby, but it wasn't that hard was it? Nice knees. Wouldn't want to damage them.' She turned to Rachel and held out a bottle of Jack Daniel's. She then took a glass, and just as I'd hoped, squeezed in between Liz and me, and lit up a readymade.

'Menthol. I've got asthma.' She coughed melodramatically. I loved it—the humour, the drama. 'I'm on sick leave, fatigue syndrome and you'd better believe it,' she announced to the room. 'Come on baby, let's rock.' She yanked me to my feet and holding me close swayed me to 'Roll Over Beethoven' in the tiny space between the bed and the desk. She'd thrown her jacket into a corner and I could feel her breasts pressing against mine. Shouting into my ear she told me she was the charge nurse at the children's ward in town, and rented a cottage in Polstead Road down the valley. She smelled of cigarettes and booze with an overlay of an unsubtle perfume that reminded me of sweet peas. She kept grinning and I kept grinning back.

The next day was a day off. I was lying on my bed reading the second volume of Proust's *À la recherche du temps perdu*. My tutor had said no one read past volume one and the madeleine so I had challenged myself to read it all from beginning to end that summer. I'd already read all of Richardson's *Clarissa* because the lecturer said even he hadn't read it. Despite the villainous handsome Lovelace, I'd found it unbearably boring. Now I was wondering if Proust intended me to dislike Marcel as much as I did.

Someone thumped on my door.

'Hey you in there, there's the phone for you.' No one ever rang us. Toll calls were too expensive. It was Suzy.

'We're driving over to the Pass. Wanna come? I'll pick you up in fifteen minutes.'

I had no idea what the Pass was, but Monsieur de Charlus, the

Duchesse de Guermantes and the unlikeable Marcel didn't stand a chance against Suzy's husky invitation.

Suzy had a large dirty brown Holden. She introduced her two brothers, John and Richard, and a cousin, Joey.

'You're driving, Richard. Here, sling those flagons and those sacks into the boot. Sit next to me in the back, Ngaio. Great she's got a hori name, eh? None of us have.'

Richard drove fast; the road was unsealed gravel and full of precipitous swerves. I was panic-stricken but also very aware of Suzy's firm warm body up close beside me. Every curve I was pressed closer. After a terrifyingly fast swoop down into a gorse and scrub covered bay we stopped. Suzy got out two flagons of beer and poured everyone a lukewarm drink with big weakly exploding bubbles, in cardboard cups. The boys upended them and disappeared into the scrub. As Suzy and I leant against the sun-warmed car I could hear the boys hallooing in the distance.

'Get 'em! There she is! Get 'em! Down your way Joey!'

They returned holding a large greyish woolly sheep struggling between them. Suzy handed them a length of rope from the boot. They roped the two rear legs together, threw the rope over a branch and heaved on it till the sheep was hanging, its front legs swinging. Then John cut its throat.

This, I had not been expecting. I watched the sheep jerking as its blood cascaded into a puddle on the ground. I was shocked. I didn't want to seem a sook so I turned away and pretended to be interested in the dark green sea. I took one glance and realised that, behind my back, the men were skinning the sheep and cutting it into chunks.

Suzy came over with two beers.

'The snotgreen sea,' I said. 'There's a writer called it that: "The snotgreen sea". "The scrotumtightening sea".'

Suzy laughed, snorted, spraying beer.

'God, that's rude. You students! It's Mum and Dad's anniversary tomorrow. The mutton's for that. Peter and Bob are getting the crays. Wanna come after your shift? I'll pick you up. Don't tell them about that sea though.' She snorted again. 'They're good

Mormons. They'd wallop us if we said anything like that.'

On the drive back, the sheep's remains in hessian sacks in the boot, Suzy put her arm over my shoulder and I shivered at its heavy warmth. Yes, she told me, she has four brothers and seven sisters. She was the baby.

'I'm the bad one, the naughty one. But that makes them love me all the more.'

The anniversary was held in a big marquee outside a small house in a Nelson suburb. Brothers and sisters and cuzzies and nephews and nieces, and, of course, the parents all hugged and kissed me. At first I automatically stiffened up as unfamiliar arms wrapped around me, and lips touched my cheek. Mine was a non-touching family. I had never been hugged or kissed by my mother or my father or my brother or my sister.

'Any friend of Suzy's is welcome here. Think of us as your home away from home.' After a meal at long paper-covered trestle tables dotted with bottles of bright orange, red and yellow soft drink, Suzy grabbed my arm.

'Come on. That's enough of this. Time for a drink.'

Suzy's house was a tiny cottage in a flat section of roughly mown grass on the way back to the hospital. I was so nervous. I lost count of how many gin and tonics I'd drunk. They tasted very ginny and not very tonicy. I was worried about what I was going to be expected to do; the only account I'd read of what I supposed was lesbian sex was in Radclyffe Hall's *Well of Loneliness* and that simply said 'and that night they were not divided'. That was not much help. Besides I disliked the protagonist, Stephen, who was called an invert and had broad shoulders and narrow hips and dressed like a man.

'Come on,' said Suzy, sounding remarkably sober, 'come to bed.'

Suzy, naked, felt soft and warm and enveloping. Voluptuous, that's the right word I thought, then I stopped thinking. We spent what seemed like hours kissing and touching and sucking before Suzy entered me and drove me into a frenzy, calling on all the unknown gods of darkness. Suzy reared above me, huge and powerful, laughing triumphantly as I, screaming, came again and again.

'That's it baby, that's it. Feel me in you, right up in you. Feel me.'

This was it; this was what it meant to make love. This was the transformational moment of my life.

When I woke I was enclosed in Suzy's arms. That part of my anatomy that I later learnt to call my cunt was wet and deliciously sore and we began kissing again. As Suzy sucked on me I pondered the fact that I'd never known my breasts and nipples were erogenous zones.

'Don't stop. Don't ever stop.'

'We won't,' murmured Suzy, nuzzling.

Suzy rang the administration, telling them I had a stomach bug and couldn't come on duty. We spent the day tangled in the sweaty sheets. Delectably sweaty sheets.

Midday Suzy made a pot of coffee, and we shared a Kit Kat bar, suck by suck. I lay out flat, trying not to move, being nibbled and licked all over. Hard not to move. 'Still, be still.'

I tried not to move as I learned the various ways of being entered, one finger, two fingers, three. As I writhed my body felt like a vast cavern, sucking in and enveloping Suzy. Except that Suzy was no longer Suzy—she'd become passionate carnality, arousal, intensity, beyond personality. I felt triumphant as I pushed her down and tried out the various ways of entering a lover. I was as excited pushing into her as I was by her making love to me. Lying back on the mattress, the sheets having long ago ended up on the floor, I saw over Suzy's round soft shoulder the thin silver sliver of a moon.

'It's night,' I whispered into Suzy's soft soft mouth. How to describe that mouth? Velvety I thought dazedly, or would satiny be better?

'Mmmmhm. Night's the time for love.' She slipped a finger ever so gently back inside me, paused, and began moving it ever so gently. 'Want more? Beg for it then, little white rabbit.'

I begged, oh yes, did I beg.

I went back on duty after one more day ill with a stomach bug. I spent every night at Suzy's cottage. Liz was first of all annoyed at the loss of her mate, and she told me any anti-Suzy gossip she could winkle out.

'She only goes for white girls—educated white girls, the more educated the better. All her family's married white. That's what the Mormons encourage them to do—how to make it in the white world. Her last girlfriend's saying all sorts of horrible things about you. She thinks you're up yourself and you're not looking after Suzy properly.'

But then Liz met a top-dressing pilot who took her flying, landing on the cool firm sand of beaches of islands in the Sounds and she stopped feeling left out.

At the end of February we drove back to Auckland.

'I'll write,' I promised Suzy.

'I'm not into writing,' said Suzy, 'but I get leave in six months.'

I hadn't finished Proust—it would be another forty years before I read of Albertine who 'loves her own sex', who meets one whom Marcel fears is a 'practicing and professional sapphist', and who mingles with the 'depraved women' of the holiday waterside town of Balbec.

Maria McMillan

Fatigue

I have to figure out fatigue.
I climb all day and spin and hold
my body in only the most treacherous

positions until I want to weep
with tiredness. I need warm food.
So now I climb. And when I can

do it no more I climb more. And some
thing stops me climbing and I override
the thing to climb again. Knowing

my body, its mass, when and how
muscles fail, the mechanics of it.
And the thing stops me and

I climb through the thing and
no matter how I try I can not climb until
I fall, over and over I try, thinking

I know what a body can do
and it can not do this.

Rope

The only thing I can possibly do
is stay here forever, hanging
on with both hands, not ever

doing the next thing. I will
find a way to loop the rope
around me so when I sleep

I will not fall. Warm clothes
will be delivered.
Blimey. The wind is everywhere.

Most things live suspended
in matter as dense as itself.
We sink to the bottom like

weighted divers.
The perfect twist.
The nest of sleeping mice.

I'm still. I must move
all my muscles in the same
moment to be this still.

I think of the rope.
The rope disappears.

Hannah Mettner

Sex dream

Last night a woman offered to give me an injection against
crossness and frustration. She was wearing those thick 50s wingtip
glasses and her hair was rolled back in complicated neatness. I
guessed she knew what she was doing. Up close I could see the
cat flick at the corner of each eye caught in a fringe of lines,
and the clumping of mascara. The ritual began . . . cut-out map
pieces of continents and countries were arranged on a Formica
table in their proper formations. *Just think*, she said, shunting
Brazil into place, *of the disruption we could be causing . . . tsunamis
up and down Africa*. She placed a small, white birthday candle
between Europe and Asia, and lit it. Being indoors, the orange
flame stood straight up, *just wait*, she said, *for an easterly*, holding
up a wetted finger. The flame veered west suddenly as if a small
child were puffing at it for a wish and Spain leapt sideways with
it as it has done many times before. I was worried, imagining tiny
people grabbing up glasses of wine and clutching at tables as their
afternoon jolted like a kicked hammock, shouting *NOT AGAIN!*
Next, the woman pulled out a small wooden hammer, like a meat
tenderiser, and began preparing my left hand by lightly pounding
it. On the underside, the knots at the base of my thumb gave way
with pops and clicks; on the top, the hammer sprang away from
small bones at awkward angles. Finally she drew the injection
and flicked it like they do in the movies. She applied it to that
vein running along the narrow bone of my middle finger and
into my wrist, next to the trapezoid. I lifted up like a kite away
from my body and migrated, with the wind, to Spain. My body
arrived somewhat belatedly, sweating, and looking resentfully
at my pitcher of Sangria; we hugged, pleased to see each other
again. Bright circles of paper lanterns rustled between leaves; the
night was opening up.

Fardowsa Mohamed

First

i was nineteen, my second year of university, skin just cleared to
reveal a face i was not yet accustomed to. i wasn't used to people
finding me beautiful apart from my hooyo—that's a good place
to start. i want to also preface this by saying: hooyo, i really
am sorry. i can imagine my aabo's sigh of disappointment from
across the ocean, just imagine his voice and his breath on the
back of my head. anyway, i was in the physics tutorial, my
multi-coloured pens circling my specific gravity, neurons deep
in a problem, trying to not make friends, when my pens all fell
on the floor. he picked them up and put them on my desk and
did not say a word. then if we fast forward for the sake of time
to when i was getting sahra from school [as the model eldest
daughter i am/was] and the toyota wouldn't start. i had no one
to call i guess so i texted him and he showed up to hooyo's
house—green eyes in a leather jacket—and did something to
the engine that i pretended to understand, out of pride [i think
he was winging it too]. sahra told me that night as i undid her
braids that she liked him, which disarmed me i guess. i showed
him my paintings in the garage on saturdays and he sat in front
of them for hours, and said nothing. somewhere between those
saturdays, quickly like the ending day, i realised that i fell in
love with that boy, just as hooyo warned. once when hooyo
and sahra were at ayeeyo's house we watched horror movies on
my floor on a mattress worn-out by children jumping on it. he
looked more delicate naked than i expected, no natural armour,
the moon illuminating him through the open window he
jumped through. my braids undone with teeth and hair rejoiced
in the crawling of new hands. and i know that's about the time
it started to sink like the last eddies of bath water. just like when
aabo left and i asked hooyo why and she said i don't know, i
can only guess. i asked him to do a lot in those six months;
things for which he did not receive the appropriate training. fix

things only surgery, science, my aabo, a time machine, another
country could fix. i fell into those wide eyes but he was just a
boy lost like me but you don't realise these things. that we are
all children:

still that little girl barefoot in the driveway

watching the hungry night feast

on the waning day

wondering

where he is.

Clare Moleta

How Far from Earth

The road is soft and lunar. It falls ahead of her across the earth—something unravelled and left behind. She is alone on its surface, weaving around the potholes, taking all the space she needs. Four thirty in autumn, at least an hour till dark. The tree shadows strung between the wet bright fields on either side.

She changes down a gear and rides steadily, breathing in the rawness of ditch water and grass, breathing out steam. Watching it float white for a heartbeat and then lose itself in the air. Before, only minutes before, she was trapped on the edge of a motorway at peak hour. Towers behind her, city somewhere ahead out of sight. Crawling with her head down, picking her way through the broken glass while the passing drivers honked and catcalled. On an uphill stretch to lights, a man leaned out of a van window and grabbed her arse and she almost came off—her body tipping over the handlebars and her front wheel bucking the curb. She fought for control while the traffic kept moving past her as if what was happening to her wasn't happening, as if she wasn't there.

But then she saw the sign and it was west, like on the map, so she turned off and this road opened up for her like a trick, like a door in a rock with lambs and green pastures on the other side. And nothing followed her through.

She rides for fifteen minutes, twenty minutes, and no cars pass her. She loses the sound of traffic, sees no figures walking towards her or away. The road runs on straight and uneven between trees and ditches, red pools of beech leaves and fences around sheep, under a pale flat sky. A blackbird drops down out of it and flies ahead of her. Her breathing settles and she claims the whole road, curving and looping around the ruts. There are a few houses to start with but then they stop and there's just field after field. Someone's estate, maybe, with this lumpy old road running through it, a country road that had been forgotten while the country went under the motorway, but is still here just as real as the car yards and diesel fumes and the towers full of shaven-headed children and all the plastic bags flapping in all the wire. She can get home this way too.

It was a one-off workshop. Just a trial, Gerry said, but they'd let her know if they wanted more. Twelve till four on a Sunday in the darts club on the ground floor of Thomas Larkin. On Wednesdays after school she ran a theatre class for twenty or thirty or forty kids in the community hall in the basement of the central tower, John Flinders, but on Sundays the hall was busy with youth group and AA and this Sunday there would be a memorial later on for the girl, the teenager. People had already started arriving when she left.

She'd been teaching the kids for two months and then she got asked to try an adult session. She said yes straight away and was terrified. The oldest kids in her kids' class were only a few years younger than her but she managed to seem like a grownup to them, maybe just by being from outside. Gerry, the community organiser, got six women signed up. When she asked he said most of them were old enough to be her mother but not to let it worry her. She didn't know if they'd change their minds when they saw her, if they'd believe she had anything to offer them. It took her a long time to prepare the class. Nothing too abstract or physical to start with, nothing that would make them feel exposed to each other afterwards when they sat waiting in the laundromat or yelled at each other's kids. But something tangible.

The central library didn't have plays but there was a small collection of screenplays and she had a few monologues already, things she'd used for auditions. She didn't know what they would have seen so she picked classics and a few American blockbusters. Nothing recent. The darts club was small and hard-lit. It smelled of tobacco and lino and cleaning fluid. While she waited for the women to arrive she held onto the small stack of paper and tried to keep her hands steady. Did breathing exercises, the quieter ones. She looked out the window at her bicycle locked and chained to a railing as close to the club entrance as she could manage. On the concrete, a bunch of kids were leaping back and forward over a stream from a burst pipe. Two women shopped from a blue van that sold batch bread and detergent and sweets and loose cigarettes. On the edge of the near green there was a burnt-out car slowly filling up with rubbish, and more small children pushing each other off a swing set. Behind them, another pre-cast concrete tower. A few floors up it, someone heaved something black over a balcony and she watched it fall to the ground, exploding rubbish. They were monologues for women but they were about men. Women wanting men or breaking up with men or having revelations about men. She hadn't done that on purpose—it only occurred to her when she ran through them in her head, looking out the window. They felt flimsy and attention-seeking and a long way from anything that mattered in the towers.

A leaf lands on her shoulder, slips down the shiny fabric of her jacket. Her lifting knee catches it for a second, rusty and rain-shaped, and then it falls and is sucked into her spokes. It had taken three visits before she realised that about the towers. No trees.

The light has shifted and fallen and a damp smell comes creeping out of the bitumen and the grass and the sluggish water in the ditches. She lets go of the handlebars to zip her jacket higher and then leans back and hangs her arms by her sides and concentrates on pumping straight down. Her hips guide the metal frame along the smoother surfaces in the road. The lower half of her is a piston but her upper body floats free and high. When she handed out the monologues, something changed in the room. She hadn't done it till halfway through, when she had a sense of each woman—her age, voice, how she carried herself, how she was in the space with the others. She tried to give each of them a piece she thought they could handle and bring something to. First it was the buzz of saying the same lines as Julia Roberts or Susan Sarandon but then they took the words and lifted them, made them live and work differently with their own voices and bodies and histories in the small room that she thought had mostly held men. She realised how little she knew about any of them and how much she'd assumed. At the end of the workshop, a woman called Sandra asked if she could keep hers, and she said yes, they all could, the monologues were theirs.

A long way ahead of her, in shadow, the road curves up and the trees close around it but here it's still flat and she can breathe easy while she pedals. She lifts her arms free of her sides, palms down, the air slicing open around them. It feels like, not flying but maybe sailing. Rowing maybe. She is the transport but she's being carried too, quietly and steadily covering the distance between the towers and Hen's mother's house. On Wednesdays there were buses from the city to the towers and back and she could walk to their flat from town, but the buses didn't run much on Sunday and not at all out to where Hen's ma lived.

Last night when she'd looked at the map, she'd traced a direct line west off the motorway and asked why hadn't they put a road through there and avoided the city altogether. Hen had shrugged and said you couldn't put a road through a graveyard. She didn't see why not—they put them through everything else. She'd thought about riding to teach the class and back through town and out again, west to Diswellstown, in time for dinner, felt the ache and stretch of the coming day and wondered if it would rain and thought about not going. But it was good to be there, to be there with him in the house where he'd been a child. And now the going is so easy, so sure, she could almost lift above the road and see it mapped.

She can't wait to tell Hen about this shortcut she discovered for herself, here, where he's seen and done everything first. And she's slow to make a place for the sound because her mind isn't on it, it isn't part of where she is now, but it keeps coming behind her until she wakes up to it and drops her arms and pulls over to the side, remembering how Hen yelled at her that time she was riding ahead of him in the dark on the back road to Diswellstown and a car came up behind them and hung back and finally barged past too close because she was doing that thing, that flying thing she did sometimes on her bike and it must have looked like she was indicating.

But this car doesn't pass. She looks over her shoulder and sees it still a way behind her, a white Hiace van moving slow, not pulling over, not overtaking. She turns back to face the road ahead of her and thinks about the man who grabbed her out the passenger window, and how she had caught up with the van at the traffic lights and he saw her coming and grinned and said something to the driver who was grinning too, and the lights changed but there were cars in front of them and she had her bike lock ready. When she lifted it he swore and started winding the window up. She hit the glass first and then the paintwork around it, chipping flakes of white. A charge through her like a concrete cutter. On the other side of the window his slack, stunned face rearranging. A young guy, younger than her, in his boss's van. He called her a psycho bitch and went to open his door on her but there was a snarl of horns behind them and the driver put his foot down and she pulled back to the side of the road and watched it go with the metal heavy in her hand and her whole body trembling.

She looks back again, quickly, but it's not a plumber's van, this one is unmarked, plain white. At this distance, in this light, she can't see into the cab at all. Thinks, fuck's sake, pass will you? She pulls right off the road, onto the strip by the ditch where the mud comes up through the grass as she rides over it. After a minute the engine revs. She concentrates on her straight line and waits for it to overtake. Hears it coming up behind her, jolting on the ruts, the gear change and the rattle of the accelerator. Then it slows again and stays where it is, just behind her.

Something switches on inside. She should look back now to see what's wrong, wave them past, but she doesn't. She can feel her pulse through the engine noise. So much noise from one car. Just her on the road with one car behind her. One van. Like the van in the stories about the girl. No houses, nobody on foot, no distant tractor in the fields, nothing watching but sheep. She leans over the handlebars and rides faster, rides as fast as she can without standing because standing means showing her arse to the driver behind her, showing the driver she has an arse. Otherwise it's so easy to take her for a boy. It happens all the time. Hen just laughs about it, she thinks it makes him proud somehow—shows him different because he doesn't need a face full of makeup. Meet a girl like that out at night, he told her once, you wouldn't know what you were going to wake up with. She pulls her hood down lower. Her throat is raw and no matter how many breaths she takes it isn't enough. But she feels herself pulling away from the van, or the van falling back. Looks ahead to where the road lifts and the trees close in. Doesn't look behind her because looking behind her would acknowledge that the van has something to do with her.

She hears the engine rev again and there's nowhere for her to go except into the ditch. Feels the force of all that steel bearing down and her own human frailty. This time it pulls alongside and keeps pace with her, blocking out the road. The urge to look and the fear of looking merge in a kind of shame that keeps her head down and her face forward but she knows she is being looked at, assessed in the uncertain light in her baggy jacket and straight-cut jeans with her hoodie pulled low, leaning over the crossbar of her stolen bike. You think I'm a boy, she screams in her head, you think I'm a boy and you keep driving. And the van passes. It passes and accelerates up the road ahead of her, towards the hill and the trees at the top of the hill, maybe fifty metres, a hundred metres. And then it pulls over at the side of the road.

The urge that hits her then is to get off the bike. As if the bike is dragging her down, making her a target. As if she could run faster than she can ride. Back the way she came? Into the fields, with the sheep? There's nowhere else—only ahead of her, the van and the rising and closing in of the road and what's on the other side of the hill. She pulls out as far as she can and changes gear. Now she stands on the pedals, arse in the air. She's on the far side of the road, approaching the van, when the back doors swing open. They open but no one got out to open them, and that means there's someone else, not just the driver, someone in the back too. Now she looks. Now she can't look away from the space between those doors a white van, seen in connection but no one gets out and she pulls level, pulls past, her legs weak and pumping, arms locked on the frame. She rides past and keeps riding and for a moment there's nothing except the sound of her gasping and the air burning in her lungs. Then she hears the doors slam and the engine start.

The van closes the distance and sits behind her again, rattles again like something's shaking loose inside. Then it overtakes her again, no hurry, pulling in closer until there's only the pressure of it and the hot diesel stink instead of air but she doesn't look, don't look. Nothing she can do would be more dangerous. If she sees the man inside, meets his eyes, then they'll be joined together and she will be complicit in whatever is happening here. Drives on up the road and pulls over. The doors open. She speeds up, swerves wide, gets past. Waits for the sound of the engine. Thinks, there's something wrong with it, with the engine, it's engine trouble, nothing to do with me. They're lost and they're checking the map, they don't see me, they don't even know I'm here. All this fear, she's on her own with it. If they knew they'd laugh at her.

But no one gets out. Not from the front, not from the back. Just the van, waiting.

The third time, she understands that she can't keep riding like this, she's getting too tired, adrenaline giving out. When she stands on the pedals her legs and arms shake, her fingers on the gears are boneless and she breathes in shallow stabs. When the doors swing open the third time, she sees how the road ends there, how it closes down to the space between the doors and leads her all the way in. There's nowhere to go but go there, leave her bike on the road and crawl in and let the doors shut behind her.

She claws back for the feeling of chasing the plumbers' van, the spitting surge though her body, the lock coming free smoothly in her hand as she pulled up alongside, but that's all gone now. Is that how they got the other girl—used up all her fight first? And was this always coming her whole life, this road running alongside every road she thought she was choosing, waiting for them to converge. Would it have mattered if she'd done something different on the motorway, or stayed in bed beside Hen this morning with last night's beer seeping out of his skin, or stuck a different map on her bedroom door when she was fourteen on the other side of the earth? Or would she have ended up here anyway.

Something carries her past the doors, past the van, keeps her legs working and her grip locked and her eyes on the trees ahead of her. Something more desperate than rage, more hopeless than fear. No end to the road it just keeps going like this. Behind her, the engine starts.

When the van passes her again, she looks. It doesn't matter now because she's already consented, there's no backing out. But the glass is tinted and all she sees in that slow second is a shape behind the wheel. She looks away, down. Each leaf that let go of its tree and lies where it fell to be buried under more leaves, red and orange or already brown. She rides over them and the smell of rot comes up like a season. She's not riding fast anymore, it's too hard, but it's their job to stop, not hers, so why can she still hear the engine? When she looks up, the van is a small white shape between the trees on the hill ahead of her. It crests the hill and goes down out of sight. She stops peddling and the bike comes to a stop almost without coasting because she's at the start of the rise. Waits. The sound of the engine comes to her quietly, then faintly, then not at all.

Carefully swings her leg over the bike, lowers the frame onto the leaves. In the middle of the road she crouches down slowly, falls forward on her knees, on her hands. A part of her listening for the van to come back, for the new rules. Part of her already being herded back the way she came. But the rest of her is on her hands and knees, just breathing, feeling her heart slow down, looking at the black tar and the places where it's broken open. Smelling earth. She thinks Gerry will ask her to take another workshop and this is what she will say to Sandra. This time try it like you've got a plane ticket in your bag and you haven't told him yet, the whole time you're talking you're thinking about when you're going to tell him.

When she looks up there will be a phone box. Not before but now, just across the road, because she needs it. Hundreds of thousands of miles from humankind and when she steps inside it still smells of piss, like every phone box in the city, but it's not broken and she finds the right coins and lifts the handset and the dial tone joins her to the world again. Even if the van comes back now they can't touch her. One of Hen's brothers answers—they bark in single syllables and she can never tell them apart. If it's the one with the motorbike then Hen can borrow that instead of asking his mother for the car but Hen's not there, he's down the Straw for a quick pint before dinner, so she tells the brother in a shaky rush and her story sounds thin and full of conjecture, lacking a punchline. When she finishes he doesn't say anything straight away. There's another voice in the background and she realises she only has half his attention. Are you there? She's trying to see him in the cramped hall where the phone is, the thin patterned carpet and the picture of Mary, no light on probably, so it's just the outline of him, and the smell of coal and potatoes and damp, his ma calling to him from the kitchen. Then he says, right so, will I pass on a message or what? And that's how she knows, how she will know, that what just happened to her wasn't serious. Wasn't anything really, just engine trouble or maybe a jammer, or else some idiots messing with her head because of the white van in the papers. That she's got herself all worked up over nothing and it's lucky she hasn't called the guards or she'd be a laughing stock. And if she asks the brother straight out to come and get her he'll do it but she will find that she can't ask him. Couldn't stand Hen thinking she was that useless.

Hen didn't want her to take the job. It was her teacher who asked her to step in for him after he'd overcommitted or got a better offer and couldn't finish up the term. She'd been training with him for more than a year, one night class a week after her shift, weekend workshops when she could afford them. She'd never taught before. He told her he'd thought of her first, thought she'd be good at it. He could have asked anyone. Hen warned her about the kids, about their parents, about the dealers and the gougers and the smackheads. You go in there, he said, talking like you do, looking like you do, they'll eat you alive. But Hen had only ever been there to buy gear himself.

There was a woman at work who was from the towers—she'd listened to her talk about it at breaks sometimes, about people there, things that happened. Sharon was a year younger than her and she lived with her boyfriend on the fifteenth floor of Michael Pearce. Said people didn't know shit about it. Said her front door was all scratched and banged up, graffitied, so no one would bother but inside they had central heating and satellite TV. Said you could see the whole city. She imagined bumping into Sharon after a class, kids running past yelling out her name, saying see you next week. And Sharon would look at her differently, something gone from her eyes. Maybe she would ask her up for a cup of tea, and they would take the lift together all the way to the fifteenth floor.

When Hen realised he couldn't talk her out of it, he told her the thing he was always telling her. She just needed to look like she could handle herself. Most of the time that was all it took. He said, don't you be there after dark though.

She gets up off her hands and knees, the cold of the road in her bones. It's darker, it will be dark soon, and the van hasn't come back. She looks up the bare road where it went, to the trees closing around the top of the hill. Somewhere on the other side is the old graveyard that backs onto Murphy's estate—she has to cut through it to get to the back road that will take her to Diswellstown. And maybe the van really just had engine trouble and she was an idiot, or maybe it's waiting for her at the graveyard, seen in connection with the deceased. But it isn't the same fear now, she can't summon it. It's a copy of fear. She could go back the way she came, all the way back to the motorway in the dark and then ride the motorway into town without lights and call Hen from the flat. She stands there trying to decide, trying to make herself do one thing or the other thing while it gets dark around her, slowly and then fully and she looks back and there isn't even a glow from the motorway. It's like she's on the moon. And nothing holds her down here. There are no towers in her lineage. Her absence will fill no hall with candles. She could just peel off the surface and float away into some dark orbit. And Hen, who spent a lifetime learning not to cry, will not cry for her.

It's too far to go back now. And if the van is waiting for her, there's nothing to stop it coming back for her either. So in the end she goes forward in the dark, not riding, just pushing the bike, with the air cutting into her lungs. They needed smoke breaks, those women. Too many for the time they had but she'd thought it mattered more that they were on side, focused and willing. And that they would have gone whether she said so or not.

When she came out to join them, because she couldn't just wait inside like she thought she was something special, Rita was saying, you saw them little skirts she wore, up to here. No better than her ma, that one.

And Sandra, you think she got in the van willing?

And Rita, shrugging, flicking ash, wouldn't've been the first time is all.

Then they saw her and the talk closed down like a lock. Is that your bike there? Sandra said, and blew smoke at it. You'd want to bring that inside.

The cold is fierce now. Her nose runs and her fingers burn. In a little while there's a bit of light from the other moon and the feeling of being alone makes her cry. Not just alone here but even on the other side of the graveyard, even if she made it to Hen's mother's house and squeezed in around the table with his noisy, scathing family and shared their food and laughed at their jokes; even if she caught Hen's eye across the table or felt his boot, or one of his brother's boots, move against her leg, she would still be on the moon.

Near the top of the hill she stops crying and gets back on the bike because the darkness between the dark of the trees could hold anything. All she can do is ride in the middle of the road and try not to breathe too hard, try to listen and be ready. As she gets to the top, the clouds over the moon pass away for a moment and the graveyard is clear in relief, below and to her left, just like the map. She sees the shape of each headstone. A low stone wall all the way around, and after the graveyard the road runs on, veering away deeper into the country. But there's a dark block of trees outside the wall, alongside it, that is easily big enough to hide a van. She waits for the sound of the engine starting up. Listens for voices or leaves underfoot, for the quiet unlatching of doors. She listens a long time but there's nothing. No sound comes up to her, no smell of exhaust, just a quiet that feels old and whole.

And something starts to uncurl inside her, begins to understand that the van is gone. Whatever they were doing, whatever it had been about, it no longer involves her. The graveyard is only as big as a small field. All she has to do is go down there and wheel her bike through the gate and between the graves, run it all the way to the back wall and lift it over. The rest of her life is there again on the other side. But when the clouds cover the moon, she knows she can't do it. Because of the black trees she can't turn her back on and how the gate might scream under her hand, because of graves she can't see anymore. She used everything up on the real fear and she has nothing left for this nameless one. Tries to think, to remember where the road went after the graveyard but all she knows is it's the wrong way, the way the van has gone. When she faces the graveyard again she is rocked with anger at how useless she is, how incapable. How much more likely to stay there until she freezes to death than try to save herself. Why did she take this road? Why did she imagine she was strong enough?

She makes her legs move up and down, turning the wheels forward, as if she can trick herself into bravery through motion. Carries herself that way out into the open. And a light comes into view. A glowing through the trees just outside the graveyard. Too late to hide. She holds entirely still and waits and watches that steady shine, thinks of Hen drinking too fast in the heat and smoke of the Straw not thinking of her but it isn't headlights it isn't torchlight. When the moon comes back there's a house down there. Small, stone up against the stone wall of the graveyard, buried in trees. Not so different really from Hen's mother's house. They will listen and tell her she was right. There will be a phone and Hen will answer and it won't be like she thought.

So she rode down towards it, smelled smoke, saw a window slippery with light. How had so much light been hidden from her? Rode faster, started to shake again. Behind her was the deep black vacuum of space but she made it to the gate and the gate was open and she half fell off her bike and left it, went up the path, past walls of ivy and a broken-down garage that was dark and almost shut. Knocked on the door and waited, and the door opened and she went in.

Stephanie de Montalk

Pain

The winds must come from somewhere when they blow
'Villanelle', W.H. Auden

1

It was a pelvic pain and it started slowly in November 2003, two weeks after a fall in Poland where I was researching a novel and promoting the Polish translation of my memoir/biography, *Unquiet World: the Life of Count Geoffrey Potocki de Montalk*. I slipped on the marble bathroom floor of a Warsaw hotel and bounced off the sharp edge of the bath, breaking three ribs on the lower left side.

I thought myself fortunate at the time. I could have hit my head, fractured my back, or ruptured a kidney about which there was concern at the Szpital Kliniczny Dzieciatka Jezus (Clinical Hospital of the Baby Jesus), to which I was whisked by ambulance and briefly admitted. I delayed my trip by train to Krakow and settled awkwardly, but gratefully, to resting the ribs and staying warm in the calm but bitingly cold northern autumn.

The pain was intermittent at first. It was also familiar. I had experienced the deep, dragging discomfort sporadically for twenty years. It was typically absent overnight and on rising, and gathered pace during the day. In 1985 a specialist, detecting tenderness at the point at which the left ischial spine (a process of the lower and dorsal part of the hip bone) enters the base of the pelvis, had diagnosed an ischial tendonitis or bursitis, explained as a complaint common in the shoulder, similar to tennis elbow, soldier's heel, housemaid's knee. 'It's usually caused by a minor but repetitive irritation,' he said. 'Weavers get it, writers, maybe, and others who sit for long periods. There's no treatment necessary. Exercise and rest as pain dictates. It could take months to come right.'

I had checked the diagnosis in a medical textbook. It confirmed a widespread condition which included a chronic form of bursitis in animals, especially horses, which lay on hard floors. I remembered that Charles Dickens was said to have suffered from ischiogluteal bursitis. I was not then a writer, but I had been sitting researching and scripting a film documentary. The symptoms made sense.

2

On my return to New Zealand in December 2003, the condition intensified. I continued to sit long hours at the computer bringing the novel I was working on—the story behind 'The Fountain at Bakhchisaray', Alexander Pushkin's *poema* of the impossible love of a Tatar khan for a Polish countess held captive in his Crimean harem—to first draft, waiting for the inflammation to recede as it had in the past, reminding myself that, given his prodigious output, clearly Dickens had pressed on regardless.

During February 2004, I gritted my teeth in cafés and restaurants, shifted from hip to hip during movies, excused myself early from social occasions, alluding to my ribs, or saying 'I've injured my back', aware that the concept of pelvic pain was difficult for many, and mention of ischial spine confusing.

By March the pain had escalated beyond any level at which I had known it before. It dragged and burned: a cat at the curtains, a coal smouldering; it needled like crushed glass; it radiated out and pressed down, a nonexistent weight from the area of the left ischial spine. On glorious Indian summer afternoons I lay on a sofa oblivious to the buzz of sun and cicadas, wondering why mainstream analgesics were having so little effect; how pain of this persistence and degree could be caused by a bursitis or tendonitis; how Dickens had continued to write.

Further consultations uncovered nothing. An MRI was normal. A bone scan picked up the three fractured ribs but found no sign of ischial enthesis. Wearily I decided that if I was to live with this unanswerable condition I should follow the example of Robert Louis Stevenson, who wrote of his recurrent respiratory illness, 'I begin to hope I may, if not at least outlive this wolverine upon my shoulders, carry him bravely like Symonds and

Alexander Pope.'

John Symonds had lived his life around tubercular symptoms. Pope, with a curvature of the spine, had failed to grow and suffered life-long headaches and a heightened sensitivity to pain. These men had sought refuge in writing. Could chronic pain be an incentive for me to do the same? Perhaps this was to be the effect of the fall and the ribs were merely collateral damage.

But the pain was too consuming. Moreover, Stevenson's burden had revived memories of John Bunyan, and Pilgrim's obstinate progress. The book—a Christmas present when I was nine— awakened, in vivid illustration, Pilgrim in a dusty blue tunic with a water flask, staff, and a creeping shape on his shoulders, weeping and trembling, crying, 'What shall I do?' It also recalled, in 'the manner of his setting out, his dangerous journey and safe arrival at the desired country', a story more concerned with the shedding of his oppression than its management.

I pushed the metaphysical direction to write aside. Aristotle had said, 'The prudent man strives for freedom from pain, not pleasure.' I needed to regain control, keep making decisions. These were medically enlightened times. Why sit blindly, albeit bravely, trying to write and hoping to get better?

3

The sunlit uplands would not easily be found. The literature on pain was blocked by theory and principle, hedged like an inaccessible poem with hidden, internal workings and attempts to explain highly individual perceptions. All it could say with certainty was that, while significant progress had been made in the alleviation of physical distress, much remained individual, incomprehensible, beyond our control.

I was well aware of the consequences of this incomplete understanding of pain and its control. Twenty-seven years previously in Hong Kong, an anaesthetic for a Caesarean section had paralysed me, rendering me unable to move a finger or open an eye; but it had also left me fully conscious, pinned to the table as if beneath concrete, from a pre-operative palpation and discussion of the baby's position, through the gagging insertion of the endotracheal tube, ripping midline incision, post-delivery ligation of the fallopian tubes and cries of constriction and pain reverberating in sound waves in my head.

The surgeon and anaesthetist had confirmed my distressed recovery-room account of their conversations in Cantonese and English, including the surgeon's remark prior to suturing that I seemed 'a bit light', and expressed horror that they had mistaken the twitching responses of my concealed consciousness for involuntary reflexes. 'Transient states of painless awakeness with incomplete recall are not uncommon,' they had said, 'especially during the light anaesthesia of Caesarean sections, but rarely at your sustained height of awareness and pain.'

In the years since, other patients have come forward, law suits for emotional trauma have been taken and compensations awarded.

More importantly, a Patient State Analyser and Bispectral Index, capable of detecting and measuring changes in brain waves during sedation, will soon enable anaesthetists to mix hypnotic and analgesic agents with greater accuracy.

Yet, for all this, the exact cause of the newly named 'Anaesthetic Awareness with Explicit Recall'—or 'Silenced Screams', as a survivor entitled her book on the subject—outside obvious equipment failure or inadequate medication, continues to elude researchers, and the phenomenon—in my case forever reminiscent of Edvard Munch's work of anguish and alienation, *The Scream*, and a matter of inward panic each time I approach the doors of an operating theatre—remains a mystery.

*

The difficulties of diagnosis and treatment posed by the hidden process of pain seemed to be especially prevalent in the assessment of chronic pain: that mysterious landscape beyond the known impact of acute and obvious tissue damage; of childbirth's pain of purpose, surgery's pain of healing and prevention of harm, and injury's intention of warning. All too frequently chronic pain languished, not readily understood in the areas of medicine and surgery: a territory of disorders, syndromes and cycles; of past experience, unique personality and the interplay of family, social and employment environments; of psychological and psychiatric attention.

It had little in common with the old Cartesian Theory of pain which likened the nervous system to a grid of electrical wires carrying signals from sites of injury to the brain, where sensations appropriate to the degree of tissue damage were recorded. It was closer to the newer Gate Control Theory of 'input modulation', which presumes that 'neural mechanisms in the dorsal horn of the spinal cord act like a gate', admitting, blocking, intensifying or reducing pain impulses before transmitting them to pain centres in the brain; that, during transmission, the signals are again modulated and pain is experienced when their arrival at the pain centres exceeds crucial levels.

Pain-gating further presumes that, if the pain gate changes or becomes damaged—as it might as a result of chronic or unrelieved pain—it stays open, even after the tissue has been treated or controlled. In such instances pain, often out of proportion to the original injury and level of harm detected by diagnostic means, and known as neuropathic pain, continues, at which stage the pain itself becomes the diagnosis or disease.

'As this long-term, unrelenting pain process continues,' a brochure on chronic pelvic pain concluded, 'as conventional treatments yield little relief, even the strongest person's defenses can break down.' The outlook was grim: limited physical and social activity, depression, displacement in the family and society.

I moved through the brochure's section on diagnostic testing (all that could be done, had been done) to 'Therapeutic Approaches': discussion of individual perception of pain in body and mind, the resultant rise of 'multiple interactive problems', the importance of patience, the assistance of mental and physical therapies, medication as 'a temporary supportive measure until other therapies kick in'.

But I was beyond patience and nebulous therapies, beyond

breathing and relaxation. I needed conclusive solutions and unequivocal medications. The bio-feedback, distraction, imagery and other transmission modulating cognitive activities could come later. The pain was intractable, intense; surely this signalled significant physical injury, as the unfashionably simple Cartesian specificity theory proposed?

4

One bleak morning, 'under the power of [Bunyan's] Giant Despair', I typed 'ischial spine', location of my supposed tendonitis, into Google. The words quickly took me to a pelvic pain forum and from there to the site of a rare and obscure disorder known as Pudendal Nerve Entrapment (PNE). I stared at the screen in disbelief. The essential symptoms matched my own. The pain was nerve related. No wonder it flared and played games. Of course it would not respond to the usual medications. Furthermore, its chronic nature probably also meant that by now the control gate and pain pathways were affected.

Just as quickly I closed the site down. The stories of fruitless visits to physiotherapists, chiropractors, osteopaths and acupuncturists; orthopaedists, gynaecologists, urologists, proctologists, neurologists, psychiatrists, even dermatologists; the well meaning but misadventurous testings and treatments were unsettling reading. The young man in North America who spoke of consulting twenty specialists in five months, and the young woman from Britain who wrote, 'I can't go on,' were by no means atypical.

However, the next morning I returned, although not to hover at the edge of Tophet. For the rest of the week, relieved and apprehensive—partly because at last the pain had a name, also because there was no certain cure—I roamed the Internet, downloading information and excluding problems, amongst them ischial bursitis, with which the condition was often confused.

I learnt that entrapment of this nerve caused, for no apparent reason, pain that was characteristically heightened by the mechanics of sitting and bending—activities that increased pressure on the pelvis and thereby the nerve. That determinants encompassed accident trauma, endometriosis, longstanding irritation and scarring of the nerve resulting from prolonged sitting, surgery and complicated childbirth, and sports-related activities like high mileage cycling, weight-lifting and rowing. Also, that discrete variations in tissue mass and nerve routes possibly explained why most people could endlessly sit, ride, or row, while the nerves of others became inflamed and, in due course in the case of an unfortunate few, confined by scar tissue and adhesions.

I was alarmed to discover that only a handful of physicians and surgeons—in the USA, Egypt and France—offered conclusive testing and treatment.

Nantes—home of the world's leading PNE neurosurgeon, Professor Roger Robert, pioneer of the trans-gluteal approach to surgical relief—seemed to be the centre of choice. In 1987, Robert, together with neurologist Jean-Jacques Labat and radiologist and pain specialist Maurice Bensignor (now deceased), concerned about 'the consistency of complaints of severe pain with sitting' expressed by sufferers of deep, chronic, pelvic pain, began to investigate the possibility of entrapment of the pudendal nerve.

A hundred years ago surgeons had severed the pudendal nerves of patients suffering this intolerable pain without knowledge of the underlying condition. But the catastrophic effects of sexual dysfunction and incontinence had quickly caused withdrawal of the procedure, and the pain to remain undiagnosed.

Initially, working with cadavers—six men and six women— Robert and his colleagues identified the area known as Alcock's canal, and sites between the two ligaments of the right and left ischial spines, as 'areas in the course of the pudendal nerve where entrapment could occur'. They found, by simulating sitting in the cadavers, that the nerve does not lie flat but 'describes a curve which drags it around the regions of the ischial spine which it straddles like a violin string on its bridge', hence the pressure applied and the pain caused by sitting and bending

The team members had confirmed their research in 1988,

in *Surgical Radiologic Anatomy*, in which they found that the clinical manifestations of entrapment—aside from pain—were few, and the character of the pain, which was 'piercing and very comparable to acute toothache', comprised 'sensations of burning, torsion or heaviness, and also of foreign bodies'. They determined that the symptoms, sometimes precipitated by a fall, could be of 'indolent' development; and, crucially, that 'activities requiring the seated position . . . are no longer available to these patients, whose mental attitude is one of chronic pain sufferers so obsessed with their miserable state as to be rapidly regarded by their doctors as psychiatric cases'.

This is a pain, summarised the web site, 'sometimes so intense that suicide is considered. But since a change of day to day habits can alleviate the pain some or a lot, people make those changes and learn to tolerate the pain that remains'. The entry further noted that, while occasionally the symptoms had been present for as long as twenty years, most seemed to be in the five-to-ten-year range, presumably because that was how long it took to come across a doctor who could correctly diagnose PNE.

The Nantes specialists reported that the non-surgical approach to freeing the nerve—a series of precise, CT (scan) guided injections of steroid into the area of entrapment—worked for some. Of surgical patients—whose progressive and relentless symptoms rendered steroid infusions impractical—up to two thirds achieved varying levels of relief from decompression and transposition of the nerve, while the rest experienced no improvement or a worsening of pain, usually because the nerve had been badly damaged. Additionally, and a potentially successful surgical outcome aside, the pain could increase for up to a year owing to the handling of the already traumatised nerve.

I checked the Comparative Pain Scale—a PNE-tailored assessment devised by an American sufferer. The scale provided for the subjective comparison of pain with clinically established levels of pain and behavioural change. It divided colour-friendly sections headed Minor Green, Moderate Yellow and Severe Pink into subgroups which ranged from the One of the 'barely noticeable pain [of] a mosquito bite, or a poison ivy itch' to the Ten of 'unimaginable' pain causing loss of consciousness.

I decided I was experiencing typically unstable pain, rising from the 'distressing' Yellow Four of 'an average toothache', to an 'utterly horrible' Pink Eight, 'comparable to childbirth or a real bad migraine headache', in minutes.

I was also of the view, having experienced all three readily treatable and short-term comparisons, that their equation with the fatigue and despair relevant to the rare and unreachable entrapment of the burning nerve was too approximate to be useful, even though the terms 'distressing' and 'utterly horrible' seemed close to the mark. And I remained unconvinced that levels of pain could be 'clinically established', for while my own, prolonged experiences of childbirth, for instance, were indeed 'utterly horrible', the experiences of others, according to personal physiology and duration of labour, might be more, or less, so. Pain, like happiness, I adjudged, can be exactly established as a zero or a ten, but only individual thresholds can measure the distance between.

Nonetheless, my options were clear. Either I consult a PNE expert, confirm the entrapment and work towards a form of recovery, or I hope for a remission, as had apparently happened in the past. Surprisingly, I chose the latter option even though early diagnosis and treatment was urged: France was hardly around the corner; the nerve might not be entrapped; the outcome of treatment was uncertain and my twenty-year history of pain rendered the odds doubly unfavourable. It was easier to stop sitting.

5

During March, April and May I strove to bring the pain under control. All the while the 'Pessimism of the Intellect' strained against the 'Optimism of the Will'—to appropriate Antonio Gramsci's activist slogan.

But, as I persuaded myself that hyper-avoidance of sitting would allow the inflammation to ease and the thinning nerve to slip free, I also agitated: to what purpose was I to stop driving, dining out, going to the cinema; to eat and write standing all day, plate perched on a sideboard, computer uncertain on a coffee table balanced on top of a work station and keyboard wobbling on a box on top of an ironing board? Unlike Stevenson, Symonds and Pope, was I being *discouraged* from writing? If so, by whom and to what end?

Was I to accept the veracity of metaphysics—described by Arthur Schopenhauer as man's 'most sublime tendency'—in which case was the pain good ghost, goblin, or ambivalent jinn? Was I to set conventional medicine against fringe disciplines, amulets and small synchronicities; to explore metaphor, myth and random events; and to embrace the dictum of fifteenth-century Austrian physician and surgeon Paracelsus that 'Magick is a Great Hidden Wisdom—Reason is a Great Open Folly?'

Or was I to pursue the fruits of philosophy: Marcus Aurelius's reasoning that 'What we cannot bear removes us from life; what lasts can be borne'; Michel de Montaigne's advice that we should 'learn to suffer whatever we cannot avoid', and his conviction that the key to living a complete life is the ability to make positive use of adversity; Friedrich Nietzsche's premise that just as 'a tree that is supposed to grow to a proud height [cannot] dispense with bad weather and storms', a fulfilled life (the attributes of which, unannounced by Nietzsche, are assumed to include courage, ambition, humour, independence and artistic dedication) is not possible without pain; or, to return to Schopenhauer, the proposal that 'we require at all times a certain quantity of care or sorrow or want, as a ship requires ballast, in order to keep on a straight course'.

The isolation from informed medical expertise was magnifying my credulity, the doubt of self-diagnosis my uncertainty.

I delivered PNE printouts to my GP, a sports medicine specialist, a neurologist, and a pain specialist—the consultant of last resort. The condition was not known to them, but, unlike medical professionals condemned on the Internet, they were keen to be informed.

In accordance with my new diagnosis, amitriptyline—in low doses a neuropathic analgesic—was prescribed. Long used as an antidepressant, amitriptyline's pain-reducing value (discovered by accident more than a decade ago) at a dose below that effective in the treatment of depression, like anticonvulsant medications such as neurontin which work in much the same way, lies in its ability to stabilise or block nerve pain receptors. The drug, taken at night, was befuddling and dried my mouth, but enabled sleep. I was also prescribed codeine, natural derivative of opium, now manufactured from morphine to which it reverts in the body, for alleviation by day. The efficacy of codeine for nerve pain was held to be uncertain: opiates, I was warned, are quick to build tolerance, can be habit- forming and provide minimal relief for only a few.

I brushed aside questions of dependence, determined an opium-related drug would work for me. Thomas de Quincey had taken tincture of opium to relieve facial neuralgia and succumbed to its 'dreams and noonday visions'. Addiction had been the lot of Samuel Taylor Coleridge too. Surely an enhanced literary output would compensate for the inevitable withdrawal and descent to reality? Moreover, I responded to the idea of using a derivative of 'the aspirin of the East', valued since antiquity: of Arabia's 'gift of God'; Greece's 'the juice'; the basis of soothing, costly, luminescent laudanum as Paracelsus had first mixed it, combining the powder he dried from the milky juice of the unripe seeds of the poppy scored in the morning with a knife, with the powdered, whisper-thin softness of gold and delicate rose of Indian pearls. The basis, furthermore, of the strong, modern, semi-synthetic narcotics (including heroin) derived from morphine; and the inspiration for thousands of synthetic opoids (like methadone and pethidine). A drug powerful enough to access the central nervous system, rather than toy with the peripheral pain receptors as the non-narcotic analgesics had done.

'Nerve pain is unlike that of trauma or surgery, in character and habit,' the pain specialist concurred, 'and chronic, unrelieved pain at your level will be difficult to control.'

He explained that changes to the nerve fibres were producing an abnormal signalling system. This was the reason amputees felt the pain of phantom limbs, and surgeons during World War II amputated early before the neurons became confused and started to send incorrect messages; and the reason only specific neuropathic drugs like amitriptyline could 'down-regulate' the receptors of damaged nerves and calm the pathways. Dosage would be a question of trial and error, he continued, codeine, at best, an ancillary tool.

I enquired about a TENS (Transcutaneous Electrical Nerve Stimulation) machine, the impulses of which block pain by confusing it, and closing a gate of transmission. 'The nerve is too deep,' he said, setting the suggestion aside.

6

The pain was indeed difficult to control. When there seemed no way forward, I was driven prone on the back seat of the car to a chiropractor for two weeks' intensive attempts at pelvic adjustment. I was soothed by heat packs and treated kindly, but to no avail, in a room overlooking a twisted tree.

I carried a handkerchief embroidered with yellow and white flowers which had been offered by a friend for prayer at her church, together with a slip of paper on which I had written 'the nerve is smooth and free in a cool breeze' in my left pocket.

I composed paragraphs of happy, healing words: words like optimism and good health; better, and best, and best step forward; violet and yellow, the colour of pansies and crocuses; orange, the colour of poppies; pink, the tinged peace of roses.

I turned my small herd of elephants and occasional ornaments on the bookshelves, so they wouldn't feel trapped, their trunks and noses facing the door.

I investigated Buddhism and pondered my accumulation of negative karma, and Zen Buddhism, which suggested that as long as I continued to be a slave to 'words and logic' I would experience 'untold suffering'.

I sought the teachings of Confucius who advised against

taking unfamiliar medicine and, if ill on the occasion of a princely visit, assuming a supine position beneath courtly robes, head facing east. The theological intelligence of C.S. Lewis, who admitted his thesis, *The Problem of Pain,* was written without personal insight of pain, from which I most usefully deduced that animals suffer less because they have no capacity to imagine the future. The Celtic wisdom of my husband's grandmother, parent of eleven children, who used say, 'You'll always be where you're meant to be,' and, 'If you're meant to be punished you will be.' The spinning thoughts of Persian mystic, Jalaluddin Rumi, who wrote in 'Enough Words':

> You must have shadow and light source both. Listen, and lay your head under the tree of awe.

I considered growing hashish, or rascals' grass, as Arabs once called it; trialling methadone; graduating to slow-release morphine.

In the lowest moments, when the pain escaped the pelvis and developed a pallid, external life of its own, when it became a cloud filling the room, closing me down, and it seemed neither words nor 'the world of men' could help me, I fantasised about oblivion. I eyed the squat, brown bottle of codeine, carried it in my pocket, counted and recounted the tiny white pills; contemplated the weightlessness of stepping late at night from a high window or bridge into the wind, curling beneath a fern into oneness with nature, sleeping in the transforming softness of moss and of gathering leaves.

Later, when the pain was less relentless, I did not find this need to surrender unreasonable or unreal. The body releases the surface memory of short-term pain. But chronic pain hides in the mind; waits, as if haunting the walls of a building or the wood of an instrument long played, storing and orchestrating sounds for the future.

As my novel—the unrequited khan, the captive countess beset by 'the heaviness which, like the night before and the day ahead, never leaves her'—languished; as the days shortened, and each evening I drew the curtains and lit and heated the house; as I repeated my encouraging mantras and paragraphs of positive words; as I read Henri Charrière's *Papillon* and Jean-Dominique Bauby's *The Diving Bell and the Butterfly*; I felt locked, without recollection of summer and little prospect of lifting spring, between Warsaw's autumn and the onset of the Wellington winter.

John (my husband) started coming home for lunch. The children brought a burner and bergamot, lavender tree and orange sweet oils; a lambskin rug for the sofa, a pair of opossum fur boots, a hand- stitched hot water bottle cover, a regular supply of dark chocolate, a pot plant, daily words of encouragement.

I absorbed the support. I achieved a measure of acceptance. The world became simpler, gifted with time and the fascination of small things. The clutter of life—deadlines, appointments, extraneous obligations—fell away. Energy and optimism slowly returned. I began to focus for short periods on writing; placating the 'animal in perpetual unrest' with the controlled stories of less immediate worlds: a modern translation of Pushkin's *poema*, a third collection of poetry. The pain held on, a cohesive influence, a necessary edge to my thinking. I was reminded that Wordsworth had compared the spontaneity of childhood expression with the measured 'philosophic mind' of later years; and that the American poet Louis Simpson had spoken of his awareness of the 'power and intelligence of things'. Pain was those later years, that power of things.

What of the neurosurgeon, Professor Robert in France, I started to wonder, as poetry—the pleasure of rhythm, the grace of words, the power of thinking in lines—cleared my mind, and the medications and constant standing tempered the pain. What of Nantes at the Atlantic mouth of the Loire, childhood home of Jules Verne; three hours by fast train, or an hour by plane, south-west of Paris?

7

Appointments in Nantes proved difficult to arrange. Emails and faxes, *Urgent et Confidentiel*, went unanswered. Key people were not available to take phone calls, their secretaries all shielding. My GP, fluent in French, spent half an hour on the phone one evening speaking to doctors in hospital corridors, and gave up. 'This is typical of things here,' commiserated a cousin in Toulouse, who had been similarly unsuccessful.

The uncertainty caused the pain to rise. I was aware that studies on wounded male soldiers and civilian patients after major surgery had revealed an interesting response to anxiety. It showed that while four out of the five civilians asked for pain medication, only a third of the soldiers requested relief, despite their greater tissue damage. The pain thresholds of the latter—free of the threat of battle—were higher than those of the civilians whose anxiety about not surviving the surgery had increased the post-operative need for narcotics.

I emailed Houston, Texas instead. Over the phone at four in the morning, I finally spoke to a knowledgeable medic: a sports medicine specialist, who had trapped his pudendal nerve in an accident and undergone surgery in France. Two years later, when he had his 'life back', he had returned to Nantes to work with Drs Labat and Bensignor and Professor Robert. As a result, in 2002 Houston offered the first expert diagnosis and treatment facility in the United States.

'Don't do anything that brings on the pain,' he advised. 'The pain is constant. Does this mean I shouldn't walk?' 'Not if it brings on the pain.'

'I've stopped sitting. Could the nerve spontaneously disengage?' 'No,' said the specialist who was happy for me to come to Houston but agreed that, financially speaking, I would be better to go to France. 'The nerve's had enough; you're at the top of the curve.'

Like Sir Richard Burton, weak and depressed having barely started the march that would lead to the discovery of Lake Tanganyika, I fretted about 'the sorry labour of waiting and reloading asses, the exposure to . . . morbific influences . . . the wear and tear of mind at the prospect of imminent failure'.

Like Burton's wife Isobel, who permanently injured her back and ankle after slipping in a Paris hotel, I might have written, 'Strong health and nerves I had hitherto looked upon as a sort of right of nature, and supposed everybody had them, and had never felt grateful for them as a blessing.'

A day later there was a message to contact Professor Robert. He spoke English, and was receptive to the symptoms I listed by phone. In due course, an email questionnaire arrived. Then, after multiple intercessions from friends who spoke French, dates for testing and surgery in August.

I completed the collection of poetry; had my hair cut, standing; on better days met friends for coffee in cafés with counters and bars.

In late July, shortly before leaving for France, the pain's base level had dropped to a Green 'blow to the nose' Three. Was this self-resolution, at last; should I cancel the arrangements in France?

I rang Atlanta, Georgia and spoke to the author of the PNE pain scale, and the website on which I had first made my diagnosis. Formerly entrapped, and freed by Professor Robert, he too had stopped sitting early and reduced his symptoms. On arrival in Nantes almost pain free he had been sent home, only to return the following year.

'It's playing hide and seek,' I said in a panic. 'It's devious and capricious. Soon I'll need it for testing and it might not be there.'

'Start sitting,' he urged. 'You should aim for at least a Three in Nantes for the tests to show cause and effect.'

8

Nantes straddles the Loire River close to the sea. The seventh largest city in France, and main city in the West, it has a population of 250,000 and a wider reach of 560,000.

'A strange city,' said a travel guide, 'born unto the river, a child of the water.'

'Once a centre of European surrealism,' said another.

Its history is marked principally by contradiction: by eighteenth-century slave trading when 450,000 Africans were shipped to America, and Nantes became France's foremost and wealthiest port; and by the 1598 Edict of Nantes: Henri IV's response to the Catholic–Protestant Wars of Religion granting the persecuted Huguenots freedom of worship and civil rights— revoked after the resumption of religious hostilities following Henri IV's assassination.

Of interest to a New Zealander, there was the 1986 Rugby Battle of Nantes, when the All Blacks were beaten 16–3 and Wayne (Buck) Shelford, at the bottom of a ruck in one of the toughest test matches of his career, tore his scrotum, displacing a testicle, and insisted the physiotherapist stitch it up at the side of the field (from where it was broadcast in close-up, live to the nation) so he could return to the game.

Jules Verne recalled his hometown—'point of departure for many a long journey'—with affection, and based much of his maritime writing on his childhood adventures there.

André Breton, the 'Pope of Surrealism', remarked that 'Nantes, alongside Paris, is perhaps the only town in France where I got the feeling that something worthwhile might happen to me'.

I travelled with John, precariously, lying and standing, sitting only for take-off and landing, protecting the nerve, attempting to maintain the pain at a tolerable level until I reached Nantes. I carried a medical letter of explanation for the airlines, and another for Customs as I was well stocked with codeine.

Between sleeping and eating I read my PNE file, pausing to picture the cadavers' quiet contribution. To be reassured by the photographs and explanatory diagrams of ligaments, muscles, fascia and vascular patterns they had made possible; the absence of supposition; the irrefutable language of anatomy. John shuddered and said, 'What the eye doesn't see,' but as a former nurse these were details I needed to know. I wanted, moreover, to be sure of my quarry. 'If you know the fighting capability of your opponents,' the fourteenth Dalai Lama said of suffering,

'. . . then you're in a much better position when you engage in the war.'

War was an apt metaphor. Be its theatre mind, body, society, or state, pain is perhaps the ultimate protection, persuasion and weapon. Aside from those rare individuals who, born without the ability to feel physical pain, tend to die young, its manifestations create the solidarity of uncertain fate and the vulnerability at the heart of life, and thereby of art, which, like the battlefields and other enduring illuminations of history, chart our struggle to define and withstand it.

We arrived at Charles de Gaulle airport at six in the morning. The reception clerk at the Sheraton, close by, astride a train station, could not check us in until noon. He gave us a key to the Club Lounge, empty, surreal, in which a buffet spread with cheeses, grapes, crackers and dried apricots, and small tables set with glasses and complimentary drinks, waited for guests who might not arrive. We opened a bottle of Badoit and watched planes take off less than 1,000 metres away.

There was an adjoining bathroom—an uncanny replica of the Warsaw scene of my fall: the same grey, mottled marble, and vertical tube lights either side of a bevel-edged mirror; the same shower over the same deep bath. I spread a towel on the floor for protection. Here, too, the hovering of unseen guests: a used ashtray and empty bottles of red raisin and grapefruit juice grouped to one side of the basin.

The suite was very quiet, with barely a hum from the air-conditioner and no hint of the workings of the airport, or of the large train station below. I lay on a narrow magazine stool with a velvet nap, my head in a soft chair. John tinkered with a samovar and tried to make tea. A lanky porter in a white jacket silently entered, and left with the empty bottles.

At twelve we took a corner table in the dining room. I stood discreetly against a wall. The pain, ever the genie, was rising, as if it knew Nantes was near, overtaking the codeine; the Australian wine; the sole, potatoes and broccoli, steamed to perfection; three

Englishmen at an adjacent table discussing pasta and olive oil with a hint of tarragon, and a married woman they all knew, who was having an affair.

Finally, entering our room, we found a voucher mistakenly inviting us to redeem 4,000 star points for a bathrobe or a bottle of Laurent Perrier Brut Champagne. Then, the telephone rang and a strange voice said, 'Oh darling, I've been trying to find you, where have you been?'

'France,' I said to John, 'is beginning to feel superstitiously appropriate and coincidental.'

That night we both dreamed of pigs: John's pig had a velvet shawl over its shoulders; mine was Dinah Hawken's favourite pet. John decided we had seen an animal resembling a pig in a TV report on flooding in Bangladesh the previous evening, and that the magazine stool in the Club Lounge accounted for the velvet napery. My connection was likely to be a couple of lines from 'Where We Say We Are', Dinah's poem of travel to the islands:

. . . I've come
for the drums, and the drumming, and the drumming of the
drums. I've come for the pig asleep in a ditch.

Nantes was the remembered France: melt-in-the-mouth fish, crusty breads and crisp vegetables; sweet tomatoes and impeccable peaches; the courteous French, their mellifluous language: it was impossible not to speak French, no matter how flawed, in the slipstream of the language.

I browsed in perfumeries, stood in the shop of *le chocolatier* where the aroma alone was sufficient, laundered our clothes using fine soaps, bought slim fitting sandals, forgot about sun block, was stopped twice in one day for directions and three times for market research.

The temperature averaged thirty degrees, but the sun had a bathing quality and the light was redemptive, golden. Our room, with its small balcony overlooking the tops of the tilleul trees in the Rue du Couedic and the potted daisies and sun-yellow awnings of the Entrecôte café, was golden. The old stone was golden. The doctors, nurses and the general population and its many dogs tucked into baskets on buses and trams and in banks, were golden. Shops closed for lunch, as expected, and didn't open on Sundays. Nobody dined before seven. The shade and early morning air were dry and pleasantly cool.

I pushed pain, at will, to one side. This was the summer I had forsaken.

In the hotel lobby and lifts I scrutinised guests for signs of nerve entrapment. A woman with an American accent stumbled over 'Bonjour' at the desk and alighted on the second floor when she meant to go to the third. She looked tired. Breakfast was delivered on a tray to her room. Was she a contender?

A friend from New Zealand, holidaying in Pornic on the coast, drove through. We spent the afternoon beside a fountain sipping martinis and toasting the synchronicity of our visits.

'I'm sleeping on saffron,' I said.

'France is the land of indulgence,' she agreed, smoking her cigarettes and tossing her newly blonde hair.

I sat, calling in la douleur for the diagnostic nerve blocks and Motor Latency Tests the following day. I was aiming for the Pink 'utterly horrible' Eight on the Pain Scale—'Pain so intense you can no longer think clearly at all, and have often undergone severe personality change'—and had photographs taken to prove it.

The CT-guided blocks were no problem: an average visit to the dentist. The thirty shocks to the deep nerve were worthy of the Inquisition, but the pain caused was short term: un mauvais quart d'heure. It produced a three-page graph and the conclusion, Il existe donc des arguments en faveur d'un syndrome canalaire du nerf pudendal bilatéral. It confirmed my diagnosis. It wasn't running my life. At the end of the day I left it, like a truculent customer, at the door of its clinic and took a taxi back to the hotel for a drink.

9

I had a gap of ten days before my consultations with Professor Robert and the all-important anaesthetist, on the afternoon before surgery.

John left for a short visit to his mother in Scotland. I was tired, and elected to stay in Nantes. The holiday season was under way. The sun was out, the streets were crowded and the canopied restaurants and brasseries beckoned. I wanted to linger over a sidewalk *pain au raisin* and *café*, the mild breeze ruffling my hair, swirling the steam from my cup, but I didn't feel brave enough to stand alone at a table. I walked to the castle—site of the signing of the Edict of Nantes—only to find the bridge across the moat blocked because maintenance was in progress. On the way back to the hotel, I lit a candle in the cool, neo-Gothic Basilica of St Nicholas and read Cardinal Newman's '*Ce que tu voudras*', which I selected from the pile of coincidentally coloured Minor Green, Medium Yellow and Severe Pink leaflets.

My cousin in Toulouse phoned. 'When John returns, come down,' he said. 'We'll take you to the country and escape the heat.'

I lay on the bed reading Robert Hass's translation of *The Selected Poetry of Rainer Maria Rilke*. In 'O Lacrimosa', Rilke had written:

Ah, but the winters! The earth's mysterious turning-within . . .
. . .
Where imagination occurs
beneath what is rigid; where all the green worn thin by the vast
summers
again turns into a new
insight and the mirror of intuition

From time to time I stood in my strappy sandals and updated my diary on the laptop which I'd positioned on the dressing table on top of the shoebox; where I also ate takeaway pastries and *tartines*—watching myself in the mirror.

The only television channel in English endlessly repeated news stories about the armed theft, from an Oslo museum, of Munch's *The Scream*; and the tallest living man who plucks the sweetest apples from the highest trees, struggles to live life at ground level and said from Ukraine, 'I must adapt to the world rather than the world to me.'

On the weather front, the east coast of Scotland was covered by a haar, and southwest Europe was having a heat wave.

The French channels carried footage of the Pope's visit to Lourdes. Jean Paul II was shown nearing the ivy-covered Grotto of Apparitions on his mobile throne. Pilgrims applauded and reached forward to absorb divine radiance. A nun spoke directly to camera about his courageous example, and a former nurse with a back injury said with conviction that she had 'a lot of faith in a cure'.

'If the Pope remains afflicted,' I said to the screen, 'how can I expect any improvement?'

I watched the long lines of pain. More than three decades earlier I had trained as a nurse. Although steroids and anti-inflammatory drugs were slowly making inroads into the treatment of debilitating inflammatory conditions, including the various forms of arthritis, derivatives and permutations of the ancient poppy had not been superseded in the management of terminal and other great physical pain. Advances had, however, been made in the *delivery* of relief: the constancy of Patient Controlled Analgesia units, for example, had replaced four-hourly injections for surgical and terminally ill patients; and epidural anaesthesia, which had revolutionised childbirth, could be substituted for general anaesthetics in abdominal and lower limb surgery and continued in the ward, or commenced during general anaesthesia, numbing the area even as the operation took place.

I remembered a woman I had nursed through the final stages of breast cancer: her name, her darkened room; her fragility and bone thin body as I sponged her, and held her against me when, unable to use a bed pan, she had made her way to the toilets. During visiting hours her husband had sat beside her bed, his head bent, asking, 'Is it time for her next injection?' When he wasn't there she had called for it as I went to and fro past her room, also longing for the regulated moment when I could unlock the Dangerous Drugs cupboard, draw up the morphine, administer the harsh intramuscular needle.

I called up my own foretaste of pain at fifteen when, following major abdominal surgery, I had learnt that empathy and a lightness of touch are not inherent in nurses; and later, perusing my medical record, that the injections that had not diffused their customary soothing warmth had contained sterile water, lest I become addicted to pethidine.

I thought about my brother, four years on, aged eighteen, dying of motorcycle injuries and rare, undiagnosed gas gangrene, asking me, as a student nurse, why the injections for the escalating pain in the stump of his amputated leg were not working.

My mother had passed away in a hospice, in the twilight sleep of a continuous morphine pump. But all may not have been as it seemed. Earlier in the course of the cancer, an idiosyncratic response to morphine had seen her hallucinate in an unbreakable nightmare. When the medication was stopped and the world returned to normal, she had preferred pain to the side effects of relief. She had asked me to watch her closely when she needed the morphine pump again, at the end. She had seemed peaceful, but what, I had agonised, of her state of mind and hidden dreams?

The next evening I couldn't find the peaches I'd bought at the supermarket. The following morning two glass tumblers were missing. In the wake of the testing, and alone in the hotel, pain, the opportunist, no longer needed, was trying to run away with me.

10

John returned. We flew south, then drove to Languedoc, and La Balbougette, my cousin's *petit manoir*.

This is sunflower country; on either side of the road, crops bow east and west, acknowledging the changing light, waiting for rain.

It is a region of spirited winds, the wild dreaming and interpretation of winds, the chronic bending of trees.

It is home to the *autan*, which makes autumn seem like spring and brings malice and happiness in the same breath.

From the eleventh to the thirteenth centuries it was a stronghold of the Cathars—believers in the greater religious purity of early Christianity's gentleness and poverty before their denouncement as heretics, their suffering at the hands of the Inquisition and the eradication of their faith.

We spent an afternoon at Carcassonne, a working walled city, once a Cathar fortress, exploring the restored ramparts and towers from which sieges were lost and repelled while the population within perished in epidemics and died of thirst in the summer's intense heat. As we were leaving, storm clouds gathered overhead funnelling thunder, rain and a midnight wind through the streets. Lanterns swayed. Tourists converged in a narrow dash to the barbican and car park. The heat wave had broken.

At La Balbougette, after the wind had died down, the shutters had stopped banging and the loggia and pool had been cleared of branches and leaves, I helped with the leisurely purchase and preparation of food. And lay as if in a field, beneath Indian lilacs, flowering laurels and the sky of the sieges, balanced between the Crusades and Inquisitions of Languedoc and the short-lived relief of the Edict of Nantes; themes of pain and transcendence.

Here pain, still skilled in the art of intrigue, spoke with a Saracen tongue, posing questions about the blending of the pain of body, mind and soul with salvation; the existence of ecstasy without agony; the influence of the middle ages when the owners of hospices—centres of enlightenment as well as curing—sought portraits of suffering for their chapels so that, in the contemplation of intensely visualised pain, the sick, wounded and possessed might be persuaded to confront and come to terms with pain, to pray and, through prayer, achieve healing belief.

I recalled the life-sized figure of Christ on the Isenheim

Altarpiece by sixteenth-century Bavarian painter Matthias Grünewald, commissioned for the hospital of the Antonite monastery in southern Alsace, where the polyptych remained until the French Revolution and the secularisation of art and healing. And the centre panel of Grünewald's masterpiece—the crucifixion—which embodied not only unimaginable suffering—graphic wounds; the grey distortion of shock, exhaustion and the body's dislocating weight; the hidden suffocation caused by the pull of the stretched arms and sockets constricting the rib cage and lungs—but also, through the symbolism of the lamb at Christ's feet, patient and sacrificial suffering as a means of redemption. On the panels either side of the pictorial disquisition, wings, supportive saints and images of the Annunciation and Resurrection were depicted, like Nantes, in the bathing, golden light of salvation.

I reflected on the heroic example of Pope John Paul II, for whom the meaning of suffering was said to be found in reminding the rest of us that we cannot control our lives, and in eliciting from those who observe pain and its process, an ennobling compassion. The view of the fourteenth Dalai Lama that suffering was unremarkable, and occurred because it was a 'part of nature and a fact of life', simply because the body existed. De Quincey, continually battling opium withdrawal, whose writings suggest a conviction that without pain the creative spirit and intellect will not fully develop. Voltaire's pragmatic Candide, who, having endured and witnessed a range of suffering, decided: 'All this was indispensable; for private misfortune makes the general good, so that the more private misfortunes there are, the greater is the general good.'

I wondered to what loss society has anaesthetised and misplaced the physiological processes of pain and its wider references—in the hasty, changing face of nursing, for example, in which machines are the first call of patients in their hours of greatest need—and whether the streamlining of alleviation—and technology-based nursing—mattered? A recent article in the *Sunday Times* had suggested it did. The writer, who suffered a chronic condition and had been admitted to a famous London public hospital where she had languished in pain and 'terrified' despite a sedative and strong painkiller, had lamented the decline in clinical expertise and absence of the 'essence of nursing'.

'Their training has robbed them of the language of compassion,' she wrote, citing the 'uber' efficiency and theoretical ethos of the new university-trained nurses.

In the end I conjectured that, new efficiencies aside, the quiddity of long-term pain—which, even as it eases seeks to return, escapes shape yet is a shaping force, causes life to lose its leniency and also its steadfast form, raises walls and during phases of relentless attack breaks those same walls down—is uncertainty. That its chronic form educes a state of closing doors: doors behind which I had found neither rampart nor crenellation, 'mirror of intuition' or rite of enlightenment and, while it would have been reassuring to believe otherwise, no new tolerance, patience or proof of learning; just a heightened sense of Time— sometimes stoic, sometimes teasing—which replied when I said, 'I am sadder and more aware, but can I *really* say I am wiser?': 'Take what comes your way. You are what you are, as you were born, as you were raised, as you will always be.'

11

A couple of days later in Nantes, in the Hôtel Dieu, a 915-bed university teaching hospital, the nerve was released from sites of severe entrapment on both sides of the pelvis. 'It's free in soft tissue in a more protected position,' said Professor Robert on his ward round the next morning.

He had performed 1,000 trans-gluteal surgical decompressions on patients, worldwide, since 1987. However, with 300,000 coronary artery bypasses carried out annually in the USA alone, PNE was hardly routine. Nevertheless, Robert reassuringly quipped, he could carry out the procedure blindfolded. Less reassuring was the state of the nerve: its long years of imprisonment and flattening, particularly on the left side. 'Until age seventy,' said Robert, 'the nerve is young.' The nerve was young enough to recover. Suddenly the accident in Poland was assuming new meaning. Without the fall and exacerbation of the pain I might unwittingly have pressed on sitting indefinitely, writing, until the expert team was no longer available, or the nerve viable.

Was the injury a *miraculum secundum naturam*; could it be one of the rare occurrences under this heading; had an event of wind and sun brought me to Nantes where poet René Guy Cadou observed he had encountered enough 'subjective coincidences' to suggest he lived in the city of Orpheus, tamer of wild animals and writer of mystical books?

*

'I need to think of the pain as a positive force,' I said to John ten days into recovery, as we lent on a table, at bar height, sharing a sesame-coated panini and raspberry tart in the Nantes Monoprix café.

In his *Second Manifesto of Surrealism* (1929), Breton had declared, 'Everything leads us to believe that there is a certain state of mind from which life and death, the real and the imaginary, past and future, the communicable and the incommunicable, height and depth, are no longer perceived as contradictory.'

The nerve, without the sedation of morphine or the restriction of scar tissue, irritated by handling, was registering pain at an intense Yellow Six, described on the Scale as 'comparable to a bad non-migraine headache combined with several bee stings, or a bad back'.

I was reminded of my poet cousin, Potocki de Montalk, and his belief in the mystical power of words. And Paracelsus, who had urged doctors to take lessons from 'old wives, gypsies, sorcerers, wandering tribes', writing, 'Resolute Imagination can accomplish most things.' 'I need to believe that pain is a welcome or appropriate presence,'

I continued. 'Like the wind after monotonous calm, or the visit of a previous but still meaningful friend; a burden, *un fardeau*, with a purpose.' The scrutiny of rationalisation and curing magic was turning full circle.

'You could convert to Catholicism,' John suggested. 'Follow the example of the Pope.'

'Or become a Buddhist—recognise that this is a physical pain, and know it is no more than a physical pain,' I said without assurance.

I walked cautiously from the café to the hospital for my final post-operative follow-up. My buttock muscles were in spasm. I felt as if I was walking through sand.

In the Service de Neurotraumatologie, a nurse, efficient in a white smock and tapered trousers, showed me to a treatment cubicle. My experience of the Hôtel Dieu had been positive. The anaesthetic had been effective; the pain of surgery contained by the intravenous administration of morphine commenced in the operating theatre as surgery still took place, and by the competence of nurses who did not speak English but were skilled in the slow arts of comfort and touch.

I lay face down as she swabbed the incisions, snipped the stitches at either end and noted a surface haematoma.

Professor Robert was called. He pressed either side of the wounds and helped me to my feet. 'Good,' he said. 'Remember that the original pain could be worse for six months, perhaps more. This is normal: the nerve has been assaulted. You may increase your medications. Don't return to work for eight weeks. Don't ride a horse or a bike.'

'The muscle spasms?'

'During surgery the muscles were forced apart with retractors. The spasms will lessen. Nature provides.'

'The flattened left nerve—will it recover?'

'It's not possible to assess the success, or otherwise, of this operation until at least a year after surgery.' He shrugged. 'I perform a simple procedure, only God knows the outcome.'

We passed from the cubicle, to the corridor where his students clustered respectfully at a distance, to the office. His secretary collated a travel authorisation and *Compte Rendu Opératoire* in French and, because of the entrapment's obscurity, a letter of explanation in English. The letter advised that all branches of the nerve were affected and concluded that only time would determine the surgical outcome and ability to fully resume the activities of daily living and employment.

In a few days I would be on the other side of the world. I was seeking a lyrical moment, a prevailing wisdom; a conclusion worthy of the journey. A journey, I was to find, that would still be testing me a year later as pain became ingrained, the capability of codeine diminished, and sitting was not possible; as I investigated a five-day continuous epidural anaesthetic to block the pain pathways and eradicate old signals still firing, and Botox injections to relax the obdurator internus muscle near the troublesome nerve; as British scientists, testing pain sensitivity in mice in the search for biochemical pathways that will better combat pain, found that rodents with a yellow fur gene mutation require lower levels of pain medication, and heartened researchers at Stanford University, using magnetic imaging, visually affirmed pain in the brain as it occurred and hailed the potential of their new technology as 'the holy grail of pain research'.

Professor Robert said, demonstrating, 'Bend and lift your knees so the nerve slides back and forth.' He held out his hand for the letter. 'The Edict of Nantes,' I murmured, the pain limited by his presence.

He clicked his pen. I asked, 'Can I sit?'

He nodded. 'You can sit—in accordance with pain.'

'How should I exercise—should I walk, can I swim?'

He spread the letter on the desk. 'Yes, but again, in accordance with pain.'

A bed was wheeled past the office, sides raised, drip stand attached, the tube running between the drip and a mechanised syringe barrel timing and dispensing relief from inside a plastic orange case.

Professor Robert paused as if in thought, or perhaps for dramatic effect. 'Pain is the leader,' he said, signing the page.

Elizabeth Nannestad

The Gold Day Has Dimmed

The gold day
has dimmed.

All that happened was the sun
went behind a cloud—
fiery was the green
among the leaves

trunks, stems
filled themselves, rose, wanting to multiply

all living things
and the earth too, the stones

were stirred
with desire.

Wherever there was water
there was light and life

and the air: well!—
you could swim in it.

The sun went behind a cloud
and all that is over now.

Emma Neale

Unlove

My friend who says her mind has frozen
My friend who says her mind has frozen—

My friend whose mind has frozen
sends me small gifts she says to keep her sane—
a cornflower-blue watch;
a box carved of light with a green latch;
a pink soapstone egg she says will one day hatch
a small, exquisite monster, its teeth sharp as love.

'It will mark you for me,' she says—
'Tiny cat nips, bee bites, gin stings—
mouth filled with time's nettled patch
you would not pluck safe for me.'

Couldn't, I have to say to her, each time.
Couldn't. Body closed as a sugar snap pea.
Mind the silk-sheathed pulse in that body.
This love that only thrives in sun-winds pocketed
by cacti, rocks, hooves, scales:
in the feral thirsts of the near-alien,
not rippled mirrors of rains, lakes, streams.

Bill Nelson

Rotational Head Injury

ever since I did the thing
I can't remember I did
we've tried to piece it together
the helmet with barely a scratch
the pine needles in bizarre places
the tendons, ropey and tender in my neck
I've asked you this before haven't I?
I keep saying as you nod, falling
into a pool of synaesthesia

ever since I did the thing
I did not do, a ropey concern
synaesthesia like tendons in bizarre places
the eye, my neck, we've tried
to keep saying this before, piece it
back together, have we been here
before? falling deep, I ask
in a pool of pine needles
have I or haven't I

I can't remember my synaesthesia
the thing I did or since
a bizarre place of us forever
the helmet with barely a scratch
tender and ropey, the neck asking
before we keep saying piece it
together, a nod to the deep, pine needle
pool, tender and falling

ever since we did the thing
I can't remember we did
I've fallen in a deep pool

asking you again and again
about the helmet, bizarre and ropey
your synaesthesia like pine needles
a tender scratch, your nod
the together we barely had
in pieces

Mikaela Nyman &
Rebecca Tobo Olul-Hossen

I love you?

Where are all the bananas when you crave one?
Takes nine months for the herb to shoot
new fruit-bearing limbs, light its purple–red
lamp, unfold ten rings
of green fingers.

> Those were the words on her Messenger screen.
> Seriously, she barely knows you, jerk!
> And you're already spouting 'I love you's?
> Doesn't he know she has met many like him?
> Those who use these words to get what they want
> words as sweet as ripe mangoes in season.

Thinking about what might transpire
in nine months.

Thinking of those thinking about
what could happen in nine months

> and all that happened.

> Okay, maybe overripe mangoes just about to go off!
> She is 25 turning 40.
> This is what people tell her.
> They tell her she is complex.
> She wonders if it's complex like a wide-woven
> Futunese mat
> or a highly strung Ambae basket, almost
> PNG-like in texture

I wish you knew how intense the taste
of that first banana after a cyclone.
Like freshly squeezed pamplemousse juice, the first
yam harvested, beyond carbs,
water, sweetness. More than potassium
and tryptophan, slight tartness of wild
berries.

Tastes sunrain and life, promises
that all will be well.

And that's why we eat another
and another
and another.

> If only she were naïve
> like a girl who just had her kaliku
> after seeing her first period and coming
> of womanhood.
> Then maybe the 'I love you's would be
> taken differently.
> For now this girl of 25 turning 40 unfriends him
> and blocks him on Messenger.

Kaliku, in Tannese, is a traditional celebration of girls from Tanna when they see their first
menstruation and enter into womanhood.

Claire Orchard

Early morning on the Sand-walk,
Down House, March 1857

Praise be for fan-tailed pigeons, for flies
who lay their eggs in the navels of animals,
and every parasite that clings to life,

for red-grouse the colour of heather,
black-grouse that of peaty earth,
for the abundance of hair on the breast of the wild turkey,

the inherited peculiarities of the horns on cattle,
for tidal floods of starlings in massed tumblings
across winter skies, for the plumed seed that is wafted.

Praise be for brown beetles diving in streams,
for the wolf pack in snow,
hard pressed for food,

for upland geese with webbed feet
who seldom go near the water, for the beak
and tongue of the woodpecker,

for humble bees sucking at red clover blooms,
for each form, lightly chalked upon a wall,
divided into great branches, oddly perfect.

Vincent O'Sullivan

When in Rome

A dog walks past the Colosseum.
He smells the fun from out here.
That must seem rather marvellous
to a dog. He has seen lions
in a hut hauled by Nubians
and thought, Christ, now there's
a challenge! He hears a tiger from
right across the Tiber, he figures
two animals went into a cage
together and now are both at once,
sizing him up through the bars of their skin.
What's Rome without excitement? He
lollops on, temples to one side, arches
the other, a street where you purchase
dogs, a street where you eat them.
A matter of logic a dog's your natural
cynic? He doubles back mid-afternoon.
The roar's lifting its quick dark rock.
So what happens if the lion loses?
He imagines a small girl
with her clay fish wouldn't half mind.

Cate Palmer

In Search of X

Only a mother could love such an ugly child. With its peeling-bark skin and rubbery lips and dull alien eyes, the toothfish will never be a conservationist flag-bearer. Let the polar bears keep that accolade: at least they make cute plush toys.

Nevertheless, Art feels a certain fondness for the toothfish. As he watches it float languidly across its temperature-controlled tub, he sometimes finds himself wondering about it: what do the lab lights look like through that thin blanket of water, those quasi-nocturnal eyes? How do the tank's tight walls compare to the ocean's mesopelagic vastness? Does the water smell different? Does it feel different? Does the toothfish have regrets?

He knows this is dangerous terrain: he's not supposed to empathise with the specimens. As far as he's concerned, the toothfish is no more than an interesting puzzle, a fish-shaped riddle, a sackful of scientific goodies. But in the perpetual white light of the Antarctic summer, everyone goes a little bit crazy. A year or two ago, they had a glaciologist who became convinced the ice was changing colour. At first it was just the usual mirages—jutting cliffs on the far horizon—but then the illusions started warping and flickering, shifting from red through green through purple and back again. He'd had insomnia for weeks, mind you, and the advent of a sleeping mask eventually turned everything back to white. But still, you never know what the endless ice, the endless daylight, the endless rotation of the same forty faces, will do to you.

The airlock sighs and Art hears the thud of boots, the rasp of a zip. A ripple creases the water's surface, and he wonders whether the fish recognises Klaus's heavy German tread. Its head seems to nod to one side as if to say *Yes*, but perhaps he is imputing intention where none exists. That's the difference between him and Klaus: Klaus assumes all creatures are automatons, and is habitually surprised that the catering staff can speak.

Klaus emerges from the vestibule and pulls off his balaclava. His sharp nose is red and scorched-looking, and as he closes the door he gives Art a curt little nod. 'There was nothing on the lines.'

Art shrugs. 'What a surprise.'

Klaus gives him a pointed look, but he doesn't say anything. He goes to his desk and pulls out the chair and sits down, peeling off his double-layered woollen socks and draping them one by one over the radiator. His feet emerge, long and white, the pinched toes like children's fingers. He swivels in his chair and fixes Art with his pale blue gaze. 'I met the journalist this morning. She is very excited to talk with us about our research. I told her she can come to our lab tomorrow afternoon.'

Art frowns. 'I thought she was here to talk to James and Rodney.'

'She is, but she is here for a whole week, and she says she may as well look at the other research while she is at the base.'

'So she's an opportunist.'

Klaus shrugs. 'She has heard about our research, and it greatly intrigues her.'

Art puts his elbows on the desk and cups his hands around his forehead. His fingers are thick and clammy against his thinning scalp. 'What has she heard?'

'She knows all about the new species. She called it the "geriatric fish".'

Art snorts. 'That's not even witty. I hope she's not planning on putting that in an article.'

'No,' says Klaus, 'I don't think so. I think she is more interested in finding out what tests we have been running.'

Art slides his head up until he can see through the gaps in his fingers. 'That's none of her business. We shouldn't be talking to the media before we've even written the preprint. It's just not good form. So I don't know who she thinks she is, but all she's going to get is a couple of pretty pictures of her "geriatric fish".' He peels his hands off his face and folds his arms on the desk. There's something odd about Klaus's expression. 'What's her name? The journalist?'

Klaus shrugs, too casually. 'Octavia.' He makes a show of flipping his socks over on the heater.

'How old is she?'

Klaus frowns. 'Why is that important? Age does not matter to whether she does her job well.'

'So she's young?'

'She is twenty-eight.'

'How on earth do you know that? Is she attractive?'

Klaus's jaw tenses, and he looks over Art's shoulder. 'If she were, it would have no bearing.' He stands up abruptly. 'I'm going to lunch.'

'You only just got back,' says Art. 'It's only eleven thirty.'

'Nevertheless,' says Klaus, 'I am very hungry.' Without looking at Art, he gathers his socks off the radiator and pulls them onto his feet one by one, gripping the desk with one hand to steady himself. Art watches the angular shoulders as they bend and straighten, the blond fuzz of hair as it winks in and out of the light, and thinks: if I were twenty-eight and female and a journalist, would I charm this man to make him talk? And then he thinks: you old fool. He watches as Klaus strides into the vestibule, as the door thuds behind him. In the tank the fish drifts, thinking its alien thoughts, and beyond that, through the triple-glazed window, the ice spreads into the distance and erupts into mountains.

*

Specimen #1 was drifting fifteen metres below the ice at Cape Vernon when Art came upon it. In the blue gloom he thought perhaps he was seeing things: this, surely, was *Dissostichus mawsoni*, but for some reason his eyes were giving it an overly bulbous head, a fan-shaped caudal fin. It took no notice of him and continued to drift along in the semi-dark, a fish-shaped patch of altered light. It was too pale. Its rough hide was almost milky, like a cataract, not brown or black or grey as *D. mawsoni* was supposed to be. He knew he should signal to Klaus, he should prepare the net, but he could not take his eyes off the fish. What if he turned to signal, and suddenly it was gone? Even then, it had an odd dignity about it: it was like a grand old dame crossing a very wide, blue street.

Klaus appeared at his elbow. He held one end of the net between his three-fingered gloves, and trailed it so Art could grab the other. Together they guided the fish into nylon mesh. Up and up they dragged it, towards the hole in the ice through which they'd found a Weddell seal poking its head the previous week, sucking air into its lungs and gazing out across the sea's eggshell lid.

The pale colouring was even more pronounced without fifteen metres of water and a two-metre sheet of ice above it. Sprawled in the net the fish looked indecent, like a dog without fur, and in the harsh light its eyes had closed to slits. Art was eager to get it into the portable tank on the back of the Hagglund; the sight of its gills opening and closing like concertinas made his throat dry.

They rode with it back to the base and eased it into the tank by the window. While Klaus took photos and compiled observations in his neat, upright hand, Art scoured the pages of *Fishes of the Southern Ocean*. There was no mention of a third toothfish species, nothing beyond the thoroughly overfished and moderately overfished Patagonian and Antarctic varieties. Had there ever been sightings of a pale, bulbous-headed mutant? No. Nothing so much as a fan-shaped tail receding into the gloom.

Two days after they brought it in, Specimen #1 succumbed to the scalpel. Art watched as Klaus's steady white-gloved hand guided the blade along ridges and flanks, across the slippery terrain of organs, as piece by piece the creature gave up its secrets. Macroscopically, it was virtually interchangeable with *D. mawsoni* and *D. eleginoides*: a cartilaginous skeleton, oily flesh, piscivorous stomach contents. But when they looked closer, at the six tiny otoliths with their tree-stump bands of opacity and translucency, they counted three-hundred-and-twenty-nine summers and three-hundred-and-twenty-eight winters. And Art found himself thinking not of fame or fortune or the thrill of discovery, but of the fish as he'd seen it down below the ice, propelling its ancient bulbous body at last into the jaws of death. Didn't it seem sad, to kill a creature that may have gone on living and living and living forever? But *sad* was dangerous. *Sad* could not be quantified. *Sad* meant he would soon be writing poems and interpreting omens and praying to some vaguely hypothesised benevolent entity in the sky.

*

'So how old is this specimen?' says the journalist, nodding her head in the direction of the tank.

'We don't know,' says Art. 'It's kind of tricky to extract the otoliths from a live specimen.'

She doesn't laugh. Instead she turns to Klaus. 'Is there a reason for keeping it here by itself? Are you doing tests on it?' She has short dark hair and eyes that could be green but are probably hazel, and she is—as Art feared—moderately attractive. On a street in a crowded city she wouldn't stand out, but this is no Times Square, no Champs-Élysées: she has raised the base's female population, temporarily, to fourteen.

'We are hoping to find a mate for it,' says Klaus. 'This one is a female. But we have not had much luck catching a male this summer.' He looks as if he's arranged himself to look casual: an ankle resting on the opposite knee, arms draped over the sides of his chair.

She smiles. 'Are you hoping to breed them?'

'Yes. That is the plan.'

'Is there a special reason for that? Something you want to look at more closely?'

Klaus's smile wavers. Art says, 'I'm sorry, but we're not at liberty to discuss that.'

She sits back in her chair. 'Oh, well I just thought it sounded intriguing—James Hurst was telling me you'd found a substance that was yielding some interesting test results, but that I'd have to talk to you about it to get the details. I know it's all a preliminary stage, but—'

'We can't discuss it,' Art says again.

She crosses one leg over the other, and Art gets a glimpse of the underside of her jeans. She looks like a woman who is used to commanding the thigh-riding power of skirts. 'So you can't even tell me what field of research it's likely to impact? I assume it'd be something to do with ageing, since the fish are so old . . .'

She is looking at Klaus, but Art speaks again. 'No, I'm sorry. It's simply a procedural thing. Legally and professionally, it would be a bad move to say anything before we've published an article.'

Her mouth—a fleshy, rather sensual mouth—is turned down at the corners. But she says, 'Would you be able to notify me first, once you're free to talk about it? If I get some photos now, we could conduct the interview over the phone.'

'Yes,' says Klaus before Art can speak, 'we would be happy to do that.' He straightens up in his chair, curls his shoulders back. 'Right now we can talk about our ongoing research, if that interests you—we are investigating the population structure of *Dissostichus mawsoni*, to determine what level of fishing is sustainable.'

'Sure,' she says. 'But do you mind if I get some photos of the fish first?' Without waiting for a response, she draws a camera out of her bag and twists the lens cap off, hooks the neckband over her head.

'Of course you may,' says Klaus. Then he adds, 'We have more specimens in the aquarium next door—they are the common Antarctic toothfish, but perhaps you are interested in photographing them also.'

'Sure,' she says again, fiddling with the camera settings. Then she raises her head, smiles. 'I would love to.'

*

Specimen #2 turned up in the general-purpose aquarium two months after Art spotted its predecessor drifting below the ice. The scientists who brought it in had been looking for a sample of transparent-blooded icefish, and they'd found their quarry—a shoal of silver mackerels in flight from a pale, bulbous-headed predator. In their haste to net the predator, they'd lost the mackerel icefish, all except one, which had already been severed above the dorsal fin by a cavernous, heavy-lipped mouth studded with small conical teeth.

Art went and had a look at the new catch after one of the icefish-hunters burst into the lab, sending a few sheets of paper scudding into the air. 'We've found another one,' he said.

Art stared at him. 'Another what?'

'Another macrocephalous toothfish,' he said, as if it was obvious. 'Come on, we've put it in a tank next door.'

Art followed him along the hallway to the aquarium, past the tanks of sea spiders and octopuses, stingrays and nudibranches. The fish was in a circular tank at the back of the room, drifting expressionlessly. It had the same pale skin and globular head as the first specimen. Art felt his pulse ascend into his throat. 'Where did you find it?' he said, in a voice that probably smacked of possessiveness. But the icefish-hunter didn't seem to notice.

'Western end of the sound,' he said. 'About ten metres down. It was chasing a shoal of mackerels. I don't know about the others, but as soon as I saw it I knew we'd found something different.'

Two weeks later, Specimen #2 joined Specimen #1 in the freezing room, reduced to a series of tissue samples in sealed capsules and carefully measured photographs. Among other things, its body gave up three pairs of otoliths, which placed its birth approximately half a century before the beginning of the Industrial Revolution, more than a hundred years before the first human stepped foot onto the ice above it.

At the end of the summer, Art, Klaus, and the tissue samples left the base in the cargo hold of a C-17. They returned to Art's alma mater, the university he'd graduated from three times and taught at for almost three decades, where Klaus had arrived as a prodigious twenty-two-year-old PhD student almost ten years earlier. Between teaching classes—Biology and Behaviour of Marine Vertebrates, Antarctic Marine Biology—they ran a series of increasingly complex tests on the tissue samples. Slowly, the possibilities narrowed. They'd hoped that isolating and comparing stretches of DNA with those of *D. mawsoni* would yield promising results, but after two months they had failed to find a sequence that differed in any significant way. It was only when they turned to proteins that the results began to get interesting. At the end of June, after a host of dead-ends and premature eurekas—almost five months before they were due to return to the ice—they found substance X.

*

After the interview, Klaus offers to walk Octavia back to her dorm. Art watches them trudge across the gravel together: two bulky red figures against the utilitarian buildings and improbable ice. Even padded and uniformed, Klaus walks like a pair of scissors: legs straight, torso bent forward, as if he has been locked in position by screws to take the force of a ubiquitous headwind.

Once they've rounded a corner, Art goes back to his desk and pops open the bottle of wine he's had on his shelf since November. He pours himself a glass and takes a vinegary sip, watches as the toothfish inscribes a bored loop around the edge of the tank and then drifts back around the other way. He is tempted to talk to it, but he will need more wine before he is brave or foolish enough to do this.

After a few minutes he hears the airlock open—a sucking sound, like a greedy kiss—and shoves the wine glass behind his computer monitor. It sloshes a little, but doesn't spill. By the time the lab door opens he is poised in front of a spreadsheet, doing his best impression of the scientist's squint, licking the last dregs of wine from his beard. But it's only the cleaner.

'Afternoon,' says the kid, grappling with the vacuum cleaner as he pulls it behind him into the room. 'Hope this isn't a bad time for me to do the floor.'

Art can't remember his name—Tim? Rob? Nick? He looks about eighteen but probably has a master's degree in psychology. In another place, another season, he probably backpacks across Europe or teaches chubby preteens how to build fires and shoot arrows and deal with hormones at some American summer camp or other. His wide grin nicks dimples into both cheeks.

Art shrugs. 'Go ahead.'

The cleaner continues to grin. 'So the journo is talking to you guys now? I just ran into Klaus walking her back to her dorm—are you finally unveiling the big discovery?'

'What "big discovery"?'

The cleaner laughs. 'Oh, I dunno. The top-secret project you're working on. I heard you discovered the elixir of youth, or something like that.'

Art's laugh comes out tinny. 'Who told you that?'

The cleaner shrugs. 'I heard some of the scientists talking about it. The squid guys—Dave and Brian.'

Art frowns. 'Well, they were probably joking. We're not discussing our research with anyone yet.'

The cleaner begins unwinding the power cord from around the vacuum cleaner, looping it expertly over his arm as it detaches in rhythmic jerks from under the hooks. 'Still,' he says as he plugs it into the wall, 'you must be onto something, if the fish are hundreds of years old—they wouldn't live that long for no reason.'

Art can feel his face overheating. 'We're just not discussing it yet,' he says again.

The cleaner's eyebrows go up. '*Okay*. Sorry I asked.' He turns on the vacuum cleaner and begins running it back and forth across the floor. The roar of sucking air is a welcome replacement for the sound of his voice.

Art turns back to his desk and pretends to type up notes. He waits as the vacuum drones and falls silent, as the outlet releases the plug, as the cord winds back around the base. 'Well, see you,' says the cleaner, and Art grunts without turning around. He hears the roll of the wheels and the click of the door, waits for the airlock to release its breath. Through the window he sees the cleaner—a humanoid shape in red Extreme Cold Weather suit and white bunny boots—clomping across the gravel. Beyond him, scissoring back towards the lab, is a figure that can only be Klaus. On the narrow stretch between buildings there is no chance their paths won't cross.

'What did you say to Tom?' is the first thing Klaus says once he's clicked the door of the lab shut. 'He said you told him to stop asking about our research.'

'He was pestering me,' says Art. He knows he must sound like a finger-pointing child, but he can't stop himself. 'All I told him was that we're not discussing it yet.'

Klaus doesn't sit down, but paces the space between his desk and the tank. 'I don't know what has gotten into you—why are you so paranoid all of a sudden?'

'I'm not paranoid,' says Art. 'I just don't think we should be under such scrutiny from people who know nothing about what we're doing and will just go spreading exaggerated rumours—'

Klaus sits down. His expression is quizzical, but not angry. 'I know it's important to keep things quiet until we are ready to publish, but to be this militant about secrecy—' He shakes his head. 'You baffle me.'

Art feels a stab of regret for the chasm that has opened between them, and for a moment he thinks of telling Klaus he will stop the paranoia, he will pull out the chess set from where it's been gathering dust under his desk and it will be just like old times. Klaus is right that he's never been this militant before— he's happily talked to other journalists about other research projects. But not *this* research. Not *this* journalist. He presses his lips together.

'There is something bothering you,' says Klaus. 'I don't know what it is, but I feel you are very bothered.' He frowns as if to chide himself for the clunky wording. 'What is it? Are you reluctant about publishing?'

Art lets out a low laugh. 'Of course I want to publish. That's ridiculous. I just hate people coming and craning over our shoulders before we've even finished testing. That's my complaint.'

Klaus's eyebrows lift. 'Really?'

'*Yes*,' says Art, with what he knows is too much urgency. 'Can you just—bear with me? Put up with my foibles?'

That gets the ghost of a smile. But then Klaus stands. 'I just came back for my sunglasses. Octavia has asked me to show her around the base.'

Art tries to sound casual. 'Well, uh—would you mind not talking to her about any of this? Just pretend you didn't hear her, if she tries to slip in questions. Talk about the fisheries project, or something.'

Klaus sighs. 'Sure. If it's that important to you, I will put up with your foibles.' He puts on his sunglasses, walks to the door, and disappears.

*

It was like the moon landing of '69 (he was fourteen, filthy, had just spent the afternoon watching an ant colony in his parents' backyard) or the terrorist attacks of 9/11 (he was forty-six, in the midst of a divorce, eating Weet-Bix in boiled water on the fold-out bed in a colleague's apartment): it was only later, once he knew how significant the moment had been, that every mundane sight and smell of that morning was sealed onto its own cluster of neurons and tucked away in the folds of his cerebral cortex. The morning he discovered X, Art was killing time before a lecture, scrolling through the test results from the tissue samples as an author flicks through his own books, not really looking for anything in particular but enjoying the accumulated bulk of scrounged wisdom. Then he spotted it: nothing a layperson would notice, just a couple of atypical numbers. He glanced through the other files with mounting excitement, spilled his coffee on the keyboard, and dialled Klaus's extension.

Klaus came over immediately and they collected the anomalies into a single file, worked their way through the proteins that had come up in the mass spectrometry tests. Sure enough, there was one that didn't seem to fit the *D. mawsoni* biochemical profile. It was an unusual combination of alpha-helix and beta-sheet, coiled and then flattened with two glutamines popped on the end like a molecular tail. It was like what they say about love at first sight (an experience that Art, sadly, has never encountered): he knew as soon as he saw it that X was something special.

If he'd been strictly scientific, he would've christened the discovery with some long-winded structural name, a hefty combination of alphas and cystines and reductases and 7s. (He did—or rather, Klaus did—on the official documents.) But X had always appealed to him, perhaps as a relic of his boyhood love for pirate maps, for burying jars of marbles and marking the spots with crossed sticks. And yet it was still scientific, still algebraic in its own way: it was precise, but also mysterious, a palimpsest of X chromosomes and x-axes and x-squared and e-to-the-power-of-x. Science, after all, was really just a glorified treasure hunt.

In vitro X displayed fascinating properties. It was an enzyme—indestructible in the reactions it catalysed—but it appeared to midwife several different reactions, as if it were changing shape for each of them, refolding its amino chains to produce a new site for the reactants to lock into. But that couldn't be possible: an enzyme, like any protein, was a fixed configuration, an origami structure stamped atomically with its own instructions for folding. Could it be that X just had several reactant sites? It was unheard of, but technically possible. A multipurpose enzyme. A biochemical skeleton key. Who knew?

They began running tests on it. If X was somehow implicated in the toothfish's bizarrely long lifespan, there had to be some way they could reproduce the cellular effects it was having. The first few tests had negligible results, but it was when they injected it into a pair of ageing mice that things began to get interesting. It wasn't that the mice got any younger, but they passed the average lab-mouse lifespan without any signs of age-related decline. Had they found it at last—the holy grail of ageing research? Nothing was conclusive at this stage. But Art couldn't resist fantasising about the possibilities: what if he injected X into his own bloodstream? Would he suddenly become young and fit and lean, like Klaus? The thought was too dangerous. And it was far too early to begin thinking about human testing, anyway. First they'd have to see the mouse test through, hypothesise a causal mechanism. Secure a patent and publish their results. Talk to the media. (Could the toothfish—homely, cold-blooded, unspectacular—be at last on the cusp of fame? Art wasn't sure how he felt about that. Perhaps it would do some good, conservation-wise. But perhaps the fish was just too ugly.)

Then November arrived, and before they had a chance to run any more tests, they were back in the cargo hold of a C-17, on their way to find more specimens, and—with any luck—to breed them for X.

*

Art finds Klaus and Octavia in the bar. It's 10pm and he hasn't seen Klaus since he left to show her around after the interview. He has a creeping suspicion of what might be unfolding: Klaus, for all his razor-sharp intellect, is a fool when it comes to flirtation.

Sure enough, they are playing pool. Octavia is bent over the table in a stance that must be calculated to enhance cleavage, and Klaus is standing beside her, a little too close but not daringly so, tapping the cue she's holding with his forefinger.

Art watches through the window for a moment, then jerks open the airlock and pulls it shut behind him. He shucks off his ECW suit and stands there in the vestibule staring at someone else's jacket, wondering if he should just give up and go back to the lab. He'll just make things awkward—he'll be like the useless extra finger on a polydactyl hand. But he pushes the door open anyway.

As he approaches the pool table, Klaus's eyes flicker, and he pulls back as if Octavia has suddenly become electric. 'Hold it back here,' he says, a little too self-consciously, and indicates where 'here' is on the cue. She shifts her hand and slides the cue back and forth across the saddle of her thumb, thrusts it forward. The balls knock.

She laughs. 'I'm so useless at this.'

'You are just unpractised,' says Klaus. He nods stiffly in Art's direction. 'You have escaped from the lab.'

Octavia straightens up. 'Come to watch me lose?'

Art tries to think of a clever comeback, but then too much time passes and he finds himself remaining silent. From the set of Octavia's lips he can see that he has lost whatever power he had in the lab: here, away from the white coats and rubber gloves of home, he is simply in the way.

He mutters something patently insincere—'Just thought I'd wind down with a drink or two'—and lurches towards the bar. He points at a bottle and says, 'Could I have one of those?'

The bartender's eyebrows go up, but he doesn't say anything. Art swipes his card and takes the bottle.

'Do you want it in a glass?'

'Oh, no—I prefer it like this.' He makes a quick escape and slides into a window booth. Outside the sun is in its usual spot, hanging ponderously just above the horizon. The beer smells sour, but he raises it to his lips anyway, taking care to keep his teeth away from the rim.

He tries to catch what Octavia and Klaus are saying—he hears her laugh, and the monotone rumble of Klaus's vowels—but all he can make out is '. . . the hill?' and '. . . not getting any better.' He hazards a glance in their direction and sees that Klaus is returning the cues to the rack. Octavia is (or has been) watching him; her eyes dart to the window when she sees he's seen her.

Klaus appears at his elbow. 'Octavia would like to climb the hill. So that's where we are going.'

'Okay,' says Art. 'I hope the view is good.' He has a feeling he's just been snubbed. He sips his beer and watches as they make their way to the door, then re-emerge a minute or two later under anonymous red padding. As they trudge towards the hill a lone skua glides onto the gravel ahead of them, and the taller figure points and says something to the shorter figure. They stand there watching it for a minute or two, and Art imagines the lecture Octavia must be receiving: skua diet, skua pedigree, skua mating . . . Suddenly the bird raises its head and ascends into the air with a single beat of its wings.

Art waits until they've turned a corner, then stands up and carries the open bottle out into the vestibule. He sets it down by a pair of boots and pulls on his ECW suit. As he clomps out across the gravel he realises he has left the bottle behind, precariously full, ready for someone else to kick over. But he can't bring himself to care. All he wants to do is lie down and go to sleep.

But instead of taking him to his dorm, his feet carry him back to the lab. Before he realises he's in the wrong place, he has stripped off his overclothes and pushed open the door, padded over to his desk, reached down to switch the computer on. He can't be bothered going back out, performing the rigmarole of the dress-up and strip-down. So he spins in his chair while he waits for the computer to boot, stretches his feet out and looks at the tank.

The toothfish is not drifting from one end to the other but lying beneath the water, completely still. Panic sloshes in his gut. Before he knows what he's doing, he is kneeling beside the tank and reaching into the water, and his hand is on the fish's dorsal fin and then on its rough cold flank. The contact is startling, and his hand reels from it. The fish is hard and unyielding but unmistakably animal. A second or two after he draws his hand away, it propels itself across the tank with more speed than he has seen since it arrived in the lab. 'Sorry,' he mumbles. The fish doesn't say anything, but lingers down the far end of the tank as if waiting for a promise that he will do better next time. *Sorry,* he says again. 'I was worried.'

He crawls over to his desk and rises up onto his knees, reaches for the wine glass still lodged behind the computer screen. It's half-full, musty-smelling. He raises it to his lips. He has the odd feeling that someone is watching him, that he is performing. For the fish? No: for Klaus. Which is ridiculous. He takes a sip of the wine, swills it around in his mouth as he's seen the wine snobs do. 'Not bad,' he says, trying the words out. 'A little tart, but I'd give it an A-minus.'

The fish is still hovering down the far end of the tank. Art shuffles around the rim and settles into a crouch beside it. 'Are you all right now?' (No answer.) 'Were you . . . you must get kind of lonely in there.' It flicks its head to one side and bumps up against the tank's wall like a docking boat, and he curses whoever it was that chose a tank with opaque walls. He would like to be able to look at the fish and feel it looking right back at him.

'Well,' he says, setting his glass on the floor, 'you *look* lonely.' He reaches out a hand and lets it hover over the water for a moment. 'We need some icebergs, don't we? Make it feel like home.' He plunges his hand in, and feels the faint sting of the salt and the not-quite-sufficient chill, and then the fish's slippery flank. A jolt goes through him but he keeps his hand there, and the fish stays in place as if stunned. 'It's okay,' he says. 'I won't hurt you.'

*

They found Specimen #3 within a week of returning to the base. It was on the second line they checked that morning—a hook and sinker strung through a cylindrical puncture wound in the ice—and when they pressed the button on the mechanical winder, they weren't expecting much to come up. They sat and waited for the line to wind, and Art rubbed at the ice with the toe of his boot, scooped up the glassy crystals and considered patting them into a ball, throwing it at Klaus. It was what Klaus had done, the first time he came to the ice—threw and tasted the snow, sculpted it into a deformed snowman, lay in it and made angel wings—but he was no longer twenty-three and dazzled by everything he saw: he was staring intently into the hole, watching for the first glimpse of whatever it was that was on its way up.

'Do you think—' he started to say, and then his eyes widened. A sound came out of his mouth, but it wasn't a recognisable word. Art looked into the hole and saw the swollen head of the fish emerging like a monstrous baby. As the tail surfaced it slammed against the sides of the hole, and the fish opened and closed its huge hooked mouth. The logistics guys—Don and Evan—were suddenly there, grabbing at the fish and helping Klaus detach it from the hook. Don scooted over to the tank and pushed it across the ice towards the hole, and Art watched dumbly while the others struggled with the fish and finally managed to lever it over the lip of the tank. It fell into the water with a decisive splash.

Klaus looked as if he wanted to grin. 'Can you believe it? Three days on the ice and this is what we find.' Finally the corners of his mouth pulled across his cheeks as if they weren't used to traversing such terrain. 'At this rate we will have a breeding pair by Tuesday.'

They didn't, but Art hadn't really expected them to. Tuesday passed, and then the next Tuesday, and the next. The fish—jostled across the ice in its portable tank, transferred to a roomier pool by the window in the lab—passed its days in silent contemplation, unaware of the fate that had met its two less fortunate predecessors. Art wondered what it thought of its new surrounds—the noises, the colours, the creatures that peered at it through the water. Did it think it had died? Gone to hell? Purgatory? An alien planet? (And what was X doing, right now, inside the fish's body? How many years had it performed its silent remedial work, tidying up old cells and stopping them from proliferating, waiting for someone—him—to discover it?)

*

At 11:30 Art trudges back to the dorm, strips off his ECW suit and drags his feet along the corridor to the room he shares with Klaus. He unlocks the door and pushes it open, hoping as he does so that his careful silence is not in vain. But both beds are empty.

He tries not to panic. Tells himself they must've gone back to the bar, must still be playing pool. But even that would be a worry: what could Klaus have told Octavia by now? He's always been a man of his word (didn't he say, 'I will put up with your foibles?' Wasn't that essentially a promise?), but it's possible that she has spun some trap that even he could not evade, some trap involving beer and cleavage and pheromones.

An image, unbidden, enters his mind: two people in a single bed, one blond and skinny-limbed, the other dark-haired and fleshier. He tries instead to picture the fish: its pale, bark-like hide; the swell of its overlarge head; the glassy orbs of its eyes. He rubs his temples. Should he go and look for them at the bar? Set his mind at ease? (But what if they aren't there? How easy would his mind be, then?) No: he'll go to bed, try to get to sleep, worry about what has happened—is happening—in the morning.

He changes into his pyjamas and slips under the snarled covers, pulls his eye mask onto his forehead. The light coming through the curtains is wan and reluctant, but he knows it will keep him awake if he gives it the chance. He flaps a hand onto the bedside table, confirms the presence of a glass of water. Pulls down the mask. Pictures the fish's yawning mouth. He imagines he is in his diving suit, gliding over the stalagmite-shaped teeth, shining his light at the back of the throat where the rubbery grey tongue descends into the tight black hole of the oesophagus.

*

Not that long ago (eight years? nine? ten?), Art was Klaus's PhD supervisor. Klaus had turned up at the door of his office one day, unslept and unshaven, fresh off the plane from Germany and still toting his luggage. He'd sent an email the week before, perfectly timed to coincide with an identical letter. Despite the stilted wording, Art had been slightly touched by the email: there was a kind of zealous enthusiasm about it that shone through despite sentences like 'It would be my great honour to undertake a PhD supervised by yourself on the evolutionary origins of Notothenioid antifreeze glycoproteins'. Art had replied that he'd be happy to discuss the proposal further; he'd expected a phone call, another stilted email, but he hadn't considered that Klaus would immediately book a flight and travel halfway across the world, take a shuttle to the university, turn up outside Art's office wilted and puffy-eyed.

Art offered him a seat, a coffee. Klaus accepted the first and declined the second. They talked about fish. Klaus was young— only twenty-two—and obviously something of a genius; he had started university at sixteen, could fit more jargon into a single sentence than any of Art's colleagues. Whether or not it had been a calculated move to turn up with his luggage—a salmon-pink suitcase with a padlock dangling from the twin tabs of the zip—

the effect he conveyed was one of oblivious homelessness, of such complete dedication to his passion—science—that everything else—food, shelter, family, friends—had drifted into irrelevance. Art knew the feeling: until a few weeks earlier, he'd been practically living in his office, returning each night to his colleague's fold-out bed with his suitcase and all that it contained—the irritating essentials of his life—crammed behind it.

They talked for three and a half hours. Klaus had clearly read the literature; he knew almost as much about antifreeze as Art did himself. Somehow the topic swerved to evolution, to the ancient split between fish and tetrapods. They discussed the coelacanths, ancient sarcopterygians whose lobed fins still resembled the primeval appendages that had once evolved into legs. And further back still were the earliest vertebrates, the jawless fish—ancestors of lampreys, equipped with sucking funnel-mouths studded with tiny teeth.

Art agreed to supervise Klaus. He asked Klaus where he was staying. Klaus seemed bewildered by the question; he hadn't given it any thought. Art offered the couch in his apartment as if he'd just thought of it. Klaus accepted.

They walked back down the hill together. Art microwaved a tin of chilli beans and lowered bread into the toaster, but Klaus fell asleep on the couch before he had a chance to eat anything. Art watched him sleeping. He'd always thought you could see something when a person was asleep that was invisible when they were awake—the defences fell away, the carefully constructed persona slipped off like a mask—and what you were left with was something pure, a glimpse of the vulnerable inner core. He'd watched his wife sleep now and then during the last few months they'd lived together, and it had comforted him, because he'd glimpsed that underneath all the animosity she really was the same woman (open, innocent, drooling slightly) he'd always known.

Asleep, Klaus didn't look like a scientist. He slept with his hands curled up against his face as if he wanted to suck his thumb, and his long limbs bent and folded beneath him like a collapsible chair. He had his mouth slightly open, and from where Art was sitting there was no sound coming out of it. He slid quietly off his stool and padded across the carpet. Knelt. Listened. Beneath the buzz of the VCR and the distant drone of traffic, he could just make out Klaus's breathing: calm and steady, each breath so long it almost swallowed two of Art's own. The veins on the backs of his hands weren't raised or bumpy, but Art could see them clearly—blue and somehow botanical— threading under the translucent skin. The hair on his head was blond, but the stubble on his chin was reddish. Was that a Viking trait? Suddenly Klaus stirred and pushed the side of his nose into the leather, and Art backed away. He went into the bedroom and pulled a spare blanket off the bed, took it back into the lounge and draped it over Klaus. Retreated to the bathroom and brushed his teeth. Changed into his pyjamas. Fell asleep thinking he'd probably wake up and find himself alone in the apartment.

But the next day Klaus was still there. He said he would find his own place soon, but he ended up staying for weeks. The apartment—which had been white-walled, cell-like—quickly became an improvised lab. They fermented sauerkraut—a vat of red cabbage, a vat of green—and Art smuggled a microscope home so they could look at the bacteria. Klaus bought a fish tank and began filling it with specimens he collected on bus trips to the south coast: a piece of concrete stuck with chitons and barnacles, a couple of starfish, a cluster of anemones. Approval came through for his PhD application, and his place at the research base for that summer was confirmed. They played marathon chess games that Klaus usually, eventually, won. Talked long into the night about antifreeze and evolution. Confessed their problems relating to women. Art told Klaus about his wife—his ex-wife—and how she'd once called him a 'cold fish' and then realised how appropriate that was, given the types of creatures he spent most of his time with—and how she'd doubled over with laughter, hadn't been able to stop. After a while he'd gone into the other room because he felt vaguely affronted and didn't know what to do, and later she'd told him that had been precisely what a cold fish would have done, and it had only made her laugh harder.

Klaus said he'd had a few girlfriends, but nothing serious. They always seemed to get frustrated with him after a few months. He didn't know the etiquette of dating: how often were you supposed to visit? What were you meant to talk about? How should you initiate getting into bed together? He made women sound like a problem that he hadn't managed to solve yet but knew there was a solution to, as if—armed with the right formula—romance would be as easy as plugging the numbers in, combining the reactants, peering through a microscope and drawing what you saw.

It was sometime during those first few months that Art began to think of Klaus as his son. He'd never had kids—the time had never seemed right, and then his wife had passed her window of biological opportunity—and he'd always dimly regretted the absence. He watched as Klaus ate his cereal in the mornings— flushed with the exertion of his 6am run, sealed to his T-shirt with sweat—and felt the stirring of something he had trouble identifying. Protectiveness? Paternalism? He felt oddly tender towards the younger man—who was really, beneath all the jargon-heavy sentences and cool self-sufficiency, just a boy. A boy who pretended he knew how to operate in the world, but really didn't. A boy on the run from something. Art had tried to ask Klaus about his past—his family, his home country, his reasons for moving halfway across the world—but Klaus always managed to brush off the questions. He was from Munich. Had two sisters. Divorced parents. And that was as far as Art usually got.

After Klaus moved out, Art did his best to adapt to solitary life. He contented himself with staying late at work in case Klaus dropped by, equipped his office with a beer fridge and chess set and under-desk supply of soup tins. He walked back to his apartment as late as he could, along slippery darkened streets and down flights of unlit steps; once home, he bumped into furniture and missed the toilet bowl as he tried to navigate without turning the lights on (they were too bright, too reminiscent of a hospital or prison; they made the place seem even emptier than it was).

Finally—after hastily brushing his teeth, splattering the faucet with foam as he spat—he pulled on his pyjamas and slipped into bed.

Years passed. Winters broken mercifully by summers, city streets giving way to endless ice. Klaus finished his PhD and started lecturing, got one promotion and then another. By thirty he had the sort of publication record most would hope for by forty. He was the golden boy of the department, well on his way to leading the field of southern ocean ichthyology. Art told himself he was proud.

*

Art wakes at quarter to nine, peels off his sticky mask and fumbles with the clock. Why didn't he hear the alarm? He flops back onto the pillow and sees that Klaus's bed is still empty, the blanket still taut under the cuff of the sheet. It's late enough for Klaus to have returned, slept, made his bed, and left again. Art hopes and doubts that this is what's happened.

He takes a gulp of water and manages to spill it down his front, props himself on his elbows and then rolls forward until his torso is upright. He feels hungover, but all he had was a couple of glasses. Even ten years ago his body would have handled the toxicity without complaint, converting ethanol to acetaldehyde and acetaldehyde to acetic acid, shrinking and re-expanding his brain while he slept. He folds the covers off his knees and swings his feet onto the floor, puts a hand on the bedside table to steady himself.

The windows shudder, and suddenly he's aware that he can hear something above and beyond the creaking of his body. He pulls the curtains and sees a grey, horizonless vista. The mountains and ice have vanished into a fog of blown snow. He can hear the wind funnelling past, doing its best to rip and punch and shatter; a storm, he's always felt, is the continent's way of purging, an attempt to swipe an unwelcome parasite off its flank. The violent fog outside is oddly congruous with the interior of his skull.

He pulls on his clothes and straps his watch across his wrist, hesitates by the door for a moment. Breakfast will have finished by now, so maybe he should just go straight back to the lab. In weather like this there won't be any line-checking; Klaus will be at his desk, flipping his socks on the heater and typing up notes for the fisheries report. (Unless he's lying in a sordid tangle of sheets and limbs, snoring off a wild night—but Art doesn't want to think about that. He pictures the fish. Yes, he'll go to the lab.)

He makes his way along the corridor to the vestibule, pulls on his ECW suit and bunny boots. As he heaves the airlock open he hears a cracking sound, and a mound of snow topples in. The wind hits his eyes and he pulls his goggles down over them, launches himself out into the blizzard, pushes his weight against the airlock and hears it seal behind him.

He takes the guide rope in his fists and wades out into the storm, hauling himself step by step across the opaque space between the buildings. He can just make out the red legs of his suit vanishing into white-booted camouflage, and ahead of him the rope twists and buckles as it fades into the blizzard. After what feels like two hundred metres but is probably only twenty, the lab building looms through the fuzzed lenses of his goggles. He stumbles against it and hooks his insensitive claws around the airlock handle, pulls it with all his weight. It lets out a surprised pop and he falls in on a drift of snow.

Klaus isn't in the lab. His computer sits untouched and blank-screened on his desk; his socks are nowhere in sight. Art wades across the floor and slumps into his chair. So. Octavia has emerged victorious. He looks at the fish. It's performing its usual routine, circling around and around the edge of the tank as if by endlessly repeating this tiny circumference it can almost believe it's swimming much further. He tries to tell himself the reason he feels betrayed is because of what Klaus might have said to her, what she might have lured out at a candid moment. But does he really care that much about X? Does it matter if she publishes something before he's ready? A bit, but not a lot. Not enough to make him feel like this.

He rests his cheek against the cool surface of his desk. From here the buttons of his keyboard are blurry and huge at one end, slivered like staples at the other. Except for the first column—Tab, Caps Lock, Shift, Ctrl—he can't see any of the labels. He should be happy for Klaus, happy that he's finally caught something other than a fish. But Klaus is naïve; he might've mistaken her advances for genuine interest, her calculated pursuit of a story for something like attraction. (Is he being unfair? Probably. What has she done, other than asking a few questions he didn't want to answer and leaning over a pool table in a slightly provocative fashion?)

He snaps his head off the desk and stands up. He'll go and find them, since there's no way he'll get any work done otherwise. He'll go and bang his fists against Octavia's door until it opens, he'll look right into Klaus's once-familiar blue eyes and say— what? I thought I knew you? I thought you were smarter than this?

He goes back out into the vestibule and pushes the airlock open, hauls himself along the rope to the dorm building. He does his best to walk sedately along the corridor to Octavia's room; when he reaches it he leans against the door for a moment, raps twice. His fingers are swelling in the warmth like sausages in danger of bursting their skins. He waits half a minute for an answer, then knocks again.

Nobody comes to the door. He feels like a fool. Of course they wouldn't still be in bed: it's nine o'clock. They'll be in the cafeteria, sipping coffee and lingering after breakfast. He goes back around the corner, past his own room, and then along the corridor that branches out from the dorm hallway. At the cafeteria door he pauses, steels himself. He's not sure what he will say when he finds them.

He pushes the door open, scans the room. He sees her immediately: she's sitting by herself at the end of a table, staring at her laptop and jiggling her knees with caffeinated urgency. Klaus is nowhere in sight.

Art feels himself deflate. But he wades past the tables anyway, comes to a stop beside her. She frowns at the screen, types a couple of words. Then she hits the full-stop key and raises her eyes to look at him. One side of her mouth twitches into a bent smile. 'Oh, hi.'

'Hi,' he says. He feels suddenly nervous. 'Pretty wild storm, huh?'

'Yup.' She's looking at him as if she's waiting. Then she exhales. 'I was thinking I'd go for a walk to Whale Rock today.' She shrugs, gestures at the empty coffee cup. 'But the gods are angry, so instead I'm indulging my vices.'

'Fair enough.' He clatters into the seat opposite her. 'This is the first Condition One we've had all season. If I were you I'd be grateful I was getting a front-row seat.' He realises, too late, that he sounds like a disgruntled grandfather. He tries again: 'I mean, this is pretty special, in the context of global weather patterns. Antarctica gets amazing katabatic winds. That means "going downhill". When you get cold air forming over a high place, it can get up to incredible velocities as it flows downward—I mean, today we're talking, oh, probably more than two hundred knots.'

Octavia nods. 'Yeah, one of the meteorologists—Luke—was telling me just before.'

'Oh.' She's looking at him curiously, as if he's a species she's never seen before. Up close her eyes are brown around the middle and green around the outside, like inverted kiwifruit. She has a dimple on one cheek. He focuses his frustration at this dimple. 'Where's Klaus?'

She frowns. 'I don't know . . . in the lab?'

He shakes his head. 'He's not there—and he's not in the dorm either. I haven't seen him since last night—not since he was at the bar.' The unspoken words—*with you*—hover in the irritated space between them.

'Well, I haven't seen him since last night either.'

'Oh.' Art's stomach lets out a hiccup of nausea. 'Well, where else could he be?'

'I don't know,' she says. She's beginning to look worried now. One of her hands unmoors from the table, flutters. 'Have you checked the main aquarium? I mean, he wouldn't be . . .'

Art stares at her. If Klaus isn't inside, then he must be outside. He stands up too fast, and his head pulses angrily. The chair teeters behind him. 'He's out on the ice.'

She's shaking her head as if she doesn't want to believe him. 'He can't be, can he? I'm sure he wouldn't have gone out in this weather—'

'He must've gone out to check the lines. Before the storm hit.' He pushes the chair back in and marches across the cafeteria. Her voice threads across the space behind him—*Wait, wait*—but then the door seals, blocks it out. He jogs along the grey corridor, past the line of dim, chattering windows. A gap surges with snow where one of them has blown out. He reaches the Search and Rescue office and knocks, twists the knob.

The desk attendant looks up. He frowns. 'Art?'

'Klaus is missing,' Art says in a rush. 'I can't find him anywhere—he must've gone to check the lines this morning.'

The other man nods. 'No need to panic. We've got it all under control.'

'You mean you know where he is?'

The other man folds his arms and parks his elbows on the desk. 'He's out near Cloudy Point. He and a couple of the logistics guys went out this morning. They saw the storm coming but Klaus had just got something on the line, and he wanted to get it up and into the tank before they left. But the weather hit them too fast.' He shrugs. 'They couldn't get the Hagglund started. We've told them to wait inside it until we can send help.'

Art sags against the wall. Along the windowsill he can see a faint dusting of snow, thickest at the pane and thinning towards the edge. 'So they're all right.'

'A bit cold, but they're doing fine.'

'Can I talk to Klaus?'

'We can't get reception right now. How about you just go back to your lab, and I'll give you a call when we've got a new development?'

Art feels himself nodding. 'Okay.' He peels his torso off the wall and walks out of the office, back along the corridor. The howling of the blown-out window seems to change pitch as he gets closer, like the warping siren of a fire truck. He can see fingers of snow grabbing through it, gusting towards the ceiling and floor, silting up to cover the glass shards.

At the door to the cafeteria he pauses for a moment, considers going in and telling Octavia. But what would he say, after breaking the news? He doesn't feel like enduring her dimple, her coolness, her practised secrecy.

So instead he trudges back to the vestibule, mechanically inserts himself into his suit and boots. He pictures Klaus in the storm: blue-lipped, shivering Klaus, hunched inside the Hagglund with the logistics crew. Have the windows held? Or is Klaus curled on the floor beneath a seat like a child playing a no-peeking game, his jacket crusted with ice that looks like shards of glass and shards of glass that look like ice? Art imagines Klaus's frostbitten hands, fused finger-to-finger in his mittens like sticky half-eaten sweets. He shakes the image out of his head, tries instead to picture the fish they found on the line. In his mind it looks identical to the fish in the lab, its serrated mouth hinged open in fright as the portable tank rocks back and forth with the motion of the storm. What could it be thinking, as the water sways? Down below the ice, it never would have encountered such elemental wrath. It would feel, he thinks, as if the earth itself were cracking open: that's the only equivalent.

In all likelihood it's nothing but a humble *Dissostichus mawsoni*, another statistic to add to their fisheries study. But there's a chance, however slim, that it could be the elusive Specimen #4—the mate they've been searching for all summer, the male that will turn the tank-bound female's eggs into swarms of X-producing offspring.

He puts his hands on the airlock handle and pushes down, stumbles out, finds himself once again in the disorienting swirl of snow. He drags himself hand over hand along the rope, to the familiar airlock in its mint-green corrugated face. He tugs at its ice-sealed lips and falls inside, onto the ankle-deep drift that cakes the carpet. Levers himself up again and unzips his suit.

Once he's hung it up he wedges the door open and steps out into the lab, seals the blown-in snow behind him. But even the lab floor has a slushy coat to it, and his socks are sodden by the time he reaches his chair. He peels them off his feet and drapes them over the radiator.

He waits in his chair for the phone to ring. Minutes pass, possibly hours. He looks at the fish. It's pressed up against the side of the tank, nudging at the corner with its lips, as if it wants to see through the wall, see him looking at it. He thinks of telling it that they might have found it a companion, a mate, but then he decides he shouldn't say anything until he's sure, until he can say with a sad knowing smile, *How would you like to have a friend? A friend of your own kind?*

The fish moves its lips as if it's filtering food scraps through its teeth, or trying to talk. 'What's that?' says Art. 'You're hungry?' He glances at his watch. Nine forty. He goes to the fridge and draws out a tray of mackerel icefish, tosses two chilled carcasses into the tank. The toothfish bites through them cleanly, swallows each piece with a decorous gulp.

Klaus deserves an apology. This is what Art imagines he will say, once the airlock has kissed shut and Klaus's heavy tread—muted by the packed snow—has thudded reassuringly into the vestibule: *I'm sorry.* He will not need to say what he's sorry for, because Klaus will know, and neither of them is very good at saying things out in the open, expressing their feelings. Klaus will thud across the floor and sink into his chair, and off will come the socks, and underneath them his feet will be so white they are almost blue, but before he warms them he will go through the motions, saddling his socks over the heater next to Art's. Art will wait until he's finished, and then he will ask about the new fish. In it will come, wheeled in its portable tank and then splashed into the pool with Specimen #3, and there will be a couple of tense moments before the two fish recognise each other—before the pheromones weave through the water and into the nares, before they know for sure that they are of the same kind.

Art and Klaus will watch the fish for a while, and then they will get talking. Evolution, X, antifreeze. Art will pull out the chess set from under his desk. Between bouts of silent concentration they will talk through lunch and dinner and into the night, and the sun will not rise or set to tell them they have been sitting too long in the same place, that they need to stretch or eat or go to sleep.

Art watches the phone. With each rattle of the windows he almost thinks he can hear it ringing. *Soon*, he tells himself. *Now.* He checks his watch. Taps his feet. Jiggles his knees. And eventually, the phone rings.

Lawrence Patchett

The Road to Tokomairiro

I

Harry was a first-rate whip. It wasn't boasting to say that, it was simply a fact. He was a top driver, a trusted one. He'd whipped the great Victorian routes and, lately, the action having shifted to Otago, he'd made the South Road his own, the Pigroot too. When the first Cobb & Co pulled into Naseby it was Harry who'd whipped the horses in, the whole town out in bunting and brass to watch his team and coach pour over the bridge. And still people looked out for him. They listened for the cornet he played; kids ran alongside his wheels. Everyone knew Harry. They knew him and trusted him—and he loved them for it in return. On the coach he was all for his passengers. He fussed over them and joked with them and took the road slowly. Some whips went hell for leather, but that wasn't Harry's way—he preferred his passengers to arrive comfortable. Harry was all for his passengers.

And on that November morning he loaded up with even more goodwill than usual, a pair of newlyweds boarding at Otokia—Mr and Mrs Ryrie, just married the previous day. They'd come up especially for the ceremony, and when Harry pulled the coach alongside to return them, they smiled up as if they adored the whole world.

'Folks, here's the happy couple I told you about,' said Harry. 'Mr and Mrs Ryrie—just married.' Then he leapt down and flung the doors open. At the sight of the newlyweds, all the passengers applauded. One man whooped out loud.

How people loved a wedding, thought Harry. Even the sourest old miser would love this couple. For a minute they just made you forget everything.

'Morning, Mr Ryrie,' he said. 'Ma'am. It all went well, I'd say. A happy time, I'd say.'

'Oh, fine, fine,' said Mr Ryrie.

His wife smiled.

'Well, congratulations, both of you,' said Harry. 'I'll take them bags for you.' He hoisted the luggage onto the coach while Mr Ryrie handed his wife inside. 'Reckon you're the happiest man on this coach, Mr Ryrie.'

'Oh, call me Marcus,' said Mr Ryrie. He was a bald and prosperous man, and he was beaming. He owned a Balclutha store.

'Reckon I'll stick with *Mr Ryrie* today,' said Harry. 'On account of your new situation—*Mrs Ryrie*, too. I'll stick with those handles today.' He shook Mr Ryrie's hand a second time, giving the moment its appropriate ceremony. Then he said, 'Well, all aboard, everyone,' and he swung the doors shut and climbed up.

A second man followed him up to the box-seat, then Mr Ryrie stepped up strongly. Reverend Keane clambered up to lie on the roof, having surrendered his seat inside to Mrs Ryrie.

'Are you comfortable up there, Reverend?' said Harry.

Keane nodded, adjusting a blanket underneath him. He was a thin and abstemious man from Lawrence. His face and hat showed above the low rails that bordered the roof.

'You hang on there, Reverend,' said Harry.

At first Keane didn't respond, but Harry waited, and at last the Reverend said, 'It's an honour to give up my seat for a bride. I don't mind at all.'

At that, Harry clapped his hands. He had a full and ready coach now. He had passengers behind, beside, and above him. It was a good feeling. He sounded his cornet, then gave the leather a long and snaking crack over the greys, just for the show of it. The coach jolted forward and, in the shaking and clatter, Harry started up a yarn with Mr Ryrie. He knew him from a store visit of a few years ago, and he'd liked him then, and he admired him and his new wife now. They were brave and patient people—already almost forty, and only just married. That showed character. It showed fortitude, and Harry admired that in a passenger. Having brought them up from Balcultha, he was glad to see them married now. It gave him a straightforward surge of pride. They were underway now: first stop, the Taieri Ferry, then the Tokomairiro horse-change, and from there, the rest—the easiest stretch—of the South Road.

It was all in order as they left the Taieri—the coach running along freely, the team alert under the reins. Beside Harry his box-seat passengers were drowsing in the jolting sleepiness of coaching, the fatigue and warmth and rhythm of the horses as they pulled and pulled spreading a lethargy through everyone.

Then it all slammed to the right and down. The coach fell and began to roll, and Harry saw two things—Reverend Keane flying off the roof and to the side, and a fore-wheel spinning away. Then the coach was rolling over, capsizing. At his periphery, Harry saw Mr Ryrie as a dark vaulting shape, swinging down from the box-seat rail like a pinioned black bag. Then Harry was jerked off the coach by the reins, the kingbolt snapping free, the team skittering and falling and speeding on, leaving the coach behind.

Harry thudded to the road and was dragged. Stones from the hooves flew at his eyes and chin.

He let them go.

Then he was prone on the road, his overturned coach behind him, his team ahead. He stood to run back towards his passengers. As he came close he could see a body on the road. It was Mr Ryrie. He was underneath the coach and pinned. The railing of the box seat was right across his chest. His head and neck were free of the box seat; the rest of his body disappeared under the coach at an angle.

Already two men were at the coach-side and lifting. Harry thundered in beside them. They heaved and were unsuccessful.

'Again,' said Harry. He strained and the coach came up, then someone was drawing Mr Ryrie out. Harry heard him moan.

'Down,' said Harry, to the other men. 'Watch your toes.'

Then he was kneeling beside Mr Ryrie. The businessman's face twisted in a grimace. His chest was queerly caved.

'Mr Ryrie?' said Harry.

The man's eyes searched up. His breathing sounded terrible.

Someone reached in a pannikin and Harry dabbed Mr Ryrie's face with water. The bald head had a smudge of dirt on the crown; otherwise it was undamaged and perfect-seeming. That chest, though—it bowed in.

'Mr Ryrie,' said Harry. 'Mr Ryrie. Keep breathing, sir.' He elbowed away someone who was trying to lean in. 'Keep breathing, sir. Keep going.'

In the distance Harry heard someone leading the women away. It was Reverend Keane. Harry saw Mr Ryrie's eyes roving up, tracing at those sounds. His neck was cradled on Harry's hand, and Harry could feel the tension in it, the effort that was going into his breathing.

'Hang on, Mr Ryrie,' said Harry. 'We're almost there.'

Mr Ryrie opened his eyes and searched up again. Through the sound of his own breathing, he must have heard something. But his eyes closed and opened again, and closed.

Harry tightened his grip against the man's neck. Inside him there was a skittering knowledge that Mr Ryrie was dying, but still he sent his voice on. 'Almost there, sir,' he said. 'Bravely on. Almost there. Keep going.'

Mr Ryrie gasped up in anguish another time; his eyes searched and closed.

'Almost there, Mr Ryrie. Almost there. Bravely on,' said Harry. It was something he'd call forward to a fading team. 'Nearly there, sir. Bravely on. Nearly there. Ah Christ, he's died.'

Mr Ryrie's face went smooth. His neck sagged against Harry's hand.

'Ah Jesus,' said Harry. 'Where's that Reverend?'

He turned to look. Above and behind him, a hoop of men was surrounding and looking down.

'Where's the Reverend?' said Harry.

'He's with the womenfolk, Harry,' said someone.

'Go and get him.'

Harry returned his attention to Mr Ryrie. The businessman was deeply gone. His eyes were open but his dead face was calm. Harry laid the bald head gently on the road. There was a jagged stone underneath—Harry lifted Mr Ryrie's head again, smoothed the road, then removed his own hat and flattened it and laid it under. He looked for Reverend Keane. He saw that lean religious man coming down. He was bringing the bride with him. The other women were along the slope, standing beyond and watching. Mrs Ryrie came closer. She had Keane by the hand. Her face was pale.

'Can I see him, please, Harry,' she said.

Harry was still on his knees. He moved back a short way. As she leaned down, Harry felt her hand rest on his shoulder. Then she collapsed in. Her hands went to her husband's face.

Harry stood up and moved back. He left her with Keane.

'I'll get my team,' he said. 'I'll see to the horses.'

He stepped along the slope. He heard Mrs Ryrie start to cry. He heard her voice climb into a terrible sound. He picked up speed towards his horses to get away from it. It was a rending noise—and as Harry came towards his team he saw his rearmost gelding had fallen. The horse was lying in a sickening shape on the road, the harness twisted half-away and tangled.

Harry ran towards it.

Already he could see from the unnatural lie of the beast that its back was broken. He knelt beside it and loosened, then pulled away the bridle, the bit clattering on the horse's teeth as Harry ripped it away. A great shuddering was in the horse, his whole hide quivering. The dust beside his nostrils snorted and sprayed.

'Ah Jesus,' said Harry. 'Ah Christ.'

He knelt beside the dying horse helplessly. He had no rifle to destroy it. He had nothing.

He looked back up the slope towards the coach. Mrs Ryrie was still beside her husband. She was sorrowing over him. She was a brave woman—Harry had seen that from the first—but now that awful sound came from her. She howled. She still had Keane by the hand. The Reverend was stooping beside her. Harry could not tear his eyes from the three of them—the Reverend standing in a crescent shape, Mrs Ryrie sorrowing over her husband. She was in so much pain. Harry could see it all coming out of her—her marriage and honeymoon, her courtship, her hope and courage, her voyaging from Scotland. Her single sunny day of honeymoon—all of it was being torn out and crushed on the road.

Harry worked methodically then. He checked no other passengers were hurt. He covered Mr Ryrie entirely with blankets. He told the men that soon they would have to walk back to Taieri. He would remain with the coach until a dray could be brought to retrieve Mr Ryrie. He asked them to see to their women, and he checked that Mrs Ryrie had a female companion to comfort her. He asked Reverend Keane to walk on to Tokomairiro to send telegrams.

He went to his team and unharnessed them, hitching them to the far side of the coach. Kneeling over the broken gelding, he made him as comfortable as he could, spoke to him, longed for a rifle to dispatch him. He cleared the dust from around his eyes and nose, then left him.

As he came back to the coach the passengers were murmuring quietly, discussing what luggage they could carry. Harry walked through and around them. Coming to the coach, he examined the axle which had shucked its nut and wheel. The axle showed only a little damage where it had crashed to the road and dragged. Otherwise there was no flaw to point to. Deep grooves spiralled down the axle, the same as every axle on every Cobb & Co.

He walked up behind the coach in search of the wheel. It was lying brazenly in the centre of the road, its spokes showing up ruddily. He lifted and wheeled it hand-over-hand towards the coach, the rim of the wheel making normal sounds on the stones.

As Harry neared the standing passengers, one of the single men leapt up to help him. Together they leaned the wheel against the coach.

'Can I help with anything else?' said the man.

'Not yet,' said Harry. 'Are the passengers all comfortable? Are they ready?'

'Yes, Harry.'

'I'll be with you shortly,' said Harry.

He walked again up the slope behind the coach. He was searching for the axle-nut that should have held the wheel on the coach. He found it in the scrappy area by the side of the road. It was not damaged. It was squat and shiny in the sun. He took this thing in his hand and gauged the distance to the coach. It was about one hundred yards. He had everything now—the wheel, the axle-nut, the harnessing—yet no clue as to what had caused the accident. There was no reason why the nut and wheel should have come off, why the coach should have crashed.

He ripped a length of his shirt-sleeve and wrapped the axle-nut inside it, then placed it in his waistcoat pocket.

He went to the men.

'Are you ready?' he said.

They were.

He turned then and found Mrs Ryrie and her companion. She was a long way from the body of her husband now, and as Harry came towards her she stood from the luggage she'd been sitting on. She was no longer crying.

Facing her, Harry felt very grave. He tried to meet her eye. 'Mrs Ryrie, do you think you could walk down with the other passengers? They will walk to the settlement. I will remain with your husband. I will make sure he is all right until we can bring him on.' It was difficult to speak—he tried to clear his throat. 'Do you want to walk on with the passengers or would you rather stay here? One of the ladies,' he gestured at her companion, 'could stay here with you, if that is what you choose.'

Something involuntary feathered over Mrs Ryrie's face, then she was calm again. 'I'll walk on now, Harry,' she said. 'Thank you.'

'Mrs Ryrie, I cannot explain this accident,' said Harry. 'There is no reason for it. I am dreadfully sorry. You know I thought your husband a very good man. It is a very bad accident.'

Mrs Ryrie reached a hand to his arm. For Harry the contact was horrible.

'Thank you, Harry,' she said. 'I know you've done all that you can.'

Harry coughed and tried to speak again, but his voice was broken. He stood sickly before her a moment more, then turned away. He walked back to her dead husband and the coach and the team. He told his passengers they could walk on now. He watched them as they lifted their luggage and went down the road, the Ryries' boxes shared amongst the men.

He waited until they were out of earshot, then he went up the slope behind the coach and lifted a great stone from the side of the road. This he cradled back down beyond the coach to the broken gelding. Holding the stone in both hands he crouched above the horse. It was still shivering, foam coming from its mouth and nostrils. Its distressed eye flickered up at Harry as he hovered above.

'I'm sorry,' said Harry.

Then at a precise point near the gelding's ear he brought the rock down once then twice, three times, four times. On the fourth blow he felt the rock crush through the skull, and the horse ceased its shuddering. He rolled the rock away and knelt again beside the horse. He smoothed its head first, then pushed both eyes closed. Then he removed all harnessing and dust from the gelding, smoothing its whole body with his hand. As he passed over the great rounded areas of skin he felt the warmth dissipating. When the whole horse was as clean as he could make it, Harry removed his own waistcoat and laid it over the horse's shoulder and mane. The laid-out garment made a pitiful shape, so he went to the coach and returned with two blankets and laid those over the gelding, retrieving his own waistcoat and buttoning it slowly.

Then he left the horse and returned to Mr Ryrie, who was covered right over. He sat beside the still body and waited for the dray to come. It was mid-afternoon and he was still five miles and more from Tokomairiro. He'd not brought the Ryries much more than a mile beyond the place of their wedding.

As he sat, he glanced occasionally at the coach that had

betrayed him. He watched over his surviving team as well, once getting up to water them with liquid he poured into his own flattened hat and held under each horse's nose. At one point he remembered his tobacco and fished it out and tried to roll and smoke a cigarette but, at the first taste, spat it out and threw it away. For the rest of the time he sat beside Mr Ryrie and stared at the road.

II

Harry was back at Taieri. It was the next day. He'd been returned there for the inquest; it was in the Taieri Hotel, in a backroom that smelled of pub. Harry sat in the middle area, the other witnesses equidistant from him. Reverend Keane was there too, and at the front were the coroner and a policeman; along the side was a jury.

The policeman stood and called the room to order. He explained how it would go. He hoped they would not be detained too long. He called Mr Ryrie's brother.

This gentleman stood at the desk and confirmed the identity of the deceased, his locality, his profession, his age. He was younger than Mr Ryrie had been—he had more hair—yet the steady certainty of his voice had something of his brother in it, and Harry felt a return of the sick constricting of his throat that he'd felt since the accident. He squeezed his palms tight together and focused on the floor, avoiding what he could see of the brother— his back and shoulders, the collar starching into his neck-hair.

Even though they weren't watching or listening to Harry, instead craning towards Mr Ryrie's brother and the sergeant, Harry felt the presence of the jury at the side of the room as the evidence was given. He felt their attention. Of all the people Harry did not want to face in that room, those members of the jury were the worst. They were all ordinary men, all local, all watching and listening obediently.

In a short while he was called and he walked to the front and stood before everyone. He listened as the policeman gave him instructions. His fingers fumbled as he reached into his chest pocket, brought his statement forward and unfolded it loudly.

'I am Harry Nettleford,' he said, then paused.

Silently the court waited for him as he cleared his throat and began again. 'I am a coach driver. I drive the Cobb & Co between Balclutha and Dunedin. I drove that coach yesterday. Before I set out from Otokia I looked over the coach and found everything was in order. There was no problem with the wheels or the axles. I checked them—no one had looked over the coach but the groom and me. The stableman—it was just the stableman and me. We did not oil the axles. There was nothing strange—nothing—'

'Nothing out of the ordinary?'

Harry glanced at the policeman.

'That's right,' he said. 'There was nothing out of the ordinary. There was nothing strange.' He returned his attention to his statement, his eyes swimming over it. He found the right place. 'Mr Ryrie was on the far box-seat corner. Another man was in between. I can't remember his name. We had got along about a mile and three quarters when the crash came.'

As Harry read through his handwritten sentences, he felt the attention of every single person in the room. He was the only person making any sort of noise. He could feel especially the presence of the jurors in their double-row at his right hand side. He felt them pressing towards him. He inched his finger along the page.

'I went looking for the axle-nut and found it down the side of the road. It was behind where the accident happened. It was about one hundred yards back. Here is the nut. You can check it. You can see it was not faulty at all. There is no way it could have caused the accident.' Harry drew the axle-nut from his waistcoat pocket and the fresh tissue he'd wrapped it in. He went to hand it to the policeman, but a sharp look passed from the coroner to the sergeant. It seemed Harry had broken some protocol.

'The court will examine it after the evidence,' said the policeman.

'Please take it from me,' said Harry. 'Please.'

The policeman glanced at the coroner, who studied Harry's

face, then nodded. The policeman came and scooped it from Harry's hand.

'Thank you,' said Harry. 'Will you show it to the jury?'

'We will, Harry.'

Harry shot a look at the jurors. They looked attentive but inexpert. A couple looked like farmhands but some were indoor men—one had a clerkly look, another was very young. They would not know what they were inspecting. 'The nut is a left-hand screw,' he said. 'That means it tightens as the wheel turns round. The thread of the screw is very deep. On Cobb & Co coaches it is deeper than on all other machinery that I know of. You will see that it's not damaged at all. The axle was perfect too—except it was damaged from where it fell on the road.'

They were staring at him. He dropped his head to his statement again. He found his place. He read on. A deeper silence worked into the room as he eliminated all possible causes for the accident—every passenger was sober; he was driving quietly. Twice he had to hack loudly to clear his throat and continue. He was sensitive to the slightest movement of the jurors out at his right; his eye shot up and searched the men each time, then came down again, his eye skittering over the paper he'd smoothed on the desk to prevent it from shaking.

As he neared the end of his evidence the blockage in his throat made it difficult to continue. He went on lumpenly for a time, then stood over his statement, his hand at his throat, unable to speak.

'Take your time, Harry,' said the policeman.

Harry did not look up. He tried to work saliva into his throat. In the quiet behind him he heard someone walking up from behind. It was Keane—the Reverend reached a cup of water forward for Harry.

'Thank you,' said Harry. He drank slowly. He set the glass down. He found his place again. 'I was not driving fast. I was going along quietly. I know that part of the road very well. Where it happened, the road is very good. It is level there.'

He bent his head more, tried to hide his face somehow. The

jury seemed to be leaning even closer, as if sensing that something conclusive was coming. 'I have no idea why this accident happened,' he said. 'I can't explain it at all. There is no reason.'

His voice was shaking; he breathed in slowly. 'I am very sorry for it. I've never had a passenger die. I had got along only about a mile and a bit more. I had checked everything and I was driving carefully. I have never had trouble on that road. I've always made Tokomairiro—I've never had—' He broke off. He pushed his palms against the desk. 'There is no reason at all why that wheel came off. There is no reason why Mr Ryrie died. I am very sorry for Mrs Ryrie.' He tried to smooth the statement on the desk but his hands were shaking badly.

He faced the officials. 'That is the end of my statement, sir.'

'Thank you, Harry,' said the policeman. 'The court will examine the coach shortly. You can stand down.'

Harry sensed the court breathing out. They sat back. They waited while Harry stood before the desk, folding his paper. Then they watched him as he walked to the back of the room.

After Harry, Reverend Keane gave his evidence. At first Harry could not lift his face to listen. He could not face anybody. He kept his eyes on the floor. But Keane's voice pulsed on. It was gentle and pushing forward, as if the Reverend was eager to comfort the coroner and the jurors, to reassure them of something. Tall and lean before the desk he gestured with his hands while his voice went on.

'I was on the roof,' he said. 'I had surrendered my seat to Mrs Ryrie. Harry Nettleford was the driver, as you know, and he was driving slowly. I can confirm he was sober—he is a good driver, I believe.' Keane did not look at Harry as he said this. He maintained eye contact with the officials and the jury as he spoke, speaking consolingly to them all. 'We had been travelling a while when the coach fell over. I was thrown from the roof and I landed on my shoulder, but I was not hurt badly at all. I was not injured—I make that clear.'

He used his hands and arms then to indicate how the coach

had fallen and the path that Mr Ryrie's body had taken, the way it lay under the box-seat railing. He was always tending forward as he spoke, swaying towards the men with the movements of his hands and the rhythm of his sentences. It soothed Harry to listen to this man as he talked and remembered so carefully.

But soon Keane was dismissed. He hesitated at the desk for a moment—he seemed to have something more to say—then, at a glance from the coroner, he turned to make his way back down. As he walked through the seats he was frowning, his eyes roving over the witnesses. Then he made eye contact with Harry, and it was shocking. In that moment, Keane's face twisted; it seemed to twitch and flare, and Harry saw that the Reverend was not comfortable at all. The surging reassurance of his voice had been a trick. Keane was distressed.

Harry stared—then Keane had walked beyond him and lowered into a distant chair. Harry returned his attention to the floor.

The evidence concluded and the jury inspected the coach, then retired. A verdict of accidental death was issued, no blame attaching to anyone. The coroner thanked the jury, thanked Harry and the other witnesses, then dismissed them.

Harry left the makeshift courtroom without looking at anybody. He went through the dark of the pub's main bar, then climbed the stairs. He had been provided with a room in the hotel for the night of the inquest, and he went up there now.

In his room a bowl of water and a towel stood on the washstand. He dipped his hands and scooped a double-handful of water against his face, letting the cold work into his skin. As he washed his face the water dripped from his fingers, making a plain and loud sound. He rinsed his face again and again.

Then he groaned and sank against the washstand. He crouched all the way down to the floor.

'Ah God,' he said. Water spilled to the floor as, sitting against the wall, he ground his hands into his eyes. He felt so dirty, so betrayed. He was covered in shame.

III

Harry was to work the South Road the next day, a young driver delivering him a coach and passengers at Taieri. From there Harry would drive on to Balclutha, the first objective being the horse-change at Tokomairiro—a distance of about seven miles, and already looming up in his mind as a very far one. That morning he'd woken to a nauseating thought of the reins in his hands, the thought that his passengers would know how Mr Ryrie had died. At breakfast he'd sat over his food, unable to force down anything but two mouthfuls of tea.

But he was ready on time. Outside the hotel, freshly washed, his hair and suit brushed, he greeted the coach when it came in, thanked the junior driver and sent him away. He introduced himself to the passengers, and was relieved to find only a small number were travelling. Then he secured the doors and walked among the team, checking the harnessing, their legs and hooves. He circled the coach, bending to double-check the axle-nuts and wheels. Finally he pulled on the luggage to ensure it could not come down.

Then he climbed to the box-seat and settled with the reins, waiting. One further passenger was yet to come. It was Reverend Keane. He had stayed in the hotel too, and over breakfast he'd asked if he might travel up on the box-seat with Harry, changing beyond Tokomairiro at Milton for the Lawrence road. When he had asked this favour Harry had tried not to look too discouraging. In truth he did not want anyone beside him, least of all the Reverend, but over breakfast he'd seen that something was very wrong with the man. The twisting discomfort Harry had seen in his face at the trial had worsened and was now tormenting him. He picked at his food while his eyes, bright and darting, continually sought out Harry's, then flashed away.

And now he stepped down from the hotel, one hand holding a suitcase, his face searching up at Harry. 'Can I come up there?' he said.

'Of course,' said Harry. He indicated the seat next to him.

But the older man hovered, his eyes going down the street as if suddenly remembering something down there.

'I'd be honoured, Reverend,' said Harry. 'Please come up.'

'Ah,' said Keane. 'Yes.'

Harry reached down his hand to help the older man. Keane was light when Harry hoisted him, and as soon as he was seated, he sat with his suitcase on his lap, staring fixedly down the road.

'Shall I take that from you, Reverend?' said Harry.

Keane did nothing to respond, so Harry lifted the suitcase and turned to stow it above, taking extra care to secure it properly. When he sat back down again he found the Reverend was still staring ahead.

With this tense, taut shape at his side, Harry's morning dread returned. He did not want to travel with Keane—but, he was ready to depart. His passengers below were settled. He had to go. It was time to play his cornet. He lifted it from its place beside him. For a moment he could not bring himself to blow into it, to make its congenial sound—but below him he could sense his passengers listening out for it, the pub-owner as well. He forced a single note through the instrument, replaced it at his side, and nudged the team forward. 'G'dap,' he said. 'Get on.'

Then the coach was in motion—and the movement relieved Harry immediately. He almost smiled. Watching over the moving team he surged with gratitude for them. They were good horses. He'd driven many times with the lead gelding and he knew its huge appetite for the work, its hungry taking of the main share of the pull. Harry loved a horse like that, a horse that would pull and pull until its own heart stopped if Harry asked him too. He gritted his teeth now against the memory of that last horse-death, the feeling of that angled stone in his hands as it passed into the wounded horse's skull.

With Keane beside him Harry went along in the clatter without speaking for some time. The road steepened and narrowed and became more difficult, then levelled and soon they were passing the scene of Mr Ryrie's fall. There was no indication now that anything had happened there, beyond a wide brown stain where the broken-backed gelding had been butchered and taken away.

Harry felt the silence beside him tighten as Keane re-crossed his legs and squirmed.

For himself, Harry had no appetite for anything—not for conversation, not for Keane's disquiet. Now that he and his team were underway he wanted only to get to Tokomairiro, to change his team and go beyond. He wanted to drive and drive.

But it was impossible to ignore the man beside him. He seemed to get more distressed by the quarter-mile.

'Are you comfortable, Reverend?' said Harry. 'Would you like another blanket?'

Keane responded to this by standing to rearrange the blanket that was already under him. He held the box-seat rail and lurched as the coach slid into a rut and corrected; then he fussed over the padding the blanket provided, pulling it this way and that. Then he sat down.

'You can sit inside, sir,' said Harry. 'You must be very uncomfortable.' Getting no response, he decided to risk a joke. 'Us whips grow gristle on our chuff, Reverend, if you'll pardon my language. Gristle and a thick hide—that's why we can sit up here so long.'

'Ah,' said Keane. He did not make eye contact with Harry and the sound he made was not a laugh. It was the sound of someone in disturbing sleep.

'All right, Reverend?'

Keane re-crossed his legs and looked straight ahead. Then with his right hand he began to worry a patch above his knee, the heel of his hand working in, again not paying attention to the process, as if unaware it was happening at all.

The coach ground its way up the hill, the horses labouring and mighty, and Harry lapsed back into silence, a little drearier than before. It was grim to think of continuing in this tension. There was an hour and more left to run before Tokomairiro, and he did not want to drive all that way with a worked-up passenger beside him. Not today.

He tried one more time. Deliberately talking slow, he looked over the trees they were passing. 'And how about your trip over,

Reverend?' he said. 'How was the Lawrence road? Before the accident, I mean.'

Keane twitched but still said nothing.

'They've improved that road, I heard,' said Harry. 'Ned was driving you, I suppose? He's a grand driver.' Harry watched more trees going by, and he nodded. 'Yes, he's a fine driver, our Ned. The best in Otago, I'd say.'

Having done this, having received no reply, he returned his attention to his horses. He began a low whistling to take some of his own tension away—and at that, as if summoned up by the high sound, Keane turned right round to look straight in Harry's face.

'It wasn't your fault. Do you know that? You heard me say that to the coroner. You heard the coroner.'

'I did,' said Harry. 'Thank you for that, Reverend. I'm grateful.'

'You heard the jury say it was a freak accident. There was no blame assigned to anyone.'

'I heard that,' said Harry.

Keane nodded and switched round to the front again and recommenced the worrying of his knee.

Harry hoped for silence now. He hoped that Keane would shut his mouth, having managed to pick up the one subject that Harry did not want to discuss today. But Keane turned towards him again.

'We could all feel guilty about that accident,' said Keane. 'Every one of us. But we have to remember it was an accident. It was nobody's fault.' The coach swayed, but Keane remained erect; somehow he didn't sway as the coach swayed. 'And there was something of God in it, too,' he said. 'I know that—I believe that. God did not turn his head away two days ago. He was there, you can depend on that. There was something of God in it—not in the accident, not the death, but in what will follow. In Mrs Ryrie—her recovery. She will not be abandoned. I know that. That's certain.'

Harry watched his dependable horses pulling along.

'Not in that accident,' said Keane, muttering on. 'No.'

Harry said nothing.

Keane touched Harry's arm. 'You cannot be burdened by it,' he said. 'Do you hear me?'

'I hear you,' said Harry.

'It was not your accident. Do you know that?'

'I do,' said Harry. 'Thank you.'

'Do you?' said Keane.

'I do.'

'So why don't you say something?' said Keane. 'Are you hearing me? Do you hear me at all?'

Harry watched him.

'Don't just sit there,' said Keane. 'Don't just *sit*. You have to hear me. I'm helping you. Have you heard me? I'm saying there is God in your accident. I'm saying it was not your fault. Absolution—I'm saying absolution. I'm speaking about a dead man. I'm talking about the dead man your coach killed. Your horses—' he flung a gesture at them '—your horses killed a man.'

This time Harry glared—glared at Keane.

'Do you hear me?' said Keane. 'I say I'm taking it from you. The coach crushed him—it killed him—' he paused at Harry's sharp intake of breath '—but you are absolved, you are—he died out here. The coach—'

Harry made a sharp movement with his hand. He gripped the reins tight.

'The coach killed him,' said Keane, resuming. 'Absolution—I'm saying—'

'Stop talking, Reverend,' said Harry. 'Stop.'

'I'm helping you. I'm—'

'I will set you down, sir. I will put you off my coach. Do not talk.'

'But there was a dead man.'

Harry pointed directly at him this time. 'I'm warning you, sir. I will set you down. Don't make me.'

Keane fell silent. Harry turned again to the road. He tried to relax the reins in his hands. He'd been gripping them so tight. After a hundred yards he glanced at Keane and saw the man was fixated on a point beyond the horses. He looked deeply perplexed by what he saw—as if he'd broken a vase out there, and could not figure out how.

Harry did not care that Keane was uncomfortable. He didn't care that the man's journey was spoiled. He was full of bile.

He watched his team as they strained up the incline.

One of his passengers shifted in the coach behind him, adjusting in their seat or swapping places, maybe trading a window seat for the middle one.

The coach rattled on, jolting, jerking.

When at last Harry's voice came, it was distant to his own ear. 'It was the worst day of my life, Reverend.'

'I understand.'

'No,' said Harry, 'with respect, sir—if you don't mind, let me say this. It was the worst day of my life. It was the worst day I could imagine.' Again he tasted bile in his mouth. He wanted to spit it out, to swill. 'I had a passenger die that day, and a gelding died too. That's the worst day possible for a whip, Reverend.'

'I know it was painful.'

'Mr Ryrie was my passenger. So was his wife. They were on my coach, and the worst thing happened to them. They were my passengers. Don't try to take that away from me.'

And now Keane turned again in his seat, as if the conversation had resumed in earnest. 'But you heard the court say it wasn't your fault. You know that for sure.'

Harry banished this with a wave. 'He was my passenger. I have to carry that, sir. I have to. I'm not proud of it—it gives me a bloody shame. But it's mine now. I have to carry it. Let me have it, please. Don't give it to God.'

'What do you mean?' said Keane.

'Just that.'

'Pardon?' said Keane. His voice had a high and panicked sound.

'You said there was God in the accident. I don't want that, sir.'

'I said there was God in Mrs Ryrie's recovery. That's what I said. Yes, that's what I said.'

'Well, frankly, I think that's poor, Reverend. I'm sorry to say that to you. I apologise. I know that you're a religious man. God knows I'm a church man too, sometimes, when I can be. But Mr Ryrie got killed. I can't see anything in that—all I can see is a dead husband, and I had a hand in his dying. I don't like it, but it's what happened, and I don't want anybody interfering with it. I don't want God. I'm sorry, sir—I'm a church man, but not in that way. Not in the get-off-Scot-free way. Not at all.'

At this Keane resumed his front-ways, fidgeting vigil, and with a stabbing desperation Harry wished the man wasn't there. He wanted so desperately to be alone with his team. He did not want Keane. He did not want to spend anything more on him— no more listening, no more sympathy.

The horses strained up a steeper section of road, and Harry leaned forward with them. Keane tended up too, his voice lifting over the coach as it creaked upward.

'You know, there's a great risk in marriage,' he said. 'A risk— yes. It's the part that says, *Till death do us part.* That's a risk, you know. Sometimes death rushes up very quickly. It rushed up very quickly for Mr Ryrie.'

'Bloody hell,' said Harry.

'That's the risk in a marriage,' said Keane. 'It's ordained that it's risky. Everybody knows that. Oh, yes, that's true.' He lifted his hand up as if the certainty was a fleeting one, one he had to catch. 'Yes it is—it's true all right. Mr Ryrie knew that, or he should have.'

'Don't say that,' said Harry.

'Oh, yes—yes it is.'

'Shut up, sir,' said Harry. 'Be quiet, sir.'

'No, I will not,' said Keane. 'I have a right.'

'You do not,' said Harry. 'This is my coach, sir. You are my guest. You are in my care. You'll do as I say.'

'No,' said Keane.

'What?' said Harry.

'Ah.'

Harry turned to Keane; suddenly the man was scratching at

his forehead and scalp, the fingernails rasping loud.

Harry's voice burst out of him. 'The Ryries were good people, Reverend. They were patient and brave. They'd waited for years. Mrs Ryrie had sailed from Scotland to find him. They'd waited all that time. They had waited and waited, and worked hard. They were married and they were happy for one day, and then they climbed on my coach and Mr Ryrie got killed, and it was over. Their marriage died in a day.'

'Oh, God,' said Keane.

'No,' said Harry. '*One day*, Reverend. Bloody one. I don't know what you call that, but I call it cruel.'

Keane did not turn to Harry this time. His head was bent away.

'They were just married, sir,' said Harry. 'That's important. They'd just got happy at last, and my coach killed the groom. That's what I've got to carry forever.'

'Oh God,' said Keane.

'Ever heard a woman cry like she did, Reverend,' said Harry, 'the way she cried that day? You remember that sound? Have you ever heard anything so bad? I don't think I have. I don't think I'll ever forget it, either. Not this side of the grave.'

Keane whispered something.

'Pardon?' said Harry.

'Ghastly—it was ghastly.'

'Maybe it was,' said Harry. 'I don't know what to call it—that sound of Mrs Ryrie's. I don't think it had a name. I just know I heard it, and I'll be hearing it forever. That's what I know. If you want to call that thing *God*, Reverend, then please keep it to yourself, sir. Don't bring it up here.' He spat on the juddering footboard. 'I'm sorry, sir, but I won't have that. This is my coach. It's my box-seat. Don't do that up here.'

'Oh God,' said Keane. 'How did that happen?'

'One day, sir,' said Harry. 'They had one day together. G'dap!' He whacked the reins with sudden ferocity and felt the surprise of the horses working back through the reins. It wasn't their fault, but they responded, and the coach jerked along a little further, a little faster, spitting stones to the scrub at the side of the road.

They were within two miles of Tokomairiro before the two men spoke again. At first Harry was too angry to care—indeed for the first while he fed his anger deliberately, hunching away from the Reverend and reliving the worst points of the argument in his mind. But as the road ran on a coachman's instinct returned and he submitted to it, glancing at Keane to find him in a worsened condition—more withdrawn, sitting in a sickle shape, his forehead showing an uneven red where he'd scratched it, in one place even breaking the skin.

Harry began calling along his team, sending up encouragement in the hope it would pull Keane from his reverie. Then he cleared his throat and began to hum an old driving song. He kept that up for fifty yards or so, and then he began, softly, to speak. 'I had this driving mate in Victoria, Reverend,' he said.

Keane jerked as if surprised by the sound.

'When I whipped there, you know,' said Harry. 'On the Bendigo. Now this mate was a diamond, sir. Very rough, though—too rough for the lady passengers. It was his language. But he was a good driver. He was called Jack, sir.'

Keane gave no sign that he was listening. Harry continued.

'We both whipped the Bendigo route at that time,' he said. 'And this was bang in the middle of the gold rush. Our coaches were full to the brim each time—passengers everywhere. G'dap!' he said, for punctuation. The horses circled their ears back without changing their pace, knowing from Harry's voice that it was not said in anger or urgency.

'One of our runs went past the Weymouth Station. Now, I don't know if you know Weymouth, Reverend, but it's a huge station.' Harry lifted his free hand to suggest an expanse of station, and as he did so he noted the pleasant fall of this section of the road they were entering, the slope down over the Tokomairiro Plain to the river. It was a stretch of road he'd loved a long time.

'Yes, it was just huge—and all beautiful pasture stretching out everywhere. A lovely station. Now at this time Mr Weymouth had a daughter up for marriage, sir. Bear in mind he was a very rich man, very powerful. This was a great run. So with this daughter came eight thousand pounds, plus a share in the station. And every lad knew about this, sir. It was all the talk down the Bendigo line—every miner and whip had a point of view on it, if you get my meaning—but this Miss Weymouth was very high and mighty. It was a grand station, and that young lady was grand too. She was well out of our reaching. She certainly wouldn't fall for no whip, sir—not in a month of Hail Marys.'

He glanced at Keane, and this time he was not troubled that the passenger was not engaged with his story. He felt better for his own sake—for himself, Harry was pleased his own story was underway.

'So one day Jack had a breakdown in his coach and I had to come through with another coach and driver, that coach taking the passengers on while I fixed Jack's broken one, and then we followed along slowly, Jack and I, towards the next horse-change. Now, as we went along, Jack was a mite sore about his breakdown, I can tell you, Reverend. He was wild. Jack was a proud man, sir, and he was near fifty by this time, and he didn't like breaking down, and he didn't like riding without passengers, either. Not as a whip, sir—he said it was demeaning.'

Harry felt the beginnings of a demand for a smoke in his mouth and hands, but he decided against it. He'd wait for Tokomairiro now.

'So we're riding along together,' he said, 'Jack swearing black and blue all the way about what he's going to do when he finds the groom who caused him to break down. He was convinced some groom had made a mistake, you see. Of course I didn't believe him at all. It was just a breakdown, sir. It was just—' Harry breathed in sharply '—just one of those things. Anyway I was riding along enjoying the scenery while Jack turned it all blue with his bad language. Finally his yapping died down, but only because Jack was getting this other idea. We were coming towards the trail for the Weymouth Station, you see, and I could see an idea working away in Jack's brain. I could see him straining away at it—just *sweating* at it, Reverend. I'm sure you can picture what I mean.'

This time Harry saw Keane's mouth twitch as if he wanted to smile. The Reverend was a little more still now, and he seemed to be listening, or at least registering the rhythmic soothe of Harry's voice, and immediately that Harry detected that change he felt perversely resentful, as if now that he was easing Keane's tension he should be able to punish him too. But that wasn't the purpose of a box-seat story, and they were only half an hour or so from Tokomairiro now. Harry could change the seating arrangements once he got there, somehow ensure that Keane sat inside. He carried on. 'Sure enough, we're driving along and making easy time when Jack says, Pull up, to his team, and Whoa.'

Again the near-most geldings of Harry's team pricked their ears, sending them back to catch what was said, then rumbled on responsibly, knowing the instruction was not for them.

'Now what's doing, I say to Jack. Why are we stopped here. I'm going up there, he says to me. I'm going up to the Weymouth Station. And straight away, I'm regretting this idea, Reverend, because I know Jack, and I know his schemes. I just know it's going to be a bad notion, this one.'

Again Harry wished for a smoke. He wanted to inhale and exhale, pause to hold the smoke in as he told his story. Smoking went so well with a tale.

'I'm off up to the homestead, he tells me. I'm off up to see about that daughter of Weymouth's. Now, remember this Jack was a tough little rooster, Reverend. He was near fifty by this time, and all weaselled up from the whip. He had half-a-dozen teeth left in his head, and he had hardly any hair. He was one tough bird. Plus he was half-mad from a whole life in the bush and on the route, sir. And I knew only trouble could come of this. So I said, Don't go up there, Jack. You'll get in trouble. You could lose your route, Mr Weymouth being such a powerful man, not to mention kin to the owner of our line. He could blacklist any whip off the Bendigo, and that would make life hard for Jack and for me. So that was my advice, Reverend. You can see I was slamming hot brakes on the idea.'

This time Reverend Keane nodded. He was certainly listening now. Harry looked across the plain to the shallow valley that signalled the Tokomairiro River and the few buildings there. He swayed with the movement of the coach as it negotiated a rut, and he thought of standing against the fire. It was not a cold morning, but the stove would be on in the stable kitchen, and there was something about standing with your back to a stove that brought great comfort to a man, even if it was in early summer, and even if it was only for a few minutes in between chores at a horse-change. 'Get along,' Harry said, to his team. 'Almost there, boys. Almost there.'

He eased his position on his seat and continued.

'But Jack was just busting with this idea,' he said. 'Between you and me, Reverend, I think Jack wanted to salvage something from the day. Maybe a little of his pride, having run his own coach off the road that day. Maybe he wanted proof that the world wasn't always so mean. He'd had a heck of time of it, Reverend, over the years—Tasmania and all. But he was a tough bird, because of it.' Harry nodded for emphasis. 'Boy was he a tough one. Anyway, I sat on that empty coach and listed all the reasons he shouldn't go up there to the station, all the things he'd risk by approaching this famous daughter. But he was all for his plan—he was fair frothing at the mouth about it. I couldn't persuade him. So he unhitches one of his team and off he goes— bareback, I mean—talking to his horse all the time, just jawing away. Practising his love-talk, maybe.'

Again Harry sensed Keane twitching with a half-smile. Enjoying that effect, Harry leaned back and worked the reins a bit, adjusting their lie across the rumps of the nearest two, getting the tension just so. He couldn't help it—adding a little flourish to the story with coaching finesse, it was second-nature now.

'Now I had nothing to do, so I sat there and waited. In fact, I believe I went to sleep for a while. And when I woke up, Jack still hadn't returned, and I began to be a little worried about this little caper of his, and what might follow straight after. I was dead certain, you see, that he'd be on the swag again, once Weymouth started trouble. I was a bit concerned for him, sir, but I thought, Well, come what may, and I had another snooze.'

Keane adjusted on his seat. His backside must have been very sore—the box-seat was hell after a few hours for passengers who weren't used to it—but Harry could see the outline of the buildings at the settlement now. They were getting closer. He pressed on more quickly with his story. 'So after a while I woke to find old Jack making his way back down the trail on his horse. He was coming along nice and slow, too—no dogs after him, no shotgun up the freckle, if you'll pardon my French—just Jack nosing along on his own. Now what happened, I say to him. What did you do? And for a beginning he's playing it all coy like he's got the secrets of the kingdom in his bag or in his brain. And I can see he's enjoying it. I can see he wants to keep on keeping it under his hat, sir. So we harness up again and drive away, and for a long time Jack's keeping mum about his little adventure. I have to press him and press him and it's driving me mad, and finally he opens up about it, and here's what he says, Reverend. The first thing he says is: Got us a mutton each, Harry. Paid my respects to the meat safe up there.'

'And he brings this out of his coat—two hunks of mutton, plus some bread to wrap it in. And he tucks in right away. I don't want any of that, I say, so Jack just tucks into mine, straight after—and he wasn't a pretty eater, Reverend. I mean he was a pig-dog, and he just bolted it down. You could fair see the food going down his neck, sir, and soon he was well and truly outside that meat. Then he starts licking his fingers and smacking his lips, making a big show out of how first-rate it tasted. So still I had to wheedle away at him to find out what happened with the daughter. Now what's the story, I said to him. Come on, Jack, tell me now, I said.'

Harry leaned towards Keane to get his full attention now.

'Here's what he told me, Reverend. He told me: It was a while before I could see Mr Weymouth, Harry, him being such a busy man with that high-falutin' farm and all that wealth just filling up his day. So I waited in one of his fancy chairs until he was ready. And when I got sick of that I made my little foray into the kitchen. And I washed my face and combed my hair to the side.' Harry paused. 'Now, that part was a little difficult to believe, Reverend. I don't think Jack ever combed his hair in his life. He just wasn't that kind of man, sir. He might have taken his hat off, maybe pushed the sweat and grease around a few times, but nothing more. What was that, sir?' said Harry.

'What?' said Keane.

'Oh, nothing, sir,' said Harry. He had heard the Reverend make a sound—perhaps a strangled cough, perhaps the beginnings of a laugh; it was impossible to tell.

Harry batted away a fly with his free hand. 'Where was I? Oh yes—at last Mr Weymouth has time to see Jack. And the first thing he says to Jack is that he's not hiring men. Did you get that, Reverend—Mr Weymouth took one look at our great romancer and decided Old Romeo was on the swag. He said to Jack, No work here, mate, better luck next time. So in other words, he flat-out dismissed him, Reverend. And soon enough he's walking away towards his study or billiards room, this Mr Weymouth. But Jack says, No, I've not come about work, sir. I've come about your daughter. I've come about Evangeline.'

Now Harry put some tension on the reins to slow up his team. He had only a few hundred yards to tell this last part of his story. The pub and horse-change were in sight now. It was not time to ease off the team yet, and Harry felt them pull strongly on, not understanding, not used to this rupture in the drive's natural rhythm, but he couldn't muff this last part of the story. He kept the tension on the reins, eased them back a way. 'So that got Mr Weymouth's attention,' he said. 'Mr Weymouth turned all the way round to face Jack, and this time he gave him the long stare. I mean he eyeballed him properly. And here's what Jack said to him—he said: Mr Weymouth, I understand your daughter comes with eight thousand pounds on the side, sir. Now, I'll admit that's a lot of money. If I had that money, it would keep me in food a long time. It's a generous price, sir—especially to a man of modest means like me. But I can spare you the expense, sir. I'll take her for four thousand pounds and a feed.'

Now Harry slapped his knee to mark the end of his story, and Keane laughed outright and loud.

'Four thousand pounds and a feed, sir,' said Harry. 'That's what Jack told him. He said, Save yourself some dough, sir, I'll take her for four thousand pounds, and you can keep the change.'

Now that it came, the Reverend's laughter had a ripping sound of release in it, and it was loud, but it was not a noise of joy. It had something else in it, a groan, and it tore out of him as he bent with his shoulders shaking, ostensibly from amusement at the story, hiding his face in his hands.

Harry talked a little more to smooth things out for the Reverend, to allow him time. 'It's good to hear you laugh, sir. It's a healthy sound.' He could see the pub-keeper's wife outside the pub now. She was waiting for the coach and the team. Harry brought his cornet up from beside him. 'I've heard a few stories on the box-seat, Reverend,' he said. 'But that's my favourite story about marriage. I'll never forget that one.'

Keane had his handkerchief at his eyes. He shook his head as Harry put the cornet to his lips and gave it the first blast. As he played his customary run of notes Harry heard the passengers murmuring inside the coach, perhaps pleasantly surprised at the time they'd made.

'Jack always quoted that little victory, Reverend,' said Harry. 'He always said that when all was said and done, at least he'd tried for marriage, and at least he'd got a decent hunk of mutton out of it. He was always saying that, later on.'

Keane did not respond. He seemed to have emptied out, now. He would find fatigue before long. Harry looked forward to stowing him inside the coach after Tokomairiro; he hoped the man would sleep once inside.

He felt the team surge ahead for the last few yards before slowing. Nearly every team did that—they loved to pour towards a stopping-point in one last great show. Harry let them do it now.

The pub-keeper's wife waved across the remaining distance and—subtly, adroitly—cocked her hip at Harry, and he was shocked to recall that lately a harmless little flirtation had sprung up between them, he and the pub-keeper's wife, a banter across the bar-room as he took his brief rest at the change. It felt squalid now, and Harry ignored it, did not crack the woman a grin in reply. Instead he gave his arrival an extra flourish in the hope it would intimidate her, keep her silent on the Ryrie score. He pulled up grandly, made the hooves and wheels scatter stones. 'Whoa,' he shouted. 'Whoa, boys.'

Then he stepped off and walked round the coach to the doors. It was his custom to open them for his passengers; he did not like people to descend from the coach unassisted. But this time he did not swing the doors open immediately. Instead he stood by the coach with the doors ajar, his eyes on the road-dust at his feet. A deep fatigue was draining through him. He was more than road-weary, but he stood a moment more, until he knew he would be all right. Then he worked his face into a cheery expression, and pulled the doors wide open. He faced his passengers. He grinned at them as they searched his face, then roved out beyond him.

'Tokomairiro, ladies and gentlemen,' he said. 'Forty minutes only, please.'

Note

Key sources include 'Inquest', *Bruce Herald*. (Volume VI, Issue 342, 16 November 1870, p. 3). Accessed 10 October 2010. <http://paperspast.natlib. govt.nz/cgi-bin/paperspast?a=d&d=BH18701116.2.8&l=mi&e=-------10--1----0-all>; and Isobel Veitch, *From Wells Fargo, California, to Cobb & Co, Otago* (Dunedin: Square One Press, 2003). The fictional story of Jack's proposal to Ms Weymouth was suggested by a reference to a similar story in Veitch's book.

Chris Price

Song of la chouette
18 July: Musée Picasso, Antibes

The bird in the hand is an owl.
The owl has the artist's eyes.
With them across alps and
over cliffs of sleeping women

it flies, looking for fissures and
platters, chair-backs and shoulders
spotting and looking and taking
in what cowers among the boulders.

At night the small round bird
balloons to voodoo mask,
a stringless kite, no jess or trace
to draw it back—yet faithful

it returns to the hangar and the man
who recalibrates the sights; grateful
and silent, he builds *le grand hibou*
in black and white. One night the owl

drops the eyes in ancient Greece.
They calmly lie and see for weeks
until the bird, on another hunt,
plucks them up in its feet.

The bird holds the eyes in its claws.
The man hoods the bird in his palm.
The blind mice run at night. The owl means
no harm. The artist it darkly serves

paints under cloudless skies.
I am the owl. You are the prize.

essa may ranapiri

cough in

it consumes it and is made by it planet and body / the human
eye is 70 to 90 percent water / the earth's surface is within that
range / 71 percent water / this water is above the land / as well
as beside the land / an island (an eye inside the land above the
land) is a subcontinental sprout of not-water in the middle of
water / boxed in by under-water and over-water / there is a body
of water drowning / a human body in water / drowning / a body
performing / a human body speaks / within a structure of islands
/ other bodies / as performative / next to expressive / the island
in the throat makes / a sound / the sound is an action / speaking
words / performative phrase see: i love you / performative phrase
see: take the bread out to thaw / performative phrase see: declared
guilty by the state of / water leaving loaf / dough boxed / the
body raises an arm out in front of it / the arm meets material
restriction / hand meets cardboard / a forest of trees thinned / the
box is leaking / wet through paper branches / water has weight
and mass / water pushes downwards / inwards / the wall of this
box is a different kind of weapon / birds kill themselves by flying
into glass windows / the metaphor of glass functions / it doesn't
function if the glass is clean / the world is not clean / the world is
created in violent eruptions / the top of a volcano peaking above
the sea / a bulb on a mushroom cloud stalk / blinking / water
seeing itself by water dead

Melissa Day Reid

The Life and Deaths of Adeline Snow
Chapter 1 of a work in progress

Adeline loves her grandparents but hates the sulphurous smell of their water, a smell she can accept in January in Montana from hot springs feeding rivers or pools, but not from a tap in a pink-tiled bathroom in the flat land of Illinois in July. When she was little, when she smelled the odour of this water for the first time, she blamed it on her grandfather. Her mother, happy to teach anytime, anywhere, told Adeline about the aquifer feeding the household water supply.

'We won't wash your hair too often while we're here,' she said. 'When I was a girl the minerals gave my hair a pink tinge.'

Adeline hates the smell of her grandparents' water, but the day has been hot and thundery, and soaking in a lukewarm tub is the only way she will cool down tonight. In a borrowed bathrobe, its orange silk pooling at her feet, Adeline has accepted help she doesn't need—she can put up her own hair to keep it dry, to keep it from turning pink (she imagines herself with hair the colour of her grandparents' bathroom walls)—but she likes the way her grandmother's hands stroke and rake through her hair, arrange and pin it in place.

'There,' says her grandmother, running those hands down Adeline's bare neck and resting them on her shoulders. 'You're all set. Hop in.'

After the bath, Adeline scrubs herself dry with a towel, slides her cool limbs into cool pyjamas, and slips between cool sheets in the room her grandmother decorated just for her when she was born. When she isn't visiting, her grandparents use it as a study, but really it's all hers: turquoise-blue and white, with a mural of a street scene painted on the wall next to the narrow bed. She appreciates the lack of cuddly characters and the colour pink.

Her parents come to kiss her, and fuss with her sheets and ask her if she had a nice day. They leave her room holding hands when her grandparents come in. Her grandfather kisses her goodnight and leaves the bedtime story to her grandmother, who produces *another* story about Brave Zaya, who lived on Earth in the time between gods and men. Adeline has outgrown Zaya, but doesn't know how to tell her grandmother this without hurting her feelings.

After the bath and the long story, Adeline has to kick away sleep. She wants to lie comfortable and happy and listen as her parents and grandparents come upstairs and disperse for the night. She seeks the cool patches of her pillows and sheets, populates the street scene with figures from her imagination, and is wide awake when the grown-ups climb the stairs for bed, and for a long time after they have switched off their reading lamps.

In the morning, she knows she slept only because she remembers her dreams.

Adeline's grandparents live in a suburb with roads that meander like the streams in everyone's backyards, streams concealed by belts of trees spared to serve as natural beauty on otherwise cleared lots. Their house is built into a hill. Visitors who enter the house by the front door can go down a flight of stairs into the finished basement, walk through the back door onto a grey flagstone patio, and cool their feet on the lawn.

Adeline's grandfather is famous for his barbecued ribs, and that's not him boasting, everyone here this afternoon calls them his famous ribs. He stands on the patio behind his vast, black barbecue and in front of a yellow road construction sign that reads *Caution! Men Cooking*, turning the ribs and painting them with his equally famous barbecue sauce. All of the guests line up so that he can tong a few ribs straight from the grill onto their plates, and as they wait, they all take it in turns to hold Adeline's elbow, crow over her height and insist she call them by their first names now she is practically grown up.

Adeline's mother has coached her: she's a young lady now and shouldn't tear around in the woods the whole time. She should charm her grandparents' guests. Trapped by her mother's brief in the small crowd on the patio, Adeline holds her eyes open until they tear up and conjures blurry visions through the moisture. The ribs everyone's eating are human. Mr Reynolds's fawn golf pants are the legs of a faun. Her grandfather would appreciate the pun.

After dinner the sky turns green as it often does before a thunderstorm. Despite the brewing weather, the guests scatter themselves over the perfect lawn for which Adeline's grandfather is also famous. Adeline moves among the clots of adults, charming her way to the woods, where the green above her head deepens and descends. Though she snakes through the trees as long as she can, she still hits the stream within a minute. She rolls up her long shorts and wades in. The glassy water parts and joins around her thighs. Clouds cap the heated air. Orange light cuts through in the west.

When her feet are numb, she returns to the bank and slips on her sandals. Crouching down to pull the back straps up over her heels, she sees her grandfather's lawn winking through the tree trunks in the green evening light. She could reach it in ten leaps. As if pursued, she used to swipe her way through the branches and shove several feet of lawn between her back and the wild boundary before she saw or felt the grass underfoot, or felt her breath heavy and fast, and her heartbeat. Now she feels safe, and a new wilderness has gone inside with the grown-ups, who have conceded the lawn to the impending rain and hail.

Weaving around the basement between women in Bermudas and halter tops, men in golf pants and Izod shirts, Adeline sees and hears the slosh of ice cubes. Her father is working the bar. She walks up to him like a customer.

'Can I please have a root beer, Dad?'

'Hey, sweetheart. There you are. How was your expedition?'

'Okay. But I think I have heat exhaustion.' Adeline raps on the bar. 'So, how about that root beer?'

'Have you asked Mom?' Adeline's father nods towards the far corner of the basement, where her mother is passing around the leftover hors d'oeuvres.

Adeline's grandmother, slipping behind the bar to fix her own drink, tells Adeline of course she can have whatever she wants and to refill her glass whenever it's empty. 'It's a party, sweetie,' she says. 'Excess is the name of the game.'

Adeline's mother looks over at the three of them, zeroes in on Adeline, points at her glass of root beer and mouths Just One. Then she waves Come Here. Adeline obeys, and her mother gathers her in, winds one arm around her hip and kisses her bare shoulder.

To a tanned blonde with frosted pink lipstick and leathery skin, Adeline's mother says, 'Can you believe this long tall sally?' and to Adeline, 'Do you remember Mrs Spinks?'

'Nice to see you again, Mrs Spinks.'

Mrs Spinks says Adeline has grown into such a beautiful young woman her father will need a shotgun to keep the boys away.

Adeline knows she is supposed to be gracious when adults say such horrible things.

'Gross,' she says.

Mrs Spinks shows her fillings when she laughs.

Later, Adeline's grandfather starts a game of Dime in the Shot Glass. Most who play miss and swig from their glasses, but when the dime drops from between Adeline's knees it rings out success. She photographs the party with her little Kodak camera, reloads twice with new film.

Winding down to sleep has never been so impossible. Moonlight leaks through the gaps between Adeline's eyelids unless she squeezes them very tightly together.

'You just overdid the root beer,' says her mother, walking her back down the hall to her own room. 'Nothing for it but to ride it out. You'll feel fine in a little while-o.'

Flicking on the light as they enter her room, Adeline slips away from her mother and over to the little table where her grandfather pays bills and her grandmother puts photographs in albums.

'Do you want to play cards, Mom?'

'Not really, sweetie. It's after midnight. Here, just hop into bed and think pleasant thoughts and you'll drift off eventually.'

Her mother pulls back the bedcovers and gestures an invitation to lie down. Adeline does not refuse the invitation, but protests as she accepts it.

'I don't have any pleasant thoughts.'

'Oh, come on. It's easy. Here, watch.' Her mother makes a dreamy, drowsy face. 'Candy canes, fairies, people in this house love me.'

'That's the best you can do?'

'Lie down.'

Adeline complies, and her mother tucks a sheet up under her chin.

After she is alone and her eyes adjust to the inadequate, suburban, moonlit darkness, Adeline feels very cross with the night, with her mother, and the sheet. She thrashes her legs until the stupid thing is bunched at the end of her bed. Her feet drift to the floor, and pull the rest of her body after them. For a cool, supine moment, she presses her cheek against the smooth wooden floor, runs her fingers over the braids and coils of the rag rug. Then she stands and goes to the window. She wants to open it and breathe in the smell of the storm that finally broke at about nine: damp earth and scant remnants of ozone.

'Who on Earth are you talking to, Adeline?'

Her amused grandfather, who pees five times a night, is sitting on the edge of her bed. The light in her room is grey. Adeline goes through all of the steps of being woken from a dream. She blinks, bends her arms to stretch her back, breathes in loudly through her nose.

'I don't remember,' she says. 'What was I saying?'

'It was unintelligible, as always.'

'What time is it?'

'I'm not sure.' He looks out the window, weighs the light with a squint. 'Five? Sorry to wake you, but it sounded like a bad dream.'

'I think it was. Too much root beer, Mom will say.'

'Sugarbeets are the root of all evil.'

'Was that supposed to be funny?'

'That *was* funny,' says her grandfather, patting her shoulder with mock condescension. 'I'm going to make a sandwich. You want one?'

'Too sleepy.' Adeline shuffles her shoulders under the covers and turns onto her side. 'But you enjoy.'

'All right, Addy.' Her grandfather kisses her on the forehead, right on her damp hairline. 'See you in the morning.'

Adeline wakes up again, to a wail of calamity. It pins her to her bed and then, unaware of having travelled, she is in the hallway looking into her grandparents' room over the top of her mother's head. Her grandfather is on the floor. Her grandmother holds one of his hands in both of hers, pleading with him in a raw, low voice. Her father kneels beside him compressing his chest, breathing into his lungs.

Her mother is on the phone, but she turns and wraps her arms around Adeline, stops her from going farther into the room.

Adeline tries not to look or, for some messed-up reason, cry. Her mother hangs up the phone and walks her slowly out into the hallway, where she can stop trying.

Adeline and her mother stand in the hallway and cry and make noises to soothe one another.

Cardiac arrest. Those are the words Adeline hears the ambulance crew say to her father and grandmother, white hot words that roll down the hallway astride her shrouded grandfather. His body goes down the stairs and out the front door but the words stay behind in the house, with the cold word dead.

On Wednesday, he will burn to ash.

Today, everyone who came to the party drops by the house again to fill a basin of sympathy and the freezer. Adeline's grandmother will not have to cook for a month. This slow gathering takes place in the living room, a more sober setting than the basement. People laugh, but not the way they did at the party. This laughter has more mass.

Adeline's father sits on the long floral couch under the picture window, guarding her grandfather's chair. Her grandmother does not advocate excess. Her mother does not wave her over from across the room to charm people, but instead keeps her close, holds her hand and doesn't try to brush away her silence.

At dinner time, the family is left alone to eat a spinach lasagne, which they heat in its disposable aluminum dish. Their appetites vary. Adeline's grandmother's is healthy. She prods Adeline's hand.

'Enjoy this meal, honey. That's what he'd want.'

After dinner, the cool trio: bath, pyjamas, sheets. Adeline's parents enter and leave her room holding hands. In between they arrange her bedclothes and kiss her, press their palms to her cheeks.

When her grandmother comes in alone and stoops to kiss her forehead, the alone part makes Adeline cry. Dry-eyed, her grandmother sits on the edge of her bed and kisses her again.

'There's one from him,' she says. She smoothes the sheet under Adeline's chin though it is folded back with precision already, and sits with her while she cries.

Afterwards, Adeline wipes her cheeks with the backs of her fingers.

'Why aren't you sad, Granny?' she says. Crying has gummed up her lips.

'Oh sweetheart, I'm very sad. It just hasn't hit me yet. And I've had a lot of practice with sadness.'

'What do you mean?'

'I'm an old woman.'

'No you're not.'

'Kind of you to say, but I'm as old as the hills. Older. Now, your story.'

Adeline's grandmother assumes the solemnity that marks the onset of storytime. Adeline is surprised she wants to tell a story tonight, considering, but she does. Every one of her stories begins 'Zaya the Divinely Beautiful did such-and-such in the time between gods and men.' Tonight the did such-and-such is 'grew tired of being alone'.

Adeline doesn't hear much past '. . . and so the Earth gave her a friend'. She is practically asleep with her eyes open. Concentration is out of the question. And anyway, she hasn't really paid attention to one of these stories since she was maybe eight or nine.

Her grandmother's knotty hands describe the actions of the story, the lined skin draping her throat wobbles with the movements of her mouth. Adeline feels on her own face an exhausted version of the attentive look she makes it wear at story time. She wishes she could explain to her grandmother the origin of this look, the love and respect that has plastered it across her face every night for the entire month of July for several years. She thinks that after recovering from the initial resentment generated by the news that Zaya is boring, her grandmother might actually feel touched. She dares herself to say something, but her grandmother is so into the story—Zaya's lover dies of a spider bite, something, something, the usual weirdness—she just can't.

And she is grateful to her grandmother for replacing thoughts of her grandfather—the terrible colour he went, the never seeing him again—with this story. But noting her gratitude is another way of remembering these terrible things. As Adeline is about to start crying again, she realises her grandmother has been looking at her for a long time without speaking, that the story is over. There is something significant in the long look.

'What?' says Adeline.

'You will travel between the Earth and the underworld?' Her grandmother sounds annoyed. 'You will have no control over when you leave the Earth and little control over when you return? The dead will take and release you as they wish? None of that sounds a little familiar?'

Adeline makes only the nn of 'No, should it?' before it *does* sound familiar. A dream she had when she was little, just after her father's grandmother died.

Her grandmother gives her a little slap on the arm.

'You weren't listening to me, were you?' she says. 'I *thought* you were wearing your pretending-to-listen face.' She shakes her head, and then gives Adeline another long look. 'I told you this story because I don't know which one of us will go with Grandad,' she says.

Adeline's recollection of the underworld lurches from dream to memory.

*

Adeline stares at the pair of eyes in the mirror on the back of the music room door. The house is quiet. Her mother and father lie in bed.

Her father says, Gingie.

Adeline wonders where her great-grandmother has gone. She didn't come into Adeline's room this morning, didn't smooth Adeline's cheeks with her hands to open Adeline's eyes. They didn't play together in Adeline's long, long closet where the ceiling slopes so that even Adeline has to sit down under the low end. Adeline turns her head back and forth and watches her irises slide along between her eyelids.

Adeline's mother and father lie in bed. Adeline cries and asks them when they will get out of bed and tells them to get out of bed now. Her mother tells Adeline they are very sad. She pulls back the covers and invites Adeline into bed. Adeline lies with her parents for a while and then she gets up and pads out of their room.

She plays on the sidewalk. She likes to run up and down in front of the chain link fence that surrounds the yard where the big black dog lives. The dog runs with her, his tongue out. He doesn't bark. When Adeline trips and skins her knees and the palms of her hands she almost cries. The dog stops running and looks at her, his ears held up. She waits for the stinging to stop and then runs with him again. Blood blooms along the front of her white knee socks.

She plays on the sidewalk. She feeds out an inch of the tape measure she found in her Christmas stocking and bends it against the plastic case. The inch snaps off in her fingers. She likes the feeling of the metal breaking and the crisp sound of it. She breaks the tape measure into sixty inch-long pieces. She will show them to her father when he gets out of bed.

Adeline's father gets out of bed. He takes her with him to the tobacconist's. The tobacconist's smells like him and is dark in the middle of the day and the carpet there is red and green and blue and black. The same old man is always at the counter and always hands Adeline the same flavour of lollipop. Nowhere else has root beer flavour, but here that's all there is. Every time she visits, Adeline tells the old man she likes root beer.

Adeline and her father walk home between piles of grey snow. He is quiet, but he holds her hand and swings it in his. When they come inside through the back door into the kitchen her mother looks up from the book she is pressing open against kitchen table.

Hello you two, she says. You both have very pink cheeks.

Adeline and her mother and father play together in the long, long closet with the sloped ceiling. Adeline leads the game but her mother keeps trying to change the rules. Gingie never tried to change things.

Where's Gingie? asks Adeline.

In heaven, says her mother. Remember what I told you about heaven?

She's dead, says her father. She's dead and buried next to Grampy in Lindley Park.

Adeline walks into the bathroom in the middle of the night. She climbs onto her little stool and looks in the mirror. She turns her head back and forth and watches her irises slide along between her eyelids. Gingie, not in heaven or Lindley Park, walks into the bathroom.

Adeline, says Gingie.

You know my name.

I know it now. I have remembered some things.

You can talk.

I have to show you something.

Down the hallway, in her bedroom, Adeline lies in bed. She stands next to Gingie and looks at herself lying in bed.

I'm dead, says Gingie. Do you know what that means?

Am I dead, too?

No. Your body is alive. Look. It's breathing. You're breathing. But your body and soul have become separated. Do you understand?

No, says Adeline.

Gingie takes Adeline's hand and they walk back out into the hallway. They walk through the living room to the front door, which Gingie opens.

What do you see? she asks.

Nothing, says Adeline.

Any colours? Grey? Black? White?

Nothing.

That's a good sign.

Do you see nothing, too?

Me? No. I can see everything. The slope in front of the log house, grassy all the way down to the road, and the bridge over Mill Creek, and Grampy waiting in the truck with his elbow poked out the open window. Gingie picks Adeline up and kisses her hair. Come on, honey.

Are we going to heaven?

No, Addy. We're going for a drive.

Gingie carries Adeline close to her body. Adeline feels movement, the pounding of Gingie's feet down a slope, her arm shifting as she opens the door of the truck. Adeline wraps her arms and legs around Gingie's seated body and presses her eyes into Gingie's collar bone. She can breathe but cannot sense air on her skin. No dust, no popping of tyres on loose stones, but she feels they are travelling along a gravel road, and she notices when they stop travelling.

Adeline lifts her head and she can see shadows. The shadows are not as frightening as the nothing.

Gingie has started to disappear and Grampy has started to appear. They look the same: like people, like clouds. Out the window, there are shadows like trees. Slowly, they grow into trees made of stone and metal, with shadows of their own. The trees crowd the bank of a silver river.

As the trees gain substance, the cloud people in the truck turn into a mist. It nudges at the windows. Adeline opens the doors of the truck and watches the mist comb itself through the branches of a tree, split and drift away.

Adeline wakes up and walks into the kitchen. Her mother and father are reading the paper and drinking coffee and there is bright, long sun shining through the windows over the sink.

*

Though the night is the summer's hottest yet, Adeline's cold limbs crawl towards her body. She lies still and tight, and tries not to overreact.

'It really happened?' The words sit her up, push her past her grandmother, stand her up, feet apart, toes gouging into the braided rug. Afraid she might shout, she leans close into her grandmother's face to whisper, and understands as she does this that she is angry. 'I went to the *underworld*?'

'With Gingie. Yes, I'm afraid you did. Mommy told me what you said happened at the time, because she was afraid you'd become obsessed with death.'

'You break this to me with a stupid *Zaya* story?' says Adeline.

Her grandmother shrugs, smiles a little to acknowledge her mistake. 'I figured, she's a kid, tell her a story.'

Adeline is still leaning into her grandmother's face. She feels hands upon her shoulder blades drawing her into a hug. She lets the tension drain out of her shoulders but keeps it in her toes. She hasn't finished being angry yet.

But she *has* finished talking. The situation is too preposterous to support questions or any further comment. Silenced, she breaks out of the hug, gently though, and lies down again, on top of the rumpled covers, facing the wall. Her grandmother lies down, too.

'Okay, forget the stupid story. I'll give it to you straight,' she says. 'I've been there seven times. The last time was about a hundred years ago.'

Still facing the wall, Adeline says, 'A *hundred* years ago?'

'Immortality is a feature of our condition.'

'You're not serious.'

'Kid, I wish I was pulling your leg. When Mommy told me what happened to you I just cried and cried.'

'Why doesn't *she* know about this?'

'Not everyone in an afflicted family is afflicted. If Mommy had it, she would have been taken by now.'

'Taken.'

'Taken and returned. We go, we come back. There's really nothing to be afraid of. It's a pain in the neck, that's all. An inconvenience.'

'I'm not *afraid*.' As Adeline says this, she hears her anger freeze into fear.

Her grandmother's hand travels down her arm. 'I'm sorry. I wanted to wait until you were older to let you in on this. Twelve isn't old enough.'

Adeline's anger comes right back. 'When would I be old enough to hear *this*? I can travel to the underworld? I'm *immortal*?'

'Good point.' Adeline's grandmother sighs, a long breath in, a long breath out. Only an immortal being would take so much time over a sigh. Adeline tries it out. Her lungs are cavernous. She and her grandmother are the same. With the out-breath, Adeline loses her anger like smoke through her nostrils. When she has finished her sigh, wrung out her lungs, her grandmother replies with another sigh, and they end up in a longest sigh contest. Adeline's tenth is longer than her grandmother's eleventh.

'Whippersnapper,' says her grandmother.

Adeline turns away from the wall and places her head in the bowl between her grandmother's shoulder and chest. 'How old are you, anyway?' she says.

'Really, really old.' Her grandmother's chest rumbles in her ear. 'I don't know exactly.'

'Wow.'

'Yeah, wow,' says her grandmother. She wraps a hand across her forehead as if she can take the temperature of her uncountable years. 'Addy, honey, what we both need right now is a good night's sleep.'

'You think I'm going to *sleep* now?'

'Want to come to my bed?'

'Yes, please. But if we talk, we have to talk about other stuff.'

'Agreed.'

'Like what life was like in the stone age,' says Adeline, scooting down to the end of the bed to get out of it.

Adeline's grandmother sweeps her legs across the quilt. Their momentum pulls the rest of her up out of bed. 'I'm not *that* old,' she says.

In the church her mother has organised for the funeral service— plenty of soaring and leaping architecture, beautiful windows— Adeline sits in a pew with just her mother and her father, between them. Her grandmother couldn't make it out the door this morning. She was crying the way she sighed last night.

Adeline sits in the pew pretending that she is a normal person. It isn't hard. The information she acquired last night will never sound true, and anyway grief insulates her from it. Her grandfather was not religious, but there he is up the front of the church in his coffin, surrounded by flower arrangements. Adeline has never seen her father cry, she's never seen him in a church, or wearing a tie. His tears and the red and blue striped silk dividing his white shirtfront stab at her heart.

While Adeline and her father cry, her mother sings and kneels and prays. She believes in the power of public rites, and rites require the performance of certain things at certain times. But she doesn't seem to hold their lack of decorum against them, and when she is allowed by the rite to sit beside Adeline, she stretches her arms around both of them, and whispers things like, 'I know, I know,' and, 'I miss him, too.' Adeline has heard these words often since Sunday night. Her father has said them to her mother, her mother has said them to her grandmother, and everyone has said them to her as they have all rattled around in the private house of grief.

When the rite has been performed to the satisfaction of the Book of Common Prayer, a recessional hymn blares out, and the six pallbearers and the coffin lead the priest and choir down the aisle, and the mourners out into the parking lot, where the hearse waits.

Adeline's grandfather was the person who taught her 'The Worms Crawl In and the Worms Crawl Out', and now the hearse that will go by, causing people to think they could be the next to die and to host worm pinochle parties, will have him inside it. She might have a chance to ask him if this is funny or not.

She sings the song in her head. All the way to the crematorium, she looks out the window of the black car her mother rented for them to ride in today and sings it, and she's still singing it when she steps out onto the gravel square in front of the low brick building that could be anything but a place where they burn dead bodies.

In the light and lily-filled chamber surrounding the oven, Adeline stops singing. Her grandfather takes his place, ready to burn, and she presses her eyes against the shoulder of her father's jacket. She doesn't want to watch the mechanics of cremation, but this part of the day is family only; there's just the three of them and if she went to wait in the lobby one of them would end up alone. Hiding her eyes isn't enough, and she has to plug her ears as well.

She imagines the inside of the oven acting like a nuclear bomb, that her grandfather will be instantly vaporised but somehow leave them a memento mori to take away. But the oven acts like an oven: slowly. And afterwards he will need processing. Her mother strokes her wrists, draws her fingers out of her ear canals and explains these things to her. They can go home now, to wait for him.

When they get home, Adeline's grandmother is drunk.

'Nice one, Mother,' says Adeline's mother. She leaves her good shoes crooked by the front door, drops her purse on the hall table and disappears upstairs.

Adeline's grandmother sips her scotch. 'This should be condoned. Expected, at least. Your father was the love of my goddamn life.' Her voice rises to a shout directed up the stairs.

Adeline's mother and grandmother *never* speak to each other this way.

'Astrid,' says Adeline's father gently, but then he loses his thread. He shrugs everything above his belt.

Adeline's grandmother pushes at the air in front of her with her drink. The ice makes noise. 'Go be with Veronica, Mark.'

He drops his shoulders, nods, and obeys.

He's only halfway up the stairs when Adeline asks, 'Do you want another drink, Granny?'

'Addy, you are the only sensible person in this family. But no, thank you. I need to think about sobering up now.'

'Can I have a sip of that one?'

Adeline's grandmother looks into her drink and then holds it out to Adeline, who takes it. As she analyses the smoky, medicinal taste, she hears her grandmother say, 'Let's get out of here.'

Outside, it's 103 degrees with what feels like 100 per cent humidity. Adeline and her grandmother drag the sprinkler on its long hose to a patch of lawn where the woods will shade their heads while their bodies lie in the sun.

Face down, Adeline's grandmother says, 'This lawn will go to the dogs now.' She has gone from 'I've had a lot of practice with sadness', to drunk and housebound over the love of her life, to ruing the demise of the perfect lawn. Adeline lies beside her, face up. The sprinkler waves back and forth, showering their legs for three seconds out of every fifteen. The day is still and the layers of leaves in the canopy are immobile except where the water reaches. Each patch of green, its hue dependent on how much tissue blocks the light, is fixed in place, giving Adeline scope to find a pattern, but there isn't one. There aren't even faces.

Her grandmother executes another of her immortal sighs and Adeline braces herself for more of the lunatic truth.

'I should tell you, the younger ones are usually taken. For their stamina.'

Adeline really, really doesn't want to talk about this stuff, but she says, 'Okay.' She thinks of Olympic gymnasts, the stoic way they wait inside their youth and training to perform uncommon feats. She tries to make her face look like that, but she can feel her chin pushing into her lower lip. She smoothes it down with her fingers.

The sprinkler still waves back and forth. There still aren't any faces in the leaves.

'Let's go down to the stream,' says Adeline, too agitated to lie on her back anymore.

Her grandmother sits up. She searches Adeline's face for a sign that all is well and evidently imagines she finds one, because she smiles brightly. 'What a grand idea,' she says. 'I never go down there, but always think that I should.'

The night begins with the cool things to cancel the heat.

Adeline lies in her bed and tries not to farewell her parents when they leave her room. They seem okay, as though their mourning has peaked.

Her grandmother comes in, jaw and shoulders tense with the wait that will end before morning. After they hear her parents' bedroom door close, Adeline and her grandmother walk down the hall to her grandparents' big bed, where Adeline pretends to almost instantly fall asleep.

She can't remember falling asleep, but when she sits up in the middle of the night, her head remains on the pillow, eyes closed. Her legs stay curled together under the covers as she stands. Her grandmother's eyelids flicker with dreaming. Her grandfather strokes her grandmother's hair. He looks up at Adeline, happy to see her and sorry about the circumstances. She feels the same way. They meet at the foot of the bed and join hands.

He says, 'Ready?'

She nods, and they leave the bedroom and go downstairs, and he opens the front door onto a nothing Adeline knows won't last.

The braided Mercury River is the only feature of the underworld that isn't the strangely purple colour of doom. It flows silver under the skeletal birds and papery insects, silver past the banks covered in wire grass where the trees of iron and stone stand. The Mercury River laps silver at the feet of the dead and the feet of those who tend the dead as they walk its braided channels.

Adeline and her grandfather walk the braided bed of the Mercury River towards the mountain, vast and bare and distant.

'How's your algebra?' he says.

'My what?'

'Come on, Addy. Stay sharp. Don't let this place get to you. How's your algebra?'

Adeline, who has been watching her feet slap the stones, kicks one into the river, feels more alive, says, 'Pretty good, actually.'

'That's the spirit,' says her grandfather. 'And then I say: Oh, yeah? So what's 5q + 5q?'

'And then I say: 10q.'

'You're welcome.'

'Hilarious,' Adeline deadpans, and then she looks at him and what she sees brings hope and guilt. 'Grandad.' She moves closer to him, takes his hand, which is cold and moist. 'You're fading.' She'll go home soon, when he is gone.

He points his hazy profile at the horizon, towards the Mountain. 'That's the way this works,' he says.

Their feet go steady along the stones.

'Have you heard the one about the two bear biologists from behind the Iron Curtain?'

'No, but I have a feeling I'm going to hear it now.'

'If you insist. They went to study grizzlies on the Kamchatka peninsula. One day, they surprised a mating pair and were eaten.

Their stunned research assistants shot the bears and opened their guts in the childish belief the biologists would spring out unharmed. But it was carnage. The Russian had been eaten by the female and the Czech was in the male.'

'Groan. Awful.'

'How is it that *my* granddaughter lacks a sense of humour?'

Adeline stumbles. Her grandfather puts an arm around her and the contact makes her teeth chatter and her chest ache.

'You're dead, Grandad.'

He twists at the waist, turning his torso as though looking in the mirror for five extra pounds. 'Does it show?'

'Funny.'

Her warmth makes him feel more dead the way his coldness makes her feel less alive. They step away from each other. The mineral clatter of their passage overtakes talk.

Rounding a bend, they come upon the main channel where the river occupies a narrow slice of its wide, stony bed. The area is as crowded as a suburban lawn after a barbecue dinner.

Those nearest Adeline and her grandfather greet them with murmurs when they enter the main channel. There are a few in the channel alive like her, but most in the channel are dead.

There are some dead who sit on the riverbed. Though the walking dead become more transparent and amorphous with every step, the seated dead still have recognisable parts and sit with their limbs knotted around their torsos. They face downriver, assailed by the birds and insects. Adeline wants to swat the birds and insects away until she realises they're administering encouragement with their beaks and wings and legs, not torture. The seated dead ignore the birds and insects. They are miserable but will endure.

It appears the wise course is to keep walking. But for the first time since Adeline and her grandfather arrived in the underworld, he stops moving. They stand together on the stones.

'Watch,' he says.

He shivers like the mesh on the bottom of a rolled snare drum, and then part of him drifts away.

'What was that?'

'My left hand, I think. No, my right. My right foot. You know what? I don't think I have parts anymore.' There is no way to see his smile. Adeline has to hear it. 'I love you, Addy. Be brave.' He expends a piece of himself brushing her cheek.

The cold doesn't make her feel less alive this time.

And then he says, 'Now, I'm sorry, but here goes my mouth.'

When the last mute scrap of Adeline's grandad becomes beads of mist on her eyelashes, when those have dried, she is alone in the landscape.

She's pretty sure this is *not* how this works. Her recently mist-beaded eyelashes are supposed to be fluttering right about now as she wakes in her turquoise blue and white room.

All she can think to do is to keep on walking.

The landscape is a finite roll of stage scenery, cranked along to create the illusion of movement while she pretends to walk as on-stage lovers pretend to ride a tandem bicycle. Trees and grass pass her, trees and grass, trees and grass. The river is a silver cloth shimmied from the wings. The mountain, a painting, vast and bare and distant, never comes closer. Every time she looks down at her feet, they seem farther away.

What her mother used to call buds open. Her feet are no longer just farther away but also partially obscured. The bangs that grazed her eyebrows when she arrived here grow to graze her breastbone.

Birds preen, roost, fly; insects scuttle, dart, clean their faces.

The scenery rolls through its repeats.

And then a bird with noisy wings alights in the bare crown of a tree on the river bank. The bird is a living thing in this world of shades, fat and glossy and not dim purple, but green and blue and bronze and red, with a snow white breast. The bird's colours stop Adeline's feet. The bird looks at Adeline. Birds don't look at people the way this bird looks at her.

The bird makes a sound that is almost like the voice of a woman talking in another room, or out on the street, beyond a window, but also like the cooing of a pigeon.

It swoops down from the tree and lands on the riverbank. Something in the noise of its wings suggests delight. Looking at Adeline all the while, the bird hops through the wire grass to the base of the tree and taps the trunk with its beak. The tree turns to wood and pops flowers out the length of its branches. It's a cherry tree. The bird flies arcs across the festooned canopy. Rains of cherry blossom pink shiver to the ground. Adeline reconsiders her resolution not to talk. This bird knows the earth. This bird knows the way out.

'Tell me what to do.'

As though dislodged by her voice, the rest of the petals fall from the tree like snow from a roof the morning after a spring blizzard. Leaves unfurl and fruit develops, mean and pale, and then ripe red. On the wing, the bird plucks a pair of cherries from a branch bowing low to the ground, lands, and proffers them most charmingly to Adeline, the movements of its generous, chivalrous head like the ticking of a second hand. The sight of food, like sunshine, makes her squint.

She leaps from the riverbed onto the bank and from the bank into the branches of the cherry tree, scooping as she goes the twin cherries from the beak of the bird. With cherries in her mouth and more in her fists, she can hear flight and birdsong, can hear buds bursting and grass growing. Juice trickles down her throat. Colour spreads like syrup across the landscape. The grey drains from the river's silver.

Adeline hasn't returned to Earth but that doesn't matter. She now inhabits a glorious approximation. She can eat. Drink. Rest. Holding pulp in her mouth is a divine luxury. She starts separating the pits from the flesh so that she can swallow what she has in her mouth and eat more.

She propels a pit from between her lips and follows it with her eyes. The pit's trajectory is intersected by a green and gold beetle the size of a matchbox, with its elytra raised like a pair of alarmed eyebrows. It whirrs into the hair by Adeline's ear and says very calmly, in a voice that sounds like hands rubbing together, 'Spit. Spit all of it out and run. Follow me. And don't look behind you.'

Adeline holds the cherries in her mouth. She slides her eyes back towards the bird. She turns her head a degree or two.

The beetle runs a barbed leg along the curve of Adeline's ear. 'Please,' it says.

It is the please—the sincerest, most desperate please Adeline has ever heard—that earns her unquestioning obedience. She reaches her hand up to her mouth and though it kills her to remove the cherries, she pushes them into her palm with her tongue. The mass of them putrefies in her hand. All the colours dim a little. A silence erupts. Through the silence, the sound the bird makes—coo-as-thunderclap—travels to the mountain and back.

Though Adeline has not walked faster than a shuffle since her bangs first brushed her eyelids, now she runs like John Colter. The beetle's frantic wings whirr a foot in front of her and the bird's noisy wings signal pursuit.

Wherever the beetle is leading her is a long way from where the beetle found her, but the bird never seems to gain on them, doesn't eat the beetle or peck out Adeline's eyes, doesn't seem to have any allies to aid in the pursuit. Adeline's panic settles down and finally disappears, and the run becomes as monotonous as her years-long walk. The chase, the escape or whatever, is ritualistic. But it has drained the underworld of colour as night drains the day. And the bird keeps making that awful sound, louder and louder.

Adeline is sure she's grown a little before the beetle finally wheels around, catches a strand of her hair with one of its front legs, and burrows in right by her ear.

'Keep going straight. The spring is just over this rise ahead. When we get there jump in and swim down without pause. You have one shot at getting out of here. Don't mess it up.'

'Why should you care if I mess it up?'

'You're taking me with you.'

Just as the beetle said, there is a silver spring about a yard in diameter below the lip of the rise. Adeline sees it just in time to prepare herself to jump, which gives her no time to respond to the beetle's declaration that it is stowing away. When Adeline's feet hit the surface of the spring, the bird makes the most awful in its series of awful sounds.

The silver liquid sucks Adeline in and pulls her under, turns her body into a dive. She thinks of cormorants, but with her human anatomy must draw her thighs up to her chest to prepare for every great push and kick hard to part the way with her head. She swims in silver, in darkness, in blackness, on and on through blackness.

Harry Ricketts

Noddy

(in mem Richard Gilmore, 1952–2010)

Noddy: that was what we used to call you
because all that scary first term,
skipping lectures and half-falling in love,
you nearly drove us mad, telling that joke.

> *One morning bright and early in Toyland*
> *Noddy woke up, got out of bed,*
> *looked out the window and said 'Hello, Sun'*
> *and the Sun said 'Hello, Little Noddy.'*

Your fair hair was always carefully brushed.
You wore ties, pink shirts, hush puppies
(I might have invented the hush puppies),
had a raspberries-and-cream complexion.

> *Then Noddy got dressed, put on his blue hat*
> *with the tinkly bell at the tip*
> *and thought he would go and see his best friend*
> *Big-Ears; so he walked out of his front door.*

Once over dinner in the Taj Mahal,
Turl Street—now also gone—you said
what a good housemaster I'd make. I sulked.
I had long hair, beads, played Pink Floyd, read *Oz*.

> *And whom should Noddy meet but Mr Plod*
> *the Policeman and Mr Plod*
> *said 'Hello, Little Noddy' and Noddy*
> *said 'Hello, Mr Plod' and he walked on.*

That first summer vac we met up in Rome,
wandered around the Piazza
Navona, got drunk, made plans, laughed a lot,
never mentioned that quick flick of your eyes.

> *And whom should Noddy meet next but Mr*
> *Golly and Mr Golly said*
> *'Hello, Little Noddy' and Noddy said*
> *'Hello, Mr Golly' and he walked on.*

By this point in the joke you'd usually
be spluttering. I wish I'd known
the 'Mad Man' you, still more the later you
who helped in drug and alcohol centres.

> *And when Noddy reached Big-Ears' toadstool house,*
> *he knocked on the door and Big-Ears*
> *opened the door and Noddy said 'Hello,*
> *Big-Ears' and Big-Ears said 'Fuck off, Noddy!'*

I like to think of you best as Thisbe
in that *Midsummer Night's Dream* in Keble
College Gardens we did after Finals.
Every night the audience would crack up

when you squeaked 'These lily lips,/This cherry
nose,/These yellow cowslip cheeks', burr-
ing dead Pyramus's lips with a finger.
By the end we were all corpsing, holding back the tears.

Freya Daly Sadgrove

Pool Noodle

the air is thick with depression
even the flies   fly very slowly

life is like aqua-jogging   but without the flotation device
and the implicit desire to exercise
also it's more the hobby of old men than old women
but old women nonetheless love to get   uhh exclusive about it
e.g. *stop laughing so* loudly *it's not even that funny* ;
crop tops are for girls who are thinner *than you* ;
you have to shave *if you want to wear a dress like that*   et cetera
it's all very manageable and I have no complaints

no one is ever allowed to be mad at me
you can make fun of me though if you want
that's my kink
o enable me   and furnish me with false gods
such as full-fat milk ; weed ; and a boyfriend

just let me work myself up for half an hour and I'll be
ready—
sexually I mean
look at the water   it's so shiny
I want to dip myself in it
like toast in the hands of a giant ill-mannered French person
life is like aqua-jogging in tomato soup :
inexplicable and disgusting
also the tomato soup is actually the menstrual blood
of eleven-year-olds
look at yourself

Frances Samuel

A new body

'Believe it or not, your lungs are six weeks old—
and your tastebuds just ten days!'
—Daily Mail headline, 2009

'Really, what do I have in common / with my body?'
—'What is a Pineal Gland' by Anna Swir

I was walking through my veins
on the scenic route
to get acquainted with my new lungs,
untainted stomach, pristine kidneys.

Not the addictive type (non-smoking)
organic yet (mindfully) anxious,
I was taking the opportunity
to admire my efforts.

But the terrain was shadowy
and there were echoes.
Here spleen   spleen   spleen—
I attempted to call my body parts to me
like small faithful dogs.
Not one organ responded.

When I reached my heart
I took a pause in chamber no. 3.

'Herb,' I said, using the first name that came to mind
because I was weary
of being surrounded by strangers.
'Why'd you have to go and change?'

I guess what I was really trying
   trying   trying
to say was: This year was going well for me
—my body and I—
we were finally getting somewhere.

And now all this red blood
where there used to be blue.

Maria Samuela

Sisters

Aunty Esther and her tribe arrive first thing on Tuesday morning.

'Hullo, my darling.' She smothers me at the front door and I'm sucked into her embrace, clamped tight against her chest, her cushiony arms wrapped round my back. The scent of the coconut oil in her hair makes me gasp. Then she holds me at arm's length to get a better look. 'Big day on Friday,' she says, meaning my birthday. I've been trying to forget it.

Her children push past us and race down the corridor.

'Kura! Tevita! Ngatokorua! No'oputa! Tua!' she calls. 'Come give your cousin a kiss.'

I'm relieved when they don't. Their howling threatens to stir the spirits of loved ones, whose faces, trapped inside framed sepia photographs, line the corridor walls. My cousins treat the hallway like an afternoon at the track. Finally they dump their bags and blankets in one of the vacant bedrooms.

Uncle Tiare follows Aunty Esther into the house, greeting Mum first in the sitting room. He catches her up on the progress of his avocado tree, filling the space in the room with his presence. 'E, reka!' he boasts. 'Everybody laughed at me, sis.'

Mum and Uncle are close like siblings. He's been part of the family long before he married my aunt, way back when they were kids with no shoes, running through my papa's taro plantation in Rarotonga. 'They said I was a foolish man to grow an avocado tree up there in South Auckland.' He's grinning. 'But two avocados I got this year, sis!' He holds up two fingers in front of Mum's face. 'Two whole bloody avocados!'

Aunty Esther shushes her husband out of the room, telling him what a foolish man he is to boast about such trivial things.

'Two whole bloody avocados!' she mocks. 'And it only took you ten bloody years!'

Mum lets Uncle brush her cheek with a kiss before he weaves his way through the house to the back door and out into the backyard, reuniting briefly with other rellies along the way.

'Two whole bloody avocados!' we hear him say.

Aunty Teina comes next.

'Auē,' she cries, seeing how much I've grown since her last visit. She fixes her lipstick after branding my cheek with a kiss. Her lips are fuller and plumper than I remember. She beckons me to her, letting me sink into her arms like they're an old, familiar La-Z-Boy. The scent of her perfume fills my head with pictures of places and people she's known—French waiters in Paris, flamenco dancers in Seville, nuns in Rome who strut the cobblestone footpaths of the Vatican City in twos and threes.

There are no restless children hanging off her designer dress knock-off—an outfit that is worlds away from her cousins' hand-me-down pants and shirts she'd grown up in when she was a boy back in the islands. And it pleases me to get to share my room with her over all my other aunts. When she teases me with her usual questions, I never feel picked on like my cousins do. But the awkwardness is still there.

'You got a boyfriend yet?' she asks in her serious voice. 'You're old enough now,' she says with a wink.

That's not true, if she means what I think she means. My cheeks flare and my tongue fishes inside my mouth, feeling for words. Aunty's eyes give off a sparkle and when she pulls me back in for another embrace I hug her back with everything I've got.

By the afternoon, when Aunty Selina gets here, we already have a full house. But that's never stopped Mum's sisters from inviting themselves over.

'Let me look at you, my beautiful goddaughter,' she cries. She holds me to her bosom and soaks my hair with tears. I panic over the halo of frizz it will make. It's all right for some people—like Tuakana, whose hair is worthy of an American shampoo commercial. People like my cousin don't worry if their aunties cry into their hair. When I was still young enough to let my mum brush my hair, it would take her thirty minutes just to comb out the knots. Several spokes would snap off the plastic comb as she raked it through, and to save on tears—both of ours—she'd sweep my hair back into a single ponytail to keep the creeping tumbleweed out of my eyes.

I recognise the little gold crucifix that rests between my aunty's collarbones. She'd given me the same necklace on the day of my First Holy Communion. That was over seven years ago now.

'Now we're truly mother and daughter in Christ,' she'd said. 'As long as you're wearing that chain close to your heart, we'll always be seen like that in the eyes of God.'

Caught up in that day's celebrations, I'd lost the necklace somewhere between the first reading and the prayers of the faithful. Mum had got upset with me, embarrassed by my clumsy ways. My First Holy Communion meant a lot to her.

Uncle Craig, Aunty's husband, carries into the house the rest of her first-class baggage. I notice the final stages of sunburn in his face, his pale skin shedding like a gecko's. Aunty steps towards me again and swallows me in her arms. She smells like tea-tree oil and feijoa.

*

When Mum was fifteen, she sailed alone to New Zealand on a ship called the *White Magnolia*. She didn't know it then, but she'd never dig her toes into the sands of Muri Beach again. Saying goodbye would become a slow-rending heartbreak. Ngatangiia, the eastside district on the island of Rarotonga where she grew up, would become distant, like a paradise in novels written by white men with brown wives and a longing to escape the rat race.

Her loneliness in those early days was eased by the wild magnolia bush that grew outside her bedroom window. It was the first time she'd seen the flower that shared its name with the ship that brought her here. It was unlike the hibiscus and frangipani blooms she'd known from her childhood, and she welcomed its strangeness. She craved unfamiliarity. The more peculiar and foreign her surroundings, the easier it became to forget what she'd come from.

The bedroom she rented in a boarding house in Newtown was furnished with a single bed and a set of bedside drawers that remained empty. She kept her clothes—three homemade dresses, two pairs of shoes, some underwear, and a secondhand winter coat—neatly folded and packed away inside her cracked leather suitcase on the polished wooden floor.

Another girl from her village helped her find work in a factory in the city. She sewed zippers onto men's trousers and later she made uniforms for the military. The factory was cold and mechanical, an artificial space where young women like her communed. In the city there were no lanky coconut trees to climb, no mangoes to pick in summer, and the sea was too open to strangers to dive for seafood. Her life became a series of clocking in and out with time cards and eating mackerel drowned in coconut cream hacked out of tin cans.

In the evenings, she'd watch the leaves from the tī kōuka flap in the wind outside her bedroom window and the red needles from the pōhutukawa tree fall like tiny spindles. The magnolia bush remained unwavering. In that bedroom, alone at night, she would sew a green and white tivaevae. The oversized petals on that bedspread were an ode to those alien flowers.

When Mum sailed to New Zealand on that giant, steel vaka, she didn't know that she'd never see her parents again. And it wasn't until years later, when she'd saved enough money for her sisters to come too, that she started to call this place home.

*

The sisters are gathered in the sitting room with the other women in the family. After the evening prayers are said, they form a ring on the mat, cross-legged on the floor with tivaevae and continental blankets draped over their laps. Bags of freshly clipped chrysanthemums are emptied onto the floor and old newspapers laid out in the centre of the coven to catch the discarded greenery.

'That's what you are,' Dad used to tease Mum about my aunts. 'A coven of witches, like the disciples of the anti-Christ.'

That made Mum the high priestess.

Aunty Teina separates the flowers. She draws attention to her manicured hands: the polish on her fingernails painted by the masters, her skin, she would say, massaged by the beating wings of angels. She sorts the flowers by size before the women begin weaving them into garlands.

Mum is centre stage. She looks radiant, surrounded by her mates, their raucous banter rising to the ceiling.

'Eh, sister,' says one of Mum's cousins, 'remember back home, when we were still girls? Remember how we used to make all the beautiful 'ei to catch the boys' eyes?' The women screech like a bat colony. I look over at Mum. Her face is serene like she's dreaming about the olden days. 'You used to catch a few eyes, eh, sis?' her cousin goes on. 'You could've had any boy in that backward village.'

Aunty Teina pipes up. 'But she wasn't a cheeky girl like you, cousin.' Again the women shriek, slapping their thighs as they thread more flowers. 'She didn't show off her beautiful 'ei like they were going out of fashion.'

'Oh but, sis,' another cousin says as the first cousin dissolves into the wallpaper, 'you remember when we first came out? You remember living in Newtown? You remember that boarding house we stayed in?' I finetune my hearing like I'm dialling in on a secret radio station. 'You remember how we snuck out at night to smoke by that ugly bush out the back?' I raise my eyes at Mum. She'd banned cigarettes from the house like they were weed. 'Remember how we dug that little hole in the ground to bury our butts in so we wouldn't get caught?' The room fills with high-pitched cackles. Mum says nothing, just smiles her Mona Lisa smile.

One by one the room fills with the beautiful garlands. The scent is overpowering. I help some of the aunties carry the flowers into the bathroom and hang the garlands from a dismantled broom handle balanced atop the shower curtain rail. When we return to the sitting room, the old newspapers and discarded greenery are disposed of and the women have settled in for a game of euchre.

'Eh, sis,' Aunty Esther accuses Mum in Cook Islands Māori. 'What's with all the bad luck in your house? How come none of us can pick up this card? What kind of curse have you put on your sisters? Why are you cheating with your black magic?'

Aunty Selina's eyes are downcast. She is silent amongst the din. It's her turn to turn down the gold-headed Jack; instead, she fingers the corner of her middle card and pauses to make sure everybody knows what that means.

'*Ooo*,' Aunty Teina jeers, her voice rising at the end.

Aunty Selina, now satisfied, withdraws the card from her hand. She returns it to the rest of the deck—placing it face down to torture the other players—and grips the handsome Jack with the tips of her fingers, bringing him back to rest against her crucifix.

'I wouldn't put that devil card so close to my chest if I was you,' Aunty Esther says. 'Not even Jesus can save you from that sunstruck-headed demon.'

I'm glad Uncle Craig isn't in the room to hear that. The freckles on his cheeks would have blended like one giant sunspot.

The other women mute their laughter, their eyes bulging. They're careful not to pick sides, but more from fear of backing the wrong sibling—the less clever sibling, the one most likely to lose—than from keeping the family peace.

It's well after midnight before the laughter in the sitting room dies down. From my bedroom I can hear the final visitors leave and the door to my parents' bedroom open and close. Aunty Selina and Uncle Craig will sleep in the sitting room this first night.

'Make sure no funny business in here,' I hear Aunty Teina say in her amplifying voice. No chance of that. Two other aunties and four cousins are also destined for that sitting-room floor. I imagine her eyeballing Uncle Craig, anyway, as they set up the foam mattresses.

Later, when Aunty Teina tiptoes into my room and slips into her nightie in the dark, I keep my eyes shut and let her inspect me. When I hear her speak in whispers, the words sliding from her mouth in one breath, I stop myself in time from answering her back. She is praying over me. It startles me. The earnestness in her voice is unnerving. But before long, her soft chanting lulls me off to sleep, and that night I dream in Polaroids.

On the Wednesday, the men are sent out on errands. Dad takes me with him to get me out of the house.

'Make sure the hall is big enough, eh. I don't want nobody to say our family is mean. Remember what happened to Nina and her lot? People say they make their guests stand out in the rain because they too cheap to hire a hall. You want that to happen to us? The shame.'

'Make sure you pick out some nice, fat pigs. I don't want people to say we too cheap to feed them. And when you order the fish, make sure it's fresh, caught that day and still flapping.'

'And when they come back,' I hear one of the aunties say as we flee the house, 'they can mow the lawns and clean out the garage. We need space for the marquee, and they're not drinking their beer in my sister's house.'

The men know better than to argue with the aunties. They pile in their cars, armed with that morning's instructions, Dad leading the convoy in his Holden Sedan. Uncle Tiare is beside him. I'm in the back seat.

The drive home is bumpier than a flight into Wellington. The three piglets are stuffed into sacks, their squirming young bodies thrown into the boot. Little hooves press into my spine through the fabric of the back seat as the piglets try to kick their way free from their burlap prisons. Blinded and bagged, their desperate squealing pierces my eardrums. I imagine the sweat running down the side of my face is a droplet of blood.

I hold my voice back, not wanting to add more drama to the day, not wanting to cause more pain. The trapped animals continue to claw at my back through the membrane of vinyl that separates us. I sit as far forward on my seat as I can, trying to trick my brain into happier places.

'Ana,' Dad calls out from the driver's seat, peering at me through the rear-vision mirror. 'You all right, girl?'

Uncle Tiare turns in his seat. 'Gee, girl, you soft or something? How else do you think we're gonna eat? We can't just live on potato salad.'

The men laugh, but Dad winks at me through the mirror.

'Kiwi girls,' Uncle Tiare teases, rolling his eyes at Dad. 'Not like proper island girls.'

At home I follow Dad and Uncle round the back of the house. Uncle carries one of the piglets still trapped in its sack while Dad carries the other two, one wriggling bag tucked under each armpit. A table made from old beer crates and a plank of wood found at the tip has been erected along the back fence to prep the meat for the umu.

'Go inside,' says Dad. I look down at the sacked piglets twitching on the makeshift table. 'It's okay. Go. Help Aunty Teina in the kitchen.'

She is buttering cabin bread biscuits. The lids of tinned corned beef are peeled back and the marbled meat is being scooped on to plates. Bowls of quartered tomatoes from the next-door-neighbour's garden and chunks of boiled taro soaking in warmed-up coconut cream are placed on the kitchen table. I slice some bread, stacking the pieces high on a dinner plate, making two spongy towers that lean to one side. I'm focused on steadying the bread, sweeping the crumbs off the Formica tabletop, when I hear the high-pitched shrieks from the backyard.

I race to the back door, opening it in time to see the blood gush from one of the piglets on to the grass. I struggle to breathe, gasping for air, just as Dad turns round to catch my eye. Blood drips from the knife in his hand. I can't move so I wait for the reprimand. Instead, Dad turns his back to me and Aunty Teina gently pulls me into the house.

There are chores for Africa, as Aunty Teina would say, and I'm grateful for it. All this hustle and bustle will take my mind off the days ahead.

'Aunty!' Aileen calls out to Mum in the next room. Kitchen drawers and cupboards fly open as she whips past them like a tempest. I can hear the other women in the sitting room keeping Mum occupied. 'Where do you keep your potato peeler, Aunty?' I pull open the cutlery drawer and dig out the peeler. She takes it from me, flicking her head in thanks. We sit down at the kitchen table, pages of old newspapers spread out to catch the potato skins.

'Better make plenty spuds,' Aunty Teina orders, as if we're making potatoes from scratch. 'We're expecting another big crowd tonight.' A ribbon of potato skin unfurls from my knife. I hold my breath to steady my knife's movements, determined to shave the whole spud in one seamless peel. When the potato skin snaps, I exhale and swallow the air with urgency.

It was Dad's idea to celebrate my birthday. 'Your family's coming from all over,' he'd said. 'Uncle Tiare and Aunty Esther and their lot. Your Aunty Mi'i and her lot from Sydney.' Two buses from Auckland will trundle down on Thursday night, and family members have been billeted out like orphaned schoolchildren. Ever since I can remember I've felt like I'm being fussed over. Treated like something breakable—precious and rare and too delicate to hold. An oddity. The special child. The one not meant to be.

When Mum found out she was pregnant, it followed years of trying and hospital visits. The doctors had taken tests, jabbing her with needles, extracting tubes of blood and having them checked in labs. But the tests showed nothing.

'We tried everything,' Mum told me. 'Even some of the old ways from home.'

'Voodoo magic,' Dad teased.

'I just learned to live with it, the thought of having no child of my own. It wasn't God's will. Not in the cards.'

When Aunty Esther got pregnant, Mum said she was happy for her. But it was hard for her to watch her younger sister fall pregnant again and again. Aunty even offered Mum one of her children to love, but Mum said she couldn't, and she loved them anyway.

Then she got pregnant.

'Oh,' Mum said. 'That day was my second-happiest. I was

more happy then than when I first met your father—'

'That was your Uncle Taki's fault,' Dad said. 'He dragged me along to that dance in Newtown. I'd just broken up with the love of my life,' he'd tease, making sure Mum could hear. 'My old girlfriend from up the Naki. We'd been together since school days. And your Uncle Taki, he thought it was a good idea for me to meet some other ladies. Take my mind off things.

'"Island girls aren't like your Papa'a girls," your Uncle Taki would say. And, man oh man, was he right!' Dad laughed. 'Your mother is out of this world. And then when your aunties arrived—'

And that's when Mum jumped in.

'And the happiest day of my life,' she'd say, 'was the day I first held you.'

The day I was born, Dad planted a magnolia shrub in one corner of the backyard. My placenta is buried deep beneath its roots. The roots took their time to take hold. Mum said it was because the plant was like me, taking its time to get ready for living. The seasons passed many times over before the florets started to bloom, so for years that plant hung naked and limp like a ragdoll.

For years I resented Mum for choosing that plant to remember my birth. Not a rose bush. Not a lemon tree. Not a native shrub of some sort. But a Frankenstein of a flower—a freak of nature. And Mum loved that plant, despite its strangeness, its slowness. Then, the year its flowers finally started to bloom, Mum found out about the cancer, and I hated that plant more. I despised its hideous flowers. They were garish and obtrusive, and it broke me to know that something so unwanted would get to live on when other things more cherished would not.

'May as well get the practice in now, cuz,' Aileen says across the table from me. 'We got that mountain of mainese to make for Friday.'

We peel two large pots of spuds for the mainese, then chop four large cans of sliced beetroot. I'm pleased we don't live in the olden days, when Mum cooked and peeled the beetroot from raw, the ruby-coloured juices running between her fingers as she sliced through its flesh with a serrated bread knife. That's how we cook the carrots still, from fresh, but the peas come frozen out of a plastic bag.

Mum taught me how to make the potato salad years ago, a recipe passed down over generations from her mother's side. The secret to the perfect mainese, she said, was in how you made the dressing. 'Don't rush with the dressing, baby. Add the oil to the egg yolks bit by bit.'

That was Mum's mantra: be patient, slow down, don't rush yourself, there's time.

The eggs are cracked on the edge of the kitchen bench and the yolks pulled away from the whites complete. Be patient, slow down, don't rush yourself, there's time.

As I dribble the oil into the bowl, the humming whisks from the electric beater churn the oil and egg yolks into dressing.

'We didn't have electric beaters back in the day,' Mum had said. 'We used to beat the dressing by hand, with a whisk your Mama Ruau kept in a cardboard box. It was one of her prized possessions, that whisk. The true secret weapon to her mainese dressing.'

I can't imagine a kitchen tool being anyone's prized possession, unless it was studded with black pearls and granted its owner three wishes.

By 5.30 in the evening more rellies have arrived. The younger cousins are a sea of faces bobbing around Mum like waves in the sitting room. She is flanked by Aunty Esther and Aunty Selina, who sit cross-legged on the floor. Aunty Teina is in the kitchen keeping an eye on the food. Flowers gifted by those who can't be here are arranged in vases and plastic buckets. They decorate the room, dwarfed only by the magnolia blooms picked that morning. Mum's green and white tivaevae, folded down to the size of a cushion, lies beneath a framed photograph of her. The bedspread and the photograph are placed at the foot of her coffin. I sit beside the couch at Dad's feet.

Once the sitting room is full, the corridor and kitchen start to hum with more visitors, the chatter filling each corner of the house. When Father O'Shea arrives to lead the Rosary, the people part like the Red Sea. He occupies the chair next to Mum, acknowledging her first, then me and Dad, then he says a 'Kia orana' to everyone else.

'Evening, Father,' Uncle Tiare calls out from the corridor. 'We've been practising our singing for you tonight, Father.' The rellies shuffle awkwardly in their seats. Tonight's singing practice was a string of ultimatums of what songs to sing, by whom, and at what volume.

'That's most excellent, Tiare,' says Father O'Shea. 'I'm looking forward to some beautiful singing tonight then.'

Aunty Esther gives her husband the look. He can thank God later that Father's in the house.

'And do we have people to say the decades of the Rosary tonight?' Father asks.

'Yes, Father,' Dad says, rubbing my shoulder. 'Ana is going to start.' I expose too many of my teeth and gums and hope I've remembered enough of the words. When Father smiles but says nothing, I try not to read anything into it.

The strumming of a guitar opens the Rosary, and Aunty Esther leads us with the evening's first hymn. Her voice cuts through the air like a whistling conch shell, which encourages the other oldies to drown her out. Soon the house is heaving with over-earnest singing, the words slowed down to magnify the gravity. The cousins whose parents are responsible hang their heads, avoiding eye contact. Only Aunty Teina, having no children of her own to shame, holds back. When it's my turn to recite the Lord's Prayer, I speak the words as fast as I think I can get away with. I've memorised them to perfection. The oldies reply in united slow-motion: 'Holy Mary Mother of *Gooooooooooood . . .*'

After the final hymn, each part of the song performed as agreed, the action moves to the kitchen. Orders are given above the clattering of plates and cutlery, and I'm swept along on my cousins' zeal. Back in my bedroom, every inch of space is filled with teenage bodies and voices.

'Hey, cuz,' Tuakana says, reaching into her tote bag. I can smell her apple shampoo. 'Help me do my hair, k?' She holds up an electric crimping iron. It dumbfounds me, the thought of deliberately making your hair like mine. My other cousins are sprawled all over the floor. This is what it feels like to have sisters.

'You want?' Tuakana asks.

'Don't need it,' I say.

'Lucky,' she says, and I read her face for irony. When I'm sure there isn't any, I watch in silence as the cousins take turns.

'How you doing tonight, cuz?' Tuakana asks.

I shrug. My struggle to find words has only gotten worse.

When one of the Auckland cousins bursts into the room screaming, I feel relief.

'Cuz,' she shrieks, looking at me.

'Cuz?' I say.

'Got my . . . *you know* . . .'

I don't know. I look over at Tuakana, feeling like a toddler.

The Auckland cousin tugs at her skirt, pulling it as far from her body as she can. 'Got any plugs, cuz? I didn't bring nothin', cuz.'

'Oh,' I say, the blood rushing to my face.

'Hang on, cuz,' says Tuakana. She digs in her bag and pulls out a box of tampons. She chucks it across the room at her, but it lands in my lap.

'Bloody nuisance, eh, cuz,' says the cousin in the doorway.

I throw the box over to her. 'Yeah, cuz.'

She takes the box and disappears down the corridor and into the bathroom.

Mum and I had the talk a few years ago, not long after I'd started Form One. I know it disappointed her that my sheets stayed as white as the day she'd cleaned them, but there was no hurrying Mother Nature. It just wasn't my time. When my friends started their periods, they'd tell me about the spotting in their underwear and the cramps, and how to place the sanitary pad into the inside of their panties, being careful to position it directly over the gusset to stop the blood from seeping out on to their clothes. Extra care was needed at school. You didn't want to be the girl with the blood patch on your uniform.

'But it does anyway,' said Sonia, my best mate. 'It leaks out the sides and stains your undies anyway. Or it gets on to your uniform and your mum makes you wash it by hand. Because if I'm old enough to have babies, she says, then I'm old enough to clean my own bloody clothes.'

I've never had to clean my own bloody clothes.

On the Thursday, I help Aunty Esther pick more chrysanthemums. We ignore the magnolia bush in the other corner. Because I know Aunty is judging my choice of flowers, I'm careful to choose only the ones with petals of a certain size—not too big that the 'ei katu will look like a floral bush is growing from the wearer's skull, but not too small, either, that it can only be seen through the eyes of the Holy Spirit. In the sitting room, the aunties prepare to make more garlands for tomorrow, trimming leaves of flax and cutting them down to size to fit the various heads.

As we hover around the chrysanthemum bush, I hear Dad and the uncles prepping the pigs behind us. The pigs hang off three metal bars of the clothesline, carefully spaced out to balance the weights. The blood has stopped dripping from their throats, but the grass is stained red where it's seeped into the dirt.

'Reckon we deserve a little something after this hard work, eh, brother,' Uncle Tiare calls out to Dad. 'Some light refreshments, I reckon, my brother. I'm starting to feel a bit thirsty over here.'

Aunty Esther swivels on her heel, snapping her head into her shoulder.

'You men aren't here to drink,' she says, the open blades of the kitchen scissors in her hand. 'What do you think this place is? The Top Tavern? *Auē.*'

The men shuffle on the spot, eyes down, lips shut. When cousin Jack arrives with the clinking flagons in the wooden crates, they take a small step away from Uncle Tiare.

'*Auē,*' Aunty cries, blessing herself with the sign of the cross.

'Auē. Auē. You men will pay for this. In the burning fires of Hell,' she says. 'Drinking in my sister's house'—she pauses to eyeball her husband—'the night before we lay her to rest!'

It wasn't easy convincing Father to let us break protocol and keep Mum at home on her final night. But the aunties are unstoppable once they've made up their minds, and we all agreed—the aunties, Dad, and I—to keep her at home. No number of Hail Marys was going to help Father with this one.

Everybody knows the drill by now. The food is prepped. The rooms are cleaned. The floors are vacuumed and mopped and dried. The ornaments and picture frames are dusted and wiped. The good plates are brought out from the cabinet in the sitting room. They're washed and dried for the elders and Father. The everyday plates for everyone else are stacked on a bench in the kitchen. Paper plates on standby. Same with the cups—good cups, everyday cups, paper cups if needed. Who's saying what prayers is decided on. Hymns are chosen and there's one quick practice. And then we wait.

Father arrives. Rosary is said. Songs are sung. Copious amounts of food are eaten. Most of the adults retreat to the garage. Then begins the drinking.

'Bring that wine over here.' Aunty Esther waves her empty glass in the air. Uncle Tiare is quick to oblige. He presses down on the plastic tap sticking out from the cardboard box. The glass fills slowly to the brim with rose-coloured booze. He fills his own glass with more beer and the two of them swig their drinks as they sing along to the strumming ukulele. Another aunty beats an old cabin bread biscuit tin with the palm of her hand. An older cousin taps a pair of spoons on his leg, which bounces to the rhythm of his foot as it taps the concrete floor. The garage is filled with spontaneous singing, the harmonies rich and un-selfconscious.

I sit in one corner of the garage with Aunty Teina, where she's keeping me entertained with more stories from the olden days.

'Your Aunty Selina,' she whispers, 'she used to *hate* your mother.' She laughs. I'm shocked at the reveal, eyeballing Aunty

Selina by the garage door. She'd sworn off alcohol since meeting Uncle Craig, so the two of them sit po-faced and silent. 'She was so jealous of your mother because your mother was the pretty one. Your mother was the smart one. The chosen one. Like *you*,' she slurs, nudging me in the side with her elbow. 'Your mother,' she says, 'was the first in the family to leave the island. The first to work in a Papaʻa job. In a factory in the city, not some plantation like the rest of us commoners.' Her laugh turns into a cackle. It delights me. 'And when she met your father,' Aunty says, her voice now lower and deeper than normal, '*auē*, your Aunty was *livid*. Absolutely livid.'

I look over at Dad, who's sitting amongst the musicians with their cobbled-together instruments. He's hidden behind half-drunk flagons piled on the table in front of him and I can hardly see his face.

'A Papaʻa man,' Aunty laughs. 'That's the first thing your Mama Ruau said when she got your Mum's letter. "My daughter is going to marry a Papaʻa man." Like your Dad was the King of England.'

Dad catches my eye. When he winks at me and the sides of his face crinkle when he smiles, I can see how Mum fell in love with him. How she let this man free her from that lonely boarding house. Even though he danced the two-step shuffle and sunburned too easily when they fished on the harbour.

'And then you came along,' Aunty says with a grin, 'and your aunty went *crazy* with the envy.'

I knew Aunty Selina couldn't have children of her own. 'It's just one of those things,' Mum had said.

'But you saved your aunty from herself,' Aunty Teina goes on to say. 'The day she became your godmother was the happiest day of her life. There was no reason to be jealous of your mother anymore, because she too had the most precious thing your mum would ever have.'

I remember the gold crucifix I'd lost that day, with my careless ways and my thoughtlessness. I hadn't realised just how much my First Holy Communion had meant to my aunt.

'Auē!' Aunty Esther calls out from the other side of the garage. The shattering sounds of glass breaking takes over the singing. I look over at the musicians' table and see Dad holding his hand to his chest. The blood stain on his T-shirt from the cut spreads into a blot.

'Dad?' I rush over to him.

'It's okay, baby,' he says. He tries to smile but the crinkles on the sides of his face have shifted to his forehead. He pulls the lower half of his T-shirt over his cut hand and hurries out of the garage. Drops of blood trickle onto the grass, mingling with the blood of the dead piglets. He makes his way across the lawn and back into the house. I follow him into the bathroom.

'It's just a little cut, baby,' he says. 'Just help me with the Band-Aid.' I help him strip off his T-shirt, which he uses to wrap his hand. 'Good thing your mum's not here to tell me off 'bout this,' he says, gesturing to the blood-stained top, trying to make me laugh.

I open the medicine cabinet and rummage for the plasters. Half-used containers of moisturisers and hand creams remind me Mum's not here to tell Dad off. Her small plastic bottle of coconut oil, an elixir for all ailments, sits in the back corner of the cupboard. Her toothbrush. Her tweezers. Her roll-on deodorant. Her nail clippers. Her sanitary pads. Her cotton balls and cotton buds. Her bobby pins. Her plastic comb. Her painkillers.

So many leftover painkillers.

'Baby?'

Dad puts one hand on my shoulder, which starts to shake with no volition. The tears fall from my eyes, blurring my sight so that when I turn round and collapse into my father's chest, all I can see is the blood-stained T-shirt wrapped round his cut hand. I hold my breath and contract my stomach muscles to keep the tears from falling but it only hurts more. In my gut and in my chest. I weep and my weeping turns into sobbing. The crying is hollow and deep and the echo of it bounces off the bathroom walls.

'Let it out, baby,' Dad says. His voice sounds like a lullaby.

I raise my head, the tears still clouding my eyesight, and catch the hazy outline of my mother's sisters in the doorway.

The aunties and I sleep in the sitting room that evening, our last evening with Mum before we bury her. Dad agrees to let us have the final night on our own. He jokes, 'All you women do is gossip, anyway.'

Aunty Teina and I lie on either side of Mum on the floor, our foam mattresses pushed up against her coffin. Some of the aunties and uncles are still in the garage, their drunken singing faint from the sitting room. I can hear the bustling in the kitchen from the other women preparing food for tomorrow.

'Sister,' Aunty Teina says, still drunk from the boxed wine. She leans over Mum, whose face looks more sunken than during the previous nights. Her cheekbones are more pronounced. The colour is draining from her face. 'We're gonna make you proud, my sister,' she says. 'We made all your favourite recipes. Pineapple pie. Donuts. Pōke. Raw fish.' Her voice starts to crack. 'And you'd be proud of your girl, sister,' she continues. 'She made the best mainese I've ever tasted. E reka!' she says, kissing her pinched fingers. 'Don't worry 'bout your girl, sister,' she says. 'I reckon she's tough as nuts.'

Mum's face has the gaunt look of a dead body days old. And the longer I look at it the more ugly it becomes. Like those magnolia flowers growing in the backyard and the ones in vases at the foot of her coffin. I hate those flowers and I hate her face. This isn't how I want to remember her.

Aunty Esther's tribe wakes first on the Friday.

'Kura! Tevita! Ngatokorua! No'oputa! Tua!' she says. 'Get up! Get ready! I don't want us to be late!' I hear my cousins racing through the house.

'Darling,' Aunty Teina says from across the room. 'How are you feeling, my love?'

After last night I expect things to be different. I look into Mum's coffin but her face is sunken and dull again.

'Won't be long now, darling,' Aunty Teina reassures me. 'The day will be over before you know it. Then you can rest.'

Dad comes into the sitting room. He leans over Mum and kisses her on the cheek, whispering in her ear. I don't hear what he says. He reaches over and gives me a hug, his cut hand dressed with a fresh plaster.

When the lid of the coffin is shut and sealed, the long wail from the aunties stabs my ears like a silver needle. We drape Mum's coffin with the green and white tivaevae and layer on top of that bunches of white magnolias. The framed photograph of Mum lies at the foot of her coffin.

I ride to the church in the hearse with Dad. When I look behind us at Mum's closed casket, the smile in her photograph is how I will remember her. It's how I saw her last night in the sitting room when the low thrumming woke me from my sleep.

*

It was the faint scent of the magnolia blossoms that I noticed first. In my mind I pictured the stalks erect and luminous, droplets of dew on delicate petals. My eyes adjusted to the semi-darkness in the sitting room. The quivering flames from the tealight candles filled the space around Mum's open casket with a warm glow. It cast a gentle light over the white magnolias placed with care on either side of her. They looked as fresh as if they'd just been picked.

They were unrecognisable, my aunts. Their breasts and bellies were swollen. Their incantations were low, and I knew that I was one of only a few who could hear them. I felt timid in their nakedness, and when they beckoned me to join them, I shied away.

'Come,' said Aunty Teina. 'Don't be afraid.'

I felt drawn to the circle, my feet pulling me towards them. I looked closer into Mum's casket. The upward curves of her lips seemed more prominent now than in the days before. Aunty Teina tugged at my nightdress, pulling it up over my neck and shoulders, discarding my underwear next until I stood nude in front of them.

'Trust us,' said Aunty, her lips motionless.

I looked down at my feet, ashamed to see myself in their eyes. And in the flickering candlelight, I noticed a trickle of blood trail slowly down my inner thigh.

'Good,' said Aunty Esther, 'she's almost ready.'

Disoriented, I fumbled for my nightdress. Something blocked my movements and I floundered backwards, falling onto one of the mattresses in a clumsy heap. The blood stain on the sheet from my period spread into a blot. Instinctively, I shoved my hand between my legs to stop the bleeding. When I felt the wetness, I panicked. I held my hand in front of me and in the soft candlelight saw the blood staining on my fingers.

A transparent image of Mum came into view from the foot of the bed. My mind began to turn over. She glowed in the dark like divinity, her lips forever pursed into that distinctive smile. Somewhere in the back of my mind my aunts recommenced their chanting.

'Mum?' I said. My own lips were still and I heard only the dull chorus of the aunties.

'Don't be afraid, my darling. Your time has come.'

I stared at the ghostly figure, longing to reach out to it.

'What do you mean? Mum? What's happening? What do you mean my time has come?' I felt tears on my cheeks. In my confusion, I forgot to tell Mum all the things I wanted to say. About the mainese I'd made. About the readings I did for the rosaries. How I'd helped Dad like I promised I would. If I could have that time again, that's what I'd do. I'd tell her those things. I'd reach over and touch her face, feel her warmth against me.

'You're ready, darling. Don't be afraid.'

The image of Mum dissipated like a sheet of ice in the sun. The aunts' chanting grew louder and louder. The words were alien but consoling. I joined the circle and let the same words fall from my mouth.

*

The day we bury Mum, I turn fifteen. I stand shoulder to shoulder with her sisters as we watch the men lower her coffin into the grave. The mat of artificial turf conceals the mounds of dirt that we will later use to bury her body. It feels natural to do so, to commit her body to the earth—like my placenta that's buried beneath that magnolia bush, beside the umu pit where we cooked today's feast, those piglets that hung lifeless from our clothesline for days.

Snatches of the green and white tivaevae peek out from beneath the magnolias on top of the casket. The flower patterns so carefully patched into that tivaevae used to bring out pity from the other women who sewed, the indistinct petals mistaken for deformed hibiscuses. As Father O'Shea scatters the first trowel of dirt over the coffin, I move beside Dad to tip the first handful of dirt into the grave.

'Ashes to ashes, dust to dust . . .' Father says.

I feel each grain of dirt as it slips between my fingers, and watch as the dirt falls into the hole in the ground. The wailing from my aunts sounds like television static, a constant hum that my ears have become attuned to. The scent of the magnolias lingers.

Aunty Esther and her tribe leave first on the Saturday morning.

'Goodbye, my darling,' she cries, hugging me tight. 'Kura! Tevita! Ngatokorua! No'oputa! Tua! Come give your cousin a kiss.'

They don't. They drag their bags and blankets out of the house and stuff them into empty spaces in their van.

Uncle Tiare says goodbye next. 'When my next lot of avocados come out, my niece,' he says, 'I'll send you a few and you can plant your own tree if you want.'

Aunty Esther overhears him. 'Eh,' she says. 'What foolishness are you filling her head with?' she cries. 'An avocado tree . . . *in Porirua!*'

She ushers the last of her tribe out the front door; Uncle Tiare trails behind them.

Aunty Teina leaves next. 'Auē,' she cries, and I sink into her arms. Now when she teases me with her usual questions, the awkwardness is gone. 'Better let your Aunty know when you get a boyfriend,' she says in her serious voice. 'You're old enough now. Do we need to have the talk before I leave?'

When I assure her we don't, the disappointment on her face is more than I can take.

Aunty Selina leaves last. 'My goddaughter,' she says, holding me for a second embrace. 'Don't forget, you can call me anytime, okay, honey?' she says. She presses into my hand a business card with Uncle Craig's name on it. The phone number is circled in red and beside it are the words 'call collect', scribbled in my Aunty's handwriting.

When she pulls me in for another hug, I feel her gold crucifix against my chest. It doesn't burn into my skin like I would've imagined once. I promise her I'll call, without moving my lips.

Uncle Craig follows her out the door with their first-class baggage.

I worry the house will feel empty once the aunties have gone. The sitting room looks like its old self again—the chairs and couch are back in their usual places; the cabinet is cleared of part-melted candlesticks. The rooms are empty of guests. There are no dead pigs hanging from the clothesline. No uncles in the garage with flagons of beer. No cousins crimping hair into tumbleweed in the bedroom. No aunties in the kitchen yelling orders at the cousins. No decades of the Rosary. No over-earnest singing. No mainese. No magnolias. No casket. No Mum.

Just home.

Kerrin P Sharpe

when the barber talks about elephants

the barber's shop boasts elephant
fezzes tea-towels photographs
cigar cases shaving mugs
never ivory and he croons elephant songs
swinging his scissors from side to side

the barber believes wild elephants
stray into cities because they remember
the jungle went on forever
and convinced the crowds are thieves
plunge into market-places plunder cars
in search of vegetation

on the world page of the morning paper
a customs officer catalogues tusks
like census exhibits thoughts of these elephants
is enough to make the barber bury his razor
even now as his scissors charge a young man's hair

a nursing elephant in West Bengal
is shot and maimed as she drinks
from the Baikunthapur River
and her bewildered baby feeds until
her mother freezes under the Indian sun

today in between customers the barber
dozes in the chair and when he wakes
the elephant on the Doulton plate is more worried

Charlotte Simmonds

I Am a Man of Many Professions,
My Wife Is a Lady of Many Confessions

I am a carpenter,
I carpent this wood.
I bore nails and nests in the chests of my trees.

My wife is a woman,
she womans this hood.
She bore children and nests in the chests of her soul.

I am a husbandman,
I husband my resources.
I keep children and money and the nests of bees.

My wife has a husband,
she husbands him well.
Our nest is well-stocked with bread, butter and coal.

I am a hunter,
in the Bavarian woods.
I pluck stags and hares from their nests in the grasses.

My wife is a gutter,
she guts a good duck,
and into the nest of her ears I pour all of my muck.

I am a fisher,
on the Sicilian shores,
I net cold cod and gannets, a roe nest if it passes.

My wife is a shagger,
she has a pet shag.
If it dives for the whiting, then in bed I'm in luck.

Tracey Slaughter

Cicada Motel

At the Cicada Motel, the woman booked me into the runt of the rooms. The caramel carpet had flecks in it the colour of cabbage tree. The bedspread was mango. She gave me a suss look, like I'd prove fly-by-night, and handed over the 17 key, fixing her glare on the palm I held out as if I had dirt all through my heartline. *My* husband *will be here*, I said, *soon*, but she just huffed like she'd won the standoff, *if you say so*, then banged her smock out through the hole-punched mosquito screen. *Husband*. The outdoor bulb sizzled with speed-of-light insects.

I'd left first. I knew it was going to take him much longer. The Cicada Motel was just somewhere to be while I waited for him to cut strings.

In the morning the sea was not the kind I was used to, just lay there and looked stale. Miles of flat grey sand pin-pricked with animal sink-holes, where dregs of silver water clicked— that close-up came later when I walked out ankle-deep. For now I just blinked out the window, a glittery reverse game of join-the-dots. He hadn't called. I tuned in to chitchat from other rooms, the sound of footfalls scuffing bored squares, the on-holiday lingo of couples being nicer to each other because they'd paid. Above the yellow sink, the mirror wore a hairline crack and smelt of ointment. I dyed my hair a bad shade to match the room and pigment wriggled into my ears. On a far-out channel folks in a black-and-white movie were tap-dancing and beseeching. It was shit reception, a choice of either violins or prophecy, a fake-tanned pastor strutting in a rhinestone vest, pumping his arm over sins of the flesh with all the holy poison he could muster. While I was waiting I starfished on the mango bed and touched myself. My scalp bled cheap bronze into the sheets. Later I made myself a bridal veil of toilet paper, and lay down quiet in the confetti of someone else's skin. I felt at home in that fruit cocktail quilt.

He did get there three days later. By that time I'd set up Monopoly from reception, and the queen spread was a landfill of tokens, houses on my cheated streets bite-size as pills. *Do not pass go*, I looked up and told him. *Do not collect. Not a thing. Not one thing.* But 17 only had one doorway, and he filled it up with his sad bulk, his hands encumbered with junk she'd fought to keep but eventually let him have, more tubs jammed in his car boot. Something alto had happened to his voice. His *wife* had happened. I pitied him, invited him in. *How did you befall me?* he said, with a soap-opera shake of his head. I was dead level with the skin he was pushing out his clothes—I grinned at the trophy and doused my grip with spit. Later I picked hotels out his spine and told him, *winner takes all.* We lay awake and listened to everything leaking.

We hadn't exactly paid top-dollar. In the Formica-fronted drawers we turned up the usual tackle of can-openers and steelos, and handy wipe-clean bedside bibles, commandments shrunk into a font my conscience couldn't decode, ultimatums from a cut-price god. On all the cups were enamelled roses like something my grandmother once said, and brown stains left runny circular ghosts round the rims. We sat up, sucking wine out of them. I liked to say unanswerable things. Like, *are hotel flies different to house flies?* Or, *why do they play the f word in songs on the radio without the k? Like just taking out that one letter makes it okay?* He demonstrated, with cartoon suck-suck hands. *Cos that's the bit that sounds like it*, he said. Then blushed like he'd never played so dirty. I slapped his fingers, then worked them inside me, laying right back in onomatopoeia.

Then he went again. All I had behind me was a life I'd had no problem leaving, so sitting on the bed at the Cicada Motel I didn't waste time looking over the past. I turned the flip-covers of the things-to-do-in-town file, clingwrapped highlights of the shithouse district, mostly takeaway joints—the pages were endorsed by grease, sweet-and-sour meals consumed by people alone on the polyester quilt. The fridge with its bony low-lit shelves cut through my sleep with a bluebottle hum. Open, it smelt like potato peel. I blinked into its budget light but could never get hungry enough to go out. If I did I'd just have to walk back staring into other people's units, dioramas in a long sad row. I'd do little rituals of housekeeping, though somehow I couldn't leave my handprints on anything. There were the guttural sounds of couples in other rooms taking an ordinary fuck. I'd squat on the grey plastic O to piss and early on I could smile—in my pants there was still a cooling stripe of his brine. To me that eddy was holy. I was at his beck and call.

The day I met him, I'd walked straight to the mall on my lunch hour and bought myself a trim black suitcase with a telescope handle. I knew what was happening—the gold zips were thick and the trunk could fold my life into it whole. On my next lunch hour I took it back—I wanted to go after him empty-handed. I did a bad tailgate tracing him home and backed under a jacaranda. I could see him cleaning the plate his wife placed in front of him, back to me, too square not to feel me looking, through French doors. The Datsun ticked in a fall of neon feathers. I could see him rinse dishes with his teen, a sulky helper in the TV strobe. Pollen warped the screen. He never once looked out, like I was zilch. By the time he walked over and got in it was dark and I was blistered by hours at the steering wheel. Finger by finger he picked away my left hand. He looked at the words on my singlet, which were so tall and white they could still be read: *Oh Lord I Have Sinned. I haven't*, he said, head-down with repentance. But I just peeled the shirt off and made sure he did.

So he came to the motel, but had to keep on going back. I should understand. It was complicated. There were logistics to leaving. And I did get it—I'd just fuck him extra hard before he left. The fringed quilt at the Cicada felt like fiberglass, and static would net all the nicks in his hard hands. I scrubbed his grip round my breast, working-class electricity, and muttered *please don't go* again. Two kids had moved into 16 and they hated each other, were outside playing tag in pink until someone wept. He said there was still so much to sort. I unlassoed him from my legs and tried to think of his wife's wellbeing. But if I said I remember one iota of compassion for her I'd be lying. At three while he was faking sleep I'd watched the silver twitch along his eyelids. I'd kissed him until our late-night whispering turned bloodshot. He felt like my birthright. When he wouldn't talk to me I went outside and played hopscotch with the bitchy girls from 16, leaping the pink chalk squares with nine-year-old kicks. In my tight shorts and topknot I looked like a princess—at least to them I did. Before he left again I bribed a View-Master off one of those kids, and fed in the notched discs as he backed out the drive, worked the spring-loaded technicolour trigger. My eyes crossed with sick fans of Disney happy-ends.

I didn't lie waiting in a slutty getup all day, some bra held together by lace and evil thoughts—but the woman at reception eyeballed me like I did, like she knew the type. And I qualified. Reception was hung with anti-fly ribbons like a melting vinyl rainbow—when you walked through it took minutes for your collarbone to shake off their sticky ricochet. The door jamb shaved my jandal, made me do a little skip up to the desk, rubbery pirouette. I needed more long-term things: an iron, a hairdryer, more of her ultra-life milk in dinky domes. And I wanted to swap games. I wanted Operation, to tweeze out the Adam's apple, pluck the funny bone. I wanted to win cash scratching out his melted heart, to not hear the buzzer going off in his face. The woman handed his flat box over with a warning that it was intact, she'd counted the bones, and pointed down the main road to the Four Square if I planned to be a longer stayer. She was staple-gunning frills of tinsel to the counter with a line of clunks. I'd forgotten a day as bad as Xmas was coming. But when I got down to the Four Square I couldn't miss it—the checkout girl was wearing a halo, a fairy-lit number-eight hoop spliced to her head band, with more wire strapped to her smock for shonky wings. She shed white feathers in the yellow bag as she packed it with the tap of single-serve things, blinking greasily at me. The kettle in 17 must have had six hundred horsepower. But none of the sachets worked. The taste of other people's yesterdays stayed at the back of my tongue. The air felt like asbestos. I tugged on the drawers just to listen to the cutlery make its aim-fire sound. When I opened doors in the dark room all the hinges sang the motel's name.

He came and went. I knew there were going to be days when we weren't quite in this together. The days I had him, I'd slow down the order that I peeled off my clothes. I tried my best to give him amnesia. It was all about timing. I'd use a pulpy tube of Revlon to paint myself an oversize grin. I'd line up pills like islands of my own tropical making, deadly getaways I just might take. *What they should stash in the drawer*, I said, *is a quick guide to not wanting to end yourself in small rented rooms*. I'd pretend to ring old boyfriends, undoing the spirals in the telephone cord with my fuckyou finger. He stared at me and smiled an unventilated smile. I promised him I'd stick a knife in the toaster. He let me bite him hard then thumb around the toothmarks, the dent-in freckles I'd left, a buckling ring-o'-rosie. Then I dabbled sorry with my tongue. When we walked the beach later, we brought home shells in casual fistfuls and left them on the sill like things we should give names.

The Lord had come and I was playing Guess Who when I saw the car waiting—so I just flicked down every face that looked like the wife, picked the blondes off in reverse order. Their clickety plastic capsize was satisfying. I thought it was him at first, here for Jesus after all—but when I realised I winched back the screen and shrugged, *might as well come in*.

His kid had nothing going for him, none of his dad's girth and heat. He scrubbed the heel of one sneaker over the laces of the other, fluoro and tryhard. In his hand he had a cracker, a tube of crimped green crêpe.

Sweet. You brought me a present.

He stared at the thing.

Mum cooked this big family dinner, he said.

Oh yeah.

Yeah, this whole awesome spread.

If it was so good why are you here, then?

I wanted to see if my Xmas wish had come true. And you'd just fucked right off.

You know, you could play nicer. Xmas spirit and that.

He's there. Dad's still there. I reckon he's staying.

Crosslegged on the mango bed I could make him look away. My shorts ended high and tight. Bull's-eye.

How even old are you? he said.

How old are you? You meant to be behind that wheel?

I'm learning. Dad's teaching me a lot of things.

Yeah? Coincidence. Me too.

I don't reckon. I don't reckon you know half of things.

Okay little boy. Go. What?

Then he started to cry, a big ruck of sobs. I watched for a while, then I tipped all the mugshots back up on the Guess Who board.

Wanna play?

He stared at me, using a fist to scrub his flushed face.

Okay, he said. You don't know my mother.

Or maybe you don't know your father.

Maybe. But I could always ask him. He is still at home.

Not for long, kid.

Yeah. Says you.

God knows why the Cicada Motel was a stop for any Xmas gig, but we heard a siren warp then, and a fire engine rigged with tinsel pulled into the carpark. Some half-cut local Santa climbed out with a swag of made-in-China presents, ho-ho-ho'ed round the units looking for kids. The checkout girl was his assistant, waving a hairy silver wand, still with the vortex of glitter cabled to her head, her white wings a wobbly scaffolding. I opened the door and watched the pink twins from 16 tweak open the sellotape on their lame gifts. The old girl from reception was blushing by the truck in her best ugly smock. Santa used his rented beard to lean in, snuggle her. She gave him a gurgle of her annual gin, and dished him a slap. I thought about sauntering over to the guy on the driver's side—in his flame-retardant hero gear he leaned out of the cab to scope the lettering on my tank: *My happy place is your happy place burning to the ground.* His grin was déjà vu. But I didn't move. Then the garish parade was pulling out.

And I'd like to tell you that I lived up to the look the old girl gave me before she trudged back to her lobby. A look that said, *suppose you're all right, considering.* I'd like to say I didn't turn back to the unit where the kid was still cluttering the tropical bed, trying to cope with the weight of his wet face. I'd like to say I was done with my nymph skin, that I let it split, and stepped out. The kid was still clutching his Xmas cracker. I latched on to the end and yanked. The bang made him flinch. I fucking loved the hint of gunpowder. I shook out the festive crap and tossed him the gag.

What's the joke.

You should know.

I slid on the pink paper crown.

Marty Smith

no horse
has equal tone
in all four hooves

the odd
sauntering sound
syncopated

like a rough unsteady
heart and I

listen
to the spaces
uneven   as what

they will find out:
I am glass, a fake
winter

I set my wall: sit
behind beneath
sharp-scraped
hooves

I block
the blue veins of
the moon

its yellow eye

Ruby Solly

Six Feet for a Single, Eight for a Double

My father leaves school to dig graves.
The first break is the hardest.
The pressure of foot on steel,
the smell of earth rising.
Koia, koia, e tau e koia.
The men sit with packed lunches,
talking about the weather
next to holes they have dug themselves.

When he leaves the job, he keeps his shovel.
Always comes home to dig for the whānau.
Koia, koia, e tau e koia.
He keeps me playing graveside,
tells me off for climbing the pile of earth.
Sends me to find things;
the grave with the lamb,
the grave with the clasped hands.

He says this is how the dead speak.
A lamb for a child,
clasped hands pulling each other up to heaven;
but this is not the only way.
The atmosphere traps us in our bodies,
holds our teeth and tongues in place.

My father says he has no rhythm,
but when he digs you see it in his body,
the flow through the earth into the feet,
contracting the calves
through the spine, to chiseled arms,
through ageing hands, into the shovel
and back into the whenua.

Koia, koia, e tau e koia.
With each beat he piles up dirt higher and higher,
making a lofty mountain
for us to bow to.

John Summers

Real life

It was like playing at real life, that first flat. Gareth, Sam and I, all students, all living there. Henry sleeping on the couch for most of the holidays. We had to go to Pak'nSave. We had to pay a phone bill and buy credit for a power manager. We took it upon ourselves to make a batch of tomato sauce. It was the cheapest place we could find and we revelled in being in a bad neighbourhood. One night Gareth and I crouched by the front window, listening to two men arguing in a car parked outside. They were burglars dividing their spoils and had come to a stalemate over bedding. 'The thing is,' one of them said, 'it was my idea to take the fucking duvet in the first place.'

The house itself was old—you could run a hand over its cream weatherboards and feel the stroke of the two-man saw that cut them. It had a red tin roof, a couple of rooms on a lean and, unfortunately, a fridge alcove in the bathroom. Next door was a newer place, a red brick unit from the sixties maybe. Another three people lived there: Rick, who was about our age and 'about to' join the army, and an older man with the strangest tattoo I had ever seen, a large yellow kiwi on the side of his face, the beak poking right into the corner of his eye. The third was a young woman I sometimes saw shopping at the supermarket where I worked part-time. She walked slowly in platform boots as if struggling to balance, and she wore miniskirts and a bandanna wrapped so tightly round her head that I had the impression she had no hair underneath.

There was a dairy on the corner, staffed every afternoon by the owner's son, still in his school uniform. They sold a terrible pie, a boule of bright yellow pastry filled with a thin brown paste. But they were only fifty cents, so I ate a couple a week. On the other side of the street was a pub. The first sound every morning was the chain on their sign dragging against concrete as someone carried it out to the footpath. It was important to advertise the fact they sold cheap jugs, even if people only ever went there for pokies.

We rented from Mrs Wilkinson, a small woman with a face puckered with worry. She was like a landlady from Dickens, prone to shrieking odd things and veering off towards hysteria during most conversations.

One day we asked her about insulation. Damp had curled our posters and softened my uni notes.

She repeated the word syllable by syllable. 'In-su-la-tion, in-su-la-tion. Why, I never heard of such a thing,' she said. 'Insulation?'

'Like a Pink Batt,' I said.

Her eyes widened, her voice rose. 'A pink *what*? Oh, my goodness no.' It was as if I had said something like 'French letter'. 'I said to Bill, in-su-la-tion. He didn't know either.'

Mrs Wilkinson we tolerated and sometimes avoided—you needed to be in the right mood to face her. But we liked Bill. He was the maintenance man, an elderly Irishman who wore a tweed cap and jacket and cream slacks but also brilliantly white running shoes, so that I found myself expecting him to break into a sprint at any minute. Bill was a character, we decided. He went about with *Best Bets* tucked under his arm. We traded the facts we learnt about him—that he couldn't drive, that he had been in cycling races a long time ago in Ireland and that he was in some sort of unmentioned relationship with Mrs Wilkinson.

At Christmas he gave me four beers. They had been a gift to him, he said, 'But it makes me sick.'

'Canterbury Draught or all beer?' I said.

'The lot of it.'

We liked him despite, or maybe because of, the work he did. His repairs were execrable, so much so they were fascinating. When the handle on the inside of the door broke off, he wedged a stout stick in its place. He wrapped a rag round this so it would be comfortable to grip, and finally he painted the whole thing white.

He was also responsible for the house's colour scheme. I found him using three tins of paint to touch up the lounge. 'I always mix my own paint,' he explained. So there was an aquamarine bedroom, a pink bathroom and a lime-green kitchen. He slathered it over the great porridgey lumps of plaster that filled the dents, or 'bruises' as he called them, that were in every wall. Even the house number on the front fence was his work, 128 painted with a four-inch brush, the numbers dribbling down the paling.

One morning I stepped up onto my bed to adjust a curtain. Stepping down, I heard a soft crunch and felt something give beneath the carpet. A rotten floorboard had finally snapped. I went looking for Bill. Both he and Mrs Wilkinson were always around. We didn't know enough then to think this was unusual, even illegal because she never gave us any notice. They'd be in the yard inspecting something or at that flat next door, a property she also owned. A couple of times she used her time there to loudly berate Rick for not doing anything with his life. His response was to lean back against the door frame and laugh, unmoved by her words.

On this day, I soon found Bill over there. He nodded across the fence. 'I've got just the thing for it.' And he ambled away.

I went back to the flat to wait. Probably I worked on an essay— two thousand words on the problems with media conglomeration or a list of all the themes and techniques that marked an Australian poet as being from this or that movement. It was scruffy work I turned in then, makeshift things like Bill's repairs. Those first couple of years of university were overwhelming, too good to be true. You mean I really get to spend my days reading interesting books and listening to people talk about ideas, going to parties and meeting girls? My mind bounced from thing to thing, never settling on an idea well enough to understand it properly, and when it came to the actual business of essay writing I tended to dash something off, scrawling longhand in a rush and only taking these notes down to the library to type up the night before due day.

There was a knock at the door. When I opened it, Bill handed me a sheet of plywood. 'You can put this over it.'

I mumbled my thanks. It wasn't the solution I had been

hoping for. 'I guess I could get a rug,' I said.

'A mat. It's a mat you want.' He told me to follow and together we went through the yard, past the battered firewood shed we used for our bikes and through the gate in the back fence. It opened into a section behind the flat next door. There was a narrow car shed and beside it a pile of rusting junk. Bill leaned into this and began to rummage, lifting away scraps of wood, a stretched coil of chicken wire, odd lengths of pipe. 'Here you are,' he said and, with a flourish, he whipped out a ragged square of Astroturf.

I would have been scratching away at my essay again when I heard the second knock on the door. And again I opened it to Bill.

He rolled his eyes. 'She wants to see it now,' he said.

Mrs Wilkinson was somewhere behind him, shouting. 'Where is it?' she said. 'Where is it?' She said this even as I led her though the lounge to the bedroom.

She went silent on seeing the hole and the sheet of ply (I had declined the Astroturf). But she was loud again as I followed her back out to the door. 'Oh, the poor boy. Holes in the floor! Living in this old place with holes in the floor. Oh, my goodness.'

Bill tried to placate her. 'He doesn't mind. He doesn't care.'

'How can he not care? Holes in the floor.'

We had come to the door and she reached for the handle. Her hand stopped before it. 'What on earth is this?'

The three of us stood there, staring at Bill's handle—a forlorn and shabby dildo emerging from the door.

Bill very quietly said, 'They needed something there.'

She spun around and jabbed a finger at his face. 'You! You did this?'

The argument began in earnest now. She berated and shouted and he muttered that same sentence again and again. At no point did they ask my opinion on either the hole or the door handle and, as soon as they stepped forward just enough, I shut the door on the pair of them.

*

It was inconvenient, all of this. Stubbing your toes on a sheet of plywood. A landlady who pretended to have never heard the word 'insulation'. Really, though, it was glorious. We were originals, or so we liked to think, dodging Riccarton's student ghetto—those flats with a pinched road sign on the porch and a PlayStation plugged into the TV. We were meeting people we wouldn't find on campus: people like those two, like the man who came down to the supermarket drunk to buy a Picnic bar and then ate it, lying on his side Roman emperor style on one of the homeware store's display beds.

We were doing the things we wanted to do. It was our time for that. I installed a cocktail cabinet in the corner of the lounge. We sometimes drank at that pub with the pokies. When I ordered a pie there the barmaid presented it to me frozen, a grey lump sliding on a plastic plate. 'Do you want it heated up?' she said. We made kava—Sam and Gareth traipsed around a craft warehouse looking for muslin cloth to strain it.

And we had parties. I brewed up a vat of home brew and shared it with friends, dragging our Salvation Army table outside on a warm but murky day and setting out bowls of pickled onions and potato chips. Oktoberfest we called it, although I think it was April.

On another occasion, an evening, we set up a stereo in the lounge, loaded CDs into the changer and hid away anything easily pocketed. We waited for everyone to come. That one was just an okay party, as far as I remember. Our friends were there, but few people I hadn't met before.

Someone must have invited Rick from next door, and late in the night I spotted him standing about, on the edge of the crowd, smiling to himself. I wandered over, a bottle of my home brew in hand, and we talked about our street, about Bill and Mrs Wilkinson. He made some remark about her, that she was a crazy old lady or something like that, and he told me it was the physical test holding him back from the army. He couldn't run the required distance fast enough and right now he was in training. I asked him about his flatmates. Those other two weren't flatmates, he said. The building was divided into three and they had a unit each.

'How does that work?' I said. 'There's only one door.' The place was small too.

'I'll show you if you want.'

The fence between our flats was shoulder height. Rick sprinted and jumped at it. His fingers scratched at the timber as he scrambled to pull himself over. A creak came from it and suddenly he was on his back, still holding a piece of rotten paling. He was more careful on the second attempt. I followed, making sure I climbed in the same place, where the boards had, this time, proven safe.

That door opened into a shared hallway, and then another door led to his single room.

'Well, it's good you have your own stove,' I said, standing awkwardly amidst the mess, looking at the caravan-style cooker close to his unmade bed.

He had to share a bathroom, he said. He reached down by the bed—everything was by the bed—to retrieve a bottle of cheap vodka from the floor. He poured me a shot glass, and took a swig from the bottle as I downed it.

Coming back through the hallway, Rick stopped to point to one of the doors and snigger. Behind it a woman was talking. She was speaking quickly and in an even tone. She was talking to herself—that young woman I had seen at the supermarket sometimes. I went to pass and to leave but Rick slammed into the door with his shoulder.

'Shut up, you fucking bitch,' he shouted.

The woman yelled back. 'Go on,' she said. 'Smash your head in. See if I care.'

Rick banged a fist on the door. 'You crazy bitch.'

'That's it. Go on, smash your head in, smash your fucking head in.'

I'd like to say I stopped him, that I pulled him away from the door and told him to leave her alone. But I didn't do any of those things. I stood rigid, sober now and queasy as he yelled once more and beat even harder on the door, his face red and the door quivering in the frame, his fist bouncing on the wood as if he might break right through it. He did this and then walked on out of the hallway, swearing to himself, forgetting I was behind him. I left too, hurrying back to our party and my friends.

We weren't the first to have parties at that flat. In the corner of the yard was a square of knee-high weeds that had been garden once. Gareth tried digging up a patch to plant lettuces, and his spade turned over sandy, ash-coloured dirt. Unhealthy and unfertile, and broken glass all through it. There were bottle caps too, pull tabs and a dried-out condom. It was archaeology digging there, all these things from the parties before us. Parties where things got smashed, where there were fights. We decided against planting anything in that soil.

It was around that time that Sam left. His mother moved back to Australia, offering her house to him and his sister. Gareth and I needed a new flatmate, and we wrote up adverts on pieces of paper, fringing the bottom so people could tear away a note with our telephone number. In some of these ads we attempted humour. I wrote one from the perspective of a conquistador—the implication being that our three-bedroom shack was an El Dorado of sorts—hoping that we would find a suitable third, another Sam who would see things the way we did and share our discoveries. Every day I came down the polished concrete steps of the university library and went straight to the noticeboard below to find that our poster, smothered by ads for desks and law textbooks, was missing only two of the little tear-away notes, the rest curling back on themselves. An Asian man came around on behalf of his friend Frank, speaking Mandarin into a cellphone as we showed him through. He started each question with 'Frank wants to know . . .' but we never heard back from either of them.

And then there was the burly, goateed guy who arrived in a van one afternoon, his long hair streaming from his backwards cap to rest on the collar of his Hawaiian shirt. Right away he was hooked. There was enough space in the room for all his computers, his only requirement.

'I've got another place to look at, but I think this place would be great. Anyway, the other one is all chicks.' He pulled a face.

The minute we heard the van rumbling away, Gareth turned to me. 'Whoa, slacker dude!' he said.

We agreed this would make him a great flatmate, adding a new and hilarious element to our flat. But that evening I checked our messages and there was his voice, shouting over the music and bar noise behind him.

'Sorry, dudes,' he said, 'but those chicks had broadband. Broadband! That's it for me.'

Finally we rented the room to Toni and her dog, Smoochie, a floppy, enormous beast with golden curls. He was so big that sitting down meant awkwardly folding his limbs, furry elbow nubs poking out in four directions. We worried about this. We had a cat after all—Mama Puss, a tortoiseshell who came with the flat. But Toni was adamant that Smoochie liked cats. And by that stage we had no choice—no one else wanted to live with us.

Toni was right. Smoochie did like cats, or at least didn't mind them. He would shamble towards Mama Puss for nothing more than a friendly sniff. She reacted with a hiss, sprinting off under the couch, but never going too far.

Toni herself was a bit of a mystery. I didn't know what she did most days. She had just finished a course and she was a dance instructor, she said, but it didn't sound like there was much work in that. Her background was another puzzle. I first assumed she was an Indian New Zealander, although she mentioned her father in Sydney and her accent sounded North American.

And once I overheard Gareth describing her to a friend: 'She's black,' he said, 'but, like, from England.'

She was smiley, friendly, maybe a little patronising. 'Silly,' she said, to correct some wrong assumption of mine, perhaps one about those dance lessons.

Her cooking was diabolical, infusing even the studs of that

house with the stink of over-broiled skate. The next day all the fixings would still be lying about the kitchen: the polystyrene pad the fish came in, the Gladwrap torn from it pornographically; half a dozen all but empty sauce bottles and smears of the offending dish across the benchtop and stove. We muttered about that amongst ourselves. For young men we were surprisingly neat, but knew we had to compromise on some things, and we appreciated her dedication to Smoochie. We loved that dog. He was a slightly mournful-looking klutz. He'd knock something over with his giant tail, then do more damage as he spun around to see what. It would be difficult finding flats, doing most things in fact, when you had an enormous animal in tow, yet Toni had made the choice to keep him.

One night I came home to find Smoochie alone. Toni arrived soon after with Steve, an American, who said, 'John, I hear you make a mean home brew.'

I offered him a glass and chatted just a little. I was obviously a third wheel. It was a date, I supposed. I made an excuse and went to bed early, trying to read one of my course texts but hearing every word of their conversation through the thin walls. I fell asleep to wake a couple of hours later with my light still on and the book open on the bed.

'I don't understand why you would think that,' Toni was saying.

'Well, you invited me over,' Steve said.

'And you thought that meant I would have sex with you?'

Steve mumbled something, and they talked on this theme for a while. My curiosity soon ran out and I lay there annoyed, wondering how uncomfortable it would be to go in there and ask them to be quiet. Finally I fell back to sleep.

Gareth was staying with his girlfriend those evenings, so the next night it was just me and Toni. I joined her in taking Smoochie for a walk. We strolled through the long, straight streets that led into Christchurch's east, and almost immediately she let Smoochie off his lead. He exploded with hairy energy, limbs firing in all directions as he took off down the street and out of sight.

'Will he be okay?' I said, nervously, never a dog owner.

'He loves to go for a run. But he always comes back.'

We walked a little, talking about Smoochie, before Toni said, 'You know Steve, who came over last night?'

'Yeah.'

'He thought that just because I invited him over I would sleep with him.'

'Really?'

'But then he went home, and he had a phone call. His mother was in hospital.' They first thought it was serious, she implied, cancer or something similarly earth-shattering, but they had then revised it to something else. She would get better. 'He called me today and told me, and do you know what he said to me? He said, I think you're an angel.'

'Ha?' I made a choked little chuckle.

Toni turned to me with a far-off, sincere expression. She was deadly serious, trying for beatific. 'He thinks I'm an angel, here to look out for him.'

My reaction was one of horror. I suddenly saw the end of our flat—it couldn't withstand this level of delusion and strangeness. 'Ha?'

Thankfully, Smoochie came running out of a driveway, knocking over someone's rubbish bin with a clatter, and she was forced to forget her story and call him back.

Steve's angel, yet he never visited again and it was the only time she would make that claim. Still my premonition was accurate. Our flat didn't last, but it was for earthly reasons, petty things that turned us against each other. Our patience with those messes in the kitchen began to fade, and we started to question the way she treated Smoochie. I'd come home to find that she had locked him, not only in the house, but in her tiny room, for the entire day. He took up as much room as the single mattress she had on the floor, and he scattered her junk—books and papers, old records (even though she didn't have a turntable)—as he burst out, anxious for space.

She didn't feed him much either, just an ice hockey puck of dog roll a day. 'He's a farm dog,' she said. 'That's all they eat.'

I was distrustful of this theory. I wondered whether she was trying to save money.

And I was chatting with Gareth in the kitchen one afternoon, when he casually opened the fridge, sliced off a hefty pink chunk and threw it to an appreciative Smoochie. 'Yeah,' he said. 'I've been doing that.'

She had been there a month. I came in, leafing through the mail. Tearing open the phone bill and happily finding that it was $37, about usual. I put it down on the kitchen counter and went to move on, when something, just a doubt, made me look again. $377! I saw now there was page after page behind it—lengthy toll calls to points throughout New Zealand but also to Sydney, America and the Cayman Islands. The account was mine. This had all been racked up in my name and now I would need to get the money out of her or fork out myself.

I carried the bill to Gareth.

His eyes widened as he leafed through those pages. 'The Cayman Islands!' he said.

We confronted her with the bill that evening. The three of us were standing in the poky lounge. This was the first time I had ever had to question someone about money like this, to have something that needed to be settled. I was ready for a confrontation, ready to drown into the swirling mud of our psychedelic carpet.

'I'll pay it,' Toni said, after flicking through the bill. 'But I didn't make all of these calls. I mean, some of them are mine, but not all of them. I didn't make this call to the Cayman Islands.'

Her saying this blunted my relief. 'Well, we didn't make them,' I said. After all, she was accusing us of making her pay for our calls. 'I don't know anyone in the Cayman Islands. Gareth doesn't know anyone in the Cayman Islands.'

'I'll pay for it,' she said, frostily. We agreed that the phone bill would be transferred to her.

'I don't want to get expensive toll calls in my name,' I said.

'Okay, okay,' she said, and at that moment the phone rang.

'That'll be the Cayman Islands,' Gareth said.

Toni glared back at him as she reached for the phone.

Next came the beer. While letting Smoochie loose, I spotted three bottles of our home brew among the flotsam on her floor. She didn't even drink—it was just something else to hoard. Gareth and I left a note on the scarred dining table: 'We have noticed that our beer has been going missing . . .'

She responded with three bottles, unopened, and another note—a torn-off piece of cardboard box, all left in the exact same place on the table. In it she apologised. She knew it was a bad thing to do. 'I don't even like beer!' (I had been right.) But it was her retribution for our insistence about the phone bill. 'I just felt so angry that you didn't trust me.' She hoped everything would be better now.

'Man, I feel really bad,' Gareth said.

'Yeah,' I said, reading the note a second time.

Finally, there were the dogs. I manoeuvred my car up our narrow driveway, an unofficial driveway without a culvert. You needed to slow, then swing in to approach the pavement front on, rolling the wheels up over it. I managed this and the very narrow space between fence and house, a couple of inches on either side of each wing mirror.

And as I came into the backyard my car was surrounded by jumping, yelping dogs. Three of them. Smoochie, of course, but two more. Terriers or something like it. Smaller but louder. They circled me, leaping up at my shins as I got out of the car. I made it to the kitchen, where I fumbled to fill and flick on the jug as I watched them through the window. First one, then the other, ran to my back wheel, cocked a leg and pissed on it. Finally, Smoochie, corrupted by these two, did the same, or at least tried to. His gangly dimensions made lifting a leg impossible and instead he crouched just beside the wheel to relieve himself, the others howling their encouragement.

Gareth walked in.

'Where did these come from?' I said, with an attempted laugh. Shocked amusement seemed the only possible reaction.

But he had chosen anger, and he misread my response as acceptance. 'Are you okay with this? Because I'm not. She said she was looking after them for someone else. It's just supposed to be for a week, and it better be. She could have told us first.'

'Yeah,' I said, still taking this in. Gareth was as angry as I had ever seen him, so I added a second, more indignant, 'Yeah!'

Over the next few days I came to share his anger. I watched Mama Puss huddling on the roof, unable to step into the yard. One of those dogs would bark all night; the slightest thing set him off. And one evening I had just gotten to sleep, much-needed sleep—I had an exam the next morning—when someone knocked on my window pane. It was Sam. He would tell me later what he saw: the front yard full of weeds, the howl of dogs and my silhouette dragging itself from bed and groping about for a dressing gown.

'What's going on? I've been trying to call you guys but there's a message saying the number doesn't work anymore.'

'She will have done that,' I said, half-asleep and unsurprised. I waved a hand towards the back of the house.

'Where are all these dogs?'

'Out the back. She's got all these dogs.'

I took Mama Puss away on a day between exams, coaxing her into a box with some cat biscuits and driving her to my mother's, where there was already one cat, but at least there were no dogs. Gareth and I made our own plans to leave. Exams were coming to an end, and we started to talk about going to Australia over the holidays. In any case, going somewhere else. Having adventures again and getting away from this flat with its messes and dogs that, despite Toni's claims, showed no sign of going anywhere.

We had already hinted to Toni that we would be leaving. When we confirmed it she said she'd stay and find another flatmate or two. I told Mrs Wilkinson by phone, and a couple of days later we went next door to see her about getting our bond back. As usual she was lurking about Rick's. I had barely seen him, avoiding him since that party. The girl next door had left and been replaced by a man who worked nights. Mrs Wilkinson was in her usual mood. Bill lingered behind her while she complained.

'It's all very well for you,' she said, 'but I'm left with things.' She went on to explain her reasons for racking up a whopping tax bill.

'What?' I said, cutting through her talk. 'What are you saying?' I just wanted to get our bond and get out.

'And you've gone and left me with that Indian girl in there. I've already got problems with an Indian man at another flat. Bill says I'll have all the Indians in Christchurch against me now.'

'All the Indians,' Bill said. 'All the bloody Indians.'

I argued some more with her, but Gareth soon intervened. Taking a more conciliatory tone, he talked through the paperwork we had done, and asked if she could do hers.

She yielded, saying, 'You'll get your money,' theatrically and with the usual hand-waving.

I went back to the house quivering and disgusted. They had been annoying before, of course, but never in a way that mattered. That flash of racism had ruined everything. Toni had ruined it too. I felt sorry for her, that we were leaving her with those two and their resentment. And I felt annoyed with myself—too stupid, too young to know that things end.

Gareth and I helped each other to move out. We borrowed his father's trailer and loaded it up with our bicycles. I slung a rope over this tangle of chains and pedals, and we were tying it all down when the boy from the corner dairy came by, in his school uniform as always. He nodded to us as he approached.

'You're losing your best customers,' I said, letting the rope slacken.

He looked back, confused.

'We're moving out.'

'You're moving out?'

'That one there,' I said, pointing to Bill's dripping 128.

'Oh, okay. Well, bye.'

Gareth and I nodded back, then exchanged bemused looks. The kid hadn't understood us. This really was goodbye. I finished knotting the rope and we got in the car and drove away.

Anna Taylor

Leaves

'I'll die if I can't go,' Ruth said, and she made an exaggerated display of her arms. The lid of the pocket mirror—which moments before she'd been using to examine the stye, forming there on her eye—splayed open too, catching the last of the evening sun; sending an arc of light up across the porch ceiling, a flutter of white down the verandah beam.

Alice gave her a small smile, though Ruth wouldn't have noticed that—the smallness of it. A smile is a smile, that's what Ruth would say.

Of course it was Alice who felt like she was dying, much of the time. The pills were supposed to ease the pain, the doctors had said, but there was nothing they could do about the tiredness. The skin on her hands was blotchy, knobs of red on the knuckles and wrist bone, and in the mornings she had to hold them—her hands—in a pail of hot water before she could open them up, the fingers having set into fists overnight. And then there were the asthma attacks to contend with, though they were currently in a lull. The winters were dreadful, but it was summer now—the mountains behind them bare of snow, the walnut trees in the paddock covered in a thick froth of leaves.

Ruth was prodding at her eye again with one finger, the bronze case of the mirror held firm in her other hand. She was younger than Alice by six years; had all the bristling robustness of their father. Ruth was stocky, well-built. *Stocky and sticky*, that's how Ruth referred to the two of them, to the differences in their shape. She had reason to be jovial about that, Alice decided, since it was Alice who had been behind the door, as they say, when the constitutions were being handed out.

*

Ruth's dress was still with the dressmaker on Deal Street. She had caught the bus to the city a month ago to buy the fabric, and had come back with yards of the stuff folded in a perfect rectangle, wrapped in a sheet of city-smelling brown paper. It was a beetle green, shot through with threads of gold, and she'd been inspired to go for that colour-tone, she said, by the poster of Doris Day in *Love Me or Leave Me*, though that dress was more teal than green, perhaps, and much more daring than anything Ruth would ever consider trying to jam herself into. She had said all this in a jumble of words and exclamations as Alice had walked a little way out to meet her, as she was making her way—her silhouette all bags and triumph—back up the drive. Doris's shoes matched the colour of her dress, exactly, Ruth had said. But the cut was too modern, too revealing.

'Fancy turning up to a dance in our little old town dressed in something like that!' she said, as if Doris Day herself would wing her way over from America, and bustle her way into the Kaik ō oura Memorial Hall. Alice had walked beside her, trying to keep her stride even, and had felt a soft, familiar tugging inside her abdomen. She had done all the jobs—milking the cow, digging potatoes for their dinner—as best she could, but now she felt the dullness of a day spent doing that, when Ruth—Ruth had been in the city, running her fingers over yards of metallic-coloured cloth. Before she had felt excited that Ruth would arrive home to see how much she had achieved, how well she'd done despite her bad hands and weak limbs, but now all she could see was dirt from the potatoes, the little lines of it under her fingernails, and the sourness of the milk that she'd spilt on her shirt, the smell of it, wafting towards her when she moved her arm in a certain way.

'And what did *you* do today?' Ruth finally said, but her face was half turned away when she asked, her eyes scanning the line of macrocarpas on the driveway, moving up towards the sky.

Their father had died at the end of that winter, suddenly—a heart attack felling him out in the paddock, as though someone had shot an arrow, sent it whistling towards his chest. When they were younger there'd been their mother's illness, both of them having to help out, and Ruth, of course, always having to care for Alice when her lungs and joints were at their worst. Ruth was thirty-two, still had a chance to claim her life. There was the farm—neither of them knew what to finally do with that—so they'd got Allen and Dick in for now, to keep it running. Ruth had made sacrifices—oh, more than you could count on both hands. Alice could never forget that. And now, Ruth's chance—Allen free of his ailing wife, thank goodness, and not too old, not really, to start again.

*

That summer was stifling, only the thinnest threads of white cloud in the sky, and in the midday heat the leaves on the bean poles drooped. Alice ferried cans of water back and forth, sprinkling it around their roots, but that only seemed to perk them up for an hour or two. The north-westerly winds were worse than they'd ever been before. Often the gales would build over the course of a day, but one night they came up out of nowhere, the branches of the walnut trees outside the house making a terrible sound—a roar—and the door of the shed at the back of the garden hurling itself against, and then away from, its frame. Ruth and Alice were just clearing away their supper dishes when the house began to shake. And then the sound of it: like a huge wave bearing down on them. They both paused, before placing their dishes in the sink.

The moon was almost full, so the sky was lit up a lurid blue. The shed door needed to be dealt to, and there was yesterday's washing still on the line.

'Don't you come out here with me,' Ruth said to Alice. 'You might snap like a twig!' She said those sorts of things good-naturedly, her eyes bright with humour, but sometimes Alice found it hard to laugh along. Who was it but Ruth, though, who ran down the hall at night whenever Alice called out; Ruth who laid her warm hands encouragingly on Alice's heaving chest. She would not say to her—how dare you say such a thing.

'I'm coming,' Alice said, and looked around for her shoes.

The wind was hot and filled with tiny airborne shards of wood (twigs *did* snap out there, as it turned out) and invisible clouds of grit. The whites of Ruth's eyes were lit up, and the leaves on the writhing walnut trees were a ghostly kind of green. Branches as thick as Alice's thigh were falling, skating across the grass. Ruth covered her head with both hands, protectively like a helmet, all the material around her body flapping maniacally. Alice held onto the verandah beam and wondered at it: the way the air had formed itself into this great noise. The cry of the wind was inside her body; her blood, she imagined, roared like that too. She could be swallowed up into that sound, lifted by it, her limbs flapping like leaves. She took one step out onto the grass, and then another. Opened her mouth to taste the wind's gritty heat.

Allen came by early the next morning, his big hands held awkwardly in front of his body. His hair was greying, but he had a smoothness around the skin of his eyes, the blue of them pleasingly light, like the irises had been mixed with a thimbleful of milk.

'How'd you fare?' he said, even though he could see, just by looking around, that the grass was strewn with branches and leaves and the green husks of hundreds of unripe walnuts. Alice and Ruth hadn't even been to see the vegetables, couldn't stand the thought of the tomatoes and bean frames tossed all over the place, everything flattened out.

'I thought of you ladies last night,' Allen said. 'Wondered if you'd be doing okay.'

He stood in the kitchen, his shoulders rolling forward slightly, as if the ceiling was too low and he was trying to fit himself in.

'I'll make you some tea, Allen,' Ruth said, and as she filled the pot, Alice noticed how she touched her other hand to her hair, patting the stray pieces back into place.

It was Alice who had befriended Allen, at first. His wife had a cancer that had got into the bone, and near the end she had to lie down all the time, plaster casts trying to hold her hips and legs together.

Alice had been bedridden for some time too, and even though moving around was like dragging her limbs through oatmeal and water, she was refusing to go back to bed. Allen's wife could have her books and magazines and embroidery patterns, she said, and she bundled them up in her sewing basket.

'You won't be needing these any time soon, Alice?' he said, but she shook her head, no.

'Well that's very kind of you,' he said, and he held the basket against his body with his big dirty hands as though it was something fragile, a creature with a quiver to it, pressed tight against the scratchy wool of his shirt.

She had watched him go down the path with it, open the door to his truck, slide the basket into the passenger seat. She had the cow and calves to check on, and walked across the grass as he pulled away from the drive. The light was bending in through his window, forming him into a perfect silhouette. The sound of the wheels against gravel; Allen's arm outstretched—hand steadying the basket—as he turned the steering wheel to move out onto the road.

Even though she had given, not lent, he brought the books and patterns back to her, one by one. There was an air about him when he did this, a kind of concentration. He would step through the French doors, bowing his head as he moved under the doorframe, and would give Alice a white smile when she offered him tea. Always, he waited for the kettle to boil, and the cups to be set on the table, with his gaze fixed on the floor. But when he drew the pattern book out from under the crook of his elbow, he would turn his body towards her, eyes on her face.

'Now she quite liked *this* one,' he would say, turning to a page, holding it open for Alice with the palm of his hand.

They would look at whatever it was, together, as if it was a discovery for them, too.

*

The house was filled with empty rooms—it was ridiculous, just the two of them living in there. Ruth said things like that, and even though Alice agreed, the thought was like something sharp in her lung. They would joke together about ways they could fill the house up. Farming small children, Ruth suggested.

'Where might we find some of those?' Alice said, and Ruth covered half of her face with her hand and laughed, the skin on her neck flooding red.

That summer they played cribbage almost every night. It was something to do with Ruth's ruffled energy—her wanting to fill the evenings up from the moment they'd finished clearing away dinner, until they went to bed.

'Crib?' Ruth said the Wednesday before the stye emerged. 'Or euchre? You choose.'

Alice was wiping down the bench; Ruth patting her hands dry.

'Crib,' Alice said. Really, she would have liked to just spend the night with a book.

She went to look for a cardigan—the lightest one with the blue trim—and when she returned the board was already laid out on the table, its little pegs by its side.

They played together, in the low light of the lamp.

Alice felt listless, didn't care about poor pegmanship, but somehow she still won. She'd been winning all week.

Ruth played dynamically, but in a rash kind of way, making errors that she never normally would have made. She seemed pleased to see Alice win—once again—and the corners of her mouth curled upwards as she shuffled the cards into a bundle and slid them back into the box.

'I don't know why,' she said, 'but I just seem to be on an unlucky streak tonight,' and then they'd caught each other's eyes. Did she feel it—that Alice was looking at her hard? There was a knowing there between them, just a flash of it, before they both turned away.

*

Months after his wife died, Allen returned a reel of embroidery cotton. He was ashamed, he said, for having kept it so long. It was the end of his working day, and Alice had been out in the garden, pinching off the curled leaves that had formed on one lack-lustre little tomato. She had been kneeling in the earth when he came up behind her. She hadn't noticed what he was holding in his hands.

'I only just came across this, Alice,' he said, his palm half open. She craned her neck. Embroidery cotton: bright green. At first she had thought it was a praying mantis—that that's what he was holding out to her.

She was down in the earth and he was standing, but it was awkward for her sometimes to get up gracefully, and so she stayed there, her toes pressed into the dirt.

'You didn't need to bring them back,' she said. 'They were hers to keep.' But then she faltered, knowing that the dead didn't get to keep anything at all.

Allen stood there, looking out at the sky. The skin around his eyes was all wrinkled up—that wasn't like him.

'I just couldn't go through it again, Alice,' he said. 'Caring for someone who was ill.' And for some reason, in that moment, her legs decided to stand up, quite of their own volition. It wasn't even that she immediately understood the implication, just that her legs knew what to do to prove, perhaps, that she did have a working body after all. She got up off the ground so suddenly, and Allen, taken by surprise, put his arms out, as if to catch her. Her shoulder collided with his chest.

Just above them, there was the sound of a wood pigeon's wings beating at the air. They both looked up. Allen's hand was pressed against the small of Alice's back.

The light had a filtered look to it, the green of the hills washed out; more yellow than green, but really hardly a colour at all. It had been the first of the summer's hot days. Was her blouse damp with sweat?

The bird was gone, and Allen's hand pulled back away from her body. Alice, too, took an abrupt step backwards, her left foot sinking down into the dark dirt of the vegetable bed. It was an awkward stance, with that one foot buried in there.

It wasn't until later that she found Ruth in a bedroom, their mother's dresses strewn across the floor. She turned towards her, and Alice knew, immediately.

'You'll never guess,' Ruth said. 'You'll never guess what Allen asked me today.'

*

The stye came up the Thursday before the dance—Ruth could feel it, she said, even before there was any sign of it; like a grain of sand was caught there, under her lid. She had come at Alice holding her lashes up against her brow, the rind of her curled back eyelid exposed.

'There's something in there,' she said. 'Can you see it?' She breathed heavily on Alice's face. Her breath smelt—what was it?—slightly sharp; metallic. Alice had never examined Ruth this closely before, or so it felt. There was the lightest sprinkling of freckles under her eyes and across the bridge of her nose, but some of the pores there were large. Veins were threaded across the white of her eye. Would Allen notice that too? A passing thought, just sliding in and then out of her again. There was no answer to that question, not one that Alice could find.

'There's nothing,' she said to Ruth. 'There's nothing in here at all.'

'Look harder,' Ruth said, and she rolled her lid right over her thumb, deftly, like handling pastry.

Alice could see it then, a tiny spot of red on that organ-pink sheen of skin.

'A stye,' she said, and Ruth exclaimed, throwing both hands in the air.

By that evening the swelling was visible, perfectly round, pregnant-looking. They sat on the porch in the last of the sun, Ruth with her mirror. She would put it down and then pick it up again minutes later; waiting for the lump to grow, or shrink.

'A watched stye doesn't boil!' she said to Alice, before lapsing into a full body slouch.

Alice looked at her own hands sitting in her lap; at the knotted thinness of them.

A falcon was circling on a current of air, right above the shadow-cast hill. It tipped its wing and dropped—fell, it seemed—before completing the same circuit, a little lower down.

'It will come to nothing,' she said to Ruth, though she knew that that wasn't entirely true.

The dress was collected on Friday, and hung alone in the empty wardrobe in their parents' room. When Allen's truck came winding up the drive that evening, Ruth collided first with Alice, and then with the china cabinet—leaving it rattling, like a quake—in her efforts to leave the room before he'd even turned off the engine.

'I'm resting,' she called to Alice, and then, from down the hall. 'Don't say why!'

Allen appeared in the glass-paned door, and when Alice opened it to him, he didn't kneel to take off his boots. He just stood there, one hand resting lightly on the frame.

The skin of his neck, she noticed, had a fine crepey look to it, a cluster of dark hair at the mouth of his shirt.

'All done,' he said to her, meaning the day, she supposed.

Alice nodded at him, lightly.

'And I just wanted to let Ruth know,' he said this, though he didn't look around for her, 'that I'll be coming by at seven tomorrow'—he paused—'to get her for the dance.' He hissed that last word, the sound almost inaudible, and Alice realised that they hadn't even acknowledged it between them, not for that whole month since he'd asked Ruth.

'She's looking forward to it,' Alice said, 'very much.' And when she smiled at him, the muscles in her face suddenly softened, as if they believed that smile, and were relieved to be able to hold it there for her, until Allen had turned to go.

*

The colour of Ruth's dress seemed to fill up the kitchen. The waist was fitted, but there was a soft cowl neckline which showed off the little dip at the base of her throat. Her shoes clattered against the floorboards as she moved in and out of the room, adjusting her hair, tugging at the hem of her skirt. They had fashioned a piece of fabric that could be a shawl, or a veil: Alice's idea. She could wear it over her hair, partially obscuring her bad eye until the lights were dimmed. When Alice suggested that, both of Ruth's eyes had filled with tears, little pools of them gathering at the base of her bottom lids. She had gripped one of Alice's hands, tight like a child, as Alice patted powder over the rheumy fullness of that eyelid.

'I'll find a clip that you can use to hold the veil in place,' Alice called to her as she rummaged through a box of their mother's things. The sound of her own voice: so bright. She put her hand to her forehead and felt the heat there, the faint pulsing under the skin.

There were dishes to do. The whole house, in fact, in a state of exhalation, scarves and bags and curlers in collapsing piles all over the floor.

The sudden quiet. And Alice sitting in the midst of it, breathing.

Outside there was the rustle of wind, the leaves of the walnut trees all moving against each other at once. She had only to do the dishes. One thing at a time. If she staggered them she could make the jobs last all night.

She turned the wireless on and then off again; tried the gramophone, but the symphony seemed harsh, filling her body up with the gnaw of its strings. Silence was best, moving around the house with bare feet and bare arms, the heat of the night settling on her skin. She scrubbed at the undersides of the pots, keen to get them clean, though they never had been before—not in her memory. Once she saw the headlights of a car rolling along the road beyond the end of their drive, and her breath seized, but the lights did not turn towards her, just moved smoothly along the road then swung away round the corner. Good, Alice told herself. It was too early for Ruth to be returning, surely.

She opened the kitchen windows to let the heat out. And then the doors—open too—the one to the verandah latched back, the front door held in place by its little iron stopper. The breeze made its way inside, cautiously at first. Then the sound of the peg bag shifting in the air was followed by a wave of movement inside the room. A pile of papers on the sideboard flapped like wings, and then fell, skidding across the floor.

Alice poured herself a glass of water; sat by the window to drink it, where she could look out at the road. Perhaps Ruth's eye might get worse, she thought. Might she slip and twist her ankle, what with her vision being so poor? That thought: like a small gasp right inside her diaphragm. Surely it was not hope that filled her body up—everything poised, as if listening for a note—before quietly deflating with the realisation of what might then unfold: Ruth being carried towards the house in Allen's arms, her bad foot swinging close to his leg. And besides, she, Alice, was not the sort of person to take refuge in the misfortune of others. No. Such a thought was ludicrous.

She went to the door to listen then, for the sound of night and trees. The way those leaves rustled, they could have been the wheeze and suck of air inside her lungs. A gust swept down the valley towards the house, and the patter of leaves moved through her body like applause. A gladness in her chest came over her so suddenly that she had to sit down. How long had the world been calling to her like this? All night those leaves had been shuffling against each other, and she had barely heard.

It was almost ten, and Alice had paced herself perfectly—after all the hours that had passed she was still occupied, still had some tidying to do. She sat on the floor surrounded by little mounds of jewellery, the odd stray stocking. The fabric of scarves and clasps on small evening bags seemed suddenly foreign to her, as if she had never seen them before. She held them in her hands, one at a time.

Their mother had loved fashionable things, had collected them, even though there was rarely anywhere to go. There were tiny geometric shapes etched into the bronze handle of a clutch. A glove with a crescent-shaped button at the base of its wrist. The red of a necktie with a shimmer to it, like sunlight on water. Alice ordered everything into assorted piles, folded the fabrics so that the edges exactly matched. She moved from room to room, her feet hardly sounding against the floorboards, putting it all away.

Sylvan Thomson

Brothers Blind

Nobody used the blind for shooting anymore. Ducks had stopped flying over that way, or maybe they never really did. At least, during the years Joseph lived in his parents' house he had never heard a gunshot split the air above the marsh. His father liked to say that a few times, before Joseph or his older brother were born, men and their quiet sons had come down the road with rifles, all dressed up in camouflage. Joseph's father said he talked to them, leaning over the gate as they passed on their way back and they had told him they had shot at nothing, had seen nothing go flying over.

Joseph first started going down to the duck blind in the middle of winter. He had just started high school in the city and his brother had left home, to go to university. It was a lonely time and when he got in from school, two buses later, he liked to go walking through the fields around his house, right down to where they sloped into the marsh and finally into the grey breadth of the sea. Joseph wore a red woollen hat on these walks which he pulled down low over his ears. He would often pick up a stick of a suitable length and swing along with it, pocking the ground beside him as he went.

He had always squinted at the duck blind if he walked down to the edge of the marshland but had never gone out to it. He thought it looked like something an animal would build, a foxes' den or a woven nest. It had a low roof held up on sapling poles, and it knelt behind a stand of sedge and toetoe. Around the blind the marshland was shaggy with reeds and glasswort. The reeds cast their needled reflections down into the brown water and when you saw them from shore, doubled up like that, they looked like seismograph readings. Joseph's father said the blind had been there since he had bought the house, back in '72.

*

The first time Joseph ever went there it was low tide and the marsh had emptied out of water. He had rubber boots on and walked carefully on the velvet mud, watching the lace crabs hurry into their holes as he went by. The mud sucked at his boot heels, and when he looked behind, silver wedges of water were gathering in each print. The blind was not deep into the marshland and you could walk there at a high tide if you had rubber boots on, as there were clumps of tussock and sod that always remained above the waterline. The sea beyond the blind was very wide and pale, a robe of worn-out silk. Joseph didn't know exactly why he went there that day, or why he never had before.

When he arrived he saw the blind was raised slightly, and sturdy looking, a different structure from what he had thought he'd seen all those times from the shore. The body of it was held up on poles like a stilt house and it was all lashed together, with a roof made the same way, laid over with mānuka brush that peeled in grey ribbons. The ribbons blew in the wind and made a coarse rustling and Joseph stood in the tussock staring. He stood like that for a while, feeling the span of the earth moving out in all directions from his feet.

It was dry when he eventually crept inside and it smelt no different from the marsh because the salty sea wind blew right through its lattice walls. It would not be dry in a storm, Joseph thought, but it was dry that day with the wood creaking and easing as he half crouched to move around inside. There was nothing in the blind apart from an upturned wooden nail box and Joseph sat down on this and stared through at the marsh outside, newly barred by the poles.

Over dinner that night he told his parents he had been walking and had gone out to the duck blind.

His father looked up from his plate, which he was swabbing with a stubbed potato. 'Anything good?' he said. 'I'm surprised it's still standing.'

'There was nothing there,' Joseph said. 'Just a wooden box.'

His mother looked stern. 'Joseph,' she said, 'please be careful the tide doesn't come in and leave you stranded.'

'I walked there on the tussock the whole way, it's not as far as it looks,' Joseph said.

His mother was always concerned with the stealthy movements of tides, the marooning of her children.

'He could sleep the night there if the tide came in,' his father said, to annoy her. 'Snug as a bug—'

'In a rug,' Joseph said, capping him and smiling.

His mother frowned. 'You'd freeze to death.'

'Men used to come down our road,' said his father.

'I know, Dad.'

'Before you were born, Joseph, you or Edward. It happened a few times. They'd go out there to shoot and come back with nothing, not a single feather. I've never seen a duck fly over since we bought this place.'

'They brought those decoy ducks with them,' his mother said.

'That's right,' his father said. 'Plastic decoy ducks. Any of those floating around out there Joseph?'

'I didn't see any,' said Joseph. He pronged a soft strip of carrot with his fork and didn't say anything else about the duck blind.

*

After his first visit Joseph started going out there whenever he could. If it was a nice day he would hurry from the bus stop to the house and put his boots on, stride down through the marshlands to the blind. He took things and left them there. He took a small wooden chest from the shed and he took binoculars. He took a camping stove and a blanket and some of his father's old westerns. He would huddle in there, wrapped in the rough blanket, which smelt of summer grass still, and read them in the fading light: *To Love a Gun*, *None but the Fast*, *No Future for Marshall Cain*, *Without a Badge*.

'What's wrong with your bedroom?' his mother said, when she caught him with new supplies. But his bedroom had nothing to do with it. When Joseph was sitting on the bus he dreamed about the duck blind. He wanted to make it watertight, lace a tarpaulin to its walls. He wanted a real rug for the floor and a set of shelves. If it was watertight he could put pictures on the wall. If it was watertight he could bring a friend out and show it to them. One day he could bring a girl.

There was only one week in the winter term where Joseph didn't go out to the duck blind. It stormed for four days and poured with rain and the marsh flooded. The sea turned the colour of milky tea, the choppy tides and rain chafing at the marsh and mixing the sea waters with the mud.

As soon as the weather cleared and the water fell away Joseph went out, worried that he had forgotten to put the binoculars into the chest or that the westerns might have turned to pulp in the rain. The marsh breathed out as he walked over it, the sun lifting steam and a warm loamy smell.

The blind was damp and steaming too, the sun drawing out curls of vapour from the wood. Some of the brush had been dislodged from the roof and had disappeared, swept out to elsewhere by the tide.

When Joseph went inside he could tell straight away that someone else had been there. There were changes that bad weather couldn't make. He saw that the chest was shifted from where he kept it flush against the wall and when he opened it the westerns were a mess, like someone had rifled through them and then tossed them back, disappointed. Fuel was spilt from the camp stove and had soaked into the wood. He could smell the naphtha singe of it, sharp above the soft smells of the rain and fresh mud.

And then there was the pig tusk. It was lying on the wooden nail box which Joseph used for a seat. He picked it up and curled his fingers around it. It was a perfect sickle shape and tarnished yellow, like nicotine teeth. He ran his hands over it and felt how it was worn sleek. He thought about how it must have been held and passed from hand to hand and held. He crouched there in his small den, the tusk in one hand. When he left he took it and the binoculars away; they were a nice pair that used to belong to his grandfather and he didn't want them stolen.

He carried the tusk in his coat pocket the next day and took it to school. On the bus he put his hand around it and grasped it firmly. He thought about the old duck hunters crouched in the blind with their quiet sons. He saw them poke the long rifles through chinks in the brush and resettle their deerstalker hats. During class he dipped his hand to his pocket again and held the tusk and after school he went back out to the blind. His mother called out to him when he was at the end of the driveway but he pretended not to hear. He thought it was conceivable that the wind had plucked her voice away and this was what he told her later, when she chided him. The binoculars hung around his neck, banging against his sternum with each step. He wanted to know that the place was as he had left it.

The shadows of gulls chased across the mud as he walked through the marsh. He saw how they were dwindling, stretching with the changing contours of the earth. When Joseph got there the blind felt undisturbed. The low, dark room was just as he had left it with the chest tucked against the wall and everything laid neatly inside. He began to think that perhaps it was someone out walking who had come in and had a careless look around on their way past, on the morning that the storm cleared. They wouldn't have thought of the things in the blind as possessions, instead they would have imagined they were discarded by the duck hunters a long time ago.

Joseph thought about this and felt better. He read for a while, a good book called *Whiskey Promises*, and then he scanned the marsh with his grandfather's binoculars. He had been seeing harriers lately, above the fields around his house. He liked how they flew with their wings firm against the up currents, turning and idling; navigating along something that he couldn't see. The very ends of their wings curled up, like a waxed moustache.

His binoculars were trained up high to find the braced shape of the harriers but as he swept across to further fields with them he caught sight of a boy on the marsh. It was a funny figure to see. The boy looked as tall as a grown man, but he was so narrow that he seemed hardly older than Joseph. He had long wisping hair like a girl's and he walked with one shoulder pitching up to his ear and dropping again.

Joseph watched through the binoculars and saw the boy advance jerkily to the marsh edge. He was a scarecrow with the stubbled fields broadening like a pan behind him. It looked like he was planning on walking straight to the duck blind and Joseph waited, tense against the wall. When the other boy got to a point where the ground went soft he stopped and kicked about idly in the reeds a bit. Then he looked up at the blind and seemed to see something. Joseph wondered if the binoculars had caught the sun and flared up. He stayed still, pressing the binoculars hard against his eye sockets. His picture of the boy through the binoculars tightened in the middle like a figure eight, draining to black around the edges. The boy looked at the blind for a while and then walked off without looking back. Joseph wondered if he didn't go any further because he was wearing good leather shoes.

As soon as Joseph saw him there on the shore he knew that it was this tall boy who had come into the duck blind. He knew that it was this boy's tusk that he was carrying in his coat. He felt sure of it and walked home thinking only about him, his long body and the funny pitching walk. No one his age had long hair, or dressed like that.

*

The next day Joseph went out to the blind again, it was a Saturday and so he left after lunch. Walking through the fields he looked behind him to see if the boy was coming. He took string with him and carried some spare planks and white paint. Again, he wore the binoculars on his chest. He was going to make a 'Keep Out' sign and as he walked across the marsh he was loaded with the planks, listing to one side with the weight of his equipment. His footprints behind him were deeper on one side, a ridge of mud pushed up by his left instep. At the blind he dropped the planks and pulled his woollen hat off, feeling heat rising from his temples. A scrape came from inside the blind, a scrape and a scuffling sound and Joseph, startled, turned to the low doorway.

He was there, the tall boy, coming out awkwardly with his head first.

'What are you doing here?' Joseph said.

'Just having a look,' the boy said. 'I left something here.' His voice was high and aggrieved sounding.

'This is my place.' Joseph tried to make his stance wider. 'I've been coming here all winter.'

'It used to be mine. My uncles built it, so did my dad.'

'That's not true.'

'It is. They're hunters.'

'There aren't any ducks here,' Joseph said. He waved an arm at the empty sky.

'Exactly, that's why I had it. Now you've got it.' The boy pushed his long hair behind his ears.

Joseph thought the boy had a strange pious face, his eyes looked like they would suit being upturned to heaven and his mouth was drawn into a pink knot. If he were at Joseph's school he would be teased for looking like a girl.

'I'll go,' the boy said. 'I thought I left something here, that's all.' He turned and began walking off.

'Wait!' Joseph called. 'What's your name?'

'Rowan,' the boy said. He had turned around.

'I'm Joseph. Did your dad really build this?'

Rowan nodded. He walked back to where Joseph stood. He seemed to be trying to control the leaping of his shoulder, tensing his jaw so a line came in his cheek.

'Is this what you left?' Joseph drew the sickle tusk from his coat pocket.

When Rowan saw it he started forward and Joseph let him take it from his open palm, feeling a small dismay as the smooth thing left him. Rowan ran his hand over the tusk almost gingerly, the way you would test the sharpness of a knife. 'So you had it,' Rowan said. But he said it to himself instead of accusing Joseph.

'Sorry,' Joseph said. 'I just wanted to know who left it.'

'I didn't mean to. I came in the storm.'

'Did your dad really help build this place?'

Rowan nodded. He was looking down at his tusk, still thoughtful. Then he looked back up to Joseph. 'He helped build it but there aren't any ducks here anymore, like you said. And you've made it better than I ever did.'

'We could share it,' said Joseph. He knew that if your father built something, you had a rightful claim to it.

'If you don't mind,' Rowan said. 'I mean, I don't.'

Then Joseph told Rowan about the harriers, how he had carried the tusk in his pocket and had seen him on the edge of the marsh in his good shoes. And Rowan told Joseph about getting caught in the storm. He said he tried to read the westerns but it was too dark, that he had tried to light the stove but the rain came in. He said he wondered about the boy who was coming out there, leaving all his things there.

Later, Rowan gave Joseph his hand to shake. His fingers were long and thin and when Joseph shook it it felt like his finger bones were loose and rolling about under the skin.

'We have to call ourselves something,' Rowan said, 'if this is going to be our place.'

There was something strange about Rowan, but Joseph thought he liked him. He talked nervously and didn't really laugh. When Joseph said something rough or teasing, the way he would talk with his brother, Rowan would frown slightly. He sat against the wall of the blind and talked instead about how you would go about angling rifles through the walls, pushing his hair behind his ears when it fell forward.

Joseph said that they could call themselves the Blind Brothers and Rowan said Brothers Blind would be better, reversing it like the Brothers Grimm. By then the sun was setting above the marsh and Joseph still hadn't gone home for dinner. The two boys leaned back against the walls and looked at each other.

'No one else can come here now,' Rowan said, 'and we're the Brothers Blind.' His eyes were grey, a strange foil colour.

Joseph remembered how that morning he had watched a grey cat pick its way across the marsh and had laughed at it, the dainty way it walked on mud. When he told her his mother had said that the cat was probably learning to catch the lace crabs.

*

After their first meeting Joseph would see Rowan in the afternoons and on the weekends. They made up ways to meet each other at the duck blind. If Joseph was to meet Rowan there he would leave a sign at the gate, usually a stick stuck up in the ground. If Joseph couldn't make it out to the blind he would take the stick and break it in half, place the two ends into a cross so Rowan would see the sign before he had walked all that distance out to the blind.

Though Rowan must have lived nearby the boys never talked about their houses. Their friendship started at the fringe of the marshes, and ended there too. Rowan was homeschooled by his mother and so could nearly always get away in the afternoon. Most days when he got home Joseph found the signal stick at his gate and, most days, he left it there instead of breaking it.

Joseph thought that it was for the best that Rowan was homeschooled because he couldn't imagine him in a normal school, folding his long legs beneath a desk or cutting his hair short. If he came pitching and tossing his way down the main drive the other boys would have no mercy.

One night at dinner Joseph's mother asked him about the boy she had seen idling at the gate, holding a long stick in his hand.

'A tall blond boy,' she said. 'Do you know him, Joseph?'

'That's Rowan,' said Joseph carelessly. 'He comes out to the blind with me sometimes.'

'Rowan,' said his mother. 'Is that Rowan Hock?'

Joseph shook his head, he didn't know Rowan's last name.

'That must be Jack Hock's son,' she said. 'He's tall like his father was, a nice face too.'

Joseph was surprised at the easy way his mother could place Rowan. He had never really thought of him as someone his parents knew of, or as part of one of the families like his that lived over the saddle, bordering the marsh.

'Is he a good friend of yours, Jo?' asked his father.

'He's all right. He's funny.'

'He's had a hard time,' said his mother.

Joseph drank his water so fast it went stiff in his throat. He didn't want to hear about Rowan like this, at least not in his mother's concerned voice.

'His father was killed hunting wasn't he?' asked Joseph's father, without looking up from his plate.

'That's what was said,' said his mother. 'But I always thought there was something funny about it.'

'I thought he was mistaken for a pig, took a bullet right through the guts.'

'We're eating,' said Joseph's mother.

'Not a nice way to go. I met him once, too. He came down with the hunters to the blind. He didn't seem the hunting sort.'

'Well the Hocks are into hunting,' said his mother. 'I wonder if he had a choice.'

Joseph excused himself and went to the bathroom, pissing out a torrent of water. When he came back in the phone was shrilling and his mother moving to pick it up. He slid into his seat.

His mother answered the phone and turned around with it held to her ear, her eyes registering surprise. 'It's Edward!' she said into the room. She flattened the fraying hairs at her hairline girlishly, leaning into the doorframe.

Joseph cleared the table slowly. His father read the newspaper, pulling the sheets tight and shaking them out after turning each page. Joseph washed the dishes like he always did, placing the plates in the rack, making a row of clean full moons. His mother's voice came through to him softly, not words but the settling and re-settling of her vowels.

When he finished the dishes he went out to the dining room.

'Edward's coming home,' said his mother when she saw him. 'He's coming home for a visit.'

'Oh,' said Joseph. 'I can show him the duck blind.'

'You can tell him about how we've banished you to the

marshland,' said Joseph's father, 'your new windy bedroom.'

'I will,' said Joseph, 'I might.'

*

'What's your brother like?' said Rowan. They were walking side by side through the marsh, passing a football back and forth.

'He's all right,' said Joseph. 'He's old.'

'How old?'

'Oh, twenty.'

'Do you like him?'

'Well he's my brother,' said Joseph. He kicked the ball to Rowan, who stopped it with his knee.

At his school Joseph had started playing soccer in the Under 15s. It was just the reserve team, but he liked it. After practice the team would wait together for their parents to come and pick them up. Joseph's father had found Edward's old shin pads and boots and had given them to Joseph. The shin pads were too big and he would undo the elastic but leave them on while he fooled around waiting to be picked up, feel them shucking up and down masterfully inside his socks.

Rowan's body would do wild things as they walked, an arm sticking straight suddenly as he ran at the ball, or his head rearing back. He could pass the ball well though, even though his body did that.

'Are you the best in the team?' Rowan asked Joseph.

'No, I'm all right though. I'm the best at being on the wing.'

'Who's the best in the team?'

'Probably Darren,' said Joseph.

Rowan liked to hear about the other boys, he wanted to know how they looked and whether they were good at school. Joseph told him that Darren would go to the A team by next season, but right then he was the star. He told Rowan how Darren had a twin sister, Melanie. They had the same curly hair and almost the same face, except hers was a sweeter version. When she came with their mother to pick Darren up from practice some of the older boys would call out 'Marry me, Melanie!' as they came in glowing from the field. Darren would run after them and hook his arm around their necks in anger, but Joseph said that he thought that Darren was proud at the same time. He told Rowan how his team called him Knuckles, because of his bony knees. It made him happy when he was flying up the side and someone would call the word out, right before the ball went hurling towards his feet.

'Do you mind?' Rowan asked. 'Being called Knuckle?'

'Knu*ckles*,' Joseph said. '*Ss*. Do you mind being called a shit sack?'

'No one does call me that,' Rowan said. He looked hurt.

'I know,' said Joseph. 'I was kidding.'

'Do Darren and Melanie look the same?'

'Yes, but Melanie's pretty.'

'Of course she is. A boy can't be pretty.'

Joseph looked at Rowan's face and thought how a boy could easily be pretty, but he would never say that out loud. 'Melanie is pretty,' Joseph said. He hefted the ball to Rowan who dribbled it thoughtfully for a while.

'And Darren's the best on the team?'

'By miles,' said Joseph. 'He'll go in the A team for sure but it's too late to switch now.'

'Does he mind?'

'Mind what?'

'Playing with the dud team?'

'We aren't the duds, you shit sack!' Joseph tackled the ball from Rowan and ran off with it, dribbling between the glasswort clumps. Gulls flew bleating overhead and Rowan launched himself after Joseph, to catch him up.

'I was making a joke,' said Rowan. He came level and grinned sidelong at Joseph.

Inside the blind they leaned back against the walls, feeling the ridges of the wood press through to their backs.

'We have to bring rifles out here,' said Rowan. 'We have to have rifles out here, poke them through the slots.' This was something he always returned to.

'There's nothing to shoot at,' said Joseph.

'We could shoot seagulls,' he said, 'or make targets.'

'We haven't got any guns.'

'There's some at my house,' said Rowan. 'My dad and my uncles, they have lots of them.'

'Do you know how to use them?'

'I've seen them used a hundred times,'

Joseph shook his head. 'There isn't anything to shoot,' he said.

Rowan opened his mouth as if to say something and then stopped. Joseph angled his head up and peered out of the vents. By then the evenings were getting lighter, the season turning toward spring. Tiny white flowers were appearing on the marsh pimpernels and he was sick of Rowan's talk about the guns. The duck blind seemed close about him, a cage, and he hunkered to a crouch and moved out of the low door.

'I'm going home,' he said, slithering out. 'We're having an early dinner.'

'Are you coming out tomorrow?' Rowan asked, still from inside the blind.

Joseph straightened up, and turned his body toward the sea. The evening was sweet and felt like a bed being made around him, the cool dome of it drifting down like a fresh sheet.

'I don't know. I've got practice tomorrow.'

Rowan followed him out and straightened up into the evening too, ending up a head and shoulders taller than Joseph. 'What about Saturday?'

'Edward's home this weekend,' he said.

They walked back together, to where the stubbled fields subsided into the marsh, and then they parted.

'Brothers,' called Rowan, when he was a stretch away from Joseph. 'Brothers Blind!'

Joseph turned and waved, but didn't say it back. He watched Rowan's tall body move away from him, hop-stepping through the needle grass.

*

After soccer practice Joseph waited with the other boys, sitting on the bleachers at the edge of the school field. He dangled his legs, looking down at where his ruddy knees disappeared into his socks.

When the station wagon pulled up to the border of the field he saw that for a surprise Edward was in the front seat. Edward wound down the window.

'Are those my boots?' he asked, as Joseph clopped up, stamping wads of grassy soil onto the concrete as he went.

'And your shin pads too,' said Joseph's father, hooking an arm out the window and giving the coach a brisk salute.

Joseph got into the back.

'Why didn't you get him new ones?' asked Edward. 'Those are too big.'

'He'll grow into them.'

'He looks like a weed,' said Edward, 'like he's got shields on his shins!'

'I like them,' said Joseph. 'They're fine.'

They drove home. Edward and his father talked about university. Joseph couldn't work out if papers were exam papers or essays. He didn't ask. He looked down at his enormous shins.

Edward had grown a dark beard. It cupped his chin and made him foreign, with his teeth chiming suddenly when he laughed. He dressed differently too. When he lived at home he just wore old T-shirts and loose jeans, spent his time disassembling bicycles in the shed, disappearing in his car on the weekends. Now he wore a buttoned shirt and tighter trousers. Joseph saw how his parents leaned into Edward's words, nodding before he had even made full sentences.

'Joseph lives out on the marsh now,' his father said after dinner. This was an old joke now, one he liked to make.

'Oh yeah?' said Edward.

'In the old duck blind,' said his father. 'He never comes home. He reeks of brine. Eats crabs for every meal.'

Edward laughed. 'I got a whiff of that in the car,' he said. He nudged Joseph who smiled tightly into his plate.

'He's made a little hut out there,' said Joseph's mother. She smiled appeasement at him. 'He won't show us it.'

'You going to take me out there, Jo?'

Joseph tucked his chin in assent.

'I'll find my old rifle,' said Edward. 'We can shoot the seagulls.'

'You wouldn't,' said his mother.

'I would,' said Edward. 'I make my own rules now.' He grinned at his mother.

Joseph looked out from under his fringe. 'You still keep your rifle here?' he asked.

The next morning Joseph woke up late. He lay in bed listening to the sounds his family made downstairs, the way the pelt of the shower could be felt in the pipes inside his wall, the measured clank of his mother putting last night's dishes away. When he got up he went directly to his bedroom window. If he angled his body right he could see down to the gate. Like he'd expected there was a long stick set in the ground at the mouth of the driveway, where the verge turned into tarmac. Rowan's doing. Joseph looked at the admonishing shape it made against the gravel.

His brother teased him for sleeping in, rustling his hair when he appeared in the kitchen. After he had eaten breakfast Joseph slipped on his father's boots that he kept beside the door and went down to the end of the driveway. His bare feet moved loosely inside the big boots, the grit inside them feeling strange on the soles of his sleepy feet. At the gate he plucked the stick from the soil and snapped it in two, laying it back down in a cross shape on the ground. Joseph thought Rowan must have come by early while he was still curled in sleep and he imagined that long figure paused at the gate, looking down the drive at the house.

Edward found the rifle in a box of his old things kept in the back of the shed. It was a long, lean shape, with potential in its length and polish. Joseph handled it carefully when his brother passed it to him, feeling unsure of what it might do of its own accord.

'You going to show me this duck blind of yours?' asked

Edward. 'We can set up like hunters.'

'Ducks don't fly over there,' said Joseph. He felt tired of explaining this.

'We can just have a go,' said Edward. 'Set up tin cans to shoot at.'

Edward looked more like his old self, wearing soft jeans he'd found in his bedroom. He had given in to being at home, the varnish slowly fading, and Joseph felt like he could nearly talk to him again.

'OK,' he said. 'But I don't want to shoot seagulls.'

'Wuss,' said his brother, but he was kidding.

They walked out along the marsh together. Edward carried the rifle and Joseph snapped off the plumy head of a toetoe and took it with him like a flag. He wore his red hat pulled down low and when Edward let him have a turn carrying the gun he swaggered with it, like a soldier.

He was anxious as they got closer to the blind, realising then that no one had ever been there apart from him and Rowan.

'I keep Granddad's binoculars out here,' he said, 'so don't tell Dad.'

'What do you use binoculars for?' said his brother. 'There's only mud to look at.'

'There's harriers here,' said Joseph. 'They hunt above the fields. I've seen them kill things.' It was true. He'd often seen them plummet down to the fields and then lift off, something held in their feet. He liked how they flew off modestly, like nothing had happened.

'We could shoot those,' said Edward.

'You can't shoot birds of prey,' said Joseph. 'It's illegal.' He didn't know if it was, but seemed likely and Edward didn't disagree.

Edward was impressed by the blind. Even though he was the same height as Rowan his big frame seemed too big for it, Joseph thought, as he watched his brother bend down and lever himself inside. Once he was in Joseph passed him the rifle and Edward eased himself over to lean against the far wall.

'This is great, Jo,' he said.

Joseph followed him in and showed him the things he kept out there, opening the chest and lifting out the camp stove, the binoculars and the blanket.

'Does Mum know you've got that out here?' asked Edward. 'She'll think you're going to set yourself on fire.'

'She already thinks I'm going to get swept out to sea.'

'This place would go up though. Like a funeral pyre.' Edward ran his hand over the wooden walls. 'Like a bier,' he said, 'like the way they burnt Achilles.'

'I don't really use the stove very often,' said Joseph.

Really, he had never used the stove but liked to have it there in case.

Edward took the binoculars and put them around his neck. He lay the rifle down on the nail box and moved forward to peer out through a chink in the walls.

'It's like a stronghold here,' he said. 'I wish we had bows and arrows.'

Joseph leaned against the wall and watched his brother scan the marsh. It did feel like a stronghold, with the two of them in there and the slim rifle laid across the nail box. The sunlight filtered into the blind through the brush laden roof and he felt its warm weight on the top of his head.

'Hang on, who's this?' said Edward. He leaned forward into the gap in the walls with the binoculars. 'Maybe it's the enemy!'

Joseph moved to his side and peered through the gap. Even without binoculars Rowan's spindly figure was clear to him. He carried something across his chest and stood at the edge of the marsh. Joseph thought of the snapped stick, waiting at the gate.

'He's got a gun!' said Edward excitedly. 'He's a weird looking kid, have a look Joseph.'

Warily, Joseph took the binoculars and looked through them. He could imagine the virtuous expression on Rowan's face, the small way he held his mouth.

'See!' said Edward. 'Do you think he'll come out here?'

'Maybe,' said Joseph. He didn't know what to say.

'He's walking, he's coming this way!' said Edward. 'I could fire a shot, give him a scare.'

'Don't,' said Joseph.

'He's got a gun too, Jo' said Edward. 'It's practically self defence.'

'Don't,' said Joseph. He watched Rowan get closer. 'I know him, that's all.'

'You know him?'

'Yeah, he's come out here a few times with me.'

'Can he take a joke?'

Joseph shrugged. 'I don't think we should shoot him, that's all.' He moved towards the entrance of the blind.

'Where are you going?'

'I'm just going to wave to him,' said Joseph. 'OK?'

Joseph stood in the mud and watched Rowan walking. When he thought he would hear him, he yelled out his name and waved. Rowan stopped and then saw him and waved back, his movements uncertain. Joseph waved again, his arm swiping. Then a gunshot split the air above the marsh and he ducked involuntarily. In his head the sound was like a tightly closed bud, flying forward. For a moment he couldn't think about who had fired and then saw the end of Edward's rifle poking upwards through the chink.

'What are you doing?' he said. Edward pushed his face out the door, grinning broadly through his new beard.

'Just making your friend jump,' he said.

Joseph looked across the salt meadow. Rowan was standing still, his face still blurred by the distance. The marsh seemed very large between them, the sedge and reeds could have been at least a hundred miles. Then Rowan moved his arms at his side, lifted and turned something.

'Holy shit!' said Edward from inside. He sounded gleeful. 'He's going for his gun!'

A second splitting shot but the bullet was angled upward and flew way over their heads. Edward moved around inside the blind.

'Don't shoot again!' said Joseph. He watched Rowan, who was still standing very still, holding the rifle out in front of him. He wondered what Rowan thought was happening; who he imagined was firing at him.

The marsh seemed silent after the shots and Joseph took a deep shaky breath, held in the smell of salt and mud. Now that the weather was getting warmer he had noticed that the marsh smelled almost sulphurous. On warm days there were constellations of tiny flies that moved above the still water. With one thing and another, Joseph didn't imagine he would come out here much longer. He saw Rowan turn around and begin walking away. His walk seemed stately, even though his shoulder skipped to his ear. The marsh broadened around him.

'He's going,' said Edward.

'Yes,' said Joseph.

'When you see him, tell him I didn't mean to scare him,' said Edward.

'I will,' said Joseph, 'I might.'

Tane Thomson

Kuki the Krazy Kea

My first real success was *Kuki the Krazy Kea*. For a while, i.e. in development stage, after the usual treatment and page-dimensioning processes, it was *Kurly the Kooky Kea*, but I was never convinced that would catch on and sales have proved me right. That bird! You could say he gave me my start in life. Yes, KKK as I call him went down very well, aside from the school teacher complaints. So, you know—all good.

Then in the early 90s Jack Lasenby brought out *Charlie the Cheeky Kea* and it was all over for Kuki.

So I wrote poems for a while.

After that I burst back onto the kidzlit scene with a YA number. Or it could have been a cross-over work, it was certainly read by several adults of my acquaintance. That was *The Rugby Girls*. The stuff those girls got up to! Then I did a picture book, *Robert the Rugby Rugrat*, with some pictures that looked as if they might be photographs.

Then I rewrote some Rider Haggard novels with many sex scenes inserted and made a lot of money.

Then I thought I would hang out with Margaret Mahy down near Christchurch, but that came to nothing. I had never used a public library in my life, all I knew was Enid Blyton, and MM as I call her was totally unimpressed by my new-found wealth, so we really had nothing to talk about; and to be honest there were just too many aspiring or minor children's writers around the place—crowds of them digging her garden, doing her washing, demanding endorsements, dressing up as pirates. I thought I would go and try Joy Cowley, but I got lost in the Marlborough

Sounds. The outboard motor just cut out. Anyway, I heard later that she was already spoken for. By an ex priest! So I gave up and went back to Tīmaru. I almost met Jack Lasenby at a festival in Christchurch but got sick of standing in the signing queue. Kate De Goldi did not answer my letters.

One day a very fat man went by on a skateboard. He did that leaping thing that people do. Well, that gave me an idea or two. Fresh material is everywhere.

Skinky the Skateboarding Skunk!

Or should that be Skanky, I wondered? Answer: *It depends on the market.*

Stanley the Stubborn Stoat.

Porky the Podgy Pūkeko.

~~*Tui the Tempestuous Tūi.*~~

Anyway, I changed my name to Tane Thomson and sales rocketed.

I moved on to *Wanda the Wonky Wētā*. Then I did some yoga classes, just to meet people, after which I wrote *Downward Dog*, the less said of which the better.

Except . . . big hit?

You bet. *Big* hit.

About this time I started having my invisibility dreams, and I wrote a sad story called *The Last Huia*, which had the whole nation in tears. At first it was about *Henry the Hopeless Huia*, but one day I was struck by a melancholy thought, and out it just poured, the whole tragedy of loss.

I wrote a story about children who had a pirate party only a real pirate came along and made them all walk the plank. Things were happy in the end, though.

Then I had the big success with *The Hairy Plane* which went around the world. He flew everywhere, with his friend the Dandy Lion, having adventures. South Pole, North Pole, the parched Sahara Desert. This made me very wealthy, of course, though I believe I wear my wealth, like my success, lightly.

The conference on my work was interesting—flattering, of course, especially the man from Canterbury University who did a Lacanian analysis of Kuki the Krazy Kea, which referred to an earlier study of my story by Patrick Evans that I had never even heard of!

Next came *Tanya the Two Timing Tūī*, which certainly sorted Tanya out. What a bitch. I had to have another invisibility dream.

But the conference gave me new confidence. I wrote letters to Elizabeth Knox, but she didn't answer a single one of them. I considered going round to her house.

Then my musical *Erewhon* became a world-wide hit.

Everything went backwards.

I mean, why don't you all fuck off.

Tayi Tibble

Diary of a (L)it Girl or, Frankenstein's Ghost Pig

When I was in Year 9, I had my first taste of irrelevant stardom by way of making the 1st XI Soccer team—a rarity for freshmen. This achievement resulted in attention: proud Kiwi slaps on the back but also some Kiwi side-eye, but both made me determined to *work hard, play hard*. However, I spent approximately 3/4 of every game benched, and it was decided that I should go play for the 2nd XI team, so I could have a go on the field.

My reputation as a glorified waterboy preceded me, and I was welcomed into the 2nd XI team like a star. I got my pick of positions and everyone always passed me the ball. The problem was that everyone always passed me the ball. The more the ball was passed to me the more aware I became of the pressure. People, whether it was warranted or not, were counting on me.

This all came to a head during a specific match against, idk, Chilton Saint James School. I captured the ball in the midfield, stepped out a player and passed the ball. The ball was passed back, and I got past another player and passed the ball. Once again the ball came back, and I made it past another two players and all my teammates were, like, *wtf!!!!* but in a good way and passed me the ball.

Having never experienced an exercise-related endorphin in my life, this was why I even bothered to play a sport. I did it for the camaraderie, the energy; all of our ur hopes, dreams, victories and regrets thick and electric in the air, like 5G. In that moment, an ancient compulsion moved me. It told me to do the mahi. I thought, āe. If the ball was passed to me, then the ball was mine. I decided to go the last stretch, take it up to the box and get that goal. I bossed up, dribbled a few paces, then immediately lost it. Some stocky blond sweeper with Dutch braids captured it and sent it right back to our defense with a single mighty horse kick. The entire team let out a unanimous, heartbreaking groan. My coach called me a ball hog, and pulled me off the field.

And ever since that match I have been haunted by a sphinx-like creature with a translucent hog body and a soccer ball head. It appears at random times, to boo at me. Once, a sexy Spanish man asked me to dance with him and because I was a redacted amount of margaritas in I did, but it wasn't very far into grinding to 'Gasolina' when he hissed at me to let him lead and dropped his hands from my waist in frustration. The thought *ball hog* slapped me off the dancefloor.

I was so terrified that I went home and visited a wise tohunga (my mum) hoping they might dip my head into a water trough, or give me some greens to sage my home. Instead they decided that I needed to confront a specific childhood trauma: my sister's first birthday.

It's late summer, 2001. February 20th, to be exact. Shavaughn Ruakere is on What Now *and my mother's ringtone is a bells and whistle version of 'Angel' by Shaggy. Nana is in the kitchen whipping cream for the cake and Aniqueja is sat on Grandad's lap, all rosy and adorable. Grandad is reading Aniqueja her new picture book, something about a duckling who wants to go rollerskating with some frogs, one of her many, many 1st birthday presents. It looks like a warm and wholesome scene, but there is a dark force in the room. The dark force is me.*

Like most traumas I have repressed it and don't remember much, but apparently I am so disturbed by jealousy, and also quite sure of my own stardom, that I am compelled to start hopping, and I mean like, literally and lamely hopping on one leg, demanding that Grandad stop playing with Aniqueja and 'look at what I can do' instead. Mum says that this was the first time she was properly embarrassed that I was her child and it certainly wasn't the last time.

I hate this story and I hate myself in this story and every time it surfaces, which it does quite often, I wish Mum had slapped me and furthermore I wish I could've been there to slap myself. At home, if I accidentally talk over someone—which is very easy to do when you're one of seven big-lipped bitches—at least two sisters will roll their eyes and say 'look what I can do' out of the corners of their mouths. It's a cheap move, like button bashing the controller while playing Tekken, because instantaneously, without getting a kick in, I am dishonoured and defeated.

TLDR: Basically, if I was MK Ultra'd by the Illuminati as I one day hope to be, 'Ball Hog' or 'Look what I can I do' would be the safe word/down phrase my handlers would use if they ever needed to brainwash me back into submission.

I've been thinking about what I can do which is apparently hogging the ball because I was at a book awards recently eating fry bread and caviar like the bougie native that I am when a friendly face materialised and asked me what it was like to be living the dream. I accidentally sucked a fish egg down my windpipe. I was highkey wrecked from being too tu meke at the Jess B gig the night before. I was also on my shy buzz and wylin' in front of Carol Hirschfeld and Stacey Morrison, the OG bougie natives. I assumed they must be referring to the food, because if the dream is a world in which Māori and Pākehā can engage in mutually beneficial and reparative relationships that enhance the world, then yes, without a doubt, fry bread topped in caviar and cream is the height of that dream, but when I said, 'Mmmm mean oi,' they said, 'How was Europe?' and 'Gee your book seems to be doing so well.' Essentially they were giving me the Kris Jenner, *You're doing amazing sweetie.*

So like the good Māori girl that I am I immediately felt shameful. If I had less melanin in my skin, my cheek would have reddened. Out of the corner of my eye I could see Frankenstein's ghost pig booing *ball hog, ball hog, ball hog* at me. I covered my mouth politely and exaggerated my chewing. I was buying time as I mentally sifted through the details of my recent trip: the Edinburgh Book Festival, the VUW Alumni reading in London, fun in Paris with Annaleese. More importantly, I thought about the photographic evidence of the trip: me laughing while straddling a cannon, me looking sunkissed while strolling the Thames, me actin' Parisian while in Paris. Then, for good measure, I thought about some of the un-instagrammable actualities of the trip like the food poisoning I gave myself cooking dead animal with salmonella tongs or the late-night drinks where I was encouraged to talk to international agents who barely acknowledged my existence, which may or may not be related to the fact that one of them also thought that Māori were extinct. I thought about all these things until finally, the big payoff for all that chewing, sifting, thinking and stalling, I swallowed and said, 'Yeah it was cool.' I heard a cricket and thought, weird time of year.

I watched that friendly face droop with disappointment. I might have seen their lip curl. They offered a polite smile, but a specific kind of polite smile that you only really give to someone you think is a real dick. I felt as though I had confirmed something for them which also confirmed it for me: the dream was wasted on me. I felt like a hog who shouldn't have been passed the ball. They peeled off and made their way towards the kiwifruit juice.

This is not the first time I have been asked this question or something similar and it's definitely not the first time I have had the same limp reaction. Weird flex but it's sort of like when I get referred to as a star or a literary it-girl. I think, *that's hot*, because I love Paris Hilton and vanity is a dark-sided Libra trait, but the thrill is also accompanied with a specific kind of awkwardness. It is an awkwardness that stems from our national allergy to tall poppies and the noxious fumes we all inhale from living in the land of the long white colonial shame; the shame of recognition, the shame of *wanting* to be recognised. Which is why every trip, literary festival, panel, reading, editorial position, hint of quasi fame that I get the slightest whiff of amongst the same ten people who attend book launches in this country, is both thrilling and terrifying; like I'm back on that soccer field. Even when I'm preparing a pic for Instagram, I find myself scoffing 'look what I can do' like a self-flagellating disciple. I think these things, fret, hesitate, wait for my coach to yell at me, but then, almost always, I upload it anyway.

TLDR: Despite not always feeling like that bitch she continues to be that bitch.

I was having a coconut gelato cocktail and a mini debrief with my e hoa Nicole recently, following the Te Hā National Māori Writers Hui. She was filling me in about a session I missed in which Patricia Grace, in conversation with Renée, mentioned that even with her most revered and popular works, like *Pōtiki*, she felt as though she had fluked it. My reaction to this was weirdly defensive. I thought *impossible* and *ridiculous*. But then I started thinking about imposter syndrome, how I've experienced it, and how it is almost impossible not to feel like an imposter when you're the only non-white voice in a journal, or brown face in a room. Or maybe, there is another brown face at the reading, but it's the bro serving the drinks and you make eye contact and the overwhelming feeling of stink makes your voice crack while you read your poem which you now recognise as having an ironic tone. You don't know how you didn't notice it before. I know because *E! True Hollywood Stories*, it happened to me.

Sometimes the most powerful revelations are the most obvious ones. It's a cool feeling, being so braindead that the smallest eureka is like being defibrillated back to life. I was fully shook as I thought about how weird vibes it would be, to be not only one of the few brown faces in a room, but the actual first brown face to pull up. Ever. In history. It occurred to me then that there was no Patricia Grace for Patricia Grace to look up to. Patricia didn't get to grow up self-identifying as one of the sleeping cousins while reading *The Kuia and the Spider* or writing essays on 'The Geranium' at high school. But I did and I am so lucky that I did. If I was in that position, writing into the dark/white world, the first published wahine writer, ever, I can easily imagine that the whakamā and imposter syndrome probably would have paralysed me.

I worry about whakamā and imposter syndrome paralysing our people, making them too afraid or inhibited to really live their best lives or at least the best lives they can under the hellskies of capitalism and party politics. I'm all about the people, and I'm all about the best lives.

At the end of 2018 I was named one of New Zealand's most fabulous people by *Viva* magazine and I can't front, I was Beyoncé x Nicki Minaj feelin' myself, because I don't serve these outfits like I'm working in a diner for nothing, and also because Kanoa Lloyd and Rose Matafeo gave me the follow back, OG bougie natives. However, in the write-up it said 'she doesn't indulge in fake modesty'. They asked me why I was so confident. I was like, *sounds fake but okay,* but what came out of my mouth was 'my mother'.

I told the magazine that she 'grounds me' and 'helps me keep my big head on my shoulders' and 'looking in the right direction'. It's true, she does, mostly by way of mocking me with tales of tantrums past, but she also encourages me to 'do the mahi' so that her own mahi pays off.

I think about all the things that my mother and foremothers have done for me, but I also think about all the things they couldn't do. I think about their lives, the stories they have told me. I think about the ways they have had to internalise their experiences of inequality and assimilate, in order to get on with minimal harassment, in order to avoid bringing attention to themselves. I think about how my mother and my Nana have never left the country. Maybe they never cared to. For a long time I didn't care to, but it also didn't seem like a possibility. It always seemed like a privilege that for whatever colonial reasons I never entertained. But now that I have been, I wonder if they ever wanted to. I feel guilty and afraid to ask.

I was sick in London, and spent the majority of that time killing the vibe. However, on the day before we were to leave for Paris, I felt a little better and caught the train to meet Annaleese at the Tate Modern. I sat outside on the grass, waiting for her to arrive and felt deliriously happy. The sun was out and I could stomach fluids—simple yet underrated pleasures. Afterwards, we walked along the river and I asked Annaleese to take a photo of me and like a good bitch she took a lot. There is one photo in particular, a b-side where I am looking off to the side, all natural and candid and unposed and upon seeing it, I didn't recognise myself at all. I saw my Nana. Another very obvious yet powerful revelation struck me and in that moment I was almost moved to tears, overwhelmed by the realisation that I am my ancestors and my ancestors are me. And despite a history of colonisation, alienation, annihilation, here they were, facing up to this notorious city, alive, Māori as, and smiling in a photo. And, even if only for a moment, I felt properly proud of myself in my entirety, all my work, history, whakapapa, I looked around just in case, but the ghost hog was nowhere to be found.

TLDR this entire essay: I feel some kind of way about being the editor of this edition of Sport *due to multiple childhood and colonial traumas, a lack of Māori representation in literature and the publishing industry generally, a culture of shame and shaming that makes people struggle with feeling deserving plus the desire to be a good humble girl that it sometimes feels in conflict with, but not necessarily exclusive to, my badgal Rihanna vibes. But also yolo, I have aroha in my heart and I'm really out here riding for our writers and our stories and our kulture with tears in my eyes like a biker with a poetic heart in a Lana Del Rey Music plus 4 kaupapa, and my campaign to #makenewzealandswagagain, more balls 4 everyone to hog I reckon, and I love our edition of* Sport.

I'm proud to present to you this edition of *Sport*. I hope you find that this edition is particularly gang, hot and flossy. Thank you to everyone who has trusted me with their mahi; your words are the only vibe check I need. In this issue, I made no concerted effort to make sure a 'wide range of diverse voices were represented' so in this issue you will find a 'wide range of diverse voices represented'. I am deeply honoured and highly hyped to include words from literary kaumātua like Patricia Grace, as well as words from fresh af writers who, in *Sport 47*, will be making their iconic sporting debut. And actually, in true ball hog fashion, it's my *Sport* debut too.

Giovanni Tiso

Badly written men

The line comes from a *Sydney Morning Herald* review of *The Story of the Lost Child*, the fourth and last chapter of Elena Ferrante's Neapolitan cycle. With but one exception the men in the story, opines reviewer Mark Twefik, 'are all needy losers whose recourse to action is either pleading, infidelity or violence.' He concludes: 'How much better would these books be if Ferrante had paid more than lip-service to the men.'

I wouldn't be the first person to observe that this statement completely misses the point of Ferrante's work. It misses in fact several points. Yes, Elena and Lila, the protagonists, are 'full of life and complexity', as Twefik puts it, while the portrayal of the men who surround them is a function of the respective roles in the lives of the two women. But that's what being a protagonist, or 'chief actor', means. You could say the same of the other women in the books, some of whom play at various times the role of antagonists.

The four novels have a first-person narrator, Elena, and another character so central at times as to almost become a first person herself, Lila. Being the story of two women whose main preoccupation, from a very young age, is to govern their own lives—a fact which would be unremarkable in a male-driven story—this first-personhood becomes not just a narratological but a thematic fact as well. Suppose Ferrante had chosen to have the books narrated by a third-person omniscient voice. Would we be tempted to assign it a gender, because of the gender of the writer or of the protagonists? And would this shift affect our desire, as readers, to spend some time in the company of the other characters, both male and female?

These questions aren't very interesting, not for us. They might have been at times during the historical time spanned by the novels, as testified by the prurient reception of Elena's own autobiographical book, written and published in the early to mid-60s, or by Lila and

Elena's childhood interest in *Little Women* and its overt moral lessons, or by the content of Elena's second book, a narrative reflection on the concept of womanhood as invented by men, from the Christian creation myth onwards. However, in contemporary Italy—the Italy in which the fictional Elena writes the cycle, firmly in the past tense, as a woman in her mid to late sixties—that the story of two women should be written, from childhood to adulthood, is unremarkable, and need not be justified.

Mr Twefik's complaint that Ferrante pays lip service to her men in this respect is a sign of the residual confusion or discomfort that undoubtedly exist, but not a criticism that should be taken seriously. I find the second part of his equation far more interesting. The men in these novels are pathetic, violent, cheating losers, he grumbles. What are we to make of it?

In the picture, my mother's best friend is posing rigidly, in a mock-military stance. She is standing in front of an apple orchard but for some reason she is dressed like a sailor. I doubt she would have come close to seeing the sea at the age of 7 or 8, when the picture was taken. The year is scribbled on the back of the photograph in my mother's hand: 1939. I like to imagine that it was Mum who took it, although I doubt that she did.

I don't have any pictures of the two of them together, but at this age they were still inseparable, as they remained even after my mother graduated from primary school and enrolled at high school in a nearby town, where she commuted by bicycle every day. Not her friend, however. The other picture I carry of her in my head is actually a description of my mother's, of how some years later this lively young woman who smiles at me in the sailor's costume used to return from the fields during the rice-picking season so utterly exhausted that her face and eyes looked lifeless, or better devoid of intelligence, like an animal's: beastly labour made flesh.

My mother and her friend grew up in the south-eastern corner of Lombardy, near the Po river, in the 'Little World' romanticised by Giovanni Guareschi in his *Don Camillo* series, which was every bit as popular fifty years ago in the English-speaking world as Ferrante's Neapolitan novels are today. Now, however, I find myself more inclined to overlay the geographically and culturally distant story of Elena and Lila with theirs. Not just because of the superficial similarities—one girl stayed in school, the other didn't; one woman got to leave her hometown, the other didn't—but because of the social order in which they were born, and that Ferrante dissects so efficiently.

While in the small rural village in the North of Italy it expressed itself in a different vernacular and through different gestures than in the big Southern city, this order was equally entrenched and archaic. My mother sometimes joked that she was born in the Middle Ages, but it wasn't really a joke in the land where farm labourers had to barter days of work for the privilege of spending the coldest winter evenings in the barn to partake of the heat emanating from the master's cows.

This order was also deeply patriarchal. My mother knew that none of the boys from land-owning families who asked her out would ever marry her; one of them talked about the land-owning girl he had set his sights on even while courting Mum. There was no need to dissimulate the fact that only the poor married for love, just as everyone knew that sex before marriage—or instead of marriage—sometimes had consequences for the women, but never for the men.

My grandfather was something of an exception: he got his girlfriend pregnant at the age of 16 and went on to marry her, even though she came from a farm labouring family and had been orphaned of her mother, while he owned no land but came from a family of tailors, which created something of a social gap. In other respects, however, he was a man of his time. He was a Fascist, like most of his contemporaries. He beat his son, like most fathers.

Meanwhile, it was from the men of their own generation that my mother and her friend had to guard against. Educated women were not prized as potential wives in a farming community, which would have helped Mum as she negotiated her way out of the Little World. Her friend, who had no such prospects, got pregnant. Her story is not mine to tell, but it is not very long and it does not end well.

I do not know who these men were, except they were clearly not the noble, laconic heroes of Guareschi's stories, just as Ferrante's men aren't the exuberant, life-loving imps of stock Neapolitan comedy. The patriarchal culture over which they presided, of which they were the agents and foot soldiers, wrote them badly. Were it they had been more complex, more nuanced. Were it they aspired to a qualitatively different life, not just for themselves but also for their wives and daughters. And oh, how much easier and happier would life have been, for my mother but especially her friend, if their recourse to action had been anything other than pleading, infidelity and violence.

I have always asked myself where my mother—who grew up during Fascism with few books and only the state radio to report on national affairs—can possibly have found the strength and the intellectual models to imagine a different life for herself, even before she took the concrete steps that turned that project into a reality. Ferrante's novels dramatise a conflict that no doubt she had to go through but that I never witnessed. By the time she had me, at the then quite late age of 40, she was a first person, in full control of her life to the extent that anyone could be, and was at peace with the world she had left behind but that we visited often.

Until the very end, that is, when she decided—or was forced by the circumstances—to go back, and spend what was to be the last year of her life in a rest home not far from the old village. Whatever social progress took place outside of those walls, it had not found its way inside, among her contemporaries, who still espoused those same values, and didn't see real worth in anything other than working the land and being part of the old order. She was back among the badly written men, although this time it was on her terms and anyway, to paraphrase Elena, her life by now had been lived, so it didn't matter.

Steven Toussaint

Mount Eden

Six pips
when the apparently real

grace relents
and the morning news begins

a mother's voice
pitchless in the day's chorale.

Grief so total
it resembles abundance

chastened
by the paradox of surplus

in a very bad year.
Exchanging

one indifferent signal
for another

you adjust
your figment's threshold

a pinnate leaf's width
on the dial

to find the season's violence
sensible again

repeated
in the weather whisperer's

impartial mysticism.
Such severe

report
like fanfare as you push

the leaves from yard to yard
all because

a little air has left the world.
The warnings turn

to traffic
and you to the sweeping under

blank façades
where later you will shake the olive

and the bay
and you will gather up

their bloodless panes
anything to stretch this needless

peace another hour.
The trees are not deciduous

enough.

Chris Tse

Infernally yours, gentleman poet in the streets
—raging homosexual in the sheets

Every gay is Halloween and the best-selling costume is
'sexy heterosexual'. Peek out your aggressively conservative
middle-class windows and you'll see the gay agenda in
action—Instagram thirst traps marching through your streets
demanding their share of free candy. Remember those novelty
pens you tip upside down and the clothes fall off a busty lady?
Tip me upside down and watch my skin fall at your feet, then
throw my homosexual skin into a rusty oil drum roaring with
the heat of a thousand flaming queens during Pride Week. I
have survived a lifetime of designing my own private Inferno—I
dare you to take it from me. And for those of you still in
doubt—of course we have an agenda! How else will smart-
casual rompers become a thing?

If you're disgusted or questioning your own skin, I invite you
to write to your MP. Write to the internet. Write and vent until
someone steps in to save us from our collective fixation on
skin—the wearing of, its propensity for itching and infection, its
unforgiveable necessity and what we argue it stands for. Make it
clear that being named 'best dressed' means nothing when you
wear your diamonds at breakfast, that we make-believe until
we make it something to obliterate. I resent nostalgia, especially
when I have a reputation to destroy. I'd rather set the crown
on fire and watch it melt, until the plastic lump in my hands
is a trophy I can take to bed with me, fusing with my skin
overnight, a shrunken inconvenience to remind me of every
single grudge I've nurtured and slept with just to spite myself.

Oscar Upperton

Department of Immigration

The second home is always in the shadow of the first.
We are far from music. We listen to the birds.
We are far from chocolate. We fast.
We are far from the sea. We dig lakes in the back paddock.

Father says, *Imagine you are in a forest.*
You have an axe. You have a knife.
What are you going to do now?

There was once a dance in a vege garden,
a boat as a present, a smooth upshoot of bubbles in a glass.
There was a way of saying that was like giving.
We do not talk this way now.

Mother says, *Imagine you are naked.*
You have one shadow between you.
What are you going to do now?

We are not committing to this horizon.
The ocean will sedately swallow us.
You can't expect us to make for that horizon.
We are just weathering a tempest here.

Father says, *Imagine you are solid.*
A stranger's hand is on your shoulder.
Imagine you are waiting.
What are you going to do now?

New transgender blockbusters

If we put on makeup the camera won't linger
and we'll change our clothes out of frame
or if we change our clothes in frame it will be done casually,
talking as we shrug T-shirts over our heads
or pulling on the spacesuit to try to fix the loose coupling
one last time. We won't die, or if we die,
we'll die surrounded by our grandchildren, handing out
    bequests
of stolen property and vowing vengeance on rival families.
We'll travel in time, and save the world,
and doom the world but not in an earthquake-causing,
crime-against-nature sort of way.
We'll have transgender friends and family members,
the frame of the film sustaining with ease the image
of trangender people talking to each other.
We'll all be very very brave
because being a person requires great bravery,
and we won't have to wear signs around our necks saying I am a
    Person.
We'll become immune to all tropes, and win every prize.
If we find a gun under the floorboards in the first act,
we will bring world peace by the fourth act.
If we open our lockets to show the platoon a photograph of our
    loved one,
we'll be guaranteed to survive until the end credits.

Rae Varcoe

Asylum Notes

If you have ever made porridge for a hundred with
the assistance of three ancient asylum patients
you'll understand how it was each Seacliff dawn
stirring the steaming, resistant oats as the light fell
on the bars, the Brick and the nurses scurrying over
the grass each draped in a red cape and wading through

a layer of mist. The cries from the Brick rose through
the window bars, ejected along with
any objects small enough to heave over
the high sills. These were the patients
whose nursing care eventually fell
into my frightened hands. It did dawn

on me, that a solitary nurse on a dark dawn
morning, moving, keys clanking, through
the dirty dayroom could in one fell
swoop on her starch stiffened person, with
even a sheet in the patient's
hand, and good timing, be easily over-

come. Even after years, I never quite got over
that fear. On night duty in the hours before dawn
I would, as instructed, 'Lavitate the patients,
Nurse', then listen to distorted voices echo through
the long corridors. Outside, there was bricked-up silence with
little interruptions as Matron's emptied bottles fell

singly into the rubbish tin. It sometimes fell
to her to admonish the inebriate admissions over
at Ladies' Reception. She always ate two fried eggs with
bacon for breakfast. On the Aga at dawn

in my turn, I would cook and deliver them through
her window. I never did master the Aga. The patients

tried to teach me that art. They had patience,
but I was distracted by the tobacco that fell
in clumps from the Zig Zag papers through
my fingers as I rolled ciggies for them. Over
the years I learned to roll with either hand from dawn
to dusk, licking, flicking, and lighting with

nonchalance. Through all this the patients
moved, some in hope, back home. Others fell
ill for always, never over it, never aware of any dawn.

Catherine Vidler

Haunted sestina

Haunted sestina beckons but offers no exit.
Spooky how a line can be so like a corridor,
words a conservatory of cobwebs,
rhythm a heartbeat knocking at the door.
The dining room table is long and dusty, its party
ages like a portrait, and isn't it spooky

how the grandfather clock has a voice, spooky
how poems don't always let you leave, the exit
drowned out by the organ's merry waltz, the party
dancing down an endless corridor,
obscuring the door,
the attic window blinded by cobwebs.

Where have all the spiders gone? Cobwebs
hang in the air like a chill, like spooky
bouquets, they're crowding the door,
and where is the exit?
An unseen person cries down the corridor:
This poem is a hall of mirrors, a party

with no guest of honour, a party
littered with deceased meanings, cobwebs . . .
Candles burn their predictions into the wall, the corridor
grins with amusement, it's spooky
how paper alone can disable an exit
and whoever heard of a house with no door?

Ghosts cluster like metaphors, clouding the door,
the cellar is swollen with monstrous memories, the party
refrains from discussing the exit.

Madam unfetters her tresses of cobwebs,
her crystal ball swarms with allusions, it's spooky
how poems are traps made for unwary words, the corridor

echoes the rap of her fingers, the corridor
shakes like a terrified door.
Lightning flashes, the reading begins with a clap, so spooky,
dead poets are risen and felled. The party
collapses, the clock tolls thirteen, countless cobwebs
weave poetry over the exit:

Haunted sestina, a party of cobwebs,
Haunted sestina, no exit, no door,
Haunted sestina, spooky corridor.

Louise Wallace

The feijoas are falling from the trees

The feijoas are falling from the trees—
a fresh bag-load every day.

Winter is on its way.
I am in the kitchen
shucking feijoas like oysters—
filling ice-cream containers to freeze.

Won't it be nice to eat them in July?
Rory is a good man, who hates feijoas.

I see a strong gust outside
and I imagine the sound of a feijoa falling.
Crashing into branches on its way down,
waiting to be plucked
from the leaves and soil.

Winter is on its way.
I try to think of how I could earn
more money; work harder, get ahead.
There is never enough
and it would be nice to get ahead.

I write a list of all the things
I need to make—
stewed feijoas, feijoa crumble—
another gust: feijoa cake.

Damien Wilkins

The World of Children's Books

This all happened on a writers' tour of the Far North. It was our day off and we drove to the top of the Island. And do you know, there really is a lighthouse up there. We walked around it. Then we went back to the van and drove to the beach for a swim. The day was hot and windless and blue.

After our swim, we sat on the beach, with our bruises. That sea, we said. We'd all been dumped by waves, sucked and tossed. You stood on the steep shelf and felt a few thousand little stones move away under you. It took some effort to stay upright.

Tina said, I didn't know Gavin was a good swimmer. Neither did I, said Kate.

But he was out beyond the breakers. You could see his feet, then his head. He was long, like a stick, careless as timber, floating and drifting.

You think he's all right? said Kate.

He's playing silly buggers, said Tina. My husband does things like that.

Then we heard the faintest shout over the surf and we walked down to the water. Carl was just coming in; his chest was scraped. He said, I've had enough of this. We said we had too. Great though, he said and we agreed. It was invigorating. It was a great violent swim full of stones and we were hungry.

Gavin's staying out there a long time, said Kate.

Carl looked out to sea; he wasn't wearing his glasses. They were up by his towel. Is he out there, he said.

Then we heard the shout again, even weaker. I don't like it much, said Kate.

No, I said. It's a bit strange he never told us he was a good swimmer.

Why don't you go and get him, Carl, we said. Do you think he's in trouble? said Carl.

Yes, we said. Hurry now.

Carl had done life saving. There was no one else in our group who could swim like that.

Every school holidays, Carl re-wrote kids' stories such as The Three Little Pigs and Cinderella for the theatre. I remember thinking, God, maybe I could do that. Carl said he made enough money from these productions to finance his other writing. A nice guy, plus with skills. Point me in the right direction, he said. I'm blind as a bat.

So we lined him up with where we thought Gavin was, and Carl ran back into the sea.

Then we watched as Carl saved Gavin's life.

When Carl brought Gavin in, we laid him on the beach. He was grey, almost metallic, and he looked older, skinnier, shinier. He was panting. We covered him up and said take it easy and you gave us a scare, Gavin.

Gavin said, I'm not sure if I'll be able to drive the van any more today.

We told him not to worry, we'd drive the van. What he had to do was rest.

In the van we were all quiet. Gavin said, I think I had another two minutes. Tops. I didn't know which way I was facing and every time I tried to look, I lost all my energy. I tried to shout but I swallowed water. How stupid it would have been. On such a beautiful day, having seen the lighthouse and everything.

I was ready to punch you, said Carl. But you were a good person to save.

What were you thinking about out there? someone said. Your life and stuff?

Gavin was a children's book illustrator, well-known. A real artisan. Famously particular, exact, diligent. The previous month, another of the top picture book artists, and a friend of Gavin's, had died. She'd lived in a house filled with dolls, which seems like a cliché about the person who devotes her life to children's books. Nevertheless it was true; Gavin had visited the house. Her work featured photo-realistic drawings of children eating ice creams or riding on their father's shoulders. These pictures often caught the child's face just before or just after some moment of pure emotion: joy or fright or surrender.

The images were very much like those recorded by cameras when the shutter is pressed too soon or too late; the photos which are discarded. Pages, then, of children whose faces showed confusion, awkward concentration, or some odd and fleeting private struggle. I always thought these books were a little creepy and hurried my own kids away from them in bookshops or libraries. She'd even written one called *A Day at the Beach*.

I was thinking, said Gavin, of my friend who died. I thought first her and now me. I said to myself, that's going to leave a big hole in the world of New Zealand children's books, for a while at least, until some new talent comes through, as it always does. Then Gavin laughed. Plus I was thinking of Tom Thumb, he said. Six months of my life I've spent drawing that Tom Thumb, almost going blind, drawing that tiny creature, peeping out from behind egg cups, running along people's fingers. Six months with a magnifying glass and a brush made up of about three fucking bristles.

Gavin never swore, or not that we'd heard him. He'd taught art in the best private schools. He was tall and somewhat immaculate.

We drove up the road away from the beach under the same blue sky we'd driven in under. Not a sign anywhere of our crisis. People were still entering the surf. We passed the outdoor shower where two women in their underwear were washing themselves. They were both blonde and tanned. It was easy to imagine them as Swedish. Carl and I looked at the women through the van's windows. Kate said to us, it's good to know that even a near-death experience doesn't change the basic male need for a good perv.

It was getting dark when we reached town. We bought fish and chips at a seaside restaurant, and sat outdoors at trestle tables that were set up on a wooden platform, a kind of pontoon thing built out over the water. It rocked gently. The sea through the wooden slats was oily black.

Fish and chips! said Gavin. I didn't think I'd want them but I do. He ate a piece of fish and smiled a bit sadly, or maybe that was just us, looking at Gavin as if he'd changed.

Thing is, Gavin, we said, worst case scenario today, *they* could have been having *you* for dinner.

We all laughed with our mouths full, full of the sea, which sounded all around us and underneath us. Then Gavin brought out a double- page spread he'd been working on from his book. He said, can you find him? Who can find him? For the first person who can find him, I'm buying them a drink. The light wasn't good for the search but we bent into the page. We leaned in close so our elbows were touching and our shoulders. And we all looked for him. We looked everywhere.

Memoir, with Electrodes

He admitted, under torture—
And they were very good
At torture—that he'd once seen
His father's penis. Attentive to his own

Testicles, they paused. Oh yes? And
What was he doing to you
At the time? I was in the bath. Go on,
What disgusting thing happened

Next? Okay, he said. Deep breath.
In real life, his father walked
Out, having had a piss. Humming
From an opera, quite an elaborate

Hum. Quite a handsome penis,
He thought, even then. Not shocking.
Comforting. That was all, a kid
In a bath, learns something.

But this wasn't real life.
He was being tortured. His prostate
Was animate. What next?
His imagination failed and he
Told the boring truth. *Zap!*

Then, as if the current carried memory
As well as pain, he remembered
Another thing: his mother's breast.
A single breast, in profile. Was he a baby?

It was full—of milk meant for him?—pale, lightly
Blue-veined. I saw my mother's breast, he told them.
Christ, you disgust us. What next with the cock and
Titties? He thought carefully. He tried to bring them

Together, this couple. He didn't know
Where they were. Perhaps they were
Dead already, somewhere. They the begetters.
It was cold outside. It was getting dark. It was begetting

Dark. But a light went on, a morning light.
Two figures skating to school, across
The frozen milky lake. She was such a good
Skater, travelling low, at first

I thought she was a boy, his father said.
The cold, the heavy coat, your
Thick swinging arms, the hat with flaps,
The rough scarf wound and wound

Concealing your chubby red face. And
At home your mother, remember, cooking—
They flared, coming to the surface
Like little doughy submarines, spitting oil —

What were they, those things we used to eat?
Those things we used to love.
Those things we used to hate.

Faith Wilson

I'm out for dead presidents to represent me

My words ain't worth shit
and since I was a girl I was told
to put my money where my mouth is.

As a brown kid in Aotearoa it was all bout
dem dollar dollar bills yo, even though they
became defunct in '91.

Before I was born, I was a nickel
in my mother's ovaries and a dime
in my dad's moneybags.

You could even say I'm made of money.

I'm your two-dollar coin
golden and baby oil shiny:
slip me into your slot machines

I'm your tatty fiver
a regular mountain climber

I'm voting for the Mana Party
with your tenner

I'm fucking Queen Elizabeth

I'm decolonising your fiddy

Preparing you for nuclear
fallout on your C Note

'Cos my words ain't worth shit
but I know how to spend my body

I'm made of money and I'm burning
bullet holes in your pockets.

Uljana Wolf

to the kreisau dogs

o the shabby raggle-taggle of village dogs: stub
tails stumpy legs mongrel muzzle at the hedge

yours is the street the dust on the asphalt edge
yours the night resounding in the valley asleep

every echo belongs to you: the flickering kick-
back of din in the hills a hierarchical snarling

a barking and baying: first Herculean then mam-
moth & abating just a chicken to tip you the wink:

whoever can't perform to order deliver the drivel is
picked off by the pack in wildfire throats the dump

is lost so cry murder etc. survey the world in this
trough master the pathways the people and me—

yours is my scent track my undaunted adventures
yours my calves   out of this shit-hole at last

postscript to the kreisau dogs

th one who says poems are like these dogs
in the thick of the village caught in their own

echo in the scraping and waiting at half moon
doggedly marking out the territory of language

doesn't know you—you bellowing hell-hounds
you cassandras of sound in the back of beyond

for behind my back you set out to stitch together
what is word and what is calf into an insolent bite

as if this leg of mine were only a page
and the order of things an exchange:

my boot here still bears the imprint of your
teeth—four prize pinches from that clinch

yes you deserve the verse that comes after
so the world sure dogs poetry   at its heel

Translated by Karen Leeder

Sonja Yelich

Arthritis the elephant

The man said he would pay happily full price.
And you said that will be fine thanks &
would you be after a receipt.

The man said he was not sure what
he would be after or before & gee
what's up with all the questions.

So you had to say don't forget your
change under the grill sir. & the talk
went back & forward through the no-smash glass.

Then he said *maps!* He would be needing a
map of the zoo to get around with. And you
had to ask for extra to the first. & *that was it* between you.

He was surprised a little by the minutiae
of drawings with arrows everywhere on
the gloss filmy paper.

3 bucks—& he was polite looking over
the standout times of 11.05 & 2
thirty for the Keeper & Animal

Displays around food.
He stopped first to spot the hedgerow
birds robbing stuff.

And passing with
Arthritis the elephant
Went by.

The second to last place people
recall him was at the iron rail
to the Galapagos Tortoise—

Which did a twisting thing with its neck
like the shape of 8 on its side.
It was a perfect day for radio reception

& he was on kilohertz. But these are
mere details & not relevant to the way
he fed himself to the lion.

Ashleigh Young

She cannot work

She cannot work when the man is in the house. She is working on a project that she has been working on for a long time, and ever since she began living with the man, the project has been moving slowly and she is no longer sure that she will finish it. In the evenings, after they watch the TV programme they both like, she and the man lie on the couch together reading or looking at their computers, and sometimes she will try, secretly, to work on her project, but after a few minutes, the man will hear her hesitant typing and look up to ask her what she is doing. She can't tell him about the project, because once, when she felt tired of his questions about it, she told him she had stopped working on it. Too many things had changed since she began all those years ago, she said, so it no longer made sense to continue, and instead she would spend her spare time on her studies. But the truth is that she has continued. All this time, she has continued, even though it is true, she supposes, that it does not make sense to continue.

Every week she looks forward to Sunday afternoon because that is when the man will go for a long ride on his bicycle. She will have the house to herself then, and she will be able to work. Nobody will creep up on her, nobody will call out to her, nobody will want to read aloud to her passages from a book or a newspaper article. She will be alone with her work and only the sounds of shuffling and scraping upstairs, where a woman and her elderly mother live. On a few unexpected occasions the man has stayed out late during the week, and she has hurried into her work at these times, but nervously, because she never knows when the man will arrive home and ask what she is doing. He has a certain way of arriving, throwing the door open as though popping the cork on a bottle, and instantly the house is reorganised because now he is at its centre, whereas before, she and her work were at the centre, and she were travelling through the centre of the work, moving slowly, very slowly towards the time when the project will be finished.

One late Sunday morning she is jumpy, thinking about her afternoon and how much progress she might make on her project. She has a feeling that today, if she works diligently, she might come close to finishing. She watches the man preparing for his ride: filling his backpack with food, spare tubes, a bottle of water. He charges his cellphone in case he has an accident and needs to call for help. When they were first living together, she would sometimes daydream that the man would have a terrible accident and not come back for a few days, and in that time she would be able to finish her project. The daydream makes her feel ashamed now, because the man is kind to her, and he does not like to leave her alone. She no longer allows herself the daydream. But even though she cares for him, and even though she knows he will go eventually and she will be alone, she grows more and more anxious for him to leave.

She goes to the spare bedroom and sits at the desk. Over and over she reads a page of her notebook where she has written a list of important tasks. The thought of finishing her project floods her with happiness. She can hear the man moving around the house, the sounds of zips on his backpack, the click of fasteners. He will be leaving in a few minutes. She hears the toilet flushing. She hears him in the kitchen, opening and closing cupboards. Soon she will hear his footsteps in the hallway. He will come into the room to kiss her goodbye, and he might stay for a while to talk to her about the route he plans to ride. On a few Sundays he has begun to talk about other things too, such as his own projects, or what might happen on the TV programme, and on those occasions he has stayed past the time when she would reasonably expect him to leave, and she has felt an increasing desperation to go into her work and has become afraid she might start pulling at her hair, or stabbing at herself with a pen, or tearing at her clothes. Then, just at the moment when her hand was losing strength from squeezing the pen so tightly, he has left her. He has walked up the steps along the side of the house, past the window of her room, to the little door that leads under the house to the dark cramped place where he keeps his bicycle out of the weather.

There was one Sunday, though, just after he walked out the door, when she heard a thump and looked up to see him pressed against her window. He was smiling at her from underneath his helmet, waving his arms above his head, and he looked like a large spider. It was as though he knew that she wanted to be alone, and was teasing her. Then he waved once more, and as always, retrieved his bicycle then slipped down the road and out to the coast and was gone for some hours.

There is no sound in the house now, even though the man is still there. Her chest has a funny feeling, as though her heart is rippling and growing larger, beginning to blur, dispersing like dye into water. As the feeling in her heart spreads into her arms, it begins to softly fizz, as though she were filled with strange debris. She is ready to go into her work to escape these feelings but she can't hear where the man is. At least twenty minutes have passed since she heard him moving about in the kitchen. The feeling is curling up into her neck and face and eyes, and she is overcome by it and afraid that she will cry out. Finally she stands. She walks into the living room. The man is sitting on the couch, in his cycling clothes, even his helmet. He is eating slices of toast. He smiles at her and says he is going soon but that he thought he should eat something first. There are still three slices of toast on his plate and she calculates that it will take him at least fifteen minutes to eat these, for he eats slowly.

She imagines running outside and throwing herself into the muddy ditch at the bottom of the garden, covering herself in cool leaves and grasses, covering herself in another feeling besides the feeling in her heart and her fear that she might stab at herself with a pen or tear her clothes apart. But instead she sits down beside the man and picks up a book that she left lying open the night before. She pretends to read as she listens to the man eating. Each chew is as loud to her as if she were inside his mouth, sliding this way and that, up and down, watching the soft, slick insides of his mouth, and his teeth, which are slightly crowded together, breaking the toast down.

After he has finished the final piece of toast he begins to talk about the ride he has planned. It is always at this moment, when he is telling her about where he will ride, that her impatience and anxiety lift away. It is easy to talk to him when he is about to leave. It is as if they are both standing at a train platform or a gate at an airport—she will go away to her work, he will go away to his ride—and the places ahead of them both, where they will not see each other, feel exciting but also places to be travelled through quickly so that they can return to each other again. In that moment, even though she wants very badly to work now, she looks forward to seeing him again.

The sound of his cleated shoes take a long time to fade as he carries his bicycle over his shoulder up the steps to the road. She waits for a few minutes, making sure. The air needs time to settle in his departure. Then she works. She works greedily, smugly. Deep inside her work, she feels her body disappear; she can travel through her work freely, with grace. She barely notices the sounds of shuffling and scraping upstairs as the woman upstairs, perhaps, tries to settle her elderly mother. She works for such a long time that when her body returns, it is in protest; she is tired and hungry. When she looks up, her eyes feel guarded, as if unsure about any sight but a page, any line that is not straight. The clock says that many hours have passed, and indeed the sky through the window is now dim. For the first time since she began to work this afternoon, she thinks about the man. He was riding all the way around the peninsula, he had said, and then over a small mountain range. He would ride into a strong headwind and on some parts of the road the waves would come up over the road. He had told her about the new lights he'd bought that were brighter than all other lights, so bright that they would light up every mark on the road and all the leaves on the trees. She decides to take the opportunity to continue to work. As the hours go by, hours and hours, and the man still does not return, and her work goes on before her, slipping always just ahead of her so that she cannot catch it, the feeling in her heart returns, but stronger. Her heart seems to ripple outwards like a puddle, spreading so far that it might fill her body completely, leaving her unable to move but for a slow throbbing. She holds herself still, finally hoping that the man might come home soon to relieve her, and as she lowers her eyes once again to her work, it is as if her work is looking out at her, pressed up against her hands, refusing to leave her.

Editors on the Storm

The changes pooled at our feet and crept up our ankles
then up to our necks. We had no choice then

but to begin swimming, and I called out to Simon, a stubborn
    dot
in the ocean. He was there, then he wasn't—

I opened my eyes in the grey fizz
to search and my contact lenses were washed away.

I'd known the rules once; now I didn't.
And I saw certain shapes, shapes

that could be nothing but writers
coming in on their boat of sorrow.

Fay Zwicky

Hokusai on the Shore

On the coast of a faraway ocean
where the sun sinks daily
a monster wave rears itself
high above a tiny figure
a young man crouched on his board.
The watchers stand fixed
on the sand and gape.

You were seventy when your wave
sprang alive. Old, ill, destitute
your money gambled away by your
grandson, your name forgotten
by the world you'd survived.
Your monster rode out
talons curved higher than heaven,
bent to envelop three boats
and their cowering oarsmen.

After all those anonymous years
beggared by petrified artefacts
your people took note, applauded,
flooded you—rewards, praise,
promises mounted. Near death
you raised life. Who among us
makes such miracles? Who keeps
a steady eye on mystery?

Quick and slow, fierce and meek,
quietly waiting came your answer:
'Until I was seventy, nothing I drew
was worthy of notice. When I'm eighty,
I hope to have made progress.'

Contributors' Notes & Acknowledgements

'The Kiss': *Sport* 36, 2008; in *Everything We Hoped For* (VUP, 2010), reprinted with permission; 'Andy—don't keep your distance': *Sport* 46, 2018, previously uncollected. *Everything We Hoped For* won the 2011 NZSA Hubert Church Best First Book Award for Fiction. **Pip Adam** is also the author of three novels: *I'm Working on a Building* (VUP, 2013), *The New Animals*, winner of the 2018 Jann Medlicott Acorn Foundation Fiction Prize, and *Nothing to See* (2020).

'Daughter': *Sport* 33, 2005; in *After the Dance* (VUP, 2005), reprinted with permission. **Michele Amas** (1961–2016) was a poet and actor. *After the Dance* was shortlisted for the NZSA Jessie Mackay Award at the 2007 Montana New Zealand Book Awards. A second collection, *Walking Home*, was published posthumously in 2020.

Chapter 2 from *Getting There: An Autobiography* (VUP, 2008): *Sport* 36, 2008, reprinted with permission. **Barbara Anderson** (1926–2013) was one of New Zealand's great writers, author of eight novels including *Portrait of the Artist's Wife*, winner of the 2003 Wattie Award. Her first book was the 1989 short story collection *I think we should go into the jungle*, which included 'Fast Post' from *Sport* 1.

'White Saris': *Sport* 33, 2005; in *Echolocation* (VUP, 2007), reprinted with permission. **Angela Andrews** has a PhD in Creative Writing from the International Institute of Modern Letters at Te Herenga Waka—Victoria University of Wellington and has worked as a doctor.

'Idiots': *Sport* 46, 2018; in *Craven* (VUP, 2019), reprinted with permission. **Jane Arthur** is a poet and bookseller (co-owner of Good Books, Wellington). She won the 2018 Sarah Broom Poetry Prize, judged by Eileen Myles, and the Jessie Mackay Prize for Best First Book of Poetry, at the Ockham NZ Book Awards 2020.

'Summer's Necrologue': *Sport* 38, 2010; in *Back With the Human Condition* (VUP, 2016), reprinted with permission. **Nick Ascroft** is a Wellington-based poet, editor and competitive scrabble-player. His most recent books are *Dandy Bogan: Selected Poems* (Boatwhistle, 2018) and *Moral Sloth* (VUP, 2019).

'Hungry': *Sport* 43, 2015; in *Some of Us Eat the Seeds* (VUP, 2015), reprinted with permission. **Morgan Bach** has an MA from the International Institute of Modern Letters at Te Herenga Waka—Victoria University of Wellington and won the Biggs Family Poetry Prize in 2013.

'The details of her nightmares': *Sport* 34, 2006; in *kōiwi kōiwi* (VUP, 2010), reprinted with permission. **Hinemoana Baker** is a poet, musician and creative writing teacher. She traces her ancestry from Ngāti Raukawa, Ngāti Toa Rangatira, Te Āti Awa and Ngāi Tahu, as well as from England and Germany (Oberammergau in Bayern). She is the author of the poetry collections *Funkhaus* (VUP, 2020), *waha | mouth* (VUP, 2014), *kōiwi kōiwi* (VUP, 2010), and *mātuhi | needle* (VUP & Perceval Press, 2004). She is currently living in Berlin, where she was 2016 Creative New Zealand Berlin Writer in Residence, and completing a PhD at Potsdam University.

'Christmas Morning': *Sport* 46, 2018, previously uncollected. **Antonia Bale** is a short story writer from Wellington. Her stories have been published in *Sport*, *Landfall* and *Turbine | Kapohou*. She has an MA from the International Institute of Modern Letters at Te Herenga Waka—Victoria University of Wellington.

'Robin Dudding 1935–2008': *Sport* 36, 2008, previously uncollected. **Fergus Barrowman** is the Publisher of Victoria University of Wellington Press.

'Self-portrait 4': *Sport* 33, 2005; in *Abandoned Novel* (VUP, 2006), reprinted with permission. **David Beach** is a Wellington poet. In 2009 he won the $65,000 Prize in Modern Letters for *Abandoned Novel*.

'Bug Week': *Sport* 40, 2012; in *Bug Week and other stories* (VUP, 2020); 'A nice night': *Sport* 42, 2014; in *Dear Neil Roberts* (VUP, 2014); reprinted with permission. **Airini Beautrais** is the author of four collections of poems and *Bug Week*, which won the 2021 Jann Medlicott Acorn Foundation Fiction Prize.

'I'll never get a poem from this neighbourhood': *Sport* 38, 2016, previously uncollected. **Miro Bilbrough** is a writer and filmmaker who grew up in New Zealand and lives in Australia. Three prose poems from *The Book of Snow and Fiction* were published in *Sport* 1, 1988, and her memoir *In the Time of the Manaroans* was published by VUP in 2020 and is forthcoming in Australia in 2022 from Ultimo Press.

'Oh, Abraham Lincoln, kiss me harder': *Sport* 40, 2012, previously uncollected. *Hera Lindsay Bird* by **Hera Lindsay Bird** was published by VUP in 2016 and Penguin UK in 2017; *Pamper Me to Hell and Back*, a UK Laureate's Choice Chapbook, in 2018; and *Irony vs Sincerity*, a Type Specimen Book for Klim Type Foundry, in 2019.

'Medical': *Sport* 34, 2006; in *Mrs Winter's Jump* (Godwit, 2007); 'It Has Been a Long Time Since I Last Spoke To You, So Here I Am': *Sport* 46, 2018; in *Lost and Somewhere Else* (VUP, 2019); reprinted with permission. **Jenny**

Bornholdt received the Prime Minister's Award for Literary Achievement in Poetry in 2020. Her recent books include *Selected Poems* (VUP, 2016), *Lost and Somewhere Else* (VUP, 2019) and the anthology *Short Poems of New Zealand* (VUP, 2018).

'Broken': *Sport* 39, 2011, previously uncollected. **William Brandt** is the author of the short story collection *Alpha Male* (VUP, 1998), which won the Montana New Zealand Book Awards Best First Book Award, and the novel *The Book of the Film of the Story of My Life* (VUP, 2002).

'Jeff Mangum': *Sport* 38, 2010; in *The Odour of Sanctity* (VUP, 2013), reprinted with permission. **Amy Brown**'s three books of poems include *The Propaganda Poster Girl* (VUP, 2008), a finalist in the Montana New Zealand Book Awards Best First Book Award, and *Neon Daze* (VUP, 2019). She has a PhD in creative writing from the University of Melbourne, and is the author of a series of children's novels, *Pony Tales*.

'What the very old man told me': *Sport* 39, 2011; in *Warm Auditorium* (VUP, 2012); 'The Pitfalls of Poetry': *Sport* 44, 2016; in *Floods Another Chamber* (VUP, 2017), reprinted with permission. **James Brown** was an editor of *Sport* in the *Great Sporting Moments* era, and has since retired to teach poetry at the IIML. His *Selected Poems* was published by VUP in 2020, and a new collection, *The Tip Shop*, will appear in 2022.

'Fifth Grade Time Capsule': *Sport* 45, 2017; in *Advice from the Lights* (Copyright 2017 by Stephen Burt. Used with the permission of The Permissions Company LLC on behalf of Graywolf Press, www.graywolfpress. org. All rights reserved), reprinted with permission. **Stephanie Burt** is Professor of English at Harvard University and taught as an Erskine Canterbury Fellow at the University of Canterbury in Christchurch during the summer of 2016–17. Burt's books of poetry and literary criticism include *Belmont* (2013), *Close Calls with Nonsense: Reading New Poetry* (2009) and *The Poem Is You: 60 Contemporary American Poems and How to Read Them* (2016).

'Thought Horses': *Sport* 40, 2012; 'All my feelings would have been of common things': *Sport* 44, 2016; in *Thought Horses* (VUP, 2016), reprinted with permission. **Rachel Bush** (1941–2016) was the author of four poetry collections, *The Hungry Woman* (1997), *The Unfortunate Singer* (2002), *Nice Pretty Things and others* (2011), and *Thought Horses* (2016).

'*Late to my appointment . . .*': *Sport* 47, 2019; in *Nostalgia Has Ruined My Life* (Giramondo, 2021), reprinted with permission. **Zarah Butcher-McGunnigle** is the author of *Autobiography of a Marguerite* (Hue & Cry Press, 2014) and *Nostalgia Has Ruined My Life* (Giramondo, 2021).

'Snow White's Coffin': *Sport* 40, 2012; in *Snow White's Coffin* (VUP, 2012), reprinted with permission. **Kate Camp** is the author of seven collections of poetry, including *Unfamiliar Legends of the Stars,* winner of the NZSA Jessie Mackay Award for Best First Book of Poetry at the 1999 Montana NZ Book Awards, *The Mirror of Simple Annihilated Souls*, winner of the New Zealand Post Book Award for Poetry in 2011, and *How to Be Happy Though Human*, published in 2020 by VUP in New Zealand and The House of Anansi in Canada. Her autobiographical essay collection *You Probably Think This Song Is About You* is forthcoming in 2022.

'Descent from Avalanche': *Sport* 37, 2009, previously uncollected. **Eleanor Catton** is the author of *The Rehearsal* (VUP, 2008), winner of the 2009 Montana New Zealand Best First Book Award, and *The Luminaries* (VUP, 2013), winner of the 2013 Man Booker Prize.

'The Last of Bashō': *Sport* 39, 2011; in *The Bengal Engine's Mango Afterglow*; (VUP, 2012); 'The Great Wall Café': *Sport* 42, 2014; in *Wonky Optics* (VUP, 2015); reprinted with permission. In 2009 **Geoff Cochrane** was awarded the Janet Frame Prize for Poetry, in 2010 the inaugural Nigel Cox Unity Books Award, and in 2014 an Arts Foundation Laureate Award. *Chosen*, his nineteenth collection of poems, appeared in 2020.

'from *The Cowboy Dog*': *Sport* 34, 2006; in *The Cowboy Dog* (VUP, 2006), reprinted with permission. **Nigel Cox** (1951–2006) was the author of six novels—*Waiting for Einstein* (1984), *Dirty Work* (1987), *Skylark Lounge* (2000), *Tarzan Presley / Jungle Rock Blues* (200), *Responsibility* (2005) and *The Cowboy Dog* (2006)—and *Phone Home Berlin: Collected Non-fiction* (2007), and in 1988 was a founder editor of *Sport*.

'To All the Boys I've Loved Before': *Sport* 47, 2019; in *AUP New Poets 6* (AUP, 2020), reprinted with permission. **Vanessa Crofskey** is a writer, performer, artist and curator of Hokkien Chinese and Pākehā descent.

'How to live by the sea': *Sport* 36, 2008; in *How to live by the sea* (VUP, 2009), reprinted with permission. **Lynn Davidson** grew up in Kāpiti, Wellington, and has recently returned to New Zealand after several years living in Edinburgh. She is the author of four collections of poetry, including *How to Live by the Sea*, *Common Land* (VUP, 2012) and *Islander* (VUP, 2019).

'Haiku': *Sport* 42, 2014, previously uncollected. **Uther Dean** is a writer, poet and comedian. He's written for the *Listener*, Radio New Zealand, *The Pantograph Punch, The Spinoff, Shortland Street* and *Power Rangers*, and co-founded the theatre company My Accomplice.

'Kissing Terry in the Rain': *Sport* 40, 2012; in *Sometimes a Single Leaf: Selected*

Poems translated and introduced by Iain Galbraith (Arc, 2020), reprinted with permission. **Esther Dischereit** (b. 1952) is a poet, novelist, essayist and dramatist. She collaborates with composers and jazz musicians and founded the avant-garde project 'WordMusicSpace/Sound-Concepts'. **Iain Galbraith**'s many translations include an English edition of W.G. Sebald's poetry, *Across the Land and the Water*, and Esther Kinsky's novel *River*. His poems are collected in *The True Height of the Ear* (Arc, 2018).

'Letter': *Sport* 36, 2008, previously uncollected. **Kate Duignan** is the author of two novels, *Breakwater* (VUP, 2001) and *The New Ships* (VUP, 2018).

'A Lonely Road': *Sport* 41, 2013; in *Empty Bones* (VUP, 2014), reprinted with permission. **Breton Dukes** lives in Dunedin. He is the author of three collections of short stories: *Bird North* (2011), *Empty Bones* (2014) and *What Sort of Man* (2020).

'Youth': *Sport* 40, 2012; in *Dinge, die verschwinden* (Kiepenheuer & Witsch, 2009; brooklynrail.org, 2010), reprinted with permission. **Jenny Erpenbeck** was born in East Berlin in 1967 and is the author of celebrated books including the novels *End of Days* (2015) and *Go, Went, Gone* (2017), and *Not a Novel: A Memoir in Pieces* (2020). She was a Writers and Readers Week guest at the NZ International Arts Festival 2012. **Susan Bernofsky** has translated many books by Jenny Erpenbeck and other writers, and is the author of *Clairvoyant of the Small: The Life of Robert Walser* (Yale, 2021).

'Woolshed Blues': *Sport* 33, 2005; in *Beauty of the Badlands* (2008), reprinted with permission. **Cliff Fell** was born in London in 1955 to a New Zealand father and English mother and travelled widely before coming to New Zealand in 1997. *The Adulterer's Bible* (VUP, 2003) won the NZSA Jessie Mackay Best First Book Award for Poetry.

'Wake': *Sport* 39, 2011, previously uncollected. **Joan Fleming** won the Biggs Family Poetry Prize in 2007. She is the author of a chapbook, *Two Dreams in Which Things Are Taken* (2010), and two poetry collections, *The Same as Yes* (VUP, 2011) and *Failed Love Poems* (VUP, 2015). She mostly lives in Melbourne, and calls New Zealand home.

'After Reading an Anthology': *Sport* 40, 2012; in *Weiche Ziele* (Haffmanns Verlag, 1994), reprinted with permission. **Robert Gernhardt** (1937–2006) was born into the German minority of Estonia in 1937, and from 1964 lived in Frankfurt am Main, where he worked as a freelance artist and writer. Translator **Richard Millington** teaches German at Te Herenga Waka— Victoria University of Wellington.

'Early': *Sport* 40, 2012; in *The Baker's Thumbprint* (Seraph Press, 2013), reprinted with permission. **Paula Green** is a poet, children's writer, critic and anthologist. Notable publications include *99 Ways into New Zealand* (with Harry Ricketts, Random House NZ, 2010) and *Wild Honey: Reading New Zealand Women's Poetry* (Massey University Press, 2020). She edits the websites nzpoetryshelf.com and, for children, nzpoetrybox.wordpress.com, and received the Prime Minister's Award for Achievement in Poetry in 2017.

'Really & Truly': *Sport* 36, 2008; in *The Lustre Jug* (VUP, 2009), reprinted with permission. **Bernadette Hall** is the author of 11 books of poems, including *The Merino Princess: Selected Poems* (VUP, 2005) and *Fancy Dancing: New and Selected Poems* (VUP, 2020), which together survey her career, as well as plays, essays and short fiction. She received the Prime Minister's Award for Literary Achievement in Poetry in 2015.

'Glass glitters better than diamond under such splintered light': *Sport* 47, 2019, previously uncollected. **Rebecca Hawkes** is a Wellington-based poet and artist with an MA in Creative Non-fiction from the International Institute of Modern Letters at Te Herenga Waka—Victoria University of Wellington. Her poetry collection 'Softcore Coldsores' is published in *AUP New Poets 5* (AUP, 2019).

'The Owners': *Sport* 41, 2013; in *Are Friends Electric?* (VUP, 2018), reprinted with permission. **Helen Heath** is the author of *Graft* (VUP, 2012), winner of the 2013 NZSA Jessie Mackay Best First Book for Poetry Award, and *Are Friends Electric?*, winner of the 2019 Mary and Peter Biggs Award for Poetry at the Ockham NZ Book Awards.

'The Pests': *Sport* 46, 2018, previously uncollected. **Zoë Higgins** works in theatre and lives in Wellington. Her work has been published in *Starling*, *JOYCE*, and *Chameleon* magazines.

'Sweet on the Comedown': *Sport* 47, 2019, previously uncollected. **Emma Hislop** (Ngāi Tahu) lives in Taranaki. In 2013 she completed an MA in Creative Writing at the International Institute of Modern Letters at Te Herenga Waka—Victoria University of Wellington. Her stories have been published in *Sport, Hue & Cry, Takahe, Ika 4, Ora Nui* and *Turbine*. She is currently working on a short story collection.

'The Garage Party': *Sport* 47, 2019, previously uncollected. **Nadine Anne Hura** (Ngāti Hine, Ngāpuhi) has a background in journalism, education policy and kaupapa Māori research. Her essays explore themes of identity, biculturalism, politics and parenting.

'hot bodies': *Sport* 47, 2019; in *How to Live With Mammals* (VUP, 2021), reprinted with permission. **Ash Davida Jane** is a poet and bookseller from

Wellington. Her first book, *Every Dark Waning*, was published in 2016 by Platypus Press.

'The Otorhinolaryngologist': *Sport* 35, 2007; 'Saudade': *Sport* 39, 2011; in *Fits & Starts* (VUP, 2016); reprinted with permission. **Andrew Johnston** is a New Zealand poet who has lived in France since 1997. He is the author of four collections of poems, including *How to Talk* (VUP, 1994) and *Fits & Starts*, both of which won the New Zealand Book Award for Poetry. His *Selected Poems* will be published in 2022.

'Flood': *Sport* 38, 2010, previously uncollected. **Hannah Jolly** completed an MA in Creative Writing at the International Institute of Modern Letters at Te Herenga Waka—Victoria University of Wellington in 2009. She grew up in the Wairarapa and currently lives in England.

'The Inertia Poem': *Sport* 46, 2018; in *There's No Place Like the Internet in Springtime* (VUP, 2018), reprinted with permission. **Erik Kennedy** lives in Christchurch. His chapbook *Twenty-Six Factitions* was published with Cold Hub Press in 2017 and *There's No Place Like the Internet in Springtime* was his first full-length collection. His second, *Another Beautiful Day Indoors*, is forthcoming from VUP in 2022.

'Tata Beach, New Year's Eve, 1974': *Sport* 42, 2014 , previously uncollected. **Elizabeth Knox** is the author of thirteen novels, most recently *The Absolute Book* (VUP, 2019; Viking Penguin US, 2021; Michael Joseph, 2021), three novellas and a collection of essays, *The Love School* (VUP, 2008). In 2019 she received the Prime Minister's Award for Achievement in Fiction and was made a Companion of the New Zealand Order of Merit. She was a founder editor of *Sport* in 1988.

'Fair Copy': *Sport* 40, 2012; in *Ins Reine* (Suhrkamp Verlag, 2010), reprinted with permission. **Michael Krüger** (b. 1943) is a poet, prose writer, translator and publisher, whose works translated into English include *Scenes from the Life of a Bestselling Author*, translated by Karen Leeder. **Karen Leeder** is Professor of Modern German Literature at the University of Oxford and was a Writers and Readers Week guest at the NZ International Arts Festival 2012.

'Tentatively Joined': *Sport* 37, 2009, previously uncollected. **Chloe Lane** has an MA from the International Institute of Modern Letters at Te Herenga Waka—Victoria University of Wellington and an MFA in Fiction from the University of Florida, and was the founding editor of Hue+Cry Press. *The Swimmers* (VUP, 2020) is her debut novel.

'Bonsense': *Sport* 37, 2009; in *The Moonmen* (VUP, 2010); Artificial Intelligence': *Sport* 44, 2016; in *Ordinary Time* (VUP, 2017); reprinted with permission. **Anna Livesey** is the author of three poetry collections, beginning with *Good Luck* (VUP, 2003). She was the 2003 Schaeffer Fellow at the Iowa Writers' Workshop. She has lived in Wellington, Beijing, Shanghai, New York, Dunedin, Wellington again and currently Auckland, where she works as a corporate strategist.

'穷人店, 富人店': *Sport* 46, 2018; in *All Who Live on Islands* (VUP, 2019), reprinted with permission. **Rose Lu** is a Wellington-based writer. In 2018 she gained her MA in Creative Writing at the International Institute of Modern Letters at Te Herenga Waka—Victoria University of Wellington and was awarded the Modern Letters Creative Nonfiction Prize. Her undergraduate degree was in mechatronics engineering, and she has worked as a software developer since 2012.

'An Englishman, an Irishman and a Welshman walk into a Pā': *Sport* 40, 2012, previously uncollected. **Tina Makereti** (Te Āti Awa, Ngāti Tūwharetoa, Ngāti Rangatahi, Pākehā) is the author of two novels, *Where the Rēkohu Bone Sings* (2014) and *The Imaginary Lives of James Pōneke* (2018), and a collection of short stories, *Once Upon a Time in Aotearoa* (2010). She also co-edited *Black Marks on the White Page* (2017) with Witi Ihimaera. Tina teaches in the MA programme of the International Institute of Modern Letters at Te Herenga Waka—Victoria University of Wellington, and is completing a collection of essays.

'From an Imaginary Notebook': *Sport* 39, 2011), previously uncollected; 'The Schoolbus': *Sport* 39, 2011); 'The question poem': *Sport* 40, 2012; in *Some Things to Place in a Coffin* (VUP, 2017), reprinted with permission. **Bill Manhire**'s most recent book is *Wow* (VUP and Carcanet, 2020).

'Dog Farm, Food Game': *Sport* 45, 2017; in *2000ft Above Worry Level* (VUP, 2020), reprinted with permission. **Eamonn Marra** is a writer and comedian who was born and raised in Christchurch and lives in Wellington. *2000ft Above Worry Level* is his first book.

'Clean hands save lives': *Sport* 39, 2011, previously uncollected. **Kirsten McDougall** is the author of three novels, most recently *She's a Killer* (VUP, 2021). 'Clean hands saved lives' won the Best Story Under 1000 Words category in the *Sport*/Unity Books The Long and the Short of It competition, 2011.

'The Harmonious Development of Man': *Sport* 40, 2012; in *Who Was That Woman Anyway? Snapshots of a Lesbian Life* (VUP, 2013), reprinted with permission. **Aorewa McLeod** taught in the University of Auckland English Department for 37 years until her retirement, and undertook the MA in creative writing at Te Herenga Waka—Victoria University of Wellington in

2011. *Who Was That Woman, Anyway?* was her first book.

'Fatigue' and 'Rope': *Sport* 41, 2013, in *The Rope Walk* (Seraph Press, 2013), reprinted with permission. **Maria McMillan** is the author of a chapbook, *The Rope Walk*, and the poetry collections *Tree Space* (VUP, 2014) and *The Ski Flier* (VUP, 2017).

'Sex dream': *Sport* 43, 2015; in *Fully Clothed and So Forgetful* (VUP, 2017), reprinted with permission. **Hannah Mettner** is a Wellington-based poet from Gisborne, and co-editor of *Sweet Mammalian*. *Fully Clothed and So Forgetful* won the 2018 Jessie Mackay Best First Book Award for Poetry.

'First': *Sport* 47, 2019, previously uncollected. **Fardowsa Mohamed** is a poet and junior doctor from Auckland. She has published work in *Landfall* and *Poetry New Zealand*.

'How Far from Earth': *Sport* 46, 2018, previously uncollected. **Clare Moleta** has an MA in creative writing from Te Herenga Waka—Victoria University of Wellington. Her debut novel is *Unsheltered* (Scribner, 2021).

'Pain': *Sport* 33, 2005; in *How Does It Hurt?* (VUP, 2014), reprinted with permission. **Stephanie de Montalk** is the author of four books of poetry; a novel; *Unquiet World*, a memoir–biography of New Zealand poet and eccentric Count Geoffrey Potocki de Montalk; and *How Does It Hurt?*, a memoir–study that was reissued as *Communicating Pain* (Routledge, 2018).

'The Gold Day Has Dimmed': *Sport* 40, 2012; in *Wild Like Me* (VUP, 2014), reprinted with permission. **Elizabeth Nannestad** worked as a forensic psychiatrist, then became a home-schooling mother. She is the author of three collections of poems: *Jump* (AUP, 1986), joint winner of the New Zealand Book Award for poetry, *If He's a Good Dog He'll Swim* (AUP, 1996) and *Wild Like Me*.

'Unlove': *Sport* 46, 2018; in *To the Occupant* (Otago University Press, 2019), reprinted with permission. **Emma Neale** is a Dunedin-based poet and novelist, and was the editor of *Landfall* 2017–2021. She is the author of six novels and six collections of poems, most recently *To the Occupant*. Her awards include the 2008 NZSA Janet Frame Memorial Award for Literature, the 2012 Robert Burns Fellowship, and the 2020 Lauris Edmond Memorial Award for Poetry.

'Rotational Head Injury': *Sport* 45, 2017, previously uncollected. **Bill Nelson** has an MA in creative writing from the International Institute of Modern Letters at Te Herenga Waka—Victoria University of Wellington. His first book of poems is *Memorandum of Understanding* (VUP, 2016).

'I love you?': *Sport* 47, 2019; in *Sista, Stanap Strong: A Vanuatu Women's Anthology* (VUP, 2021), reprinted with permission. **Mikaela Nyman** and **Rebecca Tobo Olul-Hossen**'s collaborative poetry is an ongoing conversation and exploration of the issues women face. Rebecca hails from Tanna island in Vanuatu and is working on a short story collection. Mikaela is a Taranaki-based writer with roots in the Åland islands in Finland, where her first poetry collection was published in 2019. Her first novel is *Sado* (VUP, 2020).

'Early morning on the Sand-walk, Down House, March 1857': *Sport* 42, 2014; in *Cold Water Cure* (VUP, 2016), reprinted with permission. **Claire Orchard** has an MA in creative writing from the International Institute of Modern Letters at Te Herenga Waka—Victoria University of Wellington. Charles Darwin is at the heart of her collection of poems *Cold Water Cure*.

'When in Rome': *Sport* 45, 2017; in *Things OK with you?* (VUP, 2021), reprinted with permission. **Vincent O'Sullivan** was born in 1937 and made his *Sport* debut in issue 1. His recent books include *Being There: Selected Poems* (VUP, 2015), the novel *All This By Chance* (VUP, 2018), *Selected Stories* (VUP, 2019) and *Ralph Hotere: The Dark Is Light Enough* (Penguin, 2020), which won the the general non-fiction category of the 2021 Ockham New Zealand Book Awards. *Mary's boy Jean-Jacques: a novella and six stories* (VUP, 2022) is forthcoming.

'In Search of X': *Sport* 39, 2011, previously uncollected. **Cate Palmer** has an MA in creative writing from the International Institute of Modern Letters at Te Herenga Waka—Victoria University of Wellington, and an MFA from the Michener Center for Writers, University of Texas.

'The Road to Tokomairiro': *Sport* 39, 2011; in *I've Got His Blood on Me* (VUP, 2012), reprinted with permission. **Lawrence Patchett**'s second book is the novel *The Burning River* (VUP, 2019). 'The Road to Tokomairiro' won the Best Story Over 1000 Words category in the *Sport*/Unity Books The Long and the Short of It competition, 2011.

'Song of la chouette': *Sport* 40, 2012; in *Beside Myself* (AUP, 2016), reprinted with permission. **Chris Price** teaches in the MA programme at the International Institute of Modern Letters at Te Herenga Waka—Victoria University of Wellington. She is the author of four poetry books, including *Husk* (AUP, 2002), which won the Jessie Mackay Best First Book Award for Poetry. She was the Editor of *Landfall* 1993–2000.

'Cough In': *Sport* 47, 2019; in ransack (VUP, 2019), reprinted with permission. **essa may ranapiri** (Ngāti Raukawa | takatāpui; they/them/theirs) is a poet from Kirikiriroa, Aotearoa / their second book, *echidna*, will be published by VUP in 2022.

'The Life and Deaths of Adeline Snow': *Sport* 38, 2010, previously uncollected. **Melissa Day Reid** was born in America in 1971 and moved to New Zealand in 1995. She lives in Christchurch and has an MA from the International Institute of Modern Letters at Te Herenga Waka—Victoria University of Wellington.

'Noddy': *Sport* 41, 2013; in *Half Dark* (VUP, 2015), reprinted with permission. A poet, editor, biographer, critic and academic, **Harry Ricketts** taught English literature and creative writing at Te Herenga Waka—Victoria University of Wellington until his retirement in 2021. He has published over thirty books, including the internationally acclaimed *The Unforgiving Minute: A Life of Rudyard Kipling* (1999), *Strange Meetings: The Lives of the Poets of the Great War* (2010) and *Selected Poems* (VUP, 2021).

'Pool Noodle': *Sport* 46, 2018; in *Head Girl* (VUP, 2020), reprinted with permission. **Freya Daly Sadgrove** is a Wellington-based poet, performer and bookseller, and has an MA in creative writing from the International Institute of Modern Letters at Te Herenga Waka—Victoria University of Wellington.

'A new body': *Sport* 44, 2016, previously uncollected. **Frances Samuel** has an MA from the International Institute of Modern Letters at Te Herenga Waka—Victoria University of Wellington. Her debut poetry collection is *Sleeping on Horseback* (VUP, 2014); her second, *Museum*, is forthcoming in 2022.

'Sisters': *Sport* 46, 201, previously uncollected. **Maria Samuela** is of Cook Islands descent and lives in Wellington. She has an MA in Creative Writing from the IIML at Te Herenga Waka—Victoria University of Wellington, and has been published in the School Journal and had stories translated into five Pacific languages. Her collection of short stories, *Beats of the Pa'u*, will be published by VUP in 2022.

'when the barber talks about elephants': *Sport* 45, 2017; in *Louder* (VUP, 2018), reprinted with permission. Christchurch-based **Kerrin P Sharpe** completed the Victoria University of Wellington Original Composition course taught by Bill Manhire in 1976 and since returning to writing has published four collections of poems: *Three Days in a Wishing Well* (2012), *There's a Medical Name for This* (2014), *Rabbit Rabbit* (2016) and *Louder* (2018).

'I am a Man of Many Professions, My Wife is a Lady of Many Confessions': *Sport* 35, 2007; in *The World's Fastest Flower* (VUP, 2008), reprinted with permission. **Charlotte Simmonds** is a Wellington-based poet, playwright and short story writer. Her poetry collection *The World's Fastest Flower* was a finalist in the Montana New Zealand Book Awards Best First Book Award.

'Cicada Motel': *Sport* 45, 2017; in *Devil's Trumpet* (VUP, 2021), reprinted with permission. **Tracey Slaughter** teaches creative writing at Waikato University. Her previous short story collection is *deleted scenes for lovers* (VUP, 2016), and her poetry collection is *Conventional Weapons* (VUP, 2019).

'no horse': *Sport* 33, 2005; in *Horse With Hat* (VUP, 2014), reprinted with permission. **Marty Smith** has an MA from the International Institute of Modern Letters at Te Herenga Waka—Victoria University of Wellington. *Horse With Hat* won the Jessie Mackay Award for Best First Book in the 2014 New Zealand Post Book Awards. She is writing a book about the work of the people of the racing industry.

'Six Feet for a Single, Eight for a Double': *Sport* 47, 2019; in *Tōku Pāpā* (VUP, 2021), reprinted with permission. **Ruby Solly** is a Kāi Tahu writer and musician. Her solo album *Pōneke* appeared in 2020 and her first book, *Tōku Pāpā*, and album with Tararua, *Pūaka*, in 2021.

'Real life': *Sport* 43, 2015; in *The Mermaid Boy* (Hue & Cry, 2015), reprinted with permission. **John Summers'** second book is the essay collection *The Commercial Hotel* (VUP, 2021).

'Leaves': *Sport* 40, 2012, previously uncollected. **Anna Taylor'**s short story collection *Relief* (VUP, 2009) won the 2010 NZSA Hubert Church Best First Book of Fiction Award. She has an MA from the International Institute of Modern Letters at Te Herenga Waka—Victoria University of Wellington, and won the Adam Prize in Creative Writing.

'Brothers Blind': *Sport* 39, 2011, previously uncollected. **Sylvan Thomson** is a writer from Nelson. He holds an MA from the International Institute of Modern Letters at Te Herenga Waka—Victoria University of Wellington, and an MFA from the University of Michigan's Helen Zell Writer's Program, and in 2020 was awarded the Creative New Zealand Todd New Writer's Bursary.

'Kuki the Krazy Kea': *Sport* 38, 2010; in *The Stories of Bill Manhire* (VUP, 2015), reprinted with permission. **Tane Thomson** is a writer of independent means. He once studied with Bill Manhire but got nothing out of it.

'Diary of a (L)it Girl or, Frankenstein's Ghost Pig': editorial in *Sport* 47, 2019, previously uncollected. **Tayi Tibble'**s *Pōukahangatus* won the Jessie Mackay Prize for Best First Book of Poetry in the 2019 Ockham New Zealand Book Awards and her second book, *Rangikura*, was published by VUP in 2021; both will be published internationally by Knopf in 2022/23.

'Badly written men': *Sport* 44, 2016, previously uncollected. **Giovanni Tiso** is an Italian writer and translator based in Wellington.

'Mount Eden': *Sport* 46, 2018; in *Lay Studies* (VUP, 2018), reprinted with permission. **Steven Toussaint** has studied poetry at the Iowa Writers' Workshop and the International Institute of Modern Letters at Te Herenga Waka—Victoria University of Wellington, and philosophical theology at the University of Cambridge. His previous books are *Fiddlehead* (Compound Press, 2014) and *The Bellfounder* (The Cultural Study Society, 2015). He lives in Auckland and Cambridge.

'Infernally yours, gentleman poet in the streets—raging homosexual in the sheets': *Sport* 47, 2019, previously uncollected. **Chris Tse** is the author of two poetry collections, *How to Be Dead in a Year of Snakes* (AUP, 2005), winner of the Jessie Mackay Award for Best First Book of Poetry, and *He's So Masc* (AUP, 2018), and is currently co-editing (with Emma Barnes) an anthology of LGBTQIA+ and Takatāpui writers from Aotearoa for AUP.

'Department of Immigration': *Sport* 40, 2012, previously uncollected; New Transgender Blockbusters': *Sport* 47, 2019; in *New Transgender Blockbusters* (VUP, 2020); reprinted with permission. **Oscar Upperton** was born in Christchurch in 1991, and grew up in Whangārei and Palmerston North. He now lives in Wellington. In 2019 he was awarded the Creative New Zealand Louis Johnson New Writer's Bursary. *New Transgender Blockbusters* is his first book.

'Asylum Notes': *Sport* 34, 2006; in *Tributary* (VUP, 2007), reprinted with permission. **Rae Varcoe** was born in 1944, grew up in Dunedin, worked as a blood diseases physician at Auckland City Hospital, and now lives in Nelson. She completed an MA at the International Institute of Modern Letters at Te Herenga Waka—Victoria University of Wellington in 1997.

'Haunted sestina': *Sport* 35, 2017; in *Furious Triangle* (Puncher & Wattmann, 2011), reprinted with permission. **Catherine Vidler**'s most recent books is *Wings*, a collection of visual poetry published in 2021 by Cordite Books.

'The feijoas are falling from the trees': *Sport* 40, 2012; in *Enough* (VUP, 2013), reprinted with permission. **Louise Wallace** is the author of three books of poems: *Since June* (2009), *Enough* (2013) and *Bad Things* (2017). She is an editor of *Starling*.

'The World of Children's Books': *Sport* 33, 2005; in *For Everyone Concerned & other stories* (VUP, 2007), reprinted with permission; 'Memoir, with Electrodes': *Sport* 42, 2014, previously uncollected. **Damien Wilkins** is a novelist, poet, playwright and essayist and Director of the International Institute of Modern Letters at Te Herenga Waka—Victoria University of Wellington, and was a founder editor of *Sport*.

'I'm out for dead presidents to represent me': *Sport* 47, 2019, previously uncollected. **Faith Wilson** is a Samoan/Palagi artist and writer from Aotearoa/New Zealand.

'to the kreisau dogs' and 'postscript to the kreisau dogs': *Sport* 40, 2012; in *kochanie ich habe brot gekauft* (kookbooks, 2005), reprinted with permission. **Uljana Wolf** is a poet and publisher born in Berlin in 1979. Translator **Karen Leeder** is Professor of Modern German Literature at the University of Oxford and was a Writers and Readers Week guest at the NZ International Arts Festival 2012.

'Arthritis the elephant': *Sport* 33, 2005, previously uncollected. **Sonja Yelich** is the author of two collections of poetry: *Clung* (AUP, 2004, winner of the NZSA Best First Book of Poetry Award) and *Get Some* (AUP, 2008).

'She cannot work': *Sport* 43, 2015; in *Can You Tolerate This?* (VUP, 2016); 'Editors on the Storm': *Sport* 46, 2018; in *How I Get Ready* (VUP, 2019), reprinted with permission. **Ashleigh Young** is a poet and editor at VUP. Her essay collection *Can You Tolerate This?* won a Windham-Campbell Prize from Yale University and the Royal Society Te Apārangi Award for General Non-Fiction in 2017.

'Hokusai on the Shore': *Sport* 33, 2005; in *The Collected Poems of Fay Zwicky* (UWAP, 2017), reprinted with permission. **Fay Zwicky** (1933–2017) was an Australian poet, short story writer, critic and academic primarily known for her autobiographical poem *Kaddish*, which deals with her identity as a Jewish writer. She first appeared in *Sport* in issue 7, 1991.